LIGHT
PERPETUAL

LIGHT
PERPETUAL

Book Three of
the Hussite Trilogy

ANDRZEJ
SAPKOWSKI

Translated by David French

orbitbook

Light Perpetual is a historical novel set during the Hussite Wars in Bohemia in the 1400s, a period of religious conflict and persecution. Characters in the novel may express views that some readers might find offensive.

Orbit
Hachette Book Group
1290 Avenue of the Americas
New York, NY 10104
orbitbooks.net

First Edition: October 2022
Simultaneously published in Great Britain by Gollancz

Originally published in Polish as *Lux Perpetua*

Published by arrangement with the Patricia Pasqualini Literary Agency.

Orbit is an imprint of Hachette Book Group.
The Orbit name and logo are trademarks of Little, Brown Book Group Limited.

The publisher is not responsible for websites (or their content) that are not owned by the publisher.

The Hachette Speakers Bureau provides a wide range of authors for speaking events. To find out more, go to www.hachettespeakersbureau.com or call (866) 376-6591.

Orbit books may be purchased in bulk for business, educational, or promotional use. For information, please contact your local bookseller or the Hachette Book Group Special Markets Department at special.markets@hbgusa.com.

Quote on p. v excerpted from "Dies Irae," either Thomas of Celano or Latino Malabranca Orsini, translated to English as "The Day of Wrath" by William Josiah Irons in 1849.

Library of Congress Control Number: 2022936602

ISBNs: 9780316593250 (hardcover), 9780316423755 (trade paperback), 9780316423731 (ebook)

Printed in the United States of America

LSC-C

Printing 1, 2022

Dies irae, dies illa,
solvet saeculum in favilla,
teste David cum Sibylla…

Day of wrath and doom impending,
David's word with Sibyl's blending!
Heaven and Earth in ashes ending!

O, what fear man's bosom rendeth,
When from Heaven the Judge descendeth,
On whose sentence all dependeth!

Wondrous sound the trumpet flingeth,
Through Earth's sepulchres it ringeth,
All before the throne it bringeth…

"Dies Irae," either Thomas of Celano (1200–1265) or Latino
Malabranca Orsini (d. 1294), translated to English as "The Day
of Wrath" by William Josiah Irons, 1849

Tararara, tararara, tararara dum, dum, dum…
Lacrimosa dies illa
qua resurget ex favilla
iudicandus homo reus.
Huic ergo parce Deus.

Oh my, oh my, the day of wrath is nigh, m'lords and gentle listeners, nigh is the day of wrath, an ill-fated day, a day of tears.
The Day of Judgement and of punishment is nigh. As it is written in John's epistle: *Antichristus venit…unde scimus quoniam*
novissima hora est. The Antichrist is coming, the last hour is
coming. The end of the world and of all existence is nigh…In
other words: things are bloody lousy.

The Antichrist, m'lords and dear listeners, will come from the
tribe of Dan.

He shall be born in Babylon. He shall come at the end of the
world and shall reign for three and a half years.

He shall erect a temple in Jerusalem, reign over the kings and
lay waste the Church of God. He will ride atop a fiery furnace,
performing wonders wherever he goes. Displaying his wounds,
he shall delude good Christians. He shall come with fire and
sword, and blasphemy shall be his weapon, and treachery his
arm, and destruction his right hand, and darkness his left. His
face is as of a wild beast, with a high forehead and eyebrows
grown together…

His right eye is like a star shining at dawn, his left unmoving,
green as a cat's, with two pupils instead of one. His nose is like a

chasm, his maw measures an ell, his teeth a span. His fingers are like iron scythes.

Hey, hey! And why raise a clamour at an old man, m'lords? Why so quick to browbeat him? For what, for what ills? That I frighten you? That I blaspheme? That I am a storm crow?

I make no prophecies, m'lords! I speak the truth, the pure, honest truth, as stated by the great Church Fathers. Why, and laid down in the Gospels! They are apocryphal, you say? And what of it? This whole world is apocryphal.

What do you bring, gentle maid? What foams so in those vats? Could it be ale?

Oh, first class…Świdnica ale, without doubt…

I say! But look through the window, m'lords! Do an old man's eyes deceive him? Am I mistaken or is the sun at last breaking through the clouds? Great God, yes! It marks the end of this foul, rainy weather. Indeed, just look at the light flooding the world, shining down from the skies in a bright beam. And the radiance fills the world…

Lux perpetua.

That's how you'd like it. Eternal. You could like that…

What are you saying? That since the foul weather is over it's time to leave the inn and be off? That since it's so, instead of blathering on I should quickly finish the tale? Say what happened next to Reynevan and his beloved Jutta, to Scharley and Samson at that time, a time of those cruel wars, when the lands of Lusatia, Silesia, Saxony, Thuringia and Bavaria ran with blood and were blackened by flames?

Right away, m'lords, right away. I shall tell you, for my tale is also coming to its natural ending. Though I must also tell you that if you ready yourself for a happy or joyous ending to the tale you will be sore disappointed…What? You say I frighten you again? I croak? But how, do tell, may I not croak? When such

2

dreadful things do happen in this world? When throughout Europe all one can see is the tumult of battle?

At Paris the blood is not yet dry on the swords of Frenchmen, Englishmen, Burgundians and Armagnacians. Ever is there killing and fire on the French sod, war is ever waged. It will last a hundred years, will it?

England foments with revolt, Gloucester quarrels with the Beauforts. Some evil will come of it, indeed, mark my words, between the houses of York and Lancaster, between the White and the Red Roses.

Cannons roar in Denmark, Eric of Pomerania clashes with the Hanseatic League, wages a vicious war with the Counts of Schleswig and Holstein. Zurich is in conflict with the cantons, threatens the unity of the Old Swiss Confederacy. Milan battles with Florence. On the streets of Naples mercenaries from Aragon and Navarre wreak havoc.

Sword and fire rage in the Grand Duchy of Moscow, Vasily clashes in virulent skirmishes with Yury, Dmitry Kosoy and Dmitry Shemyaka. *Vae victis!* The defeated weep crimson tears from their bloody eye sockets.

The valiant János Hunyady subdues the Turk. The children of Árpád have the upper hand! But the shadow of the Crescent hangs—like the Sword of Damocles—over Transylvania, over the valleys of the Drava, the Tisza and the Danube. The Magyars are doomed to suffer the same sorry fate as the Bulgarians and the Serbs.

Venice quails as Murad II slaughters Epirus and Albania with a yatagan dripping blood. The Byzantine Empire shrinks to the size of Constantinople; John VIII and his brother Constantine watch anxiously from the walls to see if Osman is heaving into view. Unite, Christians of the East and West, against your common foe! Be reconciled and unite!

But it's probably too late...

That day is a day of wrath, a day of trouble and distress, a day of wasteness and desolation, a day of darkness and gloominess, a day of clouds and thick darkness.

Dies irae...

King David prophesied it in the Psalms, the prophet Zephaniah foretold it, the pagan Sybil augured it. When you see a brother sending his brother to death, the young rising up against their parents, a wife deserting her husband and one nation waging war against another, when you see a great famine over the whole world, great pestilence and much ill, then you know that the end is nigh.

Eh? What are you saying? That what I describe occurs every day, repeatedly and again and again? And by no means only recently, but for centuries, over and over? Ha, both you, noble knight with the Abdank coat of arms, and you, honourable Brother of Saint Francis, are both right. You are also right, noble lords, as are you, pious monks, and you, gentlemen merchants, nodding your heads and making wise faces. You are right. There is evil and transgression everywhere. We see fratricide every day, treachery again and again and blood spilled endlessly. Behold, indeed, an age of betrayal, rape and violence, an age of ceaseless warring. How then, with this all around us, can we know: is it now the end of the world or is it not? How can one judge? What signs will show us, what *signa et ostenta*?

You still nod your heads, noble gentlemen, good burghers and pious brothers, I see. I know what you think, for I also have oft pondered on it.

Perhaps, I thought, it will come about without a sign? Without a larum? Without a warning? Simply: boom! And the end, *finis mundi*? Maybe there's no mercy? Perhaps there isn't one innocent person in Sodom? Perhaps, since we are a perverse tribe, we won't be given a sign?

Please, don't be afraid. We will. The Evangelists have promised. Both the legal and the apocryphal ones.

And there shall be signs in the sun, and in the moon, and in the stars; and upon the Earth distress of nations, with perplexity; the sea and the waves roaring. The powers of Heaven shall be shaken. And so shall the sun be darkened, and the moon shall not give her light, and the stars shall fall from Heaven. And his kingdom shall be divided towards the four winds of Heaven.

Movebuntur omnia fundamenta terrae: the earth and sea will tremble, and with them the mountains and hills. And the voice of the archangel will sound from the heavens and will be heard in the lowest reaches.

And for seven days there will be great signs in the heavens. And I shall tell you what they will be. Hark!

On the first day, a cloud will come from the north, and a bloody rain will fall from it all over the Earth.

While on the second day, the Earth will move out of her place; the gates of Heaven will open from the East and the smoke of a huge fire will obscure the whole sky. And on that day, there will be great fear and terror in the world.

Then on the third day, the abysses of the Earth's four corners will yawn and all the world will be filled with the foul stench of brimstone. And thus it shall be until the tenth hour.

On the fourth day, the sun's disc will be obscured and there will be a great darkness. The heavens will be tenebrous without sun or moon; the stars will stop shining. Thus shall it be until morning.

On the sixth day, the morning will be foggy…

Chapter One

In which Reynevan, trying to pick up the trail of his beloved, encounters much adversity. To be precise, he is accursed. At home and abroad, standing, sitting and doing his work. And Europe, meanwhile, is changing. Developing new forms of warfare.

The morning was foggy, and quite mild for February. There had been a hint of a thaw in the air all night; the snow began melting at dawn, and the prints of iron-shod hooves and the ruts made by wagon wheels filled at once with black water. Axles and swingletrees creaked, horses snorted and wagoners cursed drowsily. The column of almost three hundred wagons made slow progress. The pungent, choking smell of salt herrings hung over the column. Sir John Fastolf rocked sleepily in the saddle.

A thaw had suddenly set in after a few days of frost, and the wet snow that had been falling all night quickly melted. Water dripped from the snow lying heavily on spruce trees.

"Haaave at theeem! Kill them!"

"Haaaa!"

The noise of the sudden battle frightened some rooks. The birds flew up from leafless branches, the leaden February sky became flecked with a shifting black mosaic and the chilly, damp air was filled with cawing. The clang and thud of iron. And yells.

The fighting was short-lived but fierce. Hooves ploughed up the slush, mixing it with mud. Horses whinnied and squealed shrilly. Men uttered cries, some warlike and others of pain. It began suddenly and was soon over.

"Huzza! Cut them oooff! Cut them ooooff!"

Then again, more quietly, further off, the echo bounced around the forest.

"Huzza! Huzzaaa!"

The rooks cawed, circling above the trees. The thudding of hooves receded. The shouts died away.

Blood stained the puddles, soaked into the snow.

The wounded esquire heard the rider approaching, alerted by the snorting of a horse and the jangling of a bridle. He groaned, tried to stand up but fell back. His efforts intensified the bleeding, the crimson stream pulsating more strongly between the plates of his cuirass and flowing down the armour. The wounded man settled back harder against a fallen tree trunk and drew a dagger. Aware how feeble a weapon it was in the hand of a man who couldn't stand, whose side had been pierced by a spear and whose ankle was twisted after falling from his horse.

The approaching bay colt was a pacing horse, its unusual gait immediately visible. The bay's rider didn't have the sign of the Chalice on his chest, so wasn't one of the Hussites the esquire's troop had just been fighting. He wasn't wearing armour. Or carrying a weapon. He looked like an ordinary traveller. The wounded esquire knew only too well, though, that in the month of February *Anno Domini* 1429, no one was simply travelling in the Strzegom hills or the Jawor plain.

The rider examined him at length from the height of his saddle. At length and wordlessly.

"That bleeding needs staunching," he finally said. "I can do it, but only if you toss that dagger aside. If you don't, I'll ride off and you can cope by yourself. Decide."

"No one..." the esquire grunted. "No one will pay a ransom for me...So don't say I didn't warn you—"

"Will you toss the dagger aside or not?"

The esquire swore softly, took a big swing and flung the dagger away. The rider dismounted, unfastened his saddlebags, then knelt down beside him, holding a leather bag. He used a short folding knife to cut through the straps attaching the two parts of the breastplate to the cuirass. After removing the armour, he slashed open the blood-soaked gambeson and looked intently, bending low over the wound.

"Nasty..." he muttered. "Looks very nasty. *Vulnus punctum*, a stab wound. It's deep...I'll put on a dressing, but can do no more without help. I'll carry you to Strzegom."

"Strzegom...besieged...Hussites..."

"I know. Don't move."

"I think..." The esquire panted. "I think I know you."

"Well, I never, your face looks familiar to me, too."

"I am Wilkosz Lindenau...The esquire of Lord Borschnitz, may God rest his soul...The tournament in Ziębice...I escorted you to the tower...For you are...For you are Reinmar of Bielawa...Aren't you?"

"Aha."

"Why, it's you," said the esquire, his eyes opening wide in terror. "Christ. It *is* you."

"Accursed at home and excommunicated abroad? Indeed. It's going to hurt now."

The esquire clenched his teeth hard. Just in time.

Reynevan led his horse. Hunched over in the saddle, Wilkosz Lindenau groaned and moaned.

Beyond the hill and forest was a road, and beside it, not far away, some blackened ruins, the remains of demolished buildings that Reynevan could just about recognise as the former Carmelite monastery of the Order of Beatissimae Virginis Mariae de Monte Carmeli, which had once served as a house of correction, a place of isolation and punishment for sinful priests. And beyond it was Strzegom. Currently under siege.

The army besieging Strzegom was large; at first glance, Reynevan estimated it to be a good five or six thousand men, thus confirming the rumours that the Orphans had gained reinforcements from Moravia. The previous December, Jan Královec had led a plundering raid on Silesia with a force of almost four thousand soldiers and a proportional number of war wagons and artillery. There were a good five hundred wagons at Strzegom and as far as the artillery was concerned, it was time to put on a show. Around ten bombards and mortars roared, shrouding the artillery positions and approaches in smoke. Stone balls whistled towards the town, slamming into the walls and buildings. Reynevan knew what the targets were from the missile strikes: the Dziobowa Tower and the tower over the Świdnica Gate—the main bastions on the southern and eastern sides—along with the magnificent town houses in the town square and the parish church. Jan Královec of Hrádek was a seasoned commander and knew whom to torment and whose property to destroy. How long a city defended itself usually depended on the morale of the Patriciate and the clergy.

In principle, one might have expected a storming after the salvo, but there was nothing to suggest it.

The duty detachments were firing crossbows, hook guns and trestle guns from behind earthworks, but the remaining Orphans were lazing about around campfires and the cauldrons in the camp kitchens. Nor was there any heightened activity in the vicinity of the senior officers' tents, over which standards with the Chalice and the Pelican were waving listlessly.

Reynevan was leading his horse towards the headquarters. The Orphans he passed showed little interest in them; no one stopped them, no one shouted a challenge or asked who they were. The Orphans might have recognised Reynevan; many knew him, after all. They might just have been uninterested.

"They'll slit my throat..." muttered Lindenau from the saddle. "They'll slash me to ribbons...Heretics...Hussites...Devils."

"They won't touch you," said Reynevan, trying to convince himself as a patrol armed with bear spears and gisarmes approached them. "But to be on the safe side, say 'Czechs.' Greetings, Brothers! I am Reinmar Bielawa—do you know me? We need a physician! A medic! Call a physician please!"

The moment Reynevan entered the headquarters, Brázda of Klinštejn hugged and kissed him, after which Jan Kolda of Žampach, the brothers Matěj and Jan Salava of Lípa, Vilém Jeník and others he didn't know began to shake his hand and slap him on the back. Jan Královec of Hrádek, Hejtman of the Orphans and leader of the expedition, gave no lavish display of emotion. And didn't look surprised, either.

"Reynevan," he said, greeting him quite coolly. "Well, I never. Welcome, O prodigal son. I knew you'd return to us."

"It's time we finished it," said Jan Královec of Hrádek.

He was showing Reynevan around the lines and positions. They were alone. Královec wanted them to be alone. He wasn't certain who had sent Reynevan and with what information and was expecting confidential messages intended for his ears only. Having learned that Reynevan was nobody's envoy and was bringing no messages, his face darkened.

"It's time we finished it," he repeated, climbing up onto an earthwork and measuring with a hand the temperature of a bombard's barrel, which was being cooled with untreated animal hides soaked in water.

He glanced up at the walls and towers of Strzegom. Reynevan was still looking back at what was left of the Carmelite monastery. The place, where—an absolute eternity ago—he had first met Scharley. *An absolute eternity*, he thought. *Four years.*

"Time we finished it." Královec's voice shook him out of his reverie and recollections. "It's high time. We've done our job. December and January were enough for us to capture and sack Duszniki, Bystrzyca, Ziębice, Strzelin, Niemcza, the Cistercian abbey and monastery in Henryków, plus innumerable small towns and villages. We taught the Germans a lesson, they won't forget us. But Shrovetide is past, it is Ash Wednesday, the ninth day of February. We've been warring for well over two months and during winter months at that! We must have marched a good forty miles. We are hauling behind us wagons heavy with spoils, driving herds of cattle. And morale is falling, the men are weary. Świdnica, outside which we were encamped for five whole days, repelled us. I'll tell you the truth, Reynevan: we didn't have the force to storm it. We fired cannons, hurled fire onto the rooftops and spread terror, thinking the people of Świdnica would surrender or at least wish to parley, pay a ransom. But Lord Kolditz was undaunted and we had to leave there empty-handed. Strzegom has clearly taken heart, for it also holds out valiantly. And once again we intimidate, sow terror, fire cannons and chase around the forests with Wrocław patrols trying to beset us. But I'll be frank: we'll have to leave here empty-handed, too. And go home. For it is time. What do you think?"

"I don't think anything. You're in command here."

"I am, I am," said the hejtman, spinning around on his heel. "In command of an army whose morale is failing fast. But you, Reynevan, shrug and think nothing. And what do you do? You save a stricken German. A papist. You bring him here, ordering our medic to treat him. You show a foe mercy. Before everybody's eyes? You should have slit his throat in the bloody forest."

"You cannot be serious."

"I swore…" Královec snarled through his teeth. "That after Oława…After Oława, I vowed I would show mercy to none of them. None."

"We can't stop being people."

"People?" said the Hejtman of the Orphans, almost frothing at the mouth. "People? Do you know what happened in Oława? On Saint Anthony's Eve? If you'd been there, you'd have seen it."

"I was, and I did." Observing unemotionally the hejtman's astonished expression, Reynevan repeated: "I was in Oława. I ended up there a few days after Epiphany, soon after you left. I was in the town on the Sunday before Saint Anthony's. And I saw it all. I also witnessed the triumph that Wrocław celebrated because of Oława."

Královec said nothing for a moment, gazing from the earthwork at the bell tower of Strzegom parish church, where the bell had begun to toll, resonantly and sonorously.

"Why, you weren't only in Oława, but also in Wrocław." He stated the fact. "And now you've come here, to Strzegom. Like a bolt from the blue. You come and go. How and from where—no one knows. People have begun to talk, to gossip. To suspect."

"Suspect what?"

"Easy, easy, don't take umbrage. I trust you. I know you had important matters to deal with. When you bade us farewell on the battlefield at Wielisław on the twenty-seventh of December, we saw that you were hastening to attend to some important— extremely important—matters. How did you fare?"

"I solved nothing," said Reynevan, without concealing his bitterness. "But I am cursed. Cursed standing, working and sitting. In the hills and the vales."

"How so?"

"It's a long story."

"I adore long stories."

The fact that something uncommon would happen that day in Wrocław Cathedral was communicated to the congregation gathered within by the excited murmurings of the people standing closer to the transept and the chancel. The latter could see and hear more than the rest, who were crammed tightly into the nave and the aisles. Initially, they had to settle for guesses. And rumours borne in a swelling, repeating whisper that spread through the crowd like the rustle of leaves in the wind.

The great bell of Ostrów Tumski began to toll, hollowly and slowly, ominously and grimly, and also intermittently, since it could clearly be heard that the clapper was striking only one side of the bronze bell. Elencza of Stietencron grasped Reynevan's hand and squeezed it hard. Reynevan squeezed back.

Exaudi Deus orationem meam cum deprecor
a timore inimici eripe animam meam…

The portal leading to the vestry was graced by reliefs portraying the martyr's death of Saint John the Baptist, the cathedral's patron. A dozen prelates, members of the chapter, were emerging from the portal, singing. Attired in ceremonial surplices, grasping fat candles, the prelates paused before the main altar, facing the nave.

Protexisti me a conventu malignantium
a multitudine operantium iniquitatem
quia exacuerunt ut gladium linguas suas
intenderunt arcum rem amaram
ut sagittent in occultis immaculatum…

The murmur of the crowd suddenly grew in intensity. For on the steps of the altar had appeared in person Konrad, Bishop of Wrocław, a Piast from the line of the Oleśnica dukes. The highest-ranking ecclesiastical dignitary in Silesia, the representative of His Majesty Sigismund of Luxembourg, King of Hungary and Bohemia.

The bishop was in full pontifical regalia. Bearing a mitre decorated with gemstones, a dalmatic worn over a tunicle, a pectoral cross on his chest and a crosier coiled like a pretzel in his hand, he looked distinguished indeed. He was veiled in an aura of such dignity that you'd have thought it wasn't just any old Wrocław bishop descending the steps of the altar, but an archbishop, an elector, a metropolitan bishop, a cardinal—why, even the Roman Pope himself. Perhaps a man even more dignified and more pious than the incumbent Roman Pope. Considerably more dignified and pious. Plenty of the people gathered in the cathedral were of that opinion. As indeed was the bishop himself.

"Brothers and sisters." His booming, resonant voice, which seemed to rumble right up to the top of the high vault, electrified and hushed the crowd. The cathedral bell tolled once again and fell silent.

"Brothers and sisters!" said the bishop, leaning on his crosier. "Good Christians! Our Lord, Jesus Christ, teaches us to forgive the wayward their sins, teaches us to pray for our enemies. It is a good and merciful teaching, a Christian teaching, but it does not pertain to every sinner. There are transgressions and sins for which there is no forgiveness, no mercy. Every sin and blasphemy will be forgiven, but blasphemy against the Spirit will not be forgiven. *Neque in hoc saeculo, neque in futuro*, neither in this age, nor the next."

A deacon handed him a lit candle. The bishop extended a besleeved hand and took it.

"Reinmar Bielawa, son of Tomasz of Bielau, has sinned against the One God in the Trinity. He has committed the sins of blasphemy, sacrilege, witchcraft, apostasy. And also, when all's said and done, a common crime."

Elencza, still squeezing Reynevan's hand hard, sighed deeply and looked up at his face. And sighed again, this time more softly. Reynevan's face betrayed no emotion. It was expressionless, as though carved from stone. *His face was like it was in Oława*, thought Elencza in horror. *In Oława, on the night of the sixteenth of January.*

"The Bible speaks thus about men like Reinmar of Bielawa," said the bishop, his voice again echoing among the cathedral's columns and arcades. "If they flee from the decay of the world by knowing the Lord and Saviour, but later, yielding to it again, shall be vanquished, their end is worse than their beginnings. For it would be better for them not to know the way of justice than, having discovered it, turn away from the Holy Commandment given unto them. What is written has been fulfilled with them: the cur returns to what it has vomited up, and the swine once washed…to a muddy puddle.

"To its own puke," said Konrad of Oleśnica, raising his voice yet louder, "and to a muddy puddle has returned the apostate and heretic Reinmar of Bielawa, robber, sorcerer, violator of virgins, blasphemer, defiler of sacred places, sodomite and fratricide, perpetrator of numerous crimes; a scoundrel, who *ultimus diebus Decembris* treacherously murdered the good and upstanding

Duke Jan, Lord of Ziębice, with a knife in the back.

"Therefore, in the name of God Almighty, in the name of the Father, the Son and the Holy Spirit, in the name of all the Lord's Saints, by the power invested in us, we excommunicate the apostate Reinmar of Bielawa from the confraternity of the Body and Blood of our Lord. We sever the bond cleaving him to the bosom of the Holy Church and drive him from the congregation of the faithful!"

Nothing could be heard but panting and gasps in the silence that descended in the naves. A stifled cough. A hiccup.

"*Anathema sit!* Excommunicated is Reinmar of Bielawa! May he be cursed in his house and garden, cursed in living and dying, standing, sitting, working and walking, cursed in the town, in the hamlet and on the soil, in the fields, in the woods, in the meads and the pastures, in the hills and in the vales. May incurable ailments, pestilence, Egyptian boils, haemorrhoids, scabies and scabs fall on his eyes, throat, tongue, mouth, neck, chest, lungs, ears, nostrils, arms and testicles; on every bodily member from the top of his head to his feet. May his house, his table and his bed be cursed, his horse and his dog. May his food and beverages be cursed, and everything he doth possess."

Elencza felt a tear rolling down her cheek.

"We declare Reinmar Bielawa to be set about with perpetual anathema, to be flung into the abyss with Lucifer and his fallen angels. We number him among the threefold accursed with no hope for purgation. May *lux*, his light, for ever, for ever amen, be put out, as a sign that this excommunicate be put out of the memory of the Church and of the people. May it come to pass!"

"*Fiat! Fiat! Fiat!*" uttered the white-surpliced prelates in mournful voices.

Holding the candle away from himself with his arm outstretched, the bishop quickly turned it so that the flame was facing downwards and then released it. The prelates followed suit; the clatter of candles cast onto the floor combined with the smell of hot wax and soot from the wicks. The great bell tolled. Three times. And fell silent. The echo lingered for a long while until it faded into silence, high up under the vault.

There was an intense smell of wax and soot, and of steaming, damp, unwashed clothing. There was a cough; there was a hiccup. Elencza swallowed back tears.

The bell in the nearby Church of Saint Mary Magdalene announced the Nones with a double *pulsatio*. A moment after, it was followed by the bell of Saint Elizabeth's, only slightly late. Outside the window of Canon Otto Beess's chamber, Shoemakers Street resounded with a hubbub and the rattle of wheels. Otto Beess tore his eyes away from a painting depicting the martyrdom of Saint Bartholomew, the only decoration on the severe walls save for a shelf with candlesticks and a crucifix.

"You're taking a great risk, my lad," he said. Those were the first words he had uttered after opening the door and seeing who was standing there. "You're taking a great risk, showing up in Wrocław. I wouldn't even call it a risk. It's brazen lunacy."

"Believe me, Reverend Father," said Reynevan, lowering his eyes, "I wouldn't come here without good cause—"

"Which I can guess at."

"Father—"

Otto Beess slammed his hand down on the table and ordered him silent by swiftly raising the other. And said nothing for a long time.

"Just between you and me," he finally said, "the individual whom—owing to me—you rescued from the Strzegom Carmelite monastery four years ago, following Peterlin's murder… What did he ask you to call him?"

"Scharley."

"Scharley, ah. Are you in touch with him?"

"Not lately. But generally speaking, yes."

"Then should you meet that…that Scharley, tell him I have a bone to pick with him. He let me down sorely. The good sense and cunning he was famed for have gone to hell. Rather than taking you to Hungary, as he was meant to, he took you to Bohemia and dragged you into the Hussites."

"He did not. I joined the Utraquists myself. According to my own will and choice, preceded by a lengthy consideration of the matter. And I am certain that I acted correctly. The truth is with us. I believe."

The canon silenced him again with a raised hand. He didn't care what Reynevan believed. The expression on his face left no doubts in that regard.

"As I said, I can guess what brought you to Wrocław," he finally said, looking up. "I guessed it easily; the reasons are common knowledge. No one talks about anything else. For the last two months, your new fellow believers and brothers in faith, your confraters in the fight for the truth, your comrades and companions in the Chalice, have been laying waste to the Kłodzko lands and Silesia. For two months, your brothers—Královec's Orphans—have been murdering, burning and looting in the name of faith and truth. They have sent Ziębice, Strzelin, Oława and Niemcza up in smoke, pillaged the monastery in Henryków and plundered and ransacked half of the Nadodrze. Now, word has it, they are besieging Świdnica. Then all of a sudden you appear in Wrocław."

"Father—"

"Silence. Look me in the eyes. If you come here as a Hussite spy, a saboteur or an emissary, then leave my house immediately. Go to ground somewhere else. But not beneath my roof."

"Your words have cut me to the quick, Reverend Father," said Reynevan, meeting his gaze. "As has the suspicion that I would be capable of a base act like that. The thought that I would put you in harm's way."

"You did so by coming here. The house might be under observation."

"I was cautious. I'm able to—"

"I know." The canon cut him off bluntly. "And I know what you're capable of. Rumours travel around quickly. Look me in the eyes and tell me straight: are you here as a spy or not?"

"I am not."

"So why *are* you here, then?"

"I need help."

Otto Beess raised his head and looked at the wall, at the painting depicting pagans flaying Saint Bartholomew with huge pliers. Then he fixed his gaze on Reynevan's eyes once more.

"Oh, you do," he said gravely. "You do indeed. And more than you think. Not only in this world, but in the next one, too. You've overstepped the mark, my son. Overstepped the mark. You have grown so zealous alongside your new comrades and brothers in the new faith that you have become notorious. In particular since last December, after the Battle of Wielisław. It ended the way it had to end. Now, if I may advise you: pray, be contrite and do penance. Don sackcloth and sprinkle ashes on your head, copiously. Or you'll have no fucking chance of salvation. Do you know of what I speak?"

"I do. I was there."

"You were? In the cathedral?"

"Indeed."

The canon was silent for a time, drumming his fingers on the table.

"You've been to many places," he finally said. "Far too many,

I'm afraid. In your shoes I would curb myself. Returning *ad rem*: since the twenty-third of January, since Septuagesima Sunday, you are cast out of the Church. I know, I know what you'll say to that, O Hussite. That our Church is evil and apostatic, while yours is virtuous and true. And that you care not for anathema. By all means care not, as you will. For this is neither the time nor the place for theological debates. You didn't come here, I presume, to seek help in the matter of salvation. You think more about secular and commonplace matters, more about the *profanum* than the *sacrum*. So, speak. Tell me. Confide your woes in me. And since I must to Ostrów Tumski before Vespers, be succinct in the telling. As far as you are able."

Reynevan sighed. And told him. Succinctly. As far as he was able. The canon heard him out. After which he sighed. Heavily.

"Oh, my boy, my boy," he said, shaking his head. "You're becoming bloody repetitious. All your problems are of the same ilk. Every difficulty of yours—to express it eruditely—is *feminini generis*."

The earth shook under the stamping of hooves. The herd galloped across the field; gleaming flanks and rumps flashed past in a kaleidoscope of bay, black, grey, dun, dapple-grey and chestnut. Tails and thick manes flowed, steam belched from nostrils. Dzierżka of Wirsing braced herself against the pommel of her saddle with both hands, joy and delight in her eyes, as though she wasn't a horse trader admiring her colts and mares, but a mother, her children.

"It appears, Reynevan," she said, finally turning around, "that all your worries boil down to the same thing. Every vexation of yours, it appears, wears a frock and has a plait."

She spurred her grey to a trot and followed the herd. He hurried after her. His mount, a magnificent bay stallion, was a pacing horse and Reynevan still wasn't entirely accustomed to the unusual rhythm of its gait. Dzierżka waited for him to catch up.

"I can't help you," she said firmly. "The only thing I can do is to give you the colt you're sitting on. Along with my blessing. And a medal of Saint Eligius, the patron saint of horses, pinned to its bridle. He is a fine steed. Strong and robust. He will serve you well. Take him from me as a gift. In gratitude for Elencza. For what you did for her."

"I only repaid a debt, for what she once did for me. And I thank you for the horse."

"Apart from the horse, I can only help by giving you advice. Return to Wrocław and pay Canon Otto Beess a visit. Or perhaps you already have? While you were in Wrocław with Elencza?"

"Canon Otto is out of favour with the bishop. It appears I am to blame. It may still rankle him, and he may by no means be gladdened by my visits, which might bring him harm—"

"How caring you are!" Dzierżka sat upright in the saddle. "Your visits always threaten harm. Didn't you think about that as you rode to visit me here, in Skałka?"

"I did. But Elencza was my concern. I was afraid to let her go alone. I wanted to get her here safely—"

"I know. I'm not aggrieved that you came. But I can't help you. Because I'm afraid."

She pushed her sable calpac to the back of her head and wiped her face with a hand.

"They intimidated me," she said, glancing to one side. "They put the bloody wind up me. On the twenty-fifth of September, near Frankenstein, by Grochowa Mountain. Do you remember what happened then? I was absolutely terrified, I swear. Reynevan, I don't want to die. I don't want to end up like Neumarkt, Throst and Pfefferkorn, and then Ratgeb, Czajka and Poschman. Like

Cluger, burned to death in his home with his wife and children. I've stopped trading with the Czechs. I don't talk politics. I've given a large donation to Wrocław Cathedral. And another, just as large, for the bishop's crusade against the Hussites. Should the need arise, I'll give even more. I prefer that to seeing my roof on fire one night. And Black Riders in the courtyard. I want to live. Particularly now, when—"

She broke off, pensively twisting and bending the strap of the reins in her hand.

"Elencza…" She paused again, looking away. "If she wants to, she'll leave. I shan't stop her. But were she to wish to stay here, in Skałka…Stay…for a long while…I wouldn't have anything against it."

"Keep her here. Don't let her go off to work as a volunteer again. The girl has a heart and a vocation, but hospitals… Hospitals have stopped being safe of late. Keep her in Skałka, Madam Dzierżka."

"I shall try. But as far as you are concerned…"

Dzierżka reined her horse around and brought it so close she was touching stirrups with Reynevan.

"You are very welcome here, kinsman. Come whenever you wish. But, by Saint Eligius, have a little decency. Have some regard for that girl, a little heart. Don't torment her."

"I beg your pardon?"

"Don't pour your sorrows out to Elencza about your love for another." Dzierżka of Wirsing's voice took on a hard tone. "Don't confide in her about your love for another. Don't tell her what a great love it is. And don't make her pity you because of it. Don't make her suffer."

"I don't underst—"

"Oh, you do, you do."

*

23

"You're right, Father," Reynevan admitted bitterly. "Indeed, whenever there's a problem, it's of the female sex. And my problems are multiplying, springing up like mushrooms...But the greatest of them at this moment is Jutta. And I'm in a quandary. I have absolutely no idea what to do—"

"Well, that makes two of us," Canon Otto Beess declared gravely. "Because I don't know, either. I didn't interrupt your tale, though in places it resembled a troubadour's song, so many fanciful improbabilities did it contain. In particular, I cannot conceive of Inquisitor Grzegorz Hejncze abducting maids. Hejncze has his own intelligence and counter-intelligence service, a network of agents, and it is also common knowledge that for a long time he has been trying to infiltrate the Hussites and that he is unscrupulous. But kidnapping maids? Your story fails to convince me in any way. But then again, anything's possible."

"That is actually true," muttered Reynevan.

The canon bored his gaze into Reynevan's but said nothing. He drummed his fingers on the table.

"Today is Candlemas," he finally said. "The second day of February. Five weeks have passed since the Battle of Wielisław. I presume you've been in Silesia all this time. Where, exactly? Did you perhaps visit the convent in White Church?"

"I did not. At first, I meant to...The abbess is a sorceress, and magic might have helped in my hunt for Jutta. But I didn't go there. That other time...That other time I brought danger down on them, on Jutta and the nuns, on the entire convent. I almost caused their downfall. Furthermore—"

"Furthermore," said the canon, coldly ending Reynevan's sentence, "you were afraid to look the abbess in the eye so soon after having killed her brother. And you're right about the misfortune brought down on the convent, by God you are. Grellenort didn't forget. The bishop dissolved the convent, the Poor Clares were scattered around among various other nunneries and the abbess was sent away to do penance. Luckily for her. The Sisterhood of the Free Spirit, the Beguine Third Church, Catharism, magic… That usually means the stake. The bishop would have ordered her burned in a trice, without batting an eyelid. But there was no way he could have tried for heresy and witchcraft and then publicly executed the sister of Duke Jan of Ziębice, whom at the same time he was cultivating as a martyr in the fight for the faith, for whose soul he ordered Masses to be said and bells to be rung the length and breadth of Silesia. So the abbess got away with it and it ended with a penance. She was a witch, you say? It's also said that you are a wizard. That you know witchcraft, that you fraternise with mages and monsters. Why don't you seek their help?"

"I have."

The village of Grauweide hadn't been burned down. The village of Mieczniki, around half a mile away, was also untouched. It augured well, instilled one with optimism. Which only made the disappointment even greater and more painful.

Almost nothing remained of the convent village of Gdziemierz. The impression of nothingness and void was heightened by the snow covering the burned-down buildings in a thick layer, from whose blinding whiteness charred posts, beams and soot-blackened chimneys protruded here and there. Not much more survived of the Silver Bell Inn, located at the edge of the village. Where it had once stood, from under the snow peeped a chaotic pile of blistered beams, rafters and roof ridges resting on the remains of the stone walls and a pile of scorched bricks.

Reynevan rode all around the rubble and looked at the ruins which still aroused pleasant memories from a year before, the winter at the turn of 1428. His horse trod gingerly on the snow between blackened timbers and lifted its hooves high to step over charred beams.

A wisp of grey smoke rose almost perfectly vertically in the frosty air above the remains of a wall.

Hearing the snorts of the horse and the crunch of snow, a bearded vagabond kneeling by a small campfire raised his head and pushed back a little fur cap worn down over his brow. And returned to his previous activity of blowing on glowing embers he was shielding with the front of his coat. Nearby, at the foot of the wall, stood a blackened cooking pot, beside which lay some bagpipes, a sack and a chest strapped shut.

"Praise the Lord," Reynevan greeted him. "Where are you from? Gdziemierz?"

The tramp raised an eye, then resumed blowing.

"The people from here, where did they go? Do you perhaps know? The innkeeper, Marcin Prahl and his wife? Do you know, by any chance? Did you hear?"

The vagabond, judging from his reaction, either didn't know, hadn't heard or was ignoring Reynevan and his questions. Or was deaf. Reynevan rummaged in his pouch, wondering by how much he could deplete his modest resources. He caught sight of a movement out of the corner of his eye.

A child was sitting beneath the squat stump of a tree hung with icicles. A girl, ten years old at most, black-haired and as skinny as a small, gaunt crow. Her eyes—which were fixed on him—were also corvine: black and glassily unmoving. The tramp blew on the embers, muttered something, stood up, extended a hand and mumbled something else. Fire shot from the pile of brushwood with a crack. The Little Crow gave a cry of joy. It was a strange, whistling—quite inhuman—noise.

"Jon Malevolt," Reynevan said loudly, slowly and clearly, beginning to understand who was before him. "The beguiler, Jon

Malevolt. Where might I find him? I have business with him, a matter of life and death…I know him. We are companions."

The vagabond placed the pot on some stones arranged around the fire. And raised his head. He looked at Reynevan as though only then aware of his presence. His eyes were piercing. Lupine.

"Somewhere in these forests," Reynevan went on slowly, "live two…two ladies. Experts in, hmm…experts in the Arcane Knowledge. I'm a friend of those ladies, but I don't know the way. Might you show me the way?"

The tramp looked at him. Wolfishly.

"No," he finally said.

"What do you mean by 'no'? You don't know them? Or the way? Or perhaps you won't tell me?"

"No means no," said the Little Crow. From the top of the wall. Reynevan had no idea how on earth she had climbed up there—and unnoticed to boot—from under the tree where she had been sitting.

"No means no," she repeated in a whistle, pulling her head between her thin shoulders. Her dishevelled hair fell onto her cheeks.

"No means no," the tramp confirmed, adjusting his cap.

"Why?"

"Because." The tramp indicated the burned buildings with a sweeping gesture. "Because you lost your reason when committing this crime. Because fire and death lie before you, and behind you are smoking remains and corpses. Yet you dare ask a question, m'lord? Ask for directions? Ask the way? Calling yourself a comrade?"

"Calling yourself a comrade?" the Little Crow repeated like an echo.

"So what?" The tramp kept his wolfish eyes on Reynevan. "So what that you were there—one of us—on Grochowa

Mountain? That was then. Today, you—all of you—are infected with that crime and blood as though with the plague. Bring us not your illnesses here, stay well away from us. Begone, fellow. Begone."

"Begone," echoed the Little Crow. "We want you not here."

"And then what? Where did you go then?"

"Oława."

"Oława?" The canon suddenly raised his head. "Just don't tell me you were there—"

"On the Sunday before Saint Anthony's? Indeed I was."

Otto Beess said nothing for a long time. Eventually, the canon said, "That Pole, Łukasz Bożyczko, is the next puzzling matter in your tale. I've seen him at the Inquisitor's once, perhaps twice. He hung on to Gregory Hejncze's coat-tails, trotting after him like a dog. He made no impression on me. I'll just say this: he's about as much an all-powerful *eminence grise* as our Bishop Konrad is a pious, virtuous ascetic. He looked as though he'd have difficulty counting to three. And were I to try to paint nothing at all, I'd have him pose for me."

"I fear his appearance is meant to mislead," Reynevan said grimly. "I'm afraid of that with regard to Jutta."

"I can believe in semblances." Otto Beess nodded. "In recent days, several have been dispelled before my very eyes, stunning me with what I saw after their dispelling. But semblances are one thing and the Church hierarchy another. Neither that Bożyczko nor any other factotum would act on his own initiative without the Inquisitor's knowledge or permission. *Ergo*, Hejncze must have issued the order to abduct and imprison Jutta Apolda. And that I cannot by any means imagine. It doesn't accord in any way with my knowledge of the man."

"People change," said Reynevan, biting his lip. "Recently, various semblances have been dispelled in front of my eyes, too. I know that anything's possible. Anything can happen. Even that which is hard to imagine."

"God's truth," said the canon with a sigh. "Many things that have happened in recent years, I also previously simply could not have imagined. Could anyone have supposed that I, Provost of the Cathedral Chapter, instead of being promoted to prelate, to diocesan suffragan bishop, why, perhaps even to titular bishop *in partibus infidelium*, would be demoted to the rank of collegiate cantor? And all because of the nephew of my firmest companion, the late lamented Henryk of Bielawa?"

"Father—"

"Silence, silence." The canon waved a disdainful hand. "Don't apologise, you're not to blame. Even if I had predicted how it would end, I'd still have helped you. I would help you today, too, now, when for contact with you I risk consequences a hundredfold more severe than the bishop's disfavour, you bloody Hussite. But I am unable to help you. I have no power. I have no information, since power and access to information are inseparable. I have no informers. The faithful, trustworthy ones were found stabbed to death in lonely alleyways. Those that are left—including my servants—instead of inform-ing *for* me, inform *against* me. Father Felicjan, for example. Do you recall Father Felicjan, nicknamed Little Louse? It's he who slandered me before the bishop. And he continues to do so. In exchange, the bishop is helping him to work his way up the ladder, unbeknownst that that whoreson…Ah! Reynevan!"

"Yes, Reverend?"

"Something has occurred to me. Concerning Felicjan, in fact. Concerning your Jutta. There even seems a way to do it. Not the best, perhaps, but no other solution occurs to me at the moment.

But it needs time. Several days. Can you remain in Wrocław for a few days?"

"I can."

Saints Cosmo and Damian, the patrons of barber-surgeons, the former with a box of balsam, the latter with a flacon of healing elixir, were painted on the sign above the entrance to the bathhouse. The artist had spared neither paint nor gilt on the saintly twins, making the sign arresting; the vivid colours drew one's attention even at a distance. The barber-surgeon had been amply rewarded for his outlay on the sign painter: despite there being a number of bathhouses in Mill Street giving customers a choice, Cosmo and Damian's was usually full. Reynevan—whose eye had been caught by the colourful sign two days earlier after his visit to Otto Beess—had to book a visit in advance to avoid crowds.

The bathhouse was actually fairly deserted, probably owing to the early hour, and there were only three pairs of poulaines and three sets of clothing hanging up in the changing room, guarded by a grey-haired old man. The man was sickly-looking and shrunken, but he had a look even Cerberus of Tartarus wouldn't have been ashamed of, so Reynevan also left his raiment and cash in his care without fear.

"Teeth not troubling you?" asked the barber, rubbing his hands together, a hopeful smile on his face. "Shall we pull one out?"

"No, thank you," said Reynevan, shuddering slightly at the sight of pliers of various sizes adorning the wall of the barber's shop. Alongside the pliers was a no less impressive collection of scissors, knives, razors and blades.

"But we'll be letting some blood, won't we?" continued the barber hopefully. "Surely?"

"It's February," said Reynevan, looking at the barber-surgeon haughtily. During his very first visit, he had hinted that he was somewhat familiar with medicine, knowing from experience that physicians were treated better in bathhouses. "One shouldn't let blood in the winter," he added. "Furthermore, it's a new moon, which doesn't augur well, either."

"In that case…" said the barber, scratching the back of his head. "Just the shave, then?"

"I shall first bathe."

It turned out that Reynevan had the bathing room entirely at his disposal, since the other customers were availing themselves of the hot room, with its steam and birch twigs. On seeing a customer, the *Bademeister*—or bathhouse orderly—who was busy near the tub, slid aside a heavy cover made of oaken planks. Reynevan entered the vat without further ado, stretched himself blissfully and sank in up to his neck. The *Bademeister* slid the cover nearer to him in order to keep in the warmth.

"I have medical treatises for sale," said the barber-surgeon, who was still in the room. "Cheaply. Aegidius Corbolienus's *De Urinis*. Sigismund Albicus's *Regimen Sanitatis*…"

"No thank you. I'm limiting expenses for the moment."

"If that's the case… Just a shave?"

"After I've bathed. I shall call you."

The warm bath relaxed Reynevan; he grew sleepy and dozed off without knowing when. He was woken by the acrid smell of soap and the touch of a brush and foam on his cheeks. He felt the scrape of the razor, once, twice, three times. The barber standing behind him tilted his head back and shaved his neck and Adam's apple. The next, quite energetic movement of the razor snagged him painfully on the chin. Reynevan swore through his teeth.

"Did I nick you?" he heard behind him. "I beg your indulgence. *Mea culpa.* It's owing to inexperience. *Dimitte nobis debita nostra.*"

Reynevan recognised the voice. And the Polish accent.

Before he could do anything, Łukasz Bożyczko had shoved the oaken cover of the tub and slid it across the tub, pressing Reynevan against the side, squeezing his chest painfully.

"Indeed, you are just like marjoram, Reinmar of Bielawa," said the Inquisition's envoy. "You show up in every dish and course. Keep still and be patient."

Reynevan kept still and was patient. He was greatly helped in this by the heavy cover which was effectively imprisoning him in the tub. And by the sight of the razor, which Łukasz Bożyczko was still holding while he fixed Reynevan with a piercing look.

"We gave you instructions, I recall, in December at the Battle of Ziębice," said Bożyczko, folding up the razor. "We obligated you to return to the Orphans and await further orders. If we did not categorically forbid you from undertaking other activities—including investigating, searching and tracking—it was only because we presumed you to be intelligent. An intelligent man would have understood that such activities would not bear any fruit at all. And that if it was our wish for things to remain hidden, they would be and would remain thus. *In saecula saeculorum.*"

Bożycko handed Reynevan a towel which he used to wipe his burning face and damp forehead. He breathed out hard, mustering courage.

"What guarantee do I have that Jutta is even alive?" he snarled. "That you haven't hidden her at the bottom of some moat for all eternity? I'll also remind *you* of something: in December, at Ziębice, I didn't agree to or promise you anything. I didn't agree not to search for Jutta for one simple reason: I mean to. And I didn't agree to collaborate with you, for an equally simple reason: because I don't intend to."

Łukasz Bożyczko looked at him for a moment.

"You are excommunicate," he said finally, quite blithely. "A *significavit* was issued promising a reward for you, dead or alive. If you mean to trail around Silesia on a wild goose chase, you will be killed by the first person who recognises you. Most likely by the sorcerer, Birkart of Grellenort, who is still on the lookout for you. And even if you survive, consider this: you are of interest to us as a Hussite, as someone close to the commanders of the Orphans and the Tábor. As a private individual engaged in your own private matters and investigations, you mean nothing to us. We will lose interest in you. Shall quite simply strike you from our list. And then you will never see your Jutta again. So, take it or leave it: either collaborate or forget about the girl."

"You'll kill her."

"No," said Bożyczko, without taking his eyes from Reynevan. "We shan't. We'll return her to her parents, in accordance with the promise they were given. As per the agreement we struck, according to which we are temporarily holding the maid in isolation. For when the matter quietens down and the whole thing blows over, we'll give her back and let her parents do with her whatever they finally decide to do. And they have a dilemma, they have food for thought. A daughter infatuated, seduced and possessed by an excommunicate heretic, on top of that mixed up in the activities of the heretical sect of the Sisterhood of the Free Spirit...Cup-Bearer Apolda and his wife are thus hesitating between giving away their ignoble child in marriage and locking her away in a convent. By the by, they have decided that the convent should be as remote as possible, and the potential suitor live as far away as possible. For you, Reynevan, it's actually immaterial what they decide on. In both cases your chances of seeing Jutta again are meagre. And of having a liaison with her, none."

"Were I to obey you, what then? Would you return her to me, contrary to the promises given to her parents?"

"You said it. And guessed right, as it happens."

"Very well. What do you want me to do?"

"Hallelujah," said Bożyczko, raising his hands. "*Laetentur caeli*, may Heaven and Earth rejoice. Verily, the ways of the Lord are simple, the just walk boldly along them and swiftly reach their goal. Welcome to the straight and narrow, Reinmar."

"What do you want me to do?"

Łukasz Bożyczko's face grew grave. He said nothing for a while, biting and licking his lips.

"Your Bohemian friends, the Orphans," he finally said, "until the day before yesterday, until Candlemas, were outside Świdnica's walls. Having achieved nothing there, they headed for Strzegom and are besieging the town. Those destructive Myrmidons have ravaged the glorious Silesian lands quite long enough. So, first you will ride to Strzegom. You will convince Královec to end the siege and leave. Go back home, to Bohemia."

"How shall I achieve that? Using what means?"

"The same as usual." The Inquisition's envoy smiled. "After all, you are able to influence destiny and events. You are skilled at changing history, directing its course in quite new ways. You proved that not long ago, at the Battle of Stary Wielisław. You rid Silesia of a Piast and the Ziębice duchy of a Piast successor once and for all. Jan of Ziębice had no male heirs, and with his demise the duchy will fall under the direct rule of the Kingdom of Bohemia. Whether history will thank you for that remains to be seen. In a few hundred years. Ride to Strzegom."

"I shall."

"And will you ditch your insane searches?"

"Aye."

"Your investigations?"

"Aye."

"Do you know what? I don't fully believe you."

Before Reynevan could even blink an eye, Łukasz Bożyczko had seized him by the wrist and twisted his arm hard behind him. An open razor flashed in his hand. Reynevan struggled, but the oaken cover was still holding him fast and Bożyczko's grip was as hard as iron.

"I don't fully believe you," he drawled, dragging a copper basin towards himself. "So I'll let a little blood from you. In order to improve your health and character. Especially your character. I observe that you are governed by humours: by turns melancholy and cholera, and they derive from damp, from black and yellow secretions of bile. Those ill substances gather in the blood. So, I shall draw a little. Well, perhaps more than a little."

His hand sliced with the razor so fast that Reynevan almost lost sight of the movement. And almost didn't feel the pain. But he did feel the warmth of the blood dripping down his forearm, hand and fingers. And heard it dripping loudly into the basin.

"Yes, yes, I know," said Bożyczko, nodding. "It's an inauspicious time for bloodletting. It's winter, there's a new moon, the sun is in Aquarius and it's Friday, the day of Venus. Bloodletting weakens the body on days like this. But that's good, too. For I mean to weaken you a little, Reynevan. Remove a little of that energy which propels you in a thoroughly unsuitable direction. Do you feel it? You already grow weaker. And feel cold. The spirit is willing, but the flesh somewhat weak, isn't it?

"Don't struggle, don't fight me. You'll not be harmed, you're too valuable to us for me to put your health at risk and cause you needless suffering. Don't worry, I shall bind your arm when it's done. And I bind, believe me, better than I shave."

Reynevan's teeth were chattering from the growing cold sensation. The bath chamber danced in front of his eyes. Bożyczko's monotonous voice seemed to be coming from somewhere far away.

"Yes, yes, Reynevan. That's just how it is. Every action causes a reaction, every event has its effect, and every effect triggers further effects. In Domrémy, Champagne, for example, a wench named Jehanne has been hearing voices. What effects will flow from that? What effects will be caused in the long term by the ball from a French bombard that mutilated the face of the Earl of Salisbury last autumn at the Siege of Orléans? Or that after Salisbury's agonising death, the Earl of Suffolk assumed command of the army besieging Orléans? What influence on the fate of the world will Stanisław Ciołek's poems have, which he will write as the new Bishop of Poznań? Or the fact that Sigismund Korybut, released from imprisonment in Valdštejn Castle by the intercession of the Polish King, Władysław Jagiełło, will not return to Lithuania, but will remain in Bohemia? Or that Jagiełło and the Holy Roman Emperor Sigismund of Luxembourg will soon meet in Lutsk in Volyn in order to weigh up the fates of eastern Europe? What significance for history will have the fact that neither Jagiełło nor Witold can be poisoned, since their regular drinking of magical water from mysterious Samogitian springs protects them from being poisoned? Or, to use the trite example, that you, Reynevan of Bielawa, will persuade Jan Královec's Orphans to return to Bohemia?

"Everybody would like to know which events will exert an influence on history, on the fate of the world. Everybody would like to, but no one knows. I would, too, and I don't know, either. But believe me: I'm doing my bloody best to find out. Reynevan? Hey! Can you hear me?"

Reynevan couldn't. He was drowning.

In nightmares.

In recent times, nightmares hadn't been a problem for Elencza of Stietencron—and even if they had, it was a petty and trifling one. After spending the entire day treating the sick in the Oława hospice of Saint Świerad, Elencza was generally too weary to dream. Awoken and hauled from her bed *ante lucem*, before Matins, she and Dorota Faber and the other volunteers hurried to the kitchen to prepare breakfast, which soon had to be distributed among the patients. Then there were prayers in the hospital chapel, attending to the patients, then again the kitchen, then the laundry, the hospital ward again, prayers, the ward, washing the floors, the kitchen, the ward, the kitchen, the laundry, prayers. As a result, right after the evening *Ave*, Elencza would fall onto her pallet and sleep like a log, her hands clenching her feather-bed in an anxious presentiment of her early reveille. It was no wonder that such a lifestyle effectively deprived her of dreaming. Nightmares—once a problem for Elencza—stopped being one.

It was all the stranger that they had returned. From midway through Advent, Elencza once again began to dream of blood, killing and conflagrations. And of Reynevan. Reinmar of Bielawa. Elencza of Stietencron dreamed of Reynevan several times in such gruesome circumstances that she began to add him to her evening prayers. *Keep him—as well as me—in Your care*, she repeated under her breath, bowing her head before the altar, before the Pietà and Saint Świerad. *Give him—as well as me—strength and solace*, she prayed, gazing at the carved face of Our Lady of Sorrows. *Protect him—as well as me—in the night, be his shield and buckler, be our unsleeping refuge and stronghold. And let me see him at least once more*, she added even more quietly, so softly and secretly that neither the Intercessor nor the saint could accuse her of excessively secular thoughts.

The sixteenth of January, 1429, the Sunday before Saint Anthony's Day, proved to be just as busy as during the week, for there was unexpectedly much more to do. Czech Hussites—the main topic of conversation throughout December—marched to Oława at Epiphany and entered the town the following day. It occurred, contrary to the hopeless and alarmist predictions of some people, without the town being captured, without fighting or bloodshed. Ludwik, Duke of Oława and Niemcza, did exactly as he had a year earlier—he reached an agreement with the Hussites favourable to both sides. The Hussites promised not to burn or plunder the duke's estates, in exchange for which the duke gave sanctuary to wounded and crippled Czechs in Oława's two hospitals. Which immediately became full of patients. They ran out of pallets and bedclothes; mattresses and palliasses were laid on the floors. There was a great deal of work and nerves became frayed, which quickly affected everyone, even the usually calm Premonstratensian nuns and the usually calm Dorota Faber. Nervousness grew. Anxiety. Fatigue. And the overwhelming, paralysing fear of infection.

Elencza initially took the hubbub that woke her up as a dream. She jerked the edge of the feather-bed, her head tossing on the saliva-damp pillow. *That dream again, I'm dreaming about Bardo again*, she thought, balancing on the edge of slumber and wakefulness. *The capture and slaughter of Bardo, four years ago. Bells sounding the alarm, the blowing of horns, the neighing of horses, crashing, thudding, the wild cries of the soldiers, the keening of people being killed. Fire, lighting up the fish skins in the windows, a glimmering mosaic dancing on the ceiling...*

She sprang up and sat back down. Bells sounded the alarm. Screams resounded. The gleam of fire lit up windows. *It isn't a dream*, thought Elencza, *it isn't a dream. It's actually happening.*

She pushed open the shutters and the stench of burning and cold air filled the chamber. The nearby town square echoed with the shouts of a hundred throats and hundreds of torches twinkling with flickering lights. Shots could be heard from the

Wrocław Gate. Several nearby houses were already afire, a glow creeping into the sky over the New Castle. Flaming brands were coming closer. The ground appeared to be trembling.

"What's happening?" asked one of the volunteers in a trembling voice. "Is there a fire?"

The building suddenly shuddered, there was a cracking and clattering of the gate being broken down, then savage cries and gunfire. The clang of arms. The volunteers and nuns began to scream. *Please, not that*, thought Elencza. *Anything but what happened in Bardo. Don't scream, don't squeal, don't curl up in the corner with your head between your knees. Don't wet yourself from fear, like you did then. Run away. Save yourself. My God, where is Mistress Dorota?*

Once again, the cracking of a door being forced. The stamping of feet. The clanging of iron. Shouts.

"Death to the heretics! Kill them, whoever believes in God! Kill them!"

Elencza, hidden in the corner of the chamber, saw soldiers and an armed mob enter the hospice, saw the feverish eyes, the red, sweating faces, the teeth bared in a murderous frenzy. A moment later, she pressed her hands to her ears so as not to hear the grotesque wailing of the sick being slaughtered. She closed her eyes tightly so as not to see the viscous blood flowing down the stairs.

"Kill them! Slaughter them! Slaughter them!"

The mob thundered right past her, stinking of sweat and alcohol. The nuns in the dormitory screamed shrilly. Elencza rushed to the door leading to the laundry. The demented shrieks of women being killed continued to resound from the hospital. And the murderous cries of the killers. She heard the thudding of heavy boots as the darkness in the laundry was lit up by torches.

"A nun! A sister!"

"Hussite whore! Take her, boys!"

They seized her and threw her to the floor. She struggled as they shoved her between wooden tubs and smothered her, throwing a heavy, wet sheet over her head. She screamed, stifled by their stench and the odour of lye. She heard laughter as they tore and shoved aside her dress. As knees were forced between her thighs.

"I say! What's going on here? Stop that! At the double!"

Released, she pulled the sheet from her head. In the doorway to the laundry stood a monk. A Dominican. Holding a torch, he was wearing half-armour over his habit and had a short sword in his belt. The assailants lowered their heads and muttered.

"You amuse yourselves here," growled the monk, "while your comrades are fighting the enemies of the faith! Do you hear? Out there is the place for good Christians today! God's work awaits out there! Begone!"

The assailants slunk out, heads lowered, grumbling and shuffling their feet. The Dominican stuck the torch in a sconce and approached. With shaking hands Elencza tried to pull her dress down over her hips. Her eyes brimmed with tears, her lips trembled as she held back sobs. The monk leaned over, offered her his hand and helped her to her feet. Then punched her hard in the ear. The laundry danced in front of the girl's eyes; the floor slid away. She fell again and before she could come to her senses the monk was kneeling over her. She screamed, tensed and kicked out. He struck her powerfully in the face, seized the bodice of her dress and ripped the cloth with a powerful jerk.

"Heretical bitch..." he wheezed. "Time for your convers—"

He didn't finish. Reynevan hooked a forearm around his neck, pulled backwards and cut his throat.

They ran down the stairs and into the frosty night, into red-tinged darkness, which still resounded with shouts and the clangour of fighting. Elencza slipped on the icy steps and would have fallen were it not for Reynevan's helping hand. She glanced up, into his face, looking through tears, still stunned, still not quite sure if she was dreaming. Her legs bent under her, faltered. He noticed.

"We must flee," he uttered. "We must."

He seized her around her waist, pulled her into a niche in the wall, into the concealing gloom. Just in time. A half-naked and bloodied man ran past down the lane being chased by the wailing and yelling mob.

"We must flee," Reynevan repeated. "Or hide somewhere…"

"I…" she said, struggling to overcome her panting and the trembling of her mouth. "You…Save…Me—"

"I will."

They suddenly found themselves in the town square, near the pillory, amid the frantic crowd. Elencza looked up, straight into the face of Death. A scream of terror stuck in her throat. *It's just a sculpture*, she said to herself, trying to reassure herself, trembling. *Just a sculpture*. A skeleton representing Death carved in the tympanum above the western entrance to the town hall, grinning and wielding a scythe. *It's just a sculpture…*

Shots rained down from the windows of the blazing town hall. Firearms roared; bolts hissed from crossbows. *It's the less severely wounded Czechs*, recalled Elencza with astonishing lucidity. *The lightly wounded and convalescents were quartered in the town hall. They wouldn't agree to being disarmed…*

She tottered on, not knowing where they were going. Reynevan stopped her, squeezing her arm hard.

"We'll pause here," he said, panting, "and stand still. To avoid attracting attention. They're like predatory animals. They react to movement. And the smell of fear. If we don't move, they won't even notice us."

So they stood. Unmoving. Like statues. In the midst of Hell.

The town hall fell, the defence was breached, a yelling horde of attackers forced its way inside.

Amid the hellish wailing, people began to be thrown out of the windows, into the street, right in front of the waiting clubs and axes. Pike blades pinned to the wall a dozen living and half-dead people who had been dragged out. The dying were trampled underfoot and torn to pieces. Blood flowed in rivers, foaming in the gutters.

The streets were as bright as day from the fire. The town hall was aflame and the carved Death in the tympanum seemed to come alive in the flickering glow, grinning, snapping its jaws and brandishing its scythe. The houses on the town square's eastern frontage were ablaze, the shambles behind the town hall was on fire, the cloth hall was burning, an inferno was consuming the workshops of Walloon weavers and the wealthy stalls on Mary Street. Flames danced on the façade and roof of Saint Blaise's Hospital, devouring the beams, joists and roof timbers. Outside the hospital, the pile of corpses grew as more and more bodies were tossed onto it. Blood-soaked bodies. Lacerated bodies. Mutilated beyond recognition. The corpses were dragged through the town square by ropes tied around their necks and limbs. They were dragged towards the wells. The wells were already full to overflowing. Legs protruded from them. And arms. With fingers outspread, raised, as though calling for vengeance for the crime.

"Yea…" said Elencza, moving her numb lips with difficulty. "Yea, though I walk through the valley of the shadow of death… For Thou art with me."

She was still squeezing Reynevan's hand and felt his hand clenching into a fist. She glanced at his face. And swiftly looked away.

Drunk with fury and murder, the mob danced, sang, leaped and shook spears with heads stuck on their blades. They kicked heads around the street, tossed them around like balls. Laid them down as homage, as an offering before a group of horsemen standing in the town square. The horses, smelling blood, snorted, stamped and jangled their horseshoes.

"You will have to absolve me, Bishop," said one of the horsemen grimly, a long-haired man in a cloak, flashing gold and silver embroidery. "I guaranteed the Czechs safety with my ducal word of honour. I promised them sanctuary. Gave my oath."

"My dear Duke Ludwik, O my young kinsman," said Konrad, Bishop of Wrocław, raising himself up in the saddle, supporting himself on the pommel. "I shall absolve you whenever you wish. And as many times as you wish. Though you are *sine peccato* in my eyes and no doubt in God's also. An oath given to heretics carries no weight; a word given to a Hussite is not binding and does not obligate. We act here for the glory of God, *ad maiorem Dei gloriam*. Look: those good Catholics, those soldiers of Christ over there are expressing their love of God. Which manifests itself, indeed, through hatred for everything that is opposed to and despicable to God. The death of a heretic is glorious to a Christian. Christ benefits from the death of a heretic. And for the heretic himself the destruction of his body means hope for his soul.

"But don't think," he added, seeing that his words were making little impression on Ludwik of Oława, "that I feel no sorrow for them. I do. And I bless them in the hour of their death. Rest eternal grant unto them, O Lord. *Et lux perpetua luceat eis.*"

Another bloody head rolled towards the feet of the duke's horse. The horse took fright, jerked up its head and skittered. Ludwik tugged on the reins.

The mob wailed and yelled, combing houses in a search for the few remaining survivors. The cries of people being slaughtered could still be heard coming from the side streets. The fire roared. The bells tolled on and on with the groaning of bronze.

The carved Death in the town hall tympanum laughed scornfully and swung its scythe.

Elencza wept.

Reynevan completed his account. Jan Královec of Hrádek, Hejtman of the Orphans, leaning against a bombard, looked at Strzegom, black and menacing in the gloom, like a beast lurking in the forest. He looked for a long time. And then suddenly spun around.

"We're leaving this place," he spat. "That will be sufficient. We're leaving. Going home."

The morning was foggy and quite mild for the time of year. Preceded by patrols and a vanguard of light horse, flanked by a company of infantrymen bearing pavises, the column of wagons rolled on to the south, leaving Strzegom behind it. Down the Świdnica road. Via Rychbach, Frankenstein, Bardo and Kłodzko. Towards Homole. Bohemia. And home.

Axles creaked under the weight of their loads; the wheels ploughed deep ruts in the melting snow. Whips cracked, horses whinnied, oxen lowed. Wagoners swore. Flocks of black birds circled above the column.

In Strzegom the bells were rung.

It was the twelfth of February, *Anno Domini* 1429, the Saturday before the first Sunday in Lent, *sabbato proximo ante dominicam Invocavit.*

The hejtmans of the Orphans observed the march out from a roadside rise. The wind ruffled cloaks and billowed standards.

Morale was not good. Brázda of Klinštejn, nursing a cold, sneezed. Matěj Salava spat. The ever-lugubrious Piotr the Pole had become even gloomier than usual. Even the habitually cheerful Jan Kolda of Žampach was growling under his breath. Jan Královec observed a grim silence.

"I say! Look there!" Salava suddenly pointed at a rider he had seen, heading northwards across the snow-covered slope. "Who is that? Isn't it that wounded Teuton? Did you let him go free, Brother Jan?"

"I did," Královec reluctantly admitted. "Poor wretch. No one would have paid a ransom. May he go to Hell."

"Aye, I believe he will," Piotr the Pole rasped. "He's wounded. He won't make it to Wrocław alone, without help. He'll expire somewhere in a snowdrift."

"He won't be alone or without help," countered Jan Kolda, indicating another rider. "Ha! Why, if it isn't Reynevan on his pacing horse! You also let him leave, Brother?"

"I did. What, is he a captive? We talked. He was hesitant, I could see something was nagging at him. He finally told me he had to return to Wrocław. 'Go back, then,' I said. And that's that."

"Then may the good Lord preserve him and keep him," said Brázda and sneezed. "Let's ride, Brothers."

"Let's ride."

They descended the rise, galloped a short distance to catch up with the column and rode to the head.

Brázda reined his horse back to a trot and addressed Jan Kolda, who was now alongside him. "I wonder what news there is in the wide world—"

"Why does it bother you again?" said Kolda, turning to face him. "The world, the world. What does it mean to you?"

"Nothing," admitted Brázda. "I was just wondering, is all."

*

The morning was foggy, and quite mild for February. There had been the hint of a thaw in the air; the snow began melting at dawn, and the prints of iron-shod hooves and the ruts made by wagon wheels filled at once with black water. Axles and swingletrees creaked, horses snorted and wagoners cursed drowsily. The column of almost three hundred wagons made slow progress. The pungent, choking smell of salt herrings hung over the column.

Sir John Fastolf rocked sleepily in the saddle. The excited voice of Thomas Blackbourne—a knight from Kent—jerked him out of his slumber.

"What is it?"

"De Lacy returns!"

Reginald de Lacy, the commander of the vanguard, came to a sliding stop in front of him, so abruptly that they had to narrow their eyes against the spraying mud. Terror was painted on the face of the knight, whose chin and cheeks were covered in a fair, youthful fuzz. Terror combined with excitement.

"Frenchmen, Sir John!" he crowed, fighting to bring his steed under control. "Ahead of us! To the east and west of us! In an ambuscade! A great host!"

We're finished, thought Sir John Fastolf. *I'm finished. I'm doomed. And it was close, it was so close. We almost succeeded. We would've succeeded, had it not been for…*

We would've succeeded, thought Thomas Blackbourne. *We would have succeeded, John Fastolf, had you not got blind drunk in every roadside tavern, you despicable old sot. Had you not indulged yourself in every local brothel, you lecherous old hog. Were it not for that, the Frogs wouldn't have found out about us, and we'd have been among our fellows long ago. But now we're doomed.*

"How many…" Sir John Fastolf cleared his throat. "How many

of them are there? And who is it? Did you see their banners?"

"There'll be..." Reginald de Lacy stammered, ashamed for fleeing without having closely examined the French pennants. "At least two thousand. From Orléans, so it's surely the Bastard...Or La Hire—"

Blackbourne swore. Sir John sighed furtively. He glanced at his own men. At his five-score heavy horse. Five-score foot. At the four hundred Welsh bowmen. Wagoners and camp followers. And three hundred wagons. Three hundred stinking wagons, full of stinking barrels of stinking salt herring, bought in Paris and earmarked for Lenten provisions for the eight-thousand-strong army of the Earl of Suffolk besieging Orléans.

Herring, thought Sir John resignedly. *I'll depart this life thanks to herrings. I'll die in a pile of herrings. I'll have a grave of herrings and a gravestone of herrings. By God! All London will split their sides laughing.*

Three hundred wagons of herring. Three hundred wagons. Wagons.

"Unhitch the horses!" Sir John Fastolf bellowed like an ox, standing up in his stirrups. "Form a square of the wagons! Fasten the shafts to the wheels! Hand out bows to every man!"

He has lost his mind, thought Thomas Blackbourne. *Or not yet sobered up.* But he hurried to carry out the orders.

We'll soon find out how much truth there is in it, thought Sir John, looking at his men bustling around and the barricade created from the wagons. *In what they tell of Bohemians, about those Hussites from eastern Europe or Asia Minor or somewhere... About their victories, about the crushing defeats they have meted out to Saxons and Bavarians...About their famous leader, called... Damn it, what was it? Shishka?*

It was the twelfth of February *Anno Domini* 1429, the Saturday before the first Sunday in Lent. The sun shone brightly, burning off the low, creeping fog. He had the impression the herrings had started to smell even stronger. The thudding of hooves could be heard from the town of Rouvray to the east, growing louder.

"Bows in hand!" yelled Thomas Blackbourne, drawing his sword. "They're coming!"

Neither Blackbourne nor Sir John Fastolf had any idea they were still alive by an accident. That only a stroke of luck had saved them. That were it not for that stroke of luck they wouldn't have seen the dawn. Count Jean of Dunois, the Bastard of Orléans, had learned about the transport of herring a few days before. His thousand and a half horse from Orléans, along with La Hire, Xantrailles and the Scot John Stuart were waiting in an ambuscade at Rouvray, in order to attack the English column just before dawn and rout it. But, although he had been strongly advised against it, Dunois had based his plan on Count Clermont, who was encamped at Rouvray. Count Clermont was meant to strike first. Count Clermont was a comely young man, as fair as a maid. Who always surrounded himself with other fair young men. He had no warcraft. But he was Charles VII's cousin and therefore had to be taken into account.

Boy Clermont, as La Hire called him, naturally failed miserably. He missed the moment, squandering the element of surprise. He didn't give the order to attack, for he had been busy. Breaking his fast. After breakfast, his hair had been pomaded and curled. During this procedure, the count smiled at one of the young men in his retinue, blowing him kisses and fluttering his eyelashes. The count ignored the envoys sent by Dunois. And forgot about the English. He had more important affairs and plans.

In the confusion and bedlam, when it became clear that the moment was lost, that the English would not be taken by surprise, as Dunois swore, as La Hire and Xantrailles stood idly by waiting helplessly for their orders, John Stuart had been unable to contain himself. Along with the Scottish knighthood, he assailed the English wagons on his own initiative. Some of the impatient French charged into battle after them.

"Take aim!" yelled Dickon Wilby, the commander of the archers, seeing the armoured wedge hurtling towards them. "Take aim! Remember Agincourt!"

The archers grunted as they bent their longbows. Bowstrings creaked as they were tautened. Sir John Fastolf removed his helmet, his crest of flaming red hair gleaming like a pennant.

"Now!" he bellowed like an aurochs. "Fuck them good, lads! Fuck the buggers!"

Three salvos, three showers of arrows were all it took to send the Scots fleeing in confusion. Some managed to gallop up to the wagons, only to meet their deaths there. Javelins and gisarmes stabbed them, halberds and Lochaber axes cut them to pieces. The screams of dying men rose up into the winter sky.

De Lacy and Blackbourne, though they knew little about the Hussites and even less about their combat tactics, saw at once what had to be done. They rode out at the head of their hundred heavy horse to counter-attack and give chase. The Scots were ridden down and massacred, their dying cries echoing over the plain. On the wagons, the Welsh yelled triumphantly, cursed and stuck two fingers up as the Scots fled.

The herrings went on stinking.

Thank you, m'Lord, said Sir John Fastolf, raising his eyes heavenwards. *Thank you, wagons. Praise to you, doughty Asian Bohemians, praise to you, leader Shishka, and though your name be pagan, your warcraft is great. I'll be damned, glory to me, Sir John Fastolf, too. Pity that Bardolph and Pistol couldn't see it, witness the day of my glorious victory. Why, this battle, fought at Rouvray on the Saturday before the first Sunday in Lent,* Anno Domini *1429, will go down in history as the Battle of the Herrings. And as for me…*

Plays will be written about me for the theatre.

Chapter Two

In which Reynevan schemes in the city of Wrocław. Owing to deficits in both the theory and practice of scheming, his early successes get him into trouble—serious trouble.

Father Felicjan, once known to the world as Hanys Gwisdek and nicknamed Little Louse, currently the altarist at two Wrocław churches, would visit the Walloon settlement by the Church of Saint Maurice quite regularly; more or less once a month, usually on a Tuesday. There were several reasons. Firstly, the Walloons were known to practice fell black magic and anyone hanging around in the vicinity of their homesteads could lay himself open to its effects. For strangers, in particular anyone who came uninvited or with a hostile inclination, *vicus sancti Mauritii* was dangerous and intruders could expect consequences—one of which was to disappear without trace. Thus intruders—including agents and informers—tended not to haunt the Walloon settlement or spy in it. And that suited Father Felicjan perfectly.

The other two reasons that the twice-over altarist spent time among the Walloons were also linked to magic. And to each other. Father Felicjan suffered from piles. The complaint manifested itself not only in bloody stools and an unbearable burning sensation in the arse, but also a significant decline in male potency. The Walloons—or to be precise the Walloon prostitutes at the brothel called the Red Mill—had a magical remedy for Father Felicjan's complaint. Fumigated with magical Walloon incense, treated with an enema of magical Walloon balsams and a magical Walloon poultice, Father Felicjan could achieve—put simply and bluntly—a stiffness that just about permitted copulation. The harlots from Wrocław brothels had no intention of taking similar pains and would drive the priest away, mocking him and showing no interest at all in his suffering and worry. So Father Felicjan had to go further afield. Out of town, to the Walloon girls.

A serious impediment to his outings to Saint Maurice's was the fact that he had to leave the city walls, secretly to boot, which meant after dusk and after the *ignitegium*. Father Felicjan knew how to leave and return in secret; the problem was the three furlongs he had to cover after that. Among the cutpurses who prowled around at night outside the city walls were some who weren't afraid of the Walloons' evil reputation or the rumours of their dangerous spells. So, on his regular visits to the Red Mill Father Felicjan donned a mail shirt, belted on a short sword and carried a loaded hand cannon, and as he walked he lovingly cradled and shielded with his coat the smouldering fuse and at the same time prayed aloud in Latin—which, incidentally, he couldn't speak. Father Felicjan ascribed the fact that he never met any misfortune to his prayers. And he was right to. The boldest robbers—fearing neither the law nor God—took to their heels at the sight of the hooded oddity as he approached, clinking iron, emanating a devilish glow from under his cloak—and, to make matters worse, mumbling some sort of incoherent gobbledygook.

This time, having left the Red Mill and the Walloon *vicus*, Father Felicjan was trudging beside wattle fences at around midnight, muttering a litany and occasionally blowing on the fuse to keep it alight. The moon was full and the meadows still white with snow, so it was bright enough for Father Felicjan to walk quite swiftly, without having to worry about tripping over a pothole or falling into a cesspool, which had happened to him the previous autumn. The risk of bumping into robbers or other rogues was also diminishing, since on moonlit nights they usually abandoned their custom. Thus, Father Felicjan was striding more and more swiftly and boldly, and rather than pray, began to hum the tune of quite a secular song.

The loud barking of dogs announced his proximity to the mills and the millers' homestead on the Oława, which meant that it was only five-score paces to the bridge leading straight to the city. He passed along the causeway between the millponds and fishponds. He slowed his pace, for it was much darker among the sheds and barns, but he could already see the river shimmering in the moonlight. He sighed with relief. But speeded up, nonetheless.

The thicket rustled and a shade, an elusive shape, loomed in the shadows by the barn. Father Felicjan's heart leaped and constricted his throat. In spite of that, the altarist put the hand cannon under his arm and brought the glowing fuse to the pan. However, the darkness and his lack of experience meant that he brought it against his own thumb.

He howled like a wolf, hopped like a hare and dropped the firearm. He didn't manage to draw the short sword. He was struck on the head and tumbled into a snowdrift. While he was being tied up and dragged over the snow he was stunned and lay limp, but quite conscious. He only fainted a moment later. From fear.

In recent times, Reynevan had no reason to complain about a surfeit of good luck or fortunate incidents. Fate had by no means treated him kindly in this regard. Quite the contrary. Since the previous December, Reynevan had decidedly more cause to be worried and gloomy than joyful and euphoric.

So, he greeted the change with even greater joy, for things had begun to improve. All of a sudden, fortune began to shine on him and events to arrange themselves in a rather pleasant sequence. Quite reasonable hope had dawned, his prospects had become somewhat radiant and both his and Jutta's future presented itself in much more vivid and pleasing colours. The dismally bare and misshapen trees by the Wrocław road seemed to be cloaked in the fresh green of foliage; the grim and snow-covered wildernesses of the meadows and wetlands outside Wrocław appeared to be carpeted in a variety of sweet-smelling blossom; and the cawing of the crows pecking the frozen earth sounded like sweet birdsong. In a word, it looked as if spring had come.

The first harbinger of that intoxicating change was Wilkosz Lindenau, the wounded Wrocław esquire who had been transported with no little difficulty to his family home. The cause of that difficulty was of course his perforated side. The wound, though dressed, was festering, the esquire was burning with fever and trembling and could not have stayed in the saddle without Reynevan's help. Were it not for the medicines and spells Reynevan employed to keep the inflammation in check and fight the infection, Wilkosz Lindenau would have had scant chance of seeing the town walls or the copper helmets of the spires of Saint Elisabeth, Saint Mary Magdalene, Saint Adalbert and the other churches towering above them and soaring into the grey February sky. Scant chance of delighting in the nearness of the Świdnica Gate which led to the city. Or of sighing with relief.

"So, we're home," said Wilkosz Lindenau, sighing with relief. "And that's thanks to you, Reynevan. Had it not been for you—"

"Don't mention it."

"On the contrary," said the esquire dryly. "I wouldn't have made it without you. I am indebted to you—"

He broke off, looking at the Church of Corpus Christi, where a bell was just sounding.

"They excommunicated you for your sins," he said. "May God pardon you them. But I am alive thanks to you, and I am indebted to you for that. So I shall repay that debt. For as you see, I cheated you a little. You and your Hussites. Had they known the truth, they wouldn't have set me free, for freedom would have cost me greatly. Lindenau is my family name; I carry it in honour of the family and of my father. But my father died when I was but a tiny babe and my mater wed again soon after. Thus, in truth the only father I have ever had is Lord Bartłomiej Eisenreich. Does that name mean anything to you?"

Reynevan nodded, since the name of one of Wrocław's wealthiest patricians indeed meant a great deal. Wilkosz Lindenau leaned over in the saddle and spat a bloody clot onto the snow.

"I wouldn't say or suggest this to a criminal, a Hussite or a foe," he continued, wiping his lips. "But indeed, you do not travel to Wrocław as a foe, for I gather that a more private and personal matter brings you here. Thus, I may repay you. I shall not take you under my roof or harbour you, for you are excommunicate… But I am able to help."

"As a matter of—"

"In order to do anything in Wrocław, you need money," the esquire interrupted. "One is nobody here without money. So, having money one can solve anything, even the knottiest problem. With God's help you, too, will cope with your problem, Brother. For you shall have money. I shall give you some. Take no offence that I repay you like a true Eisenreich. Like a merchant. For I cannot do it otherwise."

"I know," said Reynevan, smiling faintly. "For I am excommunicate."

Reynevan encountered another stroke of luck just after noon. He didn't enter the city with Lindenau, having justified fears that the Świdnica Gate, which was open towards the perilous south, was under the close watch of sentries and other municipal forces. Riding along the bank of the Oława, he reached Saint Nicholas's Gate, where he mingled with peasants making for the city with various goods and livestock to sell.

He encountered no problems at the gate, since the sentries were mainly bored and indolent and the few active ones were directing their attention to exhorting bribes in the form of hens, geese or sides of meat. Soon after the bells of Saint Nicholas's Church tolled the Sext, Reynevan had put Szczepin behind him and was walking, leading his horse by the bridle, towards the town centre, now mingled with the crowd of other passers-by and wanderers heading that way.

And barely had he passed Sausage Street than he had a slice of luck. A generous slice.

"Reynevan? Can it be you?"

The person who named him turned out to be a young man in a black cloak and black felt cap. As broad-shouldered and ruddy-faced as a farmhand and with a grin as wide as a farmhand's. Carrying two large parcels under his arms.

"Achilles…" Reynevan overcame his tight throat caused by the unexpected greeting. "Achilles Czibulka!"

"Reynevan." The young man resembling a farmhand looked around, and the smile suddenly disappeared from his ruddy face. "Reynevan of Bielawa. In Wrocław, a stone's throw from the town square. Who'd have guessed it? Let's not stand in full sight, dammit. Come to my apothecary's shop. It isn't far. Here, you can carry one. Careful!"

"What are they?"

"Jars. Jars of ointment."

The apothecary's shop was indeed nearby, located in Sausage Street just by Salt Square. The sign hanging over the entrance depicted an object resembling a knobbly carrot and the word "Mandragora" painted below it dispelled any doubts. The sign was actually none too impressive, the building small and probably rarely frequented. During the time their friendship had flourished, Achilles Czibulka had possessed neither a sign nor a shop. He had been employed by Master Zachariasz Voigt, the owner of the esteemed apothecary's shop called the Golden Apple. Now Czibulka could evidently boast his own business.

"They've excommunicated you," Achilles Czibulka stated, placing the jars on the counter. "They cursed you. In the cathedral. On Septuagesima Sunday. Three weeks ago."

Reynevan had befriended Achilles Czibulka in 1419, soon after he returned from Prague, having broken off his studies after the Defenestration and the outbreak of the revolution.

At that time, Czibulka had been an assistant at the Golden Apple—with a special role. He was the *unguentarius* or employee charged with preparing ointments. Almost everything Reynevan knew about ointments he had learned from Czibulka. Both Achilles' father and grandfather had made ointments—but in Świdnica, so Achilles was a first-generation Vratislavian. He usually described himself as "Silesian, born and bred," and did so with such haughty pride you'd have thought that the Czibulkas' progenitors were wearing animal skins and dwelling in caves on the slopes of Ślęża long before civilisation arrived in the region. Czibulka's pride in his origins was accompanied, however, by an almost insufferable contempt for any nations—above all Germans—whom he described as "incomers."

Czibulka's views had often annoyed Reynevan, but that day, though, he understood that the apothecary's chauvinism might be just what he needed.

"They excommunicated you, the damned Germans," said Achilles Czibulka angrily. "You must have heard? Why, it can't have passed you by. Folk in the city were talking about nothing else. Should you be recognised in town—"

"It wouldn't be a good thing."

"Indeed not. But don't fret, Reynevan, I'll hide you."

"You'd give sanctuary to an excommunicate?"

"I don't give a fig about German anathemas!" Achilles said crossly. "We—I mean Silesian *physici* and *pharmaceutici*—must stick together, for we are one guild and one Silesian fraternity. All for one and one for all! And all of us *contra Theutonicos*, against the Germans. I vowed that, after the swine tortured Master Voigt to death."

"Master Voigt, dead?"

"Tortured him to death, the bastards. For witchcraft and devil worship. It's risible! Why, good Sir Zachariasz had studied *The Picatrix*, *The Necronomicon*, *The Grand Grimoire* and *The Arbatel* a little, had read a smattering of Pietro di Abano, Cecco d'Ascoli and Michael Scot. But witchcraft? What did he know about witchcraft? Why, even *I* am better at it than he was! Indeed!"

Achilles Czibulka deftly juggled the three jars, tossed them up, spread his arms wide and moved his hands and fingers. The jars began to move around and spin by themselves, faster and faster, describing circles and ellipses in the air. The apothecary slowed them with movements of his hands, then brought them down to land softly on the counter.

"There you go!" he said. "Magic! Levitation, gravitation.

Reynevan, you levitate, for I saw it once when you were showing off to some girls. Every second man knows some spells, wears an amulet or drinks elixirs. Is it right to torture people for that, burn them at the stake? It is not. So they can stuff their excommunication. I'll give you sanctuary. Here, over the apothecary's shop, is a small room, you'll stay there. But just don't roam around the town, for there'll be trouble."

"It so happens," muttered Reynevan, "that I must visit a few places—"

"I advise against it—"

"I must. You don't own a talisman by any chance, do you, Achilles?"

"I own a few. What kind do you need?"

"A Pantaleon."

"Ah!" The *unguentarius* slapped his forehead. "Indeed! Ha, true enough, that's a solution. I don't have one myself, but I know where to get one. It won't come cheap. Do you have money?"

"I'm due some."

"Not today, but tomorrow?" guessed Achilles Czibulka. "Very well, I'll lend it to you and you can pay me back later. You'll have your Pantaleon. And now let's go to the Moor's Head. We'll have a bite to eat and something to drink. You can tell me about your adventures. There've been so many rumours I'm dying to find out…"

Thus, before the day was over, the fortunate Reynevan was offered in Wrocław money and a hideout—the two things a conspirator cannot operate without. He also had a comrade and an accomplice. For though Reynevan greatly abridged and censored the account of his adventures, Achilles Czibulka was so impressed that immediately after hearing it, he declared his willingness to help and his complicity in everything that Reynevan was planning.

As far as Reynevan was concerned, he harboured great hopes that his winning streak wouldn't end, for he had great need of it. He had to find Canon Otto Beess. And there were risks attached to that. Otto Beess might be being followed, and his house under observation.

I'm pinning all my hopes... thought the lucky Reynevan, blissfully and happily falling asleep in the small room above the apothecary's shop, on a creaking bed, under a musty feather-bed. *I'm pinning all my hopes on the good fortune that has lately favoured me.*

And on the Pantaleon.

When Reynevan hung the amulet around his neck and activated it, Achilles Czibulka stared goggle-eyed, his mouth fell open and he took a step back.

"Jesus, Mary," he gasped. "Urgh, vile. What that bloody thing does to a fellow...Lucky you can't see yourself."

The Pantaleon amulet, a local speciality, an indigenous product of Wrocław magic, had been created with a single purpose: to conceal the identity of the bearer. To make the bearer inconspicuous. Make him unseen and unnoticed, make the eyes of the curious slide over him, without noticing not just his appearance, but his very presence.

The amulet was named after Pantaleon of Korbiela, one of Bishop Nanker's prelates. Prelate Pantaleon was famous for having such a forgettably ordinary appearance, being so grey and so repulsively bland that hardly anyone—including the bishop—noticed him or paid him any attention.

"Apparently," observed the *unguentarius*, "it's not good to wear it for too long. Or too often—"

"I know. I shall use it in moderation, with breaks in-between. Let's go."

It was Thursday, market day, and Salt Square was heaving with people bustling around noisily. It was just as crowded in the town square, where additionally something was being done to somebody on a scaffold that greatly interested the general public. Reynevan and Czibulka didn't find out what was being done to whom, for they passed through the cloth hall, and after crossing the Poultry Market came out in Shoemakers Street, which had wooden planks laid out in it.

No yellow curtain hung in Canon Otto Beess's window. Reynevan immediately lowered his head and speeded up.

"The Fuggers' Company's new house and office," he panted over his shoulder to Czibulka, who was following him. "Do you know where it is?"

"Everybody does. In New Market."

"Let's go there. Don't look back."

The Pantaleon was working impeccably and before the clerk in the office would even pay any attention to him, Reynevan had to raise his voice and bang his fist on the counter. He then had to wait for the appearance of the official of Fuggers and Company called by the clerk. And become somewhat agitated. The waiting was worth it. But not the agitation.

In terms of posture and countenance, the Fuggers and Company official more resembled a duke than a clerk or a merchant.

"Absolutely, absolutely." He smiled benignly, having listened to the matter put before him. "His Excellency Otto Beess deigned to make a…payment before his departure. Payable to the Honourable Sir Reinmar of Hagenau. Your Lordship, as I understand, is this very Sir Reinmar?"

"I am."

"But your mien does not suggest it." The official smiled even more benignly, straightening the gold-thread-embroidered cuffs of his close-fitting velvet doublet; raiment more suitable for a duke than a merchant. "Not at all. When instructing us, Canon Beess took pains to describe Reinmar of Hagenau precisely. Your Lordship doesn't answer in any way to that description. Thus, if you wouldn't mind…"

The official calmly reached inside his doublet and drew out a translucent, bluish lens hanging from a strap. He brought it to one eye and looked Reynevan up and down. Reynevan sighed. He ought to have guessed. To every spell there was a counter-spell, to every amulet a counter-amulet. The Pantaleon had a Visiovera. A Periapt of True Seeing.

"All is clear," said the official, putting the Periapt away. "Please follow me."

In the room they entered there was a large map on the wall opposite a blazing fire in a hearth. A map of Silesia, Bohemia and Lusatia. One glance was enough for Reynevan to see what the lines and arrows and circles drawn around towns and cities signified. Świdnica and Strzegom—among others—were cir-cled in red and a line heading southwards corresponded to the route of Královec's Orphans on their way back to Bohemia. The lines connecting Bohemia to Lusatia—to Žitava, Bautzen and Zgorzelec—were also conspicuous. And one thick, curv-ing arrow whose point penetrated deeply into the Labe valley, Saxony, Thuringia and Franconia.

The Fuggers and Company official was clearly tickled by his interest.

"Yesterday, on the sixteenth day of February," he said, going over and pointing, "Jan Královec and his Orphans were given a triumphant welcome in Hradec Králové. After seventy-three days of pillaging and burning, the plundering raid has ended victoriously, thus that particular line may now be erased from the map. Regarding the other lines…Much depends on the results of the conference in Lutsk, Volyn. On what Witold decides upon. On the diplomatic talents of Andrea de Palatio, the Papal Emissary. On whether the negotiations between Sigismund of Luxembourg and Prokop the Shaven in Pressburg are completed. And what do you think, sir? Shall we be wiping the red lines and arrows from the map? Or shall we be drawing new ones? What is your opinion, Sir Reinmar of Bielawa?"

Reynevan looked him in the eyes. The official smiled. The only thing he had in common with a merchant was that smile. An endearing smile, inspiring confidence. Encouraging one to entrust one's business affairs and one's money. And to share one's secrets. But Reynevan wasn't inclined to share his. The Fuggers' official understood that at once.

"Quite," he said, carelessly waving a hand, the fingers of which were laden with valuable rings. "There are matters about which we shall not speak. For the moment. Let us then get down to business."

He opened an escritoire.

"Before his departure, Canon Otto Beess," he said, looking up, "saw fit to honour us with his trust. Not without good reason. He knew that both a deposit and a secret are safe at Fuggers. Nothing will compel our company to reveal a secret once entrusted.

"Here, then, are the deposits. A letter from Otto Beess, sealed, the seal unbroken. And here are the hundred guilders deposited by Otto Beess. And another hundred that we are to pay to Your Lordship in accordance with the instructions given to us yesterday by Sir Bartholomew Eisenreich. Does Your Lordship wish to count it?"

"I trust you."

"And rightly so, if I may make so bold. And if I may advise, please do not take the entire sum at once."

"I shall decline the advice and take it all. At once and

immediately. I do not intend to return. Thus, I bid you farewell, for we shall never meet again."

The Fuggers official smiled.

"Who can know, Sir Reinmar of Bielawa? Who can know?"

Otto Beess's trust in Fuggers and Company was by no means boundless, for the canon's letter was guarded by more than a seal. The letter was written so artfully that a stranger would have made little of the contents. There was nothing in the letter that might have constituted evidence or been used in any way against the sender. Or the addressee. Even Reynevan, who knew the canon well, when all was said and done, needed some time to decipher the code.

"Achilles, do you know an inn or tavern in Wrocław with the word 'fish' in its name?" he asked without raising his head.

"There are a hundred taverns in Wrocław," said Achilles Czibulka, looking up from counting the stacks of coins. "'Fish,' you say? Let me think. There's the Pike in Mint Street and the Blue Carp in the New Town. I don't recommend the latter. Rotten food and an easy place to get a punch in the nose…Well, there's also the Gold Fish…Over the Odra, in Ołbin—"

"Near the lazar house and the Church of the Eleven Thousand Virgins," said Reynevan, still focused on decoding the letter. "*Locus virginis*, ah! Now it's clear. The Gold Fish, you say? I have to go there, Achilles. And today. After Vespers."

"Ołbin after Vespers? I strongly advise against it."

"But yet I must."

"*We* must," said the *unguentarius*, stretching so strenuously his elbows crunched. "The two of us. You might not even make it there if you go alone. Whether we shall get back in one piece is another matter. But we'll go together. "First of all, though," he said, glancing at the stacks of coins on the table, "we must safeguard the funds. You've done magnificently, magnificently, by my troth. After paying off the amulet, your fortune comes to a hundred and ninety-three Rhenish sovereigns. You kidnapped somebody, did you? Because it's about right for a ransom."

The faint light of the lamp showed that there were three assailants. They had sacks on their heads with eyeholes burned into them. One, a veritable giant, was a good seven feet tall; the second was also tall, but gaunt, his arms hanging down like a monkey's. The third was lurking in the shadows.

Father Felicjan—choking under a gag—was under no illusions. His spying and informing had harmed a great many people; thus, a great many people had reason to attack him, kidnap him and exact revenge on him. Cruel, sadistic revenge, befitting the harm his denunciations had caused. Father Felicjan was aware that the attackers would soon do various horrible things to him. The remote barn they had dragged him to was perfectly suitable for that kind of thing.

The altarist entertained neither illusions nor hopes. Nor did he have a choice other than to take a great and desperate gamble. In spite of his bound hands, he leaped up like a salmon, lowered his head like a bull and charged at the gate.

He didn't have a chance, naturally. One of the kidnappers seized him by the collar in a vice-like grip. The second struck him hard in the kidneys with something as hard as iron. The blow was so powerful that Father Felicjan was winded and lost control of his legs; so quickly and suddenly that for a moment he thought he was flying through the air. He slammed onto the dirt floor, as limp as a sack of wool.

The light of the lantern drew closer. The petrified altarist saw the third attacker through tears. That one wasn't masked. His face was ordinary and unremarkable. Very unremarkable. He was holding a long, thick, twisted leather knout. It was evidently heavy. And clinked metallically. Father Felicjan heard a clink as the assailant brought the knout close to his face.

"What you were just struck with," said the assailant, his voice sounding familiar, "was twenty golden Rhenish florins. You can be hit with the coins a few more times or take possession of them. The choice depends on you."

Reynevan had known the Gold Fish since his training at the lazar house by the Church of the Eleven Thousand Virgins. Why the tavern located near the Poznań road was so called remained the secret of the owner—or rather owners—of which the tavern had endured many, going back according to tradition to the times of Henryk Probus. You would have searched in vain for a fish—gold or otherwise—on a sign or in the decor. The tavern didn't possess a sign at all, while the decor's chief element was an enormous stuffed bear. The bear had stood in the tavern for as long as the oldest regulars could recall, with the passage of years increasingly losing out to moths. Moths were also responsible for revealing a certain mystery. The more fur they devoured, the more they uncovered seams of thick thread, revealing the animal to be a fake, skilfully constructed from several smaller bears and other more or less random elements. But that fact neither shocked nor bothered the regulars.

That evening in the Gold Fish hardly any of them were paying attention to the bear, either. All the attention of the drinkers tightly crammed into the chamber was turned towards beer and vodka, and also—in spite of Lent—joints of fatty meat. The latter, roasting over the coals, filled the tavern with a pleasant aroma and impenetrable smoke.

"I'm looking for..." said Reynevan, suppressing a cough and rubbing his streaming eyes. "I'm looking for a fellow by the name of Hempel. Grabis Hempel. I know he's a regular. Is he here today?"

"Am I my brother's keeper?" asked the taverner, peering at him through the smoke. "Look and you will find."

Reynevan was already preparing to treat the innkeeper to a similar biblical adage, but a cough from Achilles Czibulka suggested another solution. So he took from his pouch a gold florin and held it up for the taverner. The innkeeper didn't quote from the Bible again. Instead, he gestured with his head towards a corner of the tavern. Behind a table covered in demijohns and pitchers were sitting three quite freely dressed—or rather undressed—women. And four men.

They didn't get that far, for Reynevan felt something pressing him against the bar. Something large. And foul-smelling. Like the tavern's stuffed bear. He turned around with difficulty.

"New guests," said a large and tousle-haired character with his shirt hanging out of his britches, his breath smelling foully of onions and poorly digested meat. "New guests pay an entrance fee here. It's customary. So open your purse, young master, and buy the round, for we are thirsty."

The tousle-haired man's comrades—three of them—roared with laughter. One of them shoved Achilles Czibulka with his belly. That one—for the sake of variety—smelled of Lenten food. Fish, to be precise.

"Innkeeper," said Reynevan, beckoning. "Beer for these gentlemen. A mug each."

"A mug each?" the tousle-haired fellow wheezed into his face. "A mug *each*? Do you insult an Odra fisherman? A working man? Buy a barrel, you prick! You oaf! You snooty bastard!"

"Go away, good fellow," said Reynevan, squinting slightly. "Begone. Leave us in peace."

"Or else?"

"Lead me not into temptation."

"Whaaat?"

"I promised not to hit anyone during Lent."

It took some time for the tousle-haired man to put the pieces together, before he bellowed and prepared to swing a punch. Reynevan was quicker. He snatched a jug from the counter and smashed it into the tousle-haired man's face, covering him in beer and blood. Immediately, taking advantage of the momentum, he kicked the other bruiser in the crotch. Czibulka broke the nose of the third with a brass knuckle he had prudently taken with him, and punched the fourth in the solar plexus, knocking him to his knees. The tousle-haired man tried to stand up, so Reynevan whacked him in the forehead with the broken-off handle of the jug, and on seeing that it wasn't enough, hit him so hard again that only fragments of clay and glaze remained in his fist. He braced himself against the counter and drew a dagger.

"Put the knife away!" bellowed the innkeeper, running up with some servants. "Put it away, you rascal! And get out of here! I don't want to see you in here again, miscreant! Scoundrels! Troublemakers! Don't show your faces in here again! Get out, I said!"

"They started it."

"They're regulars! And you're newcomers! Strangers! Get out! *Raus! Raus*, I said!"

They were propelled, accompanied by abuse and shoves with clubs, out of the chamber. And then out of the tavern.

The drinkers found it amusing, were crying with laughter, and the wenches were cackling in shrill voices. The stuffed bear observed the incident with its one glass eye. Somebody had gouged out the other.

They didn't get far; no further than just beyond the corner of the stable. Hearing muffled steps behind them, they quickly turned around, Reynevan holding the drawn dagger.

"Easy does it," said a man they had seen inside, at a table in the corner, among the demijohns and wenches, raising a hand. "Easy does it. No false moves. I am Grabis Hempel."

"Also called Allerdings?"

"Precisely. *Allerdings.*" The man straightened up. He was tall and thin, with long arms that hung down like a monkey's. "And you are here on the canon's orders, I presume. But he only mentioned one man. Which of you is he?"

"It is I."

Allerdings examined Reynevan keenly.

"It was very foolish of you to come here asking after me," he said. "And that brawl was even more foolish. Snoopers often stop by here; they might remember you. Although, in truth, your physiognomy is…unremarkable. No offence meant."

"None taken."

"I'm going back in," said Allerdings, shrugging his skinny shoulders. "Someone may have seen me leaving with you and I'm easier to remember. We'll meet tomorrow. In Milicz Street in the Sinner's Bell beer cellar. At the Terce. And now, farewell. Begone from here."

They met. On the nineteenth of February, the Saturday before Reminiscere Sunday. In Milicz Street, in the Sinner's Bell cellar, which was usually frequented by apprentice bellmakers, and now, at the Terce, was practically empty. Right at the start, Reynevan felt the need to explain the matter at hand. Allerdings wouldn't let him.

"I know in detail what the matter is," he interrupted, before Reynevan could expand on it. "Our mutual acquaintance, Canon Beess—until recently the provost in the cathedral chapter—told me the details. He did it, I admit, only reluctantly, determined as he was to protect you and your secrets. But he knew that without the information I wouldn't be able to prepare an operation."

"Thus you know the details and have prepared an operation," Reynevan said. "So let's discuss those details. And quickly—"

"More haste, less speed, as they say," Allerdings interrupted coldly. "Before we get to the details, we ought to examine a certain matter of a more general nature. One that may influence the details. Considerably."

"Which is?"

"Whether the operation being planned makes any sense."

Reynevan said nothing for a while and fiddled with his mug.

"Whether the operation makes any sense?" he finally said. "How do you suggest we judge that? Shall we take a vote?"

"Reynevan," said Allerdings, his eyes on Reynevan, "you are a Hussite. A traitor. In this town you are an odious enemy, you are at the very heart of the enemy camp. You arouse disgust as a heretic, a turncoat, on whom anathema was laid barely four weeks ago to the tolling of bells. You are fair game here, a lamb among a pack of wolves; you have become prey to everybody, since he who kills you will gain fame, admiration, prestige, absolution of his sins, the gratitude of the authorities, a bounty—and favour with the fair sex. And they *will* catch you eventually, my lad. The magic that veils you won't save you, for magic can be overcome. If one looks carefully, one can see your true face under the disguise. If someone recognises you in the street, the mob will tear you to pieces. Or they'll take you alive and drag you to the scaffold. It will happen, since for every day you spend in Wrocław that moment draws inexorably closer. But you, instead of fleeing at once, mean to engage in some madcap schemes. So answer me, hand on heart, if you can: is there any sense in it?"

"There is."

"I understand." Now it was Allerdings' turn to fall silent for some time. "All is clear. We shall undertake any risk at all in order to rescue the maid. Any madness. Even one that will accomplish nothing."

"Nothing?"

"When I was tracking our target, I grew to know him a little. Him and his character. And I'll tell you what I think: you'll gain nothing from him. The fellow will either betray you and denounce you or deceive you and lead you up the garden path, send you to search for your Jutta in some make-believe land."

"It's our job," said Reynevan, without lowering his eyes, "to ensure he'll be too afraid to do that."

"That can be achieved," said Allerdings, smiling for the first time since the conversation began. "Very well. I've said my piece, now we ought to get down to brass tacks. So as not to waste time: making use of Canon Beess's inestimable instructions, I found out what I needed to find out. I know where, when and how. I know also that we'll need help. I swear we need a third man. And I don't mean your apothecary, for what lies ahead of us isn't a job for an apothecary. Any moment now, a fellow by the name of Jasio Kminek will appear. As you said yourself: we need our client to be afraid. And Jasio Kminek is a first-rate specialist. A veritable virtuoso at knocking out teeth."

"Then what," Reynevan raised an eyebrow, "was the point of all that oratory that came before? When you knew I wouldn't change my mind? Otherwise, you wouldn't have engaged this virtuoso."

"I felt it was my duty. And I know how to anticipate."

Jasio Kminek was a huge fellow, a veritable giant measuring over seven feet tall.

The giant greeted them, took a swig of beer and belched. He was trying gamely to act like a foolish simpleton. But when he talked, his speech gave him away. As did the flashes of intelligence in his eyes when he listened.

"We'll be working at Saint Maurice's," he said, after hearing them out. "Is it the Walloon? I try to steer clear of sorcerers."

"So you will."

"Someone to be eliminated?"

"Probably not. At most, someone will get a hiding."

"A sound one? With permanent results?"

"Can't be ruled out."

"Very well. My fee is a quarter of a grzywna in silver, or its equivalent in any coin. Agreed?"

"Agreed."

"When do we start? I'm a busy man—"

"We know. And a virtuoso."

"I work in a bakery," Jasio Kminek said emphatically. "I'll have to take leave for this. Thus do I ask: when?"

"In three days," said Allerdings. "On Tuesday. It'll be a full moon. Our client prefers Tuesdays and moonlit nights."

Father Felicjan, back pressed against the post, sighed, groaned and moaned. Feeling was slowly returning to his legs, the numbness being replaced by a growing pain. The pain was insistent enough to hamper his concentration. He had difficulty understanding what they were saying to him, so the thug with the repugnantly ordinary face standing over him had to keep repeating himself. Which clearly infuriated him.

"The Inquisition," he hissed, "abducted the maid and is holding her in secret. I'm talking about Jutta Apolda. You are to find out where she is being held."

"Good sir, how am I to do that?" Father Felicjan snivelled. "When I am a miserable worm…I'm nothing. What of it that I serve the bishop? For who am I to the bishop? A servant, a wretched servant. And what interests you, sire, is not a matter for the bishop, but the Holy Office. What ties do I have with the Holy Office, with their confidential matters? What can I know of them?"

"You can know," the thug hissed, "as much as you gain from eavesdropping, peeping and sniffing out. And it's well known that you excel in your craft. You have few equals in eavesdropping, peeping and sniffing out."

"What am I? I am but a servant. A nobody! You confuse me with somebody else."

"I do not. You are Hanys Gwisdek, commonly known as Little Louse. Currently Father Felicjan, promoted to altarist by the bishop in two churches at once—Saint Elisabeth's and Saint Michael's—as a reward for snooping and informing. True, Father Confessor? You informed *to* Canon Beess and then informed *on* him. Now you inform on Tylman, Lichtenberg, Borschnitz and others. The bishop has promised to advance your career in the hierarchy and give you further lucrative prebendaries in exchange for information. Do you think the bishop will keep his promises? When he learns the truth about you? The bishop will doubtless forgive you for whoring with the Walloon women— even during Lent. But what will he do when he finds out you also inform on him—and no less zealously? And on Inquisitor Gregory Hejncze?"

Father Felicjan swallowed loudly. And said nothing for a long time.

"What you want to know," he finally mumbled, "is a secret matter of the Inquisition. Regarding heresy. It is a great secret."

"Great secrets," said the thug, impatience audible in his voice, "can also be sniffed out. And the greater the secret, the greater the reward. Look, here are twenty Rhenish gold pieces. I give them to you, they are yours. You can keep them when I release you, with no demands exacted. If, however, you supply me with information and it satisfies me, you'll receive that sum five times over. A hundred florins, Gwisdek. That is five times more than the prebendaries you now receive annually from your two altarages. So think about it, do the reckoning. Perhaps it is worth the effort."

Father Felicjan swallowed once more and his eyes flashed like a fox's. The thug with the ordinary appearance bent over him and shone a lantern in his face.

"But know this: should you betray me..." he drawled. "Should you denounce me, should I be seized...Should any misfortune befall me, should I fall ill, be poisoned by food, choked by a fishbone, drowned in a clay pit pond or fall under the wheels of a speeding wagon...Then, Confessor, you may be sure that certain evidence will reach the people you have harmed. Whom you continue to try to harm. Included among them is Jan Sneschewicz, the bishop's assistant curate. The latter is a determined fellow, as well you know. Should he learn of certain matters... They will fish you out of the Odra, Gwisdek. Before three days pass, they will fish your swollen corpse from the Sokolnicki weir. You see that, don't you?"

Father Felicjan did. He cringed and nodded eagerly.

"You have ten days—and not a day longer—to obtain the information."

"I shall do my best...If I succeed—"

"Better that you do...Better for you. Is that clear? And now you are free, you may go. Aha, Gwisdek."

"Yes, m'lord?"

"Don't roam about after dark. I'm counting on you, so it would be a shame for you to have your throat cut around here somewhere."

*

73

The yellow curtain was still not hanging in the window of Otto Beess's house in Shoemakers Street. Reynevan hadn't especially expected to see it. He was there for a different reason. Their route simply led them along Shoemakers Street.

"Do you know where the canon went? To his home in Rogów?"

"*Allerdings*," confirmed Allerdings. "He may stay there for some time. A hostile aura has settled on him in Wrocław."

"Partly thanks to me."

"It may hurt your pride," said Allerdings, glancing at him over his shoulder, "but I'll tell you: you flatter yourself too much. If indeed you *were* the reason, you are but one of many. And not the most important. Bishop Konrad has looked askance at Canon Otto for some time now, ever searching for an opportunity to trip him up. Finally, just imagine, he has rummaged around in genealogy and decided that the canon is a Pole, and declared that he is not 'Beess' but 'Bies'—a run-of-the-mill, commonplace Polish 'Bies.' And there is no place in the Wrocław Diocese for a Polish Bies. Did the Polish Bies dream of a prelature in the cathedral? Then may he make for Gniezno or Krakow, where there are also cathedrals.

"In fact, there are several cathedrals in Poland: in Poznań, Włocławek, Płock and Lwów. And the Beess family, to be precise, are not Poles. The family originates in Croatia."

"Whether Croatia, Poland, Bohemia, Serbia or Moldova, it's all one to the bishop." Allerdings pouted. "All one damned thing. All Slavic nations. *Enemy* nations. And thus hostile to us, good Germans."

"Ha, ha. Very droll."

"I swear. And do you see the paradox?"

"I do not."

"By harming the canon, the bishop harms himself. Otto Beess was almost the only person in the Wrocław Chapter who still supported the bishop regarding papal supremacy; increasingly, the rest of the prelates and canons openly support conciliarism. Thanks to his intrigues, the bishop has rid himself of allies and things may end poorly for him. The Vatican Council in Basel approaches. That council may bring about many changes. Are you listening to me? What are you doing there?"

"Cleaning my boot. I've trodden in some shit."

After the spring of 1428, Wrocław was an island in a sea of warfare, an oasis in a desert of destruction. Even so, although fenced off from the world by the waters of the Oława and the Odra, although defended by mighty walls, the Silesian metropolis was far from basking in the blissful luxury of safety and the certainty of tomorrow. Wrocław recalled the previous spring too vividly. Its recollections were so vivid and realistic as to be almost palpable. The glow as Brzeg, Ryczyn, Sobótka, Gniechowice, Środa Śląska and the nearby Kątów burned still lived on in them. Wrocław recalled the beginning of May, when it looked down at the army of Prokop the Shaven from the city walls through eyes running from the smoke drifting from Żerniki and Muchobór as they burned. And six weeks hadn't even passed since the day the Orphans had marched downstream beside the Odra from the south, when all the bells in the metropolis had sounded the alarm of their arrival at Oława, barely a day's ride away.

Wrocław was an island in an ocean of war, an oasis in a wilderness of charred ruins and ashes. The region south of Wrocław became a fire-ravaged wilderness. Now, almost thirty thousand people were seeking sanctuary within Wrocław's walls, a city with a population of fifteen thousand in times of peace. Wrocław was crowded—not to say overcrowded. Existing in a mood of uncertainty and menace. In an aura of paralysing fear. Denunciations were commonplace.

Everybody was to blame: the bishop, the prelates, the Inquisition, the city fathers, the Patriciate, the knighthood, the merchants. Everybody. The men who cared about the safety of the city. Men who saw a Hussite spy at every doorstep and recalled the year before in horror: the gates of Frankenstein and Rychbach opened by treachery; the stronghold at Ślęża seized by trickery; the plots in Świdnica; the sabotage in Kłodzko. Men who hoped that a witch-hunt for spies would flush out the actual, real ones. And men who didn't believe in any spies, but who were very much in favour of hysterical fear. All of them encouraged informing, helping to intensify the fear and dread, which returned in the form of hatred and persecution.

After all, Hussites, traitors and witches might be lurking anywhere, in every doorway, on every corner, in any disguise. Everybody was suspicious: your neighbour, because she wouldn't lend you a sieve; the stallholder, because he gave you your change in trimmed skojeces; the carpenter, because he said nasty things about the parish priest; the parish priest, because he drank; the shoemaker, because he didn't. The cathedral lector, Schilder, should undoubtedly be informed on, because he was loitering around near a bombard on the city walls. Councillor Scheuerlein was, beyond reasonable doubt, worthy of a denunciation, because he farted terribly in the church during Sunday Mass. The city scribe, young Sir Albrecht Strubicz, was suspicious, because he had recovered after falling ill. Hans Plichta, the city guard, was suspicious, because it was enough to look at his face to guess he was a sot, a womaniser, a bribe-taker and a traitor.

The juggler-*joculator* was suspicious, because he played amusing tricks; the carpenter Kozuber was suspicious, because he laughed at those tricks. Young Jadwiga Bancz was suspicious, because she curled her hair and wore red slippers. Master Güntherode, because he took the Lord's name in vain. The tanner aroused suspicions, because he stank. As did the beggar, because he stank even worse. And the Jew, for being a Jew. And all evil, of course, is caused by the Jews.

Denunciations and delations were on the rise, the situation fuelling itself, growing like a snowball rolling down a hill. Soon, the people no one had informed on became the most suspicious. So, knowing that, some people started informing on each other. And on their closest relatives.

It would have been odd had Reynevan not been included in that deluge of denunciations.

And he was. More than once.

He was seized in Salt Square as he walked through it, dodging between stalls, heading for his breakfast. He broke his fast every day at the Moor's Head. Regularly. Too regularly.

They seized him, twisted his arms behind his back and shoved him against a stall. There were six of them.

"Reinmar of Bielau," said the leader, unemotionally, rubbing a flattened nose hideously disfigured by illness. "You are under arrest. Do not resist."

He did not. Because he couldn't. Caught by surprise, his head was muddled, it was like a dream, he was confused by what had happened. *Jutta*, he thought, feverishly and incoherently. *Jutta. The altarist Felicjan will find the place of Jutta's incarceration. But how will I contact the altarist? When I myself am in captivity? Or dead?*

A crowd gathered and grew around him.

"Go on," signalled the man with the disfigured nose. "Tie up the rogue. Bind him."

"Bind him, bind him!" A grey-haired beanpole in a leather jerkin with a drawn sword, accompanied by several armed men, forced his way through the throng. "And when you've bound him stand aside, for he is ours. We've been tracking him for several days. You were quicker, good for you, but now hand him over. Our rights take precedence."

"How so?" The Nose stood with arms akimbo. "How are they superior? This isn't Ostrów Tumski, this is Wrocław! And in Wrocław nothing ranks higher than the city council, the council governs Wrocław. I arrested the prisoner by order of the gentlemen of the council and am to deliver him to the town hall. You are right that I was quicker. And you were tardy! Your loss, you should have risen earlier. The early bird catches the worm! Thus begone, Lord Hunt. Hinder me not in my service!"

"The bishop rules Wrocław," retorted Kuczera of Hunt. "He is the proxy of King Sigismund, your master, you plebeian, and the master of your damned council. And I represent the bishop here, so beware of whom you address, you town hall lackey. And whom you send packing. I have orders to deliver the prisoner to the bishop's palace—"

"And I to the town hall!"

"This," Kuczera said angrily, "is a church matter and the town hall can keep its fucking hands off. Go on, stand aside."

"*You* stand aside!"

Kuczera of Hunt growled, panted and put his hand on his sword. At that moment, a small figure in a dull greyish smock sprang—or rather shot—from the growing and increasingly restless crowd. Before anybody could react, the figure sped on and attacked Reynevan, snatching him from the grip of the servants and knocking him over, pressing him to the ground. The astonished Reynevan looked straight into the newcomer's face. A grey, bland and quite unremarkable face. Blood was dripping from the unremarkable nose and mouth. And some kind of repulsive, sticky secretion.

"I'll sneeze snot over them," the figure murmured straight into his ear in a soft, high female voice. "And you flee..."

The town hall thugs and Hunt's men dragged the woman off Reynevan, tugging, jerking and shaking her like a rag doll. The woman suddenly sagged in their arms and rolled her eyes. She coughed spasmodically, choked and wheezed. Then suddenly rasped, spat and sneezed out snot, spraying it in great quantities in all directions. Blood and mucous thickly speckled the faces and clothing of the surrounding people.

"Blessed Virgin Mary!" howled somebody from the throng. "It's the plague! The pox! The pox!"

There was no need to repeat it. Everybody knew what *mors nigra*—the Black Death—was, everybody knew what to do in the face of the Black Death. There was a simple principle and one rule: *fuge*, run away. Everybody—market traders, passers-by, servants, the bishop's soldiers, the Nose, Hunt—fled in panic, knocking over and trampling one another. Salt Square emptied in a second.

Only Reynevan remained. A physician. Kneeling over the plague-stricken woman. Trying to open her mouth, alleviate her plight, remove the mucous and clots blocking up her throat. *There's no spell for it*, he thought feverishly and chaotically. *No spell, no charm, no amulet. No magic can cure it, or protect one from being infected by the pulmonary form of the plague. For it* was *the pulmonary form, there was no doubt, the symptoms were classic, although...She isn't febrile...Her forehead is cool...As is her body...Her chest...How is it possible? Something's not right.*

The woman with the unremarkable face pushed his hands away.

"Rather than groping me," she said calmly and clearly, "run away, you hapless idiot. Quickly. Before they realise it was an illusion."

He didn't need telling twice.

*

Had he decided on fleeing from Wrocław with no further thought, wearing just that thin jerkin, he would have pulled it off. The city was in such confusion and panic, his escape would quite likely have succeeded. But Reynevan was reluctant to give up his belongings and the bay pacing horse Dzierżka of Wirsing had gifted him. He turned out to be incapable of abandoning those material goods without a second thought or any regret. In short, materialism was his undoing. As it had been to many before him.

They seized him in the stable. They fell on him as he was saddling his horse. Resistance was out of the question. There were too many of them; he would not have fared any better had he tried to fight the hundred-armed Briareus. The highly predictable outcome was that Reynevan ended up with a sack over his head and his arms and legs bound. Then they picked him up, tossed him onto a wagon like a parcel and covered him with some soft, heavy things, probably rags.

A whip cracked, axles creaked, the wagon lurched forwards and rolled along a street lined with logs. Reynevan, pressed down by the pile of rags, swore and kicked himself.

A journey into the unknown had begun.

Chapter Three

In which the saying is confirmed: it is indeed a small world—for Reynevan keeps bumping into old friends.

The wagon that was carrying him jumped and rocked on ruts, creaking all the while as though about to disintegrate at any moment. Reynevan, who had initially interpreted the heap of rags and spiky bulrushes crushing him and barely permitting him to breathe as torture and cursed the perpetrators at length, quickly changed his opinion.

Pinned under the pile, he wasn't hitting the sides of the speeding conveyance but felt and heard the banging of other objects —probably barrels and ladders—which were chaotically flying around and rolling over him again and again. The ride was so rough that even swaddled in rags, his teeth chattered and rang as he rattled over potholes.

It was difficult to tell how long the journey lasted. A long time, in any case.

He was dragged from under the rags and tossed roughly from the wagon onto the ground. Or rather into some mud, for his clothes became wet at once. Almost immediately—and also roughly—he was tugged to his feet and the sack jerked from his head. He was shoved and felt his back hit a wheel.

They were in a ravine and snow still lay in hollows on its sides. But spring could be smelled in the air.

"Is he in one piece?" somebody asked. "Undamaged?"

"See for yourself. He's standing unaided. Hand over the money, as we agreed."

The men surrounding him differed from each other. One glance sufficed to divide them into two groups, two categories. One group could be qualified right away as urban malefactors and cutpurses, rascally members of the many gangs that terrorised the outskirts of Wrocław. It was undoubtedly they who had captured him in the stable and driven him from the city on the wagon. In order to now hand him over to the other group. Criminals also, but apparently of another class. Mercenaries.

There was no time for further analysis. He was grabbed, shoved onto a horse and his wrists tied to the pommel of the saddle. His upper arms were also bound with a rope running twice around them. The ends of the rope were taken hold of by two riders, one on the right, the other on the left. The remainder surrounded them closely. The horses snorted and stamped. He was prodded in the back with something hard.

"Off we go," he heard. "Don't try anything stupid or you'll get a hiding."

The voice behind him sounded familiar.

They avoided towns and villages, but not giving them such a wide berth for Reynevan not to be able to work out where they were. He was familiar enough with the terrain to be sure he'd seen the bell tower of the parish church of Saint Florian in Wiązów. Thus he was being taken along the Nysa road, making directly southward from Wrocław. Nysa appeared not to be their destination, however. Regarding the rest of the route there were too many options: from Nysa, five roads headed off in various directions, not counting the road they were on.

"Where are you taking me?"

"Shut your trap."

They stopped for the night on the far side of Nysa. And Reynevan recognised a friend.

"Paszko? Paszko Rymbaba?"

The mercenary who brought him bread and water stopped abruptly. Leaned over. Brushed a fair fringe from his eyes and forehead. And opened his mouth.

"By my honour," he gasped. "Reinmar? Can it be you? Ha! I thought you looked familiar...Oh, but you've changed, you have...Hard to believe—"

"Who's holding me? Where are you taking me?"

"We've been ordered not to talk," said Paszko Rymbaba, standing up straight, his voice hardening, "so don't ask. It is as it is."

"I see how it is," said Reynevan, taking a bite of bread. "You were once a knight, and now you comport yourself like a servant who's told what to do and what not to do. I even know what's behind the change, and it's a wonder you remain in Silesia. They said you all fled: Weyrach, Wittram, Tresckow, your entire old *comitiva*. That you fled far, far away, for it was getting a little too hot for you here in Silesia."

"Aye," said Paszko, scratching the back of his head, anxiously tossing a glance at the campfire where other mercenaries were devoting all their attention to a demijohn. "Aye, they were. The company went its separate ways. I was also making ready to leave them. But see, a chance to serve Lord Ungerath arose. Lord Ungerath is a wealthy man, he won't let any of his men come to harm, no fear. So I stayed, for things aren't so bad for me here in Silesia."

"What does that wealthy man want with me? How have I upset him?"

"We're not to talk."

"Just one thing," said Reynevan, lowering his voice. "One word. One name. I have to know who turned me over in Wrocław. It's not about me, in any case. Do you remember that maiden, Paszko? Kidnapped and taken to Bodak as Biberstein's daughter? The one I fled with back then? I'm fond of her, I love her with all my heart. And my question to you will decide her fate. Her life. Who betrayed me, Paszko?"

"I am not to talk. And even if I could, I know nothing in any case."

"But your commander does. Am I right?"

"No doubt," said Rymbaba, puffing up. "Sir Eberwin of Kranz is a shrewd fellow. He must know."

"Ask him, Paszko. Find out."

"I shall not: orders."

"Paszko. Didn't I come to your aid at the Battle of Lutom? The infantrymen were advancing on you, remember? They'd have stuck you like a pig had it not been for me and Samson. You are indebted. Are you a knight or not? It doesn't befit a knight to forget such debts."

Paszko Rymbaba thought for a long while. And so intensively that beads of sweat appeared on his brow. He finally brightened up and wiped his forehead.

"You saved me," he admitted, standing up straight. "But later in Bodak you jabbed me perfidiously in the side. And that beloved maid of yours kicked me in the stones and threw me down the stairs. I had headaches for a long time after that. Thus we're quits. I don't owe you anything."

"Paszko—"

"Have you finished? Then hold your hands out. I must bind them again."

"Can't you tie them a bit looser?"

"I cannot: orders."

*

They set off again at dawn, in a fog which meant Reynevan lost his bearings. He thought they were heading towards Prudnik, on the Głubczyce road, but he couldn't be certain.

Three horsemen were waiting for them at the edge of a leafless birch copse along with a tightly sealed wagon being pulled by four shaggy horses. The wagon's purpose was more than obvious, so Reynevan wasn't surprised when they shoved him inside and bolted the doors behind him. He even greeted the change with certain pleasure. He was still a captive, but at least his hands were untied.

Hooves thudded, the wagon strained and set off, its axles creaking and rattling. The only light came from a tiny grated window, which wasn't much. But it was enough to be able to see a person lying on the floor, covered with a blanket or a mantle.

"Praise the Lord, Brother," he said. "Who are you?"

The man on the floor didn't answer. The groan he gave couldn't be considered an answer. Reynevan sniffed. He approached and felt the man's forehead. It was as hot as a furnace. Feeling himself on the contrary suddenly growing cold from fear, he pulled off the blanket, reached under the sweat-soaked clothes and pressed the man's belly, then felt his neck, armpits and groin. He was searching in the faint light for the marks of blood, pus and a rash. The sick man put up no resistance, continuing to lie motionless, groaning.

"You're lucky and I'm lucky," Reynevan finally muttered, sitting up. "It's not the plague. Or smallpox. I believe."

"*Adsumus...*"

"What?" Reynevan started. "What did you say?"

"*Adsumus...*" mumbled the sick man. "*Adsumus peccati quidem immanitate detenti... Sed in nomine tuo specialiter congregati...*"

85

It's just a prayer, Reynevan reassured himself. *It's just a coincidence...*

He leaned over. The heat of the fever and an acrid smell of sweat emanated from the sick man. Reynevan placed his hands on his temples and began to slowly utter healing spells and invocations.

"*Veni ad nos...*" groaned the patient, "*et esto nobiscum et dignare illabi cordibus nostris...Adsumus...Adsumus...*"

Reynevan mumbled some spells. The sick man wheezed.

"*Ex lux perpetua,*" he said quite clearly, "*luceat eis.*"

The wagon rattled and creaked. The delirious man raved.

Reynevan was awoken by the scraping of the bolt and the creaking of the door being opened. The cold fresh air and the light shining in from the outside brought him to his senses. He squinted.

Fresh passengers were shoved into the wagon. Three men. The first, a broad-shouldered, moustachioed man in a knight's doublet, recoiled instinctively at the sight of the sick man on the floor.

"Fear not," Reynevan reassured him. "It isn't catching. A fever, nothing more."

"Get inside!" one of the mercenaries urged. "At the double! Do you need my help?"

The door to the wagon slammed shut, plunging the interior into darkness once again. The light was enough, however, for Reynevan to be sure he knew at least two of the three new arrivals sitting shoulder to shoulder opposite him. He was sure he'd seen their faces before.

"Since sad fate has brought us together," the moustachioed man began, in a cautious and hesitant voice, "let us introduce ourselves. I am Jan Kuropatwa of Łańcuchów, *miles polonus...*"

"Bearing the Szreniawa arms," said Reynevan, completing his sentence in Polish, "if I remember rightly. We met in Prague."

"Well, I'll be!" said the Pole, his suspiciously gloomy and fierce face lighting up. "Reynevan, the Prague sawbones! I remember! I thought you looked familiar, m'lord. And we're all in the shit, by the plague."

"*Adsumus*," the sick man whined loudly, rolling his head. "*Adsum…*"

"Speaking of the plague," said the other Pole anxiously, pointing at the man lying on the floor. "This one here—"

"The Honourable Reynevan is a medic, Jakub," said Kuropatwa. "He is skilled around illnesses. If he says it's not catching, we may believe him. If I may, Sir Reynevan: this good gentleman is Sir Jakub Nadobny of Rogów, of the Działosza coat of arms. And this one—"

"We've been introduced," interrupted the third man, with a thrusting, slightly crooked jaw. "Klemens Kochłowski of Wieluń, do you remember? We've had the pleasure. It was in Toszek, last autumn. We discussed…business."

Reynevan indicated he did, but only with a tilt of his head. He wasn't certain if he could go into details. And if so, how deeply. The wagon's new passengers were indeed his temporary companions in misery, but that didn't mean at all that they needed to know the facts and details of the business Kochłowski was engaged in. Which was selling horses, arms, powder and balls to Hussites.

"They caught the three of us, all on one day," said Jan Kuropatwa, clarifying things. "On the Krakow road between Bielsko and Skoczów. We had a couple of wagons, we were transporting… You can guess what. For you know what is transported along that road."

Reynevan knew. Everybody knew. The Krakow road running

through Cieszyn and the Moravian Gate—a route linking the Kingdom of Poland with Bohemia—was one of the few trade routes that fell outside the embargo imposed on Hussite Bohemia. Goods from Poland travelled practically constantly and unhindered along that road to the Kingdom of Bohemia, owing to the agreement reached between the Moravian gentry and wealthy Catholics. The Moravian Hussites didn't undertake plundering expeditions on the lands of Catholics, and the latter turned a blind eye to the shipments and convoys passing through Cieszyn. The agreement was informal and the equilibrium unstable, occasionally disturbed by some incident or other. As was apparent.

"Racibórz's men from Pszczyna captured us," continued the *miles polonus*. "It was a squad hired by that she-wolf Helena, the widow of Duke Jan. Pszczyna is hers, I mean Helena's, as a result of a widow's bequest. The old hag rules Pszczyna as a sovereign duchess and grows bolder and bolder."

"And does so illegally, the harlot," Kochłowski growled furiously. "For she does so not on her own but on Cieszyn lands! Which is against the law!"

Reynevan knew what it was all about. The gap in the blockade exploited by merchants only existed owing to the astute politics of Bolko, Duke of Cieszyn, who protected his duchy by not impeding the Hussites or interfering with their shipments. The practices of the widow, Duchess Helena, who resided in Pszczyna, and her son, Duke Mikołaj of Racibórz, differed markedly. They never passed up a chance to get under the skin of the merchants trading with Hussites, even on other people's estates.

"Plenty of our men rotted away in the dungeons of Pszczyna or were beheaded," continued Kuropatwa. "When they caught us, we thought we were doomed to end our days on the scaffold. Sir Jakub and Sir Klemens and I had already commended our souls to God...But we remained in the dungeon less than a week. They took us to Racibórz, turned us over to someone else, the Devil only knows who. And now they've shoved us in here and are taking us somewhere. Who, where, for what and in whose service, the Devil only knows."

"We know for what," Jakub Nadobny of Rogów said grimly. "To a certain death, that is sure."

"Does the name 'Ungerath' ring any bells?" Reynevan asked.

"No. Ought it to?"

Reynevan told them about his capture and the journey he had been on for the previous three days. About how the escort was probably in the service of Ungerath, a rich Wrocław patrician. Kochłowski, Nadobny and Kuropatwa racked their brains intensively. Without much effect. So they would have remained ignorant and uncertain of their fates had it not been for the new arrival to the wagon, who joined them that very day.

The new passenger was young and had fair hair, tousled like a scarecrow's. He was also cheerful and jolly, which was surprising considering the circumstances.

"If I may, m'lords," he said, smiling and sitting up, "I am Hlas of Libočany, a good Czech, a Tábor captain. A prisoner, for the time being, ha ha! Such is war, ha ha!"

Several days earlier—Hlas of Libočany, the good Czech, continued, pausing every now and then for a loud burst of foolish laughter—Sir Hynek Krušina of Lichtenberk invaded the Hradec lands. Formerly a loyal defender of the Chalice, Sir Hynek broke faith by going over to the Catholics and was now tormenting good Czechs with raids. The plundering raid on Hradec hadn't ended too well for him; his squad was defeated, dispersed and forced to flee. But Lord Krušina managed to take Hlas of Libočany prisoner.

"Such is war, ha ha," laughed the good Czech. "But I didn't tarry long in Lord Krušina's dungeon! My ransom was paid and they brought me here. And now, I overheard, they're taking me to a place near Fryštát."

"Why Fryštát? And who paid your ransom?"

"Ha, ha! Why, the same man that captured you. He who's transporting us now!"

"Who the hell is that?"

"Gebhard Ungerath. The son of Kasper Ungerath. Didn't you know? That's a good one, ha ha. See how I have to explain things to you!"

Kasper Ungerath, explained the Taborite, was a Wrocław merchant, indecently wealthy, in his lordliness so cocksure and pompous that he bought a castle in Gniechowice near Wrocław and was ruling it like a nobleman. Now a title appealed to him and he was soliciting for a coat of arms, ha ha. As part of his solicitations, he had made his sons, Gebhard and Gilbert, esquires in the bishop's army. The Taborites from Odry captured Gilbert in a border skirmish. Quickly realising what a golden goose had fallen into their grasp and what golden eggs it could lay, they demanded for the prisoner a ransom of exactly thirty thousand groschen.

"That's no mean sum, ha ha! Now do you see? Ungerath, the old skinflint, negotiated, wants to resolve the affair without parting with any cash. To gain Gilbert's freedom he will release Czech prisoners—Utraquists caught by Silesians. Ungerath has contacts, connections, debtors and quickly acquired some prisoners—meaning us, ha ha. It looks, ha ha, like we—including that half-dead character there—are valued at some four thousand eight hundred *per capita*, in the final reckoning. I'd say it's a good average price. Unless he values any of you gentlemen more highly?"

No one responded. Hlas of Libočany laughed out loud.

"We're being taken to be exchanged, gentlemen. So heads up, ha ha, our captivity will soon be over, very soon!"

The cramped conditions and fug inside the wagon made the prisoners drowsy, so they dozed almost constantly. When Reynevan wasn't sleeping he was thinking.

Who betrayed him in Wrocław?

Ruling out a simple accident—and in situations like that, accidents ought to be ruled out—it didn't leave many scenarios. Time changed people and Achilles Czibulka might have been tempted by the gold coins under the floor of the apothecary's shop; the desire to take possession of them might have been irresistible. What then could be said about Allerdings? Reynevan didn't know him at all but had grounds to consider him a hired rogue.

But of course, the prime suspect remained Pater Felicjan, Hanys Gwisdek known as Little Louse, a character to whom lying, betrayal and perfidy appeared second nature. Allerdings had warned Reynevan about him, but the latter had disregarded the warnings and bad omens. *Omnis* priest *avaritia*, ran the popular saying. Greed would stop Felicjan from betrayal, Reynevan had thought, for he stood to lose a hundred florins by doing so. That hadn't convinced Allerdings.

Allerdings might have been right, Reynevan thought in despair. *Father Felicjan might have valued his skin at more than a hundred florins and might have betrayed to save his skin. He might have betrayed to gain favour and for much more advantageous benefits in the future.*

Yes, there was much to suggest that Father Felicjan was the traitor. But if so...

But if so, Reynevan thought in despair, *the entire complicated*

Wrocław plan will come to nothing, the chances of recovering Jutta quickly vanished, my hopes dashed. Once again, I have no idea what to do or where to begin. I'm in the soup again. Back to square one again.

Assuming there's even a chance of getting beyond square one, thought Reynevan. *The cheerful Hlas may be wrong. Perhaps they won't exchange us at all? It might be as it was at Trosky Castle, where they buy Utraquists in order to subsequently execute them on the scaffold to improve the local populace's morale.*

But this time it was too much to count on being rescued by a mysterious, illusory woman.

At some point, the sick man had stopped groaning and raving. He was lying peacefully and even appeared to be feeling better. Reynevan hadn't dared to use magic in front of witnesses, so his recovery had to be put down to natural factors.

"Get out! Let's be having you! Look lively! Out of the wagon!"

The sun stung his eyes and the rush of cold air into his lungs almost knocked him unconscious. He had to grab the shoulder of Jan Kuropatwa of Łańcuchów in order to stay upright, on legs of jelly. Nadobny, standing beside him, wasn't doing any better; he was literally hanging, pale as a sheet, from Kochłowski's shoulder. The arms trader, although smallest of stature, and Hlas of Libočany turned out to be the toughest. The two of them stood firmly and most convincingly feigned courage.

"There will be an exchange of prisoners, gentlemen Hussites," Eberwin of Kranz, the mercenaries' commander, explained from the height of the saddle. "You will soon be free. You are indebted for your fate to the Honourable Gebhard Ungerath, son of His Lordship, Sir Kasper Ungerath. So bow! Low! This moment!"

Gebhard Ungerath, as stocky and ugly as a gnome, raised his

head haughtily and pouted, then reined his horse around and rode slowly away.

"Move, heretics, move! Over there, towards the bridge! Hey, over here, the sick man will have to be carried!"

"That river's the Olza," muttered Captain Hlas, suddenly growing serious. "We are somewhere between Fryštát and Cieszyn. They'll carry out the exchange on the bridge. It's something of a tradition."

They were made to stand before the bridge, surrounded by horses. The swollen Olza burbled under the bridge, washing the pillars, spilling over the fenders.

They didn't wait long before a rider appeared on the far bank. In a kettle hat, a mail hood with a short cape and a dull brownish-grey tunic worn over a brigantine, he was a typical vassal, a minor Hussite nobleman. He looked them up and down. He then described two circles with his horse before riding onto the bridge with a thud of horseshoes. He rode across to them, looking around vigilantly. Eberwin of Kranz caught up with him. They conversed for a while. Then the two men rode before Gebhard Ungerath.

"He says," said Eberwin of Kranz, clearing his throat, "that they have kept their word. They've brought young Master Gilbert. They know that instead of five—as was agreed—we have six, so, to show good will, they will free one more Silesian along with young Master Gilbert. But first he wishes to see our captives."

Gebhard pouted again and nodded his assent. The Hussite vassal, led by Eberwin, walked his horse over to the captives and glanced at them from under his kettle hat. But Reynevan bowed his head, fearful that his face would betray him.

For the vassal was Urban Horn.

He was playing to perfection the role of an insignificant and none-too-bright emissary. With gaze lowered, he mumbled something to Eberwin in hushed tones and bowed towards Gebhard Ungerath.

"You've seen what you wanted to see," Eberwin said to him, "so go back to your own. Know that we have kept our word and aren't plotting any treachery, just an honest exchange. Come on, march," he commanded the prisoners, watching Urban Horn cross the bridge and disappear into the trees. "Help that sick man!"

"Did you see?" whispered Kochłowski. "That was—"

"I know."

"What does all this—"

"I don't know. Be quiet."

A small Hussite light cavalry unit bearing red Chalices on their tunics was approaching from the other side of the river. Both parties reached the bridge at the same time. A moment later, the Hussites let two men onto the bridge. Seeing that, Ungerath's mercenaries urged their prisoners onto the bridge. The two groups began to walk towards each other. Gilbert Ungerath must have been one of the two men approaching from the left-hand bank, although neither of them was stocky or gnome-like. One of them was tall, with reddish hair; the other had a cherubic face and matching golden curls. Reynevan thought he recognised the latter. But he was busy helping Kochłowski to hold up the sick man. Whose fever had subsided and who could now walk unaided.

"*Miserere nobis…*" he suddenly said quite lucidly. A shudder passed through Reynevan. And a wave of fear. Justified fear, as it turned out.

From the trees on the left bank of the Olza emerged a good-sized cavalry unit, with bowmen, lancers and men in full armour. Spreading out into a semicircle, the new arrivals cut off the Hussites' escape route, forcing them to fall back towards the bridge.

Jan Kuropatwa swore and turned around. But Silesian mercenaries were already making for the bridge from the right bank.
They were cut off. Cornered.

"Fuck it, I see we have *Syriam ab oriente...*" Kochłowski murmured a biblical quote, "*et Philisthim ab occidente...*"

"Then we're in the shit..." groaned Hlas.

Gebhard Ungerath embraced his brother, who turned out to
be the red-haired man. Then he cast a look at the prisoners and
the Hussites. A look dripping with hatred. His face contorted
like a real gnome's.

"Thought you'd get away with it, heretics?" he said scathingly.
"That you'd save your skins? That you'd be able to strike a deal? Oh,
no, not a chance, there'll be no parleying with you, whoresons,
no deals. For you, only what you deserve, you blackguards: the
noose, the axe and the stake. And you'll be hanged, beheaded
or burned, for you'll be delivered back to where you came
from."

The recently arrived lancers and heavily armed cavalrymen
had effectively blocked the entry to the bridge on the left bank.
The knight commanding them bore crossed battleaxes on his
shield.

"As for you, accursed apostate," said Gebhard Ungerath, pointing a finger at Reynevan, "we will turn you over to the Bishop
of Wrocław. We happen to know that the bishop is dreaming of
getting you into the torture chamber. And it shall be a service to
the Church—"

"We also know," said Urban Horn, raising his head, "that this
is all in the name of service. This deceitfully hatched trick, this
entire hawker's swindle. Not even devised by you, although you
are a hawker. Your upstart papa hoped by doing so to gain fame
and land himself a knighthood. The noble Sir Hawker of Ungerath, with a broken farthing in his coat of arms. But instead of

a coat of arms, you'll have shit, Gebhard. For your plan is worth shit."

"I'll have you flayed alive for those words, heretic," Gebhard Ungerath spat furiously. "You're done for! Can't you see you're ensnared?"

"It is you who is ensnared. Look around."

In the utter silence that suddenly fell, fresh soldiers had appeared on both banks of the Olza. Numbering at least a hundred. They quickly hemmed the bridge in. From both sides.

"They are..." said Gebhard, pointing a shaking hand at the large red standard with a silver Odrowąż. "They are the knights of Lord Kravařê! Catholics! Our allies!"

"Not any longer."

Ungerath's stunned and bewildered mercenaries were disarmed without any resistance. Reynevan saw Paszko Rymbaba gazing around him with eyes wide open, unable to understand why Hussites decorated with the Chalice who had suddenly allied with armed knights bearing battleaxes in their crest were confiscating his weapons. He saw Eberwin of Kranz, as pale as a ghost, unable to comprehend why he was being disarmed and why Moravians fighting under the Odrowąż were being taken captive.

A moment later, they were all on the left bank of the Olza. While Horn was wordlessly shaking the hands of Reynevan and the Poles, the Moravians were driving into a small group and putting under guard their recent oppressors, now themselves prisoners. Standing with lowered heads, still dumbfounded, were Kranz's mercenaries, Gilbert Ungerath, and the young knight with the cherubic face. And Gebhard, with his contorted gnome's face, goggling at the incident's chief architect, a magnate dressed in splendid armour with a swarthy face and a bushy black moustache. A magnate Reynevan had seen once before.

Indeed, he thought, *it's a very small world.*

Commanding his hejtmans and knights, beneath the standard of the Odrzywąż, the crest of the Beneš family, rode up before them Jan of Kravaře, Lord of Nový Jičín, Fulnek, Bílovec, Štramberk and Rožnov, a magnate, a mighty lord, the ruler of a dominium covering an immense swathe of the north-west part of the Moravian margraviate.

"The man with the battleaxes in his arms, next to Lord Kravaře, is Silvestr of Kralice, Hejtman of Fulnek," Horn explained in hushed tones. "And the other one, with the beard, is Jan Helm."

Jan of Kravaře reined in his horse.

"Young Masters Ungerath," he said in a calm, somewhat unemotional voice, "a few words of explanation are in order. Since the time young Sir Gebhard and Sir Silvestr of Kralice, here present, devised their wily though none too honest plan, the situation has changed. And changed fundamentally, I'd say. M'lords, I was inspired by my spirit, the grace of enlightenment came to me, the scales fell from my eyes. I have seen the truth. I've understood who is in the right. I've realised who is on the side of honest Christian faith and who on the Antichrist's. Since yesterday, m'lords, since the Saturday before Oculi Sunday, I have forsaken my allegiance to Sigismund and Albrecht, received the sacrament *sub utraque specie* and sworn to uphold the Four Articles of Prague. Since yesterday, good Czechs marching under the banner of the Chalice are no longer my foes, but my brothers in faith and my allies. It is clear that I cannot allow treachery and betrayal to befall my brothers and allies. I thus declare your agreement with Lord Kralice null and void."

"Why...Why..." mumbled Gebhard Ungerath. "It's not right...It's dishonest...It's treachery...Why, it's—"

"I advise you to refrain from talk of treachery, m'Lord Ungerath," the Lord of Jičín interrupted calmly, "since the word

sounds somewhat grotesque in your mouth. And where do you
see dishonesty? Why, everything here is honest and in keeping
with divine order. Was there to be an exchange? There is one.
According to the agreement: the Czechs gave you back your
men; you gave the Czechs back theirs. To use the language of
trade so you might better understand: the reckoning comes
out even. But now I shall open an account. A quite new one.
Now, follow me, Lord Ungerath. Your father will negotiate a
ransom, for you and your brother. But before we strike a deal,
the two of you will be locked up in the Jičín tower. And with
you these other gentlemen. All of you, however many of you
there are."

Jan Helm laughed and Silvestr of Kralice joined the laughter,
slapping an armoured hand against his thigh. Jan of Kravařejust
smiled.

"I'd be a dullard, O Silesian Lords, if I didn't wring out two
thousand grzywna for the lot of you. Prokop was right, as were
you, Horn, that I would profit by going over to the Chalice! That
God would reward me! Indeed, He already is!"

"Honourable Sir Jan," Reynevan suddenly spoke. "I have a request to you. Regarding two of those knights. Please set them
free."

The magnate looked long and hard at him.

"Horn," he finally said, without taking his eyes off Reynevan.
"Is this that spy of yours?"

"Indeed."

"Bold he is. And worth so much to you that he gets away with
such boldness?"

"Aye."

"Must I take your word for it?" snorted Jan of Kravařе.

"If you prefer," said Reynevan not lowering his gaze, either,
"you may judge on the basis of facts."

98

"What facts?" said the Lord of Jičín, pouting in mockery. "I'm dying of curiosity."

"*Anno Domini* 1425, the thirteenth of September, Silesia, the Cistercian grange in Dębowiec. The council in the barn. Opposite you, Sir Jan, sat Gottfried Rodenberg, Teutonic Knight, Vogt of Lípa. On your left sat Sir Půta of Častolovice, Starosta of Kłodzko. On your right, a knight bearing on his doublet red stag's antlers, similar to the coat of arms of the Bibersteins, but with different tinctures."

"Sir Tas of Prusinovice." Jan of Kravaře nodded. "Your memory serves you well. Why, then, do I not remember you?"

"I was not with you there. I was above you. In the hayloft. Which is why I saw and heard everything. Every word that was uttered."

The magnate remained silent, twisting his black moustache.

"You are right," he said finally. "Indeed, you can be judged on the basis of facts. I judge you and find you decent. You are a resourceful rascal. The Tábor must benefit from your roguery. But my benefit, Master Spy, isn't a trifle to me, either. There would have been a profit for the Silesians you ask me for. If I release them, there will be none. And the absence of profit is a loss. Who will compensate me?"

"God," Urban Horn interrupted carelessly. "And the one temporarily deputising for him, Prokop, rightly called the Great, *director operationum Thaboritarum*. You will not make a loss, Sir Jan. You have my guarantee."

"Your guarantee is a precious thing," said Jan of Kravaře, smiling, "and grows in value. And what is more, I like the look of this Reynevan. He watched us and eavesdropped on us from the hayloft back then, dammit, so close he could have spat on Bishop Konrad's tonsure! And pissed down Legate Orsini's collar! A bold one, though a spy. Dammit, I can afford to be generous! I release those two, Lord Helm. The rest under guard! And prepare to move out, we'll soon be setting off for Jičín."

The prisoners were led away. Gebhard Ungerath yelled and cursed and Gilbert wept copious tears, heedless of the shame. Paszko Rymbaba looked back.

"Reinmar!" he called woefully. "What about me? Save me, too!"

"No, Paszko."

"But why?"

"Orders."

Reynevan turned towards the two men released owing to his intercession: Eberwin of Kranz and the cherubic young knight. Kranz looked at him grimly.

"I know why I've received this reprieve from you, Bielau," he said hoarsely. "Rymbaba told me. Let us thus not prolong this pathetic scene. Want to know how you were caught in Wrocław? By accident. And thanks to Wilkosz Lindenau's wagging tongue. He was grateful to you. Praised your goodness and nobility. Too much, too often and too loudly. May I go?"

So it wasn't Achilles or Allerdings. Reynevan sighed, greatly relieved. *And not Felicjan! So not everything is lost, Felicjan is still searching for Jutta ... Perhaps he's found her?*

"Hmm, hmm ..."

He raised his head. Eberwin had already gone and the young knight with golden curls was standing in front of him.

"M'lord," he said in a slightly trembling voice, "I confess I do not entirely understand why they freed me. I know neither your name nor your coat of arms. But you are a Hussite, so you know that the Catholic faith and knightly honour do not permit me to enter into close contact with a heretic. But know also that I am indebted to you for my release. I shall pay back the debt, I swear before God."

"You swear to a Hussite?"

"God will show me how to honour this promise, without sinning or offending the faith."

"God has heard your oath," said Reynevan, looking him in the eyes. "And I can tell you at once how to fulfil it. You will raise a toast."

"What?"

"You will raise a toast and drink to the health of the lady of my heart. Miss…Fair Nicolette. But at no other time than at your very own wedding, Sir Wolfram Pannewitz. To Miss Katharina Biberstein. Then, and only then, will I acknowledge the oath fulfilled. And you as a man of honour."

Wolfram Pannewitz paled and pursed his lips. Then blushed like a beetroot.

"I know now who you are," he said, swallowing. "For I have heard much…You wish to see me married to a maiden with a child. What reason do you have for that, eh? Perhaps that child—"

"Don't be a fool, Pannewitz," Reynevan quietly interrupted him. "Go to Stolz. Look at the little boy. And then in the looking glass. I shall not say anything more to you about it.

"God has heard," he added, loudly, for everyone to hear. "God has heard what you have vowed."

"Reynevan," Urban Horn called impatiently. "We're leaving. Don't prolong this pathetic scene."

Chapter Four

In which Reynevan loses part of his ear and most of his illusions.

"Thank you for rescuing me," said Reynevan, "but I'm not going with you. I'm returning to Silesia."

Urban Horn said nothing for a long time, watching Jan of Kravaře's detachment as it rode away. Then he turned around in the saddle. He had already rid himself of his disguise as a poor Czech nobleman and was once more the old Horn: Horn in an elegant cloak of delicate wool, Horn in a lynx calpac with a plume of heron feathers. Horn with his piercing, gimlet eyes.

"You aren't returning to Silesia," he said coldly. "You're coming with me."

"Weren't you listening?" Reynevan said in a loud voice. "Didn't it get through to you? I have to return! The fate of the person I love depends on it!"

"Miss Jutta of Apolda," Horn confirmed unemotionally. "I know."

"Oh, you do? Then you know I'll do anything in order to—"

"I know you will," Horn interrupted sternly. "The question is how much you've achieved so far."

"What are you..." said Reynevan, feeling himself pale. And then flush. "What are you driving at?"

"Hush, would you," said Horn, looking at the Poles watching

them. He urged his horse on, riding up so close that their stirrups touched. "Making your cause public won't help it. And you well know what I'm driving at. News spreads fast, rumours even faster. The news is that you were lately forced to betray. But the rumours say you've been a traitor for much longer. Since the very beginning."

"Blow that! You know me, Horn. You—"

"I do," interrupted Horn once again. "Which is why I don't lend credence to rumours. And as for news…It will have to be verified. There's no smoke without fire, so they say. For which reason, I repeat, you are not going back to Silesia. You'll come with me to Sovinec, and from there I shall immediately send you under escort to Prague. On Neplach's orders. I have to do it, you must understand."

"Listen—"

"End of discussion. Let us ride."

In the afternoon they bade farewell to the Poles and Hlas of Libočany. Kochłowski, Nadobny, Kuropatwa of Łańcuchów and the Taborite captain joined the Olomouc road which would take them to Odry. It emerged from earlier conversations that his old comrade, Dobko Puchała, was stationed in Odry with his Polish regiment. For some time Odry had been the point of conscription for volunteers from Poland and the hub for the trade of arms smuggled from Poland.

The farewell was fond. The Poles hugged and kissed Reynevan, and Kuropatwa invited him warmly to Odry, in order, as he explained it, to fight shoulder to shoulder and engage in joint operations. Reynevan couldn't have known then how quickly it would come to pass. And with what disastrous results.

Horn's unit set off westwards along the rocky Moravice valley. The eight Taborites left with the Poles and in the unit remained

seven armed Moravians, burgmen from Sovinec, the castle
which turned out to be their destination. The sick man who had
been released also rode with them. The identity of the man and
the reason Horn took him along remained a mystery. He was
still clearly unwell, sweating, coughing and sneezing. He rocked
and dozed in the saddle, while the two Moravians Horn had
assigned to him prevented him from falling off.

"Horn?"

"Yes,"

"I'm no traitor. You surely don't believe I am. Or perhaps you
do?"

Horn reined in his horse and waited for some soldiers to pass.

"The stories doing the rounds weaken my faith," he said, eyes
boring into Reynevan's. "So restore it. And convince me."

"I can guess at the source of these nasty rumours and slander,"
Reynevan exploded. "Word has spread that Jan of Ziębice seized
me in White Church, imprisoned me and tried to turn me, to
lie to Královec, to lead him into a trap and send the Orphans to
their doom—"

"You surmise correctly. Word *has* spread."

"And what of it? Did I betray them? Was Královec caught in
a trap at Wielisław? Did it end in defeat or victory? Who was
roundly defeated? Us or them?"

"That's a point for you. Go on."

"I've always been loyal to the cause of the Chalice. I worked
with Neplach. In 1427 I put him onto the trail of the plot of
Hynek of Kolštejn and Smiřický. Since then, I've had dozens of
chances to betray him. I knew a great deal, I had access to secrets,
I was party to confidential plans and strategies. I could have
turned in Tybald Raabe. I could have sold out the Vogelsang.
I could have betrayed the Chalice in 1428, before and during
the expedition, in Kłodzko, in Kamieniec and in Frankenstein.

I could have turned *you* in, Horn; I had numerous opportunities to do so. The Bishop of Wrocław would have showered me with gold. So do not make me prove my loyalty, because that's an affront to me. For there is no halfway house here, no colours or shades. Take it or leave it. You either believe me or you don't. You either trust me or you don't."

Urban Horn jerked the reins, making his snorting horse trot on the spot.

"I ought to admire your heartfelt outburst," he drawled, "but reality makes me doubt it, and your naivety. For a halfway house does exist, Reinmar. Shades do exist, and as regards colours, there is a palette, a veritable rainbow. I've already told you: I don't lend credence to the rumours, I don't believe you were an agent provocateur and a traitor from the start, that you came to Bohemia and joined us only to betray us. But you began to spy. For us, admittedly, but what difference does that actually make? You became a spy. And that is a fucking spy's lot, a spy's fate and the fucking goods in a spy's inventory: one day they finally catch you and turn you. It's normal in this trade. They kidnapped the maid you were enamoured with. And blackmailed you. And you yielded to blackmail."

"You jump quickly to conclusions. Will you manage to maintain this pace? Will I have to wait long for my sentence, too? And my punishment?"

"It's you who draws too-hasty conclusions. Much too hasty. It's time we stopped, dusk is falling. Hey, men! We'll stop here, by the trees. Dismount!"

The fire—fanned by the wind—roared and cracked, the flames shooting upwards, sparks flying above the tops of the firs. The trees soughed.

The Moravians, having finished off a plump demijohn of

slivovitz, lay down to sleep in turn, swathing themselves in cowled cloaks and sheepskins. The sick man, who had been laid down beside them, groaned, coughed and spat up phlegm. Urban Horn, yawning, used a stick to poke and move about the logs in the campfire. Reynevan was more hungry than sleepy. He was chewing some sheep's cheese, lightly toasted over the glowing logs.

The sick man choked in another coughing fit.

"Couldn't you take care of him?" Horn nodded towards him. "You're a physician, after all. It would be right to help a suffering man."

"I don't have any medicine. Should I use magic? In the presence of Calixtines? To them sorcery is a *peccatum*—"

"—*mortalium*, I know. Then something natural? Some kind of herbs or plants?"

"In February? Very well, if there are any willows here, I'll make a decoction from the bark in the morning. But his condition is improving—his fever has visibly diminished and the sweating is much reduced. Horn?"

"What?"

"I see you are taking good care of him."

"Indeed?"

"And I surmise that the exchange of prisoners was all about him, rather than me."

"Indeed?"

"Who is he?"

"Somebody."

Reynevan lifted his head and looked for a long time at the Great Bear, visible behind clouds scudding across the sky.

"I understand," he said finally. "I am under suspicion. Secrets aren't shared with the likes of me. What difference does it make if the suspicions are inflated and unproven? You don't share secrets and that's that."

"And that's that," agreed Horn. "Go to sleep, Reinmar. You have a long road ahead of you. A long, long road."

A long, long road, he repeated in his thoughts, gazing at the stars through the wind-shaken branches. *That's what he said. Thinking I wouldn't notice the sneer and ambiguity? Or quite the opposite: was he hinting at it?*

It must be a good forty miles from here to Prague: ten days' riding at a conservative estimate. A long road indeed. Leading directly into the hands of Bohuchval Neplach, known as Flutek, the head of the Tábor's intelligence service. Flutek won't easily be convinced, made to believe; that road might also be a long one. A difficult one. And painful. It's well known what Flutek does to suspects before he comes to believe them. And to those he doesn't believe.

Should I confess everything? Tell them about Jutta's kidnap, about Bożyczko, about the blackmail? Ha, perhaps I'll save my life by doing that. If they believe me. But I won't regain their trust. They'll lock me up, bury me alive in some tower or castle in a remote spot. Before I get out—if I get out at all—Jutta will be far away, married or in a convent. I'll lose her for ever.

Running away, he thought, getting up cautiously, *would be tantamount to admitting my guilt. That's how it'd be treated: as blatant proof of treachery.*

Blow it. Damn it all. There's no other choice.

The campfire died down and plunged the entire clearing in darkness. The entire camp. And the men sleeping with their heads on their saddles, shifting beneath their covers, snoring, farting, mumbling in their slumber. No one had even thought about setting a watch. Reynevan silently retreated into the darkness, among the undergrowth. Cautiously and slowly, being careful not to step on any dry twigs, he began to move towards the tethered horses.

The horses snorted as he approached. Reynevan froze, stopped dead. Fortunately, the trees were soughing and other sounds were lost in the endless rustling. He breathed out in relief. Too soon.

Someone lunged at him, knocking him over with their weight. He crashed to the ground, but before falling managed with a desperate push to turn the fall into a leap, which saved him from being seized. And saved his life. As he dodged and rolled over, he noticed the flash of a blade out of the corner of his eye. He jerked his head back and the knife that was aimed for his throat only snagged his ear, lacerating it deeply. Ignoring the sharp pain, he rolled over some roots sticking out of the ground and forcefully kicked the attacker, who was getting onto his hands and knees. The attacker swore and swung widely, trying to stab Reynevan in the leg. Reynevan spun around and kicked him again, this time knocking him over, and leaped up from the ground. He could feel the blood streaming down his collar.

The attacker also sprang up. And immediately attacked, slashing diagonally with rapid cuts of the knife. In spite of the darkness, Reynevan now knew who he was facing. The odour of sweat, fever and illness betrayed him.

The sick man wasn't so sick at all. And knew how to use a knife. He was skilled. But so was Reynevan.

He tricked his opponent with a feint, forced him to lean back. Reynevan knocked the man's wrist with his forearm, struck his elbow with his right fist, tripped him and overbalanced him with a tug to his sleeve, and for good measure struck him in the nose with the heel of his hand. The sick man howled and began to fall. As he fell, he managed to stab Reynevan in the crotch, splitting open his trousers. Only a miracle and quick reflexes prevented Reynevan from having his genitalia and femoral artery slashed. But in dodging he also tripped and lost his footing. The sick man threw himself on Reynevan like a wildcat, aiming a blow from above. Reynevan caught the assailant's wrist in both his hands. He held on with all his might, drawing in his head as the attacker struck him chaotically with his left fist.

It ended as quickly as it had started. A crowd had gathered. Several pairs of hands grabbed the sick man and pulled him off Reynevan. As they did so, he rasped, hissed and spat like a cat. He only dropped the knife when one of the Moravians brutally brought a heel down on his hand.

Urban Horn stood by with his arms folded. He observed it all in silence.

"He attacked me! Him!" yelled Reynevan, pointing at the sick man. "I went to piss and he jumped me with a knife!"

Held by the Sovinec burgmen, the sick man tried to say something, but only managed to goggle, wheeze and cough uncontrollably. Reynevan didn't waste the opportunity.

"He attacked me! For no reason! He tried to kill me! Look what a mess he's made of me!"

"Tend to him," said Horn. "At the double, you can see he's bleeding. And unhand the other, let him stand up unaided. Take away that knife. And in future, guard your weapons better. The knife belongs to one of you. He didn't have his own."

"Unhand him?" yelled Reynevan. "What do you mean by that? Horn! Have him bound, dammit! He is a killer!"

"Shut up. Let them bandage your ear, then join us over there, for a word in private. I see we need to have a serious talk."

The sick man was leaning against a tree trunk, glancing to one side. He was wiping away the blood that was still dripping from his nose. And suppressing a cough. He was sweating, and looked a sorry sight.

"He tried to kill me," said Reynevan, pointing a finger at the man. "He's a murderer. He pretended to be sicker than he was and was actually seeking out a chance to kill me. He's been planning it ever since he found out who I am."

Urban Horn crossed his arms and didn't comment.

"But now I know who he is," Reynevan went on in a calmer voice. "I had my suspicions and now I know. When we were travelling to the exchange, he was indeed ill. I treated him with magic and he was delirious. *Adsumus, Domine Sancte Spiritus, adsumus peccati quidem immanitate detenti, sed in nomine tuo specialiter congregati. Adsumus!* Does that invocation ring any bells for you?"

"Indeed," said Horn, his face unmoving. "It's a common prayer. The invocation to the Holy Spirit. Written by Saint Isidore of Seville."

"We both know whose summons it is," said Reynevan without raising his voice. "We both know who that character is. Doubtless you've known it for a long time. I just found out. Pity it wasn't from you, Horn. Your secret almost cost me my life. The bastard nearly cut my throat—"

"What?" said the sick man, overcoming his cough. "What? Was I to wait for him to cut *my* throat? I had to protect myself! Defend myself! He had begun to suspect me…And would finally have found out the truth. He would have killed me as sure as anything if he found out that—"

"—that you killed his brother," Urban Horn ended the sentence dryly. "Yes, Reinmar, your suspicions were correct. Let me introduce you. Bruno Schilling. A member of the Company of Death, the Black Riders of Birkart Grellenort. One of the men who killed your brother Peterlin."

Reynevan didn't sleep a wink until dawn. At first, the excitement and adrenaline, anger and the pain of his injured ear prevented him from falling asleep. Then came memories. And apparitions.

The Cistercian Forest, the breakneck cavalcade, the Black Horsemen screaming *Adsumus!* The knight from Grochowa Mountain: wild-eyed, deathly-blue-faced, wailing like a demon…The chase through the forest at Trosky at night…

His brother, Peterlin, stabbed and pierced by swords. And one of the men who stabbed him, who delivered the blows, who killed Peterlin, was lying, covered in a blanket, ten paces away, on the other side of the campfire, coughing and sniffing. Under the vigilant stares of the two Moravians whom Horn had instructed to guard him.

Guard him? Or perhaps protect him.

They set off in the early morning. In quite low spirits, which the weather didn't want to attune with, however. From dawn the sun had been shining splendidly and by around three o'clock it was pleasantly warm. The spring of 1429 came early.

As they rode, Reynevan ostentatiously kept himself apart and looked the other way whenever Horn tried to make eye contact. Horn quite quickly wearied of his behaviour.

"Stop bloody sulking," he drawled, trotting over. "It is as it is, you can't change the situation. So get used to it. And accept it."

Reynevan nodded towards the sick man: "Accept the fact that my brother's murderer, the blackguard who tried to kill me last night, is riding along on a black horse over there, as if nothing happened? Though he should be swinging from a bare branch?"

The sick man, riding a dozen paces ahead of them, the Black Rider, Bruno Schilling—Reynevan still couldn't decide what to call him—appeared to sense they were talking about him, for he kept glancing over furtively. The two Moravians watched him constantly.

"You ordered them, I see, to have taut crossbows at the ready," observed Reynevan. "That's not enough, Horn, not nearly enough.

I once played a part in killing one of them. Four bolts—sunk up to the fletching—were needed to finish him off."

"Thank you for the advice. But leave it to me. I know what I'm doing."

"If you knew, if you were transporting him as a prisoner to be questioned, you'd order him bound and transported in an armoured wagon, like the one we travelled in to the exchange yesterday. But you're taking good care of him, looking after him. He's a murderer. An assassin, an unthinking machine, killing to order. A member of the Company of Death that terrorises Silesia! There's no way of calculating how many people they have killed. Our people, men loyal to our cause. People who helped us and collaborated with us. And you—even though you're well aware of it—haven't even ordered him bound."

"Reynevan," Horn replied seriously, "there's a war on. We're fighting it on all fronts. It's not an ordinary war, but a religious war; there's never been one like it. A religious war differs from other wars in that men on both sides of the front often end up changing their religion. Today a Hussite, tomorrow a papist; today a Catholic, tomorrow a Calixtine. You had a clear example yesterday, in the person of Sir Jan of Kravaře. Sir Jan had been one of the bitterest enemies of the Chalice and the ideas of Huss. Along with Přemek of Opava and the Bishop of Olomouc, he represented a bastion of militant Catholicism in Moravia. You couldn't count the Hussites he has ordered burned at the stake or hanged from bare branches. And what happened today? He has changed religion and sides. The Chalice and the Tábor have acquired a powerful ally owing to that change. And you gained your freedom and your life was saved. All in all, our cause has benefited from it. We are waging a religious war. But we shall leave fanaticism and zealous fervour to the masses we send into battle. We—men of higher ideas—ought to aspire to a broader perspective. Pragmatism, laddie. Pragmatism and practicalism."

"Have I understood your analogy? That man there, that—"

"Bruno Schilling. You understood. And quickly, at that. He's no longer a Black Rider, not of the Company of Death. He's changed religion. And sides."

"A renegade?"

"Pragmatism, Reynevan, don't forget. Not a renegade, not a traitor, not Judas Iscariot, but a gain. To our cause."

"Listen, Horn—"

"Enough. That's enough, end of discussion. I didn't tell you all this gratuitously, I didn't keep coming back to pragmatism without reason. You'll soon appear before Neplach. Remember then the lesson I've just given you. Make use of it."

"But I—"

"Enough talk! Sovinec lies before us."

They didn't stay long in Sovinec. Reynevan in particular didn't stay there at all. He was given a fresh horse as soon as he passed through the gate, beside a forge resounding to the clank of metal. His new escort was also there: five extremely lugubrious foot soldiers. All in all, an hour hadn't passed before he was on the road again, and behind him the towering column of the berg-fried—the most recognisable feature of Sovinec—rising above the forested ridges of the hills, shrank in size the further away he rode.

A short time later, Urban Horn caught up with them.

"It's as if you can't part with me," Reynevan commented tartly. Horn gestured for him to fall back behind the escort. "Could it be you know something I don't? For example, that you won't see me alive again?"

Horn just shook his head and reined in his horse.

"I want to give you some advice. Parting advice."

"Say on. Don't prolong this pathetic scene. Tell me what's awaiting me in Prague. What will they do with me?"

Horn looked back, but only for a moment.

"That depends on you. On you alone."

"Could you be more precise?"

"If they turned you," said Horn, the muscles in his jaw twitching perceptibly, "Neplach will want to make use of it. He'll turn you again. It's a standard procedure. You will start feeding the enemy information. But false information. Fabricated."

"Where's the catch?"

"It's dangerous. Doubly so."

"Listen carefully," said Horn a few moments later, interrupting the long silence. "Listen carefully, Reinmar. I advise you not to run away. Running away would be proof of your guilt and your sentence would fall. Neplach is aware of how many secrets you've heard, how many of our plans and military secrets you possess. You'd know no peace. Even if you fled to the end of the world, you'd be living on borrowed time. You and anyone close to you. You might have broken down under blackmail out of fear for the fate of Miss Jutta. Miss Jutta is thus your weak point, the most tender place to strike you. Don't kid yourself that Neplach would pass up that opportunity."

Reynevan said nothing. He just swallowed and nodded. Horn also said nothing.

"I believed in the cause of the revolution," Reynevan finally said. "I had a genuine sense of mission, of the fight for apostolic faith, for ideals, for social justice, for a new, better tomorrow. I genuinely believed that we would change the old order, that we would shift the world from its ossified foundations. I fought for the cause, profoundly believing that our victory would put an end to immorality and evil. I was prepared to spill my blood for the cause of the revolution, ready to sacrifice myself, throw myself like a stone against the ramparts…And I did, like a madman, a blind man, a fool. What did you call it? Fanaticism? Zealous ardour? It fits, it fits perfectly. But now what? The zealot and the neophyte will get his just desserts; his foolish blindness and madcap passion will be the end of him, and not only he, but also those closest to him will suffer. Ha, I hope they write about it in some future chronicle, as a lesson and warning to other neophytes and fools, prepared to blindly enter the fight and lay down their lives. So they'll know what it's like."

"But it's always like this. Didn't you know?"

"I do now. And I'll remember that."

"M'Lord Houžvička!"

"What?"

"An inn! May we stop?"

Houžvička grunted and muttered.

Houžvička, the escort's commander, was a grunting, muttering fellow, right from the outset of the journey dismissing any questions by grunting and muttering. It was some time before Reynevan realised that the name wasn't Vička or Žvička, or even Ožvička. The remaining four soldiers weren't very garrulous, either, seldom even talking among themselves. One might have been called Zahradil and another Smeták, but Reynevan couldn't be certain.

"A long road ahead," grunted Houžvička, "and we're only in Libina—we haven't even reached Šumperk. We must make haste and not rest."

"You can see I'm wounded," said Reynevan, pointing to the bandage wrapped around his head. "I have to change my dressing or gangrene will set in, I'll become feverish and die here on the road. It won't please them in Prague, believe me."

Actually, the wound was healing well, the ear wasn't swollen, the pulsating pain had eased and there was no infection. Reynevan simply wanted to rest his saddle-sore backside and delight in some warm, homemade food for the first time in ages, and a breeze was blowing quite appetising aromas from the little tavern nestling at a crossroads.

"It won't please them in Prague," he said again, putting on a gloomy face. "The guilty will be called to account, no question."

Houžvička grunted and his grunting contained quite coarse epithets aimed at Prague, Praguians and being called to account.

"We'll stop," he finally agreed. "But not for long."

Inside, in the empty common room, it transpired at once that Houžvička's haste was feigned and his objections only for effect. With an eagerness equal to that of Smeták, Zahradil and the others, the escort commander threw himself at the Lenten *žur* soup, peas, dumplings and stewed cabbage, and with an enthusiasm to match his subordinates', swilled the mugs of beer being brought by the breathless servants. Seeing them finishing one mug after the next over his bowl, Reynevan grew certain the journey would be delayed. And that they would stay the night in the little tavern outside the village of Libina.

The door creaked; the innkeeper wiped his hands on his apron and hurried to greet some new customers. And Reynevan froze with his spoon halfway to his wide-open mouth.

The arrivals—there were two of them—took off cloaks bearing the marks of a long journey made in conditions of oft-changing weather. One of them was of a great height and build and the floor thudded and shook under his feet. His head was closely shaven and he had the face of a child—a dim-witted one at that. The face of the other man, who was shorter and slimmer, was adorned with a scar across his chin and a large and distinguished aquiline nose.

They sat down at the next bench and shooed away the

innkeeper who came to take their order. They silently surveyed Reynevan and the Sovinec soldiers. Obtrusively enough to attract the attention of Houžvička, who returned their stares. And muttered.

"My greetings to you, company," said Scharley slowly, twisting his mouth in the imitation of a smile. "And where is the company headed? Where, I wonder, does your road lead?"

"Prague," said Smeták before Houžvička managed to shut him up with a kick.

"And what..." Houžvička said and gulped down the large dumpling he had been eating. "And what's it to you, eh? What business is it of yours?"

"Prague," Scharley repeated, utterly ignoring him. "Prague, you say. A lousy idea, brothers. Very lousy."

Houžvička and his squad goggled. Scharley stood up, moved to their table and sat down with them.

"There's unrest in Prague," he declared, exaggeratedly modulating his voice. "Riots, disturbances, fighting in the streets. Not a day goes by without a stabbing or a shooting. Easy for a stranger to take a beating."

Samson Honeypot, who had also joined them, confirmed each statement with a vigorous nod.

"Why go to Prague, then?" continued the penitent. "It makes no sense. If I were you, I wouldn't go. And why, it's Easter soon. Where do you mean to greet the Resurrection, where will you sample the contents of your blessed Easter basket, where will you nibble on a boiled egg? In a roadside ditch?"

"Why do you care?" exploded Houžvička. "Eh?"

"Because we care for you," said Scharley. He kept smiling and Samson kept nodding. "And for your comfort, brethren in Christ. I advise you to return to your homes. And don't tell me your duties won't permit you. I shall gladly relieve you of your duty—meaning this young man. I shall buy him from you. For thirty Hungarian ducats."

He swiftly unfastened a pouch from his belt and tipped a pile of gold coins out on the table. Zahradil almost choked. The others all goggled. Houžvička swallowed loudly.

"Whaaat?" he finally managed to blurt out. "Whaaat? Whaat? You want…You want…*him*?"

"Indeed I do," said Scharley, seductively arranging his mouth and delicately smoothing down the hair on his temples. "I would like to possess him. Purchase him. I've taken a great liking to him. I adore such comely boys, particularly blonds. Why do you look at me so strangely, brother? You surely aren't prejudiced? Surely not intolerant?"

"Damn you!" roared Houžvička. "Not on your life! Get out of here! Go buying boys elsewhere! There'll be no trading here!"

"Perhaps, then," said Samson, grimacing like a moron, blowing his nose into his hand and wiping the snot onto his sleeve. He took out a cup and dice and placed them on the table. "Perhaps then you prefer to gamble? Shall we? This young man here against these thirty ducats. All on one throw. I shall begin."

The dice rolled across the table.

"A two and a one," said Samson, appearing to be worried. "That makes three. Oh dear…Oh my…I think I've lost; I surely have. What a fool I am. Your turn. Roll them, please."

Zahradil's face lit up and he held his hand out for the dice, but Houžvička slapped his hand away.

"Fucking leave it!" he roared, looking fierce. "And you, sirs, begone! And take your ducats with you! The Devil sent you here! So go to hell!"

"Lean over here," Scharley drawled, "I have something to tell you."

No one with any sense at all would have. But Houžvička did.

He leaned over. Scharley's fist struck him in the jaw and sent him flying off the bench.

At the same moment, Samson Honeypot extended his powerful arms, seized the two Sovinec men by the hair and slammed their faces down onto the table, making it bounce and overturning the dishes and mugs. Smeták, demonstrating quick reflexes, whipped a large lindenwood bowl from the table and smashed it hard into the giant's forehead. The bowl broke in two. Samson blinked.

"Congratulations, good fellow," he said. "You've pissed me off."

And punched Smeták. With devastating results.

Meanwhile, Scharley felled Zahradil with a beautiful right hook, dealt out several powerful kicks among the soldiers trying to stand up, unerringly finding their crotches, bellies and necks. Reynevan leaped onto Houžvička, who was scrambling up from the floor, but he fought back and elbowed Reynevan hard in his wounded ear. Pain and fury clouded Reynevan's eyes. He punched Houžvička once, and then a second, third and fourth time. Houžvička fell face down onto the floor. Zahradil and the other two soldiers crawled behind the bench, indicating by their raised hands that they'd had enough.

From behind the stove came the sounds of punches and the dry thuds of a skull hitting a wall. It was Scharley and Samson hitting Smeták, whom they had trapped in the corner. Smeták was screaming horribly.

"Have mercy, masters! Don't hit me! Stop it! Very well, take the lad, if you wish. I'll give him to you!"

Scharley tried the bolts one more time to check they were securely fastened, stood up and brushed the dust off his knees. The innkeeper, face flushed with distress and excitement, observed his every move, his eyes moving around nervously.

"Don't open it till the morning," said Scharley, pointing at the trapdoor in the floor. "They can stay down there. If they get angry, tell them I threatened to kill you. And as a matter of fact, there you go, give them a ducat each. Tell them it's from me, as compensation. And here, have one yourself. For the damage and the inconvenience. Oh, blow it, take two. So that you will remember us with gratitude."

The innkeeper eagerly took the money and swallowed loudly. Muffled cries, curses and dull thuds could be heard from under the trapdoor to the cellar. But the trapdoor was made of oak and sturdy.

"Never mind, noble sir," said the innkeeper hurriedly, before Scharley could speak. "Let them rant and rage. I shan't open it until tomorrow. I won't forget what you said."

"Indeed, it'd be better if you didn't," said Scharley, his expression and voice becoming a tone colder. "Samson, Reinmar, to horse. Reinmar, what's the matter?"

"My ear—"

"Don't moan and groan. If you mean to be stupid, you have to be hard."

"How did you find me? How did you know?"

"It's a long story."

Chapter Five

In which Reynevan leaves his barely recovered friends on the island of Ogygia and continues on his way. In order to soon stand before a revolutionary tribunal.

They rode. First of all, at a gallop, slowing only when going uphill and in order not to exhaust their mounts. They rode so fast earth shot out from under their hooves. But when they were around a mile from the inn in Libina, when there were hills, forests, glades and bushes between them and Libina, they slowed down. There was no point rushing.

A warm spring wind was blowing from the mountains. Samson led, having ridden to the head of the cavalcade. Scharley and Reynevan rode side by side, not trying to catch up with the giant.

"Where are we going? Scharley? Where does this road lead?"

Scharley's horse, a handsome black stallion, cavorted around, unwearied by the gallop. The penitent patted its neck.

"To Rapotín," he replied. "It's a village outside Šumperk. We live there."

"You live here?" said Reynevan, mouth open in astonishment. "Here? In some Rapotín or other? And how did you find me? How the hell—"

"It was one of a sequence of absolute miracles," said Scharley with a snort, "each one more miraculous than the last. It began three Sundays ago. The day Neplach croaked."

"What?"

"Flutek has departed this life. Passed away. *Florentibus occidit annis*. In short, he died. Of natural causes, just imagine. Some predicted the noose, others wished him the noose, all in all no one doubted that the rascal would depart this world on the gallows. But in the end, he died like a babe, or a nun. Peacefully in his sleep. With a smile on his face."

"Impossible."

"Hard to believe," Scharley agreed, "but true. There were plenty of witnesses. Including Hašek Sýkora. Remember him?"

"I do."

"Hašek Sýkora has temporarily taken over Flutek's position and responsibilities. And is, you ought to know, very favourably disposed to you. Does any reason suggest itself?"

"Two, even. Two warts, both in unpleasant and most troublesome places for a married man. I cured them using a magical unguent."

"Good Lord," said Scharley, raising his eyes heavenwards. "My heart swells when I see that there is still gratitude in this world. Suffice it to say that it was he who sent us to your aid. Ride, he said, to Sovinec and Šumperk and rescue Reynevan, he said, before they take him to Prague. Prague isn't good for him. Whatever Reynevan did, he did, were his words. The Honourable Neplach, he said, had it in for him, but the Honourable Neplach has died. I have no opinion about the scandal, he said, and once Reynevan vanishes, the scandal will die down. So may the physician vanish, may he go where he wants. If he's guilty, God will judge him; if he's innocent, God help him. A decent sort."

"God?"

"No. Hašek Sýkora. Enough chinwagging, laddie. Spur on your

horse. See how Samson has drawn away. We've fallen behind."

"Where's he hurrying to?"

"Not to *where*, but to *whom*. You'll see."

The homestead, announced by the barking of dogs and the smell of smoke, was hidden behind a birch grove and a dense black-thorn hedge, above which poked the roof of a barn. Behind the barn were a shed and a granary beneath a thatched roof; then a wicket fence beyond which was an orchard full of squat plum and apple trees; then a farmyard, a white dovecote and a well with a sweep. And a house. A large log house with a shingle roof and a porch on posts.

They had barely ridden into the courtyard than a young woman ran down the steps of the porch. Reynevan recognised her even before her headscarf had slipped off as she ran, reveal-ing luxuriant red hair. He recognised her by how she moved, and she moved as though she were dancing, gracefully, barely touching the ground, like a nymph, a naiad, or some other super-natural creature. She was dressed in a simple grey frock, calling to mind those gauzy and fantastic robes with which—for the sake of decency and also for the composition—artists covered the sensual bodies of their Madonnas and goddesses in frescos, paintings and miniatures.

Marketa ran up to Samson and the giant slipped from the saddle straight into her embrace. Having freed himself, he lifted the girl like a feather and kissed her.

"How touching." Scharley, dismounting, winked at Reynevan. "They haven't seen each other for half a day. Their yearning, as you see, was almost the death of them. What joy to be reunited after being so long apart."

"You, Scharley," began Reynevan, "will probably never be able to understand what—"

He didn't finish. Another member of the fair sex emerged from a turf-covered cellar. A more mature one. More mature in every curve, grace and inch, one might say. A Galatea or an Amphitrite, judging from her face and figure, a Pomona or a Ceres, judging from the basket of apples and cabbages she was carrying.

"Were you saying something?" asked Scharley with the face of an innocent.

"No. Nothing."

"I'm glad to see you, m'Lord Reynevan," said Mistress Blažena Pospíchalová, the widow of Mr. Pospíchal, once Reynevan's landlady in the house on the corner of Štěpán and Na Rybníčku Streets in Prague's New Town. "Make haste, gentlemen. Dinner will soon be served."

Spring is coming, Reynevan observed, walking beside Scharley along a waterlogged causeway. Water dripped from the bare trees. There was a smell of wet earth. And of something rotten.

"I arrived in Prague in the late autumn of last year, after the Austrian plundering raid," said Scharley. "I wintered at Samson's house. It has never been especially peaceful in the capital, but now, in the spring, it has become quite turbulent. And damned dangerous. A seething cauldron, one might say. The reason was the negotiations Prokop the Shaven conducted with Sigismund—"

"Prokop is parleying with Sigismund?"

"Indeed. There is even talk of peace and of recognising Sigismund as king. The conditions are his receiving of the Four Articles of Prague and the legalisation of church estates being secularised. Sigismund, naturally, would never agree to anything of the kind and will break off the negotiations. Prokop knows that perfectly well and consented to the talks in order to show that Sigismund and the Catholics are the aggressive party, seeking war and not peace. That's obvious, but not to everybody. The affair has caused an acrimonious division in Prague. The Old Town supports the talks and calls for reconciliation and for Sigismund to be crowned King of Bohemia. The New Town won't even hear of it. Preachers are feeding the flames from the pulpit. At Our Lady of the Snows, they're calling Sigismund the 'King of Babylon' and the 'Red-headed Rascal' and are inciting the people to deal with 'advocates of compromise' and 'traitors.' While in the Old Town, at the Church of Our Lady before Týn, they're appealing for extermination of the 'fanatics' and 'radicals.' As a result, Prague is split into two hostile camps. Saint Gall's, Horská and Poříčí gates have been barricaded and the streets fenced off with chevaux de frise and chains. All day and all night at the frontier, guns fire, bolts whistle and balls fly. There are regular skirmishes that end with blood foaming in the gutters. The two sides regularly search for traitors and it's extremely easy to be accused of being one. It was high time to get out of there. Blažena…Hmm…Mistress Pospíchalová announced she had inherited a house near Šumperk. And when the issue with you came about, when Sýkora told us you'd be taken via Šumperk, I took it as a sign from Providence. We left Prague without a second thought. Or a single regret."

"And now what?" said Reynevan, without trying to keep the mocking tone out of his voice. "Will you be staying here? To settle down and till the soil? Or perhaps you think about marriage?"

Scharley looked at him. With a surprisingly serious expression.

"I think, my friend, about you," he replied, equally seriously. "Were it not for you I'd have headed in quite a different direction from Prague. Down the Buda road, straight towards Hungary and then on to Constantinople, to be precise. But it turned out that first I'd have to help a comrade. To extract my comrade from the difficulties he had foolishly got himself into. But has he?"

"Scharley—"

"Has he or not?"

"He has."

"Is he in the shit? Right up to his bloody neck?"

"He is."

"Tell all."

He had to tell it twice, since after supper they met in the granary to chat and Samson Honeypot also wished to be acquainted with the course of events and with details of the shit Reynevan was in. And while Scharley only shook his head as he listened, Samson came forward at once with conclusions.

"I absolutely advise you against returning to Silesia," he began. "You would gain nothing by so doing and only put yourself in danger. You've already been unmasked and captured once in Wrocław and they'll manage it next time, too. And I wouldn't count on the altarist Felicjan. He won't find out anything, it's well beyond him. The Inquisition knows how to guard its secrets. And now it certainly won't be stupid enough to hold Miss Jutta in a place that's easy for any old venal bloody priest to find."

"So what do I do?" asked Reynevan grimly. "Go back to the Hussites? And meekly do whatever the Inquisition commands? Hoping that I'll finally satisfy them sufficiently for them to release me and hand Jutta over?"

Scharley and Samson looked at each other. Then at Reynevan. He understood.

"They'll never give her to me. Am I right?"

A meaningful silence fell.

"A return to the Hussites," Samson finally said, "only appears to be the better choice. Your account suggests that they suspect you."

"They have no proof."

"If they had, you'd already be dead," Scharley said calmly. "But if you vanish, you offer them a pretext on a plate. Your flight would be proof of your guilt. And the sentence would be immediate."

"The Hussites will be watching you," added Samson. "They'll also keep you away from secrets and classified matters. Whether you want it or not, you won't find any information that would satisfy the Inquisition."

"The Inquisition won't harm the maid," said Scharley, swiftly but without mockery. "I believe that Hejncze to be an honest fellow. And he's a university pal of yours…"

He fell silent. Spread his arms. But almost immediately recovered his aplomb.

"Chin up, Reinmar, chin up. We aren't sunk yet, we'll set sail one day. We'll find a way. Neither Homer nor Virgil mention it, but I assure you: the Trojan intelligence service had agents among the Achaeans. And they also recruited them using blackmail. And the blackmailed agents found a way to trick Troy. We shall also trick Troy."

"How?" Reynevan asked bitterly. "Do you have any ideas? Any at all? Anything's better than sitting idly by."

They were silent for a while.

"We need to sleep on it," Scharley finally said. "*De mane consilium*, tomorrow will bring an answer."

The next day didn't bring Reynevan an answer, indeed brought nothing but an aching neck. The next day wasn't especially generous to Samson and Scharley, either, it appeared, at least regarding suggestions and solutions. The giant didn't mention the conversations of the previous day at all and focused all his attention on the red-haired Marketa, both at breakfast and after it. So Reynevan and Scharley took advantage of the first opportunity to go outside and take a walk together. A long one, to a causeway marked by an avenue of crooked willows separating two empty fishponds.

"It looks like Marketa and Samson are serious," began Reynevan, nodding towards the homestead.

"It does indeed," said the penitent gravely, "as is everything with Samson. He does appear to be a creature from another world. At times, I start believing it."

"Dammit, Scharley! He's our comrade—what point would there be in his deceiving us? If he says he's a visitor from another dimension, we must believe him! Serious, expert and unquestioned authorities have puzzled over this and expressed their views on it. Bezděchovský, Axleben, Rupilius...Do you think they'd be taken in by a swindle, or fail to expose a swindle? So where do your mistrust, your lack of faith come from?"

"Because I've seen swindles in my life that even took in authorities. I have even—I confess with remorse—perpetrated several. The peccadillos of youth...But enough of that. I said I'm starting to believe. For me, that's a great deal."

"I know. And since I've mentioned him, Rupilius—"

"Forget it," the penitent cut him off dryly. "Samson doesn't want to. I've spoken to him. He's fretting a little over the promise you gave Rupilius, but he's made a decision. Rupilius, he declared, will have to cope by himself, for he—Samson Honeypot—has something more important on his mind. Something he doesn't want to give up."

"Marketa."

"Of course."

"Scharley?"

"What?"

"Hmm...Does she ever speak?"

The penitent said nothing for a moment before replying.

"Not that I've heard."

*

The following day—a Wednesday according to the calendar—yielded scant results as far as clarity and solutions were concerned. And came to nothing.

When it began to get dark, they sat down to supper, all five of them. The conversation was strained, so they spent most of the time in silence. The red-haired Adamite ate little but spent the whole meal staring at Samson, and one hand was busy the entire time touching his enormous paw. The sight of tender looks and gestures not only embarrassed the others but made them jealous. Reynevan never remembered Jutta—not even during moments of passionate intimacy—giving him such overt, visible proof of adoration. He realised that his jealousy wasn't very rational, but its barbs didn't sting any the less for that.

Blažena Pospíchalová's behaviour also stung—but this time it was his male pride that suffered. The widow devoted her complete and undivided attention to Scharley. Although she did it with restraint and without exaggerated coquetry, the erotism between her and the penitent crackled. Reynevan, meanwhile, although sparks had flown between him and the widow in times past, didn't even earn any meaningful glances. He loved Jutta, naturally, and Mistress Blažena wasn't on his mind at all. But it stung. As though a hedgehog were nesting in his bosom.

At night, when he tried to fall asleep on the rustling palliasse, profounder reflections visited him.

And after reflections—decisions.

It was still quite dark when he saddled his horse and led it out of the stable, so quietly and secretly that even the dogs didn't bark. The dawn was barely breaking when he set off. It was only just light by the time his horseshoes were thudding on the hard road.

They've found what they wanted to find, he thought, looking back at the village of Rapotín. *Both of them. Samson Honeypot has something serious. He has Marketa, his Calypso and his island of Ogygia, there in that little village. Scharley has Blažena Pospíchalová; and it doesn't matter if he stays with her or travels on to his imagined Constantinople, to the Hippodrome, Hagia Sophia and fried octopus in the tavern by the Golden Horn. It doesn't matter if he ever makes it there. It doesn't matter what happens to Samson and Marketa in the future. But it would be pointless to make them give it up, drop everything, make them head off into the world, into the unknown, in order to risk their lives for someone else's cause. On my behalf.*

Farewell, my friends.

I also have something important; something I won't give up on. I'm heading off.

Alone.

Reynevan's plan was simple: to travel to the Mezilesí pass via the Morava valley and the foot of Sněžník, and the important trade route from Hungary that led straight into the Kłodzko valley. According to his calculations he was no more than five or six miles from the pass. True, there was another variant: along the Branná valley and through the pass to Lądek, and from there along the Salt Road to Krutvald, Nysa and Ziębice. Reynevan, however, feared the second variant, for even though it led him straight to his destination, the route ran through the mountains and the weather was still fickle.

It wasn't just the weather that was perilous. Like numerous regions of Moravia, the Šumperk region resembled a veritable chequerboard then—the estates of Catholic lords loyal to Duke Albrecht bordered with the lands of the gentry supporting the Hussites—and it was difficult to stay on top of it since men changed sides and loyalties too often. The confusion was all the greater since some lords remained neutral, which meant they were indifferent regarding whom they attacked and robbed: they attacked and robbed everybody.

Scharley had shared some information with Reynevan so he knew perfectly well that he wasn't safe with anybody and that it would be best to slip through unnoticed in order not to chance upon any of the parties. Neither the Strážnický lords from Kravaře in Zábřeh who supported the Chalice nor the lords of Kunštát from nearby Lošticíce. Nor even more so the Catholics on Albrecht's side: the Šumperk Valdštejns, the lords of Zvole and the numerous vassals of the Bishop of Olomouc, who were for ever bedevilling the region with raids.

It suddenly began to snow and the snowflakes, at first delicate, grew to become enormous and wet and stuck to his eyes at once. His horse was snorting and shaking its head, but Reynevan rode on. Praying to himself that what he was taking to be the road really was.

Fortunately, the blizzard stopped as suddenly as it had started. Snow was covering the fields, turning them white, but not the road, which remained visible and distinct. Traffic even appeared on it. He heard bleating and the jingling of bells and a flock of sheep trotted out onto the road. Reynevan spurred on his horse.

"God's blessings be upon you."

"And on you, hem-hem," said the shepherd, overcoming his fear. "And on you, young lord."

"Where are you from? What's that village yonder, beyond that hillock?"

"Over yonder? That'd be a village."

"What is it called?"

"That'd be Keprnov."

"And who owns that Keprnov?"

"That'd be the monastery."

"And are any soldiers stationed there?"

"Why should there be?"

Plied with yet more questions, the shepherd told him that beyond Keprnov was Hynčice and beyond Hynčice—Hanušovice. Reynevan sighed with relief, as it appeared he was following the correct route and wouldn't get lost. He bade the shepherd farewell and went on his way. The road led him straight to a ford on the fog-bound Morava, and then clung to the right bank. He soon passed the village Hynčice, consisting of several cottages which announced themselves in advance by the smell of smoke and the barking of dogs.

A short while after, he heard a bell in Hanušovice, which turned out to be a parish church, one that hadn't been burned down. There must still have been a priest or at least a curate there, for who else would have bothered to tug on a bell rope—and in the morning, at that? Reynevan decided to pay the clergyman a visit and ask for further directions, about soldiers, about armed squads—and maybe even get himself invited to breakfast.

He hadn't yet broken his fast.

Just beyond the church he ran into a group of soldiers, five mounted, holding some riderless horses and five foot soldiers in the vestibule, in discussion with a pint-sized parish priest who was blocking the entrance. At the sight of Reynevan they all fell silent and all of them—including the priest—glared at him. Reynevan cursed his bad luck under his breath, cursed it very coarsely, using words which absolutely should never be used in front of gentlewomen and babes in arms. But he had to play the cards he had been dealt. He took a deep breath to calm himself down, sat up straight and proud in the saddle, bowed carelessly and urged the horse on at a walk towards the wattle fences and cottages, planning to gallop as soon as he was out of sight. Nothing came of it.

"I say! Not so fast, young master!"

"Me?"

"You, sir."

They blocked his way and surrounded him. One man, with eyebrows like bunches of straw, caught his horse's harness by the bit, and as his cloak fell open, he revealed a large red Chalice on the tunic he was wearing over his breastplate. A closer look also revealed the Hussite emblem on the others. Reynevan gasped softly, knowing his situation hadn't improved at all.

The Hussite with the eyebrows stared at his face and the expression on his own face—to Reynevan's astonishment—changed. From a frown to one of surprise. And from surprise to one of delight. And back to a frown.

"You are Reynevan of Bielawa, a Silesian," he stated in a tone that left no room for discussion. "A physician who treats the sick."

"Oh? And what of it?"

"I know you, so don't deny it."

"I don't deny anything. I asked what of it."

"God sent you to us, for we need a physician to treat a sick man. Without delay. So you'll ride with us. We request this of you. We request this politely."

The very polite request was accompanied by evil looks, lips being bitten and muscles twitching in jaws. And hands on belts close to sword hilts. Reynevan understood it would be better not to reject the request.

"Perhaps, though, I might learn with whom I am dealing? Where I am to go? Who is the sick man? And what ails him?"

"You'll not be riding far," interrupted the Hussite with the eyebrows, who was clearly the troop's commander. "My name is Jan Pluh. Deputy Hejtman of the field army of the Orphans of the Náchod community. You'll find out the rest in due course."

*

Reynevan wasn't overly cheered up by the fact that instead of heading for the Mezilesí pass, he had to abruptly ride in precisely the opposite direction, southwards along the right bank of the Morava. Luckily, Jan Pluh hadn't been lying and it really wasn't too far to the destination. They soon saw in the mist-filled valley a large military camp, a typical camp for Hussites on the march: a collection of wagons, tents, huts, shacks and other picturesque constructions. The war standard of the Orphans—depicting a radiating Host and a pelican pecking its own breast—fluttered over the camp. At the edge towered an impressive pile of bones and other refuse, and close by a group of women were washing clothes beside the stream that flowed into the Morava, while a pack of children were throwing pebbles into the water and haring around with dogs. As they rode past, the women followed them with their eyes, straightening their backs and wiping their foreheads with hands glistening with soapy water. Smoke and foul odours trailed among the wagons and some cows lowed sadly in an enclosure. A light snow was falling.

"Over there. That cottage there."

A skinny, pale young man was standing outside the cottage, busy pouring slops out of a pail. On seeing them, he raised his head. His expression was so doleful and forlorn that he could have posed for an illumination of the chapter about Job in a missal.

"You did it!" he cried in hope. "You've found a physician! It's an evident miracle, let us give thanks for him to God Almighty. Dismount, sire, with all haste!"

"Is the need so great?"

"Our hejtman…" said the thin young man and dropped the pail. "Our chief hejtman has fallen ill. And there's no barber-surgeon…"

"But there used to be," Reynevan recalled. "They called him Brother Albertus. He was quite an able physician."

"*Was*," said Deputy Hejtman Jan Pluh, nodding grimly. "But when we recently treated some papist captives to fire, he began to protest that it wasn't Christian and that one doesn't do that. So the hejtman went and whacked him with a battleaxe."

"And right after the funeral I was appointed physician," complained the skinny young man. "They said I know my letters so I would cope. But I can barely read and write; all I did at the apothecary's in Chrudim was write out labels and stick them on the bottles. I know bugger all about medicine. I told them, but they kept on that I'm book-learned, that there's nothing to it: if a fellow's meant to go to Heaven, the Lord God can't help him anyway; if he's fated to live, even the worst doctor won't harm him—"

"But when the hejtman himself fell ill," interrupted another of the Orphans, "he ordered us at once to ride off and search for a better physician. In truth, the Lord God smiled on us that we found you so quickly. The hejtman is in agony. You'll see for yourself."

Reynevan smelled it before he saw it. An odour so foul it almost knocked him off his feet filled the low-ceilinged cottage. The face of the stout man lying on a pallet made of planks was shining with sweat. Reynevan knew and remembered that face. It was Smil Půlpán, currently, as it turned out, Chief Hejtman of the Náchod Orphans.

"Bugger me…" said Smil Půlpán in a feeble voice, indicating that he knew Reynevan. "The little German doctor, the hejtmans' favourite. Ah well, beggars can't be choosers. Get over here, quack. Take a look. Just don't tell me you can't cure it. Don't say it if you value your life."

The stench ought in principle to have prepared Reynevan for the worst, but it hadn't. There was something on Smil Půlpán's inner thigh, perilously close to his groin. That something was the size of a duck egg, coloured blue, black and red, and looked worse than repellent. Reynevan had seen and coped with similar things, but despite that, the urge to vomit was overpowering. He felt embarrassed, but only regarding his reaction. The impulse was so slight the others hadn't noticed it.

"What is it, m'lord?" asked the apprentice apothecary from Chrudim, the field-surgeon by accident and compulsion. "Is it the plague, by any chance? What a foul ulcer…And in such a place—"

"It's certainly not the plague," Reynevan announced with conviction, preferring first of all, however, to make sure by palpating the patient's abdomen to check if he could feel the wobbling typical of buboes. He didn't. Pŭlpán howled briefly, and cursed.

"It is a carbuncle," Reynevan diagnosed confidently. "To begin with, there were a few small pimples, weren't there? They quickly became enlarged, changed into lumps, each with a yellowish pustule at its tip, which opened and then suppurated? Then they finally combined into one large, very painful canker?"

"It's as though…" The apprentice apothecary swallowed. "As though you'd witnessed it—"

"What have you been using?"

"Err…" the young man stammered. "Poultices…The womenfolk applied them…"

"Did you try to squeeze it out?" asked Reynevan, biting his lip, because he knew the answer.

"He tried, he fucking tried," Pŭlpán groaned. "I almost expired from the bloody pain…"

"I thought I could get the pus out," said the apprentice apothecary. "What was I to do?"

"Excise it."

"I forbid it…" Pŭlpán wheezed out. "I won't let you cut me… You'll carve me up, you butchers."

"A surgical operation is needed here," said Reynevan, opening his satchel. "That is the only way we can be sure of the complete *abscessus* of the pus."

"I won't let you cut me. I'd prefer it to be squeezed."

"Squeezing won't help." Reynevan preferred not to say it would make things worse. He knew that Pŭlpán wouldn't forgive the Chrudim apprentice apothecary a mistake and would take revenge on him. "The carbuncle must be excised."

"Bielawa…" said Pŭlpán, suddenly catching him by the sleeve. "They say you're a magician. So cast a spell or give me a magical decoct…Don't cut me. I'll reward you handsomely—"

"I can't cure you with gold. An operation is absolutely necessary."

"No, it's fucking not!" yelled Pŭlpán. "Do you compel me? I'm the hejtman here! Why, I'll…I give the orders! Cure me with witchcraft and remedies! Don't come near me with a knife! Touch me, you fucking quack, and I'll have you torn apart by horses! Hey, men! Guard!"

"If the carbuncle is allowed to grow," said Reynevan, standing up, "it may cause grave consequences. I tell you so that you'll know. The rest is your decision, your will. *Scienti et volenti non fit injuria.*"

"You're getting your revenge, you and your fucking Latin," Pŭlpán wheezed out. "For back then. For last year, for Silesia, for Frankenstein, for the monks we made short work of…I saw how you looked at me then. With what hatred…Now you seek revenge…"

The deputy hejtmans and captains who had entered the cottage on hearing the shouting glared at Reynevan. Then they sniffed and grunted.

"I don't know, Hejtman," muttered one of them. "But I don't suppose it'll go away by itself. Something needs doing—"

"Why did we search for a physician and bring him here?" grunted Jan Pluh. "All for naught?"

Půlpán groaned, fell back on the pillow, sweat profusely beading his cheeks and forehead.

"I shan't endure it..." he finally gasped. "Very well, go on, let the quack do his worst. But don't leave me alone with him, Brothers, keep an eye on his hands and his knife...So the scoundrel doesn't slit my throat or bleed me to death...And bring me alcohol...Alcohol, quickly!"

"Vodka will indeed be required," said Reynevan, rolling up his sleeves and checking the blade of the knife with his fingertip. "But for me. In your state, Půlpán, medicine forbids the consumption of alcohol."

"The knitting and healing of the wound will take at least a week," Reynevan instructed the field-surgeon and apprentice apothecary as he finished packing his satchel. "The patient should stay in bed and the wound must be tended to. Until it scars over, keep using poultices."

The apprentice apothecary nodded eagerly. The dopey expression of awe and admiration still hadn't left his face. The expression had adorned the young man's face from the moment Reynevan completed the operation. And wasn't about to leave it.

Reynevan was far from being smug, but he had every right to be proud of the operation. Even though, owing to the carbuncle's size, the cut had to be deep and crosswise and he hadn't dared to magically anaesthetize the patient in front of witnesses, the operation was soon over. All Smil Půlpán managed to do was to scream out and then faint, which significantly helped in the removal of the pus and the sewing up of the wound. One of the Orphan captains couldn't bear the sight of it and threw up, but the others acknowledged the surgeon's dexterity and skill with encouraging mutters, and at the end Jan Pluh even slapped him familiarly on the back.

And the apprentice apothecary kept sighing in admiration. Unfortunately, it turned out he wasn't capable of contributing anything more than that.

"You said you were using poultices. Prepared by womenfolk."

"I swear, m'lord physician. The women prepared them. And they were applied by...By Alžběta Donotková. Shall I call her?"

"Indeed."

Alžběta Donotková, a young woman probably of less than twenty, had hair the colour of linen and eyes as blue as forget-me-nots. She would have been extremely comely, were it not for the circumstances. For she was a woman of the Hussite army, a woman of marches, retreats, victories, defeats, scorching heat, freezing cold and rainy weather. And unending hard work. And she looked like all the rest. She dressed in whatever she could find, as long as it was warm, her blonde hair was hidden under a grey kerchief of coarse linen and her hands were red from the cold and cracked from the damp. But at the same time, astonishingly, something radiated from her that might be called gravitas. Dignity. Something that brought to mind the eternal feminine.

Reynevan thought he had heard the name before. But it was the first time he had seen her.

"Did you make the poultices for the hejtman? Using what?"

Alžběta Donotková raised eyes the colour of forget-me-nots at him.

"Grated onion," she replied quietly. "And crushed birch buds."

"Are you versed in healing? And herbalism?"

"Wouldn't know about that...As much as any village woman, I suppose. In any case, those poultices didn't help—"

"On the contrary," he responded. "They did indeed. You're

going to help him again now. You must apply a flaxseed pap once the dressing is removed. It's still spring, but there ought to be duckweed on the ponds. Make poultices from the juice you squeeze from it. First the pap, then the duckweed, by turns."

"Very well, m'Lord Reynevan."

"You know me?"

"I heard them talking. The women."

"About me?"

"Two years ago," said Alžběta Donotková and looked away, but only for a moment. "At the time of the raid on Silesia. In the town of Złotoryja. In the parish church."

"Yes?"

"You and your companions didn't let harm come to the Mother of God."

"Oh, that…" he said in surprise. "Was that event talked about?"

She looked at him for a long time. In silence.

"The event took place," she finally answered, slowly uttering the words. "And only that is important."

Donotková, Alžběta Donotková, he said to himself as he trotted northwards, towards Hanušovice again. People talked about her, he recalled. Gossiped. Told of a woman held in great esteem by the women who travelled with the Orphans, about a natural leader whose opinions even some of the Hussite hejtmans respected. He recalled that in those tales there was a secret, there was death and love, a great love for someone who perished. For someone whom no one could replace, who left behind him only an endless void, endless sadness and an endless sense of something unfulfilled. A story seemingly from the pages of Chrétien de Troyes or written by Wolfram of Eschenbach. Which didn't suit her coarse looks. Didn't suit at all. And because of that was probably authentic.

The wind from Sněžník fanned his face, somewhat allaying the shame he had felt when she spoke about the event in the church in Złotoryja, about the wooden Madonna. About the sculpture in whose defence he had stood, indeed; not on his own initiative, but following Samson Honeypot's example. And he didn't deserve praise for that. Nor the acknowledgement of a woman like Alžběta Donotková.

Beyond Hanušovice the road turned and continued westwards. It all made sense. He was a little over a mile from the Mezilesí pass, he estimated, and hoped to reach it by nightfall. He spurred on his horse.

They caught up with him before the evening.

He was caught by a group of ten riders, who encircled him, dragged him from his horse and bound him. His protests fell on deaf ears. They said nothing, and when he continued to protest and demand explanations, they quietened him with punches. They took him back to the Orphans' camp and tossed him, still bound, into an empty pigsty, where during the night he almost expired from the cold. They didn't respond to his shouts. The next morning, they hauled him out, quite numb with cold, and shoved him roughly to the headquarters of the Chief Hejtman. Jan Pluh and several other Orphan commanders he knew were waiting for him there.

And it was what Reynevan had suspected. And feared.

Inside, on the pallet, almost in the same position he had left him after operating on him and applying the dressing, lay Smil Půlpán. Except he was stiff. Absolutely defunct and absolutely dead. His face, as white as chalk, was horribly distorted by his goggling eyes, which appeared almost to be popping out of their sockets. And by the grimace, the lips twisted into an even ghastlier smile.

"And what do you say, physician?" Jan Pluh asked hoarsely and ominously. "How will you explain this kind of medicine to us? Can you explain it?"

Reynevan swallowed, shook his head and spread his arms wide. He approached the pallet with the intention of lifting the blanket covering the corpse, but the iron hands of the captains held him back.

"No, laddie! You'd like to destroy the evidence of the crime, but we won't let you. You killed him and will answer for it!"

"What are you talking about?" He struggled. "Have you gone mad? Killed him? That's absurd! You were all present at the operation! He was alive after it and doing well! Excising a carbuncle cannot possibly cause death! Let me examine him—"

"You miscalculated, sorcerer," Pluh interrupted him. "You thought you'd get away with it. But Brother Smil came round. He cried that he felt a burning in his lungs and guts, that the pain was making his head burst. And before he died, he accused you of magic and of poisoning."

"That's impossible!"

"And I would say it was possible. You hated Brother Smil; everybody knows it. You found a way and poisoned the poor wretch."

"You were present! You were, too!"

"You beguiled our eyes with witchcraft! We know you're a sorcerer and a wizard. There are witnesses to it."

"What witnesses? Witnesses to what?"

"That will come out at your trial. Take him away!"

The Orphans were crowded like sardines, like a swarm of locusts, on the parade ground.

"Why have this trial?" somebody shouted. "What the hell is

this pantomime for? Waste of time and effort! String up the poisoner! Hang him from a wagon shaft!"

"Sorcerer! To the stake with him!"

"Philistine!" A black-coated preacher with a ridiculous goatee beard sprang forward and spat in Reynevan's face from close up. "Abomination of Moloch! We shall send you to Hell, O scoundrel! Into the eternal fire, to the Devil and his fallen angels!"

"Kill the German!"

"Take the flails to him! The flails!"

"Silence!" thundered Jan Pluh. "We are the Warriors of God; it shall be done in accordance with God! Justly and rightly! Fear not, we shall avenge the death of our brother and hejtman, he won't get away with it! But there must be order! According to the verdict of our revolutionary tribunal! There is evidence! There are witnesses! Come on, call the witnesses!"

The crowd roared, howled and bellowed, shaking voulges and flails.

The first witness called before the court was the apprentice apothecary from Chrudim, trembling and as white as a sheet. His voice shook and his teeth chattered as he testified. The excision of the ulcer, he testified, shooting apprehensive glances at the revolutionary tribunal, was carried out by the accused Bielawa contrary to the clear wishes of Hejtman Pŭlpán, and he carried it out with extreme brutality and cruelty unbefitting of a doctor. During the operation, the accused was mumbling something under his breath, undoubtedly magical spells. Indeed, everything the accused did, he did according to the customs of sorcerers.

The crowd howled.

A few more witnesses were found, since when it's necessary, witnesses can always be found.

"A fellow told me…I forget who, but I do remember that it

was last year, at Shrovetide. He said that this Bielawa treated Neplach at White Mountain. Using witchcraft! Everybody said he used witchcraft!"

"It is known to me, your honours, that this Bielawa is in league with the Devil, that he learned spells for cheating at dice from the Devil! I heard it from one of Brother Rohač's captains, who saw it with his own eyes. It was two years ago, in the autumn…Or was it winter? I don't rightly recall…But I accuse him!"

"I swear on the grave of Brother Žižka that I saw this Bielawa during last year's plundering raid on Silesia quarrelling with our Reverend Pešek Krejčíř about some papist superstitions or other. Bielawa was looking strangely at the reverend and must have cast a spell. And then what? As a result of that spell Brother Pešek died in agony soon after."

"For he's no Czech, brothers of the tribunal, not one of us, but a German! In Hradec Králové I heard people saying that he's a Catholic spy. The papists are planting secret criminals among us to murder our hejtmans treacherously! Remember Sir Bohuslav of Švamberk! Remember Brother Hvězda!"

"And I heard, honourable commission, that this Bielawa fraternises with Praguians from the Old Town! And what are Old Towners? Traitors to the Chalice, traitors to Master Huss, traitors to the Four Articles! They desire to restore the Babylonian Sigismund to the throne of Bohemia! Without a doubt those Old Towners sent Bielawa in order to kill the hejtman!"

"Death to him!" yelled the crowd. "Death!"

There could only be one verdict, naturally, and it was arrived at very swiftly. To the overwhelming and unalloyed joy of the Náchod Orphans, Reynevan Bielawa, sorcerer, poisoner, traitor, German, Catholic spy and assassin sent by the Old Town, was found guilty of all the crimes he was accused of, in connection with which the revolutionary tribunal unanimously sentenced him to death by burning at the stake.

Obviously, he was not entitled to appeal against the sentence; before Reynevan had managed to open his mouth in protest he was seized by several pairs of strong hands and dragged, accompanied by the baying crowd, to the edge of the camp and a previously arranged huge pile of brushwood and logs. One man rolled a large barrel smelling of cabbage and another brought a lid, hammer and nails. Reynevan was lifted up and shoved by force into the barrel. He struggled and shouted so loudly his lungs almost burst, but his cries were lost among the wailing of the excited mob.

There was a deafening boom. And the air was suffused with the stench of burning powder. The crowd moved back, allowing Reynevan to see what had happened.

From the camp rode up a strange party, consisting of three war wagons. One of them was crewed by ten women of various ages, from teenagers to old women. All of them, apart from the wagoners, were armed with handgonnes and hook guns.

The muzzle of a ten-pound bombard peeped ominously from the second wagon, which was operated by four women. And it was the bombard that had just been fired: a powerful gunpowder blank. Shreds of wadding were still falling, swirling like snowflakes, in a cloud of smoke.

On the third wagon, accompanied by two women and a device concealed under a tarpaulin, stood Alžběta Donotková. She cast a sheepskin off her shoulders and a scarf from her head, and now, blue-eyed, with her tousled flaxen hair flowing behind her, she resembled Nike leading the people. Her deadly serious and menacing expression more called to mind, however, the enraged Fury Tisiphone.

"What is the meaning of this?" roared Jan Pluh, wiping flecks of powder from his face. "What is the meaning of this, Donotková? Are you play-acting? Is this a masquerade? A goose-plucking party? Who let you women pick up arms?"

"Begone from here," said Alžběta Donotková loudly, as though she hadn't heard him. "This instant! Immediately. There will be no burning. That is enough."

"Insolent woman!" yelled the goateed preacher. "O Jezebel, rabid in vain pride! You shall burn in the fire with the Philistine! But first you will taste the horsewhip!"

"Begone, all of you!" continued Alžběta Donotková, not paying any attention to him, either. "Begone, Christians, Orphans, good Czechs. Kneel, look to Heaven, pray to God, to our Lord Jesus and his holy Mother. Examine your souls. Think about Judgement Day, which is nigh. Beat your breasts, you who know not the way of peace, who have taken crooked paths. I have watched for five years as you destroyed the good inside you, as you laid in the grave what was human, as you turned this land into a charnel house. I have watched as you killed your own consciences. I have had enough; I shall not allow it any longer. In the hope that you have not killed everything inside yourselves. That perhaps a whit has remained, a tiny bit of something that is worth rescuing from destruction. For that reason, begone. While I am well disposed."

"While you are well disposed?" Pluh cried sneeringly, standing with arms akimbo. "Well disposed? And what will you do to us, maid? You've fired a blank from a cannon! And now what? You'll rend your frock and stick your arse out at us?"

In unison, the women on the wagons attached the hooks of their firearms to the sides. And Alžběta Donotková, alias the Fury Tisiphone, whipped the tarpaulin from the machine beside which she was standing. Jan Pluh involuntarily took a step back. And with him the entire mob. With a murmur of horror.

Reynevan had never seen that infamous weapon; had only heard about it. The crowd's reaction didn't surprise him. A strange construction stood on the wagon beside Alžběta Donotková. A dozen bronze barrels were attached, one beside the other, on an oaken frame and an intricate revolving mounting. It resembled a church organ and the weapon's name reflected that. Reynevan had heard tell of the "Organ of Death," capable of firing two hundred pounds of lead in the time taken to recite a *Pater noster*. In the form of sharp shot.

Alžběta Donotková raised a fuse and blew on it, making the smoking end of it glow brightly. At the sight of it, the Orphans stepped back several more paces, several tripped, several fell over, some began to withdraw for good and creep away stealthily.

"Begone, O Czechs!" Alžběta Donotková said in a loud voice. "M'Lord Reynevan, a saddled horse awaits! Don't waste any time."

He didn't need to be told twice.

He didn't spare his mount. He thundered along a valley at full speed, in a drawn-out *ventre à terre* so fast that pebbles struck by horseshoes sprayed out to the side. The horse was flecked with foam and had begun to wheeze, but Reynevan didn't slow down. He was under no illusions. He knew the Orphans would give chase.

They did. It wasn't long before he heard shouts far behind him. Not wanting them to follow him by sight in an open valley, he turned among the wickers and osiers and galloped on, splashing mud, not sparing his mount his spurs.

He rushed out onto the highway and stood up in the stirrups. He hadn't managed to confuse his pursuers, since yells and whoops were coming through the bushes. Reynevan bent forwards in the saddle and galloped. The horse wheezed, shedding flakes of foam.

He galloped past cottages and shepherds' huts, recognising the place and knowing he was close to Hanušovice. But also that his pursuers were close. A thunderous yell from many throats told him that the Orphans could now see him. A moment later he saw them. At least twenty horsemen. He jabbed his spurs into the horse and the animal, though it appeared impossible, found fresh energy. He rode onto a small bridge over a stream with a dull thud.

Two horsemen were riding like the wind from the village. One, of immense size, was whirling a heavy Flemish goedendag as though it were a hazel switch. The other, on a beautiful black horse, was armed with a curved falchion.

After passing Reynevan, Samson and Scharley were on the Orphans in an instant. With two sweeping blows, Scharley knocked two of the riders to the ground, and the third, slashed across the face, swayed in the saddle. Samson struck men and horses by turns with his goedendag, sowing terrible confusion. Reynevan reined his horse around, clenching his teeth. He had scores to settle. For the beating, for the spitting, for the barrel of cabbage. As he passed the man swaying limply in the saddle, he snatched his sword and rode into the melee, smiting left and right. He heard biblical quotations being shouted and guided by them located the pursuers' leader, the goateed priest. Reynevan forced his way towards him, fending off blows from the others.

"Hell spawn!" yelled the priest, seeing him, spurring on his horse and flying forward, brandishing his sword. "Philistine! The Lord will render you into my hands!"

They crossed swords violently once and twice and then were separated by panicking horses. And then finally by Scharley. Scharley gave no thought to honourable duels or knightly codes.

He rode up to the preacher from behind and swept his head from his shoulders with a powerful blow of the falchion. Blood spurted up in a geyser. At the sight of it, the Orphans spurred their horses and withdrew. Scharley, Samson and Reynevan took advantage of it and galloped away to the bridge. There was barely enough room on the footbridge for three horses side by side, so there was no fear that they'd be surrounded. But there were still at least three times as many pursuers. In spite of the casualties, they had no thought of retreat. Fortunately, they were reluctant to attack at once. Instead, they regrouped. But it was clear they wouldn't give up.

"Being apart from you for so long made me forget," Scharley panted. "A fellow could never get bored in your company, Reinmar."

"Look out!" warned Samson. "Here they come!"

Half of the Orphans made a frontal attack on the bridge, and the rest, forcing their horses into the water, were crossing the stream to approach from the rear. The only solution was to withdraw. And fast. Reynevan, Scharley and Samson reined their horses around and galloped towards the village, pursued by the wild cries of the Orphans.

"They won't give up!" shouted Scharley, looking back. "I don't think they like you!"

"Don't talk! Ride!"

The wind was howling in their ears as they rode onto the wide common outside the village. The pursuers spread out, meaning to surround them. To his horror, Reynevan found that he was quickly falling behind, that his mount was weakening significantly. That the wheezing horse was stumbling and slowing. Noticeably.

"My horse is failing," he yelled. "Samson! Scharley! Leave me! Get away!"

"You must be mad," said Scharley, stopping his horse in an instant and reining it around, drawing the falchion. "You must be mad, laddie."

"I don't mean to be rude," said Samson, spitting on his hand and grasping the goedendag, "but you must be extremely mad."

The Orphans yelled triumphantly as they began to close in, the snare tightening.

And it would probably have ended very badly had it not been for a *Deus ex machina*. Appearing that day in the form of fifteen heavily armed horsemen approaching at a crazy gallop from Hanušovice.

The pursuers spurred their horses and brought them to a rapid stop, in the confusion not knowing who, what, how or why. The battle cries and flashes of swords held aloft dispelled all their doubts, however. And immediately deprived them of the will and desire to continue the party. Turning around in unison, the Náchod Orphans fled, scarpered. Riding fresher horses, the new arrivals would have caught up with them without difficulty and massacred them had they so wished. But they clearly didn't want to.

"Well, well, what a fortunate twist of fate," said Urban Horn, walking his horse up. "For I have been searching for you, Reynevan, I'm on your trail. And I seem to have found you, even though it was by chance. And if I say I'm just in time, would I be mistaken?"

"You would not."

"*Salve*, Scharley. *Salve*, Samson. You're here, too? Not in Prague?"

"*Amicus amico.*" Samson Honeypot shrugged, toying with the goedendag and under his eyelids scrutinising the soldiers surrounding them. "When a friend is in need, I come to his aid. I rush to his side. Regardless of...the circumstances."

Horn understood at once and laughed.

"*Pax, pax,* O friend of a friend! Reynevan is in no danger from me. Particularly now when I hear that the honourable Flutek is at rest under a thick layer of earth. You are also no doubt aware of that. Thus, there's no sense dispatching Reynevan to Prague. Particularly since I need Reynevan's help at Sovinec Castle, to which I very courteously invite him. Very courteously."

Reynevan and Samson looked around. They were being assaulted from all sides by the smell of horses' sweat and steam coming from their nostrils, and the faces of the soldiers surrounding them were quite eloquent.

"A sojourn in Sovinec," said Horn, without taking his eyes off Scharley or the hand holding the falchion, "might be beneficial to you, too, Reinmar. If your brother's memory is indeed dear to you."

"Peterlin is dead." Reynevan shook his head. "I can't help him now. Jutta, however—"

"Help me in Sovinec," interrupted Horn, "and I will help you with regard to your Jutta. I give you my word."

Reynevan looked at Scharley and Samson and then turned his gaze to the horsemen around them.

"I'll hold you to your word," he finally said. "Let's ride."

"You can go where you will," Horn addressed Scharley and Samson, "but I would advise haste. Those men may return. With reinforcements."

"My will is to ride with Reinmar," drawled Scharley. "So kindly extend your invitation to me, too, Horn. Aha, while I think of it: thanks for saving us."

"Friends cannot be parted, I see," said Urban Horn, reining his horse around. "Ah well, I invite you to Sovinec, too. And you, Samson. Since you won't abandon Reynevan either. *Vero.*"

"*Amicus amico,*" replied Samson, smiling. "*Semper.*"

Horn stood up in the stirrups and looked towards the river in the direction the pursuers had fled, but there was no trace of them.

"The Náchod Orphans," he said gravely. "Until recently a field army, now a gang roaming the land spreading fear. These are the results of the unending ceasefire, see how harmful peace is. It's high time for a war, gentlemen, for an expeditionary raid. And in any case, we must ask brothers Kúdelník and Čapek to pay attention to that Půlpán. And keep him on a slightly shorter leash."

"That won't be necessary," said Reynevan. "Půlpán…Hmm… Půlpán's is no longer with us."

"What? What's the matter? How did it happen?"

Reynevan told him how. Urban Horn listened. Without interrupting.

"I knew," he said, when Reynevan had finished, "that your help would be indispensable to me. But I never expected it to be so indispensable."

Chapter Six

In which our heroes—presently at the Moravian castle of Sovinec—realise that one should always, in any situation, absolutely have a contingency plan up one's sleeve. To be pulled out at the right moment.

Curses, the neighing of horses and the metallic clanking of horseshoes from the courtyard came through the barred window of the tower. The Sovinec burgmen, as was customary for them, set off to patrol the pass, inspect the vicinity and extort money from the local population. A cockerel crowed with wild abandon one more time and one of the women residing at the castle yelled at her husband. A lamb bleated horrifyingly.

Bruno Schilling, former Black Rider, currently a deserter, renegade and captive, was slightly pale. The paleness was probably only caused by his recent illness. If Bruno Schilling was afraid, he was skilfully concealing it. He refrained from fidgeting on his stool and letting his eyes flick from one interrogator to the next. But he didn't avoid making eye contact. *Horn was right*, thought Reynevan. *He saw through him. Schilling isn't just any old slow-witted thug. He is a sly fox, a wily fellow and a slippery rascal.*

"Let us begin, time flies," said Urban horn, placing his hands on the table. "As we have already established, if I ask you something, you answer—concisely and to the point. I'm doing the interrogating, you're being interrogated. Is that clear?"

The lamb in the courtyard finally stopped bleating. And the cockerel stopped crowing.

"I asked you a question," Horn reminded him drily. "I don't intend to guess at your answers, so be so good as to speak them, however many questions I ask. Beginning now."

Bruno Schilling glanced at Reynevan, but quickly looked away. Reynevan didn't take the trouble to hide his dislike and antipathy. He didn't try at all.

"Schilling."

"I understand, m'Lord Horn."

"I don't see the point of this interrogation," Reynevan repeated. "This Schilling is a common thug, knifeman and killer. An assassin. The kind that is sent to eliminate somebody. You point out the prey and you slip him like a hound. And Grellenort only used the thug for jobs like that. I doubt that he let him into his confidence or revealed any secrets to him. In my opinion the rogue knows next to nothing. But he will lie, he will give false information, feed you with confabulations, pretend to be very well informed, because he realises that only by doing so is he of any worth to you. And he felt confident when you treated him like that. More like a guest than a prisoner."

From outside the window came the hooting of owls circling the tower. It appeared there was a great abundance of them in the vicinity. Which had its good sides—there wasn't a single mouse or rat in the vicinity. A hunk of bread or pancake left uneaten by the bed in the evening would still be there for a midnight snack, untouched.

"You, Reinmar," Horn threw a dog a gnawed bone, "are an expert at medicine and magic because you have studied and practised them. I am an expert at the art of interrogation. I thank you for your advice, but it would be better for each of us to stick to our specialities and do what we are best at. Agreed?"

"I have no idea how you'll fare with this renegade," said Reynevan, looking at the wine against the light of a candlestick. "But I have my forebodings. However, since you insist, I won't give you any more advice. In that case, since my advice isn't needed, what use am I to you?"

Horn began to gnaw on another bone. Scharley and Samson did likewise. Neither the giant nor the penitent joined in the discussion.

"Schilling is talking about the castle called Sensenberg," said Horn, stopping chewing for a moment, "the Black Riders' headquarters and hideout. Talking about witchcraft and spells, about elixirs, magical narcotics and poisons. I don't believe much of it and he sees that. You're mistaken to think of him as a slow-witted thug; he's a wily fox and a keen observer. He saw me send you away under escort and presumed he doesn't have to fear you now. But when he suddenly sees you beside me at the interrogation, he'll take fright. And just as well. Let him shake in his shoes a little. And you: show him hatred. Show him hostility."

"I won't have to pretend."

"Just don't go overboard with it. I've already told you: fanaticism is all very well for ignoramuses, but it doesn't befit us, men of nobler causes. Bruno Schilling had a hand in your brother's murder. But if you have revenge in mind, then he, paradoxically, can help you with it. By giving us information."

"By confabulating, you mean."

"He knows he's only alive thanks to us," said Horn, eyes flashing, "and that it was because of me that he got out of the dungeon in Kłodzko in one piece. He knows that only I can save him from Grellenort and the Black Riders, whom he has abandoned. He is only alive and safe because Grellenort knows nothing about his desertion, thinks he fell at the Battle of Wielisław. He knows that if I expose his lies, I will simply cast him out of here and announce it to the world and then his days will be numbered."

"What am I to do? Apart from showing him my hostility?"

"When he starts talking about magic at Sensenberg again, show him you're an expert and that you won't simply buy any old balderdash. If he becomes confused and tongue-tied, we'll know where we stand."

"If he's as crafty as you say, I doubt he'll let us catch him out. But I promised to help, so I shall; I'll keep my promise. Hoping you won't forget yours. When do we begin?"

"Tomorrow. First thing."

"Assassinations," said Horn, his hands still on the table, "carried out using poison, planned by Grellenort and the Bishop of Wrocław. Tell us about them, Schilling."

"Birkart Grellenort has an alchemist at Sensenberg Castle," the renegade began without a moment's delay and quite obsequiously. "He isn't a man. It's said he's lived over a hundred years. Hair as white as snow, eyes like a fish's, pointed ears, skin on his face and hands almost transparent, every vein shows through blue…"

"A Sverg," said Reynevan with a nod, seeing Horn's raised eyebrows and incredulous expression. "One of the Longaevi."

"He is called Skirfir," Bruno Schilling added quickly. "An alchemist and a mage, highly skilled. He prepares various decocts for Grellenort. And elixirs. Mainly liquefied gold. They say Grellenort's great power derives from that gold. And that he's immortal."

Horn snorted and glanced enquiringly at Reynevan.

"It's possible," confirmed Reynevan, not concealing his sudden interest, "the transformation of metals and precious stones into liquid. To be precise, into a *collodium* or colloid, with a consistency thin enough to be able to drink it."

"Drink metal?" said Horn with a look of utter disbelief. "Or stone?"

"The whole of Nature," said Reynevan, taking advantage of the chance to shine, "every thing, living or dead, every *materia prima* is imbued with the energy of creation, the original spirit, original material and formative power. Hermes Trismegistus calls it *totius fortitudinis fortitudo fortis*, the power of all powers, which can overcome every subtle thing and pervades every solid thing. Hence also a basic principle of alchemy: *solve et coagula*, dissolve and coagulate, which means the process of dissolving that energy in order subsequently to coagulate it, capture it in a colloid. One can do likewise with anything, with any substance. Including metals and minerals."

"And gold?"

"Gold, too." Bruno Schilling nodded eagerly. "Most definitely."

"A *collodium* of gold, called *aurum potabile*, is one of the most powerful elixirs," explained Reynevan, still excited. "It considerably enhances the life force and the intellectual and spiritual powers. It is also an infallible remedy for insanity, dementia and other mental ailments, particularly those caused by an excess of *melancolia*, of discharges of black bile. Making a colloid is, however, extremely difficult, and only the ablest alchemists and sorcerers are capable of doing so. And it only works in very special and rare circumstances—"

"Very well, that's enough," said Horn, waving a hand. "I don't need a concise course in alchemy. Drinkable gold aroused my curiosity and you have satisfied it. Let's return to the matter at hand. That is, poisons. And poisoning."

"One is linked to the other." The renegade wiped the sweat

from his forehead. "Skirfir prepares various elixirs for Grellenort. Liquid gold, liquid silver, liquid amethyst, liquid pearls—they are all used to enhance magical potency and abilities and strengthen the immunity of the body and spirit. We were also given some of them at Sensenberg, so I know how they work. But Skirfir also concocted poisons. Grellenort's designs were no secret. He wanted to eliminate senior Hussites, poison them, but in a way that wouldn't arouse the slightest suspicions. So it would look—"

"So it would look like death caused by a wound," said Reynevan, taking advantage of Schilling stammering. "A cut received in battle or an accident. To make it impossible to link the death with the poison. Sudden death always arouses suspicions of poisoning—there is an investigation at once and the toxin is traced back to the poisoner. But regarding the poison we're discussing, there are no symptoms, the victim doesn't feel or suspect anything. Until—"

"Until he is cut with iron," the renegade interrupted in midsentence. "Or steel. But nothing else. Death is inevitable. They called that poison 'Dux.'"

"*Dux omnium homicidarum*," Reynevan confirmed pensively. "Also *Mors per ferro*. Those are snatches of the spells used when making it. Which is why Guido Bonatti in his writings uses the name 'Perferro,' which is also the name given in the *Picatrix*... In the Latin translation, because in the original it is *khadhulu ahmar al-hajja*, which means...I don't recall what it means—"

"Never mind," Horn interjected, "for I'm not interested. Reynevan, O venerable mage, so you thus confirm such a poison exists? And works exactly as just described?"

"I confirm what is written in certain sources," said Reynevan, calming down and looking Schilling in the eyes, "but I shall not pass over what is written elsewhere. According to which the so-called Black Tincture is necessary to make Perferro—"

"Indeed, indeed, you are quite right, M'Lord Bielau," Schilling hurriedly confirmed. "I heard Grellenort and Skirfir talking about it."

"The legendary Black Tincture," Reynevan continued, without lowering his eyes, "can only be obtained by transmuting a metal called *chalybs alumen*, which is ruled by the Eighth Planet. The problem, though, is that according to many scholars that metal only exists in legend. And one need not be a scholar to know that there are only seven planets—"

"There are eight planets," the renegade swiftly countered. "I also learned that by eavesdropping. The eighth planet is called Poseidonos, and Grellenort is said to know of its existence from the Devil himself—"

"Let's leave the Devil out of it for now," Horn again interrupted. "And Ptolemy. Don't get out of line, Schilling. I'm doing the interrogating, you're being interrogated. And a moment ago *Messer* Reynevan quoted authorities that appear to somewhat refute what you are testifying. Authorities that do not lend credence to your testimony. That reject them. I warn you: telling me fairy tales may have nasty consequences for you."

"M'Lord Horn." Bruno Schilling immediately rid himself of obsequiousness. "I don't give a fig for authorities and Ptolemy can count as many planets as he wants. But I tell you that I seized tramps, beggars and other wanderers from highways and delivered them to Sensenberg for Grellenort and Skirfir's experiments. I saw them administering poison to them, and afterwards cutting them with iron. I saw with my own eyes the effect iron had on the action of the poison—"

"And how did the poison act?" interrupted Reynevan. "What were the symptoms?"

"The thing is, there were various ones. It's a merit of that poison that it's difficult to identify on the basis of symptoms: they are deceptive. Before they died, some of the victims thrashed around, others trembled, others cried that their heads and guts were burning and died so contorted that shivers ran down your spine at the sight. While others simply fell asleep and died in their sleep. With smiles on their faces."

Horn shot a telling glance at Reynevan, to stop him from reacting.

"Which of our men were given the poison?" he said and turned to look at Schilling. "When? How?"

"I know not. The poison was only concocted at Sensenberg, somebody else took care of the rest."

"But you, the Black Riders, snatched people to be experimented on. When were you ordered to do so? Until when did it go on?"

"We began," said Bruno Schilling, clearing his throat and wiping his forehead. "We began the abductions in the winter of 1425, after Candlemas, and we went on until Easter. Then we were ordered to desist."

Urban Horn said nothing for a long time, tapping his fingers on the table.

Reynevan looked at Schilling, not concealing what he thought. The renegade avoided his gaze.

A warm wind fanned their faces as they stood on the ramparts facing the direction it was blowing from, which was the south, from the Oderskie Wierchy.

"I cut myself shaving this morning," Horn said grimly.

"That's nothing," said Reynevan, reassuring him, although he was far from calm himself. "Perferro requires a more severe trauma to the tissues, has to infect the circulatory system...The lymph, and actually it is—"

"All of us," said Horn, not waiting to find out what it actually was. "All of us may be carrying it. Me, you—"

"The assassins' targets were the hejtmans, important men. I don't include myself among them."

"You are admirably humble. Pity I hear little conviction in your voice. That Smil Půlpán of the Náchod Orphans wasn't especially high-ranking, either. Not wanting to brag, I consider us to be much more important. But the best moment to administer the poison is during banquets and Půlpán most certainly feasted with high-ranking hejtmans. As did I. As did you…Ha, but you were wounded last year and you're still alive. And Schilling claimed they stopped using the poison after 1425."

"That isn't at all what he claimed. He only said they stopped snatching people for experiments in 1425. But I have proof they went on poisoning and are continuing to do so."

"Do you mean Neplach? It's obvious he was killed by that poison. But he might have taken it earlier. He never engaged in fighting, so a good deal of time might have passed before he cut himself with something iron."

"I mean Smil Půlpán. I was there when he was wounded in Frankenstein, a year ago, when an iron bolt tore off his ear. But he died a week ago, when I excised that carbuncle with a steel blade."

"Ha, indeed, indeed. And it confirms completely what you overheard in the Cistercian grange. The bishop and Grellenort planned the killings and Smiřický gave them the targets. That was in September of 1425. A month later, in October, Jan Hvězda, the Tábor's head hejtman, was shot with a crossbow bolt. The wound didn't look serious, but Hvězda didn't survive it."

"Because the bolt had an iron tip and Hvězda already had Perferro in his blood," agreed Reynevan. "And soon after, in November, Bohuslav of Švamberk, Hvězda's successor, died from what appeared to be an equally harmless cut. Yes, Horn, I had my suspicions earlier that Hvězda and Švamberk were killed with the help of black magic, and after hearing what Smiřický confessed to me, I grew certain. But so treacherously—"

"Expertly," Urban Horn corrected him. "A brilliant idea, expert execution and knowledge...And on the subject of knowledge...Reynevan?"

"What?"

"Come, come. Don't play dumb. Is there an antidote?"

"Not as far as I know. If Perferro is already in your bloodstream, it can't be flushed out."

"You said 'not as far as you know.' But perhaps there's something you don't know."

Reynevan didn't answer at once. He was thinking. He didn't intend to reveal it to Horn, but during his time with the Prague mages from the House at the Archangel apothecary's shop, he had taken medicines against poison, including ones that gave full immunity against toxins. He wasn't sure whether they also worked with Perferro. Or whether he was still immune to anything at all, since he hadn't taken the medicines for over a year.

"Well," Horn urged him. "Is there an antidote or not?"

"I can't rule out the possibility. After all, progress is being made all the time."

"Our only hope is progress," said Horn, biting his lip. "At least in this field."

Sovinec Castle had stood on a rocky outcrop of the Nízký Jeseník for a century; for a hundred years its proud and threatening bergfried had towered over the forest and frightened the local population. Two brothers, knights of the old Moravian Hrutovic family—given by the Bishop of Olomouc a fiefdom in the form of the villages Křížov and Huzová for their wartime service—built it and converted it into their family stronghold. From then on, the brothers started calling themselves the "Lords of Huzová" and used a bended shield as a coat of arms.

Having built a castle almost a mile from Huzová, they christened it "Sovinec" from the Czech word for "owl," great numbers of which nested in the neighbouring forests. And from then on began signing themselves the "Lords of Aylburk." The German name, in spite of fashion, never caught on, however, and the burg remained "Sovinec" for ever.

The castle's current owner and lord was a knight—Pavel of Sovinec—a supporter of the teachings of Huss and an ally of the Tábor. Where he was dwelling at the time of our story, in March 1429, is unknown. Now Urban Horn governed Sovinec and his vassals reigned supreme over the surrounding area.

On the Saturday before Laetare Sunday, the women of Sovinec were doing their laundry, so all morning the entire castle was permeated with the smell of wet steam and the acrid odours of lye and soap suds. Meanwhile, by noon, after Reynevan and Horn had finished another round of questioning, the entire castle courtyard was decorated with laundry hanging out to dry. It was dominated by pairs of drawers, which Scharley and Samson counted out of boredom, stopping at a hundred and nine. Since they had previously counted thirty-two vassals and foot soldiers at the castle, it turned out that there was an abundance of drawers at Sovinec, but they were rarely washed.

The friends were sitting on a woodpile in the kitchen courtyard, not far from the stable, and Reynevan, enjoying the spring sunshine and not hiding his excitement, told them about the most recent revelations from the interrogations.

"That Bruno Schilling has been telling incredible, quite unbelievable stories. About Sensenberg Castle and the Kaczawskie

Mountains. Magic has evidently been present there since the times of the Knights Templar, who built the castle. Schilling doesn't know it and can't even name it, but to a specialist like me there is no doubt that there is still present in Sensenberg a *theoda*, a *spiritus purus*, a kind of *genius loci*, the magical power of a long-dead but powerful mage. A *theoda* like that acts extremely powerfully on the *mens* of the people residing there, for it can very strongly distort the *mens* of people with lesser resistance and weaker will, or even utterly destroy it. Schilling confirmed that there were cases of *mentis alienatio*, and even cases of incurable *amentia* and *paranoia*."

"*Amentia* and *paranoia*," Scharley repeated, seemingly casually, as he contemplated the drawers. "Well, well. Who'd have thought it?"

"And in the field of alchemy," said Reynevan, warming to his theme, "I have learned about things and matters that are quite breathtaking. I've already told you about the compositional poison Perferro and I've mentioned colloidal metals. Among those metals, just imagine, is the mysterious *Potassium* described by Flamel, which is still considered by some a fantasy. The mysterious *Thallium*, which was allegedly experimented on by Arnaldus of Villa Nova, who was close to creating the philosopher's stone. Incredible, incredible!"

Scharley and Samson kept quiet, their eyes fixed on the drawers.

"Schilling also told us extraordinary and astonishing things regarding the medicines that the Black Riders use to induce trances. It is thought that the substances referred to in the works of Geber and Avicenna as *al-qili*—and which we called 'alkaloids' in Prague—possess the strongest narcotic and hallucinogenic properties. They were thought to be extracts of magical herbs, but what transpired? That they grow in any common woodland! And were none other than the common saltwort and the even more common fly agaric, *muscarius*. They are the basic ingredients of that celebrated intoxicating potion called 'bhang' mentioned in the manuscripts of Morienus. Can you imagine?"

Scharley and Samson probably could. And even if they couldn't, they didn't let it show. Neither by word, gesture nor expression.

"And the notorious, mysterious hash'eesh, which al-Hasan ibn-al-Sabbah, the Old Man of the Mountains, used to intoxicate his assassins in his mountain citadel of Alamut? Grellenort's Black Riders, as I suspected, also drug themselves with the very same hash'eesh. It is made from the resin of the flowers of a plant called in Greek *kannabis*, which is similar to hemp. As it turns out, however, there are two varieties of that medicine. One bears the name of ganja and is a beverage; it is drunk and one falls into a euphoric trance. The other—called hash'eesh—is burned and the smoke is inhaled…I know it sounds unbelievable, but Bruno Schilling promised—"

"This Bruno Schilling murdered your brother, O specialist," Scharley interrupted calmly. "It's hard for me to sympathise, since I'm an only child, but I think that if I had a brother I wouldn't chat about magic and mushrooms with his killer. I would simply break his neck. With my bare hands."

"It was you who once tried to convince me of the futility of revenge," said Reynevan, cutting him off sourly. "And I'm not chatting with Schilling, I'm interrogating him. If, one day, I make out a bill for Peterlin's death, it will be to the initiator of the crime, not some lackey. And the knowledge gained during the interrogations will come in useful to that end."

"What about Jutta?" Samson Honeypot asked softly. "How will your knowledge about *al-qili* and hash'eesh aid her release and rescue?"

"Jutta…" Reynevan stammered. "We'll soon ride to her aid. Very soon. Horn promised to help and we can't do it without his help. I'll help him and he'll help us. He'll keep his word."

"He will," said Scharley, standing up and stretching. "Or he won't. God moves in mysterious ways."

"What do you mean by that?"

"That life has taught me not to trust people too hastily and always to have a contingency plan up my sleeve."

"I'll ask you again: what do you mean by that?"

"Nothing beyond what I've said."

"M'Lord Horn?"

"Yes?"

"You promised me freedom, m'lord. If I honestly and scrupulously confessed everything."

"You haven't yet done so. In any case, why do you need freedom? Grellenort won't give up until he's tracked you down and finished you off. But he won't find you in Sovinec."

"You promised."

"I know, Schilling, I know. I promised, and I'll keep my promise. When you confess everything. So confess. How many people did you kill?"

Reynevan didn't expect the question to disconcert Schilling. He wasn't mistaken. Schilling wasn't bothered. The renegade only narrowed his eyes a little. And weighed up his answer a little longer than usual.

"I think it's probably more than thirty," he finally replied, indifferently. "I'm only counting the ones who were the main target, the ones Grellenort ordered us to kill by name. If we didn't manage to attack them alone, with no one else around… then others also died. Companions, camp followers, servants… Sometimes kin…"

"You murdered the merchant Czajka along with his wife," said Horn in a calm voice, showing he was well informed and knew all about it. "Johann Cluger and his entire family perished at home, in a fire you started, after boarding up the doors and windows."

"Things like that did happen, but seldom," the renegade admitted dryly. "We usually lay in wait until they were alone—"

"As with my brother..." said Reynevan, surprising himself with his calm. "Tell me about that murder. For you took part in it, didn't you?"

"Aye, I did." Something strange flashed in Schilling's dark-ringed eyes. "But...You need to know something...I was under the influence of ganja and hash'eesh. We all were, as usual. And then you don't know if you're awake or asleep...But I didn't stab your brother, Brother Bielau. I'm not lying. To convince you, I'll say that I wanted to, but I simply couldn't get to him. There were eight of us then, Grellenort was the ninth. He, Grellenort, struck first."

"My brother..." Reynevan swallowed. "Did he die quickly?"

"No."

"Did you kill as a group on Grellenort's orders?" said Horn, deciding it was time to intervene and change the subject. "I know he occasionally killed alone. By himself."

"Because he enjoyed it." The renegade scowled. "But in general, he wanted the suspicion to fall on others. Or to make people afraid that an unclean power was killing the merchantmen. Once, in 1425, after the Feast of Our Lady of the Snow, Grellenort commanded us to kill the master of the leathermakers' guild in Nysa—I forget his name—then ride swiftly to Świdnica and kill the merchant Neumarkt. At the same time, he, Grellenort, killed a certain Pfefferkorn by his own hand in the vestibule of the church in Niemodlin, and soon after the knight Albrecht

Bart, near Strzelin. Well, and the common folk believed it was the Evil One's doing or that he was in league with the Devil. And that was the point."

"Grellenort brought ten Riders to the Battle of Stary Wielisław," said Horn. "Apart from you, who fled like a coward, none survived that battle. How many are left at Sensenberg?"

"I didn't flee and I'm not a coward," said Bruno Schilling, unexpectedly reacting angrily. "I abandoned Grellenort because I'd been planning to do so for a long time and was waiting for my chance. For I've had enough of all those crimes. For I feared divine retribution. For Grellenort made us call out '*Adsumus*' and '*Veni ad nos*.' And we did. We cried as we killed: '*In nomine Tuo!*' And when the ganja wore off fear would seize me. Fear of God's retribution for blasphemy. And I decided to leave him… Leave him and atone…I am not absolutely evil to my core…"

He's lying, thought Reynevan and his mind's eye was suddenly filled with visions, clear and brutally vivid visions. A stifled scream, blood, the glow of fire reflected in a blade, Schilling's contorted face reflected in polished steel, his cruel laugh. Blood again, gushing in streams onto the stirrups and the pointed iron sabatons set in them, fire again, laughter again, foul curses, swords slashing the hands of people clinging to a window belching heat and flames.

He's lying. Reynevan shuddered. *Lying. He is utterly and completely evil. Only men like that are attracted by Sensenberg and Grellenort's spells.*

"You're lying, Schilling," Horn said unemotionally. "But I wasn't asking about that. How many Riders are left in Sensenberg?"

"Ten at most. But Grellenort will soon have as many as he needs at his disposal. If he doesn't already. He has ways and means."

"What are they?"

The renegade opened his mouth, intending to say something, but stammered. He glanced at Reynevan and then his eyes darted away.

"He draws people, m'Lord Horn. He attracts them to himself…Lures them, like…Aye…Like…"

"Like a moth to a flame?"

"Exactly."

The expedition that the Sovinec garrison undertook to the south must have been successful and profitable. The foot soldiers returned cheerful and were filling themselves with even more cheer. Some, judging by their slurred speech and singing, were close to becoming cheerful to the point of unconsciousness.

Three things in this world soothe a wound like honey,
Wine and girls aplenty and a pouch full of money.

"Horn?"

"Yes, Reinmar."

"How did you find out that Schilling deserted? And that Ungerath had him and wanted to exchange him for his son?"

"I have my sources."

"Very pithy. I have no further questions."

"Just as well."

"Rather than ask, I will state: Schilling was the only reason for your expedition to the Olza."

"Indeed," Horn admitted after a moment of silence interrupted by the hooting of owls. "For me. For others, the reason was Kochłowski. Were it not for Kochłowski, I wouldn't have got from Korybut either the men from Odry or the money. Kochłowski is an important figure in the arms trade. And Jan of Kravaře's change of colours and sides was simply a very fortunate stroke of luck, nothing more. Anticipating your next question: I didn't even know about you. But I was pleased to see you."

"That's kind of you."

The sounds from the courtyard had quietened down. Some of the slightly less-drunk vassals were still singing. But less jolly songs were beginning to dominate in their repertoire.

I came from the earth to the earth,
I found my good sense on the earth,
I walk on it like a lord,
I shall be buried in it…

"Horn?"

"Yes, Reinmar."

"I don't know your plans in this regard, but I think…"

"Tell me what you think."

"I think we ought to keep what we know about Perferro secret. We have no idea who may have been poisoned, and even if we did, we have no way of helping. If, though, rumours about the poison spread, then confusion, panic and fear will break out and the Devil knows what consequences there will be. We ought to keep quiet."

"You read my thoughts."

"The two of us and Schilling know about Perferro. Schilling won't leave Sovinec, I fancy. He won't get out and start gossiping."

"You fancy correctly."

"In spite of the pledge he was given?"

"Indeed. What are you getting at, Reynevan? You had a reason for starting this conversation, after all."

"You asked me for help and I helped you. Almost a week has gone by. You've stopped interrogating Schilling about matters concerning magic, while every hour and every day I spend at

Sovinec reminds me that somewhere far away Jutta is imprisoned and is hoping to be rescued. So I mean to leave. As soon as possible. After reassuring you that everything I found out here, particularly about Perferro, I shall keep secret. I shall never reveal it to anyone."

Horn said nothing for a long time and gave the impression he was engrossed in listening to the owls hooting.

"You won't reveal anything, you say. Splendid, Reinmar. I'm very glad to hear it. Goodnight."

The winter, it appeared, had yielded utterly to the spring, and there were no signs that the winter meant to fight back. It was the day of Saints Cyril and Methodius, the eighth of March, *Anno Incarnationis Domini* 1429.

Horn was waiting for Reynevan in the hunting chamber of Sovinec Castle, which was decorated with numerous hunting trophies.

"We're leaving," Reynevan began without further ado as soon as they sat down. "Today. Scharley and Samson are packing our saddlebags."

Horn was silent for a long time.

"I mean to storm, capture and burn down Sensenberg," Horn finally announced. "I mean to finish off the Black Riders, once and for all. I mean to put an end to Birkart Grellenort, after first using him to discredit and annihilate Konrad of Oleśnica, the Bishop of Wrocław. I tell you this that you might know my plans, although you certainly guessed them anyway from the questions I asked of Schilling. And I ask you straight: do you wish to take part in it? Be present? And contribute?"

"No."

"No?"

"Not before freeing Jutta. Jutta is more important to me. Nothing and no one is more important, understand?"

"I do. And now I shall tell you something. Listen. And try to understand me."

"Horn, I—"

"Just listen. I am neither Horn nor Urban," Horn began. "An acquired Christian name, an acquired surname. In actuality I am Roth. Bernhard Roth. My mother was Małgorzata Roth, a Beguine from the Świdnica Beguinage. She was murdered by Konrad, currently the Bishop of Wrocław.

"You must know what happened to the Beghards and Beguines in Silesia. Barely three years after the Vatican Council in Vienne proclaimed them heretics, Bishop Henryk of Wierzbno ordered a great witch-hunt. A hastily convened Dominican-Franciscan tribunal tortured and sent to the stake over four dozen men, women and children. In spite of that, the Beghards survived and were not disbanded either during the subsequent waves of persecution in 1330, when Schwenckefeld raged murderously, or in 1372, when the Black Death visited us. The pyres blazed and the Beghards survived. When in 1393 another witch-hunt was undertaken, my mother was fourteen. She may have survived until then because her behaviour was modest in the Beguinage; she remained inconspicuous, slaving away day and night in the hospital of Saint Michael.

"But 1411 came. The plague returned to Silesia and blame had to be urgently apportioned, but not to the Jews, for they had lost their appeal as culprits. Variety was needed. And my mother's luck deserted her. Her neighbours and fellows learned fast. During the previous witch-hunts it had come to light that denunciating was profitable; there were notable benefits. The authorities looked favourably upon it. And there was no better way to shift suspicion away from oneself.

"And more than anything there was Konrad, the first-born son of the Duke of Oleśnica. Konrad, who unerringly sensed where the true power lay, gave up ruling the duchy he had inherited and chose a career as a clergyman. In 1411, he was a provost in the Wrocław Cathedral Chapter and wanted very, very much to become a bishop. But to do so he had to distinguish himself, make a name for himself. The best way was as a defender of the faith, the scourge of heretics, apostates and sorcerers.

"And it turned out from the informers that despite his pious efforts, the Beghardian plague had survived in Świdnica, that Cathars and Waldensians still endured, that the Brethren of the Free Spirit still functioned. And again, the Dominican–Franciscan tribunal got down to work. The tribunal was zealously aided by the Świdnica torturer Jorg Schmiede, who worked eagerly and fervently. And thanks are owed to him that the vile Beguine and heretic, Małgorzata Roth, confessed to everything she was accused of. Such as praying for Lucifer's Second Coming. Carrying out abortions and doing prenatal examinations. Copulating with the Devil and a rabbi, at the same time, just imagine. And from that coupling giving birth to a bastard. That is: me. Poisoning wells and, by so doing, spreading the plague. Digging up and desecrating human remains in a cemetery. And finally, the most terrible crime: that in church, during the Elevation, she looked not at the Host but at the wall.

"To conclude: my mother was burned at the stake on the common behind the Church of Saint Nicholas and the plague cemetery. She showed remorse before her death, so they showed mercy to her. Twice over. Before the burning she was strangled and her bastard's life was spared. Instead of being drowned as the judges demanded, I was handed over to a monastery. But first of all, I was made to watch as my mother's body sizzled, blistered and finally became charred at the stake. I was nine years old. I did not weep. Since that day I have never wept. Never. Not during the two years in the monastery, where I was starved, beaten, insulted. I shed tears for the first time on All Souls' Day in 1414. On hearing that the torturer Jorg Schmiede had died, of a chill. I wept from rage that he had escaped me, that I couldn't do to him what I had devised and planned in detail during sleepless nights.

"Those childish tears changed me. The scales fell away. I understood that it is foolish to look for revenge against lackeys and hirelings, that it was a pointless waste of time to track and kill informers, false witnesses, members of the tribunal—even the head of the tribunal, the pious Piotr Bancz, lector at the Świdnica Dominican convent. I gave up those plans. Making the firm decision, at the same time, that I would do anything to get my hands on the real wrongdoer. Konrad, the Bishop of Wrocław. It isn't easy to land somebody like Konrad, a stroke of luck, a chance, is necessary. And for me this Bruno Schilling is just such a chance.

"So you must understand my reasoning, Reinmar, you must see that I can't proceed any other way. There's no smoke without fire, as it is said. I cannot rule out the eventuality that you were, indeed, turned, that you are working for the other side. Now, after Schilling's interrogations, you simply know too much for me to let you go. Because perhaps you would hurry, O noble, headstrong Lancelot, to the aid and rescue of your beloved Guinevere. Perhaps you would keep your promise and stay silent. I think—why, I believe—you would behave and act like that. But I cannot rule out other possibilities, of the kind that might thwart my plans. I can't take that risk. So you'll stay here, at Sovinec. As long as will be necessary.

"You're taking it calmly," said Horn, breaking the long silence that fell after he finished speaking. "You aren't yelling, hurling insults, or attacking me…It can be explained in two ways. The first: you're wiser. The second—"

"It's the second."

Horn stood up. That was all he had time to do. The door slammed open and Scharley, Samson and Houžvička burst into the chamber. Houžvička was holding a nocked crossbow and was aiming it straight at his former commander's face.

"The knife, Horn." Scharley's keen eyes hadn't missed anything, as usual. "Toss it on the floor."

Houžvička raised the crossbow. Urban Horn dropped the dagger—which he had managed to draw unnoticed from his sleeve—onto the floor.

"You are mistaken about me," said Reynevan. "For I, as you see, have given up being the naive idealist—by applying your wise teachings, as a matter of fact. I've gone over to calculated pragmatism and practicalism, acquired appropriate convictions and principles. Concluding that my own interests are more important than other men's, and that one should always have a contingency plan up one's sleeve. If you're going to believe in anything, it's best to believe in Hungarian gold ducats which can buy various kinds of loyalty. Your vassals don't return from their expedition for two days and your foot soldiers are under lock and key. As you soon will be. In a cell. We, however, are leaving."

"Congratulations, Scharley," said Horn, crossing his arms on his chest. "My congratulations, for I know it's your plan and your operation. By considering himself a cunning man of action, Reinmar flatters himself too much. Ah well, you win, I lose. There are three of you, not counting that turncoat with the crossbow, whom by God I shall take to task one day. But you, Scharley, have disappointed me. I thought you were a man."

"Horn," interrupted Scharley. "Get to the point. Or get into the cell."

"Would you threaten me with a cell if there were only the two of us? You and me? One against one? *Le combat singulier?* Wouldn't you like to find out what would happen then?"

Samson shook his head. Reynevan opened his mouth, but Scharley quietened him with a gesture.

"Very well, let's find out what would happen. Do you really want that?"

Horn didn't reply. Instead, he sprang forwards and kicked Scharley hard in the chest. The penitent flew back towards the whitewashed wall, slammed his back against it and quickly dodged, but Horn was quicker. He was on him, struck him in the jaw with a right hook, then a left, and Scharley fell, smashing a stool. Horn was upon him, winding up for a kick. The penitent wriggled away, caught Horn's leg in both hands and threw him to the ground. They leaped to their feet almost simultaneously. But that was the end of the fight. Horn swung and Scharley avoided the punch with a subtle, almost imperceptible movement, punched Horn hard in the chin, then slammed him with a hook, spun around and elbowed him in the face, spun again and hit him with his forearm, and then punched him, spinning the other way. After the final blow, Horn was unfit to continue fighting. Just to make sure, the penitent punched him very hard one more time, then kicked him, flooring him once and for all.

"Well, that's probably enough," he said, wiping his lip and spitting blood. "Now we know. To the cell, Horn."

"We'll lock you up separately," suggested Reynevan, who was helping Horn to stand up, with Samson's assistance. "Or perhaps you prefer to be with Schilling? You could talk. Time doesn't drag so much when you can talk."

Horn glared at him through rapidly swelling eyes. Reynevan shrugged.

"Your men will release you when they return. By then we'll be far away. And incidentally, for your information and to reassure you: I'm hastening like Lancelot to rescue Guinevere, abducted by the evil Maleagant. Other issues, including your plans, are of no interest to me just now. I don't intend—in particular—to thwart them. And I shall keep the secret. So farewell. And don't think badly of me."

"Go to hell."

In the courtyard, Scharley gave Houžvička, Smeták and Zahradil a leather package he had torn from under his saddle. It was twenty Hungarian ducats in gold, the second payment, promised and due on completion of the job. Scharley wasn't so foolish as to pay them in full up front. The Moravians leaped into the saddle without delay and galloped off into the distance.

"Their haste is understandable and advisable," commented Scharley, watching them ride away. "Their next encounter with Urban Horn might end badly. In the best case by hanging, for I can't rule out a slower death. Which I swear reminds me that we ought to get away as soon as possible."

"Rather than talk, let's ride. On we go!"

The horseshoes echoed loudly under the vault of the gatehouse. And then they were fanned by the wind, a warm wind from the Oderskie Wierchy mountains.

They set off at a gallop across the steep hillside along a track running into a valley. In the valley they rode into woodland, into a dark and musty tree-lined ravine. The ravine led them out onto a scree slope.

Where their way was barred by fifty horsemen.

One man, astride a grey, rode forward.

"Reynevan? I'm glad to see you," said Prokop the Shaven, known as Prokop the Great, the most senior hejtman of the Tábor, *director operationum Thaboritarum*. "I've been looking for you. I need you urgently."

Chapter Seven

In which we leave our heroes in Moravia for a while in order to travel—through both space and time—to the city of Wrocław. Which, as it turns out, can be a dangerous place.

"The Antichrist," the scribe, bent over a parchment, read with feeling, "shall come from the tribe of Dan."

He cleared his throat and glanced at the bishop. Konrad of Oleśnica, staring at the sunlight glinting on the slightly open window, sipped from a goblet. He gave the impression of not listening and of being quite uninterested in the prepared text. The scribe knew that was by no means true.

"Saint Irenaeus," he continued, "maintains that the Antichrist will come at the end of the world, reign for three and a half years, build a temple in Jerusalem, vanquish the kings by force, torment what is sacred and lay waste to the entire Church. According to the prophecy of the Revelation, he shall be known by the number 666 and his names shall be Evanthas, Lateinos and Teitan. Nonetheless, the martyr Hippolytus links the number 666 to the names Kakos, Olicos, Alittis, Blaueros, Antemos and Genesiricos. 666 also refers to the Turkish name of Mahometis when written using the Greek alphabet. And one may also conclude that if we subtract from 666 the number of fish Peter caught in the Sea of Galilee, and then multiply it by the number of sailors on the ship on which Paul sailed to Italy, and we divide it by the length of the ark in God's temple according to the Book of Exodus, the words 'Ioannes Hus apostata' written in Cappadocian emerge. All of which demonstrates the inordinate shamelessness of the heretics who revere that Huss. Oh, you wretched envoys of the Antichrist! The Antichrist reveals his secret in you when you reject the sacrament and the offering; when you blaspheme the One God in Three Persons and the Blessed Virgin Mary; when you deny divinity to the Son of God and attribute it to the Antichrist; when you sow all kinds of discord, crime and abomination; when you sully the whole truth of the sacred Catholic faith. May God have mercy on you!"

The scribe put down the sheet of paper and glanced nervously at the face of Bishop Konrad, which remained inscrutable.

"Good," the bishop finally said, to the relief of the scribe. "Very good. Very little to correct, indeed. Where you call the Hussites 'wretched,' add 'O Czechs, you despicable Slavic nation.' No, no, 'base and despicable...,' that's better."

"'Base, despicable and contemptible,'" corrected the Wallcreeper. "That will be even better."

The scribe paled and went as white as the sheet of paper he was holding, for he had seen what the bishop—who was sitting with his back to the window—hadn't seen. Namely, the bird that had alighted on the windowsill turning into a human being. A man with black hair, dressed all in black, with a kind of avian physiognomy. And the gaze of a demon.

"Write the homily out." The bishop's harsh order shook the scribe from his stupefaction and brought him back to his senses. "Once you've written it, take it to the chancel, have them copy it and distribute it to the churches for priests to use in their sermons. Go."

The scribe, clutching his handiwork to his belly, gave a low bow and shuffled backwards towards the door. Bishop Konrad sighed heavily, took a gulp of wine and signalled the servant boy to recharge his goblet. The servant's hands shook and the neck of the carafe jingled against the lip of the goblet. The bishop dismissed him with a wave.

"You haven't shown your face here for a long time," he said to the Wallcreeper when they were alone. "You haven't flown in through the window, haven't alarmed the servants, haven't given rise to rumours for quite a while. I was beginning to worry. Where have you been, son, and what have you been up to? Let me guess: studying devilish books and grimoires at Sensenberg? Stupefying yourself with hash'eesh and the poison of fly agaric? Summoning Satan? Venerating demons, offering them human sacrifices? Killing prisoners in their cells? Losing your subordinates, your famous Black Riders, on battlefields? Allowing traitors to get away and letting spies lead you by the nose? Go on, son, tell me. Give me your account. Brag about which of my instructions and orders you have ignored recently. And how you've been staining my reputation."

"Finished, Papa dear?"

"No, son. I haven't finished with you. But know this—I am sorely tempted to be done with you, once and for all."

"Since you're talking about it, it can't be so bad," said the Wallcreeper, grinning and lounging in an oak curule seat. "If I were really vexing you or were no longer useful, you'd finish me off quietly and without warning. And without mercy. Heedless of any blood ties."

"I've told you," Konrad said, squinting, "so don't make me repeat it. There are no blood ties between us. I may call you 'son' and treat you like a son. But you are not my son. You are the son of a sorceress, a poisoner, on top of that a *converso* whom I saved from the stake by making her a nun. The fact that I gave your mother the honour of fucking her numerous times does not in the least mean that you are the fruit of my loins, Birkart, that you sprang from my seed. I'm inclined to believe, son, that the very Devil begat you. And it's not beyond the realm of possibility that some mortal man in Lubáň could have got his paws on your mother; I'm too familiar with both convents and the temperament of your lascivious mama, which makes me certain that many a priest confessor had his way with her there. It is your character, however, that shows definitively who brought you into the world."

"Go on, Papa dear, go on. May it bring you relief."

"It would appear," continued the bishop, playing with the stem of the goblet and enjoying the expression on the Wallcreeper's face, "that you are the son of the Devil and a lewd Jewess. A perfect Antichrist, the hero of my last propaganda homily. Evanthas, Lateinos or perhaps Shitas or Twatos, I forget. Pour me some wine. You've scared away the staff, so serve me yourself. And tell me what brings you here. What do you want?"

"Nothing. I passed by to pay my respects. Ask how you are, since it behoves a son to take an interest in his parent's health. I wanted to ask—like a dutiful son—whether you need anything, Father. Perhaps you need some sort of filial help from your son? Or service?"

"Your concern is tardy—I needed you a month ago, and I truly regret that you weren't close at hand. You'll regret it, too, I think. Reynevan of Bielawa was in Wrocław. And you were once strangely fascinated by him."

The Wallcreeper's face twitched slightly. So slightly that no one who didn't know the Wallcreeper would have noticed. But the bishop did.

"A month after I excommunicated him," he continued, "two months after Wielisław, where he defeated and humiliated you, that scoundrel dares to show his heretical face in my city. But that's not all: he managed to escape. My servants are sheer fools —by Satan—fools and incompetents."

"What was he doing in Wrocław?" the Wallcreeper asked through clenched teeth. "What was he after? Was he alone or with companions? Who unmasked him and how? How the hell did he get away? Details, Bishop. Details."

"I don't give a damn about details." Konrad snorted. "What interests me is the result, and there is none. I didn't ask about details, they would only have lied to me, trying to cover up their own ineptitude. Sound out Kuczera of Hunt, perhaps you'll get something from him. And now begone. You've turned up at a bad time. I'm expecting a guest. Oswald of Langenreuth, secretary and advisor to Conrad of Dhaun, the Archbishop of Mainz. He is on his way directly from Volyn. From Lutsk, to be precise."

"I'd like to remain. Lutsk interests me, too. To some degree."

"Stay," agreed the bishop after a moment's thought. "According to the usual conditions, naturally. Meaning hop into the cage."

The Wallcreeper smiled, and the smile appeared to survive the metamorphosis in the beak of the bird that opened to squawk strangely. The bird shook its wings, its black eye glowered, it fluttered over to the gilded cage in the corner of the chamber and it alighted, ruffling its feathers, on a golden perch.

"Don't flap your wings," warned the bishop, rocking the wine in the goblet. "Or caw at untimely moments. Enter!"

"His Lordship," announced the lackey, "Sir Oswald of Langenreuth."

"Show him in. Welcome, welcome."

"Your Bishoply Eminence," said Oswald of Langenreuth, a tall, elderly, ascetically thin and richly attired man, bowing in respect. "Your Eminence as usual looks youthful, hale and full of energy. What is behind such an appearance? Witchcraft, perhaps?"

"Work and prayer," replied Konrad. "Piety and moderation. Be seated, be seated, my dear Lord Langenreuth. Sample some Alicante, brought from Aragon. And the sturgeon will soon be served. Forgive me the humble refreshments. We're fasting, after all."

A gust of wind blew in through the window. A warm and springlike gust.

"Speak, speak," said the bishop, nodding and interlocking his fingers. "What of distant Volyn? His Excellency the Papal Legate, Andrea de Palatio, was here recently. Like you, he was returning from Lutsk, but he didn't regale me with gossip, for he was hastening home at great speed. But his countenance was sour, oh, sour indeed. Just by the by, do you know what the Czechs called the council in Lutsk? The council of the three old men."

"Those three old men rule half of Europe," Oswald of Langenreuth observed tartly, "and protect the other half from a Turkish invasion. While the oldest and most decrepit of them has two sons, who ensure continuity to the dynasty founded by said old man."

"I know. The youngest is our king. And soon, God willing, will become emperor. He absolutely deserves it. Particularly after what I heard about Lutsk."

"Did the legate's sour face surprise you?" Langenreuth raised his eyebrows. "Andrea de Palatio brought some secret papal bulls to Poland. In them, His Holiness Martin V appealed to and urged King Władysław and Duke Witold to the godly undertaking and worthy hardship that is a crusade on Bohemia. Owing to—and I quote—respect for God, mercy and the good of his soul, the Vicar of Rome calls on the King of Poland and the Grand Duke of Lithuania to march on Bohemia in order to convert it, destroy it and put an end to its heretical disgrace. On behalf of the Apostolic See, the Pope permits the extermination of heretics in accordance with the rulings of the Church's holy laws. End of quotation. But what happened in Lutsk? The papal dreams of a crusade vanished like smoke. For what did our dear king, that Sigismund of Luxembourg, whom you would gladly see as emperor, do in Lutsk? He offered Witold the crown. The crown! He is making him King of Lithuania!"

"And wisely."

"An inexplicable kind of wisdom. Actually, it's the second time that the Holy Roman Emperor manifests a like wisdom. In 1420, by issuing the Wrocław sentence he infuriated Witold, owing to which we now have Korybut and his Polish regiment in Bohemia. Now, for a change, Sigismund is infuriating Jagiełło, offering Witold the crown and wresting Lithuania from Poland. The infuriated Jagiełło is on the point of abandoning all plans for a crusade to Bohemia and is liable to forge an alliance with the Hussites! Is that what you call political wisdom, Honourable Bishop? The forging of an alliance of Poland with Bohemia? Do you—you and your King Sigismund—want to have an army against you, in which the victors of the Battle of Grunwald will fight alongside the victors of the Battles of Ústí and Tachov? Last spring, Prokop stood outside Wrocław's walls. Owing to the policies of King Sigismund, an allied Czech–Polish army might arrive here next spring. And before you know it, communion *sub utraque specie* will be given in your cathedral. With the liturgy in Polish."

"Don't frighten me with the prospect of the Poles," scoffed the bishop. "They only achieve a Grunwald once every hundred years. And even when it happens, they don't know how to make the most of it. In spite of Grunwald, the Order of Saint Mary survives, it is still robust, Poland still has to take it into account. The Order watches over us all, the entire nation and the Holy

Roman Empire. Poland would long ago have assumed protection over the Hussites were she not afraid of the Order and the penalty it would have to impose on a turbulent Poland. The best way to eradicate the Czech plague is to destroy the source from which the Czechs draw their strength. Jagiełło supports heresy, quite blatantly, by simply pulling the wool over the eyes of the Pope and Europe. The legate didn't leave Poland empty-handed because King Sigismund was getting matey with Witold, but because Jagiełło never even considered a crusade and doesn't care a hoot about papal bulls. Poland has other plans, Master Langenreuth, quite different ones. Their plan is—together with the heretics—to annihilate us and to establish Slavic rule over Europe. Thus King Sigismund is acting wisely, threefold wisely, by standing in the way of and thwarting those plans. For us—the Germanic nation—it is neither Poland nor Lithuania that are the threat. It's the union that is the threat. Witold acquiring the crown means the end of the union, for a crown cannot be incorporated into a crown. By giving Witold the crown, King Sigismund destroys the union. Casting a die of discord. It may even lead, God willing, to a Polish–Lithuanian war. It might result, by the grace of God, in a partition. What? Master Oswald of Langenreuth, doesn't the prospect of a partition of Poland delight you?"

"It would," said Langenreuth, "if I were a dreamer."

"Dreams become reality," said Konrad, growing annoyed. "The Prophet Daniel says that God changes times and seasons, crowns kings and topples kings. Thus let us pray that it comes to pass. God, grant us a new Roman Empire, make Sigismund of Luxembourg our new emperor. Let our dream of Europe, of a united Europe governed by Germania, come true. *Germania uber Alles!* With the other nations on their knees. On their knees, paying homage. Or, by Satan, wiped out! Slaughtered!"

"With the heretics," said Langenreuth, nodding, "like dogs outside the walls of that New Jerusalem. A splendid vision, indeed. How regrettable that life teaches one to be a realist. Not to dream, but to look ahead, and look ahead on the basis of reality. Thus do I predict that Witold's coronation will not come about. Poland will not agree to it and neither will the Pope. Sigismund will wave it away and begin another intrigue somewhere else. Jagiełło will not partake in an anti-Hussite crusade, will not give over supporting the Czechs. And the Teutonic Knights will sit tight, for they know that otherwise one morning they may see Hussite wagons outside Malbork, Chojnice, Tczew and Danzig."

"Where did you see such a course of events?" sneered Konrad. "In the stars?"

"No," said Oswald of Langenreuth coldly. "In the eyes of the Bishop of Krakow, Zbigniew Oleśnicki. But let's drop it, that will suffice about Poland, Lithuania and the whole uncivilised East. Let us talk about our western problems. About the approaching Vatican Council. About matters of Catholic faith... *Herrgott!* What has happened to your bird? Has it lost its mind? It almost broke the window! Why don't you close the cage?"

"It's a free bird," replied Bishop Konrad gravely. "It does as it pleases. Some subjects bore it. Then it flies away."

The dun horse's shoes rang on the stones of the courtyard, the resonant echo swirling around between the walls of the bishop's residence. Douce of Pack, bent over in the saddle, pulled the reins to one side and turned her steed around, making it take small, dainty steps. As she did so, she couldn't take her fascinated eyes off the Wallcreeper, who was hurrying towards the gate. The Wallcreeper noticed her but didn't return the look. He was angry.

"He's angry," said Ulryk of Pack, Lord of Klępino, nodding. "He is as angry as hell. Fierce, it's clear."

"Fierce," confirmed Kuczera of Hunt. "How fierce he is."

"You told him everything," said Hayn of Czirne, commander of the Wrocław mercenaries, grimly. "He barely asked and you told him everything at once. About tracking that Bielawa, about the denunciations...You told him all about the investigation. But I understood you don't like him."

"For that is the truth," said Kuczera, spitting on the stone threshold and rubbing the spit under his boot. "I don't like the whoreson. But the bishop ordered me. And I don't want Grellenort as an enemy. Neither would you, believe me."

"I do," said Ulryk Pack, shuddering slightly. "Upon my word, I do."

"That Bielawa is no kin of mine," said Kuczera, as though he were excusing himself. "He has been excommunicated, which means he is finished, his days are numbered. But Grellenort cannot do much with what you told him; he won't accomplish more than us. Two Sundays ago, we happened quite by chance upon Bielawa's trail, as did the town hall constables. Quite by chance. God knows what he wanted in Wrocław or what he was plotting, where he was hiding, what accomplices he had or how many."

"Grellenort is a sorcerer," Hayn of Czirne said grimly. "Black magic will accomplish what you could not."

Hooves once again thudded in the courtyard as Douce of Pack spurred her horse into a fierce gallop. A Franciscan monk walking across the courtyard flattened himself again the wall, a page in the bishop's livery dodged behind a pillar and a scribe barely managed to jump aside, spilling and scattering an armful of documents. Czirne and Hunt looked at each other in silence. They knew something about the girl, knew what had brought Ulryk of Pack to Wrocław. Douce, a sweet wench with blue-green eyes and the mouth of an angel, had killed in Klępino two tramps and the village halfwit with a spear, for no reason at all, which had rightly angered the Klępino priest. Sir Ulryk had gone to the bishop with a supplication to try to quieten the infernal priest who was railing from the pulpit against the entire Pack family.

Hayn of Czirne cleared his throat.

"Your daughter is most bold, Sir Ulrik," he said. "In the saddle, I mean."

"God didn't give me a son," replied Ulryk, as though excusing himself. "Sometimes I think perhaps it was for the best. Nature, they say, strives for balance. If I'd had one, he'd surely have liked crocheting."

"The first thing the honourable Lord Grellenort did," reported the spy, wringing his cap in his hands, "was to question m'lord Sir Kuczera of Hunt. He used magic, in two ways. Firstly, in order to test his truthfulness. Secondly, to frighten him. But Lord Hunt wasn't to be frightened. I don't know what he told Lord Grellenort, but whatever it was, Lord Grellenort was displeased and irate."

"He's always angry," said Bishop Konrad, grimacing and drinking deep from a cup. "Go on, Grajcarek."

"After that," said the spy, licking his lips, "Lord Grellenort ran off to the town hall to question the town guard. Then he returned to the Church of the Holy Cross on Ostrów Tumski and asked the priests about the Reverend Otto Beess, but learned nothing apart from the fact that the canon had gone to Rogów on the first Sunday in Lent and was residing there. Lord Grellenort also went to the Golden Goblet tavern and questioned Lord Eisenreich's men…Apparently Reinmar Bielawa had saved his wounded stepson—"

"That I know. Tell me something I *don't* know."

"The next day, Lord Grellenort visited Honourable Lord Eisenreich himself. They spoke at length. I don't know what about; it wasn't possible to steal up so close. But I heard them shouting loudly at one another."

"Ha!" The bishop snorted. "If you could hear, it means you managed to steal up. Be heedful. Birkart is no fool and will guess that I have ordered him followed. You know he is a necromancer. If he uncovers you, you can bid farewell to your pleasant life. And the Fourteen Holy Helpers won't aid you."

"I'm not just any old spy," the man said, straightening up his meagre frame in a display of professional pride. "I've been engaged in tracking for quite some time, and I also know how to use magic, as Your Eminence well knows."

"I know," said the bishop, eyeing up the spy, "to be sure. I even meant to burn you to death for your sorcery, though I took pity on you. But be heedful with witchcraft in the city; if they catch you casting spells it'll be the stake or drowning for you. I won't defend you, because how could I defend one such as you? Witchcraft is opposed to divine and earthly law. And you aren't even a human being."

"I'm a man, Your Eminence. Well, half a man. On my mother's side."

"I don't want to hear about your mother. Even less so about your father, who was some kind of incubus or elemental. Tell me what you found out. What did Birkart do after visiting Eisenreich?"

"The Honourable Sir Bartłomiej Eisenreich, as I've already informed Your Eminence, deposited in the name of Reinmar of Bielawa a considerable sum of money at the office of the Fuggers, as a reward for saving his stepson. He must have told Lord Grellenort, for Lord Grellenort hastened there at once. But the office is soundly protected from magic on the outside. What was discussed there, I know not."

"But I know, just imagine, without your spying or spells," said the bishop, holding his cup out towards a servant who stood in an obsequious bow holding a jug, "because I know the Fuggers. Thus I also know how the conversation ended."

The carved fireplace filled the chamber with warmth. The oaken chests decorated with mouldings and maple dressers came without doubt from Danzig, the exquisite glass from Prague and the carpets and tapestries from Arras. Fuggers and Company took care how it presented itself. Because it could afford to.

"I am sorry, m'Lord Grellenort," said the official. "I'm most dreadfully sorry, but we cannot help you. Fuggers and Company does not possess the information you are asking for."

"Oh, but it does," replied the Wallcreeper, looking at a lighter square on the wall, the mark remaining after the removal of a map. "I am well aware that it does. Except that it won't give it out. Because it has made a *principium* from guarding trade secrets."

"Doesn't that amount to the same thing?" said the clerk, now smiling.

"One shouldn't use the excuse of trade secrets to cover up a situation that concerns a crime. A crime, *raison d'état* and the good of the faith. Reinmar of Bielawa, who was seen entering the company's office in February, is a criminal."

"Reinmar of Bielawa? Who might that be? Never heard of him."

"Reinmar of Bielawa," said the Wallcreeper, giving the outward appearance of calm and patience, "is an excommunicated heretic. It was declared in the churches. It is a sin not to have heard of him."

"Fuggers and Company have a blanket indulgence purchased in Rome."

"One may not give an excommunicated man even a cup of water, let alone receive him in an office and enter into business with him. Were it to reach the Holy Office—"

"Fuggers and Company," the official interrupted calmly, "will explain and put right its dealings with the Holy Office. The same way it always does. Which means quickly and smoothly. The same regards the Bishop of Wrocław. Whom you serve, Lord Grellenort."

"The Fuggers," the Wallcreeper said a moment later, "ought not to protect Reinmar of Bielawa. Since, owing to him, the company has suffered serious losses. It was he who robbed the tax collector who was transporting tax levied from you. Which—owing to that incident—you had to pay over again. It is a serious loss in your balance—"

"The company will cope with the balance. It employs book-keepers to that end."

"And the company's prestige? Why, do the Fuggers allow themselves to be robbed with impunity? Will they not exact revenge on the robbers?"

The Fuggers and Company clerk brought his hands together, interlocked his fingers and stared into the Wallcreeper's face.

"They will," he finally said. "All in good time. You may be certain of that."

"The perpetrator of the attack on the tax collector is Reinmar of Bielawa. Capturing him—"

"M'Lord Grellenort," interrupted the official. "You insult my intelligence. And in the process, the prestige of Fuggers and Company, whose best interests you claim to have at heart. Please do not return to these matters. Nor to the attack on the tax collector, nor to Reinmar of Bielawa. A person, who, as I'm trying to impress on you, we do not know at all."

"And Canon Otto Beess? Is he also someone you do not know? Or Bartłomiej Eisenreich, who deposited a considerable sum in this very office in the name of Reinmar of Bielawa?"

"Do you have any other business with me, Lord Grellenort?" said the official, straightening up. "Any other matters? With which Fuggers and Company might be of assistance? If not—"

"At one time," said the Wallcreeper, staying put in his seat, "our conversations were conducted differently. We spoke the same language and had mutually beneficial interests. Many mutual interests. You no doubt remember. Shall I remind you?"

"We remember them well," interjected the clerk. "We remember everything. Everything is in the ledgers, Lord Grellenort. Every entry, every debit, every credit. And it all balances up, to the last pfennig. Bookkeeping is the basis of order. But now… The sand in the hourglass has almost run through. Other clients are waiting—"

"You sensed the opportunity," said the Wallcreeper, still sitting unmoved in the armchair. "You sniffed out which way the wind was blowing with the curs' noses of tradesmen. Once upon a time, when it affected your profits, we were favoured. You bowed low before us, didn't spare any efforts, didn't spare bribes or payments. Thanks to us you acquired a position, thanks to us you destroyed the competition, thanks to us you grew fat. And now you fraternise with our mortal enemies, sorcerers, Hussites and Poles. Isn't it a little too soon? The wheel of fortune turns. The Antichrist is coming, they say. But have you heard of Lutsk in Volyn? Today, you consider us weak, defeated, deprived of influence, having no perspective, so you erase us from your ledgers, make reverses in your balances. You underestimate the forces that stand behind us. The powers we wield. And they are, I assure you, great powers. The greatest that nature knows. And powers that nature doesn't know."

He held out his hands and spread his fingers. At the end of each fingernail suddenly appeared a thin, blue tongue of flame, growing at great speed and changing in colour first to red and then to white. At a slight movement of his fingers the flames exploded with great intensity, veiling the Wallcreeper's hands in a seething mass of fire. The Wallcreeper poured the fire from one hand to the other and made a gesture. Fire licked the edge of the table with the mouldings and rose in a flickering curtain, dancing, almost reaching the carved beams of the ceiling.

The clerk didn't so much as twitch. Or even narrow his eyes.

"The fire of punishment," the Wallcreeper said slowly. "Fire on the thatched roof of a homestead. Fire in a goods store. The fire of the stake. The fire of Hell. The fire of black magic. The most powerful known force."

He withdrew his hands and shook his fingers. The fire vanished. Without a trace. Without the slightest smell of burning. Not leaving even a mark of charring anywhere.

The official of Fuggers and Company slowly reached out his hand to the escritoire and removed something from it; when he took his hand away, a gold coin lay on the table.

"This is a *florino d'oro*," said the official slowly. "A florin, also called a guilder. It has a diameter of around an inch, a weight of around a quarter of a lot, twenty-four carats of pure gold, on the obverse the Florentine lily, on the reverse Saint John the Baptist. Please lower your eyelids, Lord Grellenort, and imagine more of these florins. Not a hundred, not a thousand and not a hundred thousand. A thousand thousands. A *millione*, as the Florentines say. The annual turnover of the company. Please imagine, try to see with the power of the imagination, with the eyes of the soul. And then you will see and know true power.

True force. The most powerful known, omnipotent and invincible. My respects, M'Lord Grellenort! You can see yourself out, can't you?"

Although the spring sun was actively sending its beams through the narrow windows of the Church of Saint Elisabeth, the aisle was still in darkness. Grajcarek could not see the person he was talking to; even the outline of their form escaped his attention. He could only smell their odour, the faint but recognisable aroma of rosemary.

"Grellenort didn't achieve much," he said toadyingly. "In town they're saying that he is trying in vain, that he won't get his hands on Reinmar of Bielawa, because the latter is long gone and far away. When he was turned out of the Fuggers', a cruel cholera seized Grellenort and he also quarrelled severely with the bishop. The bishop forbade him from visiting the Dominicans or pestering the Holy Office, but Grellenort disobeyed. That's all I know."

The figure hidden in the darkness didn't move.

"We are very grateful to you," it said in soft, excitingly modulated female alto tones, "very grateful. May this small purse at least symbolically express how grateful."

Silver jingled. The spy bowed low and shoved the purse into a pocket. With difficulty. Because it was by no means small. But after two months of spying for her, Grajcarek had become accustomed to the rhetorical figures of the woman who spoke in an alto voice.

"At your service," he said, bowing. "If there happens to be anything else…I mean at the bishop's…If I hear any information —I shall always bring it to you."

"And you will always meet with our gratitude. While we're on the subject of information and denunciations, does the name

Apolda ring any bells? Jutta of Apolda? A girl being held by the Inquisition?"

"No, m'lady, I don't know anything about her. But if you wish, I can try."

"We do wish. And now, go in peace."

The woman who spoke in an alto voice and smelled of rosemary got to her feet and the light from the windows fell on her face. The spy immediately lowered his eyes, bowed his head. Instinct warned him that it was better not to look.

"Noble lady?"

"Yes."

"I betray the bishop and inform on him, for I am angry...But he is a clergyman, a servant of God...Will I be damned for it?"

"Is the bishop in your bad books again? What was it this time?"

"The same as always. He insults my mother. For you know, m'lady, my father was a kobold, but my mother was a good and decent woman—"

"Your mother was a Jewess," interrupted the woman with the alto voice. "Of baptised parents, but that doesn't change anything. And since you are a Jew on your mother's side, your father doesn't count; it wouldn't matter if he were a kobold, a spirit, a faun, a centaur—even a flying dragon. You are a Jew, Grajcarek. If you went to the synagogue, you would know that on Judgement Day either the Garden of Eden or the fire of destruction awaits a Jew, depending on the deeds, good or bad, committed by that Jew. Deeds written down in the Book. It is a very old Book, it's actually everlasting. When it first began to be written there were no bishops; the word wasn't even known. Thus you have nothing to worry about. If you were informing on a rabbi, oh, then there would be cause for anxiety."

*

Douce of Pack reined her horse around, spurred it to a gallop and hurled a javelin at full speed. The point pierced the gatepost with a dull thud and the shaft trembled. The girl leaned back in the saddle and slowed the horse to a trot.

"A curse," said Ulryk Pack, shaking his head. "That wench is a vexation."

"Have her married off. Let her husband worry."

"Perhaps you'll be tempted, m'Lord Czirne? Would you? Why, I'd give her to you today. And I won't stint on the dowry."

"A thousand thanks," said Hayn of Czirne and looked at the javelin stuck in the post. "But I shall decline."

"M'Lord Hunt?"

"Forgive me, but I prefer the kind that crochet."

Kuczera of Hunt shrugged.

The bell in the Dominican priory rang for Vespers. The setting sun painted the window panes red, crimson and gold.

"His Excellency the Inquisitor is absent," replied Łukasz Bożyczko in his Polish accent. "He has gone away."

The Wallcreeper had already twice tried to use black magic, had surreptitiously tried twice to frighten the deacon and force him to be compliant using spells. The spells had proved ineffective and his plan came to nothing, evidently because of protective magic. *The entire residence of the Papal Office,* thought the Wallcreeper, *and who knows, perhaps also the Church of Saint Adalbert, are probably all woven around with a blockade. For it is unimaginable that Bożyczko, that inept priest, might know or be able to use witchcraft.*

"Gone away?" he repeated. "Probably to Rome, *ad limina*? You don't have to answer, Bożyczko, it's clear that Hejncze didn't tell you where he was going. I presume he didn't reveal the purpose of the journey, either. The Inquisitor doesn't talk to just anyone. But perhaps he at least gave the date of his return?"

"Nor did His Excellency the Inquisitor consider it necessary to talk about the matter of his return." Łukasz Bożyczko's face appeared to have been carved from granite. "But the purpose of his peregrination is known to all."

"Go on, that it may also be known to me."

"His Excellency the Inquisitor is currently devoting himself to the matter of the fight against terrorism."

"Hejncze has set himself a noble task," said the Wallcreeper, nodding. "There's plenty to fight against. Hussite terrorism has become a real problem."

"His Excellency the Inquisitor," said Bożyczko, not lowering his eyes, "didn't specify what terrorism he had in mind."

"More's the pity. Because forces may combine in the fight."

"His Excellency the Inquisitor is negotiating the combining of forces with Bishop Konrad. Whom you serve, Lord Grellenort."

The Wallcreeper was silent for a long time.

"Are you content with your function, Bożyczko? Does Hejncze pay you well?"

"What is behind your curiosity in this regard?" said the deacon, the expression on his face unchanging.

"Curiosity," replied the Wallcreeper. "Pure curiosity. For it is a fascinating matter, this terrorism of which we speak. Don't you think? It removes the competition from the market, creates new jobs, drives prosperity in industry, trade and commerce, stimulates individual enterprise. Justifies the existence of numerous organisations, positions, functions and whole masses of men carrying out those functions. Those masses derive from it income, royalties, pay, prebendaries, salaries and premiums. Indeed, if terrorism didn't exist it would be necessary to invent it."

"His Excellency Hejncze spoke about it," said Łukasz Bożyczko, smiling. "Even using similar words. But in a somewhat different sense."

*

The Kapellbrücke was enveloped in a damp fog propelled by the breeze from Lake Lucerne in the east. A bell in one of Lucerne's churches tolled.

The steps of the approaching man, although clearly cautious, made a dull echo under the roof covering the bridge. The man in a grey hooded cloak leaning against the balustrade jerked up his head. And touched the haft of a knife hidden under his cloak.

The man reached him. He was also hooded. And also had one hand concealed under the flap of his hooded mantle.

"*Benedicite.*" The arrival spoke first, in hushed tones, after looking around. "*Benedicite, parcite nobis.*"

"*Benedicite,*" the man in the grey cloak replied softly. "*Fiat nobis secundum verbum tuum.*"

"Who believes he will be saved?"

"But he who does not will be condemned."

"Who does God's bidding?"

"He will have eternal life."

"Amen," said the visitor, sighing with obvious relief. "Amen, Brother. I welcome you with all my heart. Let us go on."

They went over to the eight-sided stone tower standing in the lake and almost abutting against the bridge. Water splashed beneath the planks. The fog began to disperse.

"I welcome you with all my heart." Now, his suspicions allayed, he spoke with a distinct Helvetian accent. "I confess it was a relief when you uttered the watchword in the sacred tongue of our faith. We were afraid, what can I say… Some of the *Parfaits*… They had their suspicions about you. They even thought you an agent of the Inquisition."

Grzegorz Hejncze spread his arms with a smile that was meant to signify that he was helpless in the face of suspicion and could do nothing about the slur.

"We heard that Birkart Grellenort interests you," continued the Helvetian. "I gained the agreement of the Perfect Ones, hence I shall be glad to lend you help, Brother, since I know a little something about that individual. He is currently residing in the lands of the Bohemian Kingdom, to be precise in the city of Wrocław in Silesia. He serves the bishop there—"

"I am aware of all of that," Hejncze interrupted gently. "I have travelled from Silesia. From Wrocław, to be precise."

"Ah. I see. Then it is the past that interests you, not the present. If so, we must return to 1415. To the Council in Constance. As you no doubt know, Brother, in Constance it was decreed…"

Grzegorz Hejncze had been in Constance in 1415 and knew what was decreed there. But he didn't interrupt.

"…decreed that the best way to put an end to the Great Schism would be the election of a new, unifying Pope, preceded by the voluntary resignation of all three Popes who at that time went by the titles of Gregory XII, Benedict XIII and John XXIII. The first two were compliant, but not the third. He felt powerful at that time, had the support of Frederick, Duke of Austria, and of the Burgundians, he had the financial backing of the Medici family, so he began to revolt. The cardinals didn't deliberate for long and decided to put the screws on him. According to a simple principle: resign or go to the stake. Accusations were quickly fabricated. Standard, conventional ones. Fraud, corruption, heresy, simony, paedophilia and sodomy."

"I heard about it. Everybody did."

"Indeed?" said the Perfect One, glancing quickly at the Inquisitor. "Then I shall pass over widely known facts and move to lesser-known ones. Although imprisoned and guarded no less closely than Huss had been, John XXIII fled from Constance on the night of the twentieth of March. He hid in Schaffhausen, concealed by his protector, Frederick. From there, news reached the Council that powerful magic had ensured the success of the escape. A powerful sorcerer, the Jew Meir ben Haddar, in the service of Frederick strangled the guards with poisonous miasmas and carried John away in a magical flying ship. The news was clearly spread by John himself to show the Council what powerful allies he had. In order to warn the cardinals that he wouldn't leave the Holy See without a fight, that he would act against any pontificate they elected. And thus the Great Schism, rather than being eliminated, began to grow before the Council's eyes.

"There was slight confusion among the cardinals; no one knew what to do. And then, like a devil from a box, sprang Duke Cunradus de Oels, Konrad of Oleśnica, who was accompanying the Bishop of Wrocław at the Council. Konrad was known and respected in the circles of international politics and enjoyed the great esteem of King Sigismund of Luxembourg, so the cardinals were prepared to listen to him despite his lowly ecclesiastical rank. And Konrad promised nothing less than that he would in the course of two months achieve the capture of the rebellious Anti-Pope, convey him to Constance and bring him before the Council. Under one condition: no one was ever to ask him how he did it and with whose help. And what happened? On the twenty-fifth of May, *Anno Domini* 1415, John XXIII, now known simply as Baldassare Cossa, stood before the cardinals, trembling with fear, weeping and in a shaking voice begging for mercy, promising to do anything the Council instructed.

"The joy and euphoria caused by the end of the Schism at first put everything else in the shade, but the time came when the matter began to be investigated. And what had happened during those two months was clarified. What had caused—it was asked —a seasoned fighter like Cossa to be so suddenly weakened? What had frightened the belligerent Anti-Pope? What had he seen to turn him suddenly into a drooling and pitiful wreck of a man? Why had Frederick, Duke of Austria, hidden himself away in his castle in Innsbruck and wasn't emerging from it? What had happened to the Anti-Pope's companions who had fled from Constance with him? And what had happened to the Jew, Meir ben Haddar? Because the mage had vanished without trace. From that time, May 1415, no one ever saw Haddar again."

"And all that," asked Hejncze, feigning disbelief, "was understood to have been caused by Birkart Grellenort?"

"Correct," said the Perfectus, nodding. "By Birkart Grellenort, Konrad's acolyte and confidant, his ward and—as some go so far as to claim—his bastard. A magus. A theurge. A sortilegus. A necromancer. A metamorphiser who can change shape—"

"During the Council in Constance, Grellenort couldn't have been more than—"

"Twenty years old," said the Perfectus, finishing Hejncze's sentence. "That's right. A twenty-year-old had vanquished Meir ben Haddar, a mage said to be in league with Devil. So with whom…or with what could Grellenort have been in league?"

"Didn't the Church do anything about this? Or the newly elected Pope?"

The Perfectus shook his head.

"During the Council," he reminded Hejncze, "Johannes Hus was burned at the stake and a rebellion had flared up in Bohemia. Konrad of Oleśnica was made a bishop before the Council was over. A bishop who enthusiastically quelled revolts, who ordered heretics to be dragged through Wrocław town square by horses before being burned alive. The most loyal ally of the Pope and King Sigismund, an ally in troubling times. To carp at a man for such a trifling reason as employing a sorcerer? Oh, really. The affair was covered up, swept under the carpet. Expunged from the files. Treated as if it never happened. Formally, at least."

"And informally?"

"A secret investigation was conducted. The results were kept secret, but we know what they were. At a certain moment we also took an interest in Grellenort."

"After Grellenort began to use black magic to persecute Cathars and Beguines on the orders of the Bishop of Wrocław," said Hejncze, deciding to speed up the conversation.

"In the towns of Jawor and Świdnica," confirmed the Helvetian. He pronounced them "Jauer" and "Zviniza." "We didn't do anything then, we remained utterly idle, since…Since one may not answer terror with terror. Pierre of Castelnau, Peter of Verona, Konrad of Marburg, Schwenckefeld. Terrorism is wrong and leads nowhere. That's what we think, the Good People, *Amici Dei*. Terrorism is an evil and a sin."

Which are better put on other people's consciences, not one's own, thought the Inquisitor. *Which is the reason—and the only reason— you are helping me. Only for that reason are you giving me information. Convinced that I am seeking revenge. That I'm planning an assassination attempt. An act of terror. The terror, that repulses you. But when it is carried out, you'll murmur "Deo gratias." On your knees. With your eyes raised heavenward. Free of sin. But content. Satisfied.*

The Perfectus said nothing and stared at the dark massif of Pilatus, the mountain towering over Lucerne like a crouching giant. The Inquisitor didn't hurry him.

"Grellenort was educated in Andalusia," continued the Helvetian. "In Aguilar near Cordoba."

"Alumbrados," mumbled Hejncze.

"The Enlightened Ones," said the Helvetian in confirmation. "A secret sect whose roots stretch back into the gloom of prehistory; older, some say, than the Deluge—why, more ancient than humanity itself. At first exclusively Muslim, it was opened up to Christians by Gerbert of Aurillac, Pope Sylvester II. Well-known names figure among the school's alumni. The Arabs Hali and al-Kindi, the legendary Morienus and Artephius, Joachim of Fiore, Albertus Magnus, Walter Map, Duns Scotus. William of Ockham. Michael of Cesena. Jacques Duèze, that is Pope John XXII. Grellenort is also a graduate of Aguilar, which explains the rapid pace of his magical education. But that's not all."

Hejncze raised his eyebrows.

"Someone is helping him," said the Perfectus with conviction, "supporting him magically, generating the Power for him. Unceasingly. We failed to find out who."

"Still in Wrocław?" said the Wallcreeper. "Haven't you ever thought about removing? To the country, for example?"

"I like Wrocław." The neufra's brown face melted into a parody of a smile. "Nothing compares to a city. As they say: *Stadtluft macht frei.*"

"The countryside is safer, though."

"I don't feel endangered. Do you have it?"

The Wallcreeper reached for a pouch and took from it a square-sided flacon of dark glass. The neufra's gnarled and claw-like fingers twitched, as though they were about to snatch the flacon from him. She controlled herself, pushed forward a goblet and stared spellbound at the lavender liquid slowly filling the vessel. She indicated it was enough with an impatient gesture. She seized the goblet and hesitated.

"Won't you...join me?"

"No, thank you, Kundrie," he said, not wanting to upset her, knowing how addicted she was to *aurum potabile* and how she valued every drop. "It's all for you."

"Thank you indeed, son, thank you," said the neufra, overcoming the trembling of her hand. She took a sip and her amber eyes immediately brightened up. "Well, let's get down to business. Tell me what's vexing you."

The Wallcreeper sighed. Or pretended to sigh. He didn't know his actual mother. She died in a Magdalene nunnery in Lubáň giving birth to him. He was brought up successively by a poorhouse, a parish school and the Wrocław streets. And finally, by Kundrie. A neufra. An elemental. One of the Longaevi, an Eternal.

Kundrie had never revealed her real age to the Wallcreeper, but it was known that she had been living in Wrocław for around two hundred years, bearing in mind she remembered the Mongol invasion. The Wallcreeper met her when he was seven years old. The encounter had been unforgettable. It occurred in the Fish Market, where the Wallcreeper used to hang around, hoping to steal something or catch a cat to torture. In order to exist among humans, Kundrie concealed herself under a powerful illusory spell. From a small child, the Wallcreeper revealed magical gifts and extrasensory powers; the illusion had no power over him and he saw the neufra in her natural form. The sight of her shocked and terrified him. A thing that looked like a cross between a rotten willow tree and a two-legged lizard and plodded around the middle of the Fish Market, shedding stinking lumps, was a little too much for a seven-year-old. Even a seven-year-old like the Wallcreeper.

The intensity of that first impression influenced the power of their later friendship. The neufra—a predatory and extremely cruel creature—was fascinated by the boy's cruelty. And his magical gifts. She did much to refine them and was able to do so by drawing on knowledge that extended back to the very earliest beginnings. The Wallcreeper was an eager student. At the age of eight, he was a psionic and used simple magic and telepathy with ease, able to cast spells—including spells of sickness—and turn food bad. By ten, he was able to expertly use higher magic and goetia—with whose help he learned how to kill. By the time he was twelve, he was a proficient enough mage to take up studies at Alumbrados, the school located in Aguilar near Cordoba. He was sponsored by Duke Konrad of Oleśnica, at that time a seminarist in Wrocław. The duke and seminarist suddenly recalled the Wallcreeper. For reasons that the Wallcreeper wasn't party to, but could guess at.

He returned to Wrocław in 1414. As a theurge and necromancer, he instantly became the confidant of Konrad, who by then was already the cathedral provost with great chances of the bishop's mitre. Which he received in 1418. Elevating him—and at the same time his personal sorcerer—to new heights. While Kundrie, the neufra, his adoptive mother, became the talented pupil's confidant. And advisor. The Wallcreeper—in spite of his efforts—was still only a human being, and a young one at that. And extremely arrogant. He may have been talented and ambitious, but the Highest Arcane Knowledge of native Longaevi was still inaccessible to him and he had a long way to go before becoming a true Nefandi. Kundrie—an elemental linked to the Earth—was able to filter out the forces of the Longaevi and Nefandi for the Wallcreeper's benefit. And when the Wallcreeper was unable to use the powers, she did it for him. If he asked. That is, if he was able to overcome his pride. It demanded a great deal of him, hence he rarely asked for help. And only in matters that were truly important to him.

Now, the matter in hand—Kundrie was in no doubt—was important. When he talked about it, when he discussed it, his voice was calm and cold. But he clenched his teeth. And his fists. So tightly his knuckles turned white.

"Oh, yes," she said, summing up his words, and licking the colloid from her lips. "He has got under your skin, that Reynevan

Bielawa, oh he has. He mocked you, humiliated you before the bishop, covered you in shame, forced you to flee. And you're right, my son, utterly right: if they seize him now or somebody else kills him, you will never wash off the shame. So you must capture him. With your own hands. And make sure folk remember one, single thing: his torment. Have him flayed alive. But leave the skin on his face. That always makes an impression, always. Then tan the skin and display it in public. In the town square."

She fell silent and scratched a warty cheek. She saw him clench his fists in impatience and anger. She smiled. With the studied maliciousness of a teacher who can tease an arrogant pupil who imagines he needs no more lessons and believes he can manage without them.

"Yes, indeed," she said with a smile. "Yes. I forgot. First that Reynevan needs to be caught. And that is proving a slog, isn't it? In spite of your ceaseless efforts. In spite of the necromancy carried out in the crypt under Saint Maciej's. And I always taught you, always repeated: begin by thinking, with logic. Only make use of necromancy when logic disappoints."

"Kundrie," snarled the Wallcreeper. "I know you are lonely. I know you have no one to talk to and compensate for it at any opportunity that arises. But let it go. I didn't come here to hear your swansongs."

Kundrie bristled her dorsal spines but curbed her wrath. After all, the pup was her pupil. Her son. The apple of her eye.

"You came," she said calmly, "or rather hurried here to ask for help. So go ahead and ask. Nicely."

"May I politely request," said the Wallcreeper, fire flashing in his birdlike eyes. "Very politely. Happy?"

"Extremely," said the neufra, gulping greedily from the goblet. "Let's get down to business. Let us start with logical thinking, by posing certain questions. Reynevan Bielau, I gleaned from your account, was in Wrocław twice, in January and in February. He entered the lion's den twice. He isn't a madman, nor does he have a death wish. Why would he take such a risk? What was he seeking in Wrocław, what was worth such a gamble?"

"He was seeking help. From Canon Otto Beess, his friend."

"Help with what? People are saying in town that in December, Duke Jan of Ziębice imprisoned Reynevan's beloved, a Poor Clare converse maiden. He allegedly outraged her and ordered her killed; proof of why Reynevan—mad and possessed by revenge—killed the duke at the Battle of Wielisław. Thus he avenged the maid, enjoying sweet revenge. Riding with the Hussites on the plundering raid, he could have indulged himself even more. But he travels around Silesia alone. Why?"

"Because he thinks the wench is alive and imprisoned and searches for her," said the Wallcreeper, shrugging. "He is mistaken. I also sought her, for I needed her. No, not only as bait for Bielawa. I meant to force her to testify, thus confirming the heresy of the Poor Clares from White Church. The bishop and Inquisitor Hejncze wanted to avoid a scandal and sent the nuns to do penance. But I wanted to sentence them all to the stake, and I would have with Miss Apolda's testimony. Sadly, nothing came of it. I didn't find her. Not in Ziębice, nor in the vicinity of the castles where Duke Jan usually keeps his none too willing lovers—"

"You say you needed the wench," interrupted Kundrie. "But what if somebody else did? And that somebody found her first?"

The Wallcreeper remained silent. He watched her finish the *collodium* of gold and put down the goblet, her eyes shining amber.

"Don't be cocksure, my son. Don't underestimate your opponents. Don't presume they are stupider than you. Don't deceive yourself that they can't outrun you, anticipate your actions or outsmart you. Back then in Schaffhausen, in the case of the Jew, Haddar, a similar oversight almost cost you your life. The current situation, I believe, is similar. Somebody you underestimated, who outsmarted you and got there first. Guessing that whoever has the maiden, has Reynevan. And has something to blackmail Reynevan with—"

"I understand," said the Wallcreeper, cutting her off and standing up. "Now I understand what it was all about. I suspected something of the kind, but you have put me back on the right track. Now I understand why Wrocław…Farewell, Mother. I have to go and deal with something. I'll drop by soon."

The neufra, without uttering a word, gestured with her eyes at the goblet with a lavender drop at the bottom.

"Very well. I'll bring you more."

He found Father Felicjan in the service section of the bishop's court, near the kitchen, sitting on a barrel and voraciously eating something from an earthenware bowl. When he saw the Wallcreeper, he choked on it. The Wallcreeper had no intention of wasting time. A punch knocked the bowl from the altarist's hands, then he seized the front of the man's cassock, hauled him to his feet, shook him and slammed him against the wall with such force that some copper pots fell and scattered with a clang. Father Felicjan goggled, wheezed and then coughed up and spat out the remains of a half-chewed mushroom pieróg onto the Wallcreeper's doublet. The Wallcreeper took a swing and with all his might struck the altarist in the face with a reverse blow, and then dragged Felicjan, wailing, into the kitchen courtyard, covered in feathers and silver fish scales. Felicjan lunged for Grellenort's legs and seized him around the knees, but a punch hurled him to the ground. He tried to get away on all fours, but the Wallcreeper caught up with him and kicked him hard in the backside. The altarist tumbled nose first into a pile of cabbage leaves and vegetable peelings. The Wallcreeper snatched a poker from the dumbstruck cook's assistant, struck Felicjan once and twice and then gave him a sound hiding. The altarist howled, screamed out and wept. The kitchen girls and cooks fled in panic, abandoning pots, cauldrons and kettles.

"I've been meaning to do that for a long time," said the Wallcreeper, dropping the poker and standing over the altarist. "For a long time, I've thought to give you a hiding, you rat, you scoundrel in a cassock, you fucking mendacious priest. But there was no time, until today. Treat this as an advance payment. Against what you will receive from the bishop. When he finally learns that you are informing on him to Inquisitor Hejncze."

Father Felicjan sobbed heart-rendingly.

"The bishop won't learn it from me, if that reassures you," the Wallcreeper went on, adjusting a cuff. "Because it doesn't concern me. What concerns me is something else…You spy for the Inquisition and I want to know…Hey, Brother—why do I suddenly sense fear? Do you still have something more to hide?"

"I'll tell you everything!" sobbed Felicjan. "Make a clean breast of it! I didn't do it willingly! They made me! They attacked me. Beat me up! They threatened me…That if I betrayed them, they'd kill me…I can't talk about it…"

The Wallcreeper ground his teeth. He seized the priest by the collar, pulled him up and pressed him against a vat of fish with one knee.

"Can't?" he hissed. "Well, let me help you."

He grabbed the altarist by the wrist and growled a spell. There was a hiss, and there was smoke. Father Felicjan cringed, his face turned black and a terrible yell shook the floor of the courtyard. The Wallcreeper didn't let go until he could smell burning flesh. When finally released, the altarist fell to his knees, sobbing uncontrollably, gently holding his burned hand close to his belly.

"Rub ointment into your hand and it'll be as right as rain in a couple of weeks," said the Wallcreeper, straightening up. "But your genitals, oh, it'd be much harder to heal your genitals. Talk, whoreson, before I scorch your balls. Are they dear to you? Do they matter to you? Are you fond of them? Well, then, now tell me everything. Don't conceal anything. Don't utter a single untruth."

And Father Felicjan, sobbing, weeping and blubbering, told him everything. He didn't conceal anything or speak a single untruth.

"It was Reinmar of Bielawa..." he finished, voice faltering. "An excommunicated heretic...He was disguised with a spell, but I recognised his voice...He beat me and tortured me... Threatened to kill me—"

"Inquisitor Gregory Hejncze," the Wallcreeper summarised, "the man you inform to, is holding a maiden, Jutta of Apolda, somewhere in secret. Reynevan Bielawa ordered you to find out where she is imprisoned. How is he to make contact with you? Who were his accomplices?"

Father Felicjan burst out crying. So pathetically that the Wallcreeper believed in his ignorance.

"What have you found out?"

"Nothing at all..." sobbed the altarist. "How can I? I am but a worm...How can I learn the Inquisition's secrets?"

"You are a spy of the Inquisition. Meaning Hejncze trusts you to an extent."

"I'm a miserable wretch—"

"Oh, you are, you are, no doubt," said the Wallcreeper, looking down at him in disgust. "So listen, worm. Go on spying. If you learn the place of Apolda's imprisonment, inform me. If Bielawa or one of his comrades contacts you, you will also inform me. If you do well, I shall bolster your wormlike existence with a generous reward. I shall not stint. But if you disappoint me or betray me…Then, vile worm, it won't end with some light roasting. I won't leave a span of your skin untouched. So begone, get to work, go and spy. Be off, out of my sight."

The altarist fled away stealthily, clutching his hand to his chest. He didn't look back once.

The Wallcreeper watched him go. And turned around, feeling somebody's eyes stuck onto his back.

By the stone staircase stood a girl of around sixteen. In a padded men's doublet and a beret with a plume worn at a rakish angle. Her rapaciously snub nose poorly suited her blonde locks, rouged face and doll-like mouth. Suited them badly. But didn't mar them.

She heard, thought the Wallcreeper, involuntarily feeling for the knife hidden in his sleeve. *She saw and heard everything. She didn't flee, because fear paralysed her. And now there's a witness. A quite unnecessary witness.*

The girl approached slowly, eyes still fixed on him. Eyes the colour of a mountain lake, framed by half-inch eyelashes. Those eyes betrayed no fear, the Wallcreeper finally realised, but rather delight in what had happened. Delight and a wild, unbridled, pheromone-fuelled fascination. He was surprised to feel her fascination beginning to affect him, too.

"A like-minded soul," he drawled through clenched teeth. "Attired like a boy."

Douce of Pack came even closer. She fluttered her long eyelashes.

He fell on her like a hawk. Turned her around, pushed her against the barrel, seized her by the back of her neck and bent her over viciously. Douce's beret slipped down over her eyes. The Wallcreeper dug his fingers into her blond locks, tore from her bottom the woollen *braccae* and undergarments and forced himself hard against the girl. Douce trembled with excitement. And then cried out. Loudly.

In the cry were pain and lust.

"Something is in prospect," said Grajcarek, crumpling his cap. "Various strange individuals have been seen in town. Dangerous-looking people—"

"Speak," said the bishop, impatiently. "Spit it out, by the Devil."

"There are rumours going around that m'Lord Grellenort has fallen into disfavour with many people. That many people wish him ill. Very ill, I'd say."

"That's not news to me."

"There's more." The spy coughed into a fist. "May Your Eminence forgive me for saying this—"

"I shall. Speak."

"They say some kinsmen have come to Wrocław. Relatives of the men that were killed. Of Lord Bart of Karczyn. Of Lord Czambor of Heissenstein…For people are saying that Lord Grellenort is…is guilty of those murders…"

The bishop said nothing and played with his pen.

"Your Eminence," said the spy, breaking the silence, "I think—"

"What do you think?"

"That we ought to warn Lord Grellenort. But Your Eminence certainly knows best what to do…"

The bishop said nothing, playing with his pen and biting his lips.

"You're right," he finally replied. "I do."

The bells of Saint James's had finished tolling the Compline some time before and now the monks could be heard intoning in chorus *Salve regina*. At any moment, the later bell would sound the *pulsus serotinus*; at any moment one could also expect the tolling of the *ignitegium*.

The candles in the chamber had been put out, but a faint light came from the fireplace where the logs were burning down. The red glow gave an unearthly charm to the smooth skin and slender body of Douce of Pack, lying beside him among the ruffled bedclothes. The Wallcreeper was resting on one elbow, looking at the girl, at her widely open eyes fixed on him. He recalled other fires, other eyes, other naked bodies, other violent sex heightened by pain. At sabbaths and orgies in the mountains of Harz, in the forest clearings of Pomerania, in the caves of Alpujarras and in the wildernesses of the Estremadura. When the earth trembled from the thudding of drums and when bats and owls flitted in the night air punctuated by the trilling of pipes.

A skull-like moon shone through the window.

He had needlessly begun a liaison with her. He had lured her, drawn her to him. That was a mistake. A mistake that would have to be put right.

Douce of Pack sighed and raised herself up. The Wallcreeper instinctively looked at her neck and quickly envisioned how to seize and twist it.

Two movements would suffice, he thought, *and that gleam in her eyes would die…*

Son, he suddenly heard in his head. He sat up in bed.

Son, said Kundrie, *come at once. I must show you something, something that is linked to the maiden you seek. I am waiting. Come.*

Like hell, he thought. *She's simply run out of* aurum potabile. *Ah well, I'll have to go. She's my mother, like it or not.*

"Is something the matter?" asked Douce, sitting up and brushing her hair from her forehead. The fire from the hearth flickered on her small breasts. It flashed on her wide-open eyes. "What's the matter? Are you going?"

"Yes. I'll be back late."

"Are you leaving me alone?"

"Yes, but not right this moment."

He grabbed her by the shoulders and pressed her down onto the pillows. She yielded to him, forced into subservience. And they made love with wild abandon. In the glow of the fire and the pale light of the skull-like moon.

Stadtluft macht frei, recalled the Wallcreeper, walking from the Sand Bridge down Castle Street.

The fact that numerous creatures of the night dwelt in Wrocław was no surprise to him. Some time had passed, however, since he had last wandered there after dark and during that time, as it turned out, much had changed. Indeed, he observed as he walked, it wasn't only Kundrie who sensed a whiff of freedom in the breath of the city. It was not just she, as it turned out, who felt good and at ease in Wrocław. It was not just she, as it turned out, whom the city habitat suited.

A dzanteer, surprised by a doorway, raised its long muzzle, clearly not understanding how the Wallcreeper could see it. It finally hid in the darkness, arching its back and raising its hackles.

Several urkins, puffed up in fluffy balls, were sitting under the outlet of a gutter, licking the slimy cobbles. A rapion as agile as a lizard ducked into the darkness, its claws scraping on the stones. Just further on was a wine store and a bald gnome in a leather jerkin fiddling with the padlock didn't even raise his head. His comrade, armed with a crowbar, scowled at the Wallcreeper, growling something under his breath. It was hard to say if it was a greeting or an insult.

In an alleyway leading to Narrow Street there was a sharp odour of magic and alchemy—in other words ectoplasm, saltpetre, vitriol, alum and vinegar. The gutter was clearly phosphorescing, esphilines were crawling in it, lured by the sublimational waste. Not far away, in the arcades, lurked a garou, its well-developed senses inhibiting it from attacking. It perceived the Wallcreeper's aura in time and realised it would be better not to try. Several dozen yards further on, a lamia acted similarly. The vampiress even waited until the Wallcreeper approached, and after convincing herself that he could indeed see her, greeted him with a bow, wrapped herself in a mantle and vanished, turning grey against a grey wall.

A kludder sat moaning and scratching its belly between the buttresses of the Church of the Holy Spirit. Flying drakes, alarmed by his presence, rustled and fluttered their wings on the tracery, pinnacles and turrets of the church. Just beyond the spital, the Wallcreeper saw a shining pool of fresh blood on the stones. Led by curiosity—although the matter didn't especially interest him—he used a spell to intensify his eyesight and peered into the gloom. A kalkabra crouching over a blood-soaked body and disconcerted by the spell bared its two-inch fangs and its fur stuck up on its head like a silver crown. The Wallcreeper shrugged and speeded up. As previously, it turned out it was still perilous to walk around Wrocław by night.

He crossed Market Street and entered a small square by a well. And then they fell on him. From all sides. Dressed in a way that made them almost invisible. They were remarkably fast. For men.

Only a lightning-fast dodge saved his life—at the last moment he caught the pale gleam of a blade coming for him. He seized the assailant by the front of his jerkin, spun him around and pushed him into the path of the next attacker, straight onto his sword blade. He spun away and felt steel brush his hair. He jumped clear and saw the sword of another assassin strike sparks against the iron grating. He grabbed the hand holding the sword, tugged it, unbalanced the assailant, flung him to his knees and with a swift movement of both hands immediately broke his neck. Another man lunged and thrust, but the Wallcreeper dodged the blade with a subtle half-turn, caught him by the elbow and wrist and jerked the sword out of his now limp arm. The attacker howled. Using him like a shield, the Wallcreeper thrust the sword into the next attacker's belly and leaped towards the others without waiting for him to drop. When they retreated, he turned back and with a short movement slit the throat of the man with the broken arm.

Three men were on the ground, three still on their feet.

The skull-like moon emerged from behind a cloud and the Wallcreeper attacked.

They ran behind the well, but it didn't save them. He was on them without them seeing. The first slumped to his knees, stabbed in the groin; before he managed to utter a scream, his throat was already slashed open. The second leaped to his aid, attacking in a classic swordsman's stance. The Wallcreeper let him approach to the standard distance, parried his jab and thrust, hard and sure, into his face, between his eye and nose. The man tensed up and trembled, his arms shaking spasmodically. And then slid off the blade, as limp as a rag doll.

Only one was left, lurking in the shadows. He attacked before the Wallcreeper, trying to gain the advantage. Yelling incomprehensibly and raising to strike with a strange weapon, neither a battleaxe nor a club. The Wallcreeper evaded him and stabbed. The attacker dropped to his knees. And then crashed down onto his face.

The Wallcreeper looked down at the sword. It was clear at once that the weapon was special. And expensive. Probably Milanese. There was a swordsmith's punch on the blade, small and difficult to make out in the dark. The Wallcreeper wasn't especially interested, in any case.

One of the men on the ground wheezed and trembled, scraping his belt buckle on the stone surround of the well he was using to drag himself up. The Wallcreeper was there in three strides; slashed once, twice. On the third swing, the Milanese blade groaned and snapped. He tossed away the scrap iron.

Another of the men moaned. It was the last one he had felled. The Wallcreeper approached and picked up the strange weapon. It was a cross. A large, heavy, iron cross with straight arms. A silver engraving shone on it. They were letters.

T
R
I
SIT MIHI CRUX
ADVERSUS DAEMONES
U
M
P
H
U
S

"I'm not a fucking demon," said the Wallcreeper.

He raised the cross and brought it down like a battleaxe.

He wiped his brain-spattered trouser legs with the edge of the dead man's cloak and went on his way. Through Wrocław by night. A city that could be dangerous at night.

Chapter Eight

In which, at Odry Castle, Prokop the Shaven places his trust in Reynevan, and an apparition lacking a toe prophesies the future of Gediminas's descendants.

As they rode up from the north with the current of the Odra, the town lying on the right bank was visible from a distance. A round tower with a pointed roof loomed over the castle perched on a steep rock. The castle—built according to legend by the Knights Templar—adjoined the square of the town walls and was packed with squat towers. The gilt on the bell tower of the parish church shone.

Mist trailed over the river and fog crept among the osiers and willows, which were now turning green. Prokop the Shaven stood up in the stirrups, groaned and rubbed his lower back.

"Odry is ahead of us. Let us make haste."

The sentries in the watchtower saw the detachment and shouted a request for identification. Chains rattled, the drawbridge thudded down and the portcullis grated as it rose up. They rode in with a rumble of hooves, first through the gatehouse, then into the narrow streets, among workshops, shops and merchants' houses.

"Your medicine is wearing off," moaned Prokop. "Jesus Christ, Reynevan, it hurts so much I'm about to fall from the saddle..."

"Patience. I just have to find an apothecary's shop..."

"There's one in the town square," said Bedřich of Strážnice, riding alongside. "Always used to be. Unless it's already been plundered."

The town of Odry owed its development to its location in the so-called Moravian Gate, a depression between the ranges of the Sudety and Carpathian Mountains on the route leading from the drainage basin of the Danube to the Odra and the Vistula. The route—linking the south to the north, Danzig and Toruń to Buda, Krakow to Vienna and Venice, Poznań and Wrocław to the Venetian states on the Adriatic—was naturally an important trade route along which merchants' caravans moved unceasingly.

The road had grown deserted with the rise of the Hussites, when merchants began to avoid a region constantly in flames and in revolt. The embargo did the rest. But in 1428, Dobko Puchała of Węgrów, a Polish knight of the Wieniawa arms and a celebrated veteran of Grunwald who had also vanquished the Teutonic Knights at the Battles of Radzyń and Golub—and was now an ally of the Tábor—captured Odry and settled there. Puchała and his brave Polish followers swooped down on the country like hawks, burning what they could and slaughtering anyone who resisted. Having ensconced himself in Odry, he successfully cut Olomouc off from Opava, which was in an anti-Hussite coalition, preventing Przemko of Opava and the Moravian nobility from coordinating their actions. In so doing, Puchała became a thorn in their side and the target of numerous attacks which, however, he always managed to repulse successfully. In fact, repulsing them wasn't enough for him and he attacked enemy demesnes, sowing fear and starting fires to terrify the Catholics cowering behind castle walls. Now, though, after Jan of Kravaře had gone over to the Chalice and allied with the Tábor, Puchała controlled all the roads, including the most important road for the Hussites, the Cieszyn one, along which endlessly flowed transports of weapons and groups of Polish volunteers to Odry. There were so many soldiers in Odry that the town resembled a military camp. Most of the streets were blocked by siege engines, combat wagons and bombards, delighting the children frolicking on them.

"I'm going to the castle to meet Puchała," announced Prokop. "Brother Pardus, take care of quartering the men. Reynevan, find an apothecary's shop, purchase what you need then come and bring the patient relief. And please hurry, because tardiness is liable to enrage the patient."

"Let's hope the apothecary has the ingredients—"

"He will," Bedřich assured him. "According to rumours, the town apothecary is also an alchemist and a sorcerer. He'll have all the magical ingredients, you'll see. Unless they've already executed him for witchcraft."

Prokop the Shaven had ordered Reynevan to begin treating him almost immediately after they met, in the first tar maker's hut they happened upon in an ash woodland.

The cause of the Hejtman's torment was rheumatism, *myalgia* to be precise, rheumatoid arthritis, in this case causing acute and chronic pain in the lumbar region, from which the name "lumbago"—popular among university physicians and sorcerers—derived. The causes of the ailment were only partly understood and traditional treatments usually only brought temporary respite. Magic achieved greater success; magical balsams, even if they weren't capable of curing it completely, soothed the pain much more quickly and were longer lasting. The most effective at treating lumbago were certain village healers, but those women were afraid to, because they would be burned at the stake for doing so.

Not possessing the magical components for balsams and

poultices, Reynevan was limited to laying on hands and spells, aided by the Algos, one of the miniature amulets from the casket rescued by Scharley. It wasn't much, but it ought to have brought relief. And it did. Feeling the pain weakening and fading away, Prokop groaned in joy.

"You're a miracle worker, Reinmar. Oooh. It would be good to have you permanently to hand—"

"Hejtman, I cannot stay. I must—"

"I don't give a damn what you must. I've already told you: I need you. And not just for medical reasons. I don't wish to know anything; I haven't asked you to explain why you happened to be at Sovinec and what you were doing there. I haven't asked you about the rumpus with the Náchod Orphans or about Smil Půlpán's mysterious demise. I haven't, though perhaps I should. So be quiet. You'll stay with me and we're going to Odry. Is that clear?"

"It is."

"So say nothing more about having to do something else."

Groaning, he began to put on his shirt. Reynevan looked at his broad back, at his hairless skin, as pink as a child's.

"Brother Prokop?"

"What?"

"My question may surprise you, but…have you lately received a…wound? From an iron blade? Have you cut yourself with an iron object?"

"Why do you ask? Ah, it must be to do with some sort of witchcraft…Well, I haven't. I've never been wounded in my life, not even scratched. Almost everybody in the Tábor has been wounded or died of their wounds…Mikuláš of Husa, Žižka, Hvězda, Švamberk, Kuneš of Bělovice, Jaroslav of Bukovina… But I—although I've fought many a battle—have never been scratched…It's simply luck."

"Indeed. Good luck, nothing else."

*

The apothecary's shop had survived; it was where it should have been, opposite the stone pillory in the town square. The ingredients for the lumbago balsam were found, admittedly not immediately, but only after Reynevan had recited "*Visita Inferiora Terrae*," a password of the international alchemists' community based on the Emerald Tablet. That finally overcame the apothecary's mistrust. Credit must also go to Samson Honeypot, who at a certain moment began to slaver and look like he was about to vomit. The apothecary gave them everything they asked for, on condition that they left.

The town square was teeming with soldiers. The Polish language was being spoken all around them. In its most simplified version. Consisting chiefly of blunt, soldierly words.

"Well, that's you done for," Scharley observed, staring at the domed bell in the belfry of the parish church. "Prokop's got you by the balls. He will certainly keep you close by, but there's no knowing what plans he has for you. I doubt, however, that they'll correspond to yours. He's got you, Reinmar. And us, too."

"You and Samson can always go back to Rapotín."

"No, we can't," said Scharley, pretending to be looking at some sheepskin coats on a stall. "Even if we wanted to. Prokop's men are following us—I spotted the tail they pinned on us. They'd sound the alarm at once, I vouch, the moment we tried heading towards one of the town gates."

"None of us considers Prokop a fool," said Samson. "Rumours about the shadow of suspicion falling on Reynevan must have reached him."

"Of course they have," said Reynevan, adjusting the bag with the apothecary's purchases on his shoulder. "And now he's testing us. Very well, so let's make sure the test is to our advantage.

Don't try to escape from the town for now, and I will go to the castle according to my orders and begin treating him."

Odry Castle possessed a bathhouse, a modern, stone, elegant bathhouse. But Prokop the Shaven was a traditionalist and a lover of simplicity. He preferred traditional ways, a wooden shack standing among riverside willows, where water was poured from pails directly onto hot stones and clouds of steam suffocated you. Inside the shack were benches made of rough planks which you sat on as you slowly turned red, like a crayfish in boiling water. You sat, wiping the sweat streaming from your eyelids, sipping cold ale to sooth your steam-scorched throat.

And so they sat, naked as jaybirds, pouring water onto the hissing stones, in clouds of steam, skin flushed and faces dripping with sweat. Prokop the Shaven, also called the Great, *director operationum Thaboritarum*, the Tábor's commander-in-chief; Bedřich of Strážnice, the Orebite preacher, once the most important figure in the New Tábor of Moravia; and the young Hejtman Jan Pardus, not as yet renowned for anything special. Dobko Puchała of the Wieniawa arms, renowned for a hell of lot.

And Reynevan, currently the Chief Hjetman's personal physician.

"There, take that!" shouted Prokop the Shaven, lashing Bedřich with a bunch of birch twigs. "As a penance. Is it Lent? It is. One must do penance. Have some, too, Pardus. Ouch, what the hell! Puchała, have you lost your mind?"

"It's Lent, Hjetman," said the Wieniawa, grinning, dipping the twigs in a bucket. "Penance. One in, all in. Have some, too, Reynevan! For old time's sake. I'm glad you survived that last battle."

"I am, too."

"But I most of all," added Prokop. "I and my back. Do you

know what, I might appoint him my personal physician."

"Why not?" Bedřich of Strážnice smiled ambiguously. "After all, he's trusted. Trustworthy."

"And a notable fellow."

"Notable?" Bedřich snorted. "Notorious more like. Far and wide."

Prokop looked askance at him, picked up the pail and threw water on the stones. The steam blinded them, the violent heat entering their lungs as they breathed in. And stopping the conversation for some time.

Puchała lashed himself on the shoulders with the birch twigs.

"I have also," he announced proudly, "become a notable fellow, I mean at the Wawel, as a result of the letters that Witold, Grand Duke of Lithuania, keeps sending to King Jagiełło. I've been informed at first hand, so I know what he's written about me in those letters. I am—and I quote—a scoundrel, a brigand, a pest, and I bring evil and blight. Jagiełło is threatening to execute me. He has ordered me to leave Odry because I interfere with making peace, by causing here—and I quote—*iniuras, dampna, depopulationes, incendia, devastationes et sangvinis profluvie.*"

"I recognise the style," said Bedřich. "It is Sigismund of Luxembourg, our former king. Witold's only contribution is the questionable Latin."

"Those letters," said Jan Pardus, "are a clear consequence of the conference in Lutsk, where Sigismund won over the Duke of Lithuania and moulded him to follow his wishes."

"By promising him the royal crown," said Prokop, nodding. "And other pies in the sky—actually, a great abundance of pies. Unfortunately, it appears that the *magnus dux Lithuaniae* believed in them. Witold, up until now famous for his wisdom, good sense and Lithuanian shrewdness, is letting Sigismund wrap him around his little finger. Indeed, it is the truth: *Stultum facit Fortuna quem vult perdere.* Fortune makes a fool of the man she wishes to destroy."

"It is too remarkable to my mind," Bedřich declared, "to the extent that I suspect some kind of game in this. It wouldn't be the first time for Witold and Jagiełło, as a matter of fact. Not their first deceitful game."

"True," said Prokop, pouring water over himself from the pail and shaking himself like a dog. "The problem is that the game is being played on a chessboard where we are also pieces. And if the Polish king were suddenly to step out into open play after hiding behind a rook, he's liable to start interfering with negotiations. Then we must look several moves ahead, as in a game of chess, and place our pieces on the critical squares. While we are discussing pieces…Reynevan!"

"Yes, Hejtman?"

"You will go to Silesia. On a mission."

"Me? Why me?"

"Because I am ordering you."

Prokop turned his head away. Bedřich, on the contrary, fixed Reynevan with his eyes. Pardus was rubbing his heel with a rough stone. Puchała was lashing himself on the back with birch twigs.

"Brother Prokop," said Reynevan in the silence. "You have heard too many rumours and have your suspicions, so you want to put me through a test. You ordered that me and my comrades be followed. And now this mission to Silesia. A secret mission, probably, of the kind only entrusted to the most trusted and reliable men. You consider me such? I can't think you do. I understand that. I don't understand the provocation. Neither the purpose nor the point of it."

Prokop was silent for a long time.

"Pardus!" he finally yelled. "Bedřich! A crucifix! This moment!"

"What?"

"Bring me a fucking crucifix!"

The order was carried out in no time. Prokop held the cross towards Reynevan.

"Place your fingers on it. Look me in the eyes! And repeat after me: I swear on this Holy Cross and our Lord's Passion that when I was captured by Jan of Ziębice I didn't betray anyone, nor go over to the side of the Bishop of Wrocław, and now do not serve the bishop in order to persecute my brethren, good Czechs, supporters of the Chalice, in order by betrayal to harm them basely. If I be lying, may I expire, may I be punished and devoured by Hell, but first may the severe hand of revolutionary justice catch up with me, amen."

"...captured by Jan of Ziębice I did not betray...I do not serve the bishop...Amen."

"Splendid," Prokop said. "And everything is resolved. The matter is clear."

"Perhaps to be certain we could use trial by ordeal?" said Bedřich, pointing at the red-hot stones, a malicious smile playing on his lips. "Divine Judgement using trial by fire?"

"We may," Prokop said calmly, looking Bedřich in the eyes. "At my sign, the accuser and the accused will sit down on the stones, both at the same time, bare-arsed. He who sits longest is true. Ready, Bedřich? I'll show you when."

"I was jesting."

"I was, too. And be glad of it."

"A crucifix," concluded Scharley, grimacing as though he'd drunk vinegar. "Lord, what a pitiful and vulgar spectacle. A naive, primitive, tasteless trick. You can't have believed that pantomime?"

"I didn't. But it doesn't really matter, for Prokop was by no means joking. He indeed intends to send me on a mission to Silesia."

"Did he give you any details?"

"None. He said he would when the time came."

Scharley, not even trying to outshout the Poles who were dining at the next table, stood up and waved his arms vigorously. The innkeeper noticed and summoned a serving wench who ran up with fresh mugs.

"And so you are going to Silesia," he said, blowing off the froth. "Just as you wished. And we with you, for we won't leave you all alone. Ha, we'll have to equip ourselves suitably. In the morning I shall wander around the bazaar, take a look at the goods smuggled from Lesser Poland and acquire some supplies..."

"Do you have enough funds?"

"Don't worry. Unlike you, I make sure that my participation in the Hussite revolution brings me profit. I risk my neck in the cause of the Chalice, but I observe at the same time the principle of *virtus post nummos*. Ha, it calls to mind a certain thing..."

"Go on."

"Perhaps the secret and confidential expedition to Silesia that is being prepared is a lucky coincidence? Perhaps it's the stroke of luck we've been looking for?"

"Stroke of luck?"

Scharley looked at Samson. Samson put down the stick he was whittling, sighed and shook his head. The penitent also sighed. And also shook his head.

"You recently unleashed a tirade about calculated pragmatism in front of Horn," he said, looking Reynevan in the eyes. "You claimed the euphoria had worn off, that your ardour had cooled, that you were no longer a naive idealist. Your interests rank higher than other men's in the hierarchy; those were your very words. And now an opportunity is arising to put those words into action."

"How, exactly?"

"Think."

"By betrayal, you mean?" said Reynevan in a softer voice. "Sell the Inquisition information about the mission Prokop is sending me on? Hoping that the Inquisition in its gratitude will give me Jutta. Is that your advice to me?"

"I suggest you bear it in mind. Ponder it and decide whether your interests are higher in your hierarchy. What is more important: the Chalice or Jutta? Ponder and decide—"

"Enough, Scharley," Samson Honeypot interrupted gently. "That's enough. Don't urge Reinmar to consider a course of action that has no sense. And don't urge him to make choices where there are none to make."

The moon was hiding behind the roofs of the merchants' houses. Reynevan strode boldly and swiftly, aiming for the town walls.

He turned into a side street. Instead of going on, he soundlessly slipped into the alcove of a gateway. He waited, motionless and patient.

A moment later, he heard quiet steps, the barely audible shuffling of poulaines on cobbles. He waited for the man following him to emerge from the darkness. And then he leaped on him, caught him from behind by the hood and jerked with all his strength. The man wheezed and brought both hands up to his throat. Reynevan slammed him in the ribs with the metal-edged pommel of a knife, two handsbreadths above his hip. The man gulped air and choked. Reynevan spun him around with a jerk of his shoulder, swung and struck him hard with the pommel, with the expertise of a doctor, right in the *plexus solaris*. The man in the hood wheezed and fell to his knees.

High above on a roof a cat meowed.

"Tell Prokop," said Reynevan, using the blade to lift the man's chin. "Tell Prokop that I can swear on the cross again. I can even

swear several times. But this has to stop. I don't wish to be followed. I'll kill the next spy I get my hands on. Tell Prokop—"

"M'lord—"

"What? Louder!"

"I'm not from Prokop…I'm from the castle…On orders—"

"Whose? Who ordered you?"

"His Excellency the Duke."

The gloom of the castle chapel was only dispelled by the light
of two candles burning in front of the severe altar. The flickering light reflected on the gilt of the figure of a saint—perhaps
Matthias the Apostle, for he was holding an executioner's axe.
The light barely reached the man sitting among the choir stalls.
In the darkness, it limned his physique and the cut and details
of his rich raiment. But not his face. It didn't have to. Reynevan
knew who it was.

"Greetings, physician. It's a small world. Well, we meet again,
after so long. How many years is it since the Battle of Ústí?
Three? Am I right?"

"You are, Your Grace."

The man in the choir stall sat upright. The light fell on his
face.

It was Sigismund Korybut, Lithuanian duke of the Rurik dynasty, from the tribe of Mindaugas, great-grandson of Gediminas, grandson of Algirdas, son of Dmitry Korybut and Princess
Anastasia of Ryazan, nephew of Władysław Jagiełło, famed—
when barely a youth—for his role at the Battle of Grunwald.
Now aged a little over thirty, the Lithuanian, raised among Poles
at the Wawel, embodied the worst features of both nations: be-
nightedness, narrowmindedness, duplicity, pathological ambi-
tion, hubris, savagery, unbridled lust for power and an absolute
lack of self-criticism.

The duke glowered at Reynevan beneath the floppy hair falling over his eyes and Reynevan looked at the duke. It lasted some time, during which images of the duke's short but turbulent career quickly passed through Reynevan's head.

The Czech Hussites dethroned Sigismund and needed a new king. When asked, Jagiełło and Witold declined and Korybut travelled to Bohemia as their viceroy. He arrived in Golden Prague in 1422, on Saint Stanislaus's Day.

Shouts of joy, cheering in the capital's streets. Wonderful music for pride and vanity. Suddenly, grating, false notes in the music. Suddenly shouts from the crowd: "Stranger! Begone! We don't want you!" Disappointment and anger, when instead of the royal Hrad, his residence turned out to be a small palace in the Old Town Square. Then contact with the Tábor. Žižka, with his terrifying one eye, drawled under his bristling moustaches: "Free people do not need a king." Prague: angry, dangerous, lurking and growling like an animal.

It lasted barely six months. Jagiełło—pressed by the Pope—ordered his nephew to return. Nobody stopped Korybut from leaving Prague, no one lamented his leaving. But the political games continued. A Czech mission went to Krakow with a request for Korybut to return to Bohemia as a *postulatus rex*. Jagiełło categorically turned it down. But Korybut returned, against the king's wishes. In 1424, on the Eve of the Visitation, he arrived in Prague again. He was addressed as "M'lord." Never "Your Majesty." He was an accursed *infamis* in Poland. It wasn't clear who he was in Bohemia. But Korybut wanted to be *somebody*. He plotted. Sent envoys and letters. Yet more envoys and letters. A disaster occurred in 1427.

As an eyewitness to the mishaps in Prague in 1427, Reynevan didn't understand Korybut's reasoning. He, like many, saw in the young Lithuanian a pretender to the Czech throne. So he couldn't understand at all what induced the future king of Hussite Bohemia to plot with men who saw Bohemia's future quite differently, men prepared to agree to every concession and compromise, just to be able to return to the fold of the Holy See and the bosom of Christianity. Later, after talking to Flutek and Urban Horn, Reynevan grew wiser and understood that the young duke had simply been a marionette. A puppet, whose strings were pulled not by advocates of compromise, not by Catholic lords, but by Witold. For it was Witold the Great, the Grand Duke of Lithuania, who had sent Korybut to Bohemia. Witold wanted Bohemia to be Hussite enough for it not to let Sigismund ascend the throne. A Bohemia recognising the supremacy of Rome enough for the Pope to anoint its monarch. In another words: a Bohemia of which Witold, the son of Kęstutis, could be crowned king. The crowned king of a country extending from Berlin to Brno, from Kaunas to Kiev, from Samogitia to the Crimea.

The conspiracy was uncovered—after letters were intercepted —by Jan Rokycana, a virulent foe of the advocates of compromise. On Maundy Thursday in 1427, bells were tolled and a crowd incited by Rokycana set off for the Old Town Square. Korybut, seized in the palace, could think himself lucky: although the crowd was baying for blood, he was only imprisoned and a few days after Easter moved out of Prague. By night, camouflaged to protect him from being recognised and lynched. Imprisoned in Valdštejn Castle, he remained there until the late autumn of 1428. When released—allegedly following Jagiełło's intercession —he did not return to Lithuania. He remained in Bohemia. In Odry, a guest of Puchała. Representing…

Indeed, thought Reynevan. *Representing what?*

"You look at me," said Sigismund Korybut, "and I know what you're thinking."

After a pause, he continued, "Prokop rebuffs me. Since my arrival he has barely exchanged a word with me and the conversation lasted but a moment. He honoured the burgrave with a longer one. Even the stablemen."

Reynevan said nothing.

"He cannot forgive me for Prague," growled Korybut. "But I demand respect, by the Devil! Due respect! I am a duke! A thousand Polish knights are stationed in Odry. They came on my orders! If I leave here, they will follow me! They won't stay in this godforsaken country, were Prokop even to beg them on his knees!

"Lord Jan of Kravaře," said the duke, growing irate, "accepted Holy Communion under both kinds and is currently allied with the Tábor. Who brought that about, if not I? The Lord of Jičín parleyed with me, a duke. He won't talk to Prokop at all, wouldn't extend a hand to the Taborite murderers and damned whoresons! And wouldn't even spit at the Praguian commoners! The alliance with Kravaře is down to me! And what do I receive for that? Thanks? No! Affront after affront!"

Reynevan, completely dazed, first spread his hands and then bowed. Korybut inhaled audibly.

"I was their last king," he said calmly. "The last king of Bohemia. After they shamefully drove me away, they haven't found anyone they could call and proclaim king. Although they could have had a lawful kingdom, in harmony with the Christian world, they preferred to fall into chaos.

"And my family is to blame for it all," he added bitterly. "My Uncle Jagiełło wanted me to pull his chestnuts out of the fire. And Uncle Witold used me masterfully. He constantly played me off against Sigismund, beguiling the Czechs at the same time. But it was he, Witold, who put me in touch with Rome. It was on his instructions that I swore to the Pope that I would Christianise the Kingdom of Bohemia once more and reduce the whole of Hussitism to tiny changes to the liturgy. That I would assure the dominion of the Apostolic See over Bohemia and return all the Church's demesnes to them. I promised to the Holy Father what Witold ordered me to promise. Thus it is Witold who ought to have been locked up at Valdštejn, Witold who should have been excommunicated and deprived of everything. But it was I, *I* who was excommunicated and my property confiscated. I want compensation for all of that! Compensation! I want something from that! To have something and to be someone! And I will fucking accomplish that!"

Korybut calmed himself down with a deep breath and stared at Reynevan.

"I shall accomplish it," he repeated. "And you will help me."

Reynevan shrugged. He didn't even try to feign humility. He knew well that Prokop's protection rendered him immune and that no one—not even a hothead like Korybut—would dare to insult him or lay a finger on him.

"May Your Grace not overestimate me," he said coldly. "I see no way I can be of any help to you. Unless Your Grace is in poor health. I am a physician. Thus, if your health is hindering you in carrying out your ducal plans, I'm prepared to serve."

"You know perfectly well what kind of service I want from you. Your renown goes before you. Everybody knows that you're a sorcerer, a wizard and a stargazer. A charmer, a *raganius*, as we say in Samogitia."

"According to the Articles of Prague, witchcraft is a crime punishable by death. Does Your Grace wish death on me?"

"Quite the opposite," said Korybut, standing up, moving closer and fixing him with a piercing gaze. "I wish you happiness, auspiciousness and all the best. And I offer it to you in the form of my gratitude and kindness. Has the news from Lutsk reached you? About the conflict between Witold and Jagiełło? Do you know what will come of it? I'll tell you: a sea change in Polish politics regarding Bohemia. And the sea change in Polish politics is me. I am it. I am once again in the game, physician, in the game. And it's worth backing me, know you.

"I offer you gratitude and favour, Reinmar of Bielawa. Quite different from what you have received from the Czechs, from Neplach and Prokop, who sent you to your death and turned their backs on you when you needed help. Had you given me the services you gave them, your maiden would be by your side, free. In order to rescue the lady of a man who faithfully serves me, I will burn down Wrocław or perish in the attempt. As God is my witness, it would be thus. For that is our custom, in Lithuania and Samogitia. Olgierd would have acted thus, as would Kęstutis. And my blood is of their blood. Think it over. While there is still time."

Reynevan said nothing for a long while.

"What," he finally croaked out, "does Your Grace want from me?"

Sigismund Korybut smiled. With ducal disdain.

"To begin with," he said, "you will summon a man from the beyond."

Suddenly, raised voices, cries and curses could be heard in Odry's town square. Several Poles were pushing each other around, jostling, tugging each other's jerkins, yelling at each other, shaking their fists at one another and calling each other shits, cunts and whoresons. Their comrades were trying to separate them and restore order, only intensifying the confusion in the process. All of a sudden, swords hissed from scabbards, blades flashed. A high-pitched scream rose up, there was a surge, men came together, parted and then dispersed at once. On the cobbles remained a quivering body and a spreading pool of blood.

"Nine hundred and ninety-nine," said Reynevan.

"Not a bit of it," said Scharley, snorting disdainfully. Reynevan had just told him about the previous day's conversation in the castle chapel. "Korybut was exaggerating. There are no more than five hundred Poles in Odry today. I also doubt that a single one of them would follow him if he really took umbrage and left. That Samogitian has an inflated opinion of himself. And always has, it's no secret. Reynevan, think over whether it's worth entering into collusion with him. Don't you have enough troubles?"

"You're being used again," said Samson, nodding. "Will you ever learn?"

Reynevan sighed deeply. And told them about the duke's favour and gratitude, and about the benefits that might flow from them. He talked about the meeting in Lutsk and how Lutsk would bring King Jagiełło closer to the Hussites, owing to which Korybut's card had a real chance of being a trump. He talked about how good connections with Korybut might mean saving Jutta.

Scharley and Samson were not to be convinced. It was clear from their faces.

"This question may surprise you, Your Grace, but…have you had any kind of accident lately? A wound from being cut by iron?"

"Lately? No. There are a few marks on my skin from long ago, though. But for a long time, nothing, not even a scratch. God save me. But why do you ask?"

"Oh, no reason."

"No reason, my eye. Enough of that foolishness, Reynevan, and listen carefully. I want to tell you about the diviner Budrys.

"The diviner Budrys," went on Korybut, "was actually called Angus Deirg Feidlech and came from Ireland. He travelled to

Lithuania as a bard in the retinue of an English knight, one of the numerous outlandish men who marched eastwards in order to spread the faith of Christ among the Lithuanian pagans under the standards of the Teutonic Order. In spite of the promises of the Malbork priests guaranteeing the spreaders complete divine protection, in the very first clash with Kęstutis's warriors, the Englishman was struck by a club and his brain splashed over a rock beside the Niemen, and Angus was captured, dragged to Trakai and was meant to be burned alive on a sacrificial pyre along with the other Teutonic captives. He was saved by the remarkable, quite supernaturally fiery red colour of his hair, which fascinated the priests of Perkun. It also turned out that the stranger from across the seas revered the White Triple Goddess, that he paid homage to Milde, Kurko and Żwerine. Calling the goddesses, admittedly, by the names Birgit, Badb and Morrigan, but it isn't about the names, since a goddess is a goddess. During his stay in Vilnius, in the holy grove in Lukiškės, the Irishman revealed his fortune-telling and prophetic abilities, so he was assimilated into the druid community without any difficulty. Under the adoptive name of Budrys Vażgajtis, the stranger from the Emerald Isle soon became famous as an able *vejdalotas*, or a prophesier and a soothsayer.

"Budrys," Korybut went on, "accurately foretold a huge number of events, beginning with the result of the Battle of Kulikovo and ending with the marriage of Jagiełło to Jadwiga. There was one problem: he prophesied in a hellishly meandering, impenetrable way. A son of the culture of the West, the Irishman wove into his prophecies numerous references and hidden allusions to that culture, added disguised metaphors and used Latin and other foreign languages. The Lithuanians didn't like it. They preferred less sophisticated methods of fortune-telling. If the sacred serpent poked its head out of its hole on being summoned, it was lucky, but if the snake ignored the summons and refused to poke its head out, the prognoses were bad. Jagiełło and Witold, who were somewhat more western than their tribesmen, treated Budrys more seriously and listened to his prophesies, although they leaned towards the snake in matters of national importance.

"But I always respected and admired him," said Korybut. "I wanted him to prophesy for me, make a horoscope and foretell the future. I asked him to do so many times, but the damned bastard refused. The old goat called me a careerist and spouted some nonsense about forging one's own destiny. It was only my Uncle Witold who convinced him, shortly before I left for Bohemia. The stargazer was supposed to cast the lots and make a horoscope for all of us: Jagiełło, Witold and I. But suddenly, out of the blue, he died. Fell down stone dead.

"You, Bielawa, are a necromancer and a diviner. Summon him from the beyond. May the *vejdalotas* fulfil as a spirit what he failed to do when he was alive."

Reynevan tried for a long time to dissuade the duke from the idea, but to no avail. Korybut turned a deaf ear to the difficulties linked to necromancy, about the dangers present during divination, about the risks borne by *vehemens imaginatio*, the focusing of the imagination essential for successful conjuration. He ignored mention of King Saul and the Witch of Endor. He dismissed it all out of hand, pouted his lips and finally tossed something onto the table. Something the size, shape and colour of an old dried conker.

"You're fibbing to me," he drawled. "But I also have some knowledge of witchcraft. Summoning a spirit isn't especially difficult when you have a piece of a corpse. And this a piece of Budrys Vażgajtis. They were meant to burn him at the stake, the old pagan, with a full sacrificial funeral ritual. He was lying on his catafalques, in full ceremonial dress, decorated with fir twigs, wild flowers and foliage. I crept up at night, removed the old bugger's slipper and tore off his big toe."

"You desecrated the corpse?"

Korybut snorted. "In our family, that's not all we've desecrated."

A strong wind sprang up at midnight, whistling through the cracks in the walls. In the old armoury in a distant wing of the castle, a draught laid the flame of a black wax candle flat and blew the smoke from incense smouldering on a tripod into a spiral. There was a smell of wax and an aloe suffumigation. Reynevan got down to work, armed with a hazel wand, a Python amulet and a dog-eared copy of the *Enchiridion* borrowed from the apothecary. Inside a circle drawn in chalk, a table held a looking glass and the mummified big toe, once the property and an inseparable part of the deceased Budrys Važgajtis. Contact with the spirit of the dead man was thus meant to be enabled by a combination of divination, necromancy and catoptromancy.

"Colpriziana," intoned Reynevan, describing signs with the amulet above the chalk circle. "Offina, Alta, Nestera, Fuaro, Menuet."

Korybut, hidden in the shadows, shifted anxiously. The toe inside the circle didn't even twitch.

"*Conjuro te, Spiritum humanum.* I exhort you, O spirit of Angus Deirg Feidlech, alias Budrys Važgajtis! Come!

"*Conjuro et adjuro te, Spiritum, requiro atque obtestor visibiliter praesentem.* I command you by Ezel, Salatyel and Yegrogamel! Theos Megale patyr, ymas heth heldya, hebeath heleotezyge! *Conjuro et adjuro te!*

"By Yemegas, Mengas and Hacaphagan; by Haylos! Come, O spirit! Come from the East, the South, the West or the North! I exhort you and summon you! Come! *Ego te conjuro!*"

The surface of the mirror in the chalk circle fogged over as though an invisible person had breathed on it. Something appeared in the looking glass, something like mist, a murky haze. The haze formed into a human figure before the eyes of Reynevan, who hadn't been especially convinced about the chances of the venture's success but was now staring in utter amazement. Something like a sigh could be heard. A deep, whistling sigh. Reynevan stooped over the *Enchiridion* and read aloud the formula of a spell, moving the amulet over the lines. The cloud in the mirror grew denser. And perceptibly increased in size. Reynevan raised his hands.

"*Benedictus qui venis!*"

"*Quare,*" breathed the cloud in a quiet, whistling exhalation, "*inquietasti me?*"

"*Erit nobis visio omnium sicut verba libri signati.* I command you in the name of the great Tetragrammaton, O spirit, to unseal the book of secrets and make its words comprehensible to us."

"Kiss my astral arse," whispered the ghost.

"I command you to speak," said Reynevan, raising the amulet and the wand. "I command you to keep your word. To complete the horoscope and prophesy the fates of Mindaugas's and Gediminas's generation, to be precise—"

"This thing here," interrupted the spirit from the looking glass, "isn't my big toe, by any chance, is it?"

"It is."

The smoke of the incense pulsated, rising in a spiral. The surface of the mirror grew cloudier.

"The fifth son of his father," spoke the apparition quickly, "baptised in German and Greek, a pagan in his soul, dreams of a kingdom, but by no means a heavenly one. The star Sirius rises, contrary to his designs, and the promised crown will be lost, it will be snatched by a fire-breathing Dragon, with blood in the shape of a cross sprinkled on its back. *O quam misericors est deus justus et pius!* The Dragon heralds death and the day of death is known. The papacy of the Column *anno penultimo*, the day of Venus, on that day *diluculum*.

"When nineteen and a hundred days have passed from that death, the Column will fall, yielding up its place to the Wolf. A sign shall come forth of the Wolf's papacy: when the sun enters the last house, a wind of rare strength shall blow and shall rage for ten days without respite. And when ten and a hundred days have passed after those events, the seventh son of the father will bid farewell to this world, a king and potentate, baptised by Rome but a pagan in his heart. Lured by the sweet song of the nightingale, he will expire in a small castle, *O gallicinium dies Martis* and before the Sun rises, and it shall then be *in signo Geminorum*."

"And me?" said Korybut, unable to contain himself, from the shadows. "What about me? My horoscope! The horoscope you promised!"

"You will perish by wood and iron, second son of your father," replied the apparition in a fell voice. "Your destiny will be fulfilled on *dies Jovis*, fourteen days before *Aequinoctium autumnale*. When you confront a wolf beside a holy river. That is your horoscope. I might have prophesied you something better, but you swiped my big toe. Thus this is all you will get."

"What the hell does it mean?" said the duke, springing up. "Tell me clearly, this moment! What are you thinking? You're a corpse! A stiff! I won't let you—"

"Your Grace," interrupted Reynevan, closing the grimoire. "The spirit isn't here. It's gone. Floated off where fancy took it."

The map on the table was criss-crossed with marks. The lines on it linked Bohemia to Lusatia: Žitava, Bautzen and Zgorzelec.

One line led to Opava and Silesia, towards Racibórz and Koźle; another led into the valley of the Elbe, to Saxony; another—the thickest—straight to Wrocław. That was all Reynevan saw before Prokop the Shaven covered the map with a sheet of paper and raised his head. They looked each other in the eyes for a long while.

"I have been informed," Prokop finally said, "that you are in cahoots with Sigismund Korybut. That you spend much time together, indulging yourselves in magic and astrology. I'd like to hope you aren't indulging yourselves in anything else."

"I don't understand."

"I am certain you do. But since you prefer to hear it straight, I shall oblige. Korybut is a traitor. He was on good terms with the Pope, with Jan Příbram, with Rožmberk, with Heinrich of Plauen, and with the Catholics of Plzeň. He claimed to be trying to make peace because he bemoaned the shedding of Christian blood. And I claim that to be nonsense; he can't have been stupid enough not to understand what the Pope and the Catholics were really after. Peace? Compromises? Agreements? Fiddlesticks! They wanted to divide us, make us fight among ourselves and slaughter one another, and then they would have mopped up the survivors. Korybut must have known about it, so was found guilty of treachery, went to gaol for treachery and was lucky not to be executed. And he would have resided at Valdštejn until Judgement Day, had it not been for Jagiełło's intercession and the generous ransom he paid.

"We're come to agreement now. Here in Odry, Korybut and Puchała are doing the Tábor a valuable favour, I have to admit, and thanks to the two of them we hold firm the Moravian Gate, the bastion against an alliance between Sigismund and Albrecht and a link to Poland. We've reached agreement and they have entered an alliance, created a pact. For me, Korybut has two assets. *Primo*: he has definitely bidden farewell to hopes for the Czech throne. *Secundo*: he hates Prague Old Town. Thus we are linked by common interests. While that bond endures, Korybut will be my ally and brother-in-arms. While it endures. Do you understand me?"

"I do. But…if I may comment…"

"Go on."

"Perhaps Korybut has another asset. The congress in Lutsk drove a wedge between Jagiełło and Witold, and since Sigismund inserted it, Jagiełło is looking for a means to pay Sigismund back for that. It can be assumed that Duke Korybut could be that means. It can be assumed that Korybut's prestige will improve significantly. So perhaps it would be an idea to back him?"

Prokop chewed his moustache for a while.

"An idea, you say," he finally said. "Place a wager, you say. You say his prestige is growing. Are you such a far-sighted strategist and politician? Until now, you have never revealed any talent in that respect. You were a decidedly better physician and sorcerer. So is it magic? Astrology? Is that what you and the Lithuanian engage in? If so, then I'd also like to learn what is written in the stars. What events and fates do the movements, conjunctions and oppositions of the heavenly bodies predict?"

"A new vicar will ascend to the Chair of Saint Peter," began Reynevan cautiously. "Grand Duke Witold won't live to see it, but will die in the penultimate year of Martin V's papacy. Władysław Jagiełło, the King of Poland, will outlive both Witold and Martin. He will depart this life in the fourth year of the new Pope's papacy."

Prokop said nothing.

Finally, he said, "I suppose that the prophecies, as usual, are not absolutely clear, and don't give specific dates."

"They are not," said Reynevan without blinking. "And do not."

"Ah. But Martin V, whichever way you look at it, has passed sixty; twelve years have passed since the Council. He grows weak, reportedly, so is likely to turn up his toes any moment. Ha! And Witold, you say, will turn up his even before Pope Martin knocks on the pearly gates. Ha. Fascinating. Have you heard about the horoscope that Henryk of Brzeg made for Queen Sophia?"

"I have. And I hear it isn't too auspicious for Jagiełło's sons, Władysław and Kazimierz. Misfortunes will reportedly fall on the Kingdom of Poland during their reigns."

"But they will reign," Prokop said with emphasis. "They will both reign. At the Wawel. First one, then the other."

"They are princes, so it is quite normal."

"We speak of Poland," Prokop reminded him. "Nothing is ever normal there. But never mind, horoscopes are known to be erroneous, not to mention prophecies. Ah well, nothing can hold back our curiosity about future events. While we're on the subject, what about Duke Korybut? What do the stars predict for him?"

"The stars are fortuitous for him," said Reynevan, shrugging. "At least, that's what he believes. He is predicted to die by the holy river after squaring up to the wolf. The wolf, Korybut believes, is—according to Malachy's prophecy—Martin V's successor. And the holy river is the Jordan. The duke doesn't plan to travel to Palestine, nor does he mean to square up to the Pope beside the Jordan. He believes that will ensure him a long life."

"And what do you think?"

"The spirits occasionally mock men with prophecies. And Korybut's reminds me too much of the legend of Gerbert of Aurillac, Pope Sylvester II. It was predicted that Pope Sylvester would die after celebrating Mass in Jerusalem, so he thought that if he didn't go there, he would live for ever. He died in Rome, after celebrating Mass in Santa Croce Church. That church is also called '*Gerusalemme*.'"

"Did you tell Korybut that?"

"No."

"Well don't."

The *director operationum Thaboritarum* stood up, walked across the chamber and opened the window. There was a scent of spring.

"On Monday you set off for Silesia. You have important matters to deal with there. I trust you, Reynevan. Don't disappoint me. If you do, I shall tear your soul from you."

Palm Sunday—called Flower Sunday in Bohemia—had arrived. The bells summoned the faithful to a procession and then to Mass. More precisely: to two Masses.

The Mass for the Hussites was celebrated by Prokop the Great, the commander of the army fighting in the field himself. It was held under the open sky, naturally, according to Taborite liturgy, beyond the town walls, in Carp Meadow, with the Chalice on a table covered with a modest white cloth. The Mass for Catholics, mainly Poles, was being celebrated in the town, in the Church of Saint Bartholomew, at an altar, by Father Kołatka, a parish priest from Nasiedle specially captured during the attack on Opava for pastoral reasons and abducted along with his liturgical vestments and articles.

Reynevan partook in the Hussite Mass. Scharley didn't partake in either; he had developed an aversion to religion long before—as he said—and found the rituals tedious. Samson went down to the river, had a long walk along the bank, looking at the sky, the bushes and the ducks.

Prokop the Great delivered his sermon to the crowds in Carp Meadow.

"Behold the cruel day of our Lord is nigh!" he called. "Behold a great fury and a dreadful ire in order to turn the Earth into a wasteland and wipe the sinners from it. For the star of the heavens and Orion will not shine with their light, the sun will be shadowed from the very dawn and the moon will not shine!

"And though you may multiply your entreaties, I shall not listen to them," Father Kołatka preached from the pulpit of Saint Bartholomew's. "Your hands drip with blood. Wash them clean, be pure! Remove the evil of your deeds from My eyes! Stop committing evil! Cloak yourselves in goodness! Care for justice, help the oppressed, do right by the orphan, stand in defence of the widow! Though your sins be as scarlet, they shall shine white as snow; though as red as crimson, they shall be as wool."

"The Lord," said Prokop, his deep voice rolling over Carp Meadow, "seethes with anger at all pagans and rages with indignation at their soldiers! They are doomed to destruction, given up for slaughter! Their dead lie abandoned, a stench rises from their corpses; the mountains are drenched in their blood."

"Their designs are criminal," Father Kołatka preached in a calm voice. "Havoc and destruction lie on their paths. They know not the way of peace. There is no righteousness in their actions. They have made their own paths crooked. Thus righteousness is far from us and justice does not reach us. We expected light, but behold the darkness; the rays shine, but yet we walk in the gloom. Like the blind we feel for the wall and grope as though eyeless. We stumble at noon as though it were night, though sound in body we are as though deceased.

"Your light is come," said Father Kołatka, spreading his arms out towards his congregation in the nave, "and the Lord's glory radiates above you. For behold: darkness covers the land and dense gloom enshrouds the people, but the Lord shines over you and His glory appears above you. And the people shall go to His light, and kings to the luminescence of His dawning."

The sun emerged from behind the clouds, light flooded the land.

"*Ite, missa est.*"

Chapter Nine

In which, during a secret mission to Silesia, Reynevan is subject to numerous and various tests of his loyalty. He endures it quite patiently, unlike Samson Honeypot, who is offended and gives expression to his feelings.

They dashed through the springtide land, galloping, splashing the water and mud from the softened roads.

Having passed Hradec, they forded the Moravice and reached Opava, the capital of the Duke of the Přemyslid dynasty, Přemek. There they slowed down in order not to arouse suspicion. As they rode away from the city, bade farewell by the tolling of bells for the Angelus, Reynevan realised something was wrong. He realised it partially unprompted and partially provoked by Scharley's eloquent glances. Every once in a while, he weighed up his unease and assessed it to check he wasn't mistaken. It turned out he wasn't. It was as he sensed. Something was out of kilter.

"Something is wrong. It's not as it ought to be. Bedřich!"

"What?"

"We were meant to be riding for Krnov and Głuchołazy, as Prokop ordered. North-west. But we're heading north-east. This is the Racibórz road."

Bedřich of Strážnice reined his horse around and trotted over.

"Regarding the road," he said coldly, looking Reynevan in the eyes, "you're absolutely right. Regarding the rest, you are not. Everything is in order and is as it should be."

"Prokop told us—"

"He told you," Bedřich interrupted, "but he gave me orders. I'm commanding this mission. Do you have any objections to that?"

"Perhaps he ought to," said Scharley, riding over on his handsome black horse. "Because I do."

"And perhaps," said Samson, riding up to Bedřich's right on his huge lancer stallion. "And perhaps you could muster a little frankness, Lord Strážnice? A little honesty and trust. Is that so much to ask?"

If Samson's words dumbfounded Bedřich, it was only for a moment. He tore his eyes away from the giant then looked askance at Scharley. His glance was a signal to his four men, Moravians with fierce jaws and gnarled hands. The look was enough for the Moravians to lower their hands in unison and rest them on the battleaxes hanging from their saddles.

"A little frankness, is it?" he repeated, scowling. "Very well. You first. Starting with you, giant. What are you really?"

"*Ego sum, qui sum.*"

"We're getting off the subject," said Scharley, pulling on his black horse's bit. "Will you give Reynevan an explanation? Or shall I?"

"You do it. I'd love to hear it."

"We've changed our route unexpectedly," the penitent began without delay, "in order to deceive spies, the bishop's thugs and the Inquisition. We are riding along the Racibórz road and they are doubtless looking for us outside Krnov and have doubtless set an ambush for us there. Because they've been informed that we're going that way. You informed them, Reinmar."

"Indeed," said Reynevan, taking off a glove and wiping his

forehead. "Everything is clear. It turns out the promise on the crucifix wasn't enough for Prokop. He's still testing me."

"By the Devil!" said Bedřich of Strážnice and leaned over in the saddle to spit on the ground. "Can you blame him? Would you have acted any differently in his shoes?"

"But why did he send me to Silesia? To put me to the test? Is that why we've ridden all this way, into the middle of enemy territory? For that reason only?"

"Not only," said Bedřich and straightened up. "By no means not only. But enough of that. Time is short, let's go."

"Where to? I'm asking so I can pass it on to the bishop's thugs."

"Watch your step, Reynevan. Let's go."

They rode, now not hurrying, along a waterlogged road through woodland, with two Moravians at the front, then Bedřich and Reynevan, then Scharley and Samson, and two Moravians at the rear. They rode cautiously, for it was enemy territory, after all, on the lands of the Duchy of Racibórz. The young Duke Mikołaj was a fierce enemy of the Hussites, fiercer even than his recently deceased father, the notorious Herzog, Jan the Iron. Herzog Jan hadn't even been afraid of falling foul of Poland and its powerful king in order to harry the Hussites. In 1421 he had caused a serious diplomatic incident: he seized and arrested the entire entourage of a Czech mission travelling to Krakow and threw the envoys—beginning with Vilém Kostka of Postupice—into a dungeon, stripped them down to their hose and sold them to Sigismund, who only released them after a stern diplomatic note from Jagiełło and the mediation of Zawisza the Black of Garbów. Their vigilance was thus justified. If caught by the Racibórzians, neither a diplomatic note nor mediation would have helped; they would have been hanged without further ado.

They rode on. Bedřich glared at Reynevan and Reynevan glared back at Bedřich. It didn't look like the start of a beautiful friendship.

Bedřich of Strážnice came—legend had it—from the gentry, but of the more impoverished kind. He had allegedly studied for the priesthood before the revolution. Though he didn't look older than Reynevan and probably wasn't, his wartime experiences were already long and colourful. He sided with the revolution immediately after it broke out, carried away, like many others, by the wave of euphoria. In 1421, as a Taborite preacher and emissary, he unleashed a Hussite tornado on Moravia, which had previously been loyal to Sigismund. He established the Moravian branch of the New Tábor in Uherský Ostroh, which was known chiefly for storming monasteries and burning down churches, usually with the priests still inside. After several battles with Sigismund's Hungarians, Bedřich left Moravia to the Moravians when things began to get perilous and returned to Bohemia, where he joined the Orebites, and subsequently Žižka's Lesser Tábor. After Žižka's death, he joined up with Prokop the Shaven, whom he served as an adjutant for special commissions. He gave up being a preacher, shaved his apostolic beard and moustache and transformed himself into a young man with a face straight out of holy paintings. Anyone who didn't know him would have been deceived.

"Reynevan."

"What?"

"We have things to discuss."

"Perhaps it's high time. For as you can see, this situation is pissing me off. I've had enough of it. Prokop ordered me to go to Silesia and I have meekly carried out his order. It's clear I was mistaken. I ought to have turned it down, heedless of the consequences. But now I'm here, the Devil knows why. To be tested? As an instrument of provocation? Or the object of provocation. Or only to—"

"I've already told you," Bedřich interrupted sharply, "not by any means 'only.' The idea for an unexpected change of route was mine. Prokop trusts you. In any case, he had no choice regarding the mission to Silesia. We're going to meet and negotiate with…with certain individuals. Personages, even. Those individuals set a condition, a curious and astonishing condition: they demanded that you, Reinmar of Bielawa, take part in the meetings and negotiations in person. Don't ask me why. I don't know. Perhaps you do?"

"I do not. Believe it or not, it's just as curious and astonishing to me. So much so that it smacks of another of your deceits. For you still don't trust me, do you?"

Bedřich of Strážnice reined his horse in sharply.

"I have a suggestion," he said, sitting up straight in the saddle. "Regardless of everything, let's make a truce, at least while this mission lasts. We've ventured deep into enemy territory. It will end badly if we don't trust each other, if we aren't loyal, vigilant and prepared to defend each other's arses if it comes to it. Well? Will you shake my hand?"

"I will. But from this moment on we shall be honest with each other, Bedřich."

"Agreed, Reynevan."

Next day they passed the small town of Krzanowice and reached the village of Bojanów, conspicuous for a building of severe architecture housing a convent, a branch of the Racibórz Dominican Sisters' nunnery. They were about a mile from Racibórz, Bedřich estimated.

"Let me remind you," said the latter, gathering the unit together and beginning his briefing, "that we are merchants from Elbląg, Prussia. We have been in Hungary and are returning. We are dejected after being caught and robbed by Hussites outside Odry. That's our story, if asked. I happen to know that Reynevan and Scharley speak German. How about you, giant? He who is what he is?"

"I speak with all the tongues of men, but in spite of that I am become as sounding brass or a tinkling cymbal. And my name is Samson. So you can call me that, Commandant."

In the distance they saw the walls and spires of Racibórz. First of all, before they even reached the houses outside the walls, they passed a small church, a cemetery and a gallows atop a flat hill. Several bodies in various stages of decomposition were swinging from a crosswise beam in the mild breeze.

"There are hangings even during Holy Week," observed Scharley. "Which means there's a need. Which means they're seizing people."

"They're seizing people everywhere now," said Bedřich, shrugging. "After last year's expedition people see Hussites everywhere. It's the psychosis of fear."

"The expedition didn't even come close to the Racibórz Duchy," Reynevan said. "They didn't see a single Hussite."

"Has anyone ever seen the Devil? But everybody's still afraid of him."

They rode between the smoke-veiled cottages, hearing the calls of all sorts of livestock and the sounds of people carrying out various money-making activities. A good two dozen beggars were sitting outside Saint Nicholas's Gate with suppurating stumps and ulcers showing under their rags. Bedřich tossed them a few coppers to lend credence to their appearance and cover story: they had entered the town as merchants, and among that caste there was a fashion for giving alms, donations and other, similar displays of virtue.

"Here we shall separate," he announced after they had passed through the gate and found themselves at the Dominican Sisters' convent. "I presume you know Racibórz? This is Our Lady's Street and the town square is straight down there. Odra Street runs away from it and leads to the Odra Gate. There's a tavern called the Mill Scales by the gate. You will stop there and wait for us. I mean for Reynevan and I."

"Meaning you're going somewhere else in the meanwhile," said Scharley. "Where, might one ask?"

"One might. In principle," Bedřich's answered, his face unflinching. "But is it worth it? If, perish the thought, things were to go wrong, someone might ask you for that address. Then it's better for ignorance to act as an excuse."

"If, perish the thought, something goes wrong," the penitent said calmly, "it might be necessary to save your arses. And knowledge may then turn out to be useful. As opposed to ignorance."

The preacher said nothing for a while and bit his lip.

"The town square," he finally said. "The east side on the corner of Long Street. The house at the Golden Crown."

A mistake was impossible, since the façade of the house in the eastern frontage of the town square on the corner of Long Street was graced by a magnificent relief depicting a golden crown among vegetal motifs. The door, hidden in a porch, resembled the gate of a stronghold and they had to knock on it for a long time before eliciting a reaction. While Bedřich was knocking and swearing under his breath, Reynevan glanced back to check if they were being followed. Finally, the door was opened and their introduction heard out, after which they were led inside. Reynevan gasped in amazement. The interior was identical to the one in Wrocław where in February he had picked up Otto Beess's deposit; identical in almost every detail, right down to the Danzig furniture, the fireplace and the large map on the facing wall. The clerk occupying this familiar interior also looked familiar. And no wonder, since it was the same man.

"Gentlemen, I welcome you to the splendid and wealthy town of Racibórz," said the official of Fuggers and Company, standing as he gestured for them to sit down. "Sir Bedřich of Strážnice, I believe?"

"Indeed," said the preacher. "And this is—"

"Reinmar Bielau, also known as Hagenau," the official interrupted with a smile. "I've already had the pleasure. I'm glad to see you, glad to find you have emerged unscathed from the manifold troubles that have lately afflicted you. I would request you, m'Lord Strážnice, to pass on to Hejtman Prokop the Great that I am delighted to see Sir Reinmar."

"I shall," replied Bedřich, his face betraying no emotion.

"But let me inform you, Reinmar," said the clerk, the slight smirk still playing on his lips, "that your presence here is something of a test. A trial of trust. Hejtman Prokop has decided to put Fuggers and Company to the test. The company, which gives as good as it gets, has also submitted Hejtman Prokop to a test. The tests, I can confirm, were most successful. For everybody."

"I suggest we get to the point," Bedřich said tartly. "Time is short."

"Then let us save both time and words," agreed the clerk. "Time is money, and *verbis ut nummis utendum est*. And we are talking about money, are we not? War hovers over our heads, and *nervus belli pecunia*. So speak, Lord Strážnice. What are the expectations regarding the *pecunii* of Hejtman Prokop, the commander-in-chief of the Tábor's army? What sum does the Tábor estimate for its needs? What sum will satisfy you?"

"Six million Prague groschen."

The clerk stroked his smoothly shaven chin.

"That is no small sum. I would, in fact, say it is a large one."

"Hejtman Prokop suggests the company treat it as an investment."

"War," replied the official, "is too uncertain a thing in which to invest capital hoping for future profits. Such an investment is out of the question, both for moral and ethical reasons, since Fuggers and Company, like Caesar's wife, must take care of its appearance and its reputation. So, we are left with a loan. Confidential credit. We shall therefore give you credit, which you will repay…Let's say, over the course of three years. With interest, naturally. The interest, of course, will be high. But shall be in kind."

"You mean," Bedřich raised his eyebrows, "not in cash?"

"Yes, precisely. In kind, meaning not in cash. You will pay back the received credit according to its nominal value, but the interest will come in the form of benefits."

"What benefits, exactly?"

"Before a year passes," the Fuggers official began after a moment of tense silence, "you will launch a great expeditionary raid on Thuringia. This is determined by the economic, political and military situation. The expedition's chief aim will be to plunder, but of no less import will be its secondary ones: the export of revolution and propaganda, and to sow terror by means of destroying the enemy's economic power, by crushing its morale and by thwarting its plans concerning another crusade to Bohemia."

Bedřich didn't comment, his face didn't even flinch. But his eyes said much.

"Owing to the scale of the venture," continued the official, "the Tábor will ally with the Orphans and Prague. You will ride into Saxony across the Ore Mountains, naturally, and you will head for Dresden and Meissen along the Labe valley. And there you will begin to pay back the interest on the credit that the company will give you. In the form of services. Do you have difficulty retaining facts, Lord Strážnice?"

"I do not."

"That is good. Task one: to destroy the glassworks in Glashütte."

"I see. They belong to the competition, I guess?"

"Don't guess, Lord Bedřich, for this isn't a guessing game. Or any other similar pastime. To continue: there is an iron ore mine in Lengefeld. You will destroy the drainage gear, the scoops, the launders, the crushers and mortars used for breaking up the winning, the hammers—"

"Just a moment. Once again—what do you want us to destroy?"

"Everything," said the official of Fuggers and Company, smiling only with his mouth.

"Understood."

"As part of further services," said the clerk in a cold and dispassionate voice, "you will demolish the shafts of the mine in Hermsdorf, the hammer, the smelter and all the bloomeries. You will destroy the silver mine in Marienberg. The coalmine in Freital. And the tin mine in Altenberg. Will you remember?"

"Indeed."

"Splendid. If the Tábor agrees to the terms, six million groschen will be supplied to you in the course of a month. That is everything, Lord Strážnice. Please extend my respects to Hejtman Prokop. And I shall ask Lord Bielau to remain. I have something to say to him. In private."

Bedřich bowed and cast Reynevan a hostile glance. And went out.

"Your affairs in Wrocław are going poorly," began the official when they were alone. "I know you invested your hope in the altarist, Father Felicjan. Hope is vain. The altarist will not help you, for he himself has difficulties from which it will prove arduous for him to extricate himself. Any contact at all with him at present is absolutely inadvisable. Also inadvisable are any visits to Wrocław. Or the surrounding area."

"Did Felicjan find out anything about—"

"No," interrupted the official. "Neither him, nor anyone else."

"What about my friends? Are they safe? Need I worry about them?"

"No one is safe in these times," replied the official. "And not even the mightiest of this world can afford the luxury of peace of mind. I can only inform you that Grabis Hempel, called Allerdings, is not in Wrocław, has gone away, vanished, location unknown. And no one links you with the apothecary Czibulka. And will not. In this regard, rely on the company."

"Thank you. One more thing: in February I was rescued from the Wrocław guard by a…woman…Do you perhaps know anything about her?"

The official smiled.

"Woman, Reinmar, is a flighty thing. Fugger and Company deal only with steadfast matters."

Bedřich wasn't waiting in the Crown. He'd gone somewhere. Reynevan was alone in Racibórz Town Square.

Unlike the noisy, busy suburbs, it was quiet and somehow lifeless inside Racibórz's town walls. Reynevan, not being a local, didn't know if the town was always like that or if the oppressive atmosphere of Holy Week was infecting its residents. Outside the Parish Church of the Assumption a crowd of people heading to Mass was gathering, but they hadn't been summoned by the bell: it was Maundy Thursday, so the church's bells were silent, replaced by dreadfully and ominously clattering wooden clappers.

At that moment, Reynevan was walking towards the church,

but he suddenly turned towards the town hall. He was anxious, glancing back over his shoulder every now and then to check if he was being followed. The Fuggers clerk was to blame, because he had quite categorically insisted on vigilance and suggested that Reynevan take a different route back, ideally using a magical Pantaleon amulet. Reynevan, however, no longer had the Pantaleon, which had remained in the Mandrake apothecary's shop in Wrocław. Towards the end of his stay in Wrocław, fearful of the deleterious side effects of wearing it, Reynevan had stopped using it and hid it in a palliasse. Which was probably why he was caught.

This time he preferred to be cautious almost to a fault. Instead of going straight to the company at the Mill Scales, he took a circuitous route. He entered the busy cloth hall and stopped beside a leatherworker's bench where the greatest, densest crowd was. He vigilantly observed the passers-by. None of them looked like a tail. He sighed in relief.

And almost choked when somebody unexpectedly tapped him on the shoulder.

"May the Lord be praised," said Łukasz Bożyczko. "Welcome to Silesia, Reynevan. Where have you been all this time?"

"Well, don't make me wait," Bożyczko said, hurrying him. "What news do you have for me?"

The dark yard he dragged Reynevan into smelled of sauerkraut. Vomit. And cat pee.

"Come on," said the Pole impatiently. "Show me that you are useful."

"If you managed to find me here," Reynevan said, his back pressed against the wall, "you possess much better information than me. What I know won't be of any use to you. For I know next to nothing."

"In our custody, your Jutta is in the lap of luxury, with full board and lodging. It's so warm, clean and elegant, she might be at home," continued Bożyczko, ignoring him. "Why, it's even better than at home, because the company is more interesting. That luxury doesn't come cheap, it costs us. Go on, reassure us we aren't throwing money down the drain."

"I know nothing. I have nothing to inform you about."

"You disappoint me."

"I am sorry."

"You'll be more than sorry," hissed Bożyczko. "Do you take me for a fool? I found you here since—as you correctly guessed—I have access to information. I know you are close to Prokop, to Horn, to Bedřich of Strážnice, to Korybut. You must have seen things, heard things, been a witness or a participant in something. Military plans, political ideas, alliances, ways of obtaining financial resources. You must know something."

"I know nothing."

Bożyczko stamped his foot to scare away a cat rubbing itself against his boot.

"There are two possibilities," he said. "Either you are lying, or you a fool and a sloven. In both cases you've revealed yourself to be useless; both eventualities disqualify you from being a valuable collaborator. Which is bad for you and even worse for Jutta. The luxury she has now can easily be withdrawn, and comfort replaced by discomfort. Which could soon become pain."

"You promised not to hurt her! You're breaking your pledge!"

"Then sue me."

"I know something that might interest you," Reynevan blurted out. "If the future of the world interests you."

"Go on."

"Pope Martin V will die in 1431, probably in the month of February. Four Sundays before Easter, the Conclave will elect as Pope Gabriele Condulmer, Cardinal of Sienna, who appears in Malachy's prophecy as *Lupa coelestina*, the heavenly she-wolf. Before that happens, Witold, Grand Duke of Lithuania, will die. He will die as a duke, the royal crown will not be given to him, the machinations of Sigismund will come to nothing. The death of Władysław Jagiełło, King of Poland, will come to pass in *Anno Domini* 1434, at the end of May or the beginning of June. Sigismund Korybut will outlive both his uncles."

"Where did you learn this?"

"If I said it's from a certain witch and a certain spirit from the beyond, would you believe me?"

The cat shooed away by Bożyczko meowed. For a moment, Bożyczko fixed Reynevan with his steely gaze.

"I would," he finally replied. "For what could the source be if not the beyond or witchcraft? I know something about that. Like you, I am an adept of the Secret Arcana. It's no discredit, since it was three sorcerers who were the first to greet Jesus in Bethlehem, bringing him gold, frankincense and myrrh. Thanks for the information, we shall use it without any *dubium*. But it is not enough. Not nearly enough. I want to know—"

He broke off, stood up straight, raised his head and hushed Reynevan with a glance. Reynevan listened hard, but heard nothing except the meowing of the cat, the hubbub of the nearby cloth hall and the rattling of the wooden clappers from the Church of the Assumption. He sniffed, for he thought he could suddenly make out the faint smell of rosemary amid the stench in the yard.

"What is it? Bożyczko?"

Instead of answering, Łukasz Bożyczko grabbed Reynevan by the sleeve and tugged hard. Reynevan lost his balance, tried to grab a post, but instead of that he caught hold of a person. The person—completely invisible in the dark and as lithe as a shadow—shoved him away hard. Before he fell, he saw the flash of a blade and Bożyczko lunging at the person. A blade grated against the wall, there was the sound of a blow and immediately afterwards a furious curse, a second blow, then the clatter and crack of planks breaking. There was an intense flash like lightning, and for a moment the courtyard was lit up and the air howled; the intense smell of ozone and turpentine revealed Goethic magic. Reynevan had no intention of waiting to find out who had cast the spell. He leaped up from the ground, bounded onto a woodpile, cleared the fence and rushed towards the town through the neighbouring courtyard. He was fast, but not fast enough. He suddenly felt somebody landing on his back, knocking him down and pinning him to the ground.

"Lie still," a soft, melodic female alto voice murmured in his ear. "Lie still, Reynevan."

He did as he was told. The grip weakened. The rosemary-scented woman with the alto voice helped him to his feet.

"The Inquisitor has fled, unfortunately," she said, barely visible in the gloom. "Pity. I might have managed to extract from him where Miss Apolda is being kept."

"I doubt it," he said, overcoming his amazement and the resistance of his dry throat. "I doubt you would."

"Perhaps you are rightly doubtful," the woman said. "But at least I gave him a good scare. And thumped him twice, hard, because I'm wearing brass knuckles inside my glove. I heard his teeth ring! He used magic to escape, bloody sorcerer."

"And now he'll get even with Jutta."

"He won't. And for a while he'll be too afraid to pester you."

"Who are you?"

"Not so fast, not so fast." There was a note of scorn in her thrillingly modulated voice. "I'm a decent girl, I have my principles. Coitus on the third tryst at the earliest; sharing confidences, thoughts, confessions and other intimacies on the fourth or even later. So *piano*, my boy, *piano*. It's enough for you to know I'm on your side."

"You saved my skin in Wrocław—"

"I just said—I'm on your side. I'm taking care nothing bad happens to you. As part of that I want to help you recover your beloved. To that end, I suggest a meeting in Strzegom."

"When?"

"On the third day of the month of Tammuz. In Church Street, near the school and the Knights Hospitaller commandery. Since I'm not certain how you will calculate the date, I shall stop by there for the next three days. If you really want to save your betrothed, be on time."

"Why Strzegom, exactly?"

"It's a town that's dear to me."

"Why are you helping me?"

"I have a vested interest."

"What is it?"

"For today it is this," said the rosemary-scented alto voice. "An old friend of yours will soon ask you for advice. He faces a decision, is hesitant. Make sure he stops hesitating. Confirm in him his belief that his initial thought was right and that he's acting correctly."

"I don't understand."

"But you will. Farewell, return to your companions. Well, what are you waiting for?"

"Just tell me one thing—"

"Reynevan!"

"—are you a human being? A normal…hmm…human woman?"

"Opinions are divided on that subject," she replied with a mocking giggle. "And vary."

*

They left Racibórz the following day—which was Great Friday—early, on a grey morning. Plied with questions about the destination and route of their journey, Bedřich hinted something about the Krakow road leading eastwards, but no one was surprised when, after keeping the bridge over the Odra on their right side, they headed northwards along the left bank, and when they soon reached a crossroads, instead of taking the main road to Nysa, Bedřich, without saying a word, took the road less travelled. Which led towards Koźle.

Reynevan hadn't told his companions anything about the previous evening's events. The preacher urged them on, so they rode quickly, and the town's spires and towers came into view before sunset. Reynevan had already guessed what town it would be. And when, rather than going into Koźle, they turned hard towards the west, into forest, he knew where they were heading and to meet whom. Any doubts were dispelled by the sight of a party of knights riding out towards them. He knew them, remembered their names and arms. Prawdzic. Nieczuja. And leading them…

"God keep you!" Krzych of Kościelec, of the Ogończyk coat of arms, greeted them. "God keep you, m'lords. I'm glad to see you, m'Lord Reynevan. Welcome to Głogówek. Let us make haste. Duke Bolko is expecting you. He waits impatiently, gentlemen."

The view from the walls of Głogówek Castle gave a compelling picture of the destruction and calamities that *Glogovia Minor*—until recently the pearl of Silesian architecture—had experienced as a result of the previous year's plundering raid. Located on the far side of the River Ozobłoga, the riverside buildings had simply vanished and there were almost no traces of them on the black crust of scorched earth. The castle suburb of Przedmieście Zamkowe, once crowded and vibrant, had met a similar fate. Life was slowly returning, although clear traces were also visible of the fires that had raged there a year before, on the Friday before Laetare Sunday *Anno Domini* 1428, when after first sacking the monastery of the Pauline Order in Mochów, Tábor troops—in the shape of the Czechs of Jan Zmrzlík of Svojšín and Dobko Puchała's Poles—attacked Głogówek.

It wasn't just the suburbs that had suffered then, Reynevan recalled. The gates were destroyed and the walls breached. Zmrzlík and Puchała had forced their way into the town, slaughtering and burning. Głogówek still hadn't recovered. The houses in the town square were black with soot, and the southern part of the town, in the vicinity of the Collegiate Church of Saint Bartholomew, even though it was being rebuilt, was not much more than a ruin. The Collegiate Church itself had also taken quite a pounding and the Franciscan monastery had suffered serious damage.

"A heart-rending sight, isn't it, Reynevan?" said Duke Bolko Wołoszek, resting his elbow on the wall. "But of course, you know the town was actually lucky. When in March I was parleying with you Hussites, Prokop put a stop to the burning and ordered the release of the captured townspeople. Once released, they began the rebuilding, thanks only to which the name of Głogówek hasn't vanished from the map of Silesia. But some time will pass before Prudnik, Biała and Czyżowice return to the map.

"I shall not permit further towns to share the fate of Prudnik and Biała," continued the duke. "Głogówek survived thanks to the alliance with you Hussites. Which I struck on your advice, Reinmar, comrade and companion from Prague University. I remember that. For which reason I insisted you be brought into Prokop's mission. We shall talk about that, but in the chambers, over wine. Great quantities of wine. The sight of those burned-down houses regularly arouses in me an overwhelming desire to drink myself stupid."

"I heard," said Wołoszek, rocking Hungarian wine in a goblet, "that you were excommunicated in Wrocław. Welcome to the fraternity! Now, not only are we comrades, alumni from Prague Charles University, but we are both anathema. I was banished for my alliance with you, naturally. And for splitting the skull of a priest with a little club. But I care nothing for the anathema. They can excommunicate me until Judgement Day, I don't give a hoot. In any case, comrade, the Friars Minor will bury me with pomp in the crypt of the reconstructed Głogówek convent, singing over my coffin, praying, lighting candles and burning incense. There will be full pomp and opulence. Fuck me, I wonder if the bishop will be similarly feted when he kicks the bucket, which— God willing—will happen very soon. Are you surprised I know so much about my own funeral? I have, Brother, a soothsayer, a *sortarius* and a sorcerer in my service. He is somewhat more of a farmyard sorcerer; he catches chickens and ducks, eviscerates them and reads the future from their guts. But his predictions come true, it must be admitted."

"And was it this haruspex who prophesied such a lavish funeral? Let me guess: you will die at a ripe old age? After a happy life? Famous and wealthy?" asked Reynevan. "Let me guess: you pay him generously? You provide for his family, his friends and relatives?"

"You mock in vain," said the duke and grew serious. "The prophet didn't prophesy for gain or to flatter, for he wasn't afraid to prophesy things for which I almost had him torn apart by horses. He prophesied that…Oh, it's none of your business. In any case, what is to be, will be. You can't change destiny."

"But one can direct destiny."

"And that—to be honest—is what I'm hoping," said Wołoszek. "The sorcerer, indeed, divined for me from a duck's guts a long and prosperous life, then my death as a famed and respected man followed by a sumptuous funeral. But I shan't rest on my laurels for that reason, I won't wait idly by to receive the happiness I've been divined. I want to direct destiny. The world has stopped at a crossroads, as you are only too aware. Silesia is also at a crossroads. I know up to a point what I want to do, I've almost made a decision. But before that I wanted to meet you, comrade. That's why I asked for you to be part of the mission. I trust you."

Reynevan sipped the Hungarian wine but didn't comment.

"Exactly a year ago," Wołoszek went on, "by the Stradunia, where, as today, the first shoots are appearing on the willows, you told me about a revolution. About the unrelenting chariot of history sweeping away the Old in its flight to make way for the New. You advised me to join the victors, since it is woe to the vanquished, while glory, power and might await the conquerors. You presented me with visions.

"A year has passed. Today is Easter Saturday, tomorrow Easter Day. Bedřich of Strážnice, an envoy of Prokop, has come. With an offer, a concrete proposition. I want to know: is it an honest game, Reynevan? Should I enter into an alliance with Prokop and Korybut?"

Bolko Wołoszek, Lord Głogówek, heir to the Duchy of Opole, a Piast among Piasts, fixed Reynevan with a piercing gaze.

Reynevan didn't lower his eyes.

"By allying myself with the Tábor," the duke asked gravely, "will I mount the chariot of history or descend into the abyss? What is this eagerly awaited New World that is now dawning? A paradise? Or an apocalypse that declares: 'Woe will befall the victors as much as the vanquished?' Should I ally myself with Prokop and Bedřich, with their cause and their faith? Put your hand on your heart, Reinmar, look me in the eyes, and answer as a friend to a friend, as a university comrade. Answer with one word: yes or no? I await your answer anxiously."

From sunrise, Easter Sunday greeted Głogówek with sunshine, spring warmth and birdsong. Bells rang and the Resurrection procession set off.

Surrexit Dominus, surrexit vere
Et apparuit Simoni
Alleluia, alleluia!

The procession was led by the Guardian of the Minorites, who was also the lector at the Collegiate Church. Other Friars Minor followed after him. They were followed by the knighthood, bearing mainly Polish coats of arms. They in turn were followed by the Patriciate, burghers and merchants. The small number that had remained in the ruined town, now devoid of importance.

Advenisti desiderabilis,
quem expectabamus in tenebris,
ut educeres hac nocte vinculatos de claustris.
Te nostra vocabant suspiria,
te larga requirebant lamenta...
Alleluia!

The procession reached the Franciscan monastery. Wołoszek had chosen the place deliberately. The sight of shattered, charred but mainly intact walls was supposed to communicate a message. It was meant to remind people who and what were responsible for the walls continuing to stand.

A herald dressed in a tabard with the sign of a golden Opole eagle stepped out of the procession. After waiting for the hubbub and murmuring to quieten down and for complete silence to fall, the herald unfurled a parchment hung with seals.

"*In nomine Sancte et Individue Trinitatis, amen,*" he thundered. "*Nos Boleslaus filius Boleslae, Dei gratia dominus Glogovie et dux futurus Oppoliensis, significamus praesentibus litteris nostris, quorum interest, universis et singulis.*

"We make it known, in order to ensure peace and save our lands and subjects, we vow and pledge an alliance, a brotherhood of arms and loyalty to the Community of the Tábor and all the allies of the Tábor. We vow to stand loyally beside the Tábor and fight together for peace and stability, which means to join battle with any man who is against such stability."

The colour drained from the Franciscan guardian's face and the rest of the monks and clergymen likewise paled like shrouds. Although the duke had preliminarily prepared them for what would occur, the shock did not elude them.

"As reward and compensation for this alliance, we shall give the Tábor the towns and estates specified in the annex, with the exception of those that we shall keep for ourselves. In exchange, the Tábor promises us the towns and estates specified in the annex, which are currently in others' hands and which in the fight for peace we shall confiscate from the present owners.

"*Factum est,*" finished the herald, "*in Dominica Resurrectionis Anno Domini MCCCCXXIX ad laudem Omnipotentis Dei amen.*"

Not even the faintest murmur disturbed the silence.

Duke Bolesław Wołoszek, son of Bolesław, grandson of Bolesław, great-grandson of Bolesław, Piast among Piasts, stepped forward. He was in full armour, and with a gold chain on his chest and an ermine collar on his cloak he resembled a king. To his right stood a marshal, also in full plate, and behind him a seneschal, and he was flanked by his guests, two Polish knights: one of the Leliwa coat of arms, the other of the Kornicz arms. The pale Franciscan guardian stood on the duke's left. At the rear walked a standard bearer carrying a flag with an eagle.

Before beginning, the herald once again waited for quiet.

"Let it also be known to all and sundry that to strengthen the alliance with the Tábor we hereby receive Holy Communion in the way of Christ, that is under both means, *sub utraque specie*, not compelling any of our subjects to such a Communion and guaranteeing freedom of religious expression. We also swear to uphold the Four Articles, which have been declared and accepted by free men in the Kingdom of Bohemia."

The herald stepped aside. Wołoszek took a step forward; the seneschal and the abbot remained at the back. Bedřich of Strážnice, unrecognisable in a black cassock girded with a leather belt, stepped out of the entourage. The Hussite preacher was holding a paten and a beautifully engraved gold chalice. Wołoszek raised his right arm.

"I vow that in this duchy given to me freely by God, the Word of God will be preached safely and without hindrance. I vow that the Body and Blood of Christ the Lord will be given to the faithful under both forms of bread and wine according to the rules of the Bible and the teachings of the Saviour. That papist priests will have their secular power over wealth and worldly goods confiscated and their worldly goods and wealth will be taken from them, since it hampers them in living, believing and teaching as Christ and his apostles did. And because all mortal sins and blatant offences against Divine Law will be punished. So help me, God and the Holy Cross."

On finishing, the duke knelt down. Bedřich approached, gave the duke the paten and the Host and after it the chalice with wine. Then he lifted up both vessels with both hands.

"*Fiat voluntas Tua!*"

"Amen!" answered the congregation.

Wołoszek rose to his feet, his armour grating.

"It is done at last," he said and turned towards the men standing closest. "Let's go and have something to eat. And drink."

The banquet took place in the refectory of the Franciscan monastery. The walls were covered by a spider's web of cracks and the interior still stank of burning, but the monks insisted on receiving the duke. Everybody knew why. Converted to the Chalice and the Czech faith, Wołoszek wasn't concealing his aim of driving the priests, prelates and collegiate canons from Głogówek. The Friars Minor hoped he would let them stay.

The Franciscan cooks had tried their best to outdo one another in their culinary excellence. On the table there were four splendid, enormous roast wild boars, each one stuffed with pork and sausage. Four red deer. Eight roe deer, twelve piglets, twelve blackcocks, an immense quantity of ham, smoked meats, blood pudding and cured goose breasts. This feast was completed by an array of poppy-seed cake and gingerbread. The centre of the table was taken up by an entire roast ox with gilded horns, decorated with inscriptions formed from pork rind. One proclaimed: *O IESU, SPECULUM CLARITATIS AETERNAE.* The other was extremely sycophantic: *DEIGRATIA DUX BOLKO HUIUS LOCI BENEFACTOR.*

The beverages were also impressive: four—an *exemplum* of the four seasons—barrels of Cypriot wine. Twelve—for the months in the year—kegs of Hungarian and Italian wine. An enormous number—too many to count, but probably fifty-two bottles, the same number as weeks in the year—of Moldavian and Hungarian wine, jugs of mead and a demijohn of the famous Kaunas linden-blossom mead.

The forty days of Lent had left their mark. Having sat impatiently through the *Pater noster* and *Benedic Domine* said by the pale guardian, the post-Lenten revellers fell on the food and drink like a hawk on a woodcock, like Charles Martel attacking the Arabs at the battle of Poitiers, like the Swan ravishing Leda, or the Cretan Bull ravaging Pasiphaë disguised as a cow. The table, which at first resembled a cornucopia—the inexhaustible offerings of the horn of the goat Amaltheia—began quite quickly to empty and the sight of gnawed bones started to bring more and more to mind an excavated graveyard.

Duke Bolko Wołoszek unfastened the buttons of his doublet. And belched. A long-drawn-out and lordly belch.

"The mendicant order has exerted itself," he said. "Although I incurred the costs so as not to ruin it completely. Ill times are coming for monks and priests. I shall cast them all out. Have you seen the guardian sitting over there? Such a pale face, such a sour expression. See him staring at the wall, as though he has seen Mene, Tekel and Peres there? As a matter of fact, I feel sorry for the Franciscans, for those friars are decent: all Poles and Czechs, loyal to the principles of the Saint from Assisi. They treated the sick and helped paupers. Wherever there was poverty, calamities, misfortunes, they were always there when they were needed. So I shall feel sorry to evict them. But I *shall* evict them. The New is coming, great changes, revolution, the last shall be first and *vice versa*. The innocent will suffer along with the guilty. For the New is coming and it wouldn't be up to much if it didn't start by giving the Old a good kick up the arse. Am I right, Reynevan? Right, Brother Bedřich?"

"So you are Presbyter Bedřich of Strážnice?" said one of the Polish guests, of the Leliwa arms.

"I am," said Bedřich, stopping for a moment to pick his teeth. "And you are Spytek Leliwa of Melsztyn, the Voivode of Krakow.

And you, m'lord, are Mikołaj Kornicz Siestrzeniec, the Burgrave of Będzin. As you see, not just your names and arms, but your ranks are known to me. So please let me introduce myself according to mine. On the basis of the alliance formed today and our joint operations, the whole of Upper Silesia will soon be under our control and will belong to the Tábor, Sigismund Korybut and Duke Bolesław here present. I, meanwhile, will bear the rank and title of *director*, commander-in-chief of the Tábor's outposts in Silesia."

Wołoszek, the recent convert to the teachings of Jan Huss, glanced about himself vigilantly to check whether the intoxicated state of the other revellers meant he could speak freely.

"We have divided Upper Silesia among ourselves, as you see," he said to the Poles. "Korybut will receive Gliwice, Bedřich's Taborites—Niemcza and whatever else they wrest from the bishop. The Duchy of Opole must also acquire gains, of course, and generous ones. I want the Namysłów lands, Kluczbork, Rybnik and Pszczyna. And half of Bytom, the half currently held by that fucking Teutonic Knight Konrad the White, the bishop's youngest brother. The border posts, I have been promised, will be shifted to benefit the victors. So come on then, let us conquer and shift them!"

"Perhaps tomorrow," said Mikołaj Kornicz Siestrzeniec, "for I've eaten and drunk so much I cannot stand up."

"The day after tomorrow suits us," announced Spytek of Melsztyn. "Isn't that right, Lord Bedřich? M'Lord Reynevan? So we can ride together."

Reynevan glanced at Bedřich and raised his eyebrows enquiringly. The preacher sighed.

"We're going back to Racibórz," he said, "and from there to the Krakow road."

"The Krakow road, you say. So to Poland?"

"We shall see."

"You, Reynevan, are sitting there still glum," said Wołoszek, now ruddy-faced from wine. "It's Easter, the Day of our Lord's Resurrection. Spring, changes in nature, changes in politics, the New is coming, the Old is passing, *lux perpetua* will brighten the gloom, Good is prevailing, Evil is fleeing, power is quailing. The angels are rejoicing, they are singing in the heavens, *Gloria, Gloria in excelsis*, the greyhound has whelped and the prettiest lady-in-waiting of my wife the duchess finally let me fuck her. In a word, the body rejoices, the soul rejoices, let us rejoice *tandem* all together—so Reynevan, rejoice with us, too. Rejoice, dammit! Drink; I'm drinking to you. And say what's vexing you, brother scholar."

Reynevan told them what was vexing him.

"The Inquisition has abducted your maid?" said the duke, frowning. "Grzegorz Hejncze has sunk to abduction? Unbelievable. Were it Bishop Konrad, he would stoop to anything... But Gregorius? Our comrade from Charles University? Ah well, times change; men, too. Listen, brother, you supported me, helped me with my decision, so I shall help you, too. I have sources of information, I have men—the bishop would be surprised if he knew how close they are to him. Hejncze would be surprised, too. Jutta of Apolda, you say? I'll have them keep their ears open for that name. Eventually, somebody will happen upon a trail, for nothing can be kept hidden for long, the proverb is right: *quicquid nix celat, solis calor omne revelat.*"

"Very true," Bedřich of Strážnice confirmed with a strange smile.

Marching out at daybreak had become the tradition for the mission and this time it was no different. Before the sun had properly risen above the fog, they had left Głogówek a long way behind them and were heading briskly eastwards. They soon reached a crossroads.

"Bedřich? Which way now?" asked the penitent, innocently.

"To Racibórz. And after that along the Krakow road to Zator. I told you."

"We know what you told us yesterday. I asked where we're going today."

"Don't push your luck, Scharley."

So they rode towards Racibórz and the Krakow road, in a unit which now included the two Polish knights and their esquires. And all around, spring was blooming.

"M'Lord Reynevan?"

"Yes, Lord Melsztyn."

"You are a German—"

"I am not. I am a Silesian."

"You are not a Czech," Spytek concluded. "So what, then, draws you to Hussitism? What led you to being on their side?"

"The eternal fight between good and evil. When the time came to choose, when I had to choose, I chose good."

"Had to? You could have stayed out of the fight."

"To remain neutral in the fight between good and evil is to sympathise with evil."

"Listen carefully, Mikołaj," said Spytek of Melsztyn, addressing the other knight. "Listen to what he says."

"Aye, I am," said Siestrzeniec. "I've also heard rumours. And people say you engage in witchcraft, m'Lord Bielawa. That you are a sorcerer."

"I am indeed," replied Reynevan calmly, "and it was three sorcerers who were the first to greet Jesus in Bethlehem, bringing him gold, frankincense and myrrh."

"Tell that to the Inquisition."

"The Inquisition knows."

"Perhaps we ought to change the subject," interjected Spytek of Melsztyn.

"You divided up Upper Silesia between you with great panache," said Siestrzeniec sarcastically. "Dashingly, boldly and vigorously. The Tábor, Wołoszek, Korybut. Shared out your chickens before they've hatched. What about the Polish Kingdom's interests?"

"Are they so dear to you?" asked Bedřich with no less sarcasm. "Do you care so much for them?"

"It will be difficult to carry out your plans if Poland doesn't support them. Will it be in Polish interests to support them?"

"Hard to say," Bedřich agreed. "For it's the old problem with Poland: who is in charge and what are they going to do? Jagiełło? Jagiełło's sons? Sophia of Halshany? Witold? Our old friend, Bishop Zbigniew Oleśnicki? The Szafraniec family? In Poland, whoever is in power has his own, private interests and invariably calls his own interest the good of his fatherland. That's how it's been for centuries and it will always be thus. You ask about the interest of the Polish Kingdom, Lord Kornicz. And I ask: whose specific interest do you have in mind?"

Siestrzeniec snorted and reined in his mount.

"Lord Bedřich! Why, we are but envoys in the service of dignified personages, an escort for important statesmen. We are here to escort. Statesmen are travelling there to discuss truly important matters with other statesmen."

"Other men than statesmen know what happened in Lutsk," replied Bedřich. "And other men than statesmen can see what is happening in Poland now. Bishop Oleśnicki persecutes Polish Hussites and is urging Jagiełło to launch a crusade against Bohemia. Witold will soon be crowned King of Lithuania—"

"That coronation will never happen," interrupted Reynevan. "Believe me."

"Of course it won't," said Siestrzeniec, fixing him with his gaze. "The Pope won't allow it. Or perhaps you have something else in mind?"

"He didn't," Bedřich assured them on Reynevan's behalf. "And I, sirs, still don't know in whose name these important personages are travelling to Bohemia, to a meeting of whom we're heading to Zator. And to whom am I meant to serve as an escort."

"They are travelling on behalf of the Kingdom of Poland," said Spytek of Melsztyn, knitting his dark brows. "I assure you. Say what you like, but Poland is one and its good health comes above all else. With its kings, dukes, bishops and all. And, if necessary, without its kings and bishops."

"Without them?" said Bedřich and smiled with the corners of his mouth. "Sounds like a call to rebellion, Lord Melsztyn. Do you have rebellion in mind?"

"No, not rebellion. A confederation. A shield, a refuge, a temple of our golden liberty. The privilege of our knightly estate. In order to restrain the unfavourable direction of public affairs and abuse of power, whether royal or ecclesiastical; in order to maintain control in a poorly governed kingdom, hampered in progress or simply hurtling towards its doom, violent means are needed. Bold ones. Military ones. Evil taken to the extreme requires effective medicine, because when all is said and done it must be cured, one way or another. By the sword, if necessary."

"That sounded serious."

"I know."

"Gentlemen," said Scharley, standing up in the stirrups. "The Pszczyna region is across the river."

"We must be vigilant now," said Bedřich. "Hussites and their allies are hunted mercilessly here. The Pszczyna widow pays generously for captives."

"Is she still a widow?" asked Siestrzeniec, surprised. "I heard she married Přemek of Opava."

"Přemek considered it," confirmed the preacher. "One, because marriage with the widow would have joined the Pszczyna lands to Opava. Two, because the widow is an impressive specimen of womanhood—not so young, indeed, but a vigorous and red-blooded Lithuanian. Who knows, perhaps old Přemek was afraid of falling short in bed? Suffice it to say he took some Bosnian or other as his wife and the Pszczyna widow remains just that: a widow. But such persistent rumours were circulating that plenty of people believe her to be Přemek's wife. And since the Bosnian also happens to be called Helena, some folk are confused."

"Is Helena of Pszczyna Sigismund Korybut's sister?" asked Reynevan.

"Indeed," said Spytek, "the daughter of Dmitry Korybut, son of Olgierd. King Jagiełło's niece—"

"Niece or not," Bedřich interjected, "we must avoid her at all costs. Come on, to horse. The quicker we get away from Pszczyna, the better."

"We will," said Scharley, clicking his tongue at his horse. "So far it's going like clockwork."

He spoke too soon.

"Sire!" called one of the Moravians standing guard outside the wattle fences of the tavern where they had stopped in order to purchase feed. "Sire! Some men approach!"

"Soldiers!" called another. "At least a dozen horse—"

"Form up, weapons at the ready," ordered Bedřich. "Remain calm, perhaps they will ride on."

Siestrzeniec unfastened a heavy axe from his saddle and slipped the handle into his belt behind him. Spytek slid the haft of his sword nearer his hand but hid the weapon under his cloak. The Moravians hurried to untie the horses from the hitching post. Samson shut the tavern door and leaned against it.

Scharley caught Reynevan by the arm.

"Take this."

The weapon he gave him was a crossbow of German make. A hunting weapon with a gorgeously inlayed stock and a steel lath, but quite light. Drawn using a cranequin: consisting of a ratchet working on a small toothed wheel, turned by a windlass.

Hooves thudded on the road, a horse neighed and a unit of thirteen soldiers appeared riding slowly in the direction of Pszczyna along an avenue of crooked willows.

"Will they pass us by or not?" muttered Bedřich.

They did not. They rode into the courtyard. It could be discerned at once that they weren't ordinary foot soldiers; their uniforms and weapons revealed them to be mercenaries. Reynevan saw that they were leading a captive. A man was trotting beside one of the horses, his bound hands tied to the pommel of a saddle.

The commander of the troop, a thin-faced, moustachioed man, glared at Bedřich and company. The man being led turned his head. And Reynevan's jaw dropped involuntarily.

The prisoner was Bruno Schilling. The Black Rider, the renegade, the deserter from the Company of Death.

He recognised Reynevan in an instant. His eyes lit up with a gleam, an evil gleam, and his face set in a grimace that Reynevan hadn't seen before, not once, neither during the journey from the Olza, nor during the six days of the interrogation at Sovinec. He understood at once what the grimace meant.

"They are Hussites!" yelled Schilling tugging on his rope. "Those men over there! Those ones! They are Hussites! Czech spies! Hey! Do you hear me?"

"What?" the commander of the troop asked brusquely. "What are you saying?"

"They are Hussite spies!" Schilling blurted out, almost spitting. "I know them! You are holding me captive, though I be innocent, but they are real malefactors! Arrest them! Bind them in fetters!"

Spytek of Melsztyn paled and pursed his lips; Siestrzeniec's hand immediately moved to his sword hilt. Bedřich made a signal with his eyes to the Moravians. Scharley took off his cap and stepped forwards.

"Oh, what a jester," he said cheerfully. "You've caught a loud-mouthed thief, gentlemen warriors, no two ways about it! He slanders others to save his own skin. And give him a good thrashing when you get to Pszczyna, m'lord officer, don't spare your blows on such a fellow! Let him know what slanderers can expect!"

"And who might you be?" barked the moustachioed man.

"We are merchants from Elbing," announced Bedřich of Strážnice calmly. "Returning from Hungary—"

"And I'm a grey goose."

"I give you my word."

"He is lying!" yelled Schilling. "He is a Hussite!"

"Shut your trap," said the moustachioed man. "And you, gentlemen, will have to come with us to Pszczyna, where my superiors will get to the bottom of who you are, whether real merchants or feigned merchants. Petzold, Mladota, dismount, search their saddlebags and baggage. And take their weapons from them."

"M'Lord Commander," said Bedřich and slightly moved the edge of his cloak aside, meaningfully patting a bulging pouch hanging from his belt. "Perhaps we can come to some agreement?"

The moustachioed man urged his horse forwards and looked down at them. Then his face twisted into a contemptuous smirk.

"They pay higher sums in Pszczyna for heretics. And the fact you're offering a bribe makes you a heretic for certain. You will go in fetters. And your wretched pouch will be ours in any case."

"God knows I didn't mean it to take this turn," said the preacher and shrugged.

"Which turn?"

"This one."

A soldier passed Bedřich a crossbow and he brought the butt smoothly up to his cheek. The bowstring twanged and a bolt—fired from close range—hurled the moustachioed man from his horse.

"Attack!"

Spytek of Melsztyn hacked one of the mercenaries with his sword, while Siestrzeniec fell on the others, slashing and stabbing by turns with a sword and the battleaxe. The mercenaries fought back, yelling, lowering their spears and brandishing pole-axes. Three men fell from their horses, struck by bolts from the crossbows of the Moravians and the Polish esquires; a fourth fell face down into a puddle, shot by Scharley. The rest came for them, yelling war cries. And then Samson struck.

The giant seized a heavy bench made from a log split in half and picked it up as though it was a feather. And like the cyclops Polyphemus hurling boulders at Odysseus's ship, so Samson Honeypot flung the bench at the mounted Pszczyna mercenaries. With better effect than Polyphemus had, wreaking terrible harm among the men and animals.

Reynevan, nimbly weaving among the melee, attacked Schilling. And saw something incredible.

The renegade seized the jerkin of the rider who was leading him and dragged him to ground. The mercenary, a huge fellow, resisted, pushed Schilling away and lunged at him with a knife. Schilling avoided the thrust with a slight twist of his torso, then with a sudden movement of his shoulder bent the soldier's arm and pushed his shoulder forwards, shoving the attacker's knife into his own throat. He quickly cut the cords binding his wrists on the blade of a battleaxe hanging from the saddle, mounted the horse and spurred it to a gallop.

And would have escaped had it not been for the hunting crossbow with the German lever, made in Nuremberg, exported to Krakow and taken to Odry in Moravia where Scharley bought it from a Polish arms smuggler for the quite reasonable sum of four Hungarian ducats. Reynevan rested the stock against the fence, calmly aimed and fired. Pierced in the rump, the horse squealed and kicked wildly, Schilling flew from the saddle as though from a slingshot and into a pile of wet sawdust. Reynevan was on him with a knife drawn from his bootleg. The renegade leaped up like a cat and flashed his own blade. They came together in a series of cuts, thrusts and blows.

Schilling unexpectedly lunged, jumped forward and jabbed Reynevan in the eyes with stiffly splayed fingers. Reynevan saved his sight by twisting his head and dodged a wide, sweeping cut. He parried the next slash, sparks spraying around. Schilling kicked him, at the same time making to stab from above. Reynevan managed to shield himself, but it was a feint. The renegade turned his knife around in his hand and slashed him in the thigh. The sharp stab of pain befuddled Reynevan for a moment. Which was enough for Schilling. He spun around smoothly and slashed Reynevan's arm.

"You escaped with your life in February because I was indisposed," he hissed, bent forwards. "But I recovered."

"You'll soon be indisposed again."

"Back then I only nicked your ear. This time I'll bleed you like a pig. As I did your brother."

They fell on each other, cutting and thrusting. Reynevan parried a nasty thrust, elbowed Schilling in the face, punched him again from a half-turn, kicked him in the shin, twisted his knife around and stabbed from above with all his might. There was a crunching sound and the blade plunged in up to the cross guard. The renegade struggled and jumped clear. He looked down at the hilt stuck in beside his collar bone. He seized it and pulled it out of the wound with one fluid movement. And tossed it over his shoulder.

"It didn't hurt a bit, ha ha," he said cheerfully. "And now I'll filet you. I'll pull out your guts and wrap them around your neck. And leave you like that."

Reynevan retreated, tripped and fell. Schilling jumped forwards, yelling triumphantly. Scharley appeared out of nowhere and slashed him hard across the belly with the falchion. The renegade coughed, looked down at the spurting blood and raised his knife. Scharley cut him again, this time across his right shoulder. Blood gushed two yards up in the air and Schilling fell to his knees but still didn't release the knife. Scharley smote him again. And again. The renegade fell down for a second time. The third time he stopped making any movements.

"*Terra sit ei levis*," said Bedřich, crossing himself. "May the earth…and so on. I'm almost afraid to ask…Did you know him?"

"A passing friendship," replied Scharley, wiping his blade.

"But it's over now," added Reynevan. "We'll strike him from our list of acquaintances. Thank you, Scharley. My brother also thanks you from the beyond."

"In any case," said Bedřich and grimaced, looking down at his cut hand, "this friend is responsible for the deaths of these Pszczyna warriors whose worldly remains are now being buried in a dung heap. Were it not for him we'd have lied our way out of it without fighting. Now we must flee from here and fast. Physician, could you bandage my hand?"

"One moment," said Reynevan, removing his jerkin and blood-soaked shirt. "Hold on a little longer. I'll just get a needle and thread. I need to sew myself up in a few places, too."

They rode on, without sparing their horses. Reynevan wasn't the only one to be sewn up and who was now riding, bent over in the saddle, hissing and cursing. Spytek of Melsztyn had received a slight wound in the thigh in the fight with the Pszczyna mercenaries, one of the Moravians had been stabbed in the ribs and Siestrzeniec's esquire had been hit hard on the head.

But they were all riding and holding on. They groaned and grunted but didn't slow the pace.

"Bedřich? How's your arm?"

"Just a scratch. I asked for a dressing so as not to stain my trousers. They're new."

"Have you been wounded before? With iron?"

"At the Battle of Břeclav, on the twenty-sixth, a Hungarian pike in the shin. Why do you ask?"

"No reason."

"Schilling…" said Reynevan, deciding to broach a grim subject. "If Schilling was here, it means that he escaped from prison. And that may mean…It may mean that Horn—"

"No," the penitent interrupted at once. "I don't believe it. Horn wouldn't let himself be caught unawares. But while we're about it—"

"We will have to check," Reynevan finished. "Let's take a look at Sovinec. Right after we return to Odry."

"That will be soon," said Samson Honeypot, calmly. "In three—at most four—days."

"Samson?"

"Our commandant has changed the route again. He's been

284

leading us southwards for an hour. Straight to the Moravian Gate. We'll see Skoczów any moment."

Reynevan swore extremely obscenely.

"Yes, I admit it," said Bedřich, not even batting an eyelid at the fierce recriminations. "I misled you purposefully. I never intended to go to Zator."

"Another test of my loyalty, eh?" snapped Reynevan. "I know it was!"

"If so, why do you ask?"

Thousands of frogs croaked, crawling over each other in a forest pond choked with a thick layer of duckweed.

"I have to admit," said Scharley, "you know how to get on people's nerves, Bedřich. You're extremely talented in that regard. This time, you've even managed to enrage a peaceful fellow like me. I would smash your face in just like that if I wasn't embarrassed to do it in front of foreigners."

"As for me," drawled the foreigner Siestrzeniec, "I feel personally offended by your deception. Lucky for you, m'Lord Bedřich, your clergyman's cassock protects you. Otherwise, I would teach you some manners on the duelling ground. And knock you into the middle of next week."

"Lord Szafraniec and Lord Oporów are waiting in Zator!" Spytek of Melsztyn interjected heatedly. "We were meant to lead them to Moravia and protect them on the way. Hetman Prokop promised to assist and escort the Polish mission! And we gave our knightly parole—"

"The Chamberlain of Krakow," said Bedřich, linking his fingers on his chest, "and the Deputy Crown Chancellor are already riding to Odry and will probably get there before us. They are being guided by trusted men and don't need protection. Now, since Jan of Kravaře went over to the Chalice and allied with the Tábor, the roads there are safe. So enough of this jabbering, gentlemen. To horse and let us ride!"

"Perhaps it is acceptable among you Czechs," said Mikołaj Kornicz Siestrzeniec, grinding his teeth, "to feed knights lies, to lead them up the garden path and call their speech 'jabbering.' In Poland it doesn't go unpunished. Lucky you are protected by—"

"Protected by what?" roared Bedřich, already in the saddle. "My cassock? Where do you see a cassock? And anyway, fuck that! I tell you to your face: I had my suspicions, I didn't trust any of you, so I had to put you to the test, all of you. Do you understand, Kornicz? And what of it? Did I offend your delicate Polish honour? Do you want to fight? Do you want satisfaction? Come on, then! Which of you—"

He didn't finish. Samson Honeypot rode over on his lancer's stallion, caught Bedřich by the collar and the seat of the pants, hauled him from the saddle, lifted up the yelling Czech and hurled him into the duckweed-covered pond. There was a splash, a foul smell drifted up and the frogs fell silent for a moment.

Samson waited in the utter silence for the preacher to emerge, green from the weed and spitting out mud.

"My delicate honour was offended," he said. "But this will suffice as satisfaction."

Chapter Ten

In which we visit Wrocław once again, during the days preceding Easter, for many things happen there which it would be simply a shame not to talk about.

That morning a sudden rain fell and when the sun rose, it lit a copper and gold fire on the Wrocław churches. The roof over the nave of Saint Elizabeth's Church shimmered like the Golden Fleece, the twin spires of Mary Magdalene shone blindingly, the domes and helmets of Saints Nicholas, Adalbert, Dorothy, James, the Holy Spirit, Saint Mary on the Sand and all the thirty-five Wrocław churches gleamed. A heavenly luminosity was reflected in the wet roofs of the city, a city that appeared to be now equally everlasting.

A little bell rang melodiously in the Church of Corpus Christi. Wrocław was awake and people were already bustling around near the Świdnica Gate.

It was the twenty-first of March, *Anno Domini* 1429.

Grzegorz Hejncze, *Inquisitor a Sede Apostolica* at the Wrocław Diocese, sat upright in the saddle and stretched, joints crunching.

It's good to be home again, he thought.

The bell at Saint Vincent's began to toll the Angelus. The Knights Hospitaller lowered their heads and crossed themselves. Bishop

Konrad beckoned to his servants, instructing them to charge the goblets. The immense chapter hall of the Ołbin abbey was filled with the noble aroma of Burgundy, seasoned with cinnamon, ginger and rosemary.

The singing of monks in the church could be heard.

Gratiam tuam, quaesumus, Domine,
mentibus nostris infunde;
ut qui, Angelo nuntiante,
Christi Filii tui incarnationem cognovimus…

"So," said the bishop, raising his goblet, "Johann, Prince Elector and Margrave of Brandenburg, has decided to support Silesia in the fight against heretical Bohemia and is sending us four hundred heavily armed Knights Hospitaller from the Margraviate. Who would have thought it…? For the thoughts of Johann's father, the Elector Frederick Hohenzollern, turn more often to Poland than to Silesia…But never mind. It was a noble gesture of the margrave's, worth drinking to. The good health of Margrave Johann! And your good health, m'lords!"

Baltazar of Schlieben, *Herrenmeister* of the Margraviate, reciprocated the toast. His bony hand, covered in liver spots, trembled under the weight of the goblet.

"The Hospitallers of Saint John of Jerusalem," he said in a nasal voice, "may not stand idly by in the face of a threat to the faith and the Church. We took vows and will remain true to them. We, the knights of the Brandenburg Bailiwick, pride ourselves on our loyalty to vows and monastic principles."

"Yes, indeed," proudly added Nikolaus of Thierbach, Commander of Swobnica.

"So help us, God," added Henning of Alzey, the brother of the Dytmar who fell at the Battle of Nysa, sticking his jaw out.

"Then let us drink!" urged Konrad. "To the confusion of the Hussites!"

"Down with them!" snarled Henning of Alzey.

The bishop knew that his other brother, Dytryk, had fallen at the Battle of Drahim. Fighting the Poles.

"During their stay in Wrocław, your knights will be quartered at Ołbin with the local Premonstratensians, Master Baltazar," said the bishop, addressing Schlieben. "And I shall cover all the expenses from my own casket. Where do you make for after Wrocław?"

"Legnica. To Duke Ludwik."

"Ah, naturally," said Konrad, squinting slightly. "Why, Ludwik of Brzeg is the margrave's brother-in-law. Ha, I sincerely nurture the hope that now, having under his command the celebrated weapons of the Knights Hospitaller of the Margraviate, Duke Ludwik will display greater warcraft than he has to date. For he has not in the battles with the Hussites up until now. He has only become known for his manoeuvres. And what is a manoeuvre if not a rapid retreat? But enough, enough of unpleasant matters. Your good health!"

Wiping his mouth as his glance swept over his collocutors, the bishop said, "I shall share with you some news that has lately reached us from France, along with the first-rate Burgundy we are drinking. Why, a peasant girl from Champagne, a common maid called Jehanne, a mystic and perhaps also a soothsayer, has appeared at the court of King Charles VII in Chinon. She has utterly possessed and bewitched the king. The voices of saints from Heaven, she said, have proclaimed her the saviour of France and the divine scourge of the English invaders. And do you know what? She has roused the indolent king and the entire knighthood, and even the common people. Having proclaimed her *La Pucelle*—the Virgin—they are all flocking to Orléans and her standard and the English besieging the town are trembling in their breeches with fear."

"Such a thing does not behove a maiden," said Baltazar of Schlieben, frowning. "Some new French fashions. We, too, saw a similar maid, in male attire, riding a horse and holding a javelin in the yard at your court on Ostrów Tumski, Bishop. But a maid ought not to dress as a man. It is an act against God. It is blasphemous."

"And I tell you," said the bishop, sitting upright, "that the end justifies the means. And that you don't appreciate the importance of symbolism. You can wear out your throat harping on about honour, the fatherland, faith and the Church. The people won't budge, they don't give a shit. But give them a symbol, any symbol at all, and they will follow it at once. A symbol means more than a regiment of soldiers. Which is why, who knows, perhaps I'll also search for a Jehanne like that here, in Silesia. I'll call her the Virgin, teach her about voices from Heaven, tell her to preach nonsense and bait the Hussites, dress her in armour, hand her a pennant…Perhaps it will work?"

"But it may not be so," the Grand Master repeated severely. "Male attire on a wench is a sin, debauchery, lecherous provocation and blasphemy. Wenches who wear male attire, who believe they can be equal to men, ought to be burned. Burned!"

"Of course." Konrad snorted. "Of course they should! But only once they do what is required and outlive their usefulness."

Twenty-two groschen from the bishop. Grajcarek totted it up again, sliding a finger over the table in a dark corner of the Blue Carp tavern. *Thirty from the woman smelling of rosemary. Twelve from the Inquisition. Not bloody much, those infernal priests are stingy. Twenty from the Fuggers. After deducting costs, that makes about fifty. And I need to give my wife some money to get by, four children,*

fuck it, the fifth on the way. Jesus, when will that woman start vis-
iting witches when she falls pregnant? I'll manage to put forty aside
at most. It's not much. It's still too little to go into business with my
brother-in-law and buy the mill by the Widawa from Sir Werner
Pannewitz. Lord Pannewitz, may the devils roast him in hell for his
stinginess, is asking eighty-five grzywna for the mill…I'll have to
work more. And harder. But things are getting dangerous. Inquisitor
Hejncze has returned to Wrocław, he will be making up for lost time,
they're already building pyres for after Saint Adalbert's Day. The
town's crawling with spies. Kuczera of Hunt is sniffing and tracking.
The bishop has become suspiciously courteous. As though he suspects
something.

And Grellenort. Grellenort twice looked at me strangely.

Something rustled behind him. Grajcarek shuddered and
started, reached for a knife and at the same time formed his
fingers into a magical sign.

It was a rat. Just a rat.

That evening, Konrad of Oleśnica wasn't alone in his chambers.
The Wallcreeper knew it and guessed who he would find there.
The rumour about the bishop's new lover had spread quickly
through Wrocław, quickly stopped being a rumour and became
absolutely official news. The seventeen-year-old Miss Klaudyna
Haunold wasn't the first burgher's daughter to catch the bishop's
eye and become *carnaliter copulata* as a result of that.

Klaudyna, though, was the first of them towards whom the
Patriciate behaved appropriately. Meaning, in a nouveau riche
manner. An official delegation of Wrocław patricians visited the
bishop's residence in order officially to demand financial compensation in exchange for Klaudyna's virginity. The bishop paid
without batting an eyelid. Everybody was content.

The financially regulated Klaudyna, the daughter of the

powerful Haunolds, was sitting on a Turkish stool beside the bishop, doing what she usually did, that is devouring candied fruit and exuding charm. She had let her gleaming golden hair down like a married woman and every now and then stuck out her attractive bust, clearly visible in a gown with a plunging neckline. Every time she put a piece of candied fruit between her crimson lips, she stopped in mid-motion long enough to examine and delight in the rings the bishop had given her.

"Welcome, Birkart."

"May God keep Your Eminence."

Miss Klaudyna Haunold treated him to a smouldering look with her sapphire eyes and a glimpse of an expensive slipper peeping out from the edge of her gown. The Wallcreeper knew that in her presence one could talk freely about anything at all. Nature had counterbalanced her breathtaking looks and exceptional physical beauty with certain deficits. Chiefly of the intellectual kind.

The bishop sipped wine from a goblet. Despite the late hour, he appeared to be stone-cold sober. That had become more and more common lately. The Wallcreeper made a mental note to accost the bishop's physician at the next opportunity and force him to account for it. It might have been symptomatic of an affliction. Or the result of one.

"How are you, Birkart? You haven't met with any accidents... or had any adventures lately, have you?"

"Adventures? No."

Klaudyna pinched the bishop's thigh. Konrad extended a hand and chucked her under the chin like a cat.

"I didn't have time to ask you about one matter," he said, looking up. "Your men, you know who I mean, were massacred by the Hussites at the Battle of Wielisław. How long will it take you to recruit new ones? When can one expect it?"

"The more unexpected the joy, the greater," mocked the Wallcreeper. "Please expect away, while you still have breath in your body."

Klaudyna laughed gutturally, but the bishop wasn't in the mood.

"What a jester!" he barked. "Don't joke! I need your Riders urgently; I want to be able to summon them at will! So answer when I ask you a question!"

"*Pax*, Papa," said the Wallcreeper, narrowing his eyes. "Don't be cross, it's not healthy. Wine, women and song, and anger on top of that. You'll burst a blood vessel. And they're liable to make some Pole bishop. And with regard to my answer, I'd rather it remained *inter nos*."

The bishop gestured for Klaudyna to get up and a slap on her shapely behind was the sign for her to leave them. The girl snorted, pouted her crimson lips, glared at both of them, took a handful of sweetmeats from the dish and walked off, swinging her hips alluringly.

"The Riders are now ready to respond to orders immediately," said the Wallcreeper when they were alone. "Several from the old guard are at Sensenberg. I have about a dozen new recruits here in Wrocław."

"It confirms the rumours," said the bishop, under lowered lids. "That you attract them to you using black magic, as moths are drawn to a flame. Hayn of Czirne, the commander of the mercenaries, complained that men are deserting from his company and each one is a worse scoundrel. But Knights Hospitaller? For Master Schlieben was also complaining."

"I know you're in a hurry, Papa. So I'm not fussy, I take what I can and the ganja and hash'eesh do the rest. Who else has been complaining about me?"

"Ulryk Pack, Lord of Klępino," said Konrad in a voice tinged with mockery. "But regarding another matter. It's not like you, son. You and a maiden?"

"Drop it, Bishop. And placate Pack."

"I already have. And I didn't have to make much of an effort. Returning *ad rem*: you have men at the ready. Will they be able to keep me safe? Protect me? If—contrary to your opinion— Reinmar of Bielawa *is* planning to kill me?"

"Reinmar of Bielawa isn't planning to kill you. So if you only need my men to—"

"Not only," interrupted the bishop.

They said nothing for a while. From the ladies' chambers came the yapping of an Italian lapdog and the melodious voice of Miss Haunold hurling abuse at the servants.

"An uncertain and evil time has dawned," said Konrad of Oleśnica, interrupting the silence. "And the worst is yet to come. A few heretical raids sufficed to shock Silesia. People have begun to vacillate, ready to forget the Ten Commandments, forget their values, honour, responsibilities and vows in these evil times. Weak people forget about alliances and the weakest of them begin to seek salvation in pacts with the enemy. They forget what the law, what social order and what *amor patriae* are. They lose heart. Forget about God. What they owe to God. Why, never mind God, they dare to forget what they owe me."

After a moment of silence, he continued, "One must bring people like that back to the straight and narrow. Give them a lesson in patriotism. And if that proves too little, one must—"

"Eliminate them from this vale of tears," finished the Wall-creeper, "shifting the blame onto demons or Hussite terrorists. It will be done, Bishop. Just say the word."

"That's the way I like you, Birkart," said the bishop, sighing. "Just like that."

"I know."

They both said nothing.

"Terrorism is a useful thing," said the bishop, sighing a second time. "It can solve so much! How would we cope without it? Who would we blame for everything, on what would we put the blame? *Vero*, if terrorism didn't exist, it would be necessary to invent it."

"Well, well," said the Wallcreeper, smiling. "We think alike, even down to using the same words. And yet you constantly disown me, Papa."

When they sat together at one table, gorging themselves on pike in saffron-yellow jelly, no one, absolutely no one, would have taken them for brothers. But in spite of their physical differences, they were. The older, Konrad, Bishop of Wrocław, had the appearance of a true Piast; of a mighty, ruddy-faced, hearty sybarite. The long beard and slightly sunken cheeks of Konrad Kantner, the Duke of Oleśnica, brought an eremite more to mind.

"I have nothing but vexation from the children I sired," said Konrad Kantner, reaching for another chunk of pike from the dish. "Nothing but vexation."

"I know," said the bishop. He coughed, hawked at length and spat out a fishbone. "I know how it is, brother. I know that distress."

"My Agnieszka is turning fifteen," continued Kantner, pretending not to have heard. "As you know, I'd decided to give her to Kasper Schlick. I believe the pup will go far; he has a mind fit for a chancellor. He's a good match. Emperor Sigismund promised me the *matrimonium*, everything was arranged. And now I hear that Schlick is being sought by the daughter of Count Berthold of Henneberg. That sodding liar. He's never said an honest word in his life!"

"Indeed," said the bishop, licking his fingers. "Which is why I wouldn't be overly concerned. And I think that our gracious king is lying to Count Berthold to acquire short-term gains and is leading him by the nose. Never mind. You'll see, we'll drink ourselves stupid at Agnieszka and Schlick's wedding yet."

"God willing," said Kantner, sipping from his goblet and clearing his throat. "But that's not all. The thought occurred to me, mark you, to marry my young Konrad to Barbara, the daughter of Johann, Margrave of Brandenburg. I went with the lad to Spandau at Christmas, let the youngsters get to know each other, so I thought. But young Konrad, mark you, took one look and said 'no.' Said he won't have her because she's fat. You lummox, I say to him, the little girl is only six years old, she is sure to grow slenderer with age. That is for *primo*, and for *secundo* you can never have too much beloved flesh, your bed will be full of bliss, from one side to the other, when it comes to your nuptials. But he said if he had the choice, he'd rather fill it with two or three slim ones. Can you mark the impudent pup? Who does he take after?"

"Us," guffawed the bishop. "Piast blood, brother, Piast blood. But in truth, I must tell you she isn't the best party for young Konrad. We don't see eye-to-eye with the Hohenzollerns. They dream of a union with Poland, are plotting with Jagiełło, plotting with the Hussites—"

"You exaggerate," said Kantner, grimacing. "You are furious at Fritz Hohenzollern because he married his son off to Jadwiga Jagiellonian. But it is true that the Hohenzollerns' star is in the ascendancy. One should stay close to people who are on the way up, affiliate with them. And I'll tell you something else."

"Say on."

"The stock of the Jagiellonians is also rising. Prince Władysław is five years old. Little Anna, my youngest, is also five."

"You're either jesting," said the bishop, frowning, "or you've lost your mind. With whom would you comingle Piast blood?"

"I see Piast blood returning to the Polish throne," said Kantner, sitting upright. "To the Wawel! But you are blinded by hatred. You don't see the changes around you. *Gott im Himmel!* Don't you see that the world has changed? This is about Silesia's future. The Hussites have grown in strength, we won't stop them by ourselves! We need help. Real help. Powerful help. And what are we doing? The Strzelin Union, an alliance with Bischofswerda, a conference in Świdnica, all a damned waste of time. The Six Cities, the Elector of Saxony, Meissen, do you call them allies? They each look after their own, for each of them trembles with fear before the Hussites. The Czechs are advancing; the Lusatians and Saxons will lock themselves fast away in their castles. They won't come to our rescue. Nor would we to theirs, if they were attacked—"

"What are you driving at, brother? For I see that you hint at something."

"Receive…" Kantner stammered. "Receive the envoy. Do as you wish, you are the governor of Silesia. But receive him. Be ready to listen."

"To whom: Brandenburg?" said the bishop, smiling wryly. "Or the Poles?"

"The envoy of Zbigniew Oleśnicki, Bishop of Krakow. I met him on the way. We conversed…About this and that…"

"Indeed. Who was it?"

"Andrzej of Bnin."

"I don't know him," said the bishop. "But before an audience occurs, I shall know all there is to know about him."

Andrzej of Bnin, of the Łodzia coat of arms, still not yet thirty, was a handsome, black-haired and swarthy man. A Master of the

Krakow Academy, a royal secretary, the Presbyter of Pobiedziska and the Canon of Łęczyca and Poznań, he was advancing swiftly up Poland's clerical hierarchy. Ambitious, even a little too ambitious, he was aiming at becoming at least a bishop. Oleśnicki, so the rumours went, trusted him implicitly. Which couldn't be said for everyone.

"Zbigniew Oleśnicki, Bishop of Krakow," he said, in a calm voice, "is the most ardent *candor fidei catholicae* and most staunch *persequens* of apostasy and of heresy. There is nothing more important to the Bishop of Krakow than *negotium fidei*, the fight for the faith. The bishop holds the view that the fight against heresy is equally as important—if not more so—as the fight against the pagans for the Holy *Sepulchrum*. The bishop understands what *Crux cismarina*—a crusade on this side of the sea—is. Particularly that we share the same side. The bishop asked me to say: we are on the same side of the sea. Krakow or Wrocław, we are on the same side, on the same shore. And with this wave of heresy swelling before us, the shore is liable to be flooded."

"It is not news to me," replied Konrad, Bishop of Wrocław, nodding, "that Zbigniew Oleśnicki sees and understands the menace of heresy. It is not news to me nor by any means strange. Zbigniew is gearing up to be a cardinal; and how may a future cardinal turn a blind eye to heresy? How may he be tolerant of heretics? How cannot one understand that what is happening in Bohemia is a thousandfold more important to us than the crusader states, Jerusalem, the Sacred Grave and other fripperies? For the truth is that the Hussite plague is not overseas, but here, in our own yard, so to speak. The truth is that naught but a *Crux cismarina* can save us. Thus I ask: where are the Polish forces marching on Bohemia with a crusade? Why can they still not be seen? Is it so difficult for the Bishop of Krakow to bend the impudent necks of the Szafraniec family and other Hussite accomplices? So difficult finally to bend the neck of the decrepit Jagiełło?"

"Are they your words, Your Excellency?" said Andrzej of Bnin, raising an eyebrow. "Because it's as though I were hearing King Sigismund. He pipes a similar tune. Why don't the Poles ride on Bohemia, where is Polish faith, where are the Polish regiments, blah, blah, blah. Where are the Polish regiments, you ask? They protect the borders of Greater Poland, Kuyavia, the Dobrzyn Lands from the Teutonic Knights, who are itching for the Polish army to set off for Bohemia in order to descend on Poland with fire and sword. With the blessings of your Emperor Sigismund. Zbigniew Oleśnicki, the Bishop of Krakow, future cardinal, is a good Catholic and foe of heresy. But above all he is a Pole."

"My forefather," said Konrad, pouting his lips, "was Piast the Wheelwright, my foremother was Rzepicha. Bolesław the Brave was my kinsman. As were Bolesław the Wry-Mouthed, Mieszko Tanglefoot, Henryk the Bearded. But when the time came to think about the future, my forefathers knew what to choose. They chose the Holy Roman Empire of the German Nation. They chose Europe. They chose progress and betterment. Zbigniew Oleśnicki thinks himself a Pole but serves Jagiełło. Who is a neophyte, a clandestine pagan, whose father made human sacrifices to Lithuanian devils. As a Pole, old Zbigniew ought to understand that Poland's future is not Lithuania, not Ruthenia, not the uncivilised East, but Europe. The Holy Roman Empire of the German Nation. Pass my words on to Zbigniew, Lord Bnin."

"I shall. But I doubt if he will listen to them. The Bishop of Krakow understands Polishness a little differently. He also sees the Germans and their empire a little differently. He can afford, forgive my bold words, seriously to doubt the honesty of German intentions. And has reason to do so."

"What, then," asked the bishop, sitting upright on a curule seat, "does Zbigniew want from me? Eh? Why the hell did he send you here, Lord Łodzia? Is he seeking help? Needs an ally? Against Witold, the pretender to the throne? Or perhaps against Svidrigiello, Jagiełło's younger brother, who grows ever more insolent?"

"Is an alliance such an ill thing that you talk of it with such disdain?" said Andrzej of Bnin, smiling. "Particularly here, in Silesia? Wouldn't an alliance have been useful to you a year ago, in 1428, when the Czechs reduced Silesia to ashes? Wouldn't military aid have been useful to you then? Don't you think that it may yet be useful when another Hussite plundering raid descends on you? For it is sure to; and if not today, then tomorrow. The Czechs will come and burn down what is left to burn and plunder what hasn't been plundered. Who will stand against them? One Silesian duke killed, the rest intimidated. The knighthood demoralised. The allies are scattered, no money for mercenaries. Emperor Sigismund won't come with relief. Think, O Bishop Konrad, Governor of Silesia. Wouldn't help be useful at this moment of despair? Help, or rather…intervention?"

The Bishop of Wrocław said nothing for a long time.

"I understand," he finally uttered in a slow, drawling voice. "I finally see what you are driving at. The conundrum is solved. Intervention. A Polish Army in Silesia. A crusade to Bohemia: no. But to Silesia: indeed. Over my dead body. Repeat that to Zbyszko, Lord Bnin. Over my dead body."

Andrzej of Bnin said nothing and didn't lower his gaze. Neither did Konrad.

"Polish fancies," he finally said. "Polish fantasies about Silesia. Pro-Hussites, Anti-Hussites, Roman Catholics, Orthodox Catholics; you all dream about Silesia being Poland again. You want to incorporate Silesia into the Kingdom of Poland once more. You cannot understand that one can't step into the same river twice. You disposed of Silesia yourselves, Silesia will never be Polish again. But you know that. Yet still you dream, weave fantasies. You're just waiting to wrest Silesia from my grasp!"

"In the hope of gaining what?" asked Andrzej of Bnin, smiling quite contemptuously. "What remained after 1428? Your ruins? Twenty-five burned-down towns, hundreds of settlements in ashes, scorched fields that will be barren for decades? We mean to seize Silesia from you by force, you say? Why do we need force? The Silesian princes are vying with each other to come under Polish protection. First Bolko Wołoszek of Opole, followed by Cieszyn, Głogów, Oświęcim. And others will join after the next Hussite plundering raid. Perhaps all of them?"

"Oh, but you are cocksure," said Konrad, grinding his teeth. "You self-righteous Polish prigs. It is indeed your Polish trait: self-righteousness and an utter inability to look ahead."

"History will judge our ability to look ahead," said Andrzej of Bnin, sitting upright, his features hardening, "and time will verify it. But time, with due respect, quite painfully confirmed your own abilities in this regard, honourable Bishop of Wrocław. For where is the division of Poland, a plan concocted in Pressburg with the Hungarians and the Teutonic Knights? Where are the Siewierz Lands, Sieradz and half of Greater Poland, which were meant to fall to you after the partition? And you dare to speak of self-righteousness?"

Konrad said nothing, but looked away theatrically.

"Let us then return to looking ahead," said Andrzej of Bnin, softening his voice by a tone. "I shall tell you, honourable Bishop of Wrocław, what Zbigniew Oleśnicki, *episcopus* of Krakow, predicts. And it will be the following course of events. After the next Czech plundering raid, half of the Silesian dukes will go over to Hussitism and the other half will flock to the protection of Władysław Jagiełło, King of Poland. The Pope, in order to win Jagiełło over, will deprive you of your mitre and crozier. And since ecclesiastically Wrocław falls under the metropolis of Gniezno, Zbigniew Oleśnicki will appoint your successor in the diocese and the King of Poland will approve him. And Emperor Sigismund, whom you so loyally serve? Do you think he will lift a finger in your support? Not a bit of it. He will not. But instead, will award you with the Order of the Dragon. To console you. As is his custom."

The bishop was silent for a long time. Then he turned his head.

"You have said much," he said, looking the Pole in the eyes. "You have spoken much nonsense. But in any case, it's as I said. Whether for or against the Hussites, you are all equally my enemies, your entire nation. And Zbigniew Oleśnicki is my bitterest foe."

"The Bishop of Krakow is not your foe," Bnin said slowly. "Which can easily be proved."

"How?"

"By his rendering you a favour."

"In exchange for my consent to Polish intervention?"

"To the glory of God."

"Well, well. And what service will Zbyszko render me?"

"He'll give you information."

"I'm all ears."

"The Bishop of Krakow," said Andrzej of Bnin, weighing up his words, "a good Catholic and an uncompromising enemy of heresy, has men among the Poles who serve the Hussites, as he has among the merchants who do business with the Czechs. He has obtained much information thanks to that, including one piece that is important for you. For Silesia. Concerning the Hussite espionage network operating in Silesia."

"We can cope by ourselves with Hussite spies," said Konrad, pouting his lips.

"Can you indeed?" said the Pole, smiling. "There is one man you cannot cope with."

The day didn't differ in any way from other ordinary weekdays. From the Młynówka came the curses of rafters, the thud of barrels being rolled and the rattle of hammers from the lane beside the church, the cries of stallholders from a side street, and the bleating of sheep and squealing of pigs from the shambles. The monotonous voice of the magister and the voices of the pupils repeating the lesson were lost in the hubbub of the town. Although the voices were barely audible, Wendel Domarasc knew what lessons the boys were repeating. For he had held the post of rector in the Collegiate Church of the Holy Cross in Opole. Had written the school curriculum.

Si vitam inspicias hominum, si denique mores,
Cum culpant alios, nemo sine crimine vivit.

Instinct warned him just in time. Wendel Domarasc sprang up from the table, seized the reports of the agents and tossed them into the fire. A moment before the door was broken down and flew off its hinges, the magister took a blue flacon from a dresser. He managed to drink the contents before the thugs rushing into the chamber twisted his arms behind his back, caught him by the hair and bent his head over. The rector wheezed.

"Let him go."

Although he'd never seen him before, Domarasc knew at once who the man standing in front of him was. He guessed it by the black clothing and the black shoulder-length hair. By the strange, seemingly birdlike physiognomy. And the look of a devil.

"Poisons are like women," said the Wallcreeper, raising the blue vial and turning it over in his fingers. "In two respects. *Primo*: they can't be trusted; they will betray you when you need them most. *Secundo*: they ought to be replaced often. For newer and fresher ones, because they lose all their value when they age.

"You will not flee from me into death," he added with a hideous smile. "Your stale poison won't kill you. You'll suffer at most from diarrhoea. And stomach ache. You're already getting torsions, I see. Sit him up or he'll fall over."

The bruisers searched the chamber, which they did with noticeable expertise. The Wallcreeper closed the window, cutting the chamber off from the hubbub of the street. The voices of the pupils repeating their lesson gained in strength because of it. Individual words could now be made out.

Nolo putes pravos homines peccata lucrari;
Temporibus peccata latent, sed tempore parent.

"*Disticha catonis*," said the Wallcreeper, recognising the words. "Nothing changes. For ages you've been drumming wise words into those boys' heads, over and over the same. You, scholar, were also once flogged in time to those couplets. But it turns out, you weren't beaten hard enough. The lesson wasn't learned; Cato's wisdom evaded your mind. *Temporibus peccata latent, sed tempore parent*. What, did you think you could endlessly hide your practices from us? O spy of spies, O notorious Shadow, O faceless man? Did you hope you'd remain forever unpunished? That was a vain hope, Domarasc, vain. In other words: abandon all hope. Hope is the mother of fools."

The Wallcreeper leaned close and looked the spy in the eyes. Although he was almost fainting from the intensity of the stomach cramps, Wendel Domarasc mustered the strength to look back at him. With calm, steely, disdainful eyes.

"*Spes*," he replied calmly, "*una hominem nec morte relinquit.*"

The Wallcreeper said nothing for a moment, and then smiled. Very hideously.

"Cato," he said, drawing out the words, "didn't have all the answers. His opinions concerning hope were particularly unreasonable. Clearly owing to a lack of personal experience. I presume he'd never been in the torture chambers in the dungeons beneath Wrocław town hall."

Wendel Domarasc, chief resident spy of the Hussite intelligence service in Silesia, said nothing for a long time, fighting intestinal spasms and dizziness.

"The philosopher calls..." he finally said, looking into the Wallcreeper's black eyes. "The philosopher calls patience the greatest virtue. It's enough to sit down on a riverbank and wait. Your enemy's corpse is sure to float past, sooner or later. You'll be able to take a good look at the corpse. Watch the current spin it around. Watch fish nibble it. Do you know what I'll do, Grellenort, when all this is over? I'll sit down on a riverbank. And wait."

The Wallcreeper was silent for a long time. His birdlike eyes were quite expressionless.

"Take him away," he finally spat.

Inquisitor Gregory Hejncze put his hands together and placed them beneath his scapular. The scapular, like the habit, was freshly laundered and smelled of lye. The smell was soothing. It helped him stay calm.

"I wish," said the Inquisitor in a calm voice, "to congratulate Your Eminence on the capture of the Hussite spy. That is a success. A thing of great benefit *pro publico bono*."

Bishop Konrad splashed water on his face, placed a finger against his nose and blew the contents of one nostril into a bowl. He took a napkin from the hands of the servant.

"They say," he said, wiping his face and blowing his other nostril, this time into the napkin, "that you have spent time in Rome?"

"If they say so," Grzegorz Hejncze replied and inhaled the smell of lye, "then I must have."

"How is Holy Father Martin V's health? Does he betray any symptoms? For I hear they prophesy that his days are numbered."

"Who prophesies thus?"

"Soothsayers. After leaving Rome, you reportedly travelled to Switzerland? And how is it in Switzerland?"

"It's lovely. Their cheese is excellent, too."

"And their infantry," said the bishop, shooing away the servant with the basin. He gestured to another who was holding a fur-trimmed mantle to come to him. "Their infantry is also good. Perhaps they'll loan us a thousand pikes when we launch another crusade against Bohemia? Did you talk about that with them? With the Bishop of Basel?"

"I did. They won't. A crusade—they said—will fail dismally. As usual. It's a waste of soldiers."

"Whoresons," said the bishop, wrapping himself up in the mantle and sitting down. "Stinking cheesemakers. Wine, Grzesiu? Drink, don't be afraid. It's not poisoned."

"I'm not afraid," said Hejncze, looking at the bishop over his goblet. "I regularly take a magical mithridate."

"Magic is a sin," said the bishop, chuckling. "What's more, poisons exist for which there are no antidotes and which no spells will help. I assure you there are. I'll tell you more about them another time. But now you speak. What news of Bamberg? My spies inform me that you also visited the Bishop of Bamberg. What of him?"

"I understand Your Eminence is not enquiring about his health?"

"I don't give a shit about his health. I'm asking whether he will join the crusade. Will he offer soldiers, cannons, guns? And if so, how many?"

"His Excellency Frederick of Aufsess," said the Inquisitor, his face as grave as pneumonia, "avoided an unambiguous answer. In another words, he was evasive. Oh well, evasion appears to be permanently and inextricably linked to a bishop's mitre. But the truth peeps out from behind the evasion. It peeps out—to quote the ancients—like an arse from the nettles. It is true that one's own needs are uppermost. In Franconia and Bavaria, the town mob is fomenting, the peasantry is becoming unruly. Reports emerge from France of the Virgin, Jehanne d'Arc, the holy warrior of God. Rumour has it that when *La Pucelle* is done with the English she will lead her people's army against lords and prelates. And Hussites? The Hussites are far from Bamberg, no one in Bamberg fears them, no one believes they will get that far, and even if they do, the city walls are high and formidable. In a word, Bamberg cares nothing for the Hussites. Let those who have reason to, fear them. Those are the words of His Excellency Bishop Frederick."

"To hell with him, the old ass. What about the Archbishop of Magdeburg? I believe you visited him, too."

"I did. Archbishop Gunter of Schwarzburg is too prudent to underestimate the Hussites. He doesn't rule out a crusade and calls enthusiastically for defensive alliances. He is systematically building an army; he now has more than a thousand men under his command. But certain problems, I tell you sincerely, have arisen. For the Archbishop is most irate. With you, Bishop Konrad."

"Indeed," said Konrad bluntly.

"He is irate about an individual who enjoys your good graces," continued Hejncze. "I refer to Birkart Grellenort. The archbishop presented me with a long list of charges. I won't bore you with them, for most are trivial matters: murder, rape, black magic. Also robbery: Archbishop Gunter accuses Grellenort of the theft committed in September 1425 of five hundred grzywna in taxes. But what arouses the greatest fury in the archbishop is a certain non-human, a sverg named—I believe—Skirfir, an alchemist and a sorcerer whom the archbishop wanted to torture and burn, but whom Grellenort impudently abducted. In order to make use of him."

Bishop Konrad chortled. Hejncze eyed him coldly.

"Yes, quite ridiculous," he said and nodded coldly. "And sickeningly banal. But it harms the alliance between Saxony and Silesia, an alliance essential in the face of the Hussite peril. One that is crucial to Silesia's survival. Thus I should like to know what Your Eminence intends to do in this matter."

Konrad became serious and fixed the Inquisitor with his gaze.

"What matter?" he drawled. "I don't see one. Do you, Grzesiu? Are you trying to tell me that even though he is my favourite—and according to common gossip my bastard—I ought to drive him out, curse him, declare him an outlaw, secretly imprison or eliminate him? That I ought to do so for the cause, since Birkart Grellenort is a *persona turpis*, who damages our alliances and relations with our neighbours? I might respond, Grzesiu, by saying that alliances and relations with our neighbours are damaged by idiotic, petty-minded church dignitaries who sulk like children deprived of their toys. I might, but I won't. I'll answer otherwise, concisely and to the point. If anybody—bishop, cardinal, suffragan or Inquisitor, it matters not—tries to bully Birkart Grellenort, he will bitterly regret it, by the Good Lord above."

"The Good Lord above," replied Hejncze without batting an eyelid, "sees and hears everything. With what measure ye mete, it shall be measured to you again. Woe unto them that call evil good, and good evil; that put darkness for light, and light for darkness."

"Platitudes, Grzesiu, platitudes. You parrot the Good Book like a village priest. I said, leave Grellenort alone and leave me alone. Cast the beam out of thine own eye. Or perhaps you'd prefer another biblical quotation? From the Letters to the Corinthians, maybe? Ye cannot drink the cup of the Lord, and the cup of devils: ye cannot be partakers of the Lord's table, and of the table of devils. Reinmar of Bielawa, does that name ring any bells? A heretic, whom you saved from a painful interrogation in Frankenstein by a personal intervention and sheltered until he managed to escape? You gave protection to an old friend. For he is your comrade, your companion, your mate from the varsity. Reynevan Bielawa, an excommunicated heretic and criminal, sorcerer, necromancer, a *persona turpis* indeed. You partake of the table of demons with a necromancer, O Inquisitor. Judge a man by the company he keeps. It may interest you to know that Bielawa was in Wrocław a month ago."

"Reinmar of Bielau?" asked Grzegorz Hejncze, unable to conceal his astonishment. "Reinmar of Bielau, in Wrocław? What did he want here?"

"How should I know?" said the bishop, observing him under half-closed eyelids. "It is an Inquisitor's job—not mine—to track Jews, heretics and apostates, to know what they are plotting and with whom. For I believe, Grzesiu, that you know why Bielawa came here. And what—or rather whom—he was seeking."

From the nearby Church of Peter and Paul came a dreadful, annoying clatter. During the three days preceding Easter, the bells were silent and the faithful were called to church using wooden clappers.

"Hejncze didn't know," said Grajcarek, cringing obsequiously.

"He didn't know Bielawa had been in Wrocław. Or why he was here, to what end. Grellenort was in the residence, hidden, eavesdropping, and after the Inquisitor left, he argued with the bishop. The bishop claimed that Hejncze was dissembling, that he is a cunning fox and sly devil, well versed from the Roman curia in intrigues and scheming. Grellenort, on the other hand—"

"Grellenort," the rosemary-scented woman with the alto voice interrupted pensively, "Grellenort was inclined to believe that Hejncze was really and genuinely astonished."

"He was really and genuinely astonished," repeated the Wall-creeper emphatically. "I'm absolutely certain of it. I cast a spell on him from my hiding place. He had a blockade, naturally, some kind of protective talisman, so I didn't manage to read his mind, but if he was dissembling and trying to deceive, my spell would have uncovered him. No, Kundrie, Grzegorz Hejncze didn't know about Reynevan, the news astonished him, he was surprised that Reynevan had been searching for somebody here. Thought it's hard to believe, Hejncze doesn't appear to know about Miss Apolda. Which would suggest it wasn't the Inquisition that abducted her after all."

"A hasty conclusion," said Kundrie, blinking all four of her eyelids. "Hejncze is not the Inquisition. Hejncze is but a cog in the machine. But the bishop himself is doing his utmost to discredit that cog and eliminate it. Perhaps intrigue has finally yielded success? Perhaps Hejncze has no significance in the machine now, or is of so little importance he isn't being kept informed? Perhaps things go on there behind his back?"

"Perhaps, perhaps," said the Wallcreeper, biting his lip. "I've had enough of theories. I want hard facts. Arcane Knowledge, Kundrie, Arcane Knowledge. Necromancy and goetia. I purposely sent my men to Schönau in order to steal some of Miss Apolda's personal effects, objects she had touched. You received them. And what of it?"

"I'll show you," said the neufra and rose ponderously from the curule seat. "Allow me."

The Wallcreeper thought he knew what to expect. Kundrie usually employed the Longaevi's magic. Probably discouraged by the lack of results, she was now trying the magic used by the Nefandi. The Wallcreeper looked and quickly swallowed the saliva gathering in his throat.

On the table, a long strip of skin, apparently torn from a living person, had been formed into a circle. At regular intervals along it, indicating the corners of a triangle, were a goat's horns, a mummified bat and a cat's skull. The bat had been drowned in blood and the cat had been fed on human flesh before being killed. The Wallcreeper preferred not to know what had been done to the goat. In the middle of the circle, hammered to the table with an iron stub nail, lay a severed human head, already dripping and stinking dreadfully. Kundrie had previously gouged out the eyes—the parts that rot the quickest—and smeared wax into the sockets. The skin around the head's mouth was charred, the lips hanging in twisted shreds, curled up like rotten bark. Before the head lay a pair of severed hands, also nailed to the table. Between the hands lay some kind of skinned and mutilated animal: a large rat or small dog.

"They gave me the scarf," said Kundrie, producing a scrap of grey wool, "which I prudently cut up into pieces. This is all that's left. Look."

She placed the rag between the corpse's hands. The hands twitched and fluttered and the fingers began to suddenly twist and writhe like worms, as though trying to grab the rag. Kundrie raised her hands and held them out in front of her and her fingers were overcome by an uncontrolled shaking, imitating exactly the movements of the hands nailed to the table.

"Iä! Iä! Nya-hah, y-nyah! Ngg-ngaah-Shoggog!"

The severed hands fell into a savage fury, writhing on the nails and drumming on the table. The head's charred lips moved. Instead of the words they were waiting for, a sudden blue flame burst from them; a tongue of flame, burning and at once turning the shred of grey scarf into a tiny pile of grey ash. The objects on the table froze into a macabre tableau.

"What do you say to that, son?"

"Counter-magic."

"And very powerful," confirmed Kundrie. "Somebody is interfering. Somebody doesn't want us to be tracking Miss Apolda or whatever her name is. This magic isn't typical; it has an astral, sidereal trace. Not everybody is capable of using the sidereal element…Why are you grinding your teeth, may I ask? Ah…I understand. It comes back to me. That comrade of Reynevan, the giant with the look of a halfwit. The one who made you flee at Trosky. The second stain on your honour. You claimed—"

"He was an astral being," the Wallcreeper finished her sentence coldly. "Because he is. A visitor from the astral plane. The counter-magic that is hampering us could be his work. I saw his aura at Trosky. I've never seen the like."

"No two auras are identical. And no two pairs of eyes will see the same aura identically. That is called optics. Haven't you read Vitello?"

"I don't mean the aura's colour, size and intensity," said the Wallcreeper, shrugging, "which indeed are variable and depend on the eye of the beholder. What matters is that everything, absolutely everything, in the world has three auras. Living or dead, natural or supernatural, whether from this world or the beyond, everything, absolutely everything, has three auras. Two of them —which are usually yellow and red—almost cleave to the object.

The third pulsates with many colours and hovers at some remove from the object, creating a sphere around it."

"As every schoolboy knows."

"The creature I saw at Trosky had two auras. One, brilliantly golden, was clinging to him, making him look like a statue cast in metal. The other…for there were only two…wasn't an aura in the strict sense. It was a light blue glow. Located behind him. Like a flowing cape, like a train…Or—"

"Or wings?" The neufra snorted. "Wasn't there a mandorla? Or an aureole? A halo above his head? Wasn't eternal light, *lux perpetua*, accompanying the phenomenon? For then it might have been an archangel, for example Gabriel. No, Gabriel, as I recall, was slim, quite small and comely, and the one at Trosky had, so you claim, the face of a moron and the constitution of a giant. Ha, so perhaps it was Saint Lawrence? That one resembled an ox, both in build and intelligence. They roasted him on an iron grid, over coals, *super carbones vivos*. I recall that no matter how much they roasted him he remained underdone. They had to use a mass of *carbones* before he was cooked."

"Kundrie," snarled the Wallcreeper, "I know you're lonely and have no one to talk to, but let the anecdotes go. I don't want anecdotes. I want something specific."

Kundrie bristled her dorsal spines.

"Is advice specific enough?" she hissed. "For I do have some for you. Beware of the halfwit giant. I doubt he is really an astral being, a sidereal being, there haven't been any cases of visits from the sidereal plane for decades. But other beings circulate in this world with auras similar to what you've described and are able to use the astral element. They are also eternal, like us, the Longaevi. And as dangerous as the Nefandi. Your Book calls them the Watchers, but they don't have a name. Few of them remain. But they still exist. And it is dangerous to cross them."

The Wallcreeper made no comment. He just narrowed his eyes, but not quickly enough for the neufra not to notice a flash in them.

"Stop by the day after tomorrow," she said, sighing. "Bring me some aurum. We'll try some fresh spells. Obtain a fresh head, for that one's stinking a little."

"I'll send a servant with the aurum," he replied dryly. "You can keep his head. I have no need for it."

The Easter Mass was over. The prelates and nuns walked down the centre of the nave, dressed in white robes. Their song echoed off the cathedral vault.

Christus resurgens ex mortuis,
iam non moritur:
mors illi ultra non dominabitur,
Quod enim mortuus est peccato,
Mortuus est semel:
Quod autem vivit, vivit Deo.
Alleluia!

The whole of Wrocław appeared to have thronged on Ostrów Tumski. The crush was unbelievable in the squares in front of the cathedral and the two collegiate churches; the crowd was pressing against the halberdiers who were creating a passage for the bishop, the prelates, monks and clergy walking in the procession. The procession continued from the cathedral for further Masses, first to the Church of Saint Giles and from there on to the Church of the Holy Cross.

Surrexit Dominus de sepulcro
qui pro nobis pependit in ligno
Alleluia!

The hooded woman smelling of rosemary caught Grajcarek by the sleeve and pushed him up against a wall, beyond a buttress by the baptismal chapel.

"What do you want?" she snapped. "What do you have that's so desperately urgent? I told you not to meet me during the day. Never mind on a day like this."

Grajcarek looked around, wiped sweat from his brow and licked his lips. The woman watched him attentively. The spy cleared his throat, opened his mouth and shut it again. And suddenly paled.

"Aha," said the woman, guessing at once. "So the bishop has paid you more?"

The spy stepped back, shuddered, feeling the hard resistance of the wall against his spine, and tried to draw in the air a magical character with a trembling hand. The woman was on him. She punched him with a short movement. Then shoved him against the wall with her knee.

"A good Jew doesn't betray," she hissed. "You are a bad Jew, Grajcarek."

A knife flashed, the spy choked and grabbed his throat with both hands, blood pumping between his fingers. The woman pulled his cloak over his head, knocked him to the ground and vanished into the crowd.

"Seize her!" yelled Kuczera of Hunt to his agent. "Seize heeeer!"

The crowd teemed.

Advenisti desiderabilis,
quem expectabamus in tenebris...

Burrowing into the crowd like a mole into the earth, one of the agents caught up with the woman and seized her arm. He saw yellow-green eyes. But had no time to scream as a knife flashed and severed his trachea and gullet. As another agent blocked the woman's way, the crowd swayed and closed around them. The agent wailed, his eyes glazed over, but he didn't fall, instead held upright as limp as a doll, suspended between Heaven and Earth in the throng. People began to shout and a young girl screamed shrilly as she tried to rub the blood from her white Sunday dress with stiff little hands. Kuczera of Hunt pushed his way through the crowd but found only dead bodies. Blood trodden into the cobbles. And the faint odour of rosemary.

Alleluia, alleluia!

The Resurrection procession was approaching the Holy Cross Collegiate Church.

"M'lord…" gibbered Father Felicjan, bending over in a bow. "You commanded me to inform…I am ready…May I speak?"

"You may."

"So I will…It is like this, m'lord…There was a horse fair in Karłowice…They were trading horses—"

"Get to the point," hissed the Wallcreeper. "Get to the point, damned priest. Slowly, clearly and to the point."

"Your Highness ordered me to track the maid…the one they're hiding. I was to inform you at once…I eavesdropped at the Church of Saint Adalbert…When some Inquisition agents were talking together. Dzierżka, the widow of Zbylut of Szarada, the horse trader from Skałka near Środa…She attended the horse fair in Karłowice. And a maid was with her. Pretending to be her daughter, when everybody knows that Dzierżka doesn't have one…And there was a to-do among the merchants, for many wondered about marrying the widow, since the best stud in Silesia is part of her dowry…And here was an illegitimate or adopted maid, in line to inherit—"

"To the point."

"Yes, sire. That maid, that supposed daughter, one agent said to another, appeared from nowhere, as though she fell out of the sky and into Skałka. So I thinks: Why, perhaps she's the maid what Bielawa is seeking. And Your Grace, too? The age would seem to fit…For I heard them talking…They described what the wench looks like…"

"They did, did they? I want that description. Tell me precisely and in detail."

Bishop Konrad listened. Apparently attentively, but the Wallcreeper knew him too well. The bishop was distracted, perhaps because he was sober. His attention was divided between the Wallcreeper, Klaudyna yelling in the ladies' chambers and the shouting of Kuczera of Hunt coming from the courtyard.

"Aha," he said finally. "Aha. So the maid who witnessed and survived the robbery of the tax collector is still alive. Although you've almost had her in your grasp twice, she escaped. And now, you claim, she is hiding in Skałka, on the estates of Dzierżka of Wirsing, the widow of Zbylut of Szarada."

"And we ought, I believe, to do something in that regard."

Konrad scratched the back of his head and poked a finger in his ear.

"But do what?" he asked, disdainfully pouting his lips. "Waste of time and effort. Dzierżka of Wirsing conducts herself in exemplary fashion, doesn't trade with the Hussites any longer and generously supports the Church. I don't see any reason to… But the wench? The wench is nobody. What kind of witness is she? Even if she remembers anything of those events, if she is even capable of identifying anybody, who would listen to her, lend credence to her? For it is well known that maidens imagine various peculiar phantasmagoria when the menstrual vapours assault their minds. Let us not concern ourselves with her. Let us forget about her. Let us forget completely about the misadventure that befell the tax collector. Almost four years have passed. I have forgotten. Everybody has."

"Not everybody," said the Wallcreeper, shaking his head. "The Fuggers, for example, have not. They reminded me about it recently. Believe me, Papa, they will want to get to the truth and will take harsh measures with the guilty, making use of everything they can to achieve that end. Everything. Perhaps that maid is nobody, but she is a threat."

"Well…" said the bishop, interlocking his fingers and tilting his head. "If so…Then do as you think fit."

"And you?" said the Wallcreeper, his birdlike eyes flashing. "Do you, like Pilate, wash your hands of this? It's your arse, I recall, that's on the line—you stole the taxes, it's you whom the girl's testimony may incriminate. If you wish to solve it, don't just wave your crosier around but give me an order. A specific and unambiguous one."

"Birkart," said Konrad, eyes fixed on the Wallcreeper. "Beware. Don't go too far."

They both said nothing, testing each other's resolve with their eyes. Klaudyna had fallen silent and no sounds were coming from the courtyard. Finally, the bishop sat up straight, his features hardened and he pursed his lips.

"On my orders," he said, "you will do what you do. And whatever is done, we, the Bishop of Wrocław, *volumus et contentamur*, accept and consider it as in keeping with our will and take full responsibility for it. Will that suffice?"

"Now it will."

*

The large town clock, a feature of the tower of Wrocław town hall since the times of Bishop Przecław of Pogorzela, its cogs grinding and its springs groaning, suddenly announced the ninth hour of the day with metallic strikes. Now, at the end of March, it meant that around three hours remained to sunset and the *ignitegium*.

Douce of Pack stood in the window, quite naked, her back to the Wallcreeper, leaning against the frame like a caryatid. The Wallcreeper couldn't tear his eyes away from her. He could have gazed at her like that for hours.

"Come here," he said. "Please."

She did as he asked.

"You told me," he said slowly, "that you wish to do what I do. At my side. Do you still? You haven't changed your mind? Are you ready for it?"

She nodded. Slowly.

"If you begin, there's no going back. Do you understand that?"

She nodded again. The Wallcreeper stood up.

"Put these on."

A moment later, she was standing in front of him in a black quilted gambeson, hose and high boots. He helped her don and fasten a breastplate, a gorget, spaulders, vambraces and the other elements of armour. A black headband. A black cloak with a hood.

"Sword?"

"I prefer a javelin."

"Drink this. All of it. Repeat after me: *Adsumus, Domine, adsumus peccati quidem immanitate detenti…*"

"Come to us, remain with us, please enter our hearts."

"Amen. Let's go."

"What was it? The drink?"

"A narcotic."

"It wasn't too tasty."

"You'll grow accustomed to it. Let's go. Aha. One more thing. Tell me."

She raised her head. And her eyes. The colour of the water in a deep mountain lake. Gorgeous. Enchanting. And utterly inhuman.

"What exactly is your name?" asked the Wallcreeper.

Dzierżka of Wirsing didn't know what woke her. It wasn't the barking of dogs. The Skałka dogs, perhaps frightened by a wild animal outside, had barked throughout the night. At first, it had been hard to fall asleep; later, the barking became monotonous and lost its alarming character, until it was simply background noise. So it was probably a dreadful nightmare that made Dzierżka suddenly start, sit up in bed, muscles tense, fully awake and ready for action. Certain that what she had dreaded for the last four years was happening.

The dogs weren't barking.

"Elencza! Wake up! And get dressed!"

"What is it?"

"Get up! And look lively!"

The unnatural, deafening silence was suddenly torn, rent by the scream of a person being killed in the courtyard. Other screams almost immediately accompanied it, and in the blink of an eye the entire Skałka estate resounded with yells and the thudding of hooves. And fire glimmered in the window skins.

"Elencza! Here! This way!"

Dzierżka slid a chest aside, tore a bison skin from the wall and opened a small door hidden behind it. A smell of mustiness and cold air came from it.

"Mistress Dzierżka!"

"Quickly, there's no time! The passageway will take you to a stream. Hide there and don't come out until…Until all this is over. Quickly, girl!"

"What about you? I won't leave you!"

"Into the passageway! At once! Don't you dare disobey me! Go, child, go…"

She shut the door and covered it with the hide and the chest. Then she tore a bear spear down from the wall in the anteroom. And rushed out into the courtyard.

She didn't see anything apart from the confused light of brands showering sparks around. On the very threshold a speeding horse knocked her down, hard on the ground, winding her. Iron-shod hooves struck the ground just beside her, threatening to crush her. She didn't have the strength to move. Somebody seized her and dragged her away. She recognised who it was. It was Sobek Snorbein.

"Madam…Save yourself—"

Sobek Snorbein didn't say anything else. He groaned, fell to his knees and blood gushed from his mouth. Dzierżka saw the blade of a javelin protrude from his chest. A rider flashed past, as blurred as a black nocturnal bird, and she heard a girl's cruel giggle. And a cry.

"*Adsumus! Adsuumuuus!*"

Hooves thudded all around again, there were horsemen everywhere. Black Riders.

"*Adsuumuuus!*"

A woman in a shift came running straight at her with her arms outstretched. A Black Rider swept her head off with a blow of his sword before Dzierżka's eyes. Dzierżka leaped to her feet but was struck again by a horse and knocked over. A noose jerked her up and she was pinned by iron-gauntleted hands on both sides. She hung between two horses. A third pushed against her.

"Where is the maid?"

Dzierżka spat. Something whistled and she saw stars. She cringed with the pain.

"Where is the maid?"

The horsewhip struck again, lashing her. She howled. Her scream joined others coming from the stables and the barns.

"Where is the maid?"

"You won't get your hands on her. She isn't here. She's far away."

The Black Rider bent over towards her from the saddle. She saw his eyes. Birdlike and evil.

"I've ordered your servants, stablemen, serving wenches and children locked up in the stable," he said. "I'll burn them alive in there, roast them with all your horses. I'll roast them all alive if you don't tell me where the maid is."

"You won't get her," she repeated, spitting blood flowing from her cut lips. "You won't ever find her or harm her."

The rider turned around and issued the order. Soon after, the night exploded in a hot blast, was lit up with the red blaze of a huge fire. And filled with ghastly cries and screams, voices that the roar of the conflagration was unable to drown out. The squealing of animals being burned alive. And people.

God, forgive me, Dzierżka repeated in her mind, burying her head in her shoulders under the blows of the horsewhip. *God, forgive my sin. But they would have killed Elencza. And burned the people and horses anyway.*

Fire shot up towards the sky. It was as bright as day. But Dzierżka couldn't see a thing. She was as though blind.

She was knocked over and her ankles bound together with a leather strap. A horse neighed, stamped, the strap tightened, she felt a tug and she was dragged along the ground.

"It's your last chance, horse trader." The Black Rider's evil voice came from somewhere above her. "Tell me where the maid is and I'll give you a quick death."

Dzierżka clenched her teeth. *I'll soon be with you, Zbylut,* came rapid thoughts. *I'll suffer a little, but never mind, I'll endure it. And then I'll be beside you anew.*

A shout, a whistle and the horse set off at a gallop. In Dzierżka's eyes the world became one long, flaming line. The gravel cut her skin like a rasp.

After the third turn she lost consciousness.

"She'll live," stated the monk dryly, the infirmarian from the Friars Minor monastery summoned from Środa Śląska. "She'll survive, if God permits…In time, fresh skin will grow over the wounds. Her bones and joints will knit and heal, God willing…"

"Will she be able to walk?" asked Sir Tristram Rachenau, Lord of Bukowa, biting his moustache. His son, Parsifal, was watching behind him. "Ride a horse? For she's a horse trader, horses are her life. Will she mount a horse?"

The Franciscan shook his head and glanced at Elencza.

"I don't know," he stammered. "Perhaps. Perhaps one day, by the grace of God. She is dreadfully mangled. It's fortunate, m'lord, that you and the troop arrived with help and scared away those men. Otherwise—"

"I simply helped, as befits a neighbour," snapped Tristram Rachenau. "Thus, naturally, she may stay with us. Until she recovers, is able to stand and her men rebuild Skałka. Why, it's a miracle that they broke out of that stable, otherwise they'd all have burned to death, not a soul would have survived. And most of the horses escaped from the fire. Upon my word, it's a miracle, a genuine miracle."

"It was God's will," said the Franciscan, crossing himself. "And I shall stay here, m'lord, if you permit. I must attend the patient ceaselessly, change her dressings. The maid will help me. Miss?"

Elencza raised her head and rubbed her eyelids, swollen from weeping, with her wrist.

"Indeed."

Dzierżka of Wirsing moved in bed, moaning softly beneath the bandages.

It was the thirtieth of March *Anno Domini* 1429.

Chapter Eleven

In which we return to Moravia, to the town and castle of Odry, where the Polish deputation suggests removing the obstacle to strengthening fraternal links with Bohemia, and Reynevan learns this and that about politics.

It was the fifth of April when they reached Odry.

The incident with the fugitive Schilling meant they were concerned about Horn's fate and decided to visit Sovinec on the way. But they didn't have to. The first person they met in the castle courtyard was Urban Horn himself.

When he saw them, his face darkened and his eyes blazed. He didn't make the barest gesture, just stood there calm and unmoving. Perhaps because his movements were severely limited by his thickly bandaged neck and left hand in a sling. And because it was three against one.

"Greetings," Reynevan began. "How are you?"

"As you see."

"Oh, my."

"We left you in better shape, I recall," said Scharley, winking almost imperceptibly at Reynevan and Samson. "Who did that to you?"

Horn swore, spat and glowered at them.

"Schilling," he said, clenching his teeth. "Took me by surprise, the bastard. He escaped from Sovinec."

"Escaped, oh my," said Scharley, wringing his hands theatrically. "Hear that, Reinmar? Samson? Schilling escaped! Too bad, too bad. But on the other hand, good."

"What?" snapped Horn. "What's good about it?"

"That he didn't get far," blurted out Reynevan. "We met. And Scharley here, the one with the grin, sliced him up like a Sunday roast with his sabre. The world is a more beautiful place with one less scoundrel in it. Well, Horn, no offence, let's put this feud behind us. I suggest you cheer up and let's shake hands. Well?"

Urban Horn shook his head.

"You must be in league with the Devil, all bloody three of you. He helps each and every one of you. I'd rather be with you than against you, dammit. No offence. And thanks for that bastard Schilling. Shake, Scharley. Reinmar…Ouch, Samson! Not so hard, not so bloody hard! You'll burst my stitches!"

Prokop the Shaven received Reynevan standing up. He didn't ask him to sit down.

"I sense you expect something," he began bluntly. "What is it? Gratitude for your invaluable contribution to the mission to Silesia? Thus I express my gratitude and assure you your services won't be forgotten. Will that do? Or perhaps you're waiting for an act of contrition by virtue of my having subjected you to a test of loyalty. You won't get one. In any case, you got your own back on Bedřich, I hear. It's a wonder he's forgiven you. Anything else I've forgotten to mention? But be quick, I'm busy—the Polish envoys are waiting."

"My friends want to leave Odry, they wish to visit their loved ones. Will you allow them to leave freely, without let or hindrance?"

"Scharley and that idiot? They can do what they want. They always could."

"What about me?"

Prokop looked away. He looked for a long time through the window at the clouds.

"You, too."

"Thank you, Hejtman. Here is the *decoctum*. I've prepared a whole flacon, there's plenty...Should the pains return."

"Thank you, Reynevan. Go, search for your lady. But before you go, one more thing. One question. And answer me honestly."

"Ask away."

Prokop the Shaven slowly turned his head towards him. He looked daggers at Reynevan.

"Did you inform on Domarasc in Opole? Was he caught because of you? Did you betray him?"

"I didn't betray anyone. Domarasc in particular. I have no idea who he is. I don't know anyone of that name."

"That was the answer I expected," said Prokop, his eyes still fixed on Reynevan. "The very answer. But if by some chance it wasn't like that, then...Then don't come back, Reynevan. Don't come back: flee, drop everything and flee. Because I won't forgive you for Domarasc. If it turns out it was you, that you caused it, I'll kill you. With my own hands. Don't say anything. Now go. God be with you."

They bade each other farewell outside the Upper Gate. A bitter wind was blowing from the Odra, chilling them to the marrow. Reynevan pulled a fur collar up around his ears.

"Come with us," said Scharley, reining in his black horse. "Just come with us. I understand what's still keeping you here. I feel guilty, laddie. My conscience is pricking me. I shouldn't be leaving you."

"I'll be in Rapotín soon," Reynevan lied. "Any day now. Meanwhile, send my good wishes to Mistress Blažena. And my regards to Marketa, Samson. Hug her from me."

"Naturally," said the giant, smiling sadly. "Naturally. We'll be waiting for you, Reinmar. Meanwhile, farewell and—"

"Yes?"

"Don't let them manipulate you. Don't let them use you."

"They didn't invite me to the counsel," said Sigismund Korybut calmly, but it was clear that inside he was boiling over with anger.

"They didn't invite me," he repeated. "And not a man in the Polish deputation even sent me his respects. As though I wasn't even there! As though they didn't know about me! I am their monarch's nephew, dammit! I am a duke!"

"M'lord Your Grace," said Reynevan. He cleared his throat and then began to deliver the prepared speech that Bedřich of Strážnice had given him.

"Please understand the sensitivity of the situation. King Jagiełło has announced to the entire Christian world that you are in Bohemia without his knowledge or involvement and contrary to his wishes. In Poland you are excommunicate and outlawed. Does it surprise you that the official Polish mission wants nothing to do with you? It would be grist to Sigismund's mill, a fresh pretext for Teutonic libels. They would once again declare that Jagiełło supports the Hussites, actively and with arms. For you know, Your Grace, that you are a thorn in Sigismund's side, you and your knights. He knows what power you wield and is simply afraid of you."

A broad smile lit up Sigismund Korybut's face. For a moment, it appeared that pride would split it in two. Reynevan continued the lesson he had learned by heart.

"Though you weren't invited to the counsel, you can be certain you were discussed. I am returning from Silesia, from a mission, so I know that all the plans—and they are great plans—are based on your strength, Duke. Those plans are fully cognisant of your contributions, they won't be forgotten, but will be rewarded."

"I hope so," said the duke, snorting. "Why do you think I am in Bohemia and against Jagiełło's wishes at that? There was a faction in Poland that wanted to exploit the feuds with Emperor Sigismund as a chance to rid the Slavic lands of German influence. That faction exists and grows in strength. Who do you think has just arrived in Odry? I've known for a long time about the planned annexation of Upper Silesia. And I shall support those plans. If I benefit from them, naturally, if they give me what I want. If they cut me out a kingdom from Upper Silesia. Reynevan? Will they give me what I want? What did they discuss? What did they decide?"

"You overestimate me, Your Grace. I don't have that kind of knowledge."

"Indeed? Reynevan, I'm able to repay you. Don't scorn my gratitude when your lady is still being held captive. Find out the decisions reached by Prokop and the Poles and I shall help you to free her. I have men at my command who are capable of stealing the very Devil from Hell. You'll have them at your service. If you do me a favour. Find out what the Poles were discussing with Prokop and what decisions they made. I have to know."

"I shall try."

Korybut said nothing, biting his lip.

"I have to know," he finally repeated. "For it may be that I am here in vain…That I'm just wasting my life."

Reynevan groaned and hissed, massaging his thigh. Urban Horn snorted.

"I've been cut and so have you," he said. "And not shaving this time. What did you say back then? Serious injury to the tissues. Well, he injured our tissues, the fucking bastard, cut us with iron; you with a knife, me with a scrap of metal torn from a door. In spite of that, we are both alive. Do you understand? We can be certain we weren't poisoned with Perferro, that we don't have that devilish poison in our blood. Quite a consolation, don't you think?"

"I do. Horn?"

"Yes?"

"That Polish mission. Do you know who's in it?"

"It is being led by the Chamberlain of Krakow, Piotr Szafraniec of the Starykoń coat of arms, the lord of Pieskowa Skała. Sir Piotr and his brother, Jan, recently elected the Bishop of Kujawy, are sworn opponents of Sigismund and any negotiations with him, which is why they are sympathetic to the Hussites. Władysław of Oporów, Provost of Łęczyca, Deputy Crown Chancellor, a confidant of Jagiełło, came with Szafraniec. You've met the two younger men. Mikołaj Kornicz Siestrzeniec, Burgrave of Będzin, is a client of the Szafraniec family. The Krakow Voivode Spytek is a descendant of the acclaimed Melsztyn Leliwa family. I don't know much about him. But I'm certain I shall hear more."

"What do you think they discussed in the castle? What matters did the Poles bring before Prokop?"

"Can't you guess?" asked Horn, looking him up and down. "Haven't you guessed yet?"

Prokop, as the host, welcomed the guests. The Chamberlain of Krakow, Piotr Szafraniec, gave the welcoming speech, a brief one, for shortness of breath and his six decades of life lay heavily on him. Prokop listened, but clearly with only one ear.

"First of all," he announced impatiently, "let's establish who you represent. King Jagiełło?"

"We represent…" said Szafraniec clearing his throat. "We represent Poland."

"Aha," said Prokop, looking at him keenly. "You mean you're representing yourself."

Szafraniec bristled slightly, was about to say something, but was forestalled by Władysław of Oporów, Deputy Crown Chancellor and Rector of Krakow Academy.

"We represent," he said firmly, "a faction with Poland's future at heart. And since, in our opinion, Poland's future is inextricably linked to Bohemia's, we would be glad to strengthen our connexions. We would be glad to see peace in the Kingdom of Bohemia, see reconciliation rather than havoc and the ravages of war. We desire for there to be agreement and *pax sancta*. For that reason, we also offer our mediation in the negotiations between Bohemia and the Holy See. Since—"

"Since Jagiełło has one foot in the grave," Prokop interrupted him in a calm voice. "He is decrepit and infirm. He desires to leave a Jagiellonian dynasty, ensure his sons a hereditary throne in the Wawel. But the nobility hamper that; those plans are not to their liking. Moreover, the union with Lithuania is threatened, Witold has his eyes on the crown, which Sigismund promised him, and now he gleefully rubs his hands together at the thought of how smoothly the matter had been concocted. Emboldened by this example, Svidrigiello may come up with something recklessly stupid. Meanwhile, the Pope is calling urgently for a crusade to be launched against the Hussites, which is exactly what the Teutonic Knights are waiting for. Have I left anything out, Father Deputy Chancellor?"

"I believe not," said the Deputy Crown Chancellor, this time cutting in before Szafraniec. "You covered everything, Hejtman. In particular, the council at Lutsk and that half-baked idea about the crown for Witold—"

"An idea," Mikołaj Siestrzeniec cut in, "which may turn out to be extremely beneficial for you Czechs. Not only does King Jagiełło disobey the Pope and will not join the crusade against Bohemia, but he means to form an alliance with you. Lutsk enraged him and he is itching to thwart Sigismund and give him a taste of his own medicine. He plans, I happen to know, to attack the Teutonic Knights along with you. Ha, upon my soul! An alliance of Lech and Czech, brother Slavs, fighting shoulder to shoulder against the enemy tribe of Teutons. Do you think of taking your wagons to Pomerania, Hejtman? To the Baltic? To Danzig?"

"We could leave today!" said Dobko Puchała, laughing. Jan Pardus rubbed his hands and grinned. Prokop quietened them with a look.

"The Baltic is far away," he said dryly. "It's a long journey by wagon. And what's more, through a hostile country governed by infernal priests. Who in Poland would give us a hunk of bread, feed and water our horses, when that is punishable by excommunication, infamy or the stake? I'm grateful to you, Burgrave, for informing me of the Polish king's plans. For I think: does Jagiełło have enough strength to carry out those ideas in spite of the priests? Does he have enough time? Before God calls him to Him? Forget Baltic and Danzig, noble Poles. Let's talk about geography closer to home."

"Indeed," said Piotr Szafraniec, nodding. "Much closer, even? Quite literally just over the border? It's true that the union with Lithuania is at risk, and if Jagiełło doesn't act it might mean the end of it. Perhaps, then, we should think about a new union, while there's still time. For we are Slavic folk, emerged from common roots."

"Do I hear right? Are you suggesting a union? Of Poland and Bohemia?"

"What surprises you so? You yourself offered King Jagiełło the Czech crown. Several times."

"And he declined it each time. We understood his reasons, naturally. But the Czechs won't accept a king who doesn't accept the Four Articles of Prague or guarantee freedom of worship."

Szafraniec sat upright. "United by a union, the Kingdom of Poland and the Grand Duchy of Lithuania is a power extending from the Baltic to Crimea," he said proudly. "A force which routed and annihilated the arrogant Teutonic Order at the battle of Grunwald. It is a force which holds in check the savage Tamerlanes, Mehmets and other sons of Belial. But such a powerful entity is at the same time a union of two churches, the Latin and the Greek, and inside such a powerful entity are differences in the dogma of faith: the question of *filioque*, Communion bread, the sacraments, clerical celibacy, et cetera. The Polish crown stands loyally by the Roman faith, yet Lithuania and Ruthenia have the right to practise their religion, there is absolute equality between the two creeds. The rights are the same for all the lands of the kingdom, there are no differences between the Ruthenian nobility and the Polish—"

"Whom are you deceiving, Sir Piotr?" asked Prokop, looking up and twisting his moustache, "yourself or me? Perhaps you'd like things to be so, but they are not. Lofty words about equality and tolerance sound beautiful in the mouths of scholars in Krakow lecture halls. But you won't hear those words outside; the walls of the academy muffle them. Outside university walls, theory ends and practice begins. Polish practice, that is the Roman Church. And what are Orthodox Catholics to the Church of Rome? A pagan sect, schismatics and heretics who fled from the true fold, infected by shameful errors and offences. Men of the ilk of your Oleśnicki speak loudly about the incorporation of Lithuania and Ruthenia into the Crown, even by force, and precisely owing to the inferiority of the Ruthenians and their faith. Is that your union? With nations incorporated by force?

"What guarantee is there that you will not treat us—Czechs who receive the Chalice—just the same in a union with Poland? That you won't want to convert us by force, rechristen us, bring us back to the bosom by compulsion and violence? Where's the guarantee that you won't want to transform Bohemia after the Russian fashion, using the method of divide and rule, turning us into 'bad' schismatics and 'good' Uniates? Dividing us either into the faithful who deserve respect, dignity and privileges or into dissenters whose lot is contempt, discrimination, oppression and persecution? Well? Lord Chamberlain? Answer that!"

"Not everything is ideal in Poland," Spytek answered instead of Szafraniec, who kept silent. "You are right in that, M'Lord Prokop. We also see it. And are pondering changes. I guarantee to you we are."

"Naturally, you are," said Prokop, twitching his moustache. "Now that Svidrigiello is taking action and is being supported by the Ruthenian Orthodox Church as well as the Teutonic Knights. The Orthodox Ruthenia, then, will perhaps receive a handful of privileges, as long as it doesn't support Svidrigiello. While it is needed, it will be gulled by tolerance. But later whatever Rome orders will be done to it."

"*Roma est caput et magistra* for all Christians who believe in God," said Władysław of Oporów. "The Holy Father in Rome is Saint Peter's representative, whether you like it or not. One may not enter into an open conflict—"

"One may," said Prokop, interrupting him. "One may indeed. Enough of this, Father. If I'd wanted to listen to this I'd have gone to Krakow, where you'd have tried to convert me. Then, Oleśnicki would forbid worship in the city and threaten everyone with an interdict. But we aren't in Krakow, we're in Odry.

Which means I am the host and you are my guests. With a mission whose aims I still don't know, although we have wasted plenty of time."

Silence fell for a while. It was interrupted by Piotr Szafraniec, who coughed several times before speaking.

"We won't waste your time then, M'Lord Prokop. We didn't come here to convert you. Nor to persuade you to join a union of Bohemia with Poland, for although I consider such a union a good thing, perhaps it's too early to talk about it. For Poland cannot afford a conflict with Rome, the Teutonic Knights would accuse us again of being pagans. As Poles and loyal subjects of King Władysław Jagiełło, we must take the good of Poland into account."

"Get to the point."

"It would be beneficial for Poland to strengthen its bond with Slavic Bohemia. What harm can come of that? What is hampering agreement? What obstacle lies in the way, driven into the ground like an iron wedge, dividing our lands? Upper Silesia. We can remove that obstacle, Hejtman Prokop. Remove it once and for all."

"Do you understand, Reinmar?" said Urban Horn, quickly sketching a map of the river basin of the upper Odra with a finger dipped in beer. "Upper Silesia linked to Lesser Poland is the Kingdom of Poland combined with Bohemia. Upper Silesia in the Tábor's hands and Poland occupied by the Hussites, under the formal control of Korybut, Bolko Wołoszek and the other Herzogs who lean towards Poland. Cieszyn, Pszczyna, Rybnik, Zator, Oświęcim, Gliwice, Bytom, Siewierz, Opole, Kluczbork, Wołczyn, Byczyna, Namysłów. Over sixty miles of shared border with the Kingdom of Poland. Hussite outposts less than forty miles from the lands of the Order, barely six days' march for the Tábor and their combat wagons, and the Tábor and the Orphans are simply itching to attack the Teutonic Knights. And who is against an annexation, who will protest? Sigismund? Upper Silesia is formally a Czech land, but the Czechs don't recognise Sigismund as king. The Pope? Jagiełło will declare that Silesia has been captured by the brawler Korybut without his knowledge or consent, *sine sciencia et voluntate*, and that the Polish army has occupied the Silesian border fortresses with the sole aim of creating a cordon to prevent the spread of heresy."

"Who will believe such twaddle? Such nonsense?"

"That is politics, Reinmar. Politics has two possible aims: one is accord, the other conflict. Accord is reached when one side pretends to believe in the nonsense the other side is peddling."

"I understand."

"It's time we left Odry. I'm going to Sovinec and then onwards. Schilling's escape complicated my plans; now, what is more, Prokop is sending me on a mission, a long journey. And you, Lancelot, are doubtless hurrying to your damsel in distress. Unless something has changed."

"Nothing has, I'm still in a hurry. But go by yourself. I have to stay here."

On Beltmakers Street, snuggled into the town wall, stood a grim stone building housing the municipal dungeon, torture chamber and executioner's cottage. The place spread a baleful aura over the entire nearby vicinity and whoever could, avoided it; trade and craftsmen had moved away. All that remained was a brewery, and since it brewed good ale, the dreadful location couldn't harm it. There was also, strangely, a beer cellar, with a steep staircase leading down to it. The owner had named the tavern—immune to any associations—The Hangman. The stairs led down to deep, vaulted cellars. Beer was only drunk in the one furthest from the stairs.

Reynevan approached the drinkers. Some time passed before he was noticed. And was greeted with an ominous silence.

"It's Reynevan," Adam Wejdnar of the Rawicz coat of arms finally announced. "The physician from Prague. In the flesh! Praise the Lord, sawbones! Join us, we invite you. You know everybody, I believe."

Reynevan knew almost all of them. Jan Kuropatwa of Łańcuchów, with the Szreniawa coat of arms, and Jakub Nadobny of Rogów, with the Działosza coat of arms, with whom he had quite recently shared a cell, waved greetings, as did Jerzy Skirmunt, with the Odrowąż coat of arms, whom Reynevan knew from his Prague days. Błażej Poraj Jakubowski, sitting beside Skirmunt, knew Reynevan, but didn't hurry to reveal the fact. Reynevan didn't know the others, who were eating kasha from bowls and apparently utterly absorbed in that activity.

However, he did know the ringleader of the entire *comitiva*, a grey-haired man with a craggy, pockmarked face. He remembered Fedor of Ostrog, Starosta of Lutsk, Ruthenian prince, from the time of the previous year's plundering raid on Silesia. The latter wasn't taking his small black eyes—whose piercing malevolence not even the semi-darkness of the chamber could conceal or temper—off Reynevan.

"The two eating kasha," said Wejdnar, continuing to introduce the guests, "are Sir Jan Tłuczymost of the Bończa coat of arms. And Daniło Drozd of the boyars, from the east of Poland. "Sit you down, Reynevan."

"I'll stand," said Reynevan in an official tone. "For I don't have much time, either. Duke Sigismund Korybut, whom you serve, asked me to make contact with you. You should know, gentlemen, that I rendered the duke certain services and in return he promised me *auxilium* with certain issues that are impeding me. Do I take you to be that *auxilium*, gentlemen? Will you be helping me?"

A long, sullen silence fell.

"*Nu*, well I never," said Fedor of Ostrog finally. "Why, if we haven't got this upstart German, the Devil take his mother. Listen you…*Nu*, I've forgotten his name."

"Reynevan," said Kuropatwa.

"Listen you, Reynevan, to hell with your *xylium* or *consilium*, leave them to pediments and other fucking sodomites. We are ordinary men and such French fashions disgust us. If you don't want to sit, stand, I don't give a damn either way. But tell us what they told you to say."

"What do you mean?"

"*Herrgott!* Korybut told us you knew when and by which road a transport of money, serious money, is coming to Odry. From Poland or from Silesia. The prince told us you would reveal which route they would take."

"Duke Sigismund Korybut," Reynevan replied slowly, "didn't say a word about a transport of money. And even if he had, I would certainly not share that information with you, gentlemen. It seems to me there has been a misunderstanding. I repeat, the duke promised me your service—"

"Service?" interrupted Fedor. "We are to serve *you*? Fuck you! I am a prince, the Lord of Ostrog, dammit! *Baszom az anyat!* I fuck your mother! Korybut won't order me about! Who does he think he is? Korybut, a duke in name only, a client of the Czechs!"

"I understand," said Reynevan, raising his head with a proud look. "That has been made clear. In which case, I bid you farewell, gentlemen."

"Wait," said Jan Kuropatwa, getting up from the table. "Wait,

Reynevan, why so hasty? Let's talk. You said you need help. Why, we're happy to offer you help if you also help us in our venture—"

"What venture? In a robbery?"

"And are you so honourable?" asked Nadobny. "Eh? Giving yourself airs? And what profits has soldiering brought you? What this revolution? Wounds, bruises, anathema and infamy, as it has us. Isn't it time to think about your own good, health and happiness, physician?"

"What will benefit us," Kuropatwa declared emphatically, "will also benefit you. If you help us in our venture, we will give you a cut, you'll fill your purse. Am I right, M'Lord Ostrog?"

"Farewell to you, sirs," said Reynevan, not waiting for the prince's confirmation. "God be with you."

"Where do you think you're going?" Fedor of Ostrog asked coldly. "To inform to Prokop? No, my lad, nothing doing. Take him, Kuropatwa!"

Reynevan ducked and pushed Kuropatwa onto Nadobny. As Wejdnar leaped up from the bench, Reynevan kicked him in the knee in the style of Scharley and punched him in the nose as he fell. Tłuczymost of the Bończa coat of arms went for him and seized him. Daniło, the boyar from eastern Poland, lunged across the table to assist, knocking off and smashing plates and dishes. Ostrog, Skirmunt and Jakubowski didn't move from their seats.

A knife flashed in the boyar's hand. Reynevan tore himself from Tłuczymost's embrace and reached for his own dagger, but Wejdnar pulled down on his elbow and Kuropatwa grabbed his left wrist. The peasant Daniło stabbed. But Reynevan recalled Bruno Schilling, the renegade from the Company of Death.

He tilted his torso back, feeling on his chest the elbow of the armed hand. He bent it with a quick movement of his body, twisted it, turned it around and shoved with his shoulder as hard as he could. Astonishingly, it worked, although not as he had planned. Instead of plunging into his throat, the reversed blade only slit open his cheek. The boyar bellowed like a wild thing, splashing blood over himself and everything else. Fedor of Ostrog roared.

Tłuczymost screamed and fell, struck by the pommel of a short sword. Nadobny, cut in the hand, screamed. Kuropatwa, on the receiving end of a punch and a kick, flew onto the table among the broken bowls and spilled beer.

"Run for it, Reynevan!" shouted Urban Horn, swinging his short sword and knocking Wejdnar back down with a kick. "Run for it! To the stairs! Follow me!"

Reynevan didn't need to be told twice. They heard from below the howling of the boyar. And the furious yelling of Prince Fedor of Ostrog.

"*Baszom az anyat!* I fuck your mother! I fuck your world! I fuck your mother, the fucking whore!"

"Dammit," said Urban Horn, hunching over in the saddle. "I'm bleeding. My stitches have burst from all this exertion."

"Mine have, too," said Reynevan, feeling his thigh and looking back. "I'll sort it out, I have instruments and medicines with me. But first of all, let's get away."

"Let's get away," agreed Horn. "As far away as possible. Farewell, town of Odry. What will become of us, comrade? Will you ride with me to Sovinec?"

"No. I'm returning to Silesia. Have you forgotten? My damsel, Guinevere, is in distress."

"Then rescue her, Lancelot. And the evil kidnapper, Maleagant, ought to get his just desserts. To horse."

"To horse, Horn."

They galloped away.

Chapter Twelve

In which the woman smelling of rosemary offers to help and cooperate with Reynevan, as a result of which matters take a sudden turn for the worse. The situation is saved by a legend which—like a *Deus ex machina*—suddenly emerges from a wall.

Not far from the school, opposite the building of the Knights Hospitaller commandery, a fellow in a black mantle, with long, straggly shoulder-length hair, was standing on a low wall in order to be higher than the crowd gathered in front of him.

"Brothers!" he shouted, gesticulating energetically. "The Antichrist has manifested himself! Accompanied by signs and false miracles! He is the prophesied killer of saints, who sits like a tyrant in the city of seven hills! Satan's representative and leader of Satan's minions governs in Rome, defiling the Holy See! Indeed, do I tell you: the Roman Pope is the Antichrist! An abomination sent by Hell!"

The small crowd of listeners grew and closed in. The faces of the listeners were grim; grim was their silence, evil, weighty: like the grave. This was strange, since this type of performance—quite commonplace in recent times—was usually accompanied by laughter, cheers and cries of approval, along with whistles and insults.

"What are the Roman Church and the damned clergy today?"

called the long-haired man in excitement. "They are a conspiracy of apostates and swindlers, driven only by avarice. A gang of malefactors rolling around in filth and debauchery, satiated on wealth, power, honours, attired in a semblance of sanctity and a mask of religion, making an outrageous tool of the holy name of God, an instrument for its misrule. It is the Whore of Babylon attired in crimson, drunk on the blood of martyrs!"

"Well, well," said an alto voice as soft as satin behind Reynevan. "A gang of malefactors. A drunken whore. Who'd have thought that things would come to this. Truly, a time of great changes has dawned."

He turned around. And recognised her right away. Not just by her voice. The illusion she had disguised herself with in Wrocław couldn't hide what he saw again now. The insolent, yellow-green eyes. Eyes he remembered.

"Only a year ago," she said, moving closer to him, quite unceremoniously linking an arm through his, "only a year ago the mob would have been chased away and the rabble-rouser arrested. But now look: he talks and talks. And in a busy part of the city. Has something ended? Or begun, perhaps?"

"Who are you?"

"Not now."

He felt her warmth against his side, emanating through her cloak and padded man's doublet. He also remembered her warmth from back in Wrocław, when searching for symptoms of the plague on her body. Her hair was under a hood, but it gave off the faint scent of rosemary he remembered from Racibórz.

"Verily do I tell you," said the fellow in the mantle, becoming more and more heated and raising his voice, "that the Roman Church is not the Church of Christ, but the Diocese of the Devil, a den of brigands! Hallowed laws, Divine mysteries and the incarnation of the Word are all haggled over! The indivisible

Trinity is divided into pieces. Cunning fraudsters, false prophets, deceitful priests, lying teachers, treacherous shepherds! They were prophesied to us! It was predicted: owing to them, the way of truth will be obscured by blasphemies; to satisfy their own avarice, they will sell you with duplicitous words. And look at the Roman curia, at its bulls, its false Masses and indulgences. In truth, are they not selling us? Are they not selling our souls to damnation?

"Brothers! We must distance ourselves from the scoundrels and rogues sent by the Devil. We cannot commune with them or join the abomination they are creating. For in the whole of creation there is only good and evil, believers and non-believers, light and darkness, those who are of God and those who consort with Belial against the will of God!"

"Let us not tempt fate," said the owner of the yellow-green eyes, her rosemary scent surrounding him. "All well and good talking of changes, but this world has a long way to go before it becomes ideal. There is darkness, there is light and there are those that inform. In a moment, there will be thugs from the town hall and the Inquisition's lackeys. Let's get out of here."

"Where to?"

"Out of here, I said."

"No. First explain to me—"

"Do you want to recover Jutta or not?"

"Tremble before the wrath of the Lord," they heard as they walked away, "ye, who believed the lies and closed your ears to the truth. Ye who embraced immorality and are entering debauchery. Ye, on whom the sentence of damnation has lain for long ages! Tremble and repent! For a day of wrath is nigh, a forlorn day, a day of tears. Judgement Day is nigh!"

"*Dies irae, dies illa,*" mumbled the mysterious green-eyed woman, pressing herself against his arm. "*Et lux perpetua.*"

"Where are we going?"

"To the synagogue. But don't worry, I won't try to convert you. You can be a goy until Judgement Day. But spies don't frequent the synagogue. They don't look in there. They're afraid of Jewish spells."

In the end, they didn't enter the synagogue, which was located in the north-east part of Strzegom, not far from the New Gate. Instead, they sat down on a low wall and talked, hidden behind the staircase leading to Ezrat Nashim, the women's courtyard. Reynevan felt uncertain and tense under the piercing gaze of the strange woman's eyes; yellow-green eyes like a cat's and equally inscrutable. He was decided. Having had enough of uncertainty. Enough of mysteries. And enough of being manipulated.

"First things first," he interrupted her, soon after she began speaking. "Let's begin with this. Who are you? Why did you help me in Wrocław, why did you intervene when I was arrested? Why are you here now, in order, you claim, to help me to free Jutta? Whose instructions are you executing? For it's clear you aren't doing it on your own initiative, independently, touched by human misfortune."

"And why is that so clear?" she asked, tilting her head. "Don't I look like somebody who might be moved by misfortune? First things first, you say. Agreed, as long as we can establish what comes first. I'm prepared to introduce myself. Once I give it some thought. In any case, you asked me in Racibórz in the spring. You have the right to know a little about me. And some more besides."

She pulled the hood off her head and tossed her hair, which was as black and lustrous as a raven's feathers.

"My name is Rixa Cartafila de Fonseca. You may call me Rixa. Why do you stare so?"

"I do not."

"You do. Are you looking for where my *Judenfleck* is sewn on? Would it be easier for you if my name were Rachel? Or Sara?"

"Enough,"he said, regaining his poise,"you've introduced yourself, thank you, I'm honoured, the pleasure is all mine."

"Are you quite sure it's a pleasure?"

"Oh, indeed. We shall leave that issue for now. Let's move on to the others."

"I can't tell you whose orders I'm executing. I cannot and that is final. What you know will have to suffice."

"Well, it doesn't. Your own secrets are your business. If they are personal to you, may they remain secret. But not where they concern me. You want something from me. I want to know—"

"Agreed,"she interrupted him at once."It's high time you found out. There is no way of concealing it any longer. I want from you exactly what Łukasz Bożyczko and the Inquisition want: collaboration and information. Bożyczko is compelling you to collaborate using blackmail and threats. I want to convince you to collaborate by showing you a community of interests. In principle, I already have. I've made sure nothing bad has befallen you; I've acted as your guardian angel. And now I shall help you regain Jutta. I offer my help, my immediate assistance, we can set off today. Is that little?"

"It is much. But finish, please."

"You are close to Prokop," she said, squinting. "Close to Little Prokop, Puchała, Bedřich of Strážnice, Sigismund Korybut, Královec. You know Kolda of Žampach, Piotr the Pole and Jan Čapek. They take you into their confidence everywhere and share their secrets. I also want to be party to them. Do we understand each other?"

"No."

"You will inform me about the Hussites' plans. But in detail,

Reinmar, in detail. No prophecies of Malachy, no dates of deaths or similar oracular revelations."

"You eavesdropped on us in Racibórz. Eavesdropped on me and Bożyczko."

"Indeed, I did. You impressed me then, do you know? You gave him information, but without betraying your convictions, without betraying or harming anyone. Of course, had it not been for my intervention then, Bożyczko would have forced you to disclose more significant things. And since I hampered him in his efforts, it will only be fair if you share that information with me now."

"An interesting understanding of fairness," he said, standing up. "Listen, Rixa Fonseca. I won't be your informer. You won't learn anything from me. If that is the condition of our collaboration, there won't be any."

"I'm on your side," said Rixa, also standing up. "I've proved it. I'm not persuading you to be duplicitous. I'm not forcing you to betray anybody. I want collaboration. Mutually beneficial cooperation."

"Mutually beneficial. Remarkable."

"I repeat, I'm on your side. And also on the side of the ideals you are loyal to."

"Of course." He snorted. "You support the Chalice with all your heart and love the Hussite movement, so out of love you want to spy on Prokop and infiltrate the Tábor. That is, as I see it, a refined level of politics. I know something about politics and know it has two possible aims: one is accord, the other conflict. Accord is reached when one side pretends to believe in the nonsense the other side is peddling. We two, unfortunately, are conflicted. I don't believe in the nonsense you are peddling, and don't mean to pretend that I do."

She fixed him with her eyes.

"I'm not making you believe me. I want collaboration, not belief."

"I won't be your informer, and that's that. Thank you for the help. Thank you for your efforts thus far, my guardian angel."

"Are you not perhaps forgetting something? What about Jutta?"

"You'll achieve nothing by blackmail. Farewell. God be with you."

"Quiet," she said, smiling, "or the rabbi will hear you. Reynevan, I was only teasing you."

"Say that again."

"I was teasing you. I was wondering how you would react. I'm on your side. I don't want any information from you. I won't persuade you to give up any secrets. I'll help you to find Jutta and free her without any additional conditions or obligations. Do you want to recover Jutta?"

"I do."

"We'll set off this very day."

"I have a request."

"Yes."

"Don't tease me again. Not ever again."

After they had left the town, Reynevan, deep in thought, looked back several times. *Fate has brought me here for the third time*, he thought, *the third time in the last four years. I met Scharley at the Battle of Strzegom, I saw him in action in Strzegom, when he gave those three fops a hiding. The two of us fled from Strzegom, escaping the pursuers who were sent after us. That was in the summer of 1425. I fought at Strzegom a second time four months ago, in February, on Ash Wednesday, when the Orphans' bombards and onagers hurled balls and burning missiles at the town. The marks of that bombardment are still visible. I left Strzegom to search for Jutta in Wrocław . . .*

"I searched for Jutta in Wrocław," he said to Rixa, who was riding alongside. "I searched for her in Ziębice, in White Church, in Strzelin, in Niemcza and in Oława. I used magic, but in vain. I tried intimidation and blackmail. What now? Where are we headed? What are our plans?"

"Like you," said Rixa Cartafila of Fonseca, turning around in the saddle, "I also began in Ziębice. I was aware of Duke Jan's customs. He would transport maidens to indulge himself with them and didn't like to travel far to that end. Having marked out a circle with a radius of a mile around Ziębice, it would have been possible in no more than two days to find Jutta Apolda, like Rapunzel, looking out of a tiny window in some castle or convent for her fairy-tale prince. But the Inquisition was too quick. They kidnapped Rapunzel and now you won't see her again."

He glanced at her and his expression must have spoken volumes, for she grew serious at once.

"Magic won't help, since they used protective spells," she said. "Blackmail and bribery are effective methods, but not for a coward and scoundrel like Father Felicjan. But don't worry. There are other ways. We are riding, as you noticed, along the Jawor road. In Jawor we will visit a person who is usually well informed, and we shall try to persuade them to share that information with us. But that is tomorrow. It's important that we are there in the morning, and I don't want to spend the night in Jawor, for there are too many snoopers sniffing around the inns there. Thus we will stop for the night in Rogoźnica at the Stork. It's safe and the fleas occur in reasonable and tolerable quantities. Rein in your horse. I must tell you something. And warn you."

"Yes?"

"We are posing as travelling church clerks; they don't arouse suspicion or even curiosity. As long as they behave normally. Like clerks."

"Meaning?"

"When staying at an inn they always take one chamber with a single bed. To keep costs down. Customarily."

"I understand. But what did you want to warn me about?"

Rixa laughed out loud.

The innkeeper at the Stork accepted them as two clerks without a trace of doubt or a second thought, which reinforced still further Reynevan's conviction that Rixa was using camouflaging spells and empathic magic, not to mention amulets like the Pantaleon, which she certainly had. Without the innkeeper objecting and for a reasonable price, the "clerks" were given the keys to a small room in the loft furnished with a single stool and a single bed. Without further ado, Rixa took off her jerkin and boots, tried the palliasse and flopped back down on it, gesturing for Reynevan to lie beside her.

They lay motionless. A woodworm tapped inside the wall. Mice rustled and scratched in the ceiling. Rixa Cartafila of Fonseca cleared her throat loudly.

"This is perilous," she said, looking up at the ceiling. "Two people of the opposite sex in one bed. There's a great risk of sin. And an even greater one of unwanted pregnancy. Luckily it doesn't affect us. We're safe. Protected by the law."

"Yes?"

"If a Jew is caught sinning with a Christian woman, they cut off his cock and gouge out one eye. A Christian who lies with a Jewess risks graver consequences. He is in danger of being accused of *bestialitas*, of debauchery *contra naturam*. And the stake is certain for something like that."

"Ah."

"What do you mean, 'ah'? Are you afraid?"

"No."

"You're a bold one! Or perhaps it's not courage but ignorance of the dangers? For you don't know me; don't know with whom you're sharing a bed. For I am a terrible woman. It's in my blood."

"What is?"

"Jews caused the death of the Saviour, didn't they? It is just and natural that those guilty of the Saviour's death should bear the mark of their villainy for ever and a day."

"Meaning?"

"The blood of many generations of the chosen people flows in my veins. When Jesus was being taking to Golgotha, my fore-bear Levi spat on him, and since then every Levite has had a permanent frog in his throat; he cannot cough it up. Jews of the tribe of the Gad—who I am related to—placed the crown of thorns on Jesus's head, for which reason every year foul-smelling scabs erupt on their scalps which can only be healed by rubbing Christian blood on them. And finally, the most terrible: the tribe of Naphtali forged the nails for the crucifixion, and on the advice of a Jewess by the name of Ventria—undoubtedly a forebear—blunted their points in order to increase Jesus's suffering. For that wickedness, when women of the tribe of Naphtali reach thirty-three, live worms hatch in their mouths as they sleep. But don't be afraid, my boy, sleep peacefully. I'm only twenty."

"Ought I to be afraid?" asked Reynevan, playing along. "Me? I can do even better. I'm a sorcerer, I know the *artes prohibitae*. It flows in my blood; I'm utterly pervaded with dreadful black magic. When I pee, a rainbow appears above the stream."

"Oh! You must show me."

"What's more, I'm a Hussite," he announced proudly. "During holidays, I walk around quite naked and look forward to the day when wives will be shared among men. Just to warn you, I'm also a heretic. Do you know, dear girl, anything about our practices? At our secret heretical gatherings, Satan appears in the form of a black tomcat, whose tail we—heretics and Hussites—lift and then kiss its arse one after the other."

"You might actually be kissing a Jewish arse," added Rixa, pretending to be just as serious. "For, as Pierre de Blois teaches, the Jew, following the ways of the Devil, his father, often assumes monstrous forms."

"Yes. You are right. It is possible. Goodnight."

"Goodnight, Reinmar. Sweet dreams."

They arrived in Jawor the following day. Rixa knew the way and they reached their destination without a hitch; she was clearly at ease.

"You feel at home here."

"I *am* at home," she said, laughing. "This is River Street. The person we are visiting lives here."

"And this well-informed individual," asked Reynevan, guessing. "Who would it be? What is his profession?"

"It is Maizl Nachman ben Gamaliel. He loans money at interest."

"Is he a usurer?"

"No. A financier."

The house in River Street was grand but severe, without any decoration. It resembled a small fortress. It was surrounded by a wall, the door in the large arcaded porch was equipped with a metal hasp and staple and completed by a brass knocker and a tiny window. Rixa took hold of the knocker and banged it vigorously. A moment later the window opened.

"*Nu?*" came a voice from inside.

"*Shalom*," said Rixa in greeting. "We are wanderers, here to see the honourable Maizl Nachman ben Gamaliel."

"He's not in."

"I am Rixa Cartafila of Fonseca," she said, and a sinister note was suddenly audible in her voice. "Tell the rabbi, servant. If he's not in, may he tell me himself."

They had to wait again for a few moments.

"*Nu?*"

"Rabbi Maizl Nachman ben Gamaliel?"

"Never heard of him. And he's not in."

"We won't take much of your time, Rabbi. Let us in, please. We only need some information."

"*Nu?* And what else do you need? Cash, perhaps? Perhaps my wife should make *Gefilte Fisch* for you? Perhaps you'd like to rest your weary feet here? Begone, goys."

"Rabbi—"

"Still here? Do they want me to bless them? Schmul! Bring the gun!"

"Rabbi Maizl," said Rixa, lowering her voice and holding a clenched fist up to the window. "I'd be careful with that gun. I am Rixa Cartafila of Fonseca. I wear the ring of tzaddik Chalafta."

"*Oy vey!*" came the voice from inside. "And I'm King Solomon. And I have a ring for sealing jinns in jugs. Go away, troublemakers."

"Don't call me a troublemaker, Rabbi," hissed the woman. "I am Rixa Cartafila of Fonseca. I can't believe you haven't heard of me."

"*Nu?* Maybe I have, maybe I haven't," a slightly gentler voice replied from inside. "Such times are they that a fellow can pay heed neither to his eyes nor his ears. Never mind rumours. Try going to town. See what's brewing there. Judge for yourselves: can a Jew open his door in such times? Even a Jew who might know something about somebody? No, O girl-with-the-ring-of-tzaddik Chalafta. It's unwise to open the door if there's naught but evil outside. Go and see. Find out for yourselves. *Oy*, and if you had a door, you wouldn't open it, either."

The streets of Jawor appeared strangely deserted. And silent. Something vaguely evil hung in the air—aside from the usual stench of manure and rotting meat—something that made the hair stand up on the back of the neck and sent shivers down the spine. Something that made most of the townspeople stay circumspectly at home.

Rixa knew her way around. From the town square she turned into a lane where a large and colourful sign pointed the way towards the Sun and the Moon inn. Inside, in contrast to the outside, there were plenty of people; it was quite simply packed. It was impossible to know exactly, but Reynevan guessed that the inn was playing host to at least a hundred people. On top of that, they were all talking, so their heads were filled with a steady hum of voices.

Rixa looked around cautiously, then quickly moved towards a corner where a grey-haired man in a felt hat with a slightly torn brim was sitting, his moustaches drooping into a mug of beer. The woman sat down beside him and nudged him with her elbow.

"Miss?"

"Greetings, Schlegelholz. Been here all morning?"

"My soul aches," said the grey-haired man, wiping his moustache. "I must soothe it somehow…Dreadful times… Dreadful…"

"What is happening?"

"An atrocity, an atrocity has happened. We shall all die. There's no saving us from the plague, none."

"What's the matter?"

"It'll be four days since," said Schlegelholz, taking a long draught of beer, "since a pig's head, skinned clean, was removed from the well by Saint Martin's. And just after that, Madam Kunc, the baker's wife, lost a child. It means they infected the water. With bubonic plague. They tossed an infected swine into the well."

"Who?"

"Who, who? It's obvious who. So the townsfolk have gathered and are debating. You can see for yourself, Miss."

"I see," said Rixa, pointing at a man in a patched jerkin who had just stood up on a bench and from his elevated position gestured to the gathering to be kind enough to be quiet. "That character and his company, who are they?"

"Strangers. They arrived not long ago, Queer folk."

"Jawor people," yelled the man in the patched jerkin, "I see you're letting them spit in your broth and push you around! Have you people so lost heart? Your fathers gave the Jews a little pogrom in 1420 and you should have finished them off, shouldn't have left any alive! But what do you do? They're poisoning your wells and you sit and sip beer? What else will you let the damned Jews do? Steal the Host from the church and defile it like they did in Bautzen? Allow them to draw your children's blood like in Zgorzelec?"

"Or perhaps," said another, with hair as curly as a ram's fleece, standing up, "you'll wait for the Hussites to come and for the Jews to open the gates for them, like they did in Frankenstein last year? What, didn't you know? You perhaps don't know either that the Israelites planned to turn Kłodzko over for the Hussites to sack by starting a fire in the town. Don't you know that Juda has been in cahoots with the Czech heretic from time immemorial? Didn't your priest tell you that in his sermons? That there's a conspiracy of Satan, the Jew and the Hussite? What? He didn't? Then take a closer look at your shepherd, Jawor folk. Watch what he does, listen out for what he says. There are plenty of apostates among the clergy, too, plenty of them have succumbed to Satan's instigation! If you think something's not right with your priest, inform on him! Inform your lords at once!"

More and more locals were getting up and darting stealthily towards the exit. The faces of those who remained weren't betraying undue enthusiasm.

The speakers noticed it.

"You're cowards and beggars!" shouted the man in the patched jerkin. "We ought to be informing on you! For if a man isn't against the Jews, he's clearly in league with the Devil and is just like a Jew! Jews, I say, have yielded to evil powers! The enemy hand of Juda draws the Christian away from the true faith. Would there have been Huss without the Jew? Who, if not the Jew, following the Devil's instigation, incited the Czechs to heresy? For the filthy Hussite sect models itself on nothing other than the Talmud! And is grounded in the Kabbalah!"

"After Satan," echoed the curly-haired man, "Christians have no greater enemy than the Jews. In their revolting daily prayers, they solicit our destruction, they curse us, they use their magical rites and exhortations to beg Satan, their father and God, to wipe us out. A century ago, they tried to destroy us with the Black Death. They failed; Christ proved to be stronger. And now they have brought forth the Hussites. To bring about the doom of us, Christians!"

"Let's go," said Rixa, standing up, pulling on her hood. "I've heard it before, I know it by heart. Schlegelholz, you never saw us. Is that clear? I was never here."

Before they pushed their way through to the exit, a third speaker, head shaved to the skin, hopped onto a bench.

"Do you sit by calmly, Jawor folk? Then you have piss, not blood, in your veins, if you tolerate the stinking Judaists and their damned synagogue in the town. If you allow heretics, mages, infanticides and poisoners to live among you! Thieves and usurers, bloodsuckers like the fucking chief Jew here, Maizl Nachman! He ought to have been clubbed to death long ago!"

"Well, well," muttered Rixa. "Something new at last, our patience has been rewarded. Now I know who, what and why. I know the fellow. He's a former Cistercian monk, a fugitive from the monastery in Doberlug. He's shaved his head to hide the tonsure. He's an agent of the Inquisition. It looks as though a nice little provocation is being prepared here."

"The Inquisition? Impossible," said Reynevan, growing annoyed. "Grzegorz Hejncze would never lower himself to—"

"Not Wrocław. Magdeburg. Don't look at them, don't draw attention to yourself. We're leaving."

"It doesn't concern you, Reynevan. It isn't your war," said Rixa, adjusting the mail shirt she was wearing and removing a curved backsword from her bundle. She drew it from its sheath and it whistled as she brandished it.

"I've checked, asked around," she said. "There are plenty of them. A large gang has come from Magdeburg. In addition to agents provocateurs there are also killers. Fourteen men. They'll attack as soon as it gets dark."

Reynevan unfastened his hunting crossbow, unpacked it and slung a quiver of bolts across his back. He checked his knife and additionally slipped a misericord into his boot. Rixa looked on in silence.

"It doesn't concern you," she said. "You don't have to get involved and risk your neck."

He looked her in the eyes.

"You said you wouldn't tease, I remind you. Let's go."

*

They didn't have to wait long for the Magdeburg Inquisition, who attacked right after dusk fell. Shadowy shapes, moving so fast the eye couldn't follow them, suddenly emerged from the darkness to appear outside the house in River Street. A battering ram slammed into the door. The house was at the ready and answered. There was a boom and fire spurted from the hatch in the door. There was a surge among the figures and a cry. The battering ram slammed into the door again; this time a long-drawn-out crack announced success. Rixa spat on her hand and seized her backsword.

"Now! Have at them!"

They rushed out of the lane, falling among the men crowded at the door, surprising and jostling them. Reynevan thrust quickly with his knife, Rixa smote with wide blows of her backsword. Cries and curses filled the lane.

"Inside!"

From behind the damaged hasp and staple, the hand cannon fired again, ball shot wailed. In the flash of the gunfire, Reynevan saw just before him the man with the shaven head holding a battleaxe raised to strike. He grabbed the crossbow slung over his shoulder and shot from the hip, without aiming. The shaven man groaned and slumped to the ground.

"Inside!"

The attackers also had crossbows and harquebuses. As Reynevan and Rixa rushed into the courtyard, it suddenly became bright with gunfire, bolts were hissing through the air. Reynevan, deafened by the roar, tripped on a corpse, fell into a pool of blood. Somebody running after him tripped over him and fell alongside with a clank. Reynevan hit him with the crossbow and quickly rolled away, right by the feet of the next. Just beside his head something clanged metallically against the cobbles, throwing up sparks. He jerked the misericord from his boot, leaped to his feet and thrust so hard his shoulder crunched, the four-sided blade penetrating the rings of the mail shirt with a grinding noise. The assailant howled, collapsed to his knees, dropping a heavy iron hook right on Reynevan. He caught the hook, swung and whacked the kneeling man and felt and heard the hook penetrate his skull.

"Reynevan! Here! Quickly!"

Somewhere in the courtyard there was a howl, a wheeze and a choke. Reynevan leaped to his feet and ran towards the entrance of the house. A crossbow bolt whistled just above his head. Something boomed and flashed, a fiery puddle stinking of burning fat spread over the stones of the courtyard. Another bottle smashed against the wall of the house and burning oil ran in a cascade over the cornices. A third smashed on the steps, the flames at once engulfing the two bodies lying there; blood hissed as it evaporated. More missiles flew from the entrance. It suddenly became as bright as day. Reynevan saw a bearded man in a fox fur cap kneeling behind a pillar in the porch. It could only have been the householder, Maizl Nachman ben Gamaliel. Beside him knelt a youngster, trying to load a hook gun with shaking hands. Behind another pillar stood Rixa Cartafila of Fonseca with her curved backsword, and the expression on her face made Reynevan shiver. Just behind Rixa, holding a harquebus, was...

"Tybald Raabe? You, here?"

"Duck!"

Bolts flew from the door, chipping plaster from the wall. The youngster trying to charge the hook gun screamed piercingly and curled up into a ball. Rixa retreated from the roaring fire, shielding her face with her forearm. Reynevan pulled the youngster behind a wall, helped by Tybald Raabe.

"It's looking bad," said the goliard, panting. "It's looking bad, Reynevan. They'll soon be on us. We won't repel them."

As if to confirm it, he was answered by battle cries and angry howling from the door. Fire glistened and flickered on blades.

"Death to the Jews!"

Rabbi Maizl Nachman ben Gamaliel stood up. He lifted his eyes towards the sky. And spread his arms.

"*Baruch Ata Hashem, Eloheinu,*" he called in a sing-song voice. "*Melech haolam, bore meori haesh!*"

The wall of the house cracked, exploded in an eruption of plaster, lime and mortar. From the cloud of dust emerged something that had been plastered up in the wall. Reynevan sucked in air with a whistle. And Tybald Raabe squatted down in shock.

"*Emet, emet, emunah!* Abracadabra! Abracaamra!"

The thing that emerged from the wall resembled a snowman, but made of clay, was more or less anthropoid, but in place of a head had only a slight protuberance between its shoulders. Shorter than a man of average height, it was as fat and pot-bellied as a barrel and walked on short, squat legs, its chubby arms reaching down to the ground. Before Reynevan's eyes, the hands clenched into fists as big as bombard balls.

A golem, he thought, *it's a golem. A genuine golem, the legendary clay golem, the dream of sorcerers. The dream, passion and obsession of Radim Tvrdík of Prague. Pity Radim isn't here... Pity he can't see it...*

The golem roared, or rather trumpeted like a monstrous clay flute. Fear overcame the Magdeburg gang crowded in the gateway; it was as though terror had paralysed the thugs, taken the power from their legs. They were frozen to the spot as the golem loped towards them at a rocking trot. They didn't even defend themselves when it fell among them, regularly and methodically smiting and thumping them with its huge fists. Yelling, a dreadful yelling, tore apart the night air over Jawor. It didn't last long. Silence fell. Only the oil burning in the puddles hissed.

Viscous blood mixed with brains slowly dripped down the wall by the gate.

The sun rose. The clay golem returned to its hole in the wall and stood there, merging with the stones and mortar and becoming invisible.

"I was dead and now I am alive," said Maizl Nachman ben Gamaliel sadly. "Oh, but blood has been shed. Plenty of blood. May I be forgiven for it when Judgement Day comes."

"You saved innocent people," said Rixa Cartafila of Fonseca, nodding at a portly woman hugging and cuddling three little black-haired girls. "You defended the lives of your nearest and dearest, Rabbi, from those who desired to harm them. The Lord says: Remember what Amalek did unto thee by the way, when ye were come forth out of Egypt. Thou shalt blot out the remembrance of Amalek from under Heaven. That you did."

"I did," said the Jew, his eyes flaring, then quickly dimming. "But what now? Abandon everything anew? To wander anew? Attach the mezuzah to another door anew?"

"I'm to blame," grunted Tybald Raabe. "I put you in jeopardy. Now, because of me—"

"I knew who you were when I gave you shelter," Maizl Nachman interrupted him. "I supported your cause with conviction, aware of what I was risking. Well, flight and wandering are nothing new to me."

"I don't believe it will be necessary," said Reynevan. "While they were clearing away the corpses, the locals gave quite clear opinions about the attack, saying that the gang attacked to rob you and you simply defended yourself. Surely no one in Jawor would begrudge you that. And no one will disturb you if you stay."

"Lord save us!" sighed Maizl Nachman, "Sweet naivety. What is your name? Reynevan?"

"His name is Reynevan, indeed," Tybald Raabe interjected. "I know him and can vouch for him."

"*Ay*, vouch? No need. He came to the aid of a Jew. Do I need better guarantees? I say! What's with your hand, young woman? You with tzaddik Chalafta's ring?"

"I've broken three fingers," replied Rixa coldly. "A trifle. It'll heal by my wedding day."

"What wedding day? Who would want you? You're an old, hot-headed fishwife and I'll wager anything—even my tallit— that you don't know how to cook. Give me your hand, *shikse. Jehe sh'meh raba mewarach l'alam ul'almej almajja!*"

Before Reynevan's astonished eyes Rixa's fingers straightened, the swelling immediately vanished from them and the bruising faded away. The girl sighed and moved her hand. Reynevan shook his head.

"Well, well," he said slowly. "I am a physician, Rabbi Maizl, I am also familiar with the *artes magicae*. But to be able so smoothly to cure broken joints…I am full of admiration. I wonder where I could learn to do that?"

"From me," replied the rabbi dryly. "When you have seven years free, stop by. And don't forget to get circumcised first. But now, as King Solomon said to the Queen of Sheba, let's get down to business. You wanted information from me. May I then learn of the issue?"

Reynevan succinctly stated the matter. Maizl Nachman listened, nodding, his beard rising and falling.

"It is clear," he said, "I understand. And think I may be able to help. For I know of a similar case."

He stuck a finger into his nose, had a long and zealous poke around in it, pretending not to see that Reynevan was squirming with impatience. He finally removed his finger and examined what he had extracted. Then took up his speech again.

"Such cases," he announced, "are always a possible *gesheft*; nothing makes money like information. It occurred in Legnica. Six years ago. Miss Wiryda Hornig, a merchant's daughter, was walking out with an apothecary by the name of Gałązka. Against her father's will, who had promised her hand to somebody else. And that other man reputedly had connexions with the Inquisition, with the Holy Office. And Miss Wiryda suddenly vanished.

"The apothecary Gałązka was denounced," continued the Jew, "accused of heresy and had to flee from Silesia. After a year, when the case had quietened down, Wiryda suddenly reappeared, most remorseful and most obedient, quite as though she had been in a nunnery. She meekly married the man she had been promised to.

"*Nu*, in the Qahal we thought it was worth knowing who this man was, who had such good connexions with the Office as to cause young women to disappear. And it somehow came out that Moishe Merkelin, my sister-in-law's cousin, knew a certain Yochai ben Icchak, and that Yochai's uncle, a certain Shekel, had a stepdaughter called Debora, and she found out from her friend Ester a certain thing, which Ester had heard in the women's chamber from…Dammit, I've forgotten who. It doesn't matter, in any case. The important thing is that this cousin Moishe, an avaricious and impudent Jew, demanded fifteen guilders for the information. I considered it excessive."

"Ah."

"But you came to my aid, which somewhat changes the scale of values. Now this fifteen isn't that fifteen, it's quite a different fifteen, it's a fifteen transformed beyond recognition. Now that price is quite perfect. And that avaricious cousin Moishe doesn't live in Palestine. He lives in Opole. By Moses, in five days you'll have your information. And until then: be my guest."

"Thanks, Rabbi. And regarding those fifteen guilders, I'm prepared—"

"Don't insult me, laddie."

"I shan't wait with you," said Tybald Raabe, hesitantly clearing his throat, "it's time I went, duty calls. But just let me say…If you find out what you need to find out, make haste. Make great haste. I think—"

"And I think," said Rixa, looking him in the eyes, "that you ought to stop fibbing and tell us the truth."

"I don't know anything," replied the goliard quickly, too quickly to be credible. Then avoided Reynevan's gaze.

"Tybald," Reynevan said slowly. "Last night we stood shoulder to shoulder, we looked death in the eyes together. And now you hide something from me? You knew my brother. You know me, you even vouched for me not long ago. You know I'm moving around Silesia, risking my life because my beloved is in need, I have to find and free her. She is imprisoned, and every day of captivity adds to her torment—"

"Reinmar," said the goliard, licking his lips and lowering his eyes. "The Czechs don't trust you; various rumours circulate about you…What if it gets out that I spoke to you—"

"To Lusatia or Silesia?" asked Rixa impatiently. "Which way is the expedition headed? For there's little doubt it will soon begin."

"I know nothing…But let me think…Lusatia, perhaps?"

"Well, I never," said Rixa, smiling. "That wasn't hard. It's always difficult getting started. And now some details."

"What do you want from me?" said Tybald Raabe, feigning anger. "What am I? A hejtman or what? I'm a simple agitator, they don't share strategy with me…But it's clear to anybody who looks at a map and gives it a little thought…So think a little. Which way will the Tábor go if not along the valley of the Lusatian Nysa?"

"Žitava and Zgorzelec?" asked Reynevan, thinking back to the map he'd seen at Prokop's base in Odry.

"I wouldn't rule it out…" said Tybald, clearing his throat. "I wouldn't rule out a crossing to the right bank of the Kwisa, either. Lubáň, Bolesławiec—"

"Żagań?" Rixa asked in an altered voice.

"It's possible."

"When? The date, Tybald."

"June. I'd say."

"You'd say?"

"Some are saying Saint John's Day. Others Saint Vitus's. I tend towards the latter. But who knows…?"

"Thank you, a hundred times," said Rixa, giving the goliard a somewhat warmer look. "You have helped very much, I'm utterly grateful. I'd give you a kiss, but I'm shy, I'm really quite bashful. And since you have to go, farewell."

"Farewell to you, too. Reinmar?"

"Yes?"

"Good luck. I mean it sincerely."

Five days passed in no time. On Sunday, the twelfth of June, Rabbi Nachman ben Gamaliel called Reynevan and Rixa to him.

"My sister-in-law's cousin Moishe," he began without further ado, "gladly accepted the money, as pleased as if he'd bought the Ark of the Covenant cheap. Thus I know who brought an end to Wiryda Hornig's romance by denouncing her suitor, the apothecary, and putting her into a nunnery, all because of his connexions with the Inquisition. The same man who later became Wiryda's happy husband. Otto Arnoldus, quite a well-known person, but not necessarily for his virtues. Once a councillor, now burgomeister of the town of Bolesławiec.

"Although the underlying issue was private, not political, your case has something in common with Wiryda Hornig's, Reinmar. In your shoes, I'd go to Bolesławiec and talk, if not with Burgomeister Arnoldus himself, then with his spouse. She may remember which nunnery they sent her to. There's a good chance that the Inquisition still uses the same ones."

"A hundred thanks... We must leave as soon as possible."

"Yes, yes," said Maizl Nachman quickly, lowering his voice. "I would advise haste."

"We know," murmured Rixa. "Saint Vitus is just around the corner. We set off tomorrow at dawn. I wish you good health, Rabbi Maizl."

"Farewell," said the Jew, nodding. "Thank you for everything. And you, young woman, come closer."

Rixa lowered her head. The rabbi laid his hands on her raven-black hair.

"*Jevarechecha Hashem vejishmerecha,*" he said. "May Hashem bless and keep you. May Hashem turn his face towards you and send you peace. Goodbye, Rixa Fonseka. And goodbye to you, Reinmar of Bielawa."

Chapter Thirteen

In which there is talk about dreams and their interpretation and unexpected individuals form unexpected alliances.

In Wrocław, dusk was slowly falling, the grey hour—called *inter canem et lupum*, the hour between the dog and the wolf—was setting in, when it was getting dark but before lights were lit. It was hot, damp and humid, a storm was coming. Kundrie emptied the goblet of the rest of the *aurum potabile* with a sudden gulp and licked her lips.

"And so," she said, narrowing her amber eyes, "you are going to Jawor and the Lusatian borderlands, for news about Reinmar of Bielawa appearing there has reached you. Even though the news, I gather, isn't confirmed, nor is it very certain, you drop everything and rush there blindly. And from me you demand spells and charms capable of localising a sidereal being. Although I've already told you a hundred times that it's impossible."

"Nothing is impossible," retorted the Wallcreeper. "That was the first thing they inculcated into us in Aguilar."

The neufra sighed. And then yawned, revealing a formidable set of fangs.

"Oh well," she said. "Reinmar of Bielawa, I understand that he must be removed, otherwise he will be a vexation while he still seeks revenge for his brother. I support the plan to capture him and give him a slow death, after first, if possible, torturing to death before his eyes the girl Apolda he is still searching for. The idea of revenge is reasonable, and I applaud it. But that comrade of his, that giant…That supposed visitor from the astral realm…I would, though, advise you to abandon it. To me he is a Watcher, one of the *Rephaim*. It is wiser not to fall foul of them. I'm full of very evil forebodings regarding your pursuit of him. You aren't acting rationally. Your interest in that giant begins more and more to resemble—"

"What?"

"An obsession," she finished coldly. "In quite a clinical form. You've lapsed into mania, son. It bothers me. All the more so that lately it's not your only one."

"What did you say?"

"It's not your only mania. I see and hear. But in particular, smell it."

"What?"

"Don't play the fool. I frequent the town, I hear rumours. About you and Miss Pack. And I have a good nose. For two months you've been coming here smelling of her cunt."

"Mind you don't go too far," he hissed.

"What's come over you? You've had wenches by the score. You, Birkart Grellenort, coveted and sighed over by half of the witches in Andalusia. But until now, you've never become involved with any woman, you've never lost your head over one. Beware, for you have enemies. They didn't defeat you with iron and may reach for other weapons. Hasn't it occurred to you that this Pack girl might have been planted? Perhaps they want to punish you biblically, by the hand of a woman? A maiden will bring you down—as Delilah did Samson. Or Judith with Nebuchadnezzar…Or Holofernes? I've forgotten. Your Bible is a damned convoluted read. Too many characters, too many improbabilities and blatant fabrications. I prefer Chrétien de Troyes and the other *romanceros*."

The Wallcreeper's eyes flashed. And dimmed at once.

"Every work of literature," he replied calmly, "the Bible, too, conceals a pearl of truth among a sea of fabrications. And here we return to our giant. When I catch him, I shall drag the knowledge from him; find out what is the truth and where it lies. For he hasn't supposedly, but actually, come from there, from the sidereal plane, from a place we don't know, about which we know nothing. Some people, as you know, regard that place as the province of the Highest Being, commonly known as God. Polytheists maintain that it is the domain of many gods, demigods, deities and demons. Others are of the opinion that only demons dwell there. No one knows what it's like in actuality, because although visitors have come here from that place, no one has ever penetrated it. No one, including your fellow Longaevi and your almost almighty Nefandi—"

"So you'll capture the giant," interrupted the neufra. "And what then? If he's a Rephaim, you won't get anything out of him."

"I shall. He's trapped in a material body, condemned to its flaws and limitations. In particular, he feels the pain that can be inflicted on a body. Kundrie, I shall inflict pain on that body. I'll inflict so much he'll reveal everything to me."

"Including how to reach the astral domain?"

"Or at least make contact with it," he said. And immediately sprang up from the curule seat, crossed the room in a few paces, from a coffin leaning against a wardrobe to a complete pig's skeleton, which served God only knew what purpose for the elemental.

"What can this world offer me?" he said, raising his voice. "What can it give me? This primitive world, in which everything has already been divided up, snatched and stolen, in which now *nulle terre sans seigneur.* What can I be here? What position can I achieve, what power can I assume? That of a cathedral canon? Of starosta and governor of Wrocław, or—which the bishop tempts me with—governor of the whole of Silesia? And even should I become a bishop, a cardinal and finally Pope, what is that power in the present times? Even if we manage to vanquish the Hussites, their example will live on, for one cannot annihilate an idea. Others will come after the Hussites, the fractured edifice of Rome will never recover the integrity of an immovable monolith again. Kings and princes will fall like puppets, for what kind of power is it that can be thwarted with a dose of poison or ten inches of dagger blade? And the Fuggers, eyes fixed on the power of money? They'll see money become worth less than chaff. Mages and sorcerers? They are mortal, very mortal. Longaevi? Only in name are they immortal; they will pass along with their magical power…"

Distant thunder clattered past, a counterpoint to his speech. Kundrie was silent. The Wallcreeper sighed deeply.

"Marco Polo reached Cathay," he continued. "The Portuguese sailed to *Insulas Canarias*, to Madera and the Azores, and are preparing to cross the oceans. They believe that they will find wealth and true power beyond the ocean, in a hitherto undiscovered world. They believe in the land of Prester John, in the land of the Moguls in Ophir and Taprobana, and they plan to reach them. They will stop at nothing to achieve that. I, likewise."

The neufra still remained silent, bristling and flattening her dorsal spines by turns.

"Do you know the last person to speak like that?" she finally asked, "and, interestingly, in a like context? The crazed poet and sorcerer Abdallah Zahr-ad-Dihn, the author of the book entitled *Al Azif*, which is an onomatopoeic description of the sound emitted by nocturnal insects and ghosts. In later translations, the author's name is travestied into Abdul Alhazred and the title changed to *Necronomicon*. Which caught on."

"I know."

"So you also know that Abdul Alhazred desired above all else to reach the *syderium*, that he stopped at nothing. He went to the haunted desert of Roba el-Khaliyeh, to Irem, searched for Kadath. He died a gruesome death in the year 738, in Damascus, in broad daylight; torn to pieces and devoured by a terrible demon before the eyes of many witnesses. Doesn't that temper your ardour?"

"No, it does not."

"In that case," said the neufra, rolling her eyes, "I wish you luck. Plenty of luck."

"I'm going," said the Wallcreeper and straightened up. "I set off tomorrow. Aha, Kundrie, would there be a little Perferro in your stores? I'd like to have some to hand."

"A good idea to have some within reach," said the elemental, baring her yellow fangs. "Give some to the girl, that blasted Douce of Pack. You will draw her more powerfully to you. You will gain a guarantee that she won't run away with another. And if she does, it won't be for long. Until the first laceration with iron—"

"Kundrie."

"I won't say another thing. I have a little Perferro, but not much, one dose, enough for one person. Ask the bishop, I know he has some to spare. And at Sensenberg you have Skirfir and his alchemic athanors, after all."

"The bishop won't admit to having any. And there's no way I can go to Sensenberg." Seeing her raised eyebrows, he said, "I think they are hunting me. I cannot even be certain of my Company. It's a ragbag—"

"A ragbag of scum," she finished. "A ragbag made up of

scoundrels, good-for-nothings, cut-throats and perverts. Your Black Riders. Those are the men you command, because you were only able to recruit the like. And you set off on an expedition with a rabble like that. You must be desperate, indeed."

"Will you give me the Perferro or not?"

"I shall. And I'll add something more. Something special. It ought to help in your hunt."

She opened a small chest on the table and took something from it. The Wallcreeper fought to overcome revulsion.

"Lovely, isn't it?" The neufra cackled. "It is activated with a spell. Originating in *Al Azif*, as a matter of fact, but perfected by the Nefandi and the Italian necromancers. The chirping of nocturnal insects, the rustling of their wings... It has two functions. It should indicate the whereabouts of Bielawa or his maid."

"And the other?"

"Use it when the need to kill somebody arises. So that the victim feels they are dying."

"Farewell, Kundrie."

"Farewell, son."

The first drops of rain began tapping on the roof.

A lightning bolt tore open the sky, thunder rumbled almost at once, long and drawn-out and sharp, with a crack like fabric being rent apart. The downpour intensified; a wall of water completely veiled the world.

"It's as though someone had it in for us," said Reynevan, shaking water from his collar. "Time is short and suddenly there's a cloudburst. It's a deluge."

They sat out the storm in a forest, in dense undergrowth which only gave shelter for a while; it was soon pouring steadily on them. The horses shook their manes, lowering their heads.

"The rain is easing off," said Rixa, wiping her dripping-wet nose. "The storm is moving away. It'll soon pass and then we can gallop again; the wind will dry us. And drive evil thoughts away."

The downpour didn't abate so quickly and the now softened highway prevented them from galloping or any other feats of equestrianism, hence the journey was much longer than they planned. It took them two days to reach Legnica—a town described as a second Wrocław—just as the population of ten thousand began to be summoned to Mass by the bells of all seventeen churches. Rixa knew the town well and led them without going astray. They passed the impressive, quite new, recently consecrated Collegiate Church of the Holy Sepulchre, crossed the crowded town square and the vegetable market, dreadfully muddy after the rain. They passed the stalls of tin-smiths and needle makers. Rixa reined in her horse beyond the stalls and dismounted. They were at the entry to a lane which announced itself with the intense aroma of incense, herbs and spices.

"I have something to deal with here," she explained. "I can go by myself, asking you to wait in the tavern around the corner. Or we can go together in order to strengthen our collaboration based on mutual trust."

"Let's try. And see what comes of it."

"Then let us go. I request two things. Don't ask any questions."

"And the other?"

"Don't offer any answers."

The lane—it turned out—was Mages' Lane. The stalls and benches located there mainly offered herbs, elixirs, periapts, amulets, talismans, Loreto hand bells, crystal balls, crystals, beads, polished stones, straw effigies, shells, antlers and other marvels. Reynevan had heard of the lane, which was tolerated by councillors and the Legnica clergy. There were two reasons for that: the high duties which went to the town and the fact that the goods on sale had absolutely nothing in common with true magic. A glance was enough for Reynevan to be absolutely certain of it: the goods on the stalls were dominated by charlatanism, junk and trash.

Rixa stopped in front of a counter, behind which a black-haired girl was dusting the wares. Mainly dried frogs.

"We're here to see Master Zbrosław."

The black-haired girl looked at Reynevan, fluttered long eyelashes and vanished into the back. Reynevan surveyed the stall. He was surprised to suddenly see among the innumerable dried slimy creatures a horned lizard with a spiralling curled tail. He had seen a similar one in an illustration in the *Grand Grimoire*.

"The Master will see you."

Master Zbrosław astonished Reynevan somewhat. He was certain that the vendor of dried frogs—Rixa's contact, after all—had assumed a Slavic name just for cover. But inside, in a room smelling strongly of ginger, cloves and camphor, they were greeted by a real Slav. Broad-shouldered, with fair hair and moustache and blue eyes, he was the spitting image of the legendary King Krak.

"Greetings. How may I help?"

"I'm Rixa Cartafila of Fonseca. Sent by...tzaddik Chalafta."

Master Zbrosław said nothing for a long time and tapped his fingers. He finally raised his eyes.

"The one from Oława?"

"No. The one from Oleśnica."

They smiled at one another, glad to have successfully exchanged password and countersign.

"They say you are an expert in dream books, Master Zbrosław. And apparently able to read dreams."

"God talks to us through our dreams. Dreams give us signs, strengthen us, heal and nourish our souls."

"If we can understand their significance. The venerable Rabbi Hisda would say that an unexplained dream is like a letter received but unread. And I had a dream."

"Go on."

"In my dream the town of Żagań was in great danger."

"Interesting that it was Żagań," said Master Zbrosław, fixing Rixa with his Slavic eyes, "when there are many other towns. Located closer to other...dangers. Closer to Žitava, which is said at this moment to be feverishly preparing its defence following news of a possible attack."

"Those towns can worry about themselves," said Rixa, without lowering her gaze. "They didn't appear in my dream. In my dream, Duke Jan of Żagań had a marvellous vision. The Angel of the Lord descended from the heavens and inspired him to save his land. *Seek, O Duke*, said the angel, *help from the pious Kingdom of Poland, from the Polish nation beloved of the Mother of God. Look for help from the godly King of Poland, Władysław. Rather than plot with Emperor Sigismund*, said the angel..."

"He spoke thus? With those words?"

"Those very ones," she said in a voice as cold as Saint Kinga in bed. "*Instead of plotting with Emperor Sigismund, turn your gaze, O Duke, towards Poland. Sigismund is distant, but Poland close at hand. The times are full of misery and Poland doesn't abandon its friends in need...*"

"Well, I never," said Master Zbrosław with a sigh. "A Polonophile angel, which signifies great perturbation in a dream...A dream indeed worthy of the interpreting, whatever strangeness is in it. The letter has been received...That venerable rabbi, what was his name? I fear making a slip of the tongue..."

"Hisda."

"The letter has been received, as Rabbi Hisda teaches, so it must be read. But there are two letters here, so to speak. We are dealing with a dream within a dream. You, madam, dreamed of the Duke of Żagań's dream. I wonder if the Duke of Żagań himself dreamed it—"

"He did not," said Rixa, and her tone left no doubt that it was an absolute certainty. "And here lies the problem. We must urgently inform him of the dream. I suggest we ask the local Franciscans for help with this," she added with emphasis, "that they may pass on the news to their confraters in Głogów, the ones at the Church of Saint Stanisław. Requesting that they inform the friars from Żagań."

Master Zbrosław tilted his head.

"The Church of Saint Stanisław in Głogów is not subordinate to the Diocese of Saxony," he said. "The Głogów monastery belongs to the Gniezno Diocese. The monks will inform Gniezno at once. And then they will know about everything in Krakow."

"Never mind."

"I understand."

The master led them back in front of the stall where the pretty, black-haired girl was still dusting the frogs. *Perhaps you are Zbrosław, indeed*, thought Reynevan, *but she is Rebecca*.

"What's this?" he said as an object on the counter suddenly caught his attention. "What is it? Could it be…?"

"This?" asked the Master, lifting by a string a veined stone with a spot the shape and colour of a human eye. "A Viendo amulet. Castilian-made, brought back straight from Burgos. If it's for you, three groschen. Will you take it?"

"Don't panic, Reynevan," said Rixa. "We'll make it to Bolesławiec. Raabe might have been mistaken regarding the date of the expedition and actually I doubt whether he knew it exactly."

"He might have been mistaken the other way," said Reynevan, his features tightening and hardening. "It might begin earlier. And I know how quickly they're capable of moving. Six, even seven miles a day, even over rough ground. And I know what they're capable of when they get there. I've been in a few towns they've captured. Chojnów, for example, not far from here. We must hurry, dammit!"

"And ride through the night? Senseless. We'll stop for the night—"

"And then inform somebody else about the Hussite expedition tomorrow, you mean? Rixa, Tybald trusted us. He counted on us not trumpeting it all over Silesia. While you—"

"Reynevan," said Rixa, her feline eyes flashing. "Don't lecture me. And don't meddle in my affairs."

"And may our collaboration based on mutual trust be strengthened."

"Understand that I know what I'm doing. And I'm on your side. Of which I have assured you several times and have had enough of repeating it. By informing Żagań about the danger I was also on your side. As I was in March in Racibórz when with your mediation I helped the hesitant Wołoszek make a decision."

"All the same, I'd like to know—"

"You know as much as you need to," she said, interrupting him harshly. "And you know plenty, you have eyes and ears and you're no fool. And thus may it remain."

They said nothing. From below came cries, laughter and the sounds of merriment from the tavern's common room. Mice scratched and squeaked in the ceiling, the candle flickered.

"Reynevan?"

"Yes?"

"Not without reason did I suggest we sleep here. Tomorrow I'd also prefer not to slow the pace. Do you have any medicine for women's matters?"

"You mean for your menses?"

"I mean: do you have it or not?"

He took from his satchel a box of medicine, pleased with himself that he had prudently stocked up at the apothecary's shop at the House at the Archangel.

"Take this," he said, handing Rixa an electuary in a wafer. "Drink it with wine."

"It's bitter as hell."

"Because it has aloes. It's *Hiera Picra*, called by Galen *species ad longam vitam*. It's also effective for women's ailments."

"I hope so."

The candle flickered. The mice stopped scratching.

"Rixa?"

"What?"

"The fact you come from... That you're a—"

"Jewess? Does it influence what I do? Of course."

After quite a long silence, she unexpectedly began, "My family comes from the Xanten in the Rhineland. Almost all of them were murdered in 1096. A crusade! *Deus lo vult!* The Knights Emich and Gottschalk answered Pope Urban II's call and put it zealously into practice. They began the fight for the Holy Sepulchre by massacring the Rhineland Jews. In Xanten, one boy, Yehuda, survived, apparently because he converted to Christianity. As Guido Fonseca, he settled in Italy, where he returned to the faith of his forebears, or, as you say, fell once again into *judaica perfidia*. His descendants, once again Jews, were driven from Naples in 1288. They travelled all over the world. Some of the family ended up in Bern. A Christian child vanished there in 1294. Without a trace, in unexplained circumstances. Naturally, it must have been a ritual murder, the Jews had kidnapped the child and put him into their matzoh. For that dreadful act, all the Jews were driven from Bern. My ancestor, a rabbi, called at that time Mevorach ben Kalonymos, moved to Weinheim in Franconia.

"In 1298, in the Franconian town of Röttingen, somebody reputedly desecrated the Host. An impoverished knight named Rindfleisch received a sign from God regarding that matter. The Jews are iconoclasts, the sign declared; anyone who believes in God must kill the Jews. Many believers were found; Rindfleisch soon became the leader of a horde of murderers with whom he began the worthy task. After the Jewish communities were wiped out in Rothenburg, Würzburg, Nördlingen and Bamberg it was Weinheim's turn. On the twentieth of September, Rindfleisch and his thugs forced their way into the Jewish quarter. Rabbi Mevorach and his family and every Jew—man, woman and child—was driven to the synagogue and burned alive in it. Seventy-nine people altogether. Not many, bearing in mind that Rindfleisch had killed five thousand in total in Franconia and Swabia. Often using much more elaborate ways than burning.

"Similarly, in 1319 during the revolt of the *Pastoureaux*, that is the Shepherds, my great-great-grandfather, Paolo Fonseca, a converso, was murdered with the rest of the family, those in the diaspora. The *Pastoureaux* murdered on principle the nobility, monks and priests, but they cracked down on Jews and conversos with special zeal, often with the spontaneous help of the local people. Aware of what the *Pastoureaux* did to women and children, my great-great-grandfather Paolo strangled my great-great-grandmother and his two children with his own hands while imprisoned in a dungeon in Verdun-sur-Garonne.

"My great-grandfather, Itzhak Yohanon, who settled in Alsace, lost almost his entire family in 1338, during one of the notorious massacres carried out by the peasant bands called the *Judenschläger*. One of my great-grandmothers, who had no one to mercifully strangle her, was gang-raped repeatedly by the *Judenschläger*. It is thus possible that because of it I have a little Christian blood. Does that gladden you? Me neither, just imagine."

Rixa fell silent. Reynevan cleared his throat.

"What happened...after that?"

"The year 1349."

"The Black Death."

"Precisely. The Jews were naturally guilty of the outbreak and spread of the plague, it was a Jewish plot, concocted to destroy all Christians. The Toledo Rabbi, Peyrat, you must have heard of him, sent emissaries all over Europe to poison wells, springs and brooks. So the poisoners began to be punished. On a large scale. There were plenty of my relatives among the six thousand people burned alive in Mainz and among the two thousand burned in Strasburg. My kin were among the victims of the massacres in Bern, Basel, Freiburg, Speyer, Fulda, Regensburg, Pforzheim, Erfurt, Magdeburg and Leipzig, in various of the three hundred Jewish communities exterminated in Germany. My relatives were among those murdered in Prague, and also in Nysa, Brzeg, Góra, Oleśnica and Wrocław. Since I forgot to tell you that a large part of my family came to live at that time in Silesia. And in Poland. Things were said to be better there. Safer."

"Were they?"

"All in all, yes. But later, after the plague died down. Well, there was one pogrom in Wrocław in 1360. There was a fire, the Jews were blamed for it, a few dozen were beaten to death or drowned in the Odra; no more than two from my family. It was a little more serious in Krakow, in 1407, on the Tuesday after Easter. A Christian child was found killed, naturally with the aim of obtaining blood, indispensable for baking Passover

379

matzoh. So the Jews were blamed, of course; any doubt about that was dispelled by priests from Krakow pulpits. The mob, fomented in the churches, rushed out to bestow the punishment. Several hundred Jews lost their lives, several hundred more were forced to convert to Christianity. In this way, please note, I was born a Christian two years later, to a baptised Mama and Papa. Sprinkled with the water of the baptism, I received the name of Anna in honour of the saint whose Krakow church was burned down in 1407, torched by an over-enthusiastic Krakow mob. Fortunately, I wasn't called Anna too long, for in 1410 the family fled from Poland to Strzegom in Silesia and converted back to Judaism—*judaica perfidia*! Several of my kin and a hundred and forty of our faith dwelt in Strzegom. Seventy-three of them, including my father, Samuel ben Gershom, lost their lives in the 1410 pogrom. The reason? The sound of the shofar horn being blown during Rosh Hashana was taken as a signal for an attack on the Christians. My mother, my father's sisters and I, a one-year-old baby, fled to Jawor. There, in 1420, now eleven, I watched my second pogrom, with my own eyes. Believe me, it leaves an unforgettable impression."

"I believe you."

"I don't feel sorry for myself," she said, suddenly lifting her head up. "Please note, I don't pity myself or the members of my tribe. Nor Jerusalem, nor the temple. *Uvene Jerushalaim ir hacodesh bimhera veyameinu!* I know the words, but their meaning escapes me. I don't mean to sit by the rivers of Babylon and weep. I don't expect sympathy—not to mention tolerance—from others. But you asked if it had an influence. Indeed, it did. It's better not to undertake certain things if you're afraid, if the fear of the consequences, of what might happen, paralyses you. I'm not afraid. Down through the generations I've cumulated courage...No, not courage. Resistance to fear. No, not resistance. Insensitivity."

"I understand."

"I doubt it. Let's sleep. If your medicine has the desired effect, we'll set off at dawn. If it doesn't, we still shall."

The family gathering in Sterzendorf passed off wonderfully peacefully and without incident. Almost all the matters that were meant to be dealt with were dealt with admirably quickly and successfully. Credit, it appeared, was completely due to the two leaders of the gathering, Henryk Landsberg, the canon of Niemodlin Collegiate Church, and Sir Apeczko, the senior member of the Stercza family, unanimously elected by the combined families. Thus the quarrel over land which Henryk "the Crane" of Baruth and Namysłów monastery, represented by a hot-tempered monk, had conducted for four years was resolved without the expected arguments. The wild rumpus expected by everybody between Morold of Stercza and Lanzelet of Rachenau, caused by the reputed cheating over the sale of some cattle, never occurred. Everything went smoothly between Hrozwita of Baruth and Beatrice of Falkenhayn, at odds as a result of mutual verbal abuse of one another. Cup-Bearer Berthold de Apolda, for years furious at Tomasz Eichelborn for not keeping his word over the marriage of their children, accepted the latter's apology. The last matter had deeply, very deeply, vexed Parsifal of Rachenau. Parsifal had come to the gathering with his father, Sir Tristram of Rachenau, who had started off at once with mutual pleasantries with Albrecht Hackeborn, Lord of Przewóz. It was no secret that Lord Przewóz was seeking connexions with the Rachenau family and pushing for the wedding of his daughter, Zuzanna, to Parsifal. Parsifal, however, didn't find Zuzanna Hackeborn in the least bit attractive. Whenever there was a chance to think, Parsifal thought mainly about the flaxen-haired Ofka, daughter of Henryk Baruth of Studzisko. As a matter of fact, Ofka was present at the gathering with the remaining girls whose chaperones had put them in the ladies' chamber and made them embroider on tambour frames.

The two days of the gathering passed in a flash, and there remained only one matter, albeit a difficult one, which was driving a serious wedge between the Bischofsheim and Stercza families. There appeared to be no chance of agreement. But Canon Henryk and Apeczko Stercza, the leaders, had their heads screwed on. To calm the atmosphere, the canon said a long and boring prayer in Latin, while Apeczko suggested holding a memorial wake for the peace of the souls of their relatives and comrades fallen in battle with the Hussites for the defence of the faith, in particular Heineman Baruth, Gawein Rachenau, Reinhard Bischofsheim and Jentsch Knobelsdorf, called Eagle Owl. The memorial ceremony lasted all day and all night, and the discussions were postponed until the mourners came to their senses.

Parsifal Rachenau didn't take part in the drinking session; young men who hadn't yet been knighted weren't explicitly forbidden, but neither were they encouraged. Thus Parsifal preferred to go on a tour of the embankments and stables. Suddenly, to his great astonishment, he noticed his companion, Henryk Baruth, called Starling, walking swiftly towards him and escorting...

His cousin. The fair-haired Ofka of Baruth.

"I introduce to you my comrade and brother in arms, Parsifal of Rachenau, the son of Tristram of Bukowa," panted Starling, winking pointedly. "Indeed, Ofka, it would be hard to imagine a braver man than him. I, not to boast, also fought against the Czechs—why, even against sorcerers and sorceresses. But he— you won't believe it! He fought against the hordes of the heretic Ambrož at the Battle of Náchod; the two of us against a hundred. And on the walls of Kłodzko, why, you wouldn't believe it, girl! Though wounded and bleeding, he fearlessly resisted the heretics who were storming Kłodzko. Sir Půta of Častolovice himself squeezed his shoulder afterwards!"

Crimson spots appeared on Parsifal's cheeks. And it wasn't even because Starling was lying through his teeth. Parsifal simply couldn't refrain from blushing at the sight of the maiden, her large hazel eyes and freckled, retroussé nose. They were the most gorgeous freckles Parsifal had ever seen.

"I'll leave you," said Starling quickly. "Pass the time of day together. I have important things on my mind."

He left them alone. And Parsifal, who even a minute earlier had been ready to repay his comrade with a horse and trapping, now felt he would gladly punch him in the nose. For no matter how much he wanted, he couldn't gather himself to utter a single word. Certain that maidens only lend their ears to the refined speech of troubadours and knights errant, he felt like an utter fool.

A warm wind was blowing and frogs were croaking with abandon in the moat.

"You were wounded, were you?" asked Ofka, interrupting the awful silence and wrinkling her freckly nose. "Show me where."

"No!" said Parsifal, starting. "It doesn't behove to brag," he added quickly. "A braggart is not worthy of a knight's sash."

"But you did fight?"

"Aye."

"So you are brave? Valiant?"

"It doesn't behove to—"

"Let's see how valiant you are," said Ofka, leaning over the moat. "Oh! Catch that frog for me."

"That frog there?"

"You heard me. That big one. Thank you. And now eat it."

"What?"

"Eat it. Let's see how brave you are."

Parsifal squeezed the frog in his fist. Closed his eyes. And opened his mouth.

Ofka of Baruth caught him by the hand, snatched the frog from his grasp and tossed it into the water. And blushed like a cherry.

"Please forgive me," she said lowering her head. "I didn't mean that…Not at all. They actually say I'm flighty—"

"You aren't," said Parsifal, swallowing. "You aren't flighty, m'lady. You are…"

Ofka raised her head. Her hazel eyes grew even bigger than before.

"You are beautiful."

Ofka looked long at him. And then fled.

The conference was begun again and the seemingly intractable dispute between the Bischofsheims and the Sterczas was finally resolved. Parsifal listened with half an ear. He was in another world. Daydreaming.

"We, Henryk Landsberg, Scholaster of Niemodlin Collegiate Church, testify to all believers of Christ who read this document that Burchard Mencelin, steward of the estate in Niwnik belonging to Sir Gunter of Bischofsheim, was killed by Dieter Haxt, the esquire of Sir Wolfher of Stercza. For that crime, Lord Stercza and Dieter Haxt have agreed to pay to the family of the dead man a penitential sum approved by the testifying knights of forty grzywna. Furthermore, the parish of the church in Niwnik will receive the sum of five grzywna. The surgeon who was called to help will receive nothing since his help achieved nothing. A penitentiary cross financed by the above-mentioned Esquire Haxt will be erected at the place of the crime as evidence of the pact; at the top of said cross will be engraved the murder weapon: a battleaxe. In the process, agreement has been reached between the malefactor and murdered man's family, as with the above-mentioned knights. This came to pass on the sixth of June on the Year of our Lord one thousand four hundred and twenty-nine.

"Parsifal! I'm talking to you! Are you asleep?"

He jerked up his head, wrested from a deep dream. And quailed. His visibly enraged father was walking with two knights, an older and a younger. Parsifal didn't know the younger one, who had an angular face sporting a white scar. The older was Sir Albrecht of Hackeborn, the Lord of Przewóz, Zuzanna's father.

I'm doomed, a frightened thought flashed through Parsifal's mind, *I'm done for. They'll engage me. And then marry me. Farewell, O beautiful Ofka.*

"I'm giving you to serve as page to Sir Egbert of Kassel from Kopaniec," said Sir Tristram Rachenau, talking through his nose as he always did when irked. "Sir Egbert is an experienced man of war, and war with the Hussites may happen any time. Serve him loyally, fight courageously, guard your noble honour and—God willing—you will earn your sash and spurs. Just beware, whippersnapper, not to bring shame on me and the family."

Parsifal swallowed. It had been promised to him for a long time that he would page in Kłodzko, with Sir Půta of Častolovice, side by side with his comrade, Starling Baruth. He knew his father too well, though, to voice any objections—even by the flicker of an eyelid, let alone a word. He bowed low before the knight with the scar.

"In five days," said Sir Egbert of Kassel, "you will report in Kopaniec, armed and mounted. Do you understand?"

"Yes, sir."

*

"Oooh," said Elencza of Skałka, clapping her hands on seeing him. "Parsifal! On a horse? Armed from head to foot? You're riding to war, are you?"

"Indeed," he said, puffing up slightly. "It's an order, thus I must ride. The fatherland is in need. The Hussites are said to be preparing another attack."

Elencza looked at him from under her eyelids and sighed.

She always sighs at talk of the Hussites, he observed. *Clearly not without reason. There's a rumour the girl suffered at the hands of the Hussites. Mistress Dzierżka has never spoken directly about it, but there's something behind it.*

"My way passed through Skałka," he said and sat up in the saddle, adjusting his fanciful chaperon, "so I thought to stop by. And ask about Mistress Dzierżka's health…"

"God bless you," said Dzierżka of Wirsing. "Thank you for your concern, young Master Rachenau."

She stepped over the threshold with great difficulty, leaning on a staff, every movement clearly costing her a huge effort. He noticed she was still unable to straighten her back. *It's truly a miracle she can get out of bed,* he thought, *for barely two months have passed since the attack.*

Skałka was being rebuilt, the rafters on the new stable still exposed, and work was continuing on the new barns and sheds.

"My father told me to tell you not to be afraid, m'lady," said Parsifal, tugging at his chaperon again. His mother had dressed him in it and he couldn't grow accustomed to it for anything. "You are protected by the neighbouring landfried, let anybody try to touch you and he'll have to deal with all the local knighthood."

"Thank you indeed…" said Dzierżka, straightening up, as much as she could, narrowing her eyes in pain. "Are you going to page? For whom, may I ask?"

"Sir Egbert of Kassel."

"Lord Kopaniec," said Dzierżka, who knew almost everybody in Silesia. "A valiant knight, sometimes even too valiant. A relative of the Hackeborns of Przewóz."

So it is true. Parsifal groaned to himself. *And squiring is nothing but a preliminary to my betrothal.*

"Lord Kassel," Dzierżka continued, "is also a good friend of our Inquisitor, the Reverend Grzegorz Hejncze. They are comrades. Did you know that? Well, you do now. And what do you ride, laddie, on your way to render service? A Frisian colt? A decent mount, decent...but a pack horse. You'll take a better."

"M'lady...It doesn't behove me—"

"Not another word. I am indebted to you and your father. Let me at least pay you back with a horse."

Inquisitor Gregory Hejncze paraded before the squad with Egbert of Kassel, measuring up each soldier with attentive gaze. He reined his horse in before Parsifal.

"A new one," Kassel introduced him. "Young Rachenau, the son of Sir Tristram of Buków."

"As I presumed," said the Inquisitor, nodding, "for the similarities are striking. And the horse, splendid, clearly genuine Castilian blood. From the Skałka stud, I'll wager. Given by Dzierżka of Wirsing, the widow of Zbylut Leliwa."

"The Rachenau family's Buków is adjacent to Skałka," explained Kassel. "Sir Tristram came to Mistress Dzierżka's rescue. When that attack occurred, you know—"

"I know," Hejncze cut in, looking Parsifal straight in the eyes. "Dzierżka escaped death twice. And here you are with a horse from her, lad. How strange are the twists of fate, how strange. Order the men to ride out, Egbert."

"Yes, Your Excellency."

*

387

It's as though we're riding to war, thought Parsifal. *In battle array, with arms and gear, with sword in hand, under severe military command and rules. Suffice to look at the faces of Sir Egbert and the Inquisitor, at the faces of the foot soldiers, at the Inquisition's infantry armed with crossbows. We're going to war. Last night I dreamed of blood and fire... We are sure to see fighting. And not somewhere on the border, but most probably here, in the very heart of Silesia, by the Strzegom road, heading for Bolków, near the village of...*

"The village of Chmielno," said Egbert of Kassel, pointing. "And the tavern. Just as we were informed. What are your wishes, Grzegorz?"

"Surround it."

A cock crowed. Dogs were barking. Ducks quacked, splashing in the duckpond. A blackbird was singing, bees were humming, flies were buzzing and the sun was shining joyously. And a peasant leaving the privy withdrew suddenly at the sight of soldiers and hid behind the door with a heart-shaped hole in it. A woman in a headscarf dropped her rake and fled, lifting her skirts above her calves. Children stared enraptured at the weapons, clothing and gear of the esquires and pikemen from Kopaniec who were surrounding the buildings. Parsifal took the position given to him. He wiped his sweaty hands on his cloak; vainly, for they began to sweat again at once.

"Urban Horn!" Inquisitor Grzegorz Hejncze called loudly and resonantly. "Come out!"

No reaction. Parsifal swallowed, fiddled with his belt and fingered his sword hilt.

"Urban Horn! The tavern is surrounded! You don't stand a chance! Come out of your own free will!"

"Who calls?" came a voice from inside, behind partially open shutters.

"Grzegorz Hejncze, Papal Inquisitor! And Sir Egbert of Kassel from Kopaniec!"

The door of the tavern creaked and began to open. The footmen raised their crossbows; Kassel calmed them with a gesture and a barked word.

A man dressed in a short, grey cloak fastened with a shining buckle, in a tight-fitting, braided silver doublet and high cordovan boots, stood at the threshold. The man wore on his head a black satin chaperon even more fanciful than Parsifal's, with an even longer and even more fancifully coiled liripipe.

"I am Urban Horn," said the man in the grey cloak and looked around. His eyes were piercing and there was an arrogant grimace on his lips. "And where are m'Lords Hejncze and Kassel? I see around me only common soldiers with the faces of thugs."

"I am Egbert of Kassel," said the knight, stepping forward. "And those are my men, so curtail your insults."

"And do not waste time on them," said the Inquisitor, moving alongside. "You know me, Urban Horn, you know who I am. And you perfectly understand your predicament. You are encircled; you can't break through. We'll lay hands on you, if not alive then dead. Our offer is: let us avoid bloodshed. We are not barbarians, but men of honour. Give yourself up of your own free will."

The man was silent for a while, a sneer playing on his face.

"I have under my command six Czechs and four local men, Silesians," he finally said. "All mercenaries and only linked to me by a monetary contract. They know nothing and have committed no crimes under my command. I demand that they walk free—"

"You are in no position to demand, Horn," Hejncze cut him off. "But I consent. They will be set free. As long as none stands accused of any earlier misdemeanours."

"On your knightly parole?"

"On my priestly parole."

Horn snorted, stifling laughter. He drew a dagger from a decorated sheath and—holding it by the blade—handed it to the Inquisitor.

"I lay down my arms," he said and bowed carelessly. "And at the same time offer a proposition. I was meaning to order luncheon to the side room. Instead of one duck, they can give us three, for the fowl looked appetizing on the spits. Will you accept my invitation, gentlemen? After all, we are men of honour, not barbarians."

The three men dining in the side room were assisted by only two esquires; Lord Kassel only summoned to him Jan Karwat and Parsifal of Rachenau. Karwat, because he was a bodyguard and utterly trustworthy. Parsifal, because he was new, green and had but faint understanding of what was being discussed. Parsifal had no illusions or doubts about that.

"You're having a good year, Grzegorz," said Horn, tearing flesh with his teeth from a duck held in both hands. "The arrest of Domarasc in March, and now me. While we're on the subject, is Domarasc still alive?"

"Don't turn the tables, Horn," said Hejncze, raising his eyes. "It is I who am questioning you here. I've been dreaming about this moment for four years, since you fled from me in Frankenstein."

"When fortune favoured me, it favoured me," said Horn, nodding. "And when it abandoned me, it did so for good. I dreamed of a dead fish last night, dammit, and a dream like that always predicts misfortune. It is my bad luck and misfortune that you happened to find me today. You've become accustomed to me as a Hussite intelligence agent, so it may surprise you to learn I've come to Silesia in a different role this time. As a private individual. On a matter of personal importance."

"Indeed. Well, I never."

"I came to Silesia for private revenge," said Urban Horn, ignoring the mockery. "Does it interest you to learn against whom? I shall tell you: against Konrad, Bishop of Wrocław. Isn't it a strange coincidence? After all, you, too, Grzegorz, have a bone to pick with the bishop. How does the proverb run? The enemy of my enemy—"

"Horn!" said the Inquisitor, aiming the duck's leg at him. "Let's get one thing straight. My feud with the bishop is my business. But the bishop is the highest ecclesiastical authority in Silesia, a bulwark of stabilisation and a guarantee of order. A blow aimed at the bishop is one aimed at order; you won't draw me into anything of the kind. Don't even try. I know what you personally have against him. Just imagine, I investigated the matter of the Świdnica Beguines, I'm familiar with the documents from the trial and the report from your mother's execution. While I may sympathise with you, I won't cooperate with you. Particularly since I'm not entirely convinced by your intentions. You're trying to persuade me that you are being driven by personal reasons, that you are seeking revenge, that you have come to Silesia with mercenaries to that end. When for me, you were, are and will remain a Hussite spy; you act on behalf of our enemies. So, not in order to right the world? Not for Huss, against the errors, perversions and corruption of Rome? Not from a profound conviction regarding the need for reform *in capite et in membris*? But for your own private interest, for personal revenge? It makes no difference to me. Nor to the starving beggars I saw on my way, sitting among the ruins and the smoking remains of villages. It was you who burned down those villages, Urban Horn, you who condemned those people to misery and death by starvation."

"There's a war on," retorted the spy haughtily. "And war, if you'll excuse the platitude, is cruel. Don't put the blame on me, Grzegorz. I can also show you the burned-out settlements around

Náchod and Broumov, the mutilated people there, the charred ruins and the graves of the dead, marking the routes of Catholic crusades!"

"I forgave you one platitude, the one about war. Don't shower me with more."

"Touché."

They were silent for some time. Finally, Horn tossed the duck's carcass to a dog, snatched up a mug and drained it.

"Let us leave aside the bishop and the good of the Church for a moment," he said, putting the mug down with a clatter. "What have you to say about Grellenort? My goal was not the Bishop of Wrocław—I realise that would be aiming a little high for me, biting off more than I can chew. The aim of my attack was to be the mysterious Sensenberg Castle, Grellenort's hideout. The place where the bishop's bastard blasphemes against God, conducts black magic and necromancy, where he brews poison and intoxicating decocts, where he summons forth demons and devils. Whence he sends his Riders on terrorist missions, ordering them to murder peaceful citizens. Tell me, Inquisitor, should one regard an attack on a place like that as aggression against the Church? Or perhaps the truth is as they say; that for Rome the end justifies the means, that in the fight against free thinking, heresy and reformatory movements it's permissible to harness and employ everything, even black magic?"

Now it was the turn of Grzegorz Hejncze to be quiet for a long time. Parsifal, although he only vaguely understood, fixed his eyes on Hejncze's face. He saw the muscles in the Inquisitor's jaw working, his eyes flashing and his mouth about to form a word.

"I know where Sensenberg Castle is located," Urban Horn said, ahead of him. "And how to get there."

"The Black Riders," Kassel said, "murdered Albrecht Bart of

Karczyn, who was my comrade. As regards me, I'm prepared—"

"Don't meddle in this, Egbert," said the Inquisitor, cutting him off sharply. "Please."

The Lord of Kopaniec cleared his throat and rubbed his hands together nervously. Grzegorz Hejncze silently nodded, gesturing for Horn to continue.

"This is a unique opportunity," said Horn.

Hejncze said nothing and put a hand to his forehead, shielding his eyes.

"Grellenort is not at Sensenberg," the Hussite spy went on softly. "He has gone to the Lusatian borderlands with most of his thugs to hunt for our mutual friend, the physician, Reinmar of Bielawa. For he learned that Reynevan—"

The Inquisitor took his hand away from his forehead. Horn fell silent under his gaze.

"Yes," Horn said, clearing his throat. "I admit it. It's owing to me that Grellenort found out about Reynevan. I did it—"

"We already know what you did," interrupted Hejncze.

"Reynevan will get out of trouble...He always does—"

"To the point, Horn."

"Only a few men remain at Sensenberg. With joined forces, we will make short work of them. And we can burn down that viper's nest, that hotbed of evil. We would destroy Grellenort's hideout, his centre of terror, his sorcerer's base, the source of hash'eesh and other narcotics. We would sow doubt and fear among his Riders. And quicken his downfall."

"Ha!" said Egbert of Kassel. He rubbed his hands together, glanced at the Inquisitor and fell silent.

"I've lately heard the opinion that terrorism is evil and leads nowhere," said Grzegorz Hejncze slowly. "That seems not to be in doubt. But there is, however, one thing worse than terrorism: the methods used to counter it."

There was a long silence.

"Why," the Inquisitor finally spoke, "*ad maiorem Dei gloriam*, the end justifies the means…Let us ride to Sensenberg. *Viribus unitis*…Stop, not so fast, where are you going, Horn? I haven't finished my sentence. We will make a truce, we will collaborate. But with certain conditions."

"Yes."

"Without calling our truce 'fragile,' I'll call it 'temporary.' You aren't free yet; after Sensenberg I shall want to talk to you. Carry out an exchange of information. And set the limits…for our mutual help…in the future."

"What do you mean?"

"You know very well what. You give me something and I give you something. In order for our conversations to flow more freely and discreetly, I shall lock you up. Not in prison, but in a monastery."

"If so, make it a women's one," said Urban Horn, smiling. "For example, the one where you are holding Reynevan's betrothed captive."

"What the Devil are you talking about?" said Hejncze, growing angry. "What betrothed? Now it's you peddling that nonsense. Do you claim that I…That the Holy Office abducts and incarcerates maidens? How absurd!"

"You claim it's not the Inquisition that is holding Jutta Apolda captive?"

"I do indeed claim that. Enough rot, Horn. Before us a *sanctum et gloriosum opus*: Sensenberg and the Black Riders."

"We'll deal with them, for we attack in an alliance," said Egbert of Kassel, standing up and slamming his fist on the table. "And there is strength in an alliance! To horse, with God! And if God is with us, who can stand against us?"

"*Si Deus pro nobis,*" continued Hejncze, "*quis contra nos?*"

"Or as it is rendered in the Czech tongue: *Kdyžť jest Bůh s námi, i kdo proti nám?*" said Horn, smiling.

They set off, not wasting time, at a gallop, forty-five horse, the Kopaniec unit, the Inquisitor's men and Horn's mercenaries. They rode towards the Kaczawskie Mountains; Parsifal didn't remember the way precisely, since he was in a state of constant, almost trembling excitement.

After some time, they put the last village behind them—the last sign of human existence—and found themselves in a wilderness, in a Silesia Parsifal didn't know. Convinced of the absolute triumph of civilisation, he was astonished to see an ancient forest that an axe had never touched. A rocky, barren moor criss-crossed with ravines which for many years no man had set foot on.

And then they saw it. A steep, jagged cliff. And a peak towering above it. On the peak the ruins of a castle, a miniature of a knightly castle from the Holy Land, serrated with battlements.

A winding gorge led to the castle. At its entrance, they were greeted by the sight of what remained of their predecessors. Egbert of Kassel's scowling face grew white and the battle-hardened armigers also paled. The foot soldiers crossed themselves and some even began to pray out loud. Parsifal closed his eyes. In spite of that he saw it. The sight was etched into his consciousness.

The entrance to the ravine was almost completely blocked by a huge pile of bones. By no means lying pell-mell.

Someone had taken the trouble to compose a welcoming gateway, something like a triumphal arch, out of skulls, pelvises, femurs and shinbones intertwined with ribs. A sickening odour testified to the fact that the construction was constantly being extended; some elements had been added recently.

The horses resisted, beginning to snort, struggle and stamp their hooves. There was no choice; they had to leave them. The dismounted unit set off through the ravine. Lord Kassel ordered four soldiers to guard the four tethered horses. Under the command of the esquire. And Parsifal of Rachenau.

In this way, Parsifal of Rachenau, formally an active participant in the capture of Sensenberg, didn't see any of the actual capture. In particular, he missed the sight of the gruesome death of three soldiers bespattered by Greek fire from a magical booby trap in the castle gate. He didn't see Horn's mercenaries massacring four Black Riders in the courtyard after a heavy fight. Or the Inquisitor's men, who forced their way into the alchemic laboratory, being attacked by a monstrous dwarf, gnome or other fiend, hurling flasks of caustic acid at them. Or the beast itself being burned alive in turn when flaming brands were tossed at it.

Parsifal didn't see the fierce battle that the last five Riders waged with Kassel and the Kopaniec armigers, fighting a rearguard action in the knightly hall. He didn't see them finally slaughtered, literally hacked to pieces. He didn't see the blood splashing the walls and the frescos on them: Jesus, falling for the second time under the cross, Moses with the stone tablets, Roland in his battle against the Saracens, Godfrey de Bouillon riding into Jerusalem. And Percival, kneeling before the Holy Grail.

It was evening by the time the unit returned. Inquisitor Hejncze. Urban Horn with a bandaged hand. Egbert of Kassel from Kopaniec with a head wound. And twenty-four men. Of the thirty-six who set off with them.

They rode away in silence, deep in thought. Without needless talk, without the bragging about deeds and exploits typical in such circumstances. With the feeling of a task well completed. Of the *sanctum et gloriosum opus* they had accomplished.

While the black mass of the ruins of Sensenberg Castle burned like a torch against the starry sky, belching fire from all its windows.

"I dreamed of a fire last night," said Reynevan, slinging the saddle onto his horse. "A great fire. I wonder what a dream like that could mean. Perhaps we should visit Master Zbrosław before we set off? For might it have been prophetic? Perhaps we are meant to hurry as though to a fire?"

"Let's hope not," said Rixa, tightening the girth. "Let's make do without prophecies like that, without fire and conflagrations. Particularly since the day promises to be a scorcher."

Chapter Fourteen

In which Hosts bleed and friends meet. Night falls over the town of Bolesławiec. And as we can read in Virgil, sleep overcame every living thing.

It was already warm at daybreak on the ninth of June *Anno Domini* 1429, while around three o'clock it was scorching; the heat was literally debilitating. On the ninth of June, the residents of Gelnau—a village located at the very mouth of the Nysa Gorge—who were forever looking vigilantly up towards the mountain of Warnkoppe, rising to the south, were lying in the shade, blissfully indolent and indifferent to everything.

A cry pulled them out of their torpor. A cry of terror.

"The beacon! The beeeacon!" yelled a farmer from the most distant field. As he yelled, he pointed at Warnkoppe, from the top of which rose into the sky a vertical column of black smoke.

In Jemlitz, a small town located to the south of Žitava, the parish priest of Saint Cyriacus walked through the church's nave, wiping his sweaty face on the sleeve of his cassock. He was sweating, shouting and raging at the labourers repairing the storeroom of the presbytery. Now he was hurrying to the vestry to take a rest within its cool walls. He was constantly forgetting to stop on the way, kneel down and cross himself in front of the altar, and if he ever did it was mechanically and unthinkingly. The previous night, the parish priest had been visited by a dream, an evil dream, following which he vowed not to commit any further such derelictions.

He stopped and knelt down. And began to scream. In a voice so ghastly that the labourers heard and ran from the presbytery.

The altar was covered in blood. Blood that was dripping from the tabernacle.

Hooves thudded on the Žitava highway as a mounted messenger flashed past beside a wagon, throwing up a large cloud of dust. But the woodcutter Hunsruck managed to see the rider's face twisted in fear for a split second. He knew at once what was happening.

"Jorg!" he shouted to his son. "Fly home through the trees! Tell mother to pack our belongings! We're fleeing! The Czechs are coming!"

The bells in the Churches of the Holy Cross and Saints Peter and Paul sounded the alarm. Boots thudded, iron clanked, captains shouted. The town was preparing its defence.

"The patrols are coming first," reported Sir Anzelm of Redern after returning from his reconnaissance. "Behind them is a mounted detachment of at least three hundred horse. Following the cavalry marches a great force of around six, seven thousand, with more than two hundred wagons. There are no siege engines."

"And thus they won't strike the town," said Lutpold Uechteritz, the Starosta of Žitava in relief. "Zgorzelec and its walls may also sleep soundly, I believe. But towns, castle settlements and villages will take a pounding. Some for a second time."

"In Ostritz," said Venantius Pack, the Franciscans' abbot, wringing his hands, "they have only just begun laying shingles

on the fresh rafters…The Cistercian convent is still in ruins…
Bernstadt still has not risen from its ashes…"

"Will we permit it?" called young Kaspar Gersdorf, heatedly.
"Won't we leave the walls to fight? Meet them in the field?"

Ulrik of Biberstein, Lord of Frydland and Żary, merely snorted
contemptuously. Starosta Uechteritz looked the youngster in the
eyes.

"There's seven thousand of them," he said coldly. "With what
will you face them in the field, laddie?"

"With the name of God on my lips! By God, I'll take my men!"

"I'm not stopping you."

"If you permit, I will also leave Žitava. With my men."

Lutpold Uechteritz looked back. And swallowed.

It was Birkart Grellenort, the Bishop of Wrocław's emissary.
Tall, slim, black-haired and dressed in black. Avian eyes, an evil
smile. And the look of a devil.

"Go," he said, nodding in assent. "Go, M'Lord Grellenort."

Far away, he added in his thoughts. *And don't come back. Neither you or nor your hellish horsemen.*

Reynevan detected magic. He was able to sense it. It turned out
he hadn't lost that useful skill.

They turned off the high road soon after leaving Legnica; they
were forced to by the extreme vigilance of troops and patrols,
who were stopping to search everyone and pestering people in
every possible way. The news from Lusatia caused the psychosis
regarding Hussite spies, sorcerers and Jewish saboteurs to infect
everybody in Legnica and overwhelm every sense. They wasted
an enormous amount of time leaving the town; the Chojnów
Gate was completely blocked. Only people wishing to enter
the town were questioned and searched, but anyone leaving the
town was still observed extremely suspiciously. The roads were

teeming with soldiers. A little beyond Legnica, just after joining the Via Regia, a route passing through the whole of Europe, they chanced upon a mounted unit searching travellers. They were saved from difficulties by a row caused by a merchant from Kiev travelling home, furious that the soldiers were emptying his wagons and that they couldn't understand anything he was saying to them. They were around a quarter of a mile from the customs house in Eibenmühl, where Rixa suspected there would be another control point; there was probably also a sentry post and blockade at the toll booth in Tomaszów. So, although the Via Regia offered the chance to travel quickly and comfortably, it would be more sensible to abandon the trans-European road and ride through the forests.

Night found them close to Chojnów, which, after the plundering raid of the previous year, was still rubble and ashes. Having looked in the morning at the charred remains of the town, Reynevan doubted whether it would ever rise from the ruins.

They continued to stick to dirt roads and rutted forest tracks, heading westwards. They passed—looking down from above—a poor little village in a valley by a bend in a winding river. And it was there that Reynevan sensed magic.

He felt it, smelled it in the forest scent of moss and resin, in the wind, and heard it in the nervous squawking of jays and magpies, in the rustling of leaves and the creaking of tree trunks. The anxiety, swelling in a violent wave, made him stop Rixa by grabbing her horse's bridle. Before she had time to speak, it began.

"*Adsumus! Adsuuumus!*"

Ten Black Riders flew out and charged at them across the slope from behind a bramble-covered ridge on their left.

They reined their horses around and rode downhill in a breakneck gallop, towards the river. After fording it in showers of mud, they were pinned by another five Riders emerging from the right flank. Reynevan had already managed—despite riding hard—to wind up his hunting crossbow; now he pushed the stock against his cheek and released the trigger. Mindful of earlier lessons and experience, he didn't aim at the man but at the horse. Struck with a bolt, the black stallion reared up and lost control, throwing onto the ground not just its own rider but two others, wreaking havoc among the rest, allowing Reynevan and Rixa to dart through. And now they charged, spurring their horses' sides, downhill through the valley, towards a plain and the white ribbon of the Via Regia. Clods of turf flew around, churned up by their hooves. And the pursuers bore down on them.

"*Adsumus! Adsumus!*"

More Riders—five to be precise—came charging out from the ravine on the right, so close that Reynevan saw one of them was a girl. *I know her, I've seen her before*, he thought. And hunched over in the saddle just in time as a hurled javelin brushed his arm.

"*Adsuuumuuuus!*"

With a thudding of hooves, they hurtled onto the Via Regia and drew further away in a crazy gallop. But the Riders were right behind them. Reynevan watched in horror as one of them moved towards the head, galloping with a cloak flowing out behind him like demonic wings. He knew who it was. He knew before he saw his face. Reynevan bent his head over his horse's mane and dashed on in a wild chase, following Rixa, whose bay mare was bounding like a stag. In spite of their frantic efforts, the Black Riders began to fall back. Only slightly to begin with, then more and more visibly. They were left behind but didn't let up. Reynevan knew they wouldn't desist. Rixa, too.

"Customs!" she shouted over the wind. "House!"

He understood. The control point in Tomaszów they had wanted to avoid could now be their salvation. A crowd of people could mean their survival. But there remained a considerable distance to cover. And their horses, though fleet and still not allowing the Black Riders to shorten the distance between them, weren't made of iron, after all.

Reynevan sensed magic. And heard it.

The Wallcreeper, still galloping, raised a hand and shrieked out a spell. Reynevan and Rixa's horses neighed wildly in answer.

The road ahead of them—the Via Regia running between an avenue of trees—until then as flat as a table, now suddenly reared up. Where a moment before it had been level and even, it now rose up sharply ahead. A steep hill with no end in sight.

"It's an illusion!" screamed Reynevan. "It's a spell! It's not there!"

"Tell the horses!"

There was no sense saying it. The horses slowed down on the steep incline. They climbed up it but began to wheeze, hack and shed flakes of foam. From behind came triumphant yelling.

"Across country! Leave the road and ride across the fields!"

They turned off. But the fields weren't fields, either. It was a mountain, apparently even steeper than the road.

The time has come, decided Reynevan, *for desperate measures.*

He untied from under his jerkin the string threaded through the veined stone with a spot in the shape of a human eye. Said to be Castilian, said to have been brought from Burgos, purchased in Mages' Lane in Legnica. Costing three groschen. And probably worth as much.

"*Viendo, no vean!*" he screamed, gripping the talisman in his sweaty hand, as tightly as if he meant to crush it. "*Viendo, no vean!* Over to the side, Rixa, over there! To the trees! Ride to the trees!"

"They can see us! They'll surround us!"

"Turn towards the trees!"

Something impossible occurred. Incredible and unbelievable.

The talisman reacted to the activating spell. And began to work.

They raced on towards the trees and cries followed them; cries of astonishment and disbelief. And then of fury. They didn't look back. Faces pressed against the horses' manes, they hurtled along as fast as they could. They were only slowed down when they reached the trees, the thicket, hollows and furrows. And then there was silence.

"They couldn't see us…" said Rixa, sucking in air. "They really couldn't see us…We became invisible to them…"

"They looked but they couldn't see," said Reynevan, calming his crazily beating heart with deep breaths. "This amulet…I never expected that…And if it works really well, it will confuse them even more, they'll think they can see us…in places we're not. And that may happen, because it was an extremely strong periapt…"

"Was?"

Wordlessly, he held up the string. Now without the stone, which had turned to dust after being activated.

"It only worked once." Rixa sighed. "How long will the effects last?"

"Grellenort is with them," said Reynevan, shuddering at the thought. "Let's not allow hope to delude us too much and flee while we can. Let's vanish into the forest."

"We'll change direction to confuse them further," said Rixa, pushing her dishevelled hair under her hood. "They'll be looking out for us on the roads leading to Bolesławiec. They'll think we'll circle around and return to the road. But let's ride straight southwards, as far away as we can…"

"Without delay."

She turned around in the saddle.

"Did you see that girl? The fair-haired one?"

"I did."

"It was Douce of Pack, Grellenort's lover. A Devil incarnate."

He thought back. The courtyard at Trosky Castle. The javelin lancing the carpenter's apprentice. Eyes the colour of water in a mountain lake. Beautiful and utterly inhuman. Douce of Pack.

"Let's ride."

They rode the whole day, as hard as they could without risking exhausting the horses. And as far as the wilderness, the dense forest, bogs and ravines barred by tangles of thorny branches would allow. They rode, looking back and listening out. But they heard only the drumming of woodpeckers.

In order to cover the greatest distance possible, they only stopped when the darkness absolutely precluded riding, on a relatively dry hummock, not daring to make a fire. A crescent moon, as thin as a swarf, shone above the treetops.

"Let's turn back," decided Rixa. "We must have lost them for good after all."

They rode for some time along the course of a shallow stream, the Bobrzyca, a left-bank tributary of the Bóbr, according to Rixa. The Bobrzyca flowed through Tomaszów, which lay on the Via Regia.

In Rixa's opinion, Tomaszów was to be avoided; she suggested they head west and find the road leading to the village of Warta. Reynevan relied on her knowledge of the vicinity, for the area was unfamiliar to him. He had been there during the expedition of spring 1428, but he hadn't admired the views then, nor did he remember anything now.

The presence of a settlement—possibly Warta—was betrayed

by the clattering of storks and the barking of dogs. Soon after, they heard the thudding of a working mill, then saw the mill and the millpond with a carpet of duckweed. The dogs kept barking.

"Shall we go in or avoid it?"

"We'll go in," decided Rixa. "It looks safe. And by the way, we can ask for directions. I doubt that Grellenort was here, but there's no harm in asking."

They rode between wattle fences and vegetable beds. Cautiously. But not cautiously enough.

At the very edge of the village stood a huge oak. Four bodies hung from its branches. One, clearly recently hanged, was still twitching.

A dozen soldiers were gathered around the tree, dressed in colourful—not black—raiment. The soldiers spotted them at once and rushed towards them shouting. Reynevan and Rixa turned around, only to see a knight on a horse with a caparison galloping frantically towards them from the mill. In full plate armour. And a sallet with the visor down. With a tournament shield bearing a coat of arms. And a lowered lance. Quite simply, Amadís of Gaula. Or some other knight from legend.

Rixa dodged the lance by leaning out far from the saddle. The powerful horse struck her steed and knocked it over, sending the girl rolling across the ground to the bank of the mill stream where she hit her head hard on a post. As Reynevan's horse reared up, the knight discarded the lance, drew a sword and made a powerful reverse swing; had Reynevan not jumped down he would have lost his head. The galloping horse hit him and knocked him over, and he tumbled into the mud, right under other hooves.

The battle cries gained suddenly in intensity as more riders appeared all around and Reynevan realised that other forces had joined the affray. Light cavalry in kettle hats, many with the sign of the Chalice on their breasts. There wasn't enough time, however, to dwell on the matter, for a battle was raging around him, horses were snorting and neighing, blades flashing and clanging and blood pouring. A horse's chest knocked him over again; he fell down and looked up to see a spear raised to stab him. At the same moment, the spearman flew from the saddle, struck by a Flemish goedendag.

"Samson!"

"Reynevan?"

Samson reined his horse around, shielding Reynevan from further attack. There was no need, since the attacker cowered in the saddle, stabbed by the bear spears of two horsemen sporting the Chalice. The third slashed him across the nape with a curved falchion for good measure.

"Scharley!"

"Reynevan?"

"Take them alive!" yelled the Hussites' commander, a young knight wearing a dull brownish-grey cloak over full plate armour. "Take the knights alive! Kill the common soldiers!"

The battle was over. Whoever was meant to be finished off was finished off, whoever was meant to be tied up was tied up. Reynevan, somewhat stunned, hugged Scharley and Samson, observed by the knight in the dull brownish-grey cloak from the height of his saddle. When he raised the visor of his helmet, his face looked familiar to Reynevan.

"Our hejtman," said Scharley, introducing him. "Brus of Klinštejn of the Ronovci family. The younger brother of—"

He didn't finish. One of the dead was only feigning and now leaped to his feet and went for Brus, wielding a baselard. He didn't reach him. Scharley fired a short, odd-looking gun at him from close range, tearing his head to pieces.

"Thank you," said Brus of Klinštejn of the Ronovci family, the younger brother Brázda of Klinštejn, hejtman with the Orphans. "Thank you, Brother Scharley."

Reynevan finally remembered Rixa and looked to see her getting up from the ground and shaking sand from her hair.

"Everything in order?"

"Quite in order," she replied. And suddenly her mouth contorted into a grimace and her eyes opened wide. She was looking at Samson.

"Troop, muster!" commanded Brus of Klinštejn. "We're leaving!"

"The young Lord Gersdorf will ride with us," he said to the knight with the lance, the Amadís of Gaula, who now, in captivity, without a helmet, having lost his entire legendary aura, was revealed to be a terrified pipsqueak. "Sir Kaspar of Gersdorf, the son of Sir Lothar Gersdorf. I'm expecting a hundred grzywna for you, young m'lord. At least. Troop, we are moving out! Brother Scharley, check the rearguard!"

"What have you got me into?" Rixa asked quietly, riding over to Reynevan. "Who are your comrades?"

"This is the special sabotage-reconnaissance unit of the Tábor's field army," said Scharley, having overheard.

"A punitive expedition."

"Indeed. The Tábor, a field army under the command of Jakub Kroměšín of Březovice, with contingents under Otík of Loza, the cavalry under Mikuláš Sokol of Lamberk and the Praguians of Václav Carda. Six thousand men, two hundred wagons. Our special unit serves as reconnaissance. We hunt loose horses. We catch deserters and bandits who steal the horses from us. Did you see the hanged men in the village? They were horse thieves. We tracked them for three days, but young Gersdorf was quicker and hanged them before we could. And Gersdorf and his troop were tormenting the Tábor all the way from Žitava, so Kroměšín ordered us to deal with them—"

"Where is the Tábor at this moment?"

"At Bolesławiec. Can't you hear? That's not a storm, Reinmar, they're bombards. In any case, you'll soon see for yourself, for that's where we are headed. Unless you have other plans? Perhaps this lady whom you haven't introduced, and who looks none too delighted by our company, has other plans and designs?"

"I'm Rixa Cartafila of Fonseca. My plans and designs are nobody else's business. And what should I be delighted about? That a dybbuk is riding beside me?"

She turned around and pointed an accusing finger at Samson.

"A dybbuk, ha!" said Scharley, snorting. "At last, Samson, you've met your match. She saw through you at once. A dybbuk, I swear blind, an absolute dybbuk. A demon, an evil spirit in another person's body. And to think I suspected you of being at most the Eternal Wandering Jew."

"I regret to say I'll have to disappoint you both," replied Samson Honeypot in a tired voice. "I'm not a dybbuk. Or the Eternal Jew. I'd have known it if I was."

"Let's keep near the back," said Scharley, standing up in his stirrups, checking that no one from the unit was listening or taking an interest in them. "Tell us, Reinmar, what's been happening with you. And what brings you here."

After Reynevan had finished, the penitent said nothing for a long time. The roar of cannons from the north-west was becoming more distinct.

"The Black Riders," he finally said, "have introduced themselves to the Tábor, too. Beyond Žitava, four days ago, they caught and massacred our *hlidka*, ten men; only one managed to flee. Then we found a few of them they had caught alive. They were hanging by their legs from trees. Somebody had been trying extremely hard to persuade them to testify. And then used them as targets for javelin-throwing practice.

"And you, m'lady," he said, addressing Rixa, "are the one who rescued our Reinmar in Wrocław in the winter. And you continue, I see, to support him with help, advice, strength of spirit and your endearing personality. Of your own will? Or perhaps on somebody's orders, if I may ask?"

"I'd prefer you didn't," said Rixa, looking him in the eyes. "I won't ask you about anything and I expect the same."

"I understand," said Scharley, shrugging. "But since this is an army unit, I must think something up for the purposes of our leader, Brus of the Ronovci. For should he decide to ply you with questions, m'lady—"

"I'll cope. You may call me Rixa."

Scharley spurred his horse and trotted to the head.

"How are things in Rapotín, Samson? Marketa…"

"Everything is in the best order," said the giant, grinning. "The very best. Better than I could have expected. And probably much better than I deserve. She didn't want to let me go with Scharley. She wouldn't listen to any arguments…"

"Did you have any?"

"Several. And one of them was you. Rixa, do you really have to bore your eyes into me? You've already proved your ability to see hidden things. But no matter how hard you stare you won't see a dybbuk."

"What will I see, then? I can see supernatural things. And you're supernatural."

"One of my friends," said Samson, still smiling, "is wont to say there's no such thing as supernatural beings or phenomena. Some occurrences simply go beyond what we know about nature."

"That was Saint Augustine. You knew him personally, I presume. And it doesn't surprise me at all."

"Rixa, you're making quite extraordinary progress."

"Don't tease me. Dybbuk."

Scharley trotted over and cast a severe glance over them.

"What philosophical disputes are you engaged in here? Samson? The Czechs are starting to look back. Keep your bloody identity hidden."

"I beg your pardon, I forgot myself. Will this do? I've lately been practising. Look."

Samson crossed his eyes horribly. He smiled foolishly, whimpered idiotically and drooled from the corners of his mouth. And as a climax blew a bubble from his nose. When it popped, he blew another.

"Ha!" called Rixa in genuine delight. "Very good! And I can create illusory symptoms of the plague. I spit blood and blow out snot."

"Damn you both!" said Scharley, turning around in disgust. "Come on, Reinmar. Let's leave them to their games."

"Scharley?"

"Yes?"

"That short gun you fired near the mill. What strange weapon was it?"

"This?" the penitent said, taking a weapon from a case by his saddle and showing it to him. "This, my friend, is a Prague gun, commonly called a 'treacherous hand cannon.' It's the height of fashion in Prague now, everybody's got one. As you can see, it's short enough to hide under your cloak and use suddenly, treacherously, which explains the name. Look, the slow match is stuck into a brass matchlock and it can smoulder there the whole time. I can pull the trigger with one hand, see, I bring the slow match to the touch hole and boom! Not bad, eh? You cannot stop progress, laddie."

"It can't be denied. Hear anything?"

"No."

"Exactly. They haven't fired any bombards for some time."

They rode out of the forests onto a hill from where they were able to admire the panorama. A picturesque bend in the Bóbr. And the town on the right bank.

"Before us is Bolesławiec, the Upper Gate," said Brus of Klinštejn, pointing. "It would appear we've arrived at just the right time. The town has surrendered."

The Upper Gate turned out to have been destroyed and the remains of the hasp and staple hanging from the hinges were charred, the wall and gatehouse black from soot and cracked by fire. The Taborites had clearly employed their usual, tried and tested means of breaking down the gate by burning it through. They had piled logs up at the foot of the gate, tossed several barrels of pitch and tar on top, set them alight and waited for the outcome. Which was usually surrender. As it was this time.

"We're entering. Rixa, what about you?"

"I'll wait here."

"For whom? For what?"

She didn't answer but turned away. Scharley snorted, then tossed Reynevan an ambiguous look. Seeing that Reynevan wasn't reacting, he spurred his horse and rode after the unit.

It was peaceful in the town, although the narrow streets leading to the town square were thronged with heavily armed Hussites. The Tábor were standing in close formation in the town square, around the town hall. The townspeople herded against the walls of houses looked at the aggressors in tremulous silence.

"Either Bolesławiec has come to an agreement or is about to," said Scharley, assessing the situation. "As usual, they will set a ransom and contributions in the form of billets and supplies for the army. They will reach agreement. Otherwise, everything here would have been afire."

About a dozen combat wagons were arrayed near the town hall with cannon barrels protruding from them. Among them was the hejtman's staff wagon. It was conspicuous since its sides were upholstered and the inside lined with stolen priests' chasubles. The Hejtman of the Tábor's field army, Jakub Kroměšín of Březovice himself, dressed in a short jacket decorated with gold embroidery and red leather high boots, was standing beside the wagon. He was accompanied by Otík of Loza, Mikuláš Sokol of Lamberk and Václav Carda, the commander of the Prague municipal militias. And the gaunt-faced preacher Smolík, whom Reynevan remembered from the previous year's plundering raid.

The officers' guard let them through. They walked closer. Reynevan cleared his throat.

"Hejtman—"

"Not now!" said Kroměšín, recognising him and clearly surprised, but gestured him away. "Not now, physician!"

The municipal delegation emerged from the town hall. Councillors and burghers, led by a fat priest in a cassock and a tall bearded man in a voluminous cloak with many folds like a toga and trimmed at the bottom with beaver fur. The cloak caught Reynevan's attention: its blue was the unique shade that his murdered brother Peterlin had obtained from woad and bilberry juice at his dyeworks.

The bearded man and the fat priest stopped in front of Kroměšín and bowed. The bearded man began to speak. He spoke so softly that Reynevan, Scharley and Samson, who were standing ten paces away, could only make out every fifth word. But everybody, even those standing further away, understood what was happening. Bolesławiec was surrendering. Offering a ransom, as long as the Tábor would spare them. Them from the sword, their houses from fire. Everybody, even those standing further away, also suddenly saw Kroměšín's ferocious expression. And heard his voice. His lion's roar.

"Now? *Now* you want to pay a ransom? When we are already in the town? When you are at our mercy? Too late, Bolesławiec, too late! Yesterday, when I called on you to surrender, you shouted back proudly from the walls! Do you recall what you shouted? Something about Kratzau, by any chance? I'll give you Kratzau now! You'll remember me, wretched dogs!"

The bearded man retreated a step and paled. The fat priest, on the contrary, looked as though he would fly at the hejtman's throat.

"I knew there would be no point talking to them!" he crowed. "*Excoecavit eos malitia eorum!* Damn you, heretics! Iconoclasts! Criminals! You will roast in Hell! God's punishment will fall on you!"

At a sign from Kroměšín, the Taborite soldiers surrounded the delegation, pushing the councillors against the wall. The hejtman of the field army stood before them, resting his fists on his hips.

"It will fall on you first," he said. "Now. I will punish you in God's name. Go on, Brother Smolík," he said, addressing the gaunt-faced preacher. "Speak to them. Let them hear the voice of God's truth before they depart this Earth. They won't receive salvation, in any case, wretched dogs, minions of Rome, servants of the Babylonian Sigismund. But they will bid farewell to this Earth with lighter hearts."

The preacher stood as stiff as a poker and took a deep breath.

"This is the Lord's war!" he shouted squeakily. "So He has delivered you into our hands! You ate the bread of immorality and drank the wine of violence, so the day of punishment has come. You sinned against our Lord, so your blood will be splashed like dust and your bone marrow will be like mud. You sinned, O perverse nation, exalted yourselves proudly, bowed down before the false idols of Rome, so God will defeat you and cut off your heads as David did to Goliath. God crushes the heads of His foes, the tousle-haired skull of that which acts sinfully!"

"Good," said Kroměšín. "I especially liked the tousle-haired skull. Although the bone marrow wasn't bad either. Well, boys, did you hear? Take them as God ordered and Brother Smolík has reminded us. Do to them one after the other what David did to Goliath!"

"Mercy!" howled the bearded man in the blue cloak as he was dragged from the group. "Don't kill us! Christians! Have mercy!"

The Taborites seized him, dragged him over to a wagon and rested his neck on the shaft. One of the Taborites stepped forward and swung an axe. He struck twice again, with the burgher wheezing and croaking and the blood gushing in streams. Finally, his head fell onto the blood-spattered cobbles.

The struggling priest was thrown to the ground and pressed down with knees. A six-inch nail was held against the back of his skull. And banged in with several blows of a battleaxe, right up to the head. The priest only cried out once, then just flapped and kicked his legs.

Blows rained down on the councillors crowded into the town hall portal. They were beaten with flails, balls and chains and battleaxes, hacked with swords and stabbed with bear spears. A short time later, twelve bodies were twitching in a pool of blood.

Without a word, Kroměšín gestured with a hand and before he had lowered it, six thousand Tábor warriors attacked the town of Bolesławiec yelling wildly. They slaughtered the people in the town square in no time and then massacred anybody they found in the streets. Then forced their way into houses. The people's cries joined together in one great, hellish scream and a hail of bodies began to fall from windows. The massacre continued in the streets, no mercy was shown and the cobbles were soon covered in bodies. Blood flowed like a river into the gutters, washing away soap suds and urine, slops, dung and manure.

The churches of Bolesławiec offered no protection. People hurrying to Our Lady's and Saint Nicolaus's were struck down. Massacres took place outside the Dominican Holy Cross and in the square in front of Saint Dorothy's. The Church of Saint Hedwig, where more than a hundred townspeople and clergymen were hiding, gave sanctuary for a short while. Then the Hussites forced their way in and entered the vestibule, nave and presbyter. No one survived and the church was set on fire. Bright flames and a column of smoke rose into the sky.

When it began, when the bearded man in blue was being executed, Samson took a step forwards as though wanting to interfere. When the penitent caught him by the arm, he struggled to free himself, but stood where he was, didn't move forward, didn't get involved. Didn't stop anything. He just turned around, as white as a sheet. He looked at Reynevan. At Scharley. And again at Reynevan. And then upwards, at the sky. Quite as though expecting to see something there.

"Brother!" Reynevan said, going over not to Kroměšín, but to Otík of Loza, whom he knew better. "Persuade the hejtman to stop this massacre! Where is the town's burgomeister? Otto Arnoldus! I must talk to him!"

"Why?"

"He has information of the highest import!" he lied easily, shouting above the screams of the dying. "Secret information of special significance! For the cause!"

"Then you're unlucky, you and the cause," said Kroměšín, who was listening. "Burgomeister Arnoldus is there. And his head is over there."

He pointed to the first man executed, the bearded man in the blue cloak, the one beheaded on the wagon.

"I even feel sorry for him," he added. "May the Lord give him eternal rest. *Et lux perpetua luceat ei.*"

"He…" said Reynevan, swallowing. "Arnoldus had a wife… People! Who knows her? Who knows…?"

"I do!" One of the locals spoke up obsequiously from the group serving the Taborites as guides. "They live in Customs Street. I'll show you!"

"Lead on."

They found Wiryda Arnoldus, the newly widowed wife of the burgomeister, alive. In her plundered house. Scrambling from the floor and with trembling hands trying to tidy up her torn garb and hide her nakedness with the tatters of her shredded dress and blouse. Samson audibly sucked in air. Scharley swore. Reynevan looked away.

The raping of women was punished harshly in the Tábor's field army. The military punishment Žižka established for rape was flogging or even garrotting. But, ah well, Žižka had been dead for five years and his penalties had become visibly obsolete and fallen out of use. They hadn't survived the test of time. Like many other principles and rules. Samson removed his mantle and covered the woman's shoulders. Reynevan knelt down beside her.

"Forgive me, madam," he mumbled. "I know it is a bad time… But this is a matter of life and death. One of rescuing a person in grave difficulty…I must…I must ask you a question. Please…"

The woman shook her head and entwined the fingers of both hands in her dishevelled hair. Reynevan was about to touch her shoulder but stopped himself in time.

"Please, madam," he repeated. "I implore you. I kneel before you. I know you were once imprisoned in a nunnery. Please tell me where."

She looked at him over the bruises swelling on her swollen cheeks.

"Marienstern," she said. "And now leave me alone. Begone. And may you all be damned."

Things had calmed down outside. Kroměšín gave the command to stop the slaughter and the deputy hejtmans and captains—not without difficulty—stifled the Taborites' ardour. They needed the intervention of Mikuláš Sokol's cavalry, who took the more determined to task with blows of whips, staves and spear shafts. The Warriors of God, now subdued, limited themselves only to plunder. Resting against his wagon lined with chasubles, Kroměšín watched with contentment as spoils were brought to the town square and placed in a heap.

"Well, physician?" asked Otík of Loza, who was driving off the warriors when he saw Reynevan. "Did you find the burgomeister's wife? Did you learn anything from her?"

"We must hasten to Lusatia. To the convent in Marienstern."

"We?" said Kroměšín, frowning. "You go ahead, I want nothing from you. But your comrades serve in the army, and the army is marching to Żagań. I'll soon be ordering them to march out."

"Don't give the order yet, Hejtman."

The words were uttered by a young man in a scholar's beret and a black doublet, riding a black stallion. He was accompanied by Rixa Cartafila of Fonseca and a soldier in half-armour over a quilted gambeson. The horses snorted, smelling blood, and the newcomers had to dismount. The hejtman glowered at them.

"Who are you? What is this?"

"Order anyone not involved to move away."

Kroměšín gestured everybody away, until only Carda and Otík

of Loza remained. Reynevan, who also wanted to go away, was stopped by Rixa. It didn't escape Kroměšín's attention.

"I've seen you before, I believe," said Kroměšín, eyeing up the young man in the beret. "With Prokop. They call you Piotr Preischwitz, you are the town scribe from Bautzen. And apparently a spy of ours. Go on and speak. What do you wish to tell me?"

"I am to tell you: it is not a good moment to attack Żagań."

Václav Carda laughed and Otík of Loza snorted. Kroměšín didn't react.

"Do you see what I've done to this town?" he said, making a sweeping gesture towards the bodies, the bloody cobbles, the flames and smoke over the roofs. "I have exacted revenge for the Battle of Kratzau. The Lusatians and Silesians grew big-headed, they turned our defeat at Kratzau into a symbol to cheer folk's hearts. But I shall give *them* a symbol, so that at the sound of the word 'Kratzau' even their grandchildren will soil their britches. Bolesławiec has paid. Žitava, Bautzen, Zgorzelec, Chotěbuz, Kamenec and Gubín will pay, their time will come. And Żagań will soon pay. Herzog Jan of Żagań and his brother, Henryk, were at Kratzau, they have Czech blood on their hands; that blood demands vengeance. I won't leave a single stone standing in Żagań."

"Duke Jan of Żagań and Henryk of Głogów," said Piotr Preischwitz slowly and emphatically, "approached the King of Poland for protection, promised to stand loyally by the Kingdom of Poland and support Poland in all events. And right now, a Czech mission is residing in Krakow. Prokop the Shaven; the Englishman, Peter Payne; Bedřich of Strážnice; and Sir Vilém Kostka of Postupice. They are debating about an alliance, displaying goodwill and friendship, while you, Brother Kroměšín, want to ravage and burn down a duchy under Jagiełło's protection? I was instructed to tell you: Director Prokop does not support the idea of attacking the Duchy of Żagań. He suggests accepting the ransom offered."

"I have received no ransom from Żagań."

Preischwitz looked at Rixa and then at the soldier in the half-armour. The soldier stepped forwards and spoke.

"His Lordship Duke Jan, *illustrissimus dux* and Lord of Żagań, states his diplomatic position through me. He is prepared to—"

"Eight hundred Rhine gold pieces," Kroměšín interrupted bluntly. "If he pays, I shall spare him. I have spoken. And farewell, Brother Carda, order the army into marching formation."

"Marienstern," said Rixa, pensively. "The convent of the Cistercian Sisters. That's halfway between Zgorzelec and Bautzen. Around three days' ride from here."

"Two if one pushes the horses," said Piotr Preischwitz, correcting her. "It's Via Regia, one can make good speed. And I happen to be going that way. I'd be happy to lead you."

"Then let's not waste time," Rixa decided. "Let's get as far as Nowogrodziec before dusk."

"I cannot," replied Scharley to Reynevan's enquiring expression. "Kroměšín was right, I'm serving. The Tábor wouldn't forgive me if I deserted, and desertion means the noose. The men from my own unit would haul me up onto a branch."

"I will go," declared Samson softly. "Halfwits can get away with anything. They can't treat me as a deserter, for I never enlisted. I was on Scharley's inventory. When he tells them I've vanished, it'll be as if his dog ran away."

"Godspeed, Scharley," said Reynevan, leaping into the saddle. "Be heedful of yourself."

"You be heedful. There's only four of you, while I have six thousand comrades. And two hundred wagons with artillery."

*

The sun was setting. There was a smell of burning in Bolesławiec, flames still creeping over the embers. In Bolesławiec, blood was clotting black in gutters. In Bolesławiec, some dogs howled, others were nipping at the bodies of the dead. Bolesławiec resounded with the groans of the wounded and dying, with the cries of the raped and orphaned, with the faltering prayers of those who were without hope.

Finally, the sun set and the wounded town fell silent.

Nox ruit et fuscis tellurem amplectitur alis. Night rushes down and embraces the earth with shadowy wings.

Poor Reynevan.

I'm truly sorry for him, Marketa. I'm truly sorry I couldn't help him in his misfortune in any way.

We arrived at the Cistercian convent in Marienstern after two days' ride, only to find out that Miss Jutta wasn't there. It distressed Reynevan greatly. But the fact that Jutta had been there distressed him even more. For three months, from the middle of February to Pentecost. They missed each other by barely a month.

We visited all the female convents in the vicinity. We searched at the Poor Clare convent in Seusslitz, the Benedictines' convent in Riese and the Magdalene Sisters in Lubáň. In Zgorzelec, we spoke to the Cistercian nuns from Marienthal near Ostritz, who had fled after their nunnery was burned down in 1427. We didn't find Jutta anywhere; nothing was known about her anywhere. Reynevan was completely beside himself. I couldn't help him.

I'm truly sorry for him, Marketa.

Are you too?

We returned to Prague from Lusatia; in the middle of August, Scharley also arrived there, we spent some time together, but Scharley had to return to the field army soon after. He is currently stationed somewhere near Jičín, but news is circulating about another punitive expedition, planned for after Saint Wacław's Day.

Reynevan remained in Prague, at the apothecary's shop at the House at the Archangel; he and the sorcerers there tried to find Jutta using magic, but without success. Then a plague broke out near Psáře and he—a physician by vocation—hurried to help. He didn't hesitate for a moment. He got through his dejection, didn't yield to despair. There is much truth in the statement that what doesn't kill us strengthens us.

And me?

I decided to return here to Rapotín. For how long? For as long as possible.

And then what, you ask? We shall certainly meet again, we three, no doubt soon. Fate has bound us tightly together, for better and worse. And nothing, after all, occurs without reason.

Fate bound me tightly with them, Marketa. Very tightly.

Almost as tightly as with you.

Chapter Fifteen

In which weakness of character forces Reynevan to become a hero. The heroes heroically ford the River Mulda and heroically fight a bloody battle. Their heroism is rewarded. Their weakness, astonishingly, also. Hence the moral, which the author nonetheless will refrain from delivering.

God, Great God, venerunt gentes in hereditatem tuam, *the pagans came to Your heritage again! Is it because of our sins or are we* poena peccati, *that the heretic with his sword and flaming brand keep visiting us?*

In Anno MCCCCXXIX, ipso die sancti Johannis baptiste *the Hussite brigands despoiled our beloved monastery, our scriptorium and our pride, the library! They destroyed works of the measure of Alain of Lille's* De fide catholica, *Ramon Llull's* Libre de meravelles *and Simon of Genoa's* Clavis sanationis, *treasures such as Horapollon of Egypt's* Hieroglyphica *and Pierre of Beauvais's* Bestiaire, *treatises and codices of such marvellous work as* Expositio totius mundi et gentium, De magia veterum, Liber de mirabilibus naturae arcanis, De amore, Secreta mulierum *and many others, perhaps the only copies in the world. All one can do is wring one's hands!*

Not six months passed and another attack came. Once again, the Wycliffites, Thaborienses, Orfani et Pragenses, *and led by*

Procopius Rasu*s, called, following his command*, gubernator Taboriensium communitatis in campis bellancium, *the greatest and cruellest of the apostates and heretics, indeed not a man* ex muliere natus, *but a* monstrum detestabile, crudele, horrendum et importunum. Eodem anno circa festum sancte Lucie *that Prokop and his entire invincible army*, cum curribus, cumpixidibus, cumpeditibus et equitibus marched *ad* marchionatum Misnense, *wreaking murder and conflagration. Until finally, he reached the river called the Mulda. And the winter was mild that year...*

The quill pen was dry and scratched annoyingly on the prepared parchment. The old monk chronicler dipped his quill in the inkwell.

The servants illuminated the chamber, lighting candles in all the candlesticks. The Bishop of Wrocław, Konrad, sighed in satisfaction on seeing the expression of admiration on Grzegorz Hejncze's face. He knew it was difficult to surprise the Inquisitor, let alone impress him.

"Well?" he asked proudly, content with the effect. "A pretty thing, isn't it?"

Grzegorz Hejncze cleared his throat. And confirmed with a nod of his head. He had to. It was a pretty thing. Unquestionably pretty.

The only piece of furniture in the chamber was an immense table, covered entirely by a gigantic map of Silesia and the neighbouring countries, made of sheets of fabric embroidered with silk. Although the Inquisitor had never seen the map before, he was aware of its existence. He knew it had been made and embroidered by the Dominican Sisters of Saint Catherine based on drawings by the Cistercian Sisters from Lubiąż. And that it had taken the nuns over a year to fashion it.

There were elaborately carved figures on it, since the map mainly served to track and analyse military activities. The figures had been carved by Ambroży Erler, the best woodcarver in Wrocław, according to the strict instructions of the bishop himself. The Catholic army units were portrayed as white and gold winged angels with fiery swords, and the Hussite formations were depicted as horned devils, crouching and sticking out their backsides.

Every morning the priests recreated for the bishop the current military situation, arranging the figures according to troop movements in the theatre of operations. Since the thirteenth of December, Saint Lucy's Day, that is from the beginning of the large-scale Hussite plundering raid on Meissen and Thuringia, the theatre had occupied territory between ODERA FLV and ALB FLV embroidered in blue thread, and the figures were placed by the priests in the regions indicated by the names SAXONIA, MISNIA, TURINGA and LUSATIA INFERIOR, bordered from the north by MARCA ANTIQUA, and from the south by BOHEMICA SILVA.

"If you would, Grzesiu," said the bishop, urging him. "Have a look."

The Inquisitor did. He knew the military situation, but he could enjoy the pretty figures. The devils with protruding arses were arranged in the region of Oschatz, a town that Prokop the Shaven's army had torched four days before, on the twenty-ninth of December. The Czechs were marching along the Labe towards Pirna, destroying everything in their path with iron and fire. They wreaked havoc in the mining regions of Marienberg and Freital. Then, burning down villages on their way, they reached Freiberg, Dresden and Meissen, but didn't waste time besieging fortified towns. The fast pace of the march put a spoke in the wheel of the Prince Elector of Saxony, Frederick, by forcing him and his allies into a tactical retreat. Meaning, the winged angels were now standing in a tight group north of the word LIPSIA.

"That is the River Mulda," said the bishop, running a finger along the blue line dividing the devils from the angels. "Prokop wants to march to Saxony, so he must cross it. He will most probably do it somewhere here, in the region of Grimma. Elector Frederick could make use of it. During the crossing, he could crush the heretics, could drown them in the Mulda like cats. He simply has to use his head and muster up the courage. Do you think, Grzesiu, that the prince elector will use his head?"

"I have grave doubts," said the Inquisitor, raising his eyes, "regarding both the young prince elector's head and his courage. So far, he hasn't displayed much bravery in this campaign. Were I to search for classical comparisons, I wouldn't compare him to Julius Caesar. Rather to Quintus Fabius Cunctator."

"But among his closest advisers? Couldn't anybody prudent and valiant be found in his circle? No Caesar? I'm not thinking about the Margrave of Meissen, he is even nicknamed 'the Pliant.' Nor Johann, the Prince Elector of Brandenburg, for he's a fanatical character. Who else among them has the balls?"

"The churchmen, naturally," said Grzegorz Hejncze, smiling. "Some, at least. Certainly Gunter of Schwarzburg, Archbishop of Magdeburg."

"I expected you to mention him," said Konrad, nodding. "Yes, Archbishop Gunter is a person capable of seeing the chance presented by the Hussites crossing the Mulda. He would be able to make use of the advantage, would be able to help Frederick plan and launch an attack. But we cannot speculate or rely on chance; Gunter must be told. Somebody has to ride like the wind to Leipzig with a message."

The Inquisitor looked at the bishop pointedly and coughed into his fist.

"I know," said Konrad, scowling as though he'd drunk vinegar. "I remember the Archbishop of Magdeburg bears a grudge against me for Grellenort. So I am compelled to rely on you, O Inquisitor. Gunter will listen attentively to your suggestions, he holds Inquisitors in high esteem, supports their work and actively participates in it. *Crescit cum magia haeresis et cum haeresi magia*, a day without a pyre is a wasted day; that is his motto. The results are there to be seen; for you won't find a witch or a Jew in a radius of five miles from Magdeburg. I envy him. And regret things aren't like that in Wrocław…Don't take it to heart, Grzesiu."

"I don't. Let's get to the point."

"Do you have somebody for a mission like that?" asked the bishop, tearing his eyes away from the map. "Somebody who will go to Saxony, to Gunter of Schwarzburg. A man who is loyal, reliable and trustworthy?"

"I do. And since I predicted that he would be needed I brought him with me. He's waiting in the anteroom. Shall I summon him?"

"Do."

"If Your Eminence permits. Deacon Łukasz Bożyczko. A man whom I trust completely."

The waters of the Mulda were greyish-brown and foaming, so swollen that the reed belt was almost entirely underwater, with only a bristling comb protruding above the current. The riverside trees were submerged to almost halfway up their trunks. A wagon tipped over on its side had stopped against one such trunk. Another conveyance was resting against a tussock a bit further away, upturned, with only its wheels showing above the water.

"The third was carried away entirely," said the senior roadman.

"The river took it before we got into the main current. We managed to get the rest out."

"Aye, it must be admitted," said Jan Královec, riding his horse right to the bank, its forehooves in the water, "that the river is carrying plenty of water. And is bloody fast."

"A mild winter, rain instead of snow," said Jakub Kroměšín of Březovice, Hejtman of the Tábor's field army, nodding. "It will be just the same at the other fords."

"So is the River Mulda going to stop us in our tracks?" said Prokop the Shaven, reining his horse around and casting a look at the hejtmans. "Is this bit of wet water to thwart our plans? Brothers! I want to hear your opinions! And decisions!"

The senior roadman said nothing for a long time, weighing up what to say. Nobody hurried him. Everybody, including Reynevan, knew that he had vast experience. He had covered the Tábor's combat trail with his unit of engineers almost from the beginning, and had achieved fame in 1424 when, by a bold crossing of the Labe, he had led Žižka out of an encirclement at the Battle of Kostelec. He had created clearings in the forests at Tachov and Retz, made a crossing over the marshes of Moravia out of tree trunks, built bridges on the Sázava and the Odra, and got wagons across the Nitra, the Kwisa, the Bóbr, the Regen and the Naab.

"We shall cross it," he said, finally relieving the tension with a dry and matter-of-fact statement. "But not with a triple column, because that draws too much weight of water. We need to do it one at a time, one wagon after the next, in a row, using safety ropes."

"A crossing in a single column will take at least a day," said Jíra of Řečice, Hejtman of the Orphans, weighing up his words. "That's a long time."

"Our number will slowly grow on the far bank," confirmed

Kroměšín grimly, "and slowly decrease on this side. The Saxons will cotton on and strike us where there'll be fewest of us at a given moment. They could give us a damn good hiding."

"Especially pinned by the river," added Sir Vilém Kostka of Postupice, an experienced warrior, a participant in the war that Poland waged with the Teutonic Order in the years 1410-1414. "To be pinned against a river is to invite annihilation."

"A decision!" snapped Prokop, tugging his moustache. "What are your suggestions?"

"We shall say a Mass!" said Preacher Markolt, eagerly. "We are the warriors of God, God will listen to us. Let's celebrate a Mass, asking for the water to subside."

Prokop froze with his hand on his moustache and looked at the priest for a long time.

"Any other ideas?"

"We deliberate in vain," said Ondřej Keřský of Římovice tersely, after previously saying nothing. "We must cross the Mulda. If the roadbuilder says we cross in a row, in a row it is."

"But we must ensure," said Kroměšín, firmly, "that the Saxons don't find out about the crossing. For if the curs do—"

"We'll be done for," finished Královec.

"Oh, Reynevan!" said Prokop, snatching a towel from the barber and wiping the rest of the foam from his freshly shaven face. "I'm glad you are here. Did you bring the ointment?"

"I did."

"Just in time," said Prokop, waving away the barber and pulling a shirt on over his head. Now shaven, he smelled of Italian soap from Savona.

"My lower back hurts like hell," he said, sitting down on the pallet and turning away. "Rub that magical ointment of yours on my skin. The pain stops me from gathering my thoughts," said the hejtman, allowing Reynevan to apply the ointment. "And I must think now. You were by the river today and saw how things are. Crossing won't be easy, and during such a crossing we'll be like a snail without a shell; any old sparrow can peck at us. You understand, don't you? Well? Reynevan?"

"Of course I do."

"Ooh," groaned Prokop. "That remedy, that ointment, is just heavenly, the pain subsides like magic. What would I do without you, physician? Don't go away, Reynevan. Don't get lost or wander off."

Reynevan shuddered, sensing a strangely ominous note in his voice. The director of the field armies glanced at the commanders present and gave Kroměšín a sign. The latter put down the knife he was using to carve undercooked meat from the ribs of a roast ram, stood up, walked over to the door of the cottage, glanced outside and checked nobody was eavesdropping. The remaining hejtmans also stopped eating for a while, their faces grave and unmoving. Reynevan rubbed in the ointment.

"And so, Brother Hejtmans," said Prokop, scratching his freshly shaven cheek, "I have decided. We cross the Mulda the day after tomorrow at dawn. Upstream, using the ford near Kössern. Not a word to anyone. The information is not to leave this chamber."

The campfires of the Tábor and the Orphans glowed bright all the way to the horizon. The smell of various soldierly vittles rose from the cauldrons hanging above the coals, but Reynevan found it none too appetising, despite his hunger. He walked, deep in thought, towards the farm buildings that the Hussites hadn't burned down, in order to keep a small piece of roof over their heads. He expected to find Scharley and Samson there.

Suddenly a dainty figure emerged from behind a passing wagon. He smelled the faint scent of rosemary.

"Rixa?"

She materialised beside him, snugly wrapped up in a cloak with a close-fitting hood. She got down to business at once. Her voice was determined and harsh.

"Where and when will Prokop be crossing the Mulda?"

"I'm glad to see you, too."

"Where and when will be the crossing be? Don't make me repeat myself."

"But please do, if you'd be so kind. I'd finally like to hear whose cause you serve. I'd finally like to be certain."

"I know you were present when they took the decision about the crossing," Rixa continued as though she hadn't heard him. "There are three fords on the Mulda. One here, near Grimma. Another downstream, in Dornau. The third upstream near the village of Kössern. Which one did Prokop choose? Tell me, Reynevan, I don't have much time."

"Nothing doing."

"Listen," she said, her feline eyes flashing in the light of a torch, glowing like a real cat's. "This is important. You don't know how important. I have to know. Tell me, or—"

"What?"

Rixa didn't have time to answer, didn't have time to react with a word, a gesture or an action. A shadow suddenly dashed out from behind a wagon. Reynevan heard the dull thud of a blow, Rixa groaning softly and the sound of a body falling. He tried to react but wasn't quick enough. He heard the sound of a spell being uttered, detected the smell of ozone, typical for magic, and felt paralysis immediately overcoming him.

"Be quiet," hissed Łukasz Bożyczko. "And don't do anything you might regret."

"You've killed her."

"Don't be foolish," said the deacon, pushing Rixa with his foot and sliding the brass knuckles from his fingers. "I was only getting my revenge for Racibórz. She broke two of my teeth then. I took her sex into consideration, not wanting to spoil her looks with a scar or a bruise, so I thumped her in the back of the head. But enough of trifles, I'm here on an important mission. Where is Prokop going to cross the Mulda?"

"I don't know."

"And do you know that your ignorance may have very ill consequences," said Bożyczko after a brief silence, "for Jutta of Apolda?"

"Begone," said Reynevan, breathing out hard. "*Apage.* Begone, go away. I won't let anyone frighten or blackmail me any longer. There is a limit."

"True. And you've reached it. I warn you in earnest not to cross it."

"I don't believe in your threats. The Inquisition won't dare to harm Jutta."

"The Inquisition won't. But I will. Enough of this, time is short. Reynevan, I warn you, I'm serious—don't doubt that I'll do what I say I will do. I won't hesitate. You must decide. If you tell me the location of the crossing, you will regain Jutta, I'll give her back to you. Otherwise, you will never see the girl alive again. Stay calm, stay patient and don't make me harm you or your Jewess. I'm standing with my heel on her throat, I can crush her windpipe at any moment. And I'll kill you, too, if you do anything stupid. And then I'll have Miss Apolda killed. Decide and fast. Time is running out."

Several Taborites passed, hardly paying them any attention. Fights, tussles and score-settling on the periphery were nothing special, part of everyday camp life. Reynevan could have cried out, naturally, or called for help. But he didn't.

"Will you free…" he said hoarsely. "Will you free Jutta? Will you give her to me? Promise me."

"I swear on my soul's salvation. Where will the crossing be?"

"Upstream from Grimma. In Kössern. The day after tomorrow at dawn."

"If you're lying to me, your Jutta dies."

"I'm telling the truth. I've made a decision."

"And a wise one," said Łukasz Bożyczko.

He vanished into the gloom.

A short while after, Rixa groaned and moved. As she got up onto her knees, she groaned again, grabbing her head in a sudden movement. She saw Reynevan.

"Did you say…? she said, choking. "Did you tell him where?"

"I had to. Jutta—"

"I'll kill…" she said, jumping to her feet and staggering. "I'll kill the bastard!"

"No! He has Jutta! You can't!"

He tried to seize her by the elbow. Rixa pulled her arm free, caught him by the wrist and twisted. He screamed in pain. She stuck out a foot and threw him to the ground over her hip. Before he could get to his feet, she had disappeared into the darkness.

He walked towards the middle of the camp like a blind man, staggering and stumbling. Several times he ran into one of the Taborites, several times he was called a drunk idiot and a prick, several times he was shoved hard. He paid no attention to it.

"Reynevan!" said the next man he bumped into, who grabbed him by the shoulders and shook him. "Hey! I've been looking for you!"

"Scharley? Is it you?"

433

"No. It's Saint Perpetua. What the bloody hell's wrong with you? Pull yourself together!"

"I must…I have to confess something to you…To you and Samson…Something has happened…"

Scharley grew serious at once and looked around.

"Come with me."

They listened to him in their quarters, chewing roast turnip, a large store of which they had gathered. After he finished, they said nothing for a long while. Samson sighed several times, spreading his arms in a gesture of resignation. But without saying a word. Scharley was thinking hard.

"Well," he said finally, his mouth full of turnip. "I understand you, Reinmar, for in your shoes I'd have done the same. The thing with life is that blood is thicker than water. I praise your choice. You did what was right in the given situation. What was right."

Samson sighed and shook his head. It didn't bother the penitent. He swallowed some turnip.

"You did right," he repeated. "And they will probably hang you for it, for that is usually the fate of people who do right."

A moment later, he added, "There are two ways of getting out of this predicament. But since you don't want to run away, only one remains. We must become heroes. I even know where, when and how."

Dawn was breaking over the Mulda, which was murky with fog. The swollen waters churned in whirlpools; waves broke over the banks. A haze rose from the water.

From the foggy wetlands emerged a unit of soldiers, at least three hundred horse. It was being led by Jan Zmrzlík of Svojšín, Lord of Orlík Castle, wearing full armour covered in a short tunic decorated with his well-known and celebrated coat of arms, three red bars on a silver field. He was followed on his right by Předbor of Pohořílek, a Moravian, and on his left by Fritzold of Warte, a Helvetian mercenary from the canton of Thurgau.

Jan Zmrzlík reined his horse around, turned to face his army and for a while appeared to be about to exhort them with a speech. But all that needed to be said had already been said. About God. About the cause. About sacrifice. About the mission. And about what was riding on the unit. On them.

The fate of the entire army and the entire operation depended on them, on the unit. They were to cross the Mulda, reconnoitre the left bank, march swiftly to Kössern and capture the ford. And hold it. Protect the crossing. At all costs.

"Keep close to me and Samson in the river," said Scharley, nudging Reynevan with his knee. "That water looks vile."

"Time to begin," said Jan Zmrzlík, beckoning. "May God be with us, brothers!"

He was the first to urge his horse into the river. Behind him, without hesitation, hastened Předbor and Warte, after them Reynevan, Scharley and Samson, after them several dozen others, then the rest, stirring the water up white. When their horses' hooves lost contact with the river bed, they began swimming.

The current struck the swimming horses straight ahead, and then lifted, turned and began to carry them downstream. Gripping his horse's mane tightly, Reynevan watched horrified as several cavalrymen were swept away into the fog. He spurred his horse. Water splashed him, Samson struck out towards him, supported him, Scharley joined him and the three of them resisted the current. The remaining horsemen also began to gather into groups to bolster each other. In spite of that, every now and then a man and his horse were carried away; a man would cry

435

out and a horse would squeal. They were in the centre of the river; the current was tremendously strong there.

"Hold on! Hold on!" shouted Zmrzlík. "We're almost there!"

Carried by the river, they crossed two-thirds of it to where the current was a little weaker. But the horses were also weaker and despair could be heard in their panicked snorting. And they still hadn't touched bottom. The water was above the riders' thighs and reaching their waists and only the horses' raised heads were showing above water. Once again, a rider was taken, once again a horse was carried off, frothing up the water in its dying convulsions, wheezing before the water flooded its lungs.

The nightmare was suddenly over. The river became shallow, the horses neighed wildly on feeling solid ground beneath their hooves, and they found the remains of their strength to struggle out through the bog, bulrushes and reeds. Jan Zmrzlík's unit had crossed the Mulda. There he was, dripping water, standing on a hilltop, counting the survivors. The sun shone through the fog like a pale gold coin.

Having counted the men, the hejtmans formed up the column. The scouts had already gone ahead, one to the forests in the west, a second in a curve through the fishing villages to the north, and a third with the current, straight towards the ford by Kössern. But Zmrzlík had no intention of waiting for their return. He led his men out of the wetlands onto drier ground and ordered the march to begin. They urged their horses into a walk. The sun rose higher and higher, but it was soon hidden behind clouds blown by a strong wind. Fine snow began to fall.

The first scout returned. To the west—no one, he reported, not a sign of the enemy. The fierce expression remained on Zmrzlík's face.

They were almost level with Kössern when the scout sent

downstream returned. It was deserted, no soldiers, he reported. Morale improved visibly.

They reached the ford. A signal was given with a pennant and in no time an answer arrived from the right bank. A short while later, the forest on the far bank was teeming with men leading wagons and horses to the ford. And then the final scout returned, the one sent furthest away. Scharley cleared his throat pointedly, looking Reynevan up and down. Samson sighed. Zmrzlík also knew—before the report was given.

"They're coming! They're coming, Brother Zmrzlík! A great force!"

"And so it is treachery!" said Předbor of Pohořílek grimly. "We've been betrayed!"

"So it would appear," confirmed Zmrzlík dispassionately, standing up in the stirrups. "Form up!"

"Can we defend the crossing? There are fewer than three hundred of us!"

"It must suffice," said Zmrzlík, looking down at him. "Battle array!"

They lay in wait, hidden in a pine grove. Only whispers could be heard. Muttered prayers.

"Reynevan?"

"Yes, Scharley?"

"Don't go looking for death. We're supposed to be heroes. But not dead ones. Is that clear?"

Reynevan didn't answer; he was biting his lip.

The fog hanging over the wetlands muffled the sounds; the soft ground deadened the thudding of hooves. First, they heard the neighing of a single horse. Then the clanking of iron. And then at once they saw.

"Four hundred horse at most," said Zmrzlík in hushed tones.

"Fear makes cowards of us all. And they're marching slowly, slug-gishly. As if not to battle..."

"There's an eagle's wing in the emblem on the banner," said Předbor of Pohořílek. "The arms of Sir Hanusz Polenz, Land-vogt of Lusatia. Why are there Lusatians here? And why but four hundred of them?"

"It's the vanguard," said Zmrzlík. "The Elector of Saxony and all his men must be marching just behind him. When they arrive, they'll crush Prokop at the ford. We must stop them. Warn them! Sound the trumpet!"

A trumpet blared and along with its first tone a hundred handgonnes and harquebuses rang out. Hidden behind wattle fences and cottages, the marksmen, now dismounted, rained a hail of balls and bolts on the column, wreaking havoc among the Lusatian array. Zmrzlík's hundred horse fell on the be-wildered enemy from the right flank, while another hundred, under Fritzold of Warte, struck from the rear. The marksmen, once again mounted, penetrated the left flank. Mighty cries and clanging filled the field.

Reynevan flew out in front of all the others, was the first to attack the Lusatians, the first to knock a foe from the saddle. He cut into their ranks, wielding his sword like a madman. Scharley was fighting right beside him, smiting with his falchion, with Samson on the other side, striking with his goedendag, knocking over riders and their mounts. The Tábor cavalry, although more lightly armoured and smaller in number, had the advantage of momentum and surprise. And ferocity. Blows rained down on the stunned Lusatians as the deafening boom of armour being hewn rose above the battle cries and the screams of the wounded.

Sir Jan Zmrzlík, the Lord of Orlík, outdid all his subordinates in his bravado and warcraft. He forced his way into the Lusatian ranks and raged terribly, though methodically, hacking to the right and left with a battleaxe. Breastplates and shields cracked like clay pots beneath his precisely aimed blows, spaulders were dented, rerebraces riven, and split sallets and bloodied houn- skulls flew yards up in the air. The Lusatians began to retreat and flee before the terrible warrior and on seeing it, others also began to run away. Particularly since battle cries were now resounding from the ford as the first Taborites to cross came rushing to their aid.

But no one came to help the Lusatians. This didn't escape Zmrzlík's attention.

"Have at them!" he roared. "Kill them, kill them! Don't let them flee!"

His voice, although loud, was lost among the clanging and uproar. But they fell on the Lusatians in any case. Until the latter began to retreat in large numbers. Finally, to start running away in panic. Some of the Hussites gave chase, the rest killed off those who remained and were crammed into small, tight groups, defending themselves desperately. The fiercest and most effec- tive resistance was being put up by one group, commanded by a knight in full armour on a barded horse.

"Heretics, curs!" howled the knight from under his sallet's raised visor, brandishing a large sword to the left and right. "Here! Come on! I challenge you to single combat, one against one! Who will meet me? Come here, one of you!"

Scharley rode over to Reynevan and pushed into his fist the "treacherous" hand cannon, fuse glowing.

"Go on," he panted out, "since he's asking."

Reynevan wiped blood and sweat from his eyes. He trotted over, raised the harquebus and shot the knight straight in the face. That sufficed.

"Have mercy!" said the Lusatians, laying down their weapons one after the other. "Mercy! We surrender!"

"Don't kill any high-ranking officers!" yelled Předbor of Po-hořílek, wounded and swaying in the saddle. "Bind them! Remember the ransom—"

He choked, unable to utter anything else.

Jan Zmrzlík trotted up to the hillock and dismounted from his blood-spattered horse. He wiped the gore from his face. He glanced at the field where his three hundred horsemen had decimated and routed four hundred elite Lusatian horse. He knelt down.

"*Non nobis…*" he said, putting his hands together and raising his eyes towards the sky. "*Non nobis, sed nomini Tuo, Domine, da gloriam…*"

Others, seeing it, began to kneel, too.

Reynevan dismounted, swayed and caught hold of a stirrup. Then bent forward and threw up.

"It is a fine thing to be a hero," observed Samson, breathing heavily. "If it wasn't for the fear. How do you feel, Reinmar?"

Reynevan puked again. Samson didn't repeat the question.

Scharley trotted over and also dismounted. Waiting for Reynevan to recover.

"*Veritas Dei vincit,*" he said. "I don't know how, but *vincit*. I don't know how it came to pass that ten Saxon regiments weren't waiting here for us. It must indeed have been divine intervention. Or somebody got the fords mixed up."

"Neither one, nor the other," Reynevan replied sombrely. "Rixa rode down and finished off Bożyczko. Sending Jutta to her doom in the process, sending her to her death…"

Samson, standing alongside, shook his head. He finally pointed towards the crossing. And at the approaching forces.

Accompanied by Kroměšín, Keřský and the other hejtmans, Prokop the Shaven rode up, dressed in a sable calpac and a cloak with a wolf-fur collar worn over a quilted and studded brigantine. He was grinning broadly as he surveyed the battle-field. He dismounted and embraced Jan Zmrzlík tightly.

"*Non nobis*," said the Lord of Orlík, modestly bowing his head. "This glory is not thanks to us, but to God...Our men fought valiantly...Unsparingly...Why, like these three, for example. Many fell..."

"The sacrifice will not be forgotten," promised Prokop. He smiled with approval at the sight of Scharley splashed with blood and the still-panting Samson. He saw Reynevan. Grew serious. And walked over.

"Forgive me," he said dryly. "I had to. I didn't believe in your be-trayal, but they insisted. The suspicions had to be dispelled. And they were. We will cross here, at Kössern, without sustaining any losses. And the Elector of Saxony, the Landgrave of Thuringia and the Brandenburgians have assembled all their forces at the ford near Dornau, ten miles from here, and are waiting for us. And only this man did I tell about the crossing at Dornau."

He pointed. Reynevan saw a man tied between two horses being led. He recognised him, but only with difficulty. No face could be discerned, only a mask of congealed blood. It was Prokop's personal barber. The one with the Italian soap.

"I've known better barbers, too," said Prokop, looking on dis-dainfully. "Be sure, Brother Kroměšín, that he has confessed everything. About accomplices, contacts and so on."

"He has."

"I don't believe so. He still has his legs, I see. And can stand on them. Make more efforts."

"Yes, sir."

Prokop jumped into the saddle, reined his horse around and glanced towards the river where the Tábor was crossing. Five hundred cavalrymen under the command of Mikuláš Sokol of Lamberk had already crossed and ridden off to protect the bridgehead. Now the artillery was crossing. Wagons carrying dismantled trebuchets and onagers, and cannons of various kinds and calibres emerged in turn from the waters of the Mulda. The newest, breech-loading foglers on wooden mounts. Light six-pound bombards, slender culverins and cannons. Medium-sized bombards firing missiles the size of a human head. Finally, three fifty-pounders were hauled out of the river. They had been christened "Freedom," "Equality" and "Brotherhood" by the preachers, but the gunners called them among themselves "Kasper," "Melchior" and "Balthazar."

"I see that the credit from the Fuggers was invested wisely," muttered Scharley, examining the guns with an expert eye. "Now I know why I destroyed those mines at Marienberg and Freital—"

"Keep quiet about that, Prokop's looking."

"Reynevan," said the *director operationum Thaboritarum*, taking an interest in them again. "I see you are not only a good doctor, but that you also fight bravely. You served well; you deserve a distinction. Tell me how I can reward you. Or at least satisfy you."

"The usual," Scharley casually cut in. "Like at the Battle of Kolín two years ago. Give us leave, Hejtman. For our private interests, naturally. We have a private matter—one of vital importance—to deal with. We'll sort it out and return to take up our duties to God and the fatherland."

"Your words sound unpatriotic, Brother Scharley," said Prokop, scowling.

"Patriotism couched in words," retorted the penitent, "is a refuge for scoundrels and good-for-nothings."

Prokop the Shaven turned his head away. He looked towards the river where cavalryman Otík of Loza was urging the Taborite wagoners across. Then he turned his horse towards the road.

"*Bene*," he said as he rode away. "You have your leave."

The Tábor went to its battle positions right after the crossing, forming itself into detachments covered on the flanks by shield-bearers. Infantry—flailmen and marksmen—marched from the ford, singing.

Jesus Christ, benevolent priest,
One God, with the Father and the Spirit,
Your benevolence, our reward!
Lord, have mercy!

"One day," said Rixa Cartafila of Fonseca, who had approached unnoticed behind Reynevan. "One day they'll ask me, too. What can we reward you with, they'll ask, for your toils and sacrifice? You serve loyally, they'll say, never asking for anything; not honours, nor rewards. Ask, they'll say, and what you wish for will be given you. I have a ready answer, do you know? I'll tell them I want to wear only women's dresses to the end of my days. I want only to gaze into the fire of my oven and fear only that my challah might burn. I want a husband, a decent Jew; wealthy widowers preferred. That's what I'll say when they ask."

"You killed Bożyczko."

"No, I didn't. I didn't chase him down."

"So how the hell—"

"—did the Hussites cross successfully, because Frederick's army isn't here, but at Dornau? You tell me."

You shed your blood for us,
Redeemed us from eternal death,
Forgive us our trespasses!
Lord, have mercy!

"Reynevan?"

"Yes."

"I was furious with you."

"I know."

"If Bożyczko had…If the Saxons had known the actual location of the crossing, if they had defeated Prokop at the river, if a slaughter had occurred…My first reaction was to kill you. Or if not kill you, then at least punish you severely. I decided to conceal—"

"Conceal what? Rixa!"

"I didn't ride down Bożyczko. After that blow, my head was spinning, I threw up. And that scoundrel can use translocational spells, can travel through space. He fled without difficulty. The only thing I managed to do was to intercept his information to you. Your traitor's payment, I thought, your Judas's pieces of silver. I resolved to punish you. By concealing it."

"Tell me!"

"Your Jutta is in Cronschwitz. In the Dominican convent."

The sun set. And lit up the horizon in fiery-gold crimson.

The crossing of the Mulda had to be stopped at dusk. It was a fearful night. Barely half the army—ten thousand men with five hundred wagons—had made it to the left bank.

When night fell, the sky in the north-west was lit up by a red glow. Frederick II of the House of Wettyn, the Elector of Saxony, was burning down the suburbs of Leipzig. So they wouldn't serve the Hussites in the event of a siege of the city.

It was the only act that the elector had the courage to carry out. Before a hurried retreat north with his army.

The following day, the eighth of January, the rest of Prokop's army crossed. The Orphans' field army, five thousand soldiers under the command of Jíra of Řečice. The Orphans' municipal militias under the command of Jan Královec. The Praguians of

Sigismund Manda of Kotenčice. Finally, the rearguard, the cavalry detachment of Czech nobility supporting the Hussites. In total, a thousand and a half horse and more than eight thousand foot with wagons.

The Hussites had made it to the left bank of the Mulda. Saxony, Thuringia and Osterland were at their mercy. In their clutches.

Black smoke rose up in clouds behind the distant hills. It was the suburbs of Leipzig still burning.

"*Principes Germaniam perdiderunt*," said the Wallcreeper, tugging on his snorting horse's reins and pointing at the smoke. "The princes have brought this country to its doom, given it up for the invaders to sack. Five heretical armies are marching on Thuringia, Pleissenland and Vogtland, to transform those lands into an ashen wasteland. Indeed, the whole land thereof is brimstone, and salt, and burning! That it is not sown, nor beareth, nor any grass groweth therein, like the overthrow of Sodom, Gomorrah, Admah and Zeboim."

"*Gladius foris, pestis et fames intrinsecus*," said Łukasz Bożyczko grimly, also quoting from the Bible. "The sword is without, and the pestilence and the famine within. He that is in the field shall die by the sword; and he that is in the city, famine and pestilence shall devour him."

"And they could have defeated them during the river crossing," said the Wallcreeper, shaking his head. "Routed, slaughtered, drowned them. How was it possible? They evidently had information from spies about the location of the crossing. Did you not know anything, Deacon? You were reputedly close to the princes and the bishops, you came from Silesia with some sort of mission, I won't ask what, and in any case, you won't tell me. But you were there, weren't you, when decisions were being considered. Tell me why they made such a bad and disastrous one?"

Bożyczko raised his eyes and brought his hands together, without untangling them from the reins.

"The will of Heaven," he said. "Perhaps the Lord punished the princes with madness and blindness. Perhaps *amentia et caecitas* fell on them like a punishment?"

The Wallcreeper looked at him askance, certain he'd detected a note of scornful mockery. But Bożyczko's face was an absolute picture of piety, sincerity and humility, the combination lending his physiognomy an air of dim-wittedness.

"Don't you have anything else to tell me?" he asked, not taking his eyes off the deacon. "Don't you know anything? Don't you suspect anything? Even though you were with the princes? And perhaps you even saw the spy?"

"I am a priest," replied Bożyczko. "It doesn't behove me to interfere in secular matters, *nemo militans Deo implicat se negotii secularibus*. And now, m'lord, permit me to leave. I must hasten to Wrocław. And perhaps you are also returning there? We could ride together, it would be more pleasant, according to the proverb: *comes facundus in via—*"

"*Facundia* is not favouring me of late, I'd be a poor travelling companion," interrupted the Wallcreeper, bluntly. "Furthermore, I have a few matters to deal with here."

"I imagine you do," said Bożyczko, taking a quick glance at the unit of Black Riders formed up behind them. "Then I bid you farewell, Lord Grellenort. May God give you…what you deserve."

"Thank you for the blessing, O servant of God," said the Wallcreeper, reaching into a saddlebag and taking a canteen from it. "I also wish you luck…congruous to your piety. Drink with me in that intention."

Grellenort drank first. Bożyczko watched him intently. Then took the canteen and sipped from it.

"Fare you well, m'Lord Grellenort."

"And you, m'Lord Bożyczko."

Douce of Pack trotted over and stopped beside the Wallcreeper with her javelin resting across the saddle. The two of them watched the deacon on the dun nag disappear behind the treeless ridge of the hill.

"Now all we need do is wait," said the Wallcreeper, interrupting the silence. "Sooner or later he'll cut himself with iron. It doubtless surprises you," he went on, undismayed by the girl's silence, "that I devoted the last dose of Perferro to that damned priest. Minus the sip I had to take to avert suspicion. Why did I do it? Call it a foreboding."

Douce didn't reply. As a matter of fact, the Wallcreeper wasn't certain if she understood. It didn't bother him.

"Call it a foreboding," he repeated, reining his horse around and indicating to the Riders to march out. "Intuition. A sixth sense. Say what you like, but I have my suspicions about that Bożyczko. I suspect he's not who he pretends to be."

Chapter Sixteen

In which the reader finally learns what happened through the entire previous year to Guinevere, Lancelot's beloved, who was abducted by the evil Maleagant. By which we mean Jutta, Reynevan's beloved.

At that time, four novices, two *ancillae Dei*, four converses and four maidens from good homes were residing in the Dominican convent in Cronschwitz. That number fluctuated, since some girls left and others arrived. The arrival of a new one was always a sensation. This new one stood out. The maids' faces grew alike so quickly that each new arrival immediately caught the eye. This new one also stood out by her posture: she hadn't yet learned to stoop and humbly bow her head, owing to which she stood taller. Her voice also betrayed her, clashing with the whispers of the others. Naturally, the rigors of the convent swiftly eliminated any differences, levelling them out like a roller, but for some time the new arrival was the season's sensation.

The girl who was quartered in the dormitory on the Eve of John the Baptist's Day, had—in Jutta's opinion—all the qualities of the season's sensation. She was extremely pretty; her shapely figure couldn't even be marred by the gruesome sack called there a "habit." Her chestnut hair lay in a playful curl on her forehead and roguish sparks played in her hazel eyes, as though contradicting the embarrassed expression on her pleasantly oval face.

The girl sat down on the bed assigned to her, the only vacant one in the dormitory. As luck would have it, it was next to Jutta. Who at that moment was sweeping the dormitory.

"I am Weronika," said the new arrival softly. And obediently. The ban on using surnames was the first thing that was drummed into the converses' heads. And if a converse's head wasn't her strongest suit, the prohibition was drummed into her using other means.

"I am Jutta. Welcome and make yourself comfortable."

"Decent bed," said Weronika, jumping up and down on it several times to test it. "The one in Weissenfels was much worse. I hope no one died in it."

"This month? No. If you don't count Kunegunda."

"Dammit!" exclaimed Weronika and stopped jumping. "What did she die of?"

"They say it was her lungs," said Jutta, smiling with the corners of her mouth. "But I think it was boredom."

Weronika looked at her for a long time and sparks flickered in her eyes.

"I like you, Jutta," she said finally. "I'm lucky. I'll pray for the late Kunegunda today, in gratitude for freeing up her bed for me. Am I as lucky with my neighbour on the left?"

"If you're fond of halfwits, yes."

Weronika snorted. And immediately grew serious.

"I truly like you."

"You truly don't waste time."

"Because it's silly to do so," said Weronika, looking her in the eyes, "when you meet a kindred spirit. After all, it doesn't happen every day. Cronschwitz isn't my first nunnery. Is it yours?"

"No, not mine, either."

"You're still cool," Weronika remarked with an air of sadness. "Still mistrustful and prickly. Either you're very new here, or they've kept you here for a long time."

"I've been held in this convent since the twentieth of May," replied Jutta gently. "But I've been captive since the end of last December. Forgive me, but I don't want to talk about it."

The events of December 1428 were etched in Jutta's memory as a series of violent but semantically distinct images. It had begun the day the neighing of horses, cries and the cracking of the gate being broken ruptured the sleepy calm of the Poor Clares' convent in White Church. She had been in the refectory when the soldiers burst in, seizing her and dragging her out into the courtyard. Then the images began.

Reynevan in fetters, struggling in the arms of the soldiers. The abbess with her lips bloodied from punches, her books—her pride and joy—being consumed by fire on a huge pyre. The nuns and converses in tears.

Then Ziębice, a town she knew well, a familiar castle, the familiar knightly chamber. Duke Jan of Ziębice, whom she knew, dressed—fashionably as usual—in an embroidered doublet, *mi-parti* and poulaines with extremely long toes. Jan of Ziębice, regarded as an example and as the epitome of knightly virtue, once so courtly towards her mother and so generous to her father, who once honoured her with a compliment. And suddenly the epitome of knightly virtue with froth on his lips tears her clothes from her, and in front of everybody in the chamber strips her naked and gropes her, threatens her in vile fashion with shame and torture. And all in order to blackmail and intimidate Reynevan, her beloved, her lover, her Aucassin, her Lancelot, her Tristan, who is watching it all with his face contorted and as white as a fish's belly, with eyes from which it appears any moment will spurt blood mixed with tears of fury and humiliation. And that same Reynevan, the same, but simultaneously somehow unfamiliar, agreeing to terrible, horrible, contemptible, disgraceful things in a quite unfamiliar, unnatural voice. He agrees to them in order to save her.

She didn't hear all that Reynevan agreed to. Duke Jan ordered his soldiers to remove her. She fought back, it didn't help, they dragged her into the cloisters and the corridors. Her dress and chemise were torn to her waist, her breasts exposed. The soldiers, naturally, couldn't let a chance like that pass them by. Barely had they reached a secluded place than they pushed her against a wall. One pressed a stinking hand to her mouth and the rest pawed her, cackling with laughter. She trembled in disgust and shook spasmodically, which excited them and made them redouble their efforts. Their laughter and coarse comments finally attracted someone more important, blows fell on the soldiers, Jutta heard the sounds of slaps and dull punches. Released, she slumped to the floor and fainted.

She came to in a dark, empty cellar reeking of rancid wine. She squeezed herself into a corner, pulled her knees up to her chin and hugged them tightly. She froze in that position. For a long while…A very long time.

When she was led out of the cellar, she was sore and stiff, dazed like a corpse with rigor mortis. She had absolutely no idea what was happening to her, not even terror could break through the mist that had enveloped her senses, swaddled her in a thick layer of something soft and impenetrable.

There was suddenly the fresh night air; cold, almost freezing. At first, it appeared it would bring her to her senses, but that was an erroneous impression.

A whip cracked. Horses whinnied. The world began to shake.

*

When she came to it was day. A sunny, frosty day. The court-yard of an inn or homestead, the snorting of fresh horses being hitched up, steam belching from their nostrils. Ravens cawing. A rooster crowing.

"Miss Apolda."

A man, short, keen-eyed. A stranger. Completely unknown to her.

"If you would change, Miss," he said in a strange accent. "I beg your indulgence, but it doesn't befit you to be seen in such torn garments. It is shameful, on top of which it attracts the eye unduly. Please put these things on."

A rooster crows. A dog barks. A horse being harnessed snorts.

"Do you hear me, Miss? And understand me?"

A whip cracks, the horses whinny. The wagon bounces and thuds on the frozen ground. The cold clears her head. Her thoughts become sharper.

"Miss Apolda. We shall make a stop here. Please, do not—"

She burst into tears. And wailed. Her nose was running like a child's, and like a child she smudged the tears over her face with a shaking hand. Through the tears she saw him grimace. He threw the reins to a servant boy, put his arm around her and led her towards a building. He said something. She wasn't listening. She was busy planning.

She jabbed him in the ear with her elbow, wriggled out of his grasp and kicked him hard in the crotch, and when he curled up, she kicked him again in the side of the head. She punched the servant in the eye and he sat down, holding his face. She bounded across the courtyard, pushed over another servant, snatched the reins from him, jumped into the saddle and, kicking and hitting, forced the horse into a gallop. The horseshoes thudded on the frozen ground. She bent her head towards the mane and flew like an arrow towards the gate.

I've escaped, she thought. *I'm free.*

He caught her just beyond the gate, jerking her from the saddle with a sharp tug. She struggled in vain; his grasp was like iron. *By what miracle*, she thought, *by what miracle is he here?*

"This miracle is called translocation," he hissed, squeezing her arm in his grasp. "The ability to move through space. I'm a sorcerer. That can't be anything new to you, since your lover is one, too. Don't struggle."

"Let go…It hurts—"

"I know. It also hurts where you kicked me. You took me by surprise. You dulled my vigilance by pretending to be a crybaby. It won't happen again. You won't do that a second time. Believe me and don't even try it."

He pulled her up and shoved her into the servants' arms. Firmly, but not brutally.

"I saved you from Duke Jan's grasp," he said, turning his head away as though wanting to demonstrate his superior indifference. "I snatched you from Ziębice. I'm taking you to a place where for some time you will remain hidden from the world. Don't ask me by what right."

"By what right?"

"It's in your interests to remain hidden for some time. The convent in White Church had acquired notoriety, excessive notoriety. The cult of the Great Mother, the Sisterhood of the Free Spirit, Waldensian rituals, Arabic magic. Believe me, it will be better for you to disappear for a while."

"Better for whom?"

He didn't answer. He waved a hand, turned around and walked away.

*

453

Weronika wasn't to be dissuaded. They talked again three days later, on Sunday. When Jutta was sitting on the plank in the *necessarium* after Mass, Weronika entered, hitched up her habit and sat down unabashed over the hole beside her.

"Don't be cross," she said in anticipation. "Are you angry with me that I seek your company? Whose company should I seek? That of those idiotic converses?"

"It's embarrassing," said Jutta, not looking at her but at a crack in the wall. "It is truly embarrassing."

"*Pardieu*, Jutta, you and I are cut from the same cloth. I'll wager we're stuck here for similar reasons. You don't like being alone, I see it, which is why you react like this. I'll be like that in a month. Let's help one another. You'll help me, I'll help you."

"Indeed?"

"You help me and I'll help you," said Weronika, lowering her voice. "Because…Jutta, this is my third nunnery. I've had enough. I shall lose my mind here. I want to escape. And I have a suggestion: let's escape together. The two of us."

Jutta was still staring at the crack in the wall. But nodded in spite of herself.

Weronika's efforts yielded success, it must be admitted. Jutta had calmed down and after four days the girls began sitting beside each other to embroider tapestries. After a week they had grown closer, and after two they began to confide in one another. Weronika's surname was Elsnitz; her parents had estates near Halle. The Dominican convent in Cronschwitz, it turned out, was her third in a row; she had previously been held at the nunneries of the canonesses in Gernrode and the Poor Clares in Weissenfels. She had been locked up, she claimed, on her parents' instructions, as a punishment for immoral love. When Jutta finally decided to tell her own story, Weronika's mouth fell open in awe.

"By Saint Veronica, my patron!" she cried and held her hands to her cheeks. "It's just like a romance! Conspiracies and spying! Robberies and kidnappings! Heresy and magic! Dukes, brigands and sorcerers! Is your lover really a Hussite and a sorcerer? Oh, my. Well, my story pales into insignificance, it's paler than the fish we had for lunch yesterday! To think I was put here by a fool who wanted me for marriage!"

"What do you mean?"

"The son of my neighbours, impoverished relatives. A distant cousin. We used to meet…I was inflamed, so…You understand. For six months, time passed blissfully; now in a haystack, now in the hayloft of the stable, and when we managed to—in my parents' marriage bed. As regards me, to be honest, I was much fonder of the activity itself than of my cousin, and I was thinking of changing the object of my interests. But my foolish cousin didn't understand what it was all about, he thought it was a great love and hastened to my parents to ask for my hand. Everything was revealed. Marriage was out of the question, my father and mother wouldn't even think about it, but were dismayed enough to lock me up with the canonesses. While my cousin's parents sent him to Malbork, to the Order of Saint Mary, so the Lithuanians have probably already caught the drip and made a drum out of his skin. Thus there's no hope he will ride up on a white charger to rescue me. And yours?"

"What about mine?"

"Your lover, the celebrated physician, sorcerer and heretic. Will he come on a white charger to free you?"

"I don't know."

"I understand," said Weronika, nodding. "Oh, I do. You mentioned it. He's a Hussite, a man of ideas. Loyal to ideals. First and foremost, to his ideals. Meaning there's no use waiting for the white charger. We'll have to take things into our own hands, for

I don't mean to embroider tapestries until the end of my life. I'm already sick at the sight of them. Jutta? Have you yet thought of—"

"Of what?"

"Have you thought of escaping?"

"Yes, I have."

She had made her first escape bid towards the end of January. A mundane matter had decided it: the cold. She couldn't stand the cold; it made her unhappy. In the Magdalene nunnery in Nowogrodziec the only heated room was the calefactory; of course, it was also warm in the kitchen. Jutta joyfully greeted the days when she had kitchen duty or worked in the calefactory making parchment or ink. But those were rare moments of happiness, and afterwards she had to return to praying. And spinning, which in Nowogrodziec was done on an industrial scale. The convent functioned like a manufactory, unceasingly, with a three-shift system. Spinning was cold, the floor and walls made the room into an ice house. Jutta had had enough of it. At the first opportunity she hid inside a pile of kitchen scraps earmarked for being thrown out.

The prioress closed the book she was reading: Walafrid Strabo's *Liber de cultura hortorum.*

"Well, and how are we feeling now?" she asked without anger, more with reproach. "How do we feel after being hauled out of a compost heap? Was it really worth it?"

Jutta pulled a cabbage leaf from her hair and rubbed the slime from a rotten turnip off her ear and cheek.

And raised her head proudly. Sister Leofortis noticed it.

"It's no use talking to her," she decided. "Let me take her to the stable, Mother. Twenty lashes should get her out of these contrary moods."

"Think over what would have happened if you had succeeded," said the prioress, paying no attention to the nun. "Let's suppose you did. You crawl out of the compost heap during the night and are as free as a bird. Where do you go? You don't know the way, after all. Do you ask somebody? Who? You're a solitary girl without a guardian. Do you know what a solitary girl without a guardian is? A sexual toy for anyone who wants to play. For every village farmhand, every peasant, every wanderer. And for a gang of cutpurses—dozens of which roam around here—you are a toy for a longer period of time. For the whole gang. Until they tire of you; until, depending on what they do with you, you become a bruised rag, a misfit with a face swollen from the beatings and the tears, who can barely drag its feet along. Did you take all that into consideration when planning your escape? Did you take that risk into account? Answer me, for I'd like to hear."

Jutta jerked her head away and carrot peelings fell from her hair.

"She is blind to everything," said Sister Leofortis, pointing an accusing finger. "She thinks only of one thing. Her lover. And there's no ill road to get to a lover."

"Were you really so blind?" asked the prioress, not taking her eyes off Jutta. "I have been informed, I know this and that about you and your beloved. Your parents—people of considerable status—will never accept that union. Do you intend to live in sin, without your parents' blessing? Why, it cannot be done. It's against the will of God."

"Her paramour is a Hussite, an excommunicate dissenter," interjected Leofortis. "What do her parents mean to her, what does God mean to her? She prefers a life of misery. As long as she's with him!"

"Is that right? Answer! You will answer me, Miss!"

Jutta pursed her lips.

Ludmilla Prutkow, prioress of the *Poenitentes sorores Beatae Mariae Magdalenae* convent in Nowogrodziec, spread her arms.

"I give up," she said, "Sister Leofortis—"

"Twenty lashes?"

"No. Bread and water for a week."

"About a week after Shrovetide some strange men came to Nowogrodziec to visit me. Although they were taciturn, I guessed they were the servants of the man with the strange accent. They drove me in a covered carriage for a few days, transported me to the Cistercian nunnery, which turned out to be Marienstern in Lusatia. Seeing myself further and further away from home, I was desperate. I felt I had to escape. I discovered a small window with a loose grille in the *lavatorium*. It was high up, I needed at least three sheets tied together. One of the converses seemed to be decent. I let her into the secret and she—"

"Informed on you at once," Weronika easily guessed.

Zofia of Schellenberg, Prioress of the convent in Marienstern, was rarely seen by the nuns, practically only during Masses at the nunnery. Word had it that she was totally preoccupied with her life's work, the story of the reign and deeds of Frederick I Barbarossa.

"What, I wonder, irked you so much about our cenobium that you decided to flee from it?" she said and interlocked her fingers on her scapular and rosary beads. "Tending the carp in the fishponds? Don't you like carp? I'm sorry, the convent must live on something. And aside from the fish? What other harms befell you? What was so terrible here that you wanted to flee it by jumping from a high wall? What annoyed you, Miss Jutta?"

"The boredom!"

"Oh, the boredom. And beyond our walls, in your erstwhile

secular life, what was so engrossing? What did you fill your days with, what were your daily diversions? Hunting? Drinking and fighting? Gambling? Tournaments? War? Outlandish journeys? Eh? What was so fascinating about your former life? What did you have there that you don't have here? Well? You can embroider on a frame and spin on a wheel as much as you like here. Here you can freely gossip and twitter about trifles with better effect than at home, for the company is more intelligent. What then do you lack? A man?"

"Perhaps," she replied impudently. "That springs to mind at once."

"Oh! Ah, so we've known sinful delights. And you desire a man? Well, that could be a problem here. The sisters somehow cope, that's what ingenuity is for. I won't encourage you, but neither do I prohibit it—"

"You misunderstand me, it's not that. I love and am loved. Each moment I'm away from my beloved is like the twist of a dagger plunged into my heart."

"What?" said the prioress, cocking her head. "What? The twist of a dagger? Plunged into your heart? Dammit, girl! You're gifted. You could be a second Christine of Pisan or Hildegard of Bingen. We shall supply you with parchment and quills, a whole barrel of ink, and you can write and write—"

"I want to be free!"

"I see. Freedom. Unbounded freedom, no doubt? Wild and anarchic? In imitation of the Waldensians? Or the Czech Adamites?"

"You mock needlessly. I'm talking about freedom understood in its simplest form. Freedom without walls or bars!"

"And where would you seek that? Where can we, women, be freer than in a nunnery? Where are we allowed to study, read, debate, express our thoughts freely? Where are we allowed to be ourselves? The bars you pulled out, the wall you planned to jump from, don't imprison us. They protect us—us and our freedom. From the world, where women are numbered among household chattels. Worth a little more than a milking cow, but considerably less than a charger. Don't deceive yourself that your lover, for whom you risked complicated fractures, is any different. He is not. Today he loves you as Pyramus loved Thisbe, as Érec loved Énide, as Tristan loved Isolde. Tomorrow he'll flog you with a rod when you speak out of turn."

"You don't know him. He's different. He—"

"Enough!" said Zofia of Schellenberg, waving a hand. "Bread and water for a week."

Jutta was leafing through Galen's *De antidotis* at a lectern. It was a dull work, but it reminded her of Reynevan. Weronika had dug out a lute from a chest shoved into a corner and was strumming it. There were two illuminators apart from them in the *scriptorium*, as well as converses and novices being trained in the art, all gathered around the plump Sister Richenza. Sister Richenza, quite a simple individual, had an agreement with Jutta and Weronika: a pact of mutual absence of interference.

Weronika crossed her legs and rested the lute on her knee.

"*Ben volria mon cavalier...*" she began and then cleared her throat. And then sang with abandon.

Ben volria mon cavalier
tener un ser e mos bratz nut,
q'el s'en tengra per ereubut
sol q'a lui fezes cosseiller;
car plus m'en sui abellida
no fetz Floris de Blanchaflor:

eu l'autrei mon cor e m'amor
mon sen, mos houills e ma vida!

"Quiet, Miss! That's enough of that row!"

"We aren't even allowed to sing," grunted Weronika, putting down the lute. "Jutta? I say, Jutta!"

"Yes?"

"How did things go with that physician of yours?" asked Weronika, lowering her voice.

"What do you mean?"

"You well know what. Put your book down and come over here. Let's gossip. That—you know—cousin of mine...Just listen...The first time...It was a cool day in October, so I had woollen hose beneath my skirts. Very close-fitting. But that ass..."

The convent was changing her. A year before, Jutta would never have imagined listening undaunted to vivid tales describing the intimate details of somebody else's love life. Neither had she ever, ever, thought that she would share with anybody the intimate details of her own relationship with Reynevan. But now she knew that she would. She wanted to.

The convent was changing her.

"And when it was over, imagine, Jutta, the ass asked me: 'How was it for you?'"

"What are you whispering about?" asked Sister Richenza with interest. "You two, noble misses? Eh?"

"Sex," Weronika replied insolently. "So what? May we not? Is it prohibited?"

"No, it isn't."

"Oh, it's not?"

"It isn't," said the nun, shrugging. "Saint Augustine teaches: *Amore et act*. Love and do as you please."

"Oh, really?"

"Oh, really. Whisper on."

News from the world struggled to penetrate the convent walls, but from time to time it managed. Soon after Saint Michael's Day came the news of the Hussites' invasion of Upper Lusatia, about the ten thousand Czechs under the command of the terrible Prokop, the sound of whose name struck terror into hearts. People talked about the attack on the Celestine convent in Oybin, about the storming of Bautzen and Zgorzelec, which were repulsed at the cost of many casualties, about the sieges of Žitava and Chotěbuz. Voices trembling in terror spoke of the slaughter of people during the capture of Gubín, about the bloody massacre in Kamenec. Rumours multiplied the burned-down towns and villages into hundreds and spoke of thousands of victims. Weronika listened in suspense, then with a gesture summoned Jutta to the *necessarium*, where for a long time they had gone to confer.

"Perhaps that's our chance," she explained, sitting down over a hole in the plank. "The Czechs might enter Thuringia from Saxony. Confusion will break out; refugees will appear on the roads. It's always possible to join a group of travellers. We wouldn't be alone. With a little luck we'd be able to reach them."

"Reach whom?"

"The Hussites, naturally. You said your beloved is a notable figure among them. It's your chance, Jutta. Our chance."

"Firstly, we know only rumours," Jutta observed soberly. "There was panic in June, too, people talked of thousands of Hussites making for Žitava and Zgorzelec. But it ended in insignificant skirmishes on the Silesian-Lusatian borderlands. It might be the same this time."

"And secondly?"

"I saw the results of Hussite plundering raids in Silesia. When they march, the Hussites kill and burn everything in their path. If we happen upon a bloodthirsty mob, we're finished; the name 'Reynevan' won't save us. Some of the higher-ranking officers might know him, but the common soldiers won't have heard of him."

"Then it's our job to avoid common soldiers and find officers," Weronika said, getting up from the board and letting her habit down. "And it's possible to do so. Let us then wait for events to develop, Jutta, and keep an eye out for an opportunity. Are we agreed?"

"Yes, we are. We'll wait and keep our eyes open."

Events were indeed developing; at least, the shreds of information and rumours reaching Cronschwitz suggested that.

Soon after Saint Lucy's Day the convent was electrified by news of another attack, of a powerful Hussite army that had invaded Thuringia via the Ore Mountains, along the Labe valley. Weronika glanced meaningfully at Jutta and Jutta nodded.

All that remained was to wait for an opportunity. One came quite quickly. As though on cue.

Guests often appeared in Cronschwitz, in the form of high-ranking secular men or senior officials in the ecclesiastical hierarchy. The Dominican convent was important in Thuringia, and the voice and opinions of the prioress—a member of a notable family—were also heeded. During Jutta's stay there, the convent was visited personally by Anna Schwarzburg-Sondershausen, the wife of the landgrave. The archbishop's assistant curate from Mainz, the scholaster of Naumburg, the abbot of the Benedictine abbey in Bosau and sundry wandering prelates from various —occasionally very distant—dioceses visited Cronschwitz. The

463

rule—which was in fact the prioress's accomplishment—was that every guest would deliver a sermon or a lecture to the nuns. The subjects of the lecture were various: transubstantiation, salvation, the lives of the Saints and the Church Fathers, the exegesis of the Bible, heresies and errors, the Devil and his doings, the Antichrist. All in all, the subject was unimportant; what mattered was for it to be a distraction. Furthermore, some of the speakers were as handsome and manly as hell and for a long time supplied the nuns with fuel for sighs and daydreams.

That day, the nineteenth of December 1429, on the Monday after the last Sunday of Advent, *ad meridiem*, when the winter sun was exquisitely dyeing the stained-glass window depicting the martyrdom of Saint Boniface, four people appeared before the nuns gathered in the chapter hall. The stately Constance of Plauen, the prioress of the convent. Piotr of Haugwitz, the convent's confessor, the canon of Zeitz. An elderly, tall, ascetically thin gentleman, a priest, but dressed in the secular manner in a doublet of Venetian brocade. And finally, a younger, fair-haired man of Reynevan's age, in the attire of a university lecturer, with a pleasant face, sparkling eyes and hair as wavy as a maid's.

"Dear Sisters," said Constance of Plauen, looking like a queen in the bright light of the stained-glass window. "We are graced today by the visit of the Reverend Oswald of Langenreuth, Canon of Mainz, a close associate of our archdiocese's good shepherd, the Reverend Konrad of Daun. Having been invited, the canon will share his teachings with us. These teachings, I emphasise, concern certain secular matters, hence are mainly directed at the maidens who are temporarily residing here, as well as the *sorores* and converses who will not endure here and will return to the world. But I believe this knowledge won't do any harm either to those of us who have taken our vows, since knowledge can never do any harm and there is never too much of it. Amen."

Canon Oswald of Langenreuth stepped forward.

"We are imperfect," he began after a pregnant pause and a dramatic wringing of the hands. "We are weak! Prone to temptation. All of us, regardless of age, intelligence and sex. Nonetheless, mark ye well, Sisters, that womenfolk are much more, infinitely more at risk of temptation. For insofar as the Creator made man imperfect, He made woman the most imperfect creature among the beasts. Having granted her the ability to produce life, at the same time He left her at the behest of desire and lecherousness. Left her at the mercy of suffering. For the wise Albertus Magnus said: Lecherousness and desire are as afflictions, whoever they seize will suffer..."

"I should say," murmured Weronika.

"...and will be powerless. Great strength is needed to resist desire. But what is woman? Woman is weak! She has no soul and her body is powerless against desire, is prey to it. Even in marriage there is no escape from lust. How can one resist it when one must be obedient and subservient to one's husband? According to the letter of the Bible? The Book of Genesis says: Thy desire shall be to thy husband, and he shall rule over thee. Wives, submit yourselves unto your own husbands, as unto the Lord, teaches Paul in his letter to the Ephesians.

"How then, you ask, is one to be?" continued the canon. "What to do? Submit and sin carnally? Or resist one's husband and sin by disobedience? Know you, dear Sisters, that this dilemma has a solution, and it is owing to the teachings of the great Doctors of our Church and learned theologians.

"Thomas Aquinas says: If your spouse, driven by lust, desires your body and demands carnal commerce, you must dissuade him from that, acting zealously, but wisely. But if that yields no fruit, and it usually does not, you must submit to him, in order that by committing a lesser sin you protect your spouse from a greater.

For if unsatisfied, he is liable to run to a brothel with his lust or, God forgive, commit the sin of adultery with another man's wife. Or seize some young boy and…May the Lord's saints have mercy! Then you see, Sisters, that it is better to sacrifice yourselves than put your spouse at risk of a cardinal sin. He who protects his neighbour from a sin is doing good. Doing a good deed!"

"It's worth knowing," murmured Weronika. "I shall remember that."

"Be quiet," hissed Jutta.

"One must nonetheless take heed that there is no wantonness in it. The theologian William Auxerre says: Great delight accompanies carnal commerce, but he who does not experience pleasure has not committed a sin. But, regrettably, that seldom happens."

"Damned seldom," whispered Weronika.

"Then the one thing that can be advised is to pray. Pray zealously and continuously. But under one's breath, quietly, so as not to offend the husband during copulation, for to offend one's husband during copulation is not only a sin, but is also boorish."

"Amen," whispered one of the nuns.

"As you see, Sisters," the prioress said gravely, "it is a knotty matter. Our second distinguished guest, Nicholas of Cusa, a theologian, scholar from Heidelberg University, a *decretorum doctor* from the University of Padua, a canon in Trier, where he is secretary to that archbishop, will expound more about that for you. A man young in years but greatly renowned for his piety and wisdom."

The young man Reynevan's age stood up. And stepped forward. He put his hands together. The stained-glass window with Saint Boniface bathed him in a beautiful light.

"A cherub," muttered Weronika. "I'll probably dream of him tonight."

"I'm already dreaming of him," whispered a novice behind Jutta. Other girls quietened her with hisses.

"Dear Sisters in Christ," began the young theologian in a gentle voice. "Permit me. I shall not teach you, being far from omniscient myself, nor warn you, being not without sin myself. Let me simply share with you what I have in my heart."

The expectant silence appeared to fill the entire hall.

"A truly godly person lives in contemplation," said Nicholas of Cusa. "Free of earthly things, he turns with reverence towards eternal goodness. Then the clouded sky becomes unveiled. Suddenly, radiance flowing from God's love pierces the open heart like a flash of lightning. In its brilliance, God's Spirit talks to our hearts, saying: I am yours and you are Mine, I dwell in you and you dwell in Me.

"Two people who love each other are bound by similar ties. The desire of one is the desire of the other. His desire is your desire…"

A slight expression of alarm appeared on Canon Langenreuth's face. While the faces of many of the nuns, including the prioress's, were painted with wistful smiles.

"…for if love flows from God, truly from God, there is nothing impure in it. Pure love and desire are like light, like *lux perpetua*, like nature unsullied by the sin of the Garden of Eden.

"O Sister, my Sister, one among many! Wait, wait patiently, endure in piety and prayer until the day comes when the brilliance of love will blaze, when he who you will favour with love will appear. A *suavissimus* full of allure will lead you to a *hortus conclusus* of delight. Longing and then ecstasy. The power of love will intoxicate you, plunge you into perfect joy. The spirit, full of joy, will serve the one it loves all the more ardently since it does not conceal its nakedness before the nakedness of its innocence."

The anxiety on Langenreuth's face was more and more

467

apparent. The nuns, meanwhile, were sailing off in reveries at an alarming rate.

"He will name you his betrothed, a love which is better than wine! And the smell of thine ointments than all spices! And he will tell you: *Quam pulchrae sunt mammae tuae soror mea…*"

"If this is *devotio moderna*," whispered a novice at the back, "then I'm enrolling for it."

"Let us get up early to the vineyards; let us see if the vine has budded, whether the grape blossoms are open and the pomegranates are in bloom. There I will give you my love. And your breasts…"

"O Saint Veronica, my patron saint…I shan't bear it…"

"…your breasts, which are *mandragorae dederunt odorem*, are a fruit, you shall say, which I have laid up for you, my love. And the *commixtio* of sex will be fulfilled, the *unio mystica* will come true. What is natural will be fulfilled, in the face of God, Who is Nature. Amen. Peace be with you, my Sisters."

Constance of Plauen exhaled audibly. Oswald of Langenreuth sighed heavily.

Canon Haugwitz wiped the beads of perspiration from his forehead and tonsure.

"This is our chance," said Weronika. "We can't waste it."

They were talking, hidden in a chamber behind the bakery. Their usual place for conferring was taken, since one of the youngest converses had diarrhoea and was endlessly occupying the *necessarium*.

"Don't shake your head and don't make faces," said Weronika, wrinkling her nose. "That theologian is our chance, believe me. Why, you heard how he spoke and of what. He has but one thing on his mind, Jutta, I guarantee you. The entire convent heard his speech, everybody saw the look in his eyes.

And it expressed precisely what you and I constantly think about."

"Speak for yourself!"

"Have it your way. I am speaking for myself. And for the rest of the convent, including the Reverend Mother Plauen. No, I have no intention of waiting until one of the girls beats us to it and jumps into bed with him. The lustful theologian will help us to escape, Jutta. We only need to go to him in the guest house and win him round. I have two straws here. Go on, draw one. The short straw goes and persuades him."

"What are you..." said Jutta, recoiling as though she hadn't been offered two straws but two vipers. "You can't—"

"The short straw goes," Weronika repeated firmly, "and wins Cusa around. It won't be difficult. I think decent, solid *fellatio* should do it. With breasts, which *mandragorae dederunt odorem*. But if it turns out not to be enough, it will be necessary to move to a full programme of *commixtio* of the sexes. Nakedness before nakedness *et cetera*. Come on, we're wasting time. The short straw runs into the *hortus conclusus* and the long straw will be packing our things in the meanwhile."

"No," said Jutta, bridling. "No."

"What do you mean, no?"

"I can't...I love Reynevan—"

"And that's why you want to escape. Why you *must* escape."

She's right, thought Jutta, *she is absolutely right. I've been captive for more than a year, it's a year since the attack on White Church. I've been in the Dominican convent in Cronschwitz for seven months, it's only a question of time before some strange men come to carry me off and take me to another, more remote, convent. They'll separate me from Weronika and I can't escape alone. She's right. It's now or never.*

"Give me a straw, Weronika."

"I understand. Which one did you draw? The long one! So it's the short one for me, my patron saint heard my silent prayers. Pack our bags, Jutta. And I'll hurry to the guest house. And the theologian Mikołaj, who is waiting there *suavissimus* and full of allure."

Jutta, packed and dressed for the road, was waiting in the bakery. It was a new moon and the December night was as dark as the very bottom of Gehenna.

Weronika returned well after midnight. Flushed, sweaty and out of breath. She was wearing a fur-trimmed cloak and carrying a bundle. *She did it*, thought Jutta, *she really did it.*

They wasted no time. They ran across the courtyard very fast to the guest house and entered the darkness of the hall. Nicholas of Cusa was waiting for them, a finger on his lips indicating that they should keep quiet. He led them to the stable, where servants were saddling two horses by the faint light of a torch. Jutta put on a sheepskin she was given, pulled on the hood and leaped into the saddle.

Nicholas of Cusa dismissed the servants. Then hugged Weronika and kissed her. The kiss went on. And on. For quite some time.

Jutta, impatient, cleared her throat pointedly.

"It's time you went, *sorores*," said Nicholas of Cusa, coming to his senses. "It's time. Let's go."

"Who goes there?" growled Brunwart, the secular monastery menial, guard and porter of the guest house. "Who the Devil is out at night? A pox on you."

He recognised the canon, fell silent and bowed low. Without a word, Cusa pushed into his hand a clinking purse. Brunwart bent over in a bow.

"Open the gate. Let my servants through, I'm sending them on an urgent matter. And keep your trap shut."

"I swear…Your Reverence…"

The night was as dark as the bottom of Gehenna. Cold.

"That road leads to Weid. That one goes to Zwickau and then on to Dresden. Farewell, dear Sisters. May God lead you, and take you happily to your loved ones."

"Farewell…dear Mikołaj."

The horseshoes clattered on the stones.

Chapter Seventeen

In which *Anno Domini* 1430 begins, and a great search is going on in the war-torn lands of Saxony, Thuringia and Upper Franconia.

It took Reynevan, Scharley, Samson and Rixa two hours to reach the road leading to Altenburg from the ford in Kössern. Snow had begun to fall, but in spite of that they rode swiftly, led by Reynevan, feverish and excited by the proximity of Jutta. The Hussite army, meanwhile, having been divided up into five regiments, was marching towards Naumburg and Jena, methodically burning down every village and *oppidum* on its way. The horizon in the west blossomed with plumes of smoke made ragged by the wind.

Reynevan drove them on, at first forbidding them even from pausing for the night, even wanting to ride in the dark. In order to stop him, absolutely compelling arguments were necessary. The horses needed rest and fodder, and additionally they were in a foreign and hostile country, they could get lost, lose their way in the gloom and snowstorms, the consequence of which might be a delay much more serious than those few hours of rest. So they made a stop at an empty barn at the edge of a village. Which also looked deserted.

The horizon to the west and north glowed in the darkness.

They sat around a tiny campfire. In complete silence. For a while.

"Reinmar," said Rixa, barely visible in the dark. "We must clear up one thing. Bożyczko intimidated you by threatening to harm Jutta and wrung out of you information about the location of the crossing. Am I right?"

"What is your point, Rixa dear?" said Scharley, almost invisible in the dark.

"Prince Elector Frederick was waiting in the wrong place, *ergo*: he didn't know. He didn't know the truth. He acted on false information. My point is, I wish to ask you a question, Reinmar, as follows: what did you tell Bożyczko?"

"A lie, of course, he told him a lie," said Scharley from the darkness. "What else could he have told him?"

"A lie would come out," said Rixa, not giving up. "And Jutta would have to pay for it. Am I to believe, Reinmar, that you took such a risk?"

"The Elector of Saxony wasn't waiting with the army at Kössern," said Scharley on Reynevan's behalf again. "He was waiting near Dornau, so he was waiting in error. You said so yourself. Isn't that proof enough for you?"

"I'm not interested in proof, but in the truth."

"The truth has various faces," said Scharley, seizing Reynevan, who was about to speak, by the arm. "What face does yours have, Rixa Cartafila? Before Bożyczko hit you with the brass knuckles, you were robustly and stubbornly demanding from Reinmar information about the location of the crossing. What information were you waiting for: genuine or false? How did you intend to exploit the information, whom did you plan to give it to? And in what form—as information or disinformation? Is it worth pursuing this?"

"I want to know the truth."

"You're stubborn."

"It's in my blood. I'll keep nagging: we are heading towards the Dominican convent in Cronschwitz, because Bożyczko secreted Jutta of Apolda there. We know it, since I intercepted the information meant for Reynevan. When Bożyczko sent that information, the actual location of the crossing was already known. It was also known then that Frederick had been misled and on the basis of that disinformation he committed a disastrous military error. In spite of that, Bożyczko gave Reynevan Jutta. He behaved like a decent blackmailer. He carried out his part of the pact, handed over what he was using for blackmail after receiving that which he wished to gain by blackmail. What, then, I ask one more time, did Bożyczko gain? Information or disinformation?"

"Let me reply one more time," said Scharley. "What difference does it make? It's the result that matters."

"Not only. Loyalty to one's principles also matters."

"Rixa, dear!" The person who spoke after a longer silence was none other than Scharley again. "I also had ancestors. I also have a heritage. In my family, various pearls of wisdom and adages, some short, some long, some that even rhyme, are passed down from generation to generation. 'You can't get blood out of a stone.' 'A fool and his money are soon parted.' 'Don't put the cart before the horse.' There was a huge number of those saws, among which one especially stuck in my mind. It went as follows: 'Loyalty to principles is nothing more than a convenient excuse for apathetic clots floundering in idleness and lethargy to do nothing, since any kind of action surpasses their powers and invention.' In order to live with it, those clots have made a virtue out of their incompetence. And vaunt it."

"Splendid. And truth?"

"What about it?"

"What is truth?"

"Truth," said Samson Honeypot in a calm voice, "is the daughter of time."

"Conceived," said Scharley, finishing off the sentence, "in an accidental, short-lived romance with coincidence."

It was the late morning by the time they reached Cronschwitz. It was noon by the time knocking on the gate and then hammering on it had exhausted and wearied them. And even when they were almost hoarse from calling, the iron-bound convent gate remained tightly locked. And the stone edifice of the Dominican *cenobium* remained as it was: cold, lifeless and silent.

"We are here for Miss Jutta of Apolda! With her parents' authorisation!"

"*Pax vobiscum, sorores!* The Archbishop of Magdeburg sent us! Open up!"

"I am a priest! *In nomine Patris et Filii et Spiritus Sancti! Credo in Deum Patrem omnipotentem, Creatorem caeli et terrae!*"

"We are good Catholics! We swear on the Holy Cross!"

"We'll donate to the convent fif– no, a hundred guilders!"

"Jutta! Say something! Are you there? Juuuttaaah!"

The iron-bound gate emanated icy cold and the hostile scent of rust. The convent was silent. As the grave. Like the stones of the wall surrounding it.

"The nuns are inside," concluded Scharley, when, resigned, they had retreated to a nearby forest. "We only have one recourse. The Tábor is active nearby—that smoke is coming from somewhere near Gera, and Altenburg, which we passed yesterday, is also probably afire. I'll ride over there, bring back a hundred boys and we'll take the convent by storm."

"They'll plunder the convent. And the nuns won't be safe, either."

"They had their chance."

"I'll go to the convent again," said Reynevan, pursing his lips. "Alone, this time. I'll fall to my knees at the gate. I'll beg—"

Samson suddenly bounded like a tiger into the dry thicket and dragged out a short and very unshaven individual by the collar.

"Let me go," groaned the individual. "Let me go. I'll tell you everything."

"Who are you?"

"Brunwart, m'lord. A servant at the convent. 'Eard you yelling something outside the gate. But in vain, because that maid isn't there."

"Speak! Tell me what you know!"

"Did you say something about money…"

They rode east along the Chemnitz road. Excited by the information he had obtained, Reynevan was leading again and again forcing the pace.

"They fled from the convent," he repeated one more time, once they had slowed down. "Jutta and another maiden. A priest, the other girl's lover, helped them to escape—"

"Let's hope it was the other girl's," said Rixa, mugging roguishly and falling silent at his angry look.

"They rode east, towards Dresden," he continued, "along the Via Regia. It's obvious that they are heading home…We must catch up with them."

"They left the convent over a week ago," observed Samson. "If we're to believe the servant. They're a long way ahead. And my horse…I don't want to worry you, but there's something wrong with his gait."

"No wonder," said Rixa, snorting. "It's no joke carrying such a giant. How much do you weigh, dybbuk? Twenty-five stone?"

"We must find him a fresh horse," said Scharley, standing up in the stirrups. "I can hear yours, too, Reinmar, wheezing like a pair of bellows. We need new steeds. What do you say to those?"

He pointed towards the forest, from which a procession of peasants was just emerging along a track.

The peasants—around a dozen of them—were leading some horses. And they were dressed—or rather dressed up—very strangely. And very untypically for peasants.

"I know those horses," said Reynevan. "And those black cloaks. And those black visors—"

Before he had finished speaking, Scharley and Rixa were already urging their horses into a gallop.

In spite of wearing enormous slippers, the peasants displayed the fleetness of deer and the agility of mountain goats. Having abandoned the loot they were carrying, they loped through the thicket and snow-filled hollows with the grace of antelopes, sped away so swiftly the pursuers had no chance of catching them. Scharley and Rixa only managed to catch one of them, the most advanced in years and probably suffering from flat feet, which Reynevan diagnosed on the basis of his waddling gait.

Dragged by the collar, the peasant cried, yelled, begged for mercy and called on God; all of it very incoherently and practically incomprehensibly. Fortunately, Scharley knew the secret of talking to the residents of rural hamlets. He kicked the peasant hard in the arse, making him suddenly straighten up, after which he punched him in the nape. The result was instantaneous.

"It weren't us, it weren't us!" said the flat-footed peasant, his speech taking on human features. "It wasn't us what killed 'em, *schwöre bei Gott*, not us. They killed each other, killed each other! We only stripped the bodies of their clothing...We caught their horses and took 'em...*Um Gottes Willen!* Good m'lord... Why, last Sunday they stole everything, them knights. Didn't leave a single hen…By Saint Genevieve…So when we found them bodies—"

"Bodies? Where? Take us."

Fallow land, covered in bushes and snow, spread out beyond the forest. Snow mixed with blood had been churned up by horses' hooves and was dotted with the dark patches of corpses. Around twenty of them.

The peasants hadn't managed to strip even half the number, hence identifying the bodies presented no difficulties. At least four of the dead were wearing black cloaks, black armour and black hounskulls, familiar to everyone as the attire and distinctive features of Birkart Grellenort's Black Riders. The others looked like mercenaries.

Only Rixa rode over the bloody snow and around the battlefield, attentively inspecting the bodies, details and tracks.

"It happened yesterday," she said on returning. "There were fifteen mercenaries—all dead. There was a smaller number of Grellenort's Riders, three were killed. Two of them were finished off with misericords. Grellenort was clearly in a hurry."

"Which way?" asked Scharley. "Where did he go?"

"South. Lucky for us, or we'd have run into him."

"What's he doing here?" said Reynevan, calming his frisky horse. "What's he looking for?"

"Us," replied Samson dryly. "Let's be under no illusions."

"Christ," said Reynevan, paling. "He came from the east. Jutta—"

"No," Rixa cut him off. "Definitely not. Let's go."

They set off, Samson and Reynevan riding on fresh black horses and leading two riderless ones.

Rixa looked back one more time.

"I recognised one of the men they finished off," she said, grimacing. "He served in Wrocław under Hayn of Czirne. A thug, a murderer and a molester of little girls. It confirms that in his determination, Grellenort gathers and recruits whoever he can find: scoundrels, degenerates and utter scum. It confirms one more thing," she added. "The rumour of the destruction by the Inquisition of their legendary castle at Sensenberg. Grellenort doesn't have a headquarters any more, nor the Arabian narcotics for his underlings.

"Once horrors of the night," she said, spitting. "The Company of Death, the Demons of Midday inspiring superstitious fear. Now a pack of demoralized rogues, incurring losses in any old skirmish. And despatching their own wounded. I'd call that ruination."

"Fallen angels," said Samson, "are no less dangerous."

"You talk like a dybbuk, O dybbuk."

"He's right," interrupted Scharley. "However low Grellenort may have fallen, I'd rather not run into him. Neither him nor his Riders. I've already had that questionable pleasure."

"And who hasn't?" snorted Rixa. "To horse!"

The knight, to whom they were taken, was shaving outside a blue and white tent of heavy canvas. On seeing them, he straightened up arrogantly and wiped his face. His nose, Reynevan noticed, was swollen, and his entire left eye socket was one great bruise.

"I am Gers of Streithagen," he announced sourly. "Lord of the burg of Drachenstein. The *pfleger* here. I'm keeping guard. When the Hussites come from Freital, I won't let them cross the river, so the heretics will get a thrashing from me. Perhaps you don't believe me?"

"We do," Scharley assured him. "We have no choice."

"Who might you be?"

"Travellers."

"The duty for crossing the bridge is three groschen per horse."

"We shall pay it," said Rixa, calming Scharley, who was enraged by the exorbitant fee. "We shall pay, Noble Sir knight."

"First of all, we'd like to ask you something," interrupted Reynevan. "This is the only bridge hereabouts and whoever is heading for Chemnitz and the Via Regia has no choice but to go this way. And everybody must come before you, Sir Knight. Did two maids ride this way? Travelling by horse and unaccompanied?"

The knight paled and his bruise grew a shade darker. This didn't escape Scharley's attention.

"And those maids, what are they to you?" Gers of Streithagen drawled between clenched teeth. "Companions? Relatives? Lovers, perhaps?"

"Not a bit of it," said the penitent with a stern expression. "We're pursuing them in order to punish them. On the orders of the parish priest of Saint Nicholas in Jena. They are harlots and robbed the latter while rendering their services. Tell us, please, did they ride this way or not?"

"They did. But…They turned back."

"What!" Reynevan exploded. "What do you mean, turned back? Why? Please, Sir Knight, speak a little more coherently!"

"What do I hear? You dare to order me?" said Gers of Streithagen and stood legs akimbo. "Me, a nobleman? You urge me too forcefully, young sir! You lie about the maids, you cannot deceive me, you are in league with them. And look to me like Hussite spies! For why else would you be heading eastwards? Towards Freital and Marienberg, where the Hussites are burning and destroying the mines, from where these refugees are coming? Those wenches of yours are certainly spies, too, were also heading east before they fled towards Plauen. I am the *pfleger* here, I defend folk from heretics—"

"We see. By charging them three groschen a horse."

"I am arresting you!" said Gers of Streithagen, paling even

more. "I am arresting you, you varlets. I'll soon take the red-hot irons to you; you'll confess the truth to me in no time. Hey, men, to me! Arrest them!"

Scharley reached under his cloak for the treacherous hand cannon. Rixa was quicker. She took a step forwards. Her face contorted. She choked, coughed, wheezed and rasped. And then spat and sneezed, spraying blood and snot around. Straight into the face of the knight. And his men-at-arms. And the rapidly arriving halberdiers.

"*Heilige Maria, Mutter Gottes!*" howled one of the *pfleger*'s bodyguard, wiping the bloody snot from his face. "It's the plague! The pestiiileeence!"

"Save me, Saint Roch!"

Every last one of them bolted, the bridge thudding beneath their feet.

Only *Pfleger* Gers of Streithagen remained, motionless and staring in disbelief. Scharley lunged forwards and kicked him below the knee. As the *pfleger* dropped to his knees, the penitent broke his swollen nose with a punch.

"To horse!" shouted Rixa, leaping into the saddle. "To horse, company!"

Soon they were galloping along the highway. To the west. Back the way they had come.

"There's a crowd up ahead," Weronika warned. "Cover your face."

Like Jutta, she was wearing a *calotte*, a cap covering her hair. Now she pulled on a hood and bowed her head. Until that moment their disguise had worked, no one had seen through it, forced themselves upon them or accosted them. No one had questioned them or even taken special interest in them. They had been travelling without difficulty for several days already, even though the roads weren't empty; on the contrary, occasionally they were simply thronged. As they were now, in the proximity of Zwickau.

A river wound through a valley and the road led to a bridge, which was blocked by a queue of wagons waiting to be inspected. For some time, the traffic on the road from east to west had far outnumbered the vehicles travelling the other way. They knew why. They had been told by a hawker from the Annaberg region, the jovial husband of a mousy wife and the father of an un-countable mass of children they had met the previous day. The camouflage hadn't deceived the hawker, who, addressing them as "noble misses," explained that the exodus from the west was the result of a Hussite plundering raid and the terrifying rumours of Hussite atrocities. The main Hussite forces were bearing down on Meissen and Oschatz. But beyond Freiberg, gangs were ma-rauding, burning and destroying mines and foundries. They par-ticularly had it in for mines and foundries, the devils. They had burned down Hermsdorf, Marienberg, Lengefeld, Glashütte and Freital…

"What's that tent made of?" Weronika snorted. "Stuff for feather beds?"

The thick, blue and white striped fabric of the tent close by the bridge and the toll booth really did call to mind the material used for making bed linen. A banner wet from the snow hung forlornly on a pole stuck into the ground. Soldiers were bustling around and halberdiers stood like dummies.

They rode up to the bridge, where a tense exchange was in progress. It turned out that a unit of soldiers had stationed itself at the bridge and was collecting payments from travellers for passage by force. It was cold and was snowing, and while most of the refugees were paying up without a murmur, from time to time a braver individual would arrive and question the legality of the toll. And that had just happened. The refugee was yelling and fulminating. Children were crying. The soldiers were swearing and shaking their fists.

Jutta and Weronika rode up to the bridge with their hooded heads lowered, trying to attract as little attention as possible. Unfortunately, few travellers were heading eastwards. And each one attracted attention. Their road was suddenly blocked by a large warhorse, a bay lancer's destrier. Astride it was a knight in a beaver-fur cap and a coat worn over a gambeson.

"Halt. What do we have here? Hoods down!"

There was no way out.

"By the head of Saint Pancras!" said the knight, grinning and slamming his fist against his pommel. "Why, two maids!"

There was no use in denying it.

"I am Gers of Streithagen," announced the knight. "Lord of the burg of Drachenstein. The *pfleger* for this region. I'm keeping guard here. When the Hussites come I shan't let them cross the river; the heretics will meet their match with me. And who might you be, ladies? And why are you in disguise?"

"Not everyone we encounter is a noble knight, O noble Sir Knight," Jutta mumbled meekly. "There are those who do not respect the fair sex."

"And my sister and I are hastening," Weronika added beseechingly. "Noble sir, please let us through."

"Hastening? Doubtless to your paramours? Who are doubtless yearning to see you? Yearning for kisses?"

"We are hastening to our mama and papa. We are heading home."

He looked down at them from his destrier and an ugly smile crept over his face.

"Please follow me, misses. To my tent. I'll write you out a safe conduct. It'll come in useful should someone pester you."

Inside the blue and white tent, apart from full Milanese

armour on a stand, was a table, a folding chair and a camp bed. The lord of the burg of Drachenstein got down to business without further ado.

"Time to pay for the crossing, wenches," he said, his face contorting lewdly and pointing at the bed. "You first. Come on, undress. Off with your things."

"Noble sir—"

"Am I to call my men to help me?"

Weronika looked pleadingly at Jutta. Jutta sighed and shrugged. With trembling fingers, Veronika began to unfasten her buttons. Gers of Streithagen's eyes were fixed on her cleavage. Jutta wrenched a vambrace and gauntlet from the Milanese armour and slammed it straight into his nose. And when his hands came up to his face, she kicked him in the crotch as hard as she could.

Gers of Streithagen curled up and sat down hard on the camp bed, which collapsed under his weight. Weronika hit him with the folding chair. Jutta then put her hand inside the armoured gauntlet, clenched her fist and swung. And hit him with all her might, so hard her shoulder crunched.

They exited the canvas tent as if nothing had happened. The halberdiers didn't even look in their direction, too absorbed by another row on the bridge.

A moment later they were in the saddle. And galloping as fast as they could to the west.

Back the way they had come.

The following day, a blizzard broke out which slowed them down considerably. Reynevan raged helplessly. Rixa was worried, suspecting that the *pfleger*—humiliated before his subordinates' eyes—might come after them. Scharley thought it unlikely; the extortion on the bridge was too lucrative to abandon. And even if he did, the blizzard would also slow down any pursuers. So they rode on, gulping wind and snow, or sheltered each time the snowstorm made riding completely impossible.

The weather only improved after a few days. And then the howling wind stopped muffling the thunderous roar of cannons coming from somewhere in the west.

They speeded up, heading towards the intensifying sound of cannon fire and soon saw with their own eyes the cannons firing and what they were firing at.

"The town and castle of Plauen," said Scharley, pointing.

"What force is besieging it? The Tábor or the Orphans?"

"Let's find out."

It turned out it was the Tábor doing the besieging; the field army under Prokop the Shaven and Jakub Kroměšín. It took some time before they got through the burned remains of the cottages outside the castle, constantly being accosted by guards, and reached the hejtmans. Prokop, astonishingly, wasn't complaining of pain and didn't order Reynevan to treat him. Neither did he allow Reynevan to get a word in.

"This is Plauen," he said, pointing to the town smoking after the bombardment. "The seat of Heinrich of Plauen, the leader of the Plzeň landfried. Among the Czechs few names are so detested. It was from here that the sorties to our borderlands set off, when Plauen's mercenaries committed unspeakable atrocities. It was Heinrich of Plauen who invented the term *bellum cottidianum*—or daily battle. He also put that term into effect, sending out sorties almost daily, burning, pillaging and hanging. He didn't expect us to ride up to those walls. Neither did he expect those walls to tumble."

As if to stress the weight of those words, from the trenches a heavy cannon was fired with a deafening boom and a ball slammed into the wall, raising dust. At the same moment, a trebuchet brandished its mighty arm and sent a half-hundredweight boulder into the centre of the town. A catapult standing in position hurled a flaming barrel of pitch on a similar trajectory, accurately, for smoke rose up from the roofs at once.

"For by fire and by His sword the Lord will judge all flesh," said preacher Markolt, who was present at the conversation. "And the slain of the Lord shall be many."

"Amen," Prokop finished the sentence. "The raids and forays and this *bellum cottidianum* are costing the Czechs too much. Plauen and the others are burning fields and robbing crops while Prague is starving. That must stop. I'll show them terror.

"After the storm," he finished, biting his moustache, "I'll turn the town over to be looted and the population to be slaughtered. Our warriors are sharpening their knives."

"Even," Scharley asked with a sneer, "if they offer a ransom?"

"Indeed."

"Especially," Markolt interjected again, "since they didn't—"

"I won't hold back the warriors." Prokop cut him off. "They'd probably kill me if I tried. I know what you want, physician. Plenty of refugees took shelter in Plauen, you suspect that your lady may be among them. But I cannot help you. This is war."

"Hejtman—"

"Not another word."

Scharley and Samson drew Reynevan away. They held him back when he was itching to steal into Plauen, beyond the walls. They had a hard time convincing him it would be suicide.

The bombards fell silent soon after noon. The onagers and trebuchets stopped hurling missiles. A thundering signal rang out from the trumpets. Unfurled pennants and standards fluttered. Battle cries resounded. Five thousand Taborites charged to storm Plauen.

It was all over in two hours. They scaled the walls with ladders and destroyed the gates with battering rams. They crushed the resistance and put the defenders to the sword. They showed no mercy.

By the third hour, they had captured the castle and slaughtered all the defenders. Soon after, the Dominican convent—the final point of resistance—fell.

And then the massacre began.

Before it grew dark, Plauen was in flames and rivers of blood were flowing through the streets and hissing from the fire. The fires turned night into day, but the murderous work didn't stop, the cries of the dying didn't abate until dawn.

Reynevan, Scharley, Samson and Rixa waited on the far side of the river, by the causeway of the road leading south towards Oelsnitz and Cheb, suspecting that fugitives might flee that way. Their hunch was borne out as some fugitives even appeared, with blackened faces, wounded, panicked and stupefied by fear. Rixa and Scharley looked around, Reynevan and Samson called. In vain. Jutta wasn't among the people who managed to leave Plauen.

Reynevan remained deaf to arguments. He struggled free of his comrades and set off for the town. With a firm resolution. He wandered among the burning houses, trying to enter the blocked streets. What he saw made him turn back. He gave up. The bodies piled up in the town were too numerous, and most of them were already charred, already turned to ash along with the town.

Jutta, he thought in horror, *might have been in those ashes*.

Hope remained that she hadn't been there.

The following day, another snowstorm broke out, so violent that it all but prevented Jutta and Weronika from riding on. They had to seek shelter. By a stroke of luck, they found a shepherd's hut.

The weather cleared up in the morning. The sky brightened. Enough for them to be able to see columns of smoke. Almost the entire sky to the north and west was blackened by smoke so dense that darkness soon veiled the earth. It was as though the prophecy of the Apocalypse was coming true.

"And the fifth angel sounded," whispered Jutta, "and I saw a star fall from Heaven unto the Earth and to him was given the key of the bottomless pit. And he opened the bottomless pit; and there arose a smoke out of the pit, as of a great furnace; and the sun and the air were darkened by the smoke of the pit."

Weronika said nothing.

Before two days had passed, the roads were teeming with refugees. It wasn't difficult to find out what was happening. One only had to ask.

"The Hussites are marching from the north," said Weronika, repeating the news she picked up from the refugees. "Burning everything in their path, marching on Naumburg, Jena and Gera, and apparently they have already been seen near Altenburg. That means they reached Leipzig, turned back and headed for Thuringia and Vogtland. It's hard to believe, but it is nonetheless the truth. The lecherous *pfleger* on the bridge outside Zwickau will be surprised when they approach him from behind and seize his fat arse. And we must head north in this situation," she said. "Towards Altenburg. In order to meet the Hussites."

"Let's ride."

"Let's ride. And pray that we encounter your beloved. Or somebody who knows him."

The further north they went, the more smoke there was, and at night the glow of fire marked burning villages and *oppida*. The further north they went, the more fugitives there were and the greater was the panic on the highway. They witnessed a damaged wagon empty of its goods that was blocking the road being mercilessly shoved off it by other refugees, deaf to the wagoner's yells, the pleading of his woman and the lamentations of their children. Some time elapsed before finally a few of the last travellers decided to offer them help.

Which turned out to be their undoing.

There was a thudding of hooves, yelling and whistling as a cavalry unit came galloping over the brow of a hill. The riders bore red Chalices sewn on to their tunics.

"Hussites!" said Weronika in delight. "Jutta, do you see? They're Hussites."

In a sudden presentiment, Jutta seized her by the arm and gripped it tightly. They led their horses into a thicket of roadside pines. Not a moment too soon.

The riders bearing the Chalice spurred their horses and with wild cries charged at the refugees. They fell on them, stabbing with bear spears and hacking with swords, showing no mercy, until the roadside snow was stained red. The wounded were finished off amid squealing. One man, caught by a noose, was dragged to and fro over the road. One woman who was spared death was thrown to the ground and her clothes were torn off.

"O Blessed Mary…" whispered Jutta, cowering in the pine wood. "O Blessed Eternal Virgin…We flee beneath Your care…"

Weronika's lip was trembling. The woman screamed horrifyingly.

Suddenly hooves thudded again and more riders appeared over the brow of the hill. They—Jutta observed in horror—were riding black horses and were dressed uniformly in black, wearing black cloaks, armour and helmets. They descended on the

Hussites robbing the wagons at full gallop. Blades clanged and once more the air vibrated with yells.

And Jutta suddenly saw him.

She knew him from tales. She remembered him from White Church, where she had seen him threatening the abbess, tugging her around, beating the bound Reynevan. When she had been transported under guard in the wagon on Duke Jan of Ziębice's orders, he had looked in at her several times and she recalled his cruel smile. She remembered the black, shoulder-length hair. The birdlike nose. And the gaze of a devil.

Birkart Grellenort.

"Let's get away," she uttered. "And swiftly."

Weronika didn't protest.

The dying screamed.

"There's a town up ahead," said Weronika, pointing. "The refugees say it's Plauen. Most of them are fleeing there. They say the only safe place is within its walls. What do you think, Jutta? You don't want to head north and meet the Hussites any longer, do you? We aren't trying to make contact with them now. Perhaps it's for the best. I've seen for myself how contact with them ends."

"I won't travel north for anything," said Jutta, shuddering at the recollection. "Grellenort is there. Anything but him. I want to stay away from him. As far away as possible."

"Isn't Plauen far enough away? Aren't we going to stay here?"

"No," said Jutta, shuddering at a sudden vague foreboding. "Not here, Weronika. Please."

"As you wish, it's your decision. We'll see if it's the right one."

There had once been a village on the snow-covered terrain; the remains of clay chimneys stuck up and black squares of scorched ground indicated where the cottages and sheds had once stood.

At the edge of the burned-out village sat several ragged peasants of various ages and both sexes. They sat motionless like dolls, like roadside carvings of saints. Their eyes were unseeing and vacant.

"It's a hideous thing," said Rixa in the silence. "A hideous thing, war in the wintertime. *Der böse Krieg*, they call it. If they burn your cottage down in the summer at least the forest can feed you, leaves give some protection against the cold and you can gather food from the fields. But in winter you're doomed. Waging war in the winter ought to be banned."

"I'm with you there," said Scharley, nodding. "I hate taking a shit in a frost."

"Look there!" called Weronika. "What's that?"

"Where?"

Weronika rode up to the roadside shrine and tore off a slip of paper nailed to it.

"Take a look."

"'*Fratres et sorores in fide*, blah, blah, blah,'" read Jutta. "'Do not believe the loathsome priests or your masters…Recant your obedience to your King Sigismund, for he is no king but a scoundrel and *desolator Christi fidelium, non exstirpator heresum, sed spoliator ecclesiarum omnium, non consolator, sed depredator monachorum et virginum, non protector, sed oppressor viduarum et orphanorum omnium*…' It's a Hussite pamphlet; I've seen them before. It's aimed at the literate, which is why it's in Latin."

"Hussite emissaries are clearly abroad," said Weronika, with emphasis. "If we happen upon them…"

"Of course," Jutta guessed. "The emissary must know Reynevan, must have heard of him, at least. If we ask him, he'll take us to the Hussite commanders, protect us from marauders…But where can we search for him?"

"Where there are people. In a town."

491

*

Nestling in a picturesque valley among picturesque hills, the town of Bayreuth looked like a picturesque haven of peace. And indeed it was. The gates were manned but open, and the flocks of fugitives were neither stopped nor searched to any extent. First of all, the girls headed without any difficulty to the town hall and then to the parish church of Saint Mary Magdalene.

"Even if we don't find a Hussite emissary in Bayreuth, let's stay here," said Weronika, sighing as she cleared a path for herself and Jutta through the throng. "Look how many people are seeking shelter. Trudging along hard roads has been a torment, I've had enough. I'm hungry, frozen, filthy and short of sleep. And above all I want to go home."

"Me, too. Don't moan."

"I'm telling you, let's stay here. Even if we don't find him."

"I think we just have. I think your patron saint has really inspired you. Look."

A man in a jerkin, a skirt with a serrated edge and a goliard's hood from which strands of grizzled hair stuck out was standing on one of the wagons blocking the square. The wagon was surrounded by quite a large crowd, mainly the poor: *servi*, beggars, cripples, prostitutes, vagrants and other local *pauperes*, including vagrants, pilgrims, vagabonds. Generally speaking, a noisy, mouthy and repugnant rabble.

The goliard in the hood was speaking, attracting the crowd's attention with his raised voice and gesticulations.

"Many vile and outrageous lies are being told about God-fearing Czechs. That they murder and rob. That is a lie! They only fight to defend themselves and kill in battle those who are invading their lands, bent on destruction. When that happens, they defend themselves, their faith, their homes, their wives and children. And whoever dares to attack them incurs harm.

But they keenly desire for a cessation to wars and killing, an end to bloodshed, for divine and sacred reconciliation to come about.

"Know you that the Czechs call on dukes, masters and all imperial cities and towns to gather for peace negotiations, to put an end to the disgraceful shedding of blood. But your dukes, masters and prelates don't want to set aside their pride and arrogance! For it is not their blood, but yours that's being shed!"

"He is right!" cried a voice from the crowd. "He speaks the truth! Down with the lords! Down with the clergy!"

"Where is your king? Where your dukes? They have fled, leaving you to your fate! Do you wish to fight for such men? Lay down your lives for their wealth and privilege? O good people, citizens of Bayreuth! Give up your town! The Czechs are not your enemies—"

"You lie, godless heretic!" shouted a monk in an Augustinian habit from the crowd. "You're a despicable liar!"

"Good folk!" chimed in somebody from the *mediocres*, the town commoners of the middle class. "Don't listen to the traitor! Seize him."

The crowd fomented. Others also took up the appeals of the monk and the commoner, but the mob shouted them down and shoved them away, making good use of staffs, sticks, fists and elbows. The proletariat swiftly retook the square.

"Did you see how they wanted to stop up my mouth?" the emissary began again. "Do you see how the truth pains those damned priests? They preach deference to the Church and the lords. They call Czechs 'heretics'! But is there any greater heresy than to distort the word of God according to your own whims? For that is what the prelates do by distorting the word of Christ. Perhaps I'm wrong? Perhaps you challenge that, monks?"

"They do not! It's the truth! The truth!"

Some halberdiers marched into the square, thudding and stamping; the hooves of cavalry boomed on the cobbles. The mob swayed and began to yell. The goliard vanished from the wagon as though blown away by the wind.

"Over there," said Weronika, catching sight of him. "After him, quickly."

The emissary stealthily dashed beyond the wagons and hid in an alleyway. They ran after him. He was waiting for them, concealed around the corner. He seized Jutta by the arm and shoved her against the wall, pushing a knife to her throat. Weronika screamed softly, being strangled from behind by another man in a grey mantle who had appeared out of nowhere behind her.

"A maid?" the emissary said, looking under her hood and loosening his grip slightly. "By the Devil! You're maids!"

He gave a sign for the man in the mantle to slacken the strap he was garrotting Weronika with. He was a youngster, sixteen at most.

"What urged you to follow me? Speak, and swiftly!"

"We seek contact with the Hussites," Jutta stammered out.

"What?" he said through clenched teeth and again pressed his knife to her neck. "What the hell?"

"We've escaped from a convent," said Jutta in a faint voice, aware that her explanation sound extremely improbable. "We want to get to the Hussites. My...My betrothed...My betrothed is among the Hussites..."

The goliard let her go. And took a step back.

"What is his name?"

"Reynev...Reinmar Bielawa."

"Saint Clare, O guardian of agitators," said the emissary, gasping. And held his head in his hands. "You are Jutta of Apolda," he said forcefully. "I've found you. Saint John, O Baptist of our

Lord Jesus Christ in the waters of the Jordan! Saint Cecille, O patron saint of musicians! I've found you! I, Tybald Raabe, have finally found you!"

Chapter Eighteen

In which mercy is not given, there is no pity, there is no compassion. And medicines and amulets prove powerless.

The town of Kulmbach was afire. Plassenburg Castle, towering above them, which the Orphans were unable to capture, was now like a ship sailing on a sea of flame, borne on turbulent waves of fire.

At first, when they were riding up, Reynevan hadn't intended to contact the Orphans, had feared that recollections of Smil Pŭlpán and the conflict with the Náchod contingent were still alive among them, and that in spite of the good relationship he had with Prokop and the Tábor hejtmans, he might encounter hostility from the Orphans. The Orphans' preachers, led by Little Prokop, kept accusing him of witchcraft and were spreading rumours that he might be an agent provocateur. Hence Reynevan decided to give Kulmbach a wide berth and ride straight to Bayreuth.

Fate thwarted his plans. Riding around the besieged town, they ran into a large cavalry troop which found them suspicious. Their explanations were ignored. They were taken prisoner and delivered to the Orphans' headquarters under armed escort. To the company's immense relief, they happened upon hejtmans they knew and were on good terms with. They were greeted by

Jan Kolda of Žampach, who was cheerful as usual, and their old comrade, Brázda Ronovic of Klinštejn.

Following the storm, Kulmbach had already been captured and sacked; now fires were being lit and flames already raged on the roofs as dense smoke crawled and climbed into the sky.

"No," replied Kolda on being asked. "No, Reynevan, I have no information about any maidens. For why should I? It's war—a great disorder that no one can control. To the east of us marches the Tábor, that is Prokop and Kroměšín; to the west the municipal militias of Královec and Zygmunt Manda's Prague militia. And between us forays and maverick units are operating, gangs, leaderless groups and deserters are marauding…I advise you to rescue your maidens as quickly as you can. If they are between the armies, things look bleak."

Scharley ground his teeth. Reynevan's face was white. Brázda saw it.

"While we're on the subject of gangs and marauders," he quickly interjected, "it might be worth showing them. What do you say, Jan?"

"Why not."

Nearer the edge of the camp, among wagons heavily laden with loot, six corpses had been laid out on a tarpaulin. Six bodies, quite badly mutilated. Five of them—Reynevan's heart almost stopped—had on them the remains of black armour and black cloaks.

"Black Riders," said Kolda, pointing. "The Black Regiment. That rings a bell to you, doesn't it? Rumours about them have reached you, too. But wanting to follow us all this way, to Germany?"

Scharley looked on inquiringly, indicating the sixth corpse. That one was dressed in ordinary clothing. But his head was almost completely burned, as though it had been put into an oven and held there for a long time.

"Aye, indeed," said Brázda, swallowing. "The Black Cloaks, it appears, followed us almost from the ford. Our patrols kept disappearing and then we would find them slaughtered. But always one on a branch. Hanging by his legs. Over a fire. They're were clearly interrogating them. And when your head's in a fire you'll talk. You'll tell them everything."

Jan Kolda hawked and spat.

"It finally needled us," he said, "so we set an ambush. We fell on them, but they fled and we seized only these five. What are they looking for, Reynevan? What do they want to know, burning men with fire? What can you tell us about this?"

"Nothing. Because I'm in a great hurry."

When the black cat dashed right in front of his horse's hooves, Jakub Dancel ought to have turned back to Bayreuth. Jakub Dancel, however, only treated the cat to a coarse word and continued on his way. For if he had returned, Tybald Raabe would have shamed him for believing in superstitions. And the comely Weronika of Elsnitz might have, horror of horrors, reviled him as a coward.

Jakub Dancel rode on along the Kulmbach road, where he was expecting to come across Hussites. Had he not done that, had he turned back, he would have had—despite the war raging around him—a chance of living to seventeen.

They surprised him, a force of over a dozen horse, and surrounded him. One of them snatched the reins from him. A girl with blue, inhuman eyes knocked him from the saddle with a blow of a javelin. When he tried to stand, she struck him with the shaft and knocked him down.

The man standing over him had black, shoulder-length hair. A birdlike nose. An evil smile. And the gaze of a devil.

"I'll ask you a question," he hissed like a snake, "and you will reply. Have you seen two unaccompanied maidens on the road?"

Jakub Dancel shook his head at once. The black-haired man smiled hideously.

"I'll ask you again. Have you seen them?"

Jakub Dancel shook his head. Closed his eyes tightly and pursed his lips. The black-haired man stood up straight.

"String him up on a branch," he ordered. "And kindle a fire."

"I don't know where Reynevan is now," said the goliard emissary. He had introduced himself to the girls as Tybald Raabe. He was accompanied by two assistants, the second as young as the first.

"Five Hussite armies entered Upper Franconia," he explained, "each operating independently. I suspect Reynevan to be in the Tábor army, which is marching here via Hof and Münchberg. I'll also send word there. With that young man there, Jakub Dancel."

The young man, Jakub Dancel, glanced over at Weronika and blushed. Weronika fluttered her eyelashes.

"We, however, will wait here, in Bayreuth," continued the goliard.

"Why must we wait?" asked Jutta. "Why can't we ride straight to the Hussites with Master Dancel?"

"It's too perilous. Around here are prowling gangs, marauders and deserters. And the mercenaries are no better than them. The local knights, even *pflegers*, are afraid to stand up to the Czechs, but are still inclined to pillage and take it out on unarmed people and women—"

"We know."

"And the Czechs, hmm…" stammered Tybald Raabe. "Some lower-ranking commanders…God forbid you fall into their hands…Miss Jutta, Reynevan would never forgive me if I found you and then lost you.

"We shall wait here, in Bayreuth," he said, ending the discussion.

"I am certain the town will surrender. I have been operating here for several days, inciting the poor. The Patriciate are shaking in their shoes now, afraid of the Hussites on that side of the walls and of the mob on this side. Word has reached them from Plauen, and Hof…About massacres and fires. Bayreuth, you'll see, will surrender and pay a ransom. And when the Czechs enter, I'll hand you over into the care of the hejtmans. You'll be safe."

The candle flame flickered.

Reassured, bathed and fed, Jutta and Weronika first wept at length, reacting to the horror of their escape. Then they cheered up.

"There were moments I stopped believing," said Weronika, laughing and tightening the pegs of a lute found among Tybald's things in his clandestine quarters near the town walls. "I stopped believing we'd make it. I thought we'd come to a sorry end. If not ravaged with our throats slit by marauders, then in a ditch, expiring from the hunger and the cold. Admit it…"

"I admit it," said Jutta. "I also had moments like that."

"But that's all behind us! Ha! We've survived! Time to think about ourselves. That Jakub Dancel. Just a boy, but a pretty one. His eyes are sweet. Simply sweet. Don't make faces. You've now almost recovered your beau, you're almost in his arms. And what about me? Still alone."

Seulete sui et seulete vueil estre,
Seulete m'a mon douz ami laissiee;
Seulete sui, sanz compaignon ne maistre,
Seulete sui, dolente et courrouciee,
Seulete sui…

The candle flame flickered more strongly.

"Hush," said Jutta, suddenly jerking up her head. "Did you hear that?"

"No. What was it?"

Jutta gestured for her to be quiet.

And in Bayreuth the bells suddenly began tolling.

The door crashed open and Tybald Raabe rushed in.

"We must flee!" he yelled. "The Hussites are here! Quickly, quickly!"

On the street they were carried away by a river of refugees bearing them towards the centre. From the north came loud shouts and gunfire; the night sky was tinged with a red glow. They ran, already feeling waves of hot air and inhaling the stench of burning. On their heels were screams, the wild and ghastly screams of people being killed.

"They took the town by surprise," panted Tybald. "They scaled the walls. The town is doomed...Look lively, look lively..."

They were almost separated outside the parish church where the panic-stricken mob wrested them apart for a moment, taking them in different directions. Jutta was pushed, and as she fell she struck a buttress, was winded, by a miracle didn't fall down— if she had she would have been trampled. Tybald suddenly found himself beside her, clutched her to him, protected her, taking pokes and punches. Weronika screamed horrifyingly as the crowd carried her away. The emissary rushed to her, dragged her out of the crush, trembling, with a vacant stare and torn sleeve.

"This way, this way! Behind the vestry!"

Beside them, a woman and a child were knocked over and trampled before they had time to cry out.

Weronika was jostled and fell down, splashing into the mud.

They lifted her up and she screamed, looking around vacantly. She could barely walk and they had to drag her.

Flames were already rising over Bayreuth, with alarming speed jumping from roof to roof, from thatch to thatch. Columns of sparks shot up into the sky. And screaming rose above the roar of the inferno. The last fugitives rushed out of the streets leading to the town square pursued by Hussites. The conflagration was reflected as a thousand flashes on a thousand blades. The screaming of people being killed assaulted the ears.

They slaughtered methodically and unhurriedly, driving the crowd towards the parish church. When the church was full, fires were lit. The choir stalls were soon ablaze and the flames quickly spread to the crowded nave, the choir and the altar as the church's interior became an immense hearth. Anyone who tried to escape from the flames was stabbed with spears.

Thick streams of blood flowed along the streets leading to the river. Splashing in the bloody mud, the Hussites drove the people there.

The massacre went on.

Weronika recovered and they could run again. And they ran. As fast as they could.

Panic-stricken people teemed around the gate, where fighting and shouts and curses were coming from a nearby stable. Tybald rushed inside without a second thought. A moment later, he appeared with his other assistant, Paweł Ramusz, leading four struggling horses. Blood was dripping down Ramusz's cheek.

"Into the saddle! And to the gate! To the gate!"

Two men attacked Weronika as she was mounting the horse. They were yelling and grabbing at her clothes, trying to drag her from the horse. Tybald Raabe lashed one with his whip and Jutta kicked the other in the face. Beside them, Ramusz was lashing the mob with a knout. Weronika was trembling, the chattering of her teeth audible over the hullabaloo raging around them.

"To the gate! And the bridge!"

The roaring, incandescent fury of the raging element was hot on their heels. A wind suddenly stirred and fanned the flames, and in no time the town of Bayreuth became a single huge blaze. The surface of the moat gleamed like a red mirror. The silhouettes of riders flickered against a backdrop of flames.

"Spur the horses!" shouted Tybald Raabe, looking back. "Ride, as fast as you can!"

They fled, forcing the horses into a gruelling gallop. They didn't look back.

They galloped along the bank of the river glistening in the starlight. They didn't slow down until the horses began to wheeze and the forest track vanished into the darkness.

Jutta, suddenly feeling cold on the nape of her neck, stood up in the stirrups and listened out.

"We're being followed," she said in a trembling voice.

"Impossible…" said Tybald, also looking back. "I can't hear anything—"

"They're following us," Jutta repeated. "We must fly!"

"We'll ride the life out of the horses—"

"Would you prefer them to beat the life out of us?"

A hazy and cold dawn rose and it turned out that Jutta was right. On a distant hilltop loomed the shapes of riders. A faint cry reached them through the mist.

"*Adsuuumuuus!*"

"Damn it!" spat Tybald, spurring his horse. "It's Grellenort! Gallop, girls, gallop!"

The four of them spurred their mounts into a madcap gallop

down the hill, among sparse and leafless birch trees. They rode into a ravine, horseshoes ringing on stones. Thin ice on puddles cracked beneath them.

"Gallop! Don't slow down!"

"*Adsuuumuuus!*"

Beyond the ravine spread out a ploughed field, the snow lying white in furrows. Beyond the field was a blue-tinged forest. There was no need for commands or encouragement. Heads pressed to manes, they rode at a gallop. Clods of earth shot out from under their hooves.

But the pursuers were already close, their shouts indicating that they were now in eyeshot. Jutta looked back. Over a dozen riders were closing in, stretched out in a line. One of them was leading, at the head. She knew who it was.

They hurtled into the forest, forced their way through the thicket, lashed by snow-covered fir branches. And came out right at a crossroads. One road led into a ravine and the other into a forest.

"We'll split up!" yelled Jutta. "It's our only chance! I'll take the ravine; you go that way!"

"Jutta! Noooo!"

"I can't," panted the goliard. "I can't allow it. I'll go alone—"

"I'm the best rider here. And without you we won't get to the Hussites. Ride!"

There was no time either for argument or for tender farewells. Jutta spurred her horse and galloped into the ravine.

For a good two hours they didn't hear any sounds of pursuers behind them, but in spite of that, Tybald Raabe didn't dare slow the pace even for a moment, not until the pale sun reached its zenith.

"We'll stop…" he panted out. "And dismount. We must let the

horses rest…I don't think they're following us any more…I think we made it. Jutta—"

His voice stuck in his throat. Weronika burst out crying.

"She's the best rider among us…" uttered the goliard. "The best…She'll cope…"

Sobs were shaking Weronika's body.

"We must get help," Tybald decided. "We are close to the road leading to Kulmbach and Kronach, the Hussites must be nearby. Weronika, please stop…"

Weronika couldn't. She was sobbing louder and louder. And although tears are usually in vain, offer no help and don't improve one's predicament, this time it was different. The bushes rustled. A horse whinnied. And four riders rode into the clearing.

"Reynevan!" yelled the goliard. "Scharley! Samson!"

"That weeping was a good idea," said the penitent, greeting them. "If you hadn't been we would have ridden past."

As he talked, a deathly pallor covered Tybald's face. But Reynevan stayed calm. Or understood that he couldn't hold any grudges or grievances against the goliard, or he simply wasn't in the mood for grudges or grievances. It was probably the latter, for after listening, he instantly leaped to his feet and mounted his horse.

"We must ride!" said Tybald, also springing up. "We must ride to her rescue without delay! I'll show you the way! Give me one of those spare horses, mine won't manage even another furlong—"

"What about her?" asked Rixa, pointing at Weronika, face red from crying and nose still running.

"She can ride with us."

"No!" screamed Weronika of Elsnitz at the top of her voice. "I won't! Not for anything! I've had enough, enough, I can't take any more! I want to return to my convent! I want to go back to my conveeeent!"

"Very well," said Tybald, nodding. "Ramusz will accompany you to Cronschwitz. Farewell, Miss."

"Rescue...Jutta..."

"We shall."

A fence loomed up in front of Jutta. She urged the horse to jump and cleared it. She landed on a level dirt floor, between the cottages and shacks of a deserted village. On her left she saw a large granary; on her right, the torn sails of a windmill on a hillock showing faintly in the fog.

The horse snorted and wheezed, its bit and bridle entirely covered in froth, its neck hot, wet and slippery. But the pursuers weren't slowing, the Black Riders' horses weren't weakening; she could still hear cries and the tramping of hooves behind her.

She galloped towards the granary, for she thought she saw behind it a thicket that might give her at least temporary cover. And only cover could save her. She had no chance in a race. She cleared more wattle fences, but the horse slumped down onto its rump, seemingly about to fall. But it bravely got up.

Only to suddenly squeal. And buck, buck so fast that Jutta flew from the saddle. Having first seen out of the corner of her eye a javelin stuck into the side of her steed quite close to her calf.

She tumbled straight into some dry brambles and for a moment was snagged by the curved, prickly thorns. By the time she had struggled free, covered in scratches, it was too late, the Black Riders were surrounding her on all sides. She bolted, nimbly weaving between their horses. They easily overtook her, knocked her down in the gallop, so hard that the impact against the packed dirt floor winded and paralysed her. She was lying on her back, looking up at the suddenly dark, overcast sky. Around her, horses snorted and hooves boomed.

"Miss Jutta of Apolda."

He looked down at her from his saddle with his birdlike eyes. Smiling cruelly.

"We haven't seen each other for a long time," he said malevolently. "Just over a year has passed since our encounter at White Church. I've missed you. Go on, take her."

Two Riders jerked her up from the dirt floor. They weren't wearing helmets and she saw their faces, pale, as silver as ghouls', their vacant, dark-ringed eyes and the foam at the corners of their mouths. She suddenly quailed. In a horrifyingly certain presentiment that this time there could be no escape.

They dragged her over against the wall of a tumbled-down shed. Grellenort was already waiting there. And the fair-haired girl with blue, inhuman eyes.

"I had other plans for you," announced Grellenort. "I wanted to take you to Wrocław. Having first seized your lover, Reinmar Bielawa, I meant to force-feed him pieces of flesh I would have carved from you before his eyes, from various places. By cauterising the wounds, it would have been possible to drag it out for at least a fortnight. I planned to end with your internal organs. But time is against me and history is against me; the world has taken unforeseen turns. Thus I shall bid farewell to you here and now. I shall leave you here."

Two Riders grabbed Jutta by the hands and arms and lifted her up so that she was suspended, her toes barely touching the ground. Douce of Pack tore open her jerkin and blouse, uncovered her neck and seized her by the hair behind her neck. The Wallcreeper approached and took from his cloak a flat, elongated box. Jutta was close to fainting from fear and was unable to utter a sound, her throat tight with dread. But when she saw what the Wallcreeper was taking from the box she screamed. She screamed hysterically and struggled in the hands gripping her.

The object he took from the box was a desiccated hand. It was small, like a child's, but with inhumanly long fingers ending in hooked claws. The hand's dry skin was covered in small holes, resembling tiny molehills. They were left by the maggots that had hatched in the rotting tissue and completely devoured it, leaving the bones covered in withered skin and criss-crossed with tendons. Although it was mummified, the hand still stank repulsively of rotting flesh.

The Wallcreeper approached. Jutta felt the overwhelming desire to faint. But could not. She looked on, hypnotised.

"*Per nomen Baal-Zevuv, dominus scatophagum,*" intoned the Wallcreeper, raising the hand and bringing it close to her face. "*Per nomen Kuthulu, Tsadogua et Azzabue! Per effusionem sanguinis!*"

He scratched her neck with a dry claw. Drawing blood. She tried to scream but only managed to croak. He scratched her again. And again.

"Iä! Azif!"

A strange, hissing murmur, a susurration and a chirrup re-sounded, like hundreds of insects rustling their wings. The horror made even some of the Black Riders step back. The Wallcreeper brought the hand close to Jutta's face.

"*Adiungat Yersinia tibi pestilentiam!*"

He gave a sign for her to be released. She fell softly, quite limp. And a moment later contorted in a fit of vomiting.

He looked down at her for a while. Then beckoned to his men.

"It is done," he said. "Let us go… What is happening?"

"Hussites!" One of the Riders galloped over from the wattle fences. "A large troop! They're close!"

"Hide," shouted the Wallcreeper, pointing at the barn and the sheds. "We'll sit it out. Make sure the horses don't neigh."

*

The wind blew, the windmill on the hillock creaked, its sails revolving.

Children, let us sing to God,
Honour Him and sing His praises

A cavalry unit, two hundred and fifty armed men with the Chalice on their breastplates, rode by in a column along the road near the deserted village. At the head was Jan Zmrzlík of Svojšín, Lord of Orlík Castle, wearing full armour and a tunic decorated with his coat of arms: three red bands on a silver field.

"A village," said Fritzold of Warte, a mercenary, a Helvetian from the canton of Thurgau, pointing. "And a windmill on a hill-ock. Shall we burn it down?"

"No," decided Zmrzlík. "It's not worth leaving a trail of smoke. There's a well by the village green so we'll water the horses. And then continue on to Bamberg."

The Hussites were in no hurry and a good two hours passed before they left the green. Silence finally returned. Outside, the wind occasionally blew, whistling through cracks in the granary. Occasionally the sails of the windmill on the hillock creaked.

"They must have gone," confirmed the Wallcreeper. "Let's head outside and leave this place."

One of the Riders opened the gate wide. To find himself look-ing right down the barrel of the Prague hand cannon.

"Praise the Lord!" Scharley greeted him.

And shot him between the eyes.

At the sound of the shot, two Riders rushed out of the stable on foot. One fell, a bolt from Reynevan's crossbow plunging into his eye through the crack in his visor. Samson whacked the other so hard with his goedendag that the man's sallet collapsed and split open like an egg.

The giant forced his way into the barn, swinging the iron-bound club, and the Riders retreated before him, fleeing towards the walls. But only for a moment, for it was still five against one. Swords and daggers gleamed.

But Samson seized the post holding up the ridge beam. Veins stood out on his forehead as he tugged the post with all his might, like the original Samson. And just as the original Samson knocked down the pillars of the temple of Dagon in Gaza, so Samson Honeypot broke and knocked down the post in the barn. The ridge beam broke with a terrible crack and the rafters snapped like twigs. And the entire roof and the hayloft, the entire immense weight of old timber, everything, like the temple of Dagon on the Philistines, collapsed on the Black Riders, crushing and smashing them before they even had time to scream.

Only one leg was still sticking out from the pile of beams and rafters, one leg in a black greave and a black sabaton. It stuck out and twitched.

Samson was gasping for breath, unable to utter a sound. He tugged on Reynevan's arm.

There was still work to be done.

The Black Riders were crowded by the entrance to the granary. Rixa knocked one over, firing into him two balls from the harquebuses handed to her by Tybald. But some others had got out into the green and the Wallcreeper and the rest, already mounted, rode out and followed them. One of the horses immediately reared up and fell down—Reynevan was already waiting on the battlefield with his hunting crossbow. Tybald shot another horse with a handgonne, himself almost losing his life doing so when one of the Riders galloped up behind him with sword raised, only for Samson to hurl the goedendag at him and knock him from the saddle. Tybald fell on the man like a hawk and stabbed him under his gorget with a short sword. Meanwhile, Rixa stabbed another on the ground.

Scharley fearlessly ran in front of the Wallcreeper, slashing his horse across its forelegs. The horse crashed into the ground muzzle first; the Wallcreeper flew from the saddle and rolled across the dirt floor. Douce of Pack screamed piercingly, reined her horse around and went for Scharley, javelin in hand. The penitent didn't panic, didn't run, but waited with the falchion held in both hands. Douce stood up in the stirrups and wound up to throw. At that moment, a bolt from Reynevan's crossbow hit her horse in the neck. The horse reared. Douce fell and slammed onto the ground.

The Wallcreeper sprang up, dashed to the last of the Riders, knocked him from his horse and leaped into the saddle. He saw Samson running towards him, saw Rixa and Tybald reloading hand cannons. With a sudden movement he raised both hands, made a complicated gesture with them in the air and screamed out a spell. A ball of fire emerged from his palms and quickly began to swell.

Seeing what was about to happen, they all rushed for cover. But the Wallcreeper wasn't aiming at anyone in particular: he simply tossed the flaming ball upwards, where it exploded with a thunderous crack.

Taking advantage of the confusion, the Wallcreeper galloped over to Douce who was getting to her feet, pulled her up onto the horse and galloped away, towards the hillock where the windmill stood. Rixa fired the handgonne at them but missed.

Reynevan did not.

Struck by a bolt, the black stallion squealed, bucked and threw off both riders. The Wallcreeper and Douce bolted. Douce was limping.

Reynevan seized one of the horses running around the yard and leaped into the saddle, giving chase. The Wallcreeper turned around, seeing the horse's teeth just above his head, and howled with fear. But he nimbly dodged, raised a hand and shouted a spell. A stream of sparks, fiery needles, shot from his fingers. The horse neighed and reared up. Reynevan fell off, smashing the pickets of a fence as he fell. The Wallcreeper grabbed the reins and jumped into the saddle. And sped away.

Douce of Pack stood at the top of the stairs leading to the windmill. With a drawn short sword, hair flowing freely and teeth bared. An inhuman growl came from her throat, something like the fierce cry of a furious she-cat.

Scharley's mouth was already open to order her to throw down her weapon and surrender, but Rixa stopped him, shaking her head. She looked Scharley in the eyes and he understood.

There would be no mercy.

They grabbed the door torn from a pigsty by Tybald and used it as a shield as they climbed the stairs. They pushed Douce against the door, shoved her inside and dashed in after her.

The wind blew, the mill's sails moved around, the mechanism of the gears rumbled into motion.

Scharley caught Douce by the arm and prised the sword from her fingers. Douce struggled free and drew a knife. Rixa struck her with the hilt of her backsword. And shoved her. Straight into the driveshaft, the axles and toothed gears.

A faint wind was blowing.

The oaken cog of the gears caught Douce's arm, pulled her in with a crunching sound, like a wolf seizing something in its teeth. A bone snapped. Douce howled. She tried to struggle free, but the cogs held firm. The wind blew again lightly, the mechanism moved, the gear turned and was now pressing against Douce's chest. Douce howled so loudly that dust was blown from all the cracks.

Scharley and Rixa looked at each other. They shrugged. And went out.

Tybald was waiting by the steps. A little further off, Samson was helping a limping Reynevan put one foot in front of the other.

"Well?" asked Tybald, nodding towards the windmill. "Well?"

"Nothing," replied Rixa coldly. "We're waiting for the wind."

An approaching gale could be felt in the air. The Wallcreeper was already far away. Now he stopped and reined his horse around. He looked back.

Listened. The distance was considerable but he could hear.

"Don't leave me! Don't leave me! Don't leave me all alone!"

The Wallcreeper's face didn't twitch. And a moment later a large bird flew up from the saddle, flapping its wings.

It took off, rose and flew up into the sky, into the low clouds. Out of eyeshot.

"Don't leeeeea—"

The wind blew. The windmill's sails shuddered. Then moved, with evident effort as they overcame the obstruction. And then began to turn easily, without any hindrance.

Rixa and Tybald drove the last of the Riders, unarmed, bareheaded, to the door of the tumbledown shed. The Rider dropped to his knees, begging for mercy. But that day no mercy was being shown. Tybald caught the Rider by the hair and Rixa stabbed him under the chin with a short movement, driving the blade in up to the cross guard. The man fell, in convulsions, against the door, opening it with his weight. Rixa, hearing something, looked inside.

"Reynevan!" she screamed horrifyingly. "Reynevan! Come here! Quickly!"

"Oh, Jesus Christ!" said Tybald, also looking in and then retreating. "Oh, Jesus Christ…"

Scharley and Samson came running up. Reynevan was quicker. He rushed inside, pushing the goliard away and almost knocking Rixa over.

Lying inside on the straw was…

"Jutta!"

He rushed over to her and fell to his knees. Caught her by the shoulders.

What he first sensed was wet heat. She was so feverish as to be almost on fire. Her eyes were closed and she was trembling, shaking in shivers.

"Jutta! It's me. I'm here! Jutta!"

"Reynevan…" she said, opening her eyes. "Reynevan?"

He hugged her. And then felt the dreadful icy cold of her hands. He looked and went numb. The skin of her hands was blue, becoming indigo towards her fingers, and her fingers themselves were a deep shade of crimson.

With trembling fingers, he opened her blouse. And though he tried, was unable to suppress a groan of desperation.

Jutta's arms, breasts and belly were blue and densely covered in blisters and pustules. New ones were erupting almost in front of his very eyes. Some had already burst and blood was dripping from them. Jutta began to tremble and shake spasmodically. Reynevan covered her and wrapped her in a cloak. She looked at him vacantly.

"Reynevan…I'm cold…"

He covered her with another cloak that Samson handed him. Jutta gripped his hand tightly. She tried to say something, but almost choked on blood. He tilted her head so she could spit it out.

"What's the matter with her?" Scharley asked softly. "What ails her? What's that dreadful blue colour?"

Reynevan bit his lips and pointed to the girl's neck, to the cuts, the parallel cuts, already swollen and suppurating. He stood up and drew Scharley and Samson to one side.

"They wounded her," he uttered. "And infected her. Infecting her with—"

"With what?"

"It's..." His voice was stuck in his throat. "I think it's...They've poisoned her blood magically. Infecting her blood and making it fester...According to Avicenna...The Salernitans call it *sepsis*...The blue colouration comes from internal effusions. Her blood is seeping through her veins and forming clots... And it's spreading through her body...Purulent abscesses are forming...She now has symptoms of gangrene..."

"A remedy?"

"There is no remedy for blood poisoning...Not that anyone knows—"

"Don't say that, dammit. You're a physician. Try something!"

First the fever, he thought, kneeling down, *I have to reduce the fever... Then a strong antidote will be necessary... Something to suppress the infection...*

With shaking fingers, he unfastened the buckles of his bag, emptied out the contents and began feverishly rummaging through them. With an overwhelming sense of powerlessness. With a growing conviction that nothing he possessed could cure Jutta or even help to relieve her suffering. That all his remedies *contra malum* were fit for nothing, that *diacodia* and *electuar* were fit for nothing, that *sotira*, *antidota* and *panacea* were fit for nothing. *Artemisium*, *hypericum* and *serpillum* were all fit for nothing; the butterbur, carline thistle and all the other medicines he carried around in his bag were fit for nothing.

515

Amulets, he thought, *Telesma's amulets. Not many are left.* Gemma rutila, *which can staunch bleeding.* Venim *from lapis-lazuli, effective against venomous bites*...Aquila, *eagle stone, which purifies the blood...But all of them should be used immediately and they cut her hours ago...The magical blood poisoning is spreading like lightning...Perhaps one of the amulets will work...God, make one of them work...*

The amulets didn't work. They were too weak. They had no chance of fighting what Jutta had been infected with.

Spells. He knew a few. Bent over, he recited the spells in turn, overcoming the growing dryness in his mouth. He made magical gestures and signs, fighting to overcome the trembling of his hands.

The spells didn't work. Reynevan raised his eyes and hands.

"*Magna Mater*..." he mumbled. "O Mother of the Gods... You, the only one who defends and protects us...O Mother of the Sun, whose body is white from the milk of the stars! *Elementorum omnium domina*, O Lady of Creation, Provider for the World! O Guardian of the Sea and Sky, all the Gods and Powers, *aeterne caritatis desideratissima filia, aeterne sapientie mater gratissima, sub umbra alarum tuarum protege nos.* I humbly entreat you to give me the power of a medicine that will restore health. Save her, I beg you. Let her live."

No miracle occurred.

Jutta began to choke and spit blood; it was also spurting powerfully from her nose now. He lifted her head and tilted it. And looked on powerlessly.

"How..." said Scharley, barely audibly. "How will she—"

"Her body will be destroyed from the inside."

"How long will it—"

"A long time."

"Reynevan..." said Jutta, suddenly seizing him by the hand.

There was almost no strength left in her utterly dark blue fingers. "Reynevan," she repeated almost lucidly. "I want...to go to the sunlight..."

They all hurried to help. Picked her up, carried her out of the barn and laid her down on a makeshift bed of cloaks. The sun wasn't shining. There were low, leaden-grey clouds.

Once again, blood began streaming from her nose, and her blood-soaked hose testified to bleeding from the digestive tract and the reproductive organs. She began to be racked by convulsive shivers. She trembled for a long time.

They looked on helplessly.

"Reyne..." she said, spitting blood. "Reynevan..."

"I'm with you."

"You are..." she said, looking at him almost lucidly. "You are... That is good..."

She groped feebly for his arm. Then for his hand. Her fingers and fingernails were now quite black. Her feet likewise.

"It is now time...Montségur..."

"What are you saying? Jutta?"

"Montségur...It still exists...*Endura* and *consolamentum*... I would like to...hear...a voice from there..."

Reynevan shook his head, looking at his friends enquiringly. Scharley spread his arms.

"Let me," said Samson.

He knelt down beside Jutta and took her blackened hand.

"*Benedicite,*" he said softly. "*Benedicite, parcite nobis.*"

"*Parcite nobis,*" she whispered back. "For all my sins...I ask for forgiveness..."

"*De Deu e de nos vos sian perdonatz,*" said Samson. "*E nos preguem Deu que les vos per do.*"

Jutta appeared to be trying to smile, but a paroxysm of pain contorted her blue face into a ghastly grimace. Blood flowed from her nose and the corner of her mouth. Blood was now seeping through all the cloaks covering her.

"Reinmar," said Samson, standing up. "It is time. Let it happen."

"I don't understand."

"Jutta will go on suffering for at least a dozen hours before she dies," said the giant in a lowered voice as he approached. "Will you permit it?"

"What are you saying? End her suffering? Samson…I am a doctor! I am a Christian…God forbids…Divine law—"

"A law that makes someone suffer? When we could end her suffering? You know nothing about God, laddie, you don't know Him at all. Instead, you make of Him a cruel fanatic. You offend Him by so doing. It is unseemly."

"But—"

"You are a physician. Treat her suffering."

Scharley took Rixa by the arm and led her away. Tybald Raabe followed them.

Samson and Reynevan knelt down beside Jutta, Samson on her left, Reynevan on her right. Before they knelt down, Jutta had been unconscious but now she regained consciousness.

"Reinmar…"

"I love you," he whispered with his mouth by her ear. "I love you, Jutta."

"I love you, too. I am ready."

"*Pater sancte,*" said Samson softly, "*suscipe ancillam Tuam in Tua iusticia et mitte graciam Tuam e Spiritum Sanctum Tuum super eam.*"

"*Lux in tenebris lucet,*" she whispered in a clear voice. "And the light shineth in darkness…And the darkness comprehended it not."

And when she uttered that, the clouds suddenly parted. And the setting sun shone through them. And there was light.

And so it was that Reinmar of Bielawa, physician, opened the casket with amulets, a gift from Jošt Dun, called Telesma, the wizard from Prague. So it was that Reinmar took an amulet from the casket. The one that was buried the deepest, the singular one, small and inconspicuous, the one that should never be used, because it could only be used in absolutely, extremely final circumstances, in a hopeless, dead-end situation. And so it was that Reinmar embraced Jutta and brought the amulet to her temple and uttered a spell that ran: "*Spes proxima.*" And so it was that Jutta sighed in relief and then smiled and relaxed.

And Jutta was no more.

All that remained was her name, an empty word which there was no point in even uttering.

Chapter Nineteen

In which what was meant to happen, happens. And the words of the visionary prophet Isaiah, son of Amos, spring to mind: We wait for light, but behold obscurity. For brightness, but we walk in darkness.

On the first day, his kingdom was divided towards the four winds of Heaven. The Earth was moved from its place, the gates of Heaven opened and the smoke of a great fire blotted out the horizon. The sun was turned to darkness, and the moon to blood. From each side gazed out despair and horror. And there was sorrow. And there were tears. And there was a dreadful, overwhelming solitude.

On the second day, there was a great darkness. Stars fell from the sky. Chasms of earth groaned from the four corners of the world. The chasms disintegrated among moans, the Earth and Sea trembled, and along with them the hills and the mountains. And effigies of true and false gods tumbled, and with their fall all the peoples disdained life in this world.

The heavenly firmament was rent from East to West. And suddenly luminosity—*lux perpetua*—arose. And from it came the voice of an archangel and it was heard in the lowest depths. *Dies irae, dies illa...*

Mors stupebit et natura,
cum resurget creatura,
iudicanti responsura.
Liber scriptus proferetur,
in quo totum continetur,
unde mundus iudicetur.

On the third day...
On the third day came Samson. And with him Scharley, Rixa and Tybald.

"Enough, Reynevan. That will suffice, O friend. You have bewailed her, mourned her with dignity and in a seemly manner. But now be upstanding and pull yourself together."

Smoke rose over the land of the Bavarians and from all sides the wind bore the smell of burning. In the main, though, military activities had ceased, and rumour had it that negotiations had begun. Frederick, Margrave of Brandenburg, reputedly came in person to negotiate with the hejtmans at Beheimstein Castle near Nuremberg, which had been captured and turned into the Hussite headquarters. It might have signalled the end of the plundering raid, since the Germans were ready to pay ransom. In order to speed up their decision, Prokop ordered the Hussite columns to march on Sulzbach and Amberg in the Upper Palatinate, which seriously disconcerted Count Palatine Johann of Neumarkt.

All the rumours turned out to be true. The negotiations were crowned with success. The Margrave, the Count Palatine and Nuremberg all paid up. The punitive expedition was over. Orders were issued, the Hussite army concentrated outside Pegnitz and Auerbach began its march home in two columns. But they didn't think to be idle on their way. Marching along the southward road, the column formed up to attack Kynžvart, another castle belonging to the detested Heinrich of Plauen. Prokop led the northward column on a strenuous march towards Cheb.

The army reached Cheb on Saturday, the eleventh of February, in the late afternoon, almost at dusk, attacking at once the villages and settlements surrounding the town. The entire castle town was in flames and Jan Zmrzlík's cavalry troop made sure that not one of the surrounding homesteads remained intact. Reynevan had pulled himself together and convalesced but did not partake in the burning and killing. Along with Scharley, Samson and Rixa, he stayed close to Mikuláš Sokol of Lamberk, who remained with the reserve unit.

Tybald Raabe had left them, heading eastwards before they even set off for Pegnitz.

Night soon fell but was as bright as day from fires. And noisy. The hammers and axes of carpenters banged unceasingly as trebuchets were set up and chevaux de frise constructed. Gunners yelled and sang as they affixed bombards and mortars to wooden mounts. Taborite soldiers shouted outside the walls, promising the defenders of Cheb hideous deaths, and the defenders answered the Taborites with promises of even more gruesome deaths, vile insults and the threat of being shot at.

"Reinmar?"

"Yes, Samson."

"Are you bearing up? How are you feeling?"

"Very poorly."

"I needn't have asked."

They were sitting by a small campfire, kindled behind a tarpaulin stretched between poles, which protected it from the February winds. They were alone, as Scharley and Rixa had wandered off somewhere. As they had been wont to do lately. Finally,

Rixa came to bid them farewell and set off for Silesia.

"Something's vexing me, too..." the giant unexpectedly stammered. "I've been tormented recently by thoughts of the real Samson, the one from the Benedictine monastery. I can't rid myself of the conviction that I did him harm. I left him... There..."

"You aren't to blame," Reynevan replied gravely. "It was Scharley and I, and our foolish exorcisms, our trifling with things that shouldn't be trifled with. You tried to put right our error, tried many times; no one could accuse you of inactivity. It didn't succeed, oh well, that's God's will. And now...Now the situation has changed. You have responsibilities. You can't abandon Marketa. You'd break the girl's heart if you left her alone now. I understand it might be unpleasant for you, I know you and how much you care about other people's happiness. But now you'd have to choose: either Marketa, or the convent simpleton. It is clear to me whom you ought to choose. It is obvious. And don't tell me it's not very moral."

"It isn't very moral," said Samson, sighing. "Not very moral at all. Because now it's too late for any kind of choice. More than four years have passed since that event. Back there...In the vale of darkness...No man could have endured that, no human psyche could have withstood it. The real Samson is dead or is quite out of his mind. We shan't be able to return him to the world now. That fact, regrettably, burdens my conscience."

"Listen—"

"Don't say anything."

The roof timbers of the cottages outside the castle cracked as they burned down, the wind bearing foul odours and blasts of heat.

"The fate of the monastery simpleton," said Samson, interrupting the silence, "was by no means sealed the moment

I saw Marketa. Back then, near Kolín, in the card tricksters' roadhouse—"

"You did then what you had to do. I remember your words. What we witnessed in the gambling den precluded indifference and inaction. Thus, what had to happen, happened."

"That's true. But only later, in Prague, did I yield to my feelings. The day she smiled at me for the first time. *Quando mi volsi alsuo viso ridente…*

> *Art and nature, which tempt one*
> *Whether in a living shape or a drawn work,*
> *In order through the senses to dominate the soul*
> *Gathered together they did not have so much Power*
> *like that wonder which I was dazzled with,*
> *When I saw joy in her eyes.*

"And such a glow emanated from her," Samson was neither reciting, nor speaking, "as though happy God had entered her face. And captured my soul…Ah well…Excuse me. I know it is a banality, a trifle, but I can't help it. But I ought at least to restrain myself and not trumpet it. But perhaps it was fortunate? Perhaps it is a good introduction to what I want to tell you?"

"What do you want to tell me?"

"That I'm leaving."

"Now?"

"Tomorrow. It will be the last time. Cheb is the last town I will enter with you. I would leave today, but something holds me back. Tomorrow, however, I shall finish with this once and for all. I'm leaving. Returning to Rapotín. To her. Come with me."

"Why?" Reynevan asked bitterly and with effort. "Why would I go back there? What or who is there for me? Jutta is dead. I loved her and she has departed. What is left? I have also read

Dante Alighieri. *Amor condusse noi ad una morte*, love led us to one death. I await nothing else. So I can just as easily await it here, in this army. In the midst of this slaughter."

Samson was silent for a long time.

"You are in darkness, friend," he finally said. "In a darkness worse than the one the real Samson passed into. It has befallen both of us. We wait for light, but behold obscurity. We wait for brightness, but we walk in darkness. Like the blind, we feel for the wall and grope as if sightless. We stumble at noon as though it were night; though sound in body, it is as if we were deceased. And we long for the light. For luminosity. You chose the wrong quotation from Alighieri. I'll tell you the right one. *Sta come torre ferma...*

> *Be as strong as an unbending tower,*
> *Though winds do pound against its peak.*

"No more strength is left in me. Where there is no hope, there is no strength."

"Hope always lives. Hope is light eternal. *Lux perpetua. La luce etterna.*

> *O luce etterna che sola in te sidi,*
> *sola t'intendi, e da te intelletta*
> *e intendente te ami e arridi!*

"I am too weary to muster any optimism."

"Goodnight, Reinmar."

"Goodnight, Samson."

It began at dawn. Bombards roared, foglers and cannons boomed, mortars thundered, the arms of trebuchets creaked and a hail of missiles fell on Cheb. The entire foreground was covered in a dense veil of white smoke.

Protected by pavises and barricades, the Taborites approached the walls in a tight array, but Prokop hadn't given the order for the storm. It was known that the hejtman wanted to avoid losses and preferred the town to surrender and pay a ransom; the heavy bombardment was meant only to soften up the defenders. Hence neither black powder nor balls were spared.

But Mikuláš Sokol, emboldened by the sluggish resistance from the south side, attacked on his own initiative. A barrel of powder was placed at the gate, and when it exploded a storm unit charged in.

Inside, beyond the gate, at the entrance of a street, a counter-attack pinned down the assailants. A company of defenders clashed with a company of attackers. Both sides were armed mainly with polearms: halberds, gisarmes, voulges, pikes and bear spears, giving the impression of two hedgehogs colliding with each other. They joined battle roaring and yelling; roaring and yelling they pulled back, leaving several bodies on the cobblestones. They lowered their shafts and struck again, with a clanging and a grinding. It appeared from the exchange of insults that it was Czechs fighting Czechs.

"*Psí hlavy!* Curs!"

"*Zkurvysyni!* Bastards!"

Reynevan seized a discarded voulge and was about to wade into the confusion when Scharley held him back with a firm grip.

"Don't play the hero!" he shouted over the uproar of battle and the thunder of the cannons. "And don't look for death! Fall back, fall back, to the gate! They'll soon repel us! Beware of marksmen in those windows! Do you see?"

Reynevan saw. He dropped the voulge, seized a crossbow, aimed and fired. A crossbowman fell from the window on the first floor, pierced by a bolt. Reynevan cocked the crossbow and loaded another bolt.

"Fight!"

"Have at them!"

In front of the gatehouse, between burning houses, the two units bristling with iron came together again, sliding in the blood. Shafts cracked as they struck each other, the soldiers yelled and the wounded wailed. Samson suddenly stood up straight, utterly exposing himself to the missiles.

"Can you hear it?"

"What?"

"We can't hear anything!" yelled Scharley. "Fall back! Prokop won't give us support! We must get out of here before they kill us!"

"Can you hear it?"

At first, the battle's roar drowned everything out. But then what Samson heard reached their ears, too.

The crying of children. The high-pitched and wretched crying of children. From a nearby house which was already blazing.

Samson made to take a step forward.

"Don't do it!" yelled Scharley, paling. "It's death!"

"I must…It cannot be otherwise."

He ran. After moment's hesitation, they rushed after him. Reynevan was almost immediately shoved back and blocked by Taborites retreating after another skirmish. Scharley was forced to dodge the iron spines of the advancing defenders. Samson had vanished.

The Taborites lowered their voulges and bear spears, yelled and attacked the defenders. The two units struck each other with force, stabbing each other. Blood flowed over the cobbles.

And then Samson Honeypot emerged from the burning building.

Carrying a child in each arm. About a dozen pale, silent children were following him, huddling to his thighs and clinging to his clothing.

And suddenly in front of the gatehouse the roar of battle was extinguished, like a flaming brand shoved into the snow. The shouting stopped. Silence fell and even the wounded stopped groaning.

Samson walked slowly between the two units, leading the children. As he walked, weapons were lowered before him, were laid down at his feet. At first seemingly unwillingly, then more and more eagerly. The murderous blades of halberds and gisarmes, the blades of voulges and partisans, the blades of bear spears and corseques, the blades of spears and the slender points of pikes were lowered, clinking against the cobbles. They were lowered before Samson. They bowed down before him. Honouring him. In complete silence.

Walking through the iron avenue, Samson reached the gate. Scharley, Reynevan and several Czechs ran forwards, seized the children and pulled them away. Samson stood up straight and sighed deeply, with relief.

It was as if the spell had fallen from the men fighting by the gatehouse and they fell on each other again, yelling. And one of the gunners in a window hooked his gun onto a windowsill and brought the smouldering fuse to the touch hole.

Samson staggered and groaned softly. And tumbled to the ground. Face down.

A single glance was enough for Reynevan. He raised his head. And shook it. Feeling his lips beginning to tremble uncontrollably.

"Dammit, Samson!" yelled Scharley, kneeling beside him. "Don't do this to me! Don't do it to me, dammit! Don't you dare!"

Samson's eyes glazed over. Blood spouted in pulses from the wound, staining the snow.

That same Sunday, Father Homolka, parish priest of Saint John the Baptist's in Šumperk, chose as the topic of his sermon the story of Tobias of Nineveh, Tobias ever faithful to God, Tobias the old and blind. The parish priest talked about how the son of Tobit, Tobias the Younger, was sent by his father to the town of Rages in Media, and not knowing the route journeyed there with a hired guide and a dog.

Mrs. Blažena Pospíchalová yawned furtively. Hearing a sigh, she glanced over at Marketa, who was standing beside her. The red-headed girl had her mouth slightly open and appeared to be drinking in the preacher's every word. Didn't she know the Book of Tobit? Was it really the first time she'd heard that parable? *No*, thought Mistress Blažena, *she simply enjoys stories like that. Long, complicated and charming stories about journeys and obstacles being overcome. Parables, fables, fairy tales that—though terrible on the face of it—always end well. Plenty of folk like listening to such tales, and not without reason do priests choose them for their sermons. People aren't so bored by them.*

The preacher, certainly aware of how much folk like to hear about journeys, spun a vivid tale about the trek of Tobias the Younger, the guide and the dog through the plain of Media. He talked about the fish caught in the River Tigris, about the heart, liver and gall bladder of that fish, removed on the advice of the guide. About how Tobias the Younger met Sarah, Raguel's daughter in Ecbatana, the capital of the Medes, and how a beautiful and sincere love bound the two young people together. Mistress Blažena stifled a yawn. She knew more fascinating love stories. Marketa sighed and licked her lips.

And the preacher, his voice cracking with excitement, told of the curse placed on Sarah. About the deceitful spirit Asmodeus, who treacherously murdered all the men that the girl fell in love with. About how, on the good advice of the guide, Tobias drove out the evil spirit using incense from the heart and liver of the fish he had caught, and how he was wed with Sarah in a happy marriage. About how, after returning to Nineveh, the guide restored Tobias the Old's sight using gall from the fish. How great was the joy and gratitude, what a wedding...

"And when the wedding was over," called Father Homolka excitedly from the pulpit, "Tobit said to his son, Tobias: *Think about giving a payment to the man who accompanied you!* And he answered him: *Father, how large a payment should I give him? For after all, he brought me home safely, freed my wife and cured you...*"

"Freed..." Mistress Blažena heard a very soft whisper. "Cured..."

"Marketa? Is that you?"

"Cured him..." the girl whispered with clear difficulty. "And brought him home hale..."

"Marketa! What's the matter?"

The people in the nave raised their heads on suddenly hearing a rustling, like the rustling of feathers, like the flapping of wings. Voices, soft cries and sighs reverberated among the congregation. Everyone looked upwards. The preacher lost his thread for moment, and only a moment later returned to the sermon and the parable. And to the answer the guide gave to Tobit and Tobias.

"I shall reveal before you the entire truth, hiding nothing. It is beautiful to keep a king's secret, but to manifest the works of God is most praiseworthy."

The rustling grew in intensity. Marketa moaned loudly.

"I am one of the seven angels that stand in readiness and enter before the Lord's majesty. Fear not! Peace be with you! Worship

God for ever and ever! I do not deserve credit for being with you, it was the will of God. But I—"

"No!" Marketa screamed in despair. "No! Don't go! Don't leave me all alone!"

"And I ascend to the One that sent me. Tell of everything that befell you."

"He is leaving," groaned Marketa in the embrace of Mistress Blažena. "Now…This moment…He is leaving. For ever… For ever!"

It appeared to Blažena Pospíchalová that the stained-glass window suddenly shattered in a great brilliance and that a great luminosity flooded the altar and the presbyter. It appeared to her that she heard the flapping of wings and the rustling of feathers right over her head; it appeared to her that it would tear the wimple from her head. It only lasted a moment.

"And he was gone," said the priest, finishing the sermon in complete silence. "They stood up, but none could see him any longer."

Two tears rolled down Marketa's cheeks.

Just two.

The Taborites were driven out of the town and the gate was barricaded. They began to shoot from the walls again. There was no chance of Samson being carried, but some Czechs brought pavises and covered with them the wounded man and the others who were with him.

"*Expectavimus lucem…*" said the giant suddenly. "*Et ecce tenebrae…*"

"Samson…" When Scharley spoke, his voice caught in his throat.

"What had to happen, has happened…Reinmar?"

"I am here, Samson. Hold on…We'll carry you—"

"Let it go. I know."

Reynevan wiped his eyes.

"Marketa… *O luce etterna* …"

Samson's voice was so faint they had lean close to hear his words.

"Describe it," he suddenly said quite clearly. "Describe all that has befallen you."

They said nothing. Samson tilted his head to one side.

"*Consummatum est,*" he whispered.

And those were the last words he uttered.

And the sun was turned into darkness, and the moon into blood. From each side despair and horror peeped out. And effigies of true and false gods tumbled, and with their fall all the peoples disdained life in this world.

The heavenly firmament was rent from East to West. And suddenly luminosity—*lux perpetua*—arose. And from it came the voice of an archangel and it was heard in the lowest depths.

Dies irae, dies illa.
Confutatis maledictis,
flammis acribus addictis,
voca me cum benedictis…

Reynevan wept unashamedly.

From Cheb and Kynžvart, the old chronicler monk from the Augustinian monastery in Żagań scratched with his quill, *Prokop's victorious army returned home in the month of February, on Tuesday* ante festum sancti Matthie, *celebrating it with a triumphant entry into Prague. And there was much to celebrate. They had taken notable captives and were bearing loot and spoils on three thousand wagons, some so heavy that they needed to be pulled by ten, twelve and even fourteen horses. And what they were unable to take,* destruxerunt et concremaverunt, *they destroyed, making of it embers and ashes. In Meissen, Saxony and Thuringia, twenty towns were burned down and two thousand villages depopulated. And in Upper Franconia there was nothing even left to count; just one great desert remained.*

And it was later said in Prague and the whole of Bohemia that it was such a splendid ride that even the oldest folk could not recall when the Czechs had accomplished something of the like.

And may God absolve their sins.

Reynevan did not witness the splendour of the triumphant parade. He rode into Prague, indeed, but lying on a wagon, unconscious, burning from fever.

He was ill for a long time.

Chapter Twenty

In which Reynevan makes his final decision. For like the Apostle Paul in the Second Epistle to the Corinthians, old things had passed away and all things were become new. And *lux vitae*, the light of life, was waiting for those who had made the right choice.

The extremely mild winter of 1429 and 1430 passed smoothly and almost imperceptibly into a mild spring. Already in early March the sky was teeming with a great multitude of birds returning from the south. Starlings arrived earlier than usual; storks clattered on their rooftop nests earlier than usual. Wild geese gaggled, cranes squawked and all sorts of winged beasts chirped. Ponds, bogs, marshes and ditches resounded with the massed croaking of frogs. Alder buds split open, pussy willow was abundant, meadows bloomed white and yellow with wind-flowers and marsh marigolds.

Reynevan rode alone through the Opava lands along a high-way rutted by wheels and horseshoes, trodden by soldiers' boots. In the tracks of the twelve-thousand-strong field army of the Tábor, which had marched there barely a week earlier.

Around noon, he heard the chiming of a bell. He spurred his horse, following the sound, and soon after he saw on a rise a small wooden church with a spire, quite intact. Without a second thought he reined his horse around towards it. Much had changed in him over the previous weeks.

In that respect, too.

He dismounted, but didn't enter the chapel, although the bell was still tolling the Angelus from the belfry. He approached the entrance and fell to his knees three paces before it. *Jutta*, he thought. *Jutta.*

Agnus Dei qui tollit peccata mundi.

Requiem aeternam dona ei, et lux perpetua luceat ei. In memoria aeterna erit iusta ab auditione mala non timebit.

O God, I fall and I cannot go on. I am paralysed and unable to rise. Heal me and lift me up in the name of Your mercy. Send me the grace of peace. And grant her eternal rest.

Agnus Dei qui tollit peccata mundi. Ad te omnis caro veniet.

"Amen," said a voice, shaking him out of his reverie. "Amen to your prayer, wanderer. Peace be with you."

In the entrance to the church stood a priest, short and stout, wearing a sheepskin jerkin over his cassock, with a tonsure shaved down to a narrow strip of hair above his ears. He was resting on a forked staff as though on a crutch, and his face was graced with a large bruise.

"Peace be with you," he repeated, speaking with obvious effort and gasping for breath. "You pray in the open air. Are you a Hussite?"

"I am a doctor," said Reynevan, standing up. "I help the suffering and bring them relief. And since you are suffering, I may help you, too. Who did that to you?"

"My neighbours."

The priest's trunk was covered with bruises, which merged into a single large, blue-black contusion on his right side. The priest

535

hissed and moaned under Reynevan's hand as he examined him, groaning, sighing and sucking in air. Despite that, he kept up a constant stream of chatter.

"First of all…They burst in here yelling and raging. That the Roman Pope is the Antichrist…And that my faith is a dog's faith. Faith, I replied, is grace, we do not choose faith. I received what came to me. Without complaint. But they…Instead of joining a theological dispute with me, they punched me in the head and then began kicking me. But they didn't kill me…Did not burn down the church…Or the surrounding villages… Which means it may be true what people say…That our Duke Přemek has entered into a pact with the Hussites. And in exchange for the freedom to march through Opava they will not burn or plunder—"

"You have three broken ribs," said Reynevan, with no thought of explaining to the priest the complexities of Přemek of Opava's pact with the Tábor. "But the lungs are intact. I shall give you a compression dressing and medicine to ease the pain. I shall also leave you a remedy that will speed up the knitting of the bones. As long as it doesn't bother you that it is magical. Does it?"

"Ha," said the priest, looking curious. "A Hussite and a physician—and a sorcerer to boot. What's in that brew?"

"You don't need to know. And don't want to."

"But is it black magic? Will it put my immortal soul at risk?"

"Take precautions. Mix it half-and-half with holy water."

"You knelt at the church door," said the priest, looking Reynevan straight in the eyes. "You consider the war you are fighting in, the war you are heading to, a *bellum justum*. But you are aware that you may not cross the threshold of a church with the blood of a neighbour on your hands, even if it was spilled in a just war, before doing penance. Do I guess right?"

"You do not. Take the medicine regularly. After *matutinum*, at noon and before *concubium*. Farewell, I am going."

"You are going…" said the priest, grimacing as he felt his bandaged side. "Alone, through a land whose citizens have been severely harried by your brothers in faith, severely enough to arouse in them sinful thoughts of vengeance. I cannot even vouchsafe for my parishioners. Indeed, I have taught them to love their neighbours, but in recent years theory has diverged considerably from practice. It is possible that the local people will want to discuss religion with you in the same way that the Hussites did with me; I mean with fists and boots. Are you not afraid?"

"I am not," replied Reynevan, a little too quickly and a little too frankly. "I've stopped feeling fear."

"Oho," said the priest, noticing Reynevan's tone and glancing at him keenly. "I know that state of mind. And not by any means from reading the Good Book. I didn't hear the words of your prayer," he added, "but I am certain that at one time I said similar. Often and long enough that I felt the urge to utter the word 'litany.'"

"Indeed?"

"Sadly," said the clergyman, gravely. "I have known the burden of loss, I know how heavily it can weigh on one. Such that one can neither stand nor raise one's head. *Praesens malum auget boni perditi memoria*; the memory of lost happiness heightens one's present misery. But we shall all be transformed. At the sound of the last trumpet, for the trumpet will blow and the dead will be raised incorruptible, and we shall be transformed. For that which is corruptible must take on incorruptibility, and that which is mortal must take on immortality."

"Eschatology. Something more?"

"Indeed. Reconciliation with God."

"Penance?"

"Reconciliation. For in Christ, God reconciled the world with itself, disregarding people's sins, but putting in us the word of atonement. So if someone remains in Christ he is a new creation. Old things have passed away and behold, all things are become new. Whomsoever chooses the right path will have *lux vitae*, the light of life."

"Life is darkness. *In tenebris ambulavimus*, we walk in darkness."

"We shall be transformed. And there will be light. Would you like to confess your sins?"

"No."

The border between the duchies should have been marked by posts, stones, mounds or other signs. Reynevan didn't see any. In spite of that, it was easy to say where Opava—whose herzog had reached agreement with the Hussites—ended. And where the Duchy of Racibórz—which had always been hostile to the Hussites—began. The border was delineated by smouldering fires. The blackened, burned-out remains of villages that had existed, but were no more.

He rode out of the forests straight into a large expanse which was a single, huge battlefield. The ground was covered with hundreds of corpses—of both men and horses—and the stench of muck, black powder, blood and sickly decay. Reynevan had seen plenty of battlefields and reconstructed the course of events with ease. Around four days earlier, the knighthood of Racibórz, Karniów and Pszczyna had tried to stop the Tábor, striking the marching column from the flank. Familiar with that tactic, the Hussites shielded themselves with pavises, drew their wagons into a wall and decimated the attackers with a hail of balls and bolts, and then attacked themselves, from both flanks, clenching the Racibórz men in an iron pincer movement. And then dealt with any survivors of the clash. Reynevan saw at the edge of the battleground a pile of mutilated bodies, saw bodies hanging from trees on the boundary of the field.

Local peasants roamed the churned-up earth, stripping the corpses, their stooped posture and nervous movements calling to mind animals. Or flesh-eating demons fearful of the light.

Reynevan spurred on his horse. He wanted to join the Tábor army before dusk.

He wasn't afraid of getting lost. Smoke from fires showed him the way.

His meeting with the leaders of the punitive expedition turned out to be onerous. Reynevan was accustomed to it, because he had experienced it many times over the previous few months. He had experienced the pitying looks, the faltering words, the sympathetic nods. Had experienced the comradely embraces and slaps on the back. He had heard many exhortations to bear up and not buckle under. Which made him feel both weak and want to buckle up, although a moment before he had—it appeared—felt perfectly all right.

Things were no different now. Jakub Kroměšín, the expedition commander, sent him a sympathetic look. Hejtman Jan Pardus nodded and shook his hand in friendship. Dobko Puchała slapped him on the shoulder, hard and warmly, restraining himself, fortunately, from exhortations. Duke Sigismund Korybut behaved haughtily, barely allowing himself a reaction. Bedřich of Strážnice acted naturally.

"I'm glad you're better," he announced, leading Reynevan to the edge of the camp, towards the line of sentry posts. "I'm glad you've recovered. In February I didn't know what had knocked you off your feet: illness or misfortune. I was afraid that it might break you, destroy you or cast you into apathy, drive you away from life and reality. But here you are and that's all that matters. We're creating history here, changing the fate of Europe and the world. You've been through too much with us for you to leave us now."

Reynevan didn't comment. Bedřich looked him straight in the eyes, for a long time, as though expecting a response. Hearing none, with a sweeping gesture he pointed at the glow of fires lighting up the sky in the east and south.

"All we needed was a week," he said, "to terrorise Racibórz by fire and sword, to put the fear of God into Duke Mikołaj and blockade the widow, Duchess Helena, in Pszczyna. Any day now we'll be joined by Bolko Wołoszek, and we'll jointly attack the Duchy of Koźle, the lands of Konrad the White. And when we capture the borderlands, when we seize the castles, the regular Polish Army will invade as planned to take Zator, Oświęcim and Siewierz. Upper Silesia will be ours. Why aren't you saying anything?"

"I have nothing to say."

"But I do," said Bedřich, turning to face him and looking him in the eyes again. "As has been agreed, I will assume the function of director of the Silesian Tábor outposts. For we mean to establish ourselves here, settle here permanently and solidly. I'd like to have you beside me, Reynevan. I'm offering it to you now, before Wołoszek or Korybut do. You don't have to respond at once."

"Very well. Where is Scharley?"

"Over yonder," said Bedřich, pointing at the far-off glow. "He is busy reducing the economic health of the Duchy of Racibórz. He's been promoted. He is commanding a special unit. They call them the Fire Starters."

Two days later, on Laetare Sunday, in the early morning, preceded by a ten-horse foray, Bolko V Wołoszek, Duke of Głogówek, heir to Opole, recently become a follower of Hussitism, joined the plundering raid. Riding under a gonfalon with a train with the golden Opole eagle on the silk sheet and under the multicoloured pennants of the Opole nobility, the young duke led fifty lances of knighthood with mounted archers and five hundred foot soldiers, mainly spearmen. While a powerful and stout fifty-pound bombard rode proudly at the end of the Opole procession. Jakub Kroměšín smiled at the sight: it was a precious acquisition for his siege artillery, which chiefly consisted of foglers and twelve-pounders.

Wołoszek looked proud and grave in his Milanese armour. He was not manifesting his neophytism in any way, wasn't sporting any emblems of his new religion. Among the Opole knighthood, numerous men were, however. Whether it was sincere or ingratiating, some of the knights had decorated their shields, tunics and horses' caparisons with crimson Chalices, and there were also crowns of thorns and Hosts. Typical Hussite symbols could also be seen on the Opole infantry's pavises.

Bedřich of Strážnice, a born propagandist, had noticed it and immediately used it to his advantage. Less than an hour went by before he was celebrating a Hussite Mass on the camp common under the open sky. After which the preachers gave communion *sub utraque specie* almost until the evening to anyone willing.

The changeable wind bore the smell of burning from all sides.

Reynevan didn't participate in the evening's council of leaders. Firstly, because he hadn't been invited, and secondly, because he was still trying to find a way to go and meet Scharley. Dobko Puchała talked him out of it. When, with the aim of pissing, he had left the barn where the council was taking place.

"Drop it," he said over his shoulder, pissing in the corner. "Only God knows where Scharley is now, you won't find him. The smoke from fires won't help you, because they're moving quickly to avoid being followed. And to create the illusion that there are more of them than there are."

It was noisy in the barn, the commanders were arguing and yelling at each other. It was probably about zones of influence, because the names of towns kept being shouted out: Gliwice, Bytom, Niemcza, Kluczbork, Namysłów, Rybnik.

"I've heard that three days ago Scharley was torching villages near Rybnik," said Puchała, hopping and shaking his member, "but I don't advise searching for him there, physician, you're more likely to encounter Racibórz forces and you'll get short shrift from them. Wait for Scharley here, he should be with us any day. For we march tomorrow or the day after. We're heading for Koźle. And Konrad."

Scharley didn't come and the invasion of the Koźle lands took place two days later. The allied army was raring to go, ready to invade the lands of the hated Konrad the White; Bedřich and his preachers took efforts to carry out an effective propaganda campaign, presenting the Koźle duke as a bloodthirsty monster, guilty of numerous crimes committed during the crusades and invasions of Bohemia. In actual fact, it was the Bishop of Wrocław, Konrad the Elder and the Duke of Oleśnica, Konrad Kantner, who had taken part. Konrad the White's guilt was established simply by the fact that he was their brother. In any case, mistakes were inevitable with such a gaggle of Konrads.

On the morning of the twenty-eighth of March, the Hussite Army stood arrayed. The Tábor's white, triangular standard with *Veritas vincit* and the Chalice was fluttering in the breeze, with Bolko Wołoszek's Opole eagle on a tailed gonfalon alongside. Korybut also ordered his *banerium* unfurled, at which point it turned out he was riding into battle under the sign of the Pogoń. As was customary, Czech, Silesian and Polish field preachers rode out before the array. The soldiers bared their heads and began to loudly pray. The field resounded with the rumbling of many languages.

Bedřich of Strážnice rode out in front of the men. Now, not only by his posture and voice did he imitate Prokop, but he was even dressed like Prokop, in a typical calpac, brigantine and cloak with a wolf-fur collar. He brought his horse to a sliding stop just like Prokop and raised his hand just like Prokop.

"Warriors of God!" he called thunderously, just like Prokop. "Faithful Slavs! Here before you is the domain of the enemy of God and the one true faith! Here before you are the lands of your enemy, a cruel and fierce enemy, on whose hands the blood of the faithful and pious is not yet dry! An enemy who led crusading hordes against us in order to kill God's truth! Now the time for vengeance is come!

"Vengeance, vengeance on the enemy! The Lord is the God of retribution when He says: And I will punish Bel in Babylon, and I will bring forth out of his mouth that which he hath swallowed up! And Babylon shall become heaps, a dwelling place for jackals, an astonishment. I will drive out its people and I will dry up her sea and make her springs dry! The Lord sayeth: I will bring them down like lambs to the slaughter, like rams with he-goats! To the slaughter! To slaughter and destruction! Thus go onward! Do the will of God and make His Word deed! Onward! Onward into battle!"

Clanking with iron, blades bristling, over a mile long, numbering one thousand three hundred horse, eleven thousand foot and four hundred wagons, the punitive expedition entered the Koźle lands in a column.

*

For all its high-flown declarations and fiery ardour, the army did not do much. The Tábor field army, capable of marching eight miles a day, crawled like a tortoise through the Koźle lands, only covering the four miles to Koźle by the thirtieth of March. The forays sent ahead burned and plundered villages and small towns.

To begin with, Koźle was treated to a fifty-pound stone from the Opole bombard, unerringly hitting the roof over the nave of the parish church. That was enough for the town to surrender and it was immediately seized by Bolko Wołoszek. This led to quarrels among the commanders, for it turned out that Korybut also had his eye on Koźle. The conflict was resolved by dividing up the ransom paid by the citizens of the town. As part of the agreement, Wołoszek began a joint operation along with Kory-but: they went on a raid to Krapkowice, Otmęt and Obrowiec. The castles and lands there belonged to Duke Bernard, Woło-szek's uncle. The foray was intended—as the young Hussite duke put it—to frighten the old goose and show him who was actually in charge in the Opole region.

Meanwhile, Pardus and Puchała continued plundering Duke Konrad's lands, destroying them by fire and sword. But not all of them. Kroměšín's headquarters outside Koźle had become some-thing like an office before which a queue of petitioners formed every day. Knights, burghers, priests, monks, millers and the wealthier local peasants came to make their payments. Whoever paid saved his property and belongings from fire. Kroměšín hag-gled like an old money-lender and his coffers overflowed with cash.

Reynevan wasn't the only one to look on in disgust.

On the Tuesday after Passion Sunday, Poles, consisting of a troop of two hundred volunteer horse from Lesser Poland, joined the plundering raid. They passed through the Cieszyn region on the way, burning, pillaging and plundering. Bolko, the Duke of Cieszyn, until recently having maintained judicious neutrality, had gone senile in his old age and let himself be duped by Sigismund's favours and declared war on the Hussites. So war was what he and his land got.

The Lesser Poland Poles, mainly poor noblemen who didn't flaunt coats of arms, were led by a knight dressed in full plate armour with a gaunt face and the unmoving eyes of a killer. After introducing himself to Kroměšín as Rynard Jursza, he handed him a letter. Kroměšín read it and his face brightened up.

"It's from Sir Piotr Szafraniec," Puchała told Korybut. "He writes that Lord Siestrzeniec has assembled a regiment of soldiers in Będzin, and that regular Polish units are at the ready. But he doesn't say when they will be arriving…M'Lord Jursza! Didn't the Lord Chamberlain of Krakow order you to give a spoken message?"

"No. Nobbut gave the letter."

The Lesser Poland Poles marched alongside in array. And singing.

If I had wings like
a gosling
I'd fly to Silesia to see my Jasiek…

"What is that idiotic song?" asked Puchała, annoyed. "It's fucking wistful, like a bride's unbraiding ceremony. What is it?"

"M'Lord Chamberlain of Krakow ordered us to sing," said Rynard Jursza, squinting his eyes. "For reasons of propaganda, he said. Reminding us that this is Upper Silesia. And that we are returning to our ancient lands and to the motherland."

"To the motherland, the motherland," Dobko growled with hostility. "Let it be. But if you really must, sing the *Bogurodzica*."

*

Two wagons trundled along with the Poles from Lesser Poland. One was weighed down with loot, the other was carrying wounded men. Dreadfully mutilated. Two died just after arriving, two others were fighting for their lives and the condition of the other four was grave. Reynevan and the field surgeons had their hands full.

The wounded were from Scharley's unit.

"Oh well," said Bedřich of Strážnice, spreading his arms, "if you insist, I won't keep you here. I'm reluctant to let you risk your life far away on raids, but I understand you want to meet your friend. This is even a fitting occasion, for I am sending Scharley replacements after the Pszczyna men gave them such a hiding that only he and five others escaped with their lives. Riding in company you won't lose your way and will be safer. It's even fortunate, because—"

"Because?"

"Another man will go with you," said Bedřich, lowering his voice. "A certain individual. It is a secret; I forbid you from talking to anyone about him. But it is fortunate that you know him."

"I do?"

"Indeed. I'm just waiting…Ah, and here he is."

Reynevan was struck dumb to see who was entering the headquarters.

The clerk from Fuggers and Company took off his ornately embroidered cloak and handed it to a servant. Underneath, it turned out, was a quite unwarlike costume, although an ordinary one for a clerk. The narrow black velvet doublet reached hips clothed in close-fitting blue and red *mi-parti*, with the loins covered by a padded codpiece which dramatically emphasised his

546

manhood. The codpiece was called a *braguette* in French. Scoffed at by level-headed men, it was the height of fashion among dandies and fops.

"Good day," said the clerk and greeted Reynevan with a bow. "Canon Otto Beess was asking after you. I'm glad to be able to reassure him and inform him about your good health."

"I would be grateful."

"And tell him that misfortune hasn't broken you. For it has not, I trust?"

"I'm bearing up."

"I am glad to hear it," said the official, adjusting his cuffs. "Oh well, there's a long road ahead of us—we must, I hear, ride to somewhere near Ujazd, and it would be good to arrive there before sunset. I suggest we set off, Reinmar. If you are ready."

"I am," said Reynevan, standing up. "Farewell, Bedřich."

"What do you mean by 'farewell'?" asked the preacher, frowning.

"I meant to say: till the next time."

"Reynevan?"

"Aye."

"Ah. What a stroke of luck. I was just thinking about you."

Scharley looked warlike and dashing. He was wearing a mail shirt over a leather jerkin, an iron bevor around his neck, and his forearms were protected by vambraces. At his left hip he had a falchion, at his right a dagger, and a six-sided mace shoved into a wide belt. He hadn't shaved for several days and when he embraced Reynevan his cheek was as prickly as a hedgehog.

"I've been thinking about you," he said, moving Reynevan away to arm's length. "And do you know what I've been thinking? That beyond reasonable doubt you'll turn out to be a thorough pillock. That having only just recovered from your illness, you will abandon the peaceful and snug apothecary's shop at the House at the Archangel, where I left you. That like an utter fool you'll mount a horse and come here. When did you actually rise from your bed?"

"A week after Shrovetide."

"Then you're still convalescing. You ought to rest, slowly regain full strength and not join a war. A war where in your state you're as lost as a fart in a hurricane. You still haven't recovered, laddie. Jutta's death almost killed you and Samson's death almost finished you off. It was hard for me, too, though my hide's much tougher. But you…Why did you come here? To recruit me to exact revenge on Grellenort?"

"Revenge won't bring back Jutta. I leave her to God."

"So why are you here? To fight for the cause? For a new, better world? To die for it? Or for the cause to finish up with dysentery in a field hospital? Is that what you want?"

"Not any longer," said Reynevan, lowering his head. "At first I did. But then I cooled down. I pondered a few things. I came here, joining the expedition, for one reason: to bid you farewell. To greet you, embrace you and thank you for everything. For the last time. Scharley, I'm leaving."

The penitent didn't answer. And didn't give the impression of being surprised. Rather he looked like he had been expecting a declaration of that kind.

"I've had enough," said Reynevan, breaking the silence. "Quite enough. Do you know what Samson said to me, back then, in February, outside the walls of Cheb? When he decided to leave us and return to Marketa? He used the words of the prophet Isaiah. We expected light, but behold the darkness; the rays shine, but yet we walk in the gloom.

"For the last two months I've been thinking about his words. Realising that they apply to me. That like a blind man I'm feeling for a wall and seemingly groping my way along. That I stumble at noon as though at night. That it's as though I were deceased.

"On my travels I met a priest who reminded me about yet more words from the Bible, from the Gospel of Saint John. *Ego sum lux mundi, qui sequitur me non ambulabit in tenebris sed habebit lucem vitae.* I've had enough of wandering in the shadows, I need the light of life. Briefly: I renounce the world, for without Jutta there's nothing for me in it. I'm going far away, as far from Bohemia, Lusatia and Silesia as possible, for everything here reminds me of her…"

He fell silently under the penitent's gaze. And it blew away the pathos like a gust of wind.

"Vodka didn't help me," he uttered. "Brothels didn't help me. I can't fall asleep. And if I do, I awake soon after with the pillow wet, my face covered in tears like a child. When I shave, the soap dries on my face and I stare at the veins on my wrist with a razor in my hand. Can I live like this?

"I shall enter a monastery, Scharley. To make peace with the Creator. Say something."

"What is there to say?" asked Scharley, looking at him keenly. "I'm able to recognise a severe personality crisis, even if you're concealing it deeply. I don't mean to dissuade you from your idea—why, from a purely pragmatic point of view I'll tell you you're acting sensibly. In your spiritual and mental state, it's dangerous to fight in a war, because that demands concentration, a cool head and complete conviction regarding the rightness of the deeds and acts being carried out. Dammit, I'm your friend, and the lesser of the two evils would be to see you in a monk's habit rather than in a common grave."

"So you support me, then?"

"No. I said: the lesser of two evils. But before you go and take your monastic vows, I have a request for you. It's the last thing we'll do together. Help me in the matter of that dandy from the Fuggers. Agreed?"

"Very well, Scharley."

"We'll pass over needless preliminaries," said Scharley, passing over needless preliminaries. "Let's get to business at once. I know who you are, m'lord. For last year I destroyed with fire some mines and foundries in Saxony. As you instructed."

"That will make communication easier," said the clerk from the Fuggers, holding Scharley's gaze. "Since the business I bring today is the same as that in Saxony. And similarly lucrative. You'll destroy the building I designate and there will be *lucrum* in it for you."

"Is that all?" asked the penitent, curling his lip. "Such a trifle? And why do you approach me with it and not Kroměšín? Not Puchała, Korybut or Wołoszek?"

"Because," said Reynevan, carelessly interrupting in mid-sentence, "Sigismund Korybut or Wołoszek might assert their rights to that building. The Poles who are about to enter Silesia might stake a claim. For, I believe, the building is on lands that have been divided up in advance and already allotted to somebody."

The clerk's gaze was steady this time, too. He didn't respond, but merely smiled.

"It's clear as the day to me," said Scharley. "One fire more, one less. What is this about?"

"About a lead glance mine. Also known as galena, it's an ore used for smelting lead. The mine is called Bleiberg and is in the southern suburb of Bytom."

"You suspected correctly," said the penitent, glancing at Reynevan. "Konrad the White's property. Which Wołoszek is making a claim for. And which he would no doubt prefer to seize with other working mines."

"The mine in Bleiberg is not being worked," said the Fuggers official, adjusting the cuffs of his doublet. "Galena is not being extracted from it at present, owing to groundwater having flooded the galleries. At this moment, expert miners specially brought over from Flanders are working on removing the water from the shafts. You will drive them out, burn the winding gear and destroy the pumping equipment—"

"And the water will then flood the mine irreversibly. And it will be permanently unworkable. Is that everything?"

"No," said the clerk. "There is another target. The village of Rudki on the Kłodnica. There is an *officina ferraria* on its western border. An iron furnace, smithy and lime kiln. You are to burn it all down. To the ground."

"To get to the places you mention," Scharley observed, "we would have to stage a raid deep into enemy territory, passing through their positions and patrols. That's risky. Extremely risky."

"That has been calculated into the *lucrum* on offer. And proportionally, I believe."

"We'll be the judge of that. When you state the sum."

"The sum is not the thing."

"Ah. What is, then?"

"The *lucrum* I refer to is being transported in a black wagon. Which may even be the same one as previously."

"Once again, please."

"The money," said the Fuggers official, folding his arms, "belongs to the person who, in September 1425, ordered the robbery on the tax collector and the theft of the money he had collected. That same black wagon, which was snatched from under your nose then, is now carrying treasure to Otmuchów, a stronghold whose walls are meant to guarantee safety and be protection from robbery. I know the wagon's route and I know it has a small escort so as not to attract attention. What do you think, m'Lord Scharley? Wouldn't it be a perfect chance for revenge? Wouldn't it be a piece of historic justice and moral recuperation to rob the robber of what he robbed? If you undertake the task I am commissioning, the wagon will be yours, I'll place it in your hands, you will intercept it before it reaches its destination. You must make a swift decision. And something tells me I know what it will be."

The bells of Bytom were sounding the alarm. The buildings of Bleiberg mine were burning, smoke completely blotting out the sky. As the fire devoured the sheds, the blazing tower with the winding gear collapsed in an explosion of sparks. Shapes of riders flashed among the flames, destroying and setting light to whatever they could. They were the Fire Starters, Scharley's sabotage-storm unit, crack Polish and Moravian horsemen.

What am I doing here? wondered Reynevan. *What am I doing here?*

The bells tolled, the fire raged, the mine disappeared in the fire. Reynevan and the Fuggers clerk watched from the edge of a forest on a hillside.

"Bytom," said Reynevan, nodding, "will utterly collapse because of this loss."

"That's the whole point," said the clerk, looking at him as though in surprise. "For it to collapse."

"Who did the shaft belong to?"

"Of what interest is it to you? Let's go. There's no need to stay."

"Let's go," said Reynevan, turning around in the saddle. "Let's go, Samso—"

He froze, his words stuck in his throat. There was no giant rider on a huge horse beside him, though he could have sworn that there *had* been, that a moment before Samson had been on his right-hand side. But no one was there.

"Did you say something?" asked the official. "Reinmar?"

"Let's go."

They rode through trees, down the left bank of the small river called the Kłodnica. Ten of them: Reynevan, the clerk and four of his servants, and an escort of four Fire Starter soldiers. Around noon, they noticed a large cloud of smoke rising above the wall of forest to the north, around half a mile away.

"It's Scharley," Reynevan guessed without difficulty. "The next building. The *officina ferraria*. In the village of Rudki, if I remember rightly. A great deal of smoke, so the foundry is also large. Who did it belong to? Oh, yes, I forgot. It's of no interest to me."

"It belonged to us. To the Fuggers."

"What?"

"It's a Fuggers foundry," said the clerk, shrugging. "Scharley has just set fire to the company's property. War damage, Reinmar, affects everybody, everybody incurs losses. It would be suspicious if the Fuggers were an exception. We were going to close the foundry in any case, it was failing. You look peculiar, Reinmar. As though struck dumb. Curious. I hear you've been warring these last five years, and yet there are still things that astonish you?"

"There still are. But fewer and fewer."

"What explains your presence here?" Reynevan decided to risk asking. "In forests full of wolves and bandits, during a war and in the smoke of fires? Exposed to risk, to discomfort and hardships? You got up from the desk behind which you usually direct the world and left your luxurious office. Why?"

"One loses touch with real life behind a desk," replied the official a moment later. "Hiding behind documents, one stops seeing the real world; behind invoices, bills of exchange and letters of credit, one stops seeing the living person. Routine sets in—and routine is a fatal thing. Furthermore, it's good to have some excitement from time to time. Experience adventure and the taste of risk. Feel the blood flowing more swiftly in the veins. Feel—"

He didn't finish. A group of horsemen hurtled out at them from the undergrowth. Some of them were wearing white cloaks. With black crosses.

Reynevan just managed to wind up the lever of his crossbow and fire from the hip. The bolt passed through the neck of the horse charging at him; it reared and tumbled down with its rider. Others attacked them, brandishing weapons. Beside him, a Fire Starter swayed in the saddle on being slashed with a sword. Reynevan managed to seize his battleaxe, brought it down hard on the helmet of one of the attackers, hit him again before their horses parted and saw blood spurting from the dented hounskull. At that moment, blood splashed his face as the riders in white cloaks and crosses mercilessly carved up the Fuggers servants who were putting up meagre resistance. Wounded Fire Starters tumbled to the ground one after the other.

"Alive!" yelled a knight in enamelled armour, clearly the commander. "Take them alive!"

The Fuggers clerk was dragged from his horse. Two men attacked Reynevan, one snatching the battleaxe from him. The other, a youngster with wide-open eyes, tried to dislodge him from the saddle with the pommel of his sword. Reynevan wrested the weapon from him, seized it with both hands, by the blade and the cross guard, and struck him under the spaulder, feeling the blade penetrating the rings of the mail shirt. The youngster screamed and hunched up. Reynevan spurred his horse, but it was too late. He was surrounded on all sides. They caught him. One of the Teutonic Knights, ignoring the order to take the prisoners alive, aimed a stab at his throat. But he didn't complete the blow. He was too slow.

Yelling resounded and the ground trembled under hooves as riders galloped at speed into the clearing. It was the Fire Starters, black with soot, led by Scharley with falchion raised.

The battle was over in no time. Before you could say *Christe redemptor omnium*, the last of the Teutonic Knights was churning up the sand with his spurs in his death throes. The others, wounded, begged not to be killed.

"I throw myself on your mercy," said the knight in the enamelled armour, arrogantly, when he was brought before Scharley. "I am Magnus of Meurs, a guest of the Order of the Virgin Mary. I'll pay a ransom—"

Scharley made a short gesture. One of the Fire Starters took a swing and whacked the knight with the butt of his battleaxe. His head split like a pumpkin into three pieces, each one flying in a different direction. Correctly treating that as encouragement, the Fire Starters began to slaughter the remaining captives.

Reynevan knelt beside the youngster, the one he had stabbed. He stemmed the bleeding using Alkmena's spell, which was immediately effective. The blade had miraculously missed the vital elements of the circulatory system and both the *arteria axillaris* and the *arteria brachialis* were intact. Reynevan concentrated and sealed up the axillary vein. The youngster groaned, pale as a sheet.

"Move aside, m'lord," said one of the Fire Starters, standing over them. "I don't want to cut you by mistake when I finish him off."

"Begone."

"Not a single witness should remain," said the Fuggers clerk. "Not one. Don't be foolish, Reinmar. Rein in your charitable inclinations, this isn't the time or the place for them."

Reynevan sprang up and punched him in the face. The clerk fell over on his back like a log, groping around with his arms and staring vacantly.

"May that improve your taste of adventure," said Reynevan, trembling with fury. "And may your blood flow more swiftly. Now begone. I'm treating him and you're in my light."

"You heard what he said," Scharley instructed the Fire Starter, in an extremely forceful and grim voice. "Get away from him. And you, m'lord clerk, stand up and come with me. We have some talking to do. The job's finished, it's time I was paid back. You owe me some information."

Reynevan turned away and began suturing and applying a dressing. The wounded youngster was trembling, moaning and clenching his eyelids tightly.

He was moaning so pitifully that Reynevan decided to anaesthetise him with another spell. So strong that the boy's eyes rolled up and he went limp.

The clearing emptied and the Fire Starters rode off into the forest. Then Scharley returned. Alone.

"Your quick temper might have cost me dearly," he said coldly. "I didn't expect you to punch him in the face right away. Fortunately, our Fugger is a man of affairs, a true professional. On top of that, I think he has taken a fancy to you."

"In short," said Reynevan, standing up, wiping his hands on some linen, "a man of affairs turned the convoy with the black wagon over to you. But even if he hadn't, you wouldn't have lost out. You wouldn't have made any money, but you wouldn't have lost anything, either. So don't talk to me about costs."

"You don't understand, my friend," said Scharley, linking his hands on his chest. "You don't know everything. And perhaps that's for the best, considering you intend to don a monk's habit.

What about the boy? Will he live? Has he given up the ghost? Is he dying?"

"He'll die if we leave him here."

"And you, a step away from your vows, won't burden yourself with such a sin," guessed Scharley. "So you'll take him back to his own. And they'll string you up, since they have in their ranks some outstanding specialists straight from Malbork who are expert at hanging captives."

Scharley approached the wounded youngster and stood over him. He cowered in fear.

"Who are you? What's your name?"

"Parsifal…" groaned the youngster. "Parsifal of Rachenau…"

"How did you get here? Where are the Oleśnica forces? How large are they? How many soldiers did the Order of Saint Mary send to help you?"

"Leave him in peace, Scharley."

"Listen, *nomen omen* Parsifal," said Scharley, leaning over the wounded boy. "Your patron saint, Saint Parsifal, was watching over you today. The entire sacred Round Table and Saints George and Maurice were watching over you. If you get out of this alive, light a few candles in church and ask your father to pay for a few Masses. You met with great fortune today, great luck, greater than if you had found the Holy Grail. You happened upon a physician. Were it not for him, your mouth and eyes would be full of fragrant spring earth. Remember the physician, Parsifal. And say a few prayers for him. Will you?"

"I will, m'lord."

Joining forces, pushing and pulling, they got the wounded Parsifal of Rachenau into the saddle, while he groaned and moaned like the damned.

Then Scharley took Reynevan aside.

"I won't dissuade you from your idea," began Scharley. "But I shall ask you for form's sake: will you postpone your plans until a later date? In order to rob the black wagon with me?"

"No."

"Consider it thoroughly. The character from the Fuggers told me what we are likely to find on the wagon. You wouldn't have to look for other people's monasteries. You could found your own and be its prior. Doesn't that tempt you?"

"No."

"Too bad. Then off you go. Hint number one: the Duke of Oleśnica's army is most probably on the Pyskowice-Toszek border, but its patrols will already be in the region of Rudki. The smoke will guide them. Take Parsifal there and try not to get caught."

"I shall."

"Hint number two: head eastwards, towards the Polish border, and cross the Przemsza as quickly as you can. You'll be safer in Poland than in Silesia."

"I know."

"Hint number three: regarding your future as a monk. If you really decide to undertake such a radical act, be aware of its practical aspect. Monasteries, convents and religious orders are by no means institutions with their doors open to tramps and strangers; even less so are they asylums for criminals and outlaws on the run. Otherwise, every brigand by the name of Madej would escape punishment by becoming Brother Madius and taunt justice from behind the monastery gates. From my own experience I'll tell you, friend, that entering the gates is much more difficult than leaving them. In short, you don't have a chance without connexions."

"What are you driving at?"

"Well, I do have some, if that interests you," announced Scharley calmly. "In Poland. Ten miles beyond Wieluń—"

"Wieluń," said Reynevan, shaking his head, "is a little too close."

"Too close? What would suit you, then? Drohiczyn, perhaps? Or Vitebsk? For beyond them is only *Ultima Thule*. But I can't help you there. Don't make faces, Reynevan. Listen: ten miles beyond Wieluń, on the River Warta, lies Sieradz, the ancient settlement of the Lechitic tribe of the Sieradzanians, currently the capital of the voivodeship. There you will find a monastery of the Knights of the Holy Sepulchre, called the Miechowians in Poland. It so happens that since 1418 I have been on splendid terms with the parish priest there. The superiors of the branch monasteries are called among the Miechowians 'provosts' and the monasteries 'parishes.' The provost in Sieradz is called Wojciech Dunin. In 1418, his name was Adalbert Dohn and he wasn't yet a provost. And in short, thanks to me he can still enjoy life. He is thus indebted to me—"

"Tell me straight. It's about the revolt in Wrocław on the eighteenth of July 1418."

"I shall tell you straight," said Scharley, squinting. "Yes. It is. Years have passed but that matter still hangs over me. And will continue to do so, considering that Fuggers and Company know about it."

"Damn. Was that why you spoke of costs?"

"It was. They have me by the balls and may thus count on my discretion. So be discreet, too, Reinmar."

"Naturally. Count on me."

"In a few days," said Scharley, smiling, "I shall have the black wagon. And the money being carried in it, which I shall divide up judiciously. I shall buy myself peace and the complete absolution of my sins. I shall buy some officials and numerous influential friends. But don't tell anybody anything, not even Provost Dunin in Wieluń, when you mention me. And when you do mention me, they'll receive you there and let you take your vows. It's quiet and peaceful in Sieradz; they have a spital so it's just perfect for you. My heart will also be lighter, to tell you the truth, calm in the knowledge that you are there. That you are safe and not roaming through the world. Do it for me, friend. Head northwards after you cross the Przemsza. Go to Sieradz."

"I'll give it some thought," said Reynevan. Having already thought it through, having decided and being completely convinced of the correctness of the decision he had taken.

"Thus…And so…" said the penitent, shrugging and clearing his throat. "Dammit, I can't stand and watch you…So I shall bid you farewell, rein my horse around, jab him with my spur and ride away. Without looking back. And you will do as you wish. When you wish. Farewell. *Vale et da pacem, Domine.*"

"Farewell," Reynevan replied a moment later.

Scharley didn't look back.

Chapter Twenty-One

In which there is a discussion about a symbol and its extraordinary import. In which Reynevan, having committed evil, tries to correct his error and wash away his guilt with blood. And Zbigniew Oleśnicki, the Bishop of Krakow, changes the course of history, doing so *ad maiorem Dei gloriam*.

Thus comes death, thought Parsifal Rachenau, vainly trying to prevail against the overwhelming cold, lethargy and sleepiness. *I'm going to die. I'll part company with life here, in these wild forests, without a priest, without the sacraments and without even a funeral, and neither my father nor my mother will know where my bleached bones are lying. Will the beautiful Ofka of Baruth shed even a single tear for me? Will she think of me longingly? Oh, what an ass I was not to declare my love to her! Why didn't I fall at her feet...?*

And now it is too late. Death approaches. I shan't ever see Ofka again.

His horse tossed its head and as Parsifal swayed in the saddle, he felt a twinge of pain and became fully awake. *It stinks of smoke*, he thought. *And fire.*

Something was burning here...

"Rudki's just beyond the trees," said a voice beside him. The rider to whom the voice belonged melted in Parsifal's feverish eyes into a dark shape, vague and demonic.

"You should find your comrades over there. Keep to the track and don't fall from the saddle. Farewell, laddie."

It's that barber-surgeon, thought Parsifal, making every effort to keep his eyelids from drooping. *The physician with the strangely familiar features. He saved me and dressed my wounds…And people said that Huss's followers are worse than the Saracens, that they show no quarter and kill mercilessly…*

"M'Lord…I am grateful…Thank you…"

"Thank the Lord. And say a prayer from time to time. For the lost soul of a sinner."

Birds sang, frogs croaked, clouds floated across the sky and the Przemsza wound among the wetlands. Reynevan breathed a sigh of relief.

A little prematurely.

There were eight horses in front of the tar kiln, including one beautiful black and one extremely beautiful grey. A thin trickle of smoke curled up from the thatched roof. Reynevan immediately reined around his steed. The eight horses didn't belong either to the tar maker or to peasants; battleaxes, hatchets and clubs were hanging from the saddles, so their owners were military men. He meant to steal away quietly before they noticed him. But it was too late.

A character wearing a brigantine and carrying an armful of hay emerged from a small barn. On seeing Reynevan he dropped the hay and yelled. Another man—as similar as his twin—ran out of the barn and they both went for him, yelling. Reynevan seized the crossbow hanging from his saddle, grabbed the windlass by the crank and wound. The toothed wheel grated awfully, something crunched, the crank broke off and the lever snapped. His faithful crossbow, made in Nuremberg, smuggled from Poland to Bohemia and purchased by Scharley for four Hungarian ducats, had broken.

This is the end. The thought flashed through his mind as he spurred his horse. *The end*, he thought as they pulled him from the saddle. *The end*, he was certain, as they pressed him to the ground, seeing the flash of a curved shoemaker's knife.

"I say! I say! Let go of him! Drop him! He's one of us! A comrade."

It can't be, thought Reynevan, lying motionless and staring up at the sky. *This doesn't happen in real life. Such things only occur in knightly romances. And not all of them.*

"Reynevan? Are you hale?"

"Jan Kuropatwa? Of Łańcuchów? Of the Szreniawa coat of arms?"

"It is I. Ooh, Reynevan, you look rotten. I barely recognised you."

There were other familiar faces in the company. Jakub Na-dobny, Jan Tłuczymost and the Lithuanian Skirmunt. And the ringleader of the entire band, the Ruthenian warlord Fedor of Ostrog himself. Whose small black eyes were fixed on Reynevan in a malevolent stare.

"Why are your eyes jumping so from face to face?" said the prince finally. "Are you looking for the boyar, Daniło, whom you slashed with a knife in Odry? You look in vain. The Slo-vaks killed him by the River Váh. *Herrgott*, you're in luck, for he harboured grudges. But I don't. Even though you fucked up in Odry, I forgive you like a Christian. I'll release you; I won't hold you. But first of all, let's drink to reconciliation. Pour the mead, Kondzioł. Mikoszka, I'm talking to you. Nu, your good health!"

"Good health!"

"And where exactly are you headed, Reynevan?" asked

Kuropatwa, wiping his moustache. "I ask, for perhaps you'll ride with us?"

"I'm heading north," said Reynevan, preferring not to be too frank.

The Pole wasn't to be brushed off.

"Where, precisely?"

"Wieluń."

"Oh! Why, we're also heading that way. Ride with us, it's more pleasant in a *comitiva*. And safer. Well, Fedor? Shall we take him?"

"It's all one to me. If he wants, let him. Good health!"

"Good health!"

They rode northwards, along the green Przemsza valley.

Prince Fedor Fedorovich Ostrogski from Ostrog, the Starosta of Lutsk, was leading. Behind him, on a beautiful grey, rode Jan Kuropatwa of Łańcuchów of the Szreniawa coat of arms. Behind him was Jakub Nadobny of Rogów of the Działosza coat of arms. Jan Tłuczymost of the Bończa coat of arms from somewhere in Greater Poland. Jerzy Skirmunt, a Lithuanian from a family recently honoured by being granted the Polish Odrowąż coat of arms. Achacy Pełka, whose Janina coat of arms was doubtful enough to invite derision. The brothers Melchior and Mikoszka Kondzioł of a dubious coat of arms, dubious family and clearly dubious reputation.

Reynevan's mental state meant that it didn't matter at all to him; little mattered. He did experience some surprise to see Ostrog. He had heard rumours and gossip, according to which the prince had once again betrayed the Hussites and offered his services to Sigismund of Luxembourg. It was meant to have happened the previous year, shortly after that stormy meeting in Odry when knives were drawn. Rumour had it that Sigismund had taken Fedor as an agent provocateur and ordered him imprisoned along with his entire company. Why, some even said he had been executed in the town square in Pressburg, and one could even find eyewitnesses able to describe the beheading in picturesque detail. And now—to Reynevan's astonishment—here were the executed men riding blithely along the Przemsza's green valley. In other circumstances, Reynevan might have been suspicious, might have thought twice about joining this questionable group. But those were the circumstances. Things were the way they were.

To the west, in the region of Gliwice and Bytom, black columns of smoke were rising into the sky. There was no sense of panic in the villages they passed and nor were there any refugees on the tracks. The local people clearly had faith in their dukes, Konrad the White and Kazimierz of Oświęcim, trusting that they would defend their lives and property, for after all it was for that eventuality that they extorted duties from them. Irrespective of their actual plans in this regard, the dukes made a good impression. The further north they went, the more striking was the presence of soldiers. Every now and then a proud trumpeting of horns was heard, and several times they saw armed detachments on the horizon, galloping with unfurled pennants. Fedor's cavalcade kept to unused roads and tracks, owing to which during the two-day ride they didn't chance upon any army detachments or patrols. Danger was ever-present, however. Reynevan, despite his resignation, felt anxiety. If caught by mercenaries they could be strung up on the first branch, and he wasn't exactly thrilled at the thought of bidding farewell to the world quite like that.

The prince's company appeared to scorn danger. Ostrog and his comrades rode their horses at a lazy walk, yawning or killing boredom with foolish chat.

"Heed, company," said Jakub Nadobny, turning around in the

saddle. "Why, we're like something out of legend. Slav brothers! A Pole, a Ruthenian and a Czech!"

"A Pole, a Ruthenian and a Teuton," said Fedor Ostrog, grimacing. "Where do you see a Czech here?"

"Reynevan sides with the Czechs," said Tłuczymost. "And speaks Czech."

"Fedor curses in Hungarian, but he's not Hungarian," said Skirmunt from the back. "And Reynevan isn't a German, he's a Silesian."

"A Silesian," spat Fedor. "Neither one thing or the other. But the greater part German."

"And you," Kuropatwa asked Reynevan, "what do you think of yourself as?"

"What difference does it make to you?" said Reynevan, shrugging.

"None," agreed Kuropatwa.

"Well," said Nadobny, happily, "didn't I say, straight out of legend? A Pole, a Ruthenian and makes no difference."

"Hi, Nadobny, what happened to your brother Hińcza? Did he really bed Queen Sophia?"

"Not a bit of it," Nadobny said, bridling. "A lie and a libel! He was innocent when Jagiełło ordered him imprisoned in Chęciny. That's why I followed Korybut to Bohemia, to spite the king for his unjust treatment of Hińcza, keeping him chained at the bottom of a dungeon like some cur."

"Are you jesting? For they say Hińcza was fucking somebody at the Wawel."

"He was," admitted Nadobny. "But it wasn't the queen, it was one of her ladies-in-waiting. Szczukowska."

"Which one?" asked Kuropatwa, who was clearly in the know, curiously. "Kasia or Eliszka?"

"Now that I think about it," said Nadobny, pondering on it, "probably both."

The following day they reached Lubliniec, a small town on the road from Siewierz to Olesno, a route vital for the trade between Silesia and Lesser Poland. The members of the company rubbed their hands and rejoiced noisily at the prospect of the Lubliniec taverns and the beer brewed there; however, to their disappointment, Fedor Ostrog ordered them to stop for the night far from buildings and strictly forbade them from showing themselves. He headed for the town, accompanied by Jan Kuropatwa. Towards the evening, as darkness was falling. Promising to return at dawn.

At first, the matter didn't especially shock Reynevan. Prince Ostrog was after all a warlord, troublemaker and mercenary in various people's pay, involved in the kind of affairs and misdemeanours that had to be sorted out secretly and after dark. Some time later, though, curiosity got the better of him, particularly when an opportunity arose. For the company disregarded the prince's instructions. Leaving Skirmunt and Reynevan to guard the camp, they set off towards the nearby villages in search of alcohol, vittles and possibly sex. After Skirmunt fell asleep, Reynevan mounted his horse and quietly headed for Lubliniec.

Smoke trailed over the darkened town, dogs barked and oxen bellowed. The only illuminated building was the thatched complex of the inn, where many lights burned in spite of the late hour, and numerous people were milling around noisily. Reynevan quite quickly spotted Kuropatwa's eye-catching grey and Ostrog's black next to it. Lurking in the darkness, he intended to move closer, when suddenly a rather large party escorting a wagon arrived at the tavern with a tramping of hooves and a clanking of iron. The household servants poured out into the

courtyard with torches, and after leaving the wagon, a sump-
tuously attired, well-built, ruddy and knightly-looking man
stepped into the circle of light cast by the brands. A man in
an overcoat trimmed with sable fur, slightly younger, of equally
knightly height and posture and slightly chubby-cheeked, came
out onto the tavern steps to greet him. Reynevan gasped. He
knew both of them.

The traveller was Konrad, Bishop of Wrocław. The man greeting him was Zbigniew Oleśnicki, Bishop of Krakow. The bishops
entered the building after exchanging greetings. Soldiers and
the servants with flaming brands surrounded the building in a
tight cordon, while mounted archers set off to patrol the vicinity.

Reynevan, stroking his horse's muzzle, stepped back into the
darkness. He had to return to camp. There wasn't the slightest
chance of stealing up and eavesdropping on the dignitaries.

"Polish fantasies," said the Bishop of Wrocław. "Polish fantasies
about Silesia. The cat is finally out of the bag. Heretics, apostates and Polish dissenters allied with them have plundered the
Duchy of Racibórz, laid waste the Koźle region, burned down
Krapkowice, Brzeg and Ujazd, robbed and destroyed the Cistercian monastery in Jemielnica, attacked Bytom, and are now
marching on Gliwice and Toszek. And now the Polish Army is
stationed on the border, in preparation for an armed intervention and the annexation of Upper Silesia. But you, O Bishop
of Krakow, rather than curse the pagan-king in Krakow, rather
than burn at the stake the Szafraniec, Zbąski and Melsztyński
families and other Polish henchmen of heresy, *you* arrange a
meeting with me, wanting to negotiate and conclude a contract.
Of what kind? Regarding what? A year ago, I told your envoy,
Bnin of the Łodzia coat of arms, that I would not ask for Polish
intervention. Never."

"The Polish Army will not march into Silesia until King Władysław issues the order."

"A laughable guarantee! Jagiełło is a senile old fart. He listens to what is whispered into his ears."

"Indeed," agreed Zbigniew Oleśnicki. "And various things are whispered by various individuals. Including supporters of heresy, Ruthenian schismatics and men who would gladly see Lithuania separate from Poland. And your king, Sigismund of Luxembourg, aids them, infuriating Jagiełło by promising the crown to Witold."

"King Sigismund may offer the crown to whomsoever he wishes," said Konrad, proudly raising his head.

"He will be able to when he becomes emperor, something that is by no means certain. For the time being, King Sigismund is putting the Catholic Church at risk owing to his particularistic and short-sighted interests. And owing to the mission the Church is planning to undertake in the East. A Christian, civilisational and evangelical mission."

"A mission to be dispatched by Poland? The Messiah and chosen nation, the bulwark of Christianity? Your sin is that of pride, Zbigniew, Polish pride. The mission of which you speak could just as easily be carried out by Witold—when he becomes king."

The Bishop of Krakow slipped his hands into the sleeves of his overcoat.

"If crowned, Witold won't do anything," he responded. "He cares not about the mission or Rome. He cares solely about power. The Holy See is aware of that, for which reason it will not sanction Witold's coronation. The Holy See knows that it can only rely on Poland in the East, both in the fight against the Schism and against heresy. Whoever weakens Poland by destroying its union with Lithuania is hostile not only to Poland, but also to the Church."

"Soothsayers give the present Pope no more than a year, and his successor may love the Poles less. Particularly when he finds out who is a true Christian and who is not. Who secretly supports and arms the heretics and who fights against them, destroys them with fire and iron, putting a categorical end to the heretical abomination."

"Aha!" Oleśnicki guessed immediately. "You are preparing another Crusade? Are you in such haste to receive a beating? For the Czechs will tan your hides once more. You'll have to flee from there in panic again, in shame and dishonour, disgraced before the entire Christian world like last time. It's time to start thinking. About how if you allow the heretics to vanquish you, you strengthen them."

"It's you who strengthens them. You Poles, by giving them your support. If you were to invade with us—"

"If it was up to me," the Bishop of Krakow interrupted, "the Polish Army would invade Bohemia tomorrow. I abhor heresy and would love to see it brought to heel. But one must take into account public opinion. According to public opinion, the Czechs are Slavs, our brethren, and one does not march into a fraternal country under arms. *Vox populi, vox Dei*—Polish intervention in Bohemia would be a political misstep with unpredictable consequences. Thus Polish intervention in Bohemia will not occur."

"But will in Silesia, eh?"

"Only should Jagiełło issue the order. I, the *episcopus cracoviensis*, am doing everything to make sure he doesn't. Doing everything to hold in check and tame the pro-Hussite faction. Help me with that, O Bishop of Wrocław. Influence Sigismund to stop incitement regarding Witold and giving him the crown."

"What do you need?" asked the Bishop of Wrocław, spreading his arms. "After all, you have already dealt with Witold. You deftly caught the envoys who were carrying the crown to him and you've led King Sigismund up the garden path. Witold has settled for the Order of the Dragon and resigned himself to the fact that *magnus dux* is the apex of his career."

"Witold has not and will not agree to that. Sigismund knew what he was doing by opening up that Pandora's Box of ambitions in Lutsk. Now Witold won't rest until he takes Lithuania out of the union. He is a threat to Poland."

"The greatest threat to Poland," said the Bishop of Wrocław, snorting, "are the Poles themselves. That has always been and will always be true. But I am prepared to negotiate. But negotiations must be *ut des*: I give, so that you may give. But you don't want to give anything, won't cede anything. What does that leave us with?"

"And what ought I to cede? And what would I receive in return?"

"You give something, I'll give something. *Clara pacta, boni amici.* Listen, O Bishop of Krakow—one day a cardinal, the chaplain of the chosen nation. If you leave Silesia in peace, I'll leave you the East, the evangelical mission and the conversion of the schismatics. I'll let you be the bulwark. Witold is indeed causing damage, unravelling what you have for so long and diligently woven. Which means he is indeed a threat. And will be for as long as he lives. And if he...stopped living? Suddenly and unexpectedly?"

Oleśnicki said nothing for some time.

"It doesn't befit me to listen to this," he finally responded. "It absolutely does not. Moreover, I believe purely theoretically that the trouble would be in vain. Witold is too well protected for an assassination attempt to succeed. Neither could he be poisoned. He has serving him numerous Lithuanian sorcerers, and only drinks water from mysterious Samogitian springs. He is immune to poison."

"To *known* poisons," Konrad corrected him. "Only to known ones. For unknown ones also exist, poisons about which no one has heard—even in Venice, never mind in some Hyperborean Samogitia. And as it is said: *Ignoti nulla curatio morbi*. In Duke Witold's shoes I'd beware, for he may not survive the year if we come to agreement."

"And is there a chance?"

"Will you hinder the Polish army invading Silesia? Will you stop supporting the Hussites, Wołoszek and Korybut?"

"Those matters are at the discretion of the King of Poland. I am not he."

"Indeed? I've heard other views. I've heard you don't hesitate to reprimand Jagiełło, you're even wont to dress him down. That's nothing new, the Polish Church was always the power behind the throne, don't try to persuade me otherwise. And Poland also has the nobility, lords, estates and the people, which the king has to take into account. Don't fib, Bishop Zbigniew. *Clara pacta, boni amici!* Will you, in exchange for the friendly favour I shall render unto you in the matter of Witold, make sure that the Czech Hussites will stop receiving support from Poland? Even more so: that they will become hated in Poland. Hated by everybody, from the king down to the meanest serf?"

"Will you advise me how? Since you're so wise."

"Now it is I who doesn't wish to listen," said Konrad, chuckling. "Conspiracies, provocation? It doesn't befit a clergyman, a simple toiler in the Lord's vineyard. News from France reaches Poland, I presume, Zbyszek? News about Jehanne d'Arc, called *La Pucelle*? About how she liberated Orléans from a siege? And defeated the English at the Battle of Patay? Brought about the coronation of Charles VII at Reims Cathedral? About her besieging Paris?"

"And what of it?"

"*La Pucelle* is a symbol. And symbols are key. You cannot

underestimate their significance. And now another parable: in 1426 and 1427, the Hussites carried out two other forays into Austria. The first time they attacked the Cistercian monastery in Zwettl, the second, the convent in Altenburg. As is their custom, they murdered the monks, sacked the monasteries and set them on fire. Nothing new, I hear you say. But you're in error. In both cases, the Czechs smashed the organ into matchwood, destroyed the bells, splintered the altars. They knocked the heads off statues or destroyed them. They desecrated holy paintings and cut them to ribbons. They committed similar iconoclasm in the Bavarian monasteries of Walderbach and Schonthal in 1428, and in Silesia the same year."

"And what of it?"

"It's a symbol. During wars everybody murders, burns and robs, it's normal and is the order of the day. But only emissaries of the Devil knock the head off a figure of Saint Florian, smear shit over a portrait of Saint Ursula and chop up a miraculous Pietà into splinters. Only the hordes of the Antichrist raise their iconoclastic hands against symbols. And emissaries of the Devil and hordes of the Antichrist are hideous and hated. By everybody. From the king down to the meanest serf."

"I understand," said Zbigniew Oleśnicki, nodding. "And I admit that you are right. Regarding symbols."

"I would even have the men to do it," said the Bishop of Wrocław, smiling. "A select band, rescued from the noose. Prepared to do anything. To any designated symbol. All that remains is for you to designate them, O Bishop of Krakow. Do we understand each other?"

"We do."

"What then? Are we agreed? *Clara pacta, boni amici?* Zbyszek? And your answer?"

"*Clara pacta.*"

*

Ostrog and Kuropatwa actually returned earlier than they had promised, before the fourth night hour, and in the morning gave the signal to march out. To Reynevan's slight amazement, Prince Fedor didn't lead them to the Siewierz road, but ordered them to head east, straight into the red rays of the rising sun. And after barely two miles of riding along the highway and then fording a stream, he ordered them to leave the road and ride cross country.

"That river was the Liswarta, if I'm not mistaken," said Reynevan, trotting over to the prince. "Where are we headed? If I may ask?"

"You'll see when we get there."

"Stay calm, physician," said Kuropatwa, electing for a slightly kinder tone. "You'll see. Everything will be as it should."

Reynevan shook his head but said nothing. He reined back his horse, to go to the rear of the party.

They rode on. The sun was high when the terrain became unpleasant, boggy and sticky. They left one swamp to immediately ride into another, crossing numerous marshy valleys and stream after stream overgrown with crooked willows. It was beside one of them that Reynevan saw the Washerwoman.

No one else saw her apart from him, from his position at the rear some way behind the others. At first, she wasn't there; there was a bright, sunlit patch on a dry willow trunk stripped of bark. And suddenly the Washerwoman appeared where the patch had been. She was kneeling by the willow, bent over the stream, with her arms up to her elbows in the water. Slender to the point of thinness under a clinging white dress. Her face completely veiled by a curtain of dark hair, which reached down to the water and swayed in the current. With rhythmic, ghoulishly slow movements she washed a blouse or shift, rubbing and squeezing it.

With each movement, clouds of dark red blood billowed from the shift. The entire stream was flowing with blood and bloody foam.

Reynevan jerked his head up and turned around. But Samson wasn't beside him. Although he felt his presence, although he would have sworn he had heard him whisper, Samson wasn't there. There was a wind, a sudden, fell wind, which rattled the greening branches of the willow and rippled the surface of the water, making it glisten. Reynevan narrowed his eyes. When he opened them, the Washerwoman was gone. There was a white patch of willow trunk stripped of bark.

But the river was still dark with blood.

In the afternoon they arrived at drier ground, between some flat-topped hills. And then they saw some isolated, higher hills, light in colour.

Almost white. In the sunshine, almost snow-white.

A church tower rose up into the sky from the hilltop.

"*Clarus Mons*," said Jakub Nadobny of Rogów shortly. "Jasna Góra. The Pauline monastery by Częstochowa."

The Pauline Order's *cenobium*, funded almost half a century earlier by Władysław of Opole, was getting closer and closer. They could see the two-winged *claustrum* and church with its buttresses. They could even hear the monks singing.

"Is this our destination?" asked Reynevan. "The monastery? We're going to the monastery?"

"Indeed," replied Fedor of Ostrog, with his hand on a war hammer stuck into his belt. "Why? Don't you approve?"

"It's Easter today," said Nadobny. "We're visiting a sacred edifice."

"For we are most godly," added Kuropatwa of Łańcuchów.

Although his voice sounded serious, Jan Tłuczymost snorted and the Kondzioł brothers chuckled.

"Ride on," Ostrog cut them off. "Don't talk."

They were getting nearer and nearer to the monastery.

Benedicta es, caelorum regina,
et mundi totius domina,
et aegris medicina.
Tu praeclara maris stella vocaris,
quae solem justitiae paris,
a quo illuminaris.

Reynevan reined back his horse to let Jerzy Skirmunt, who was bringing up the rear, draw level. The young Lithuanian gave him a brief, frightened glance.

"Things are beginning to look ill here, friend," he muttered. "There's a whiff of the noose. What to do, eh?"

"It's too late for anything," said Reynevan, angrily and bitterly.

"What will you do?"

"Stay out of the way. And not take part. If possible."

Te Deus Pater, ut Dei mater
fieres et ipse frater,
cuius eras filia,
sanctificavit, sanctam servavit,
et mittens sic salutavit,
Ave plena gratia!

At the gates, they dismounted, and a small group of pilgrims fled at the sight of them. If Reynevan had entertained any doubts before, the sight of weapons being drawn dispelled them. Melchior and Mikoszka Kondzioł threw off their sheepskins and rolled up their sleeves. Achacy Pełka spat into his hand and seized a large battleaxe. Kuropatwa of Łańcuchów walked up and banged his sword hilt against the gate, once and twice.

"Who's there?" The voice of the gatekeeper was old and trembling.

"Open up!"

"What do you mean: open up? To whom?"

"Open up! And look lively! We are here by order of the king!"

"What do you mean?"

"Open the gate, you whoreson!" roared Fedor of Ostrog. "And be quick! Or we shall break it down with our axes!"

"What is this?"

"Slide back the fucking bolt, now!" yelled Kuropatwa. "While we are still tranquil!"

"Have mercy! This is a sacred place!"

"Open up, dammit!"

The bolts made a grinding sound. The brothers Kondzioł immediately charged the gate, striking it with such force that both leaves flew wide open, knocking down the gatekeeper and his assistant, a young monk in a white Pauline habit. Tłuczymost, Pełka and Jakub Nadobny rushed after them into the courtyard. The gatekeeper, lying on the ground, caught Nadobny by the edge of his cloak. Fedor Ostrog smote him across the temple with a war hammer.

"An attaaaack!" bellowed the young monk. "It's an attaaack! Brigands! Broooothers!"

Kuropatwa pinned him to the ground with a stab of his sword. The door to the chapter house opened and then immediately shut, the lock clanging. Pełka leaped forward, destroyed the hinges with two blows of his battleaxe, rushed inside and a moment later thudding and screams could be heard. Ostrog and the others ran towards the church. In the portal and vestibule, several white-habited Pauline monks blocked their way. One held out a crucifix towards the prince, almost touching his face.

"In the name of the Father, the Son and the Holy Spirit! Stop! This is a sacred place! Do not take this sin onto your consc—"

Fedor smote him with the war hammer, Melchior Kondzioł struck another monk with his battleaxe and Mikoszka stabbed a third with his sword. Blood bespattered the wall and the baptismal font. Tłuczymost pressed a fourth monk against the wall and raised a knife. Reynevan caught him by the arm.

"Hey!" said the Pole, struggling. "Let go of my sleeve!"

"Leave him, we are wasting time! The others will reach the loot ahead of us!"

There was a frantic chase through the nave and choir. The brothers Kondzioł were pursuing the Pauline monks, slashing and hacking them, blood staining their white habits, spotting the floor, splashing onto the choir stalls and the *antepodium* of the altar. Ostrog ran after one of them into a chapel, and almost at once a bloodcurdling scream resounded from inside. Kuropatwa was holding another by his habit, jerking and shaking him.

"*Armarium!*" he roared, showering the monk's face with spittle. "*Armarium*, you damned priest! Lead me to the strongroom or you die!"

The monk sobbed, shaking his head. Kuropatwa threw him onto his knees, tied a rosary around his neck and began to strangle him.

The fleeing Pauline monks rushed straight into Reynevan and Tłuczymost. Reynevan punched one, knocked another over with a kick and shoved a third hard against a stone pillar. Tłuczymost guffawed and joined in, dealing out blows to the monks trying to stand up. The brothers Kondzioł leaped at them, one wielding a battleaxe, the other a sword.

"Leave them!" shouted Reynevan, blocking their way and

spreading his arms. "They've had a beating! I've given the friars a good hiding! Come on, swiftly, to the treasure, the treasure!"

The brothers reluctantly obeyed him. They and Tłuczymost leaped onto the altar, seized the monstrance and the crucifix, gathered up candlesticks and pulled off an embroidered altar cloth. Ostrog, soaked in blood, rushed out of the chapel, lugging an icon wrapped in a cloak. Nadobny ran out after him, carrying silver votive offerings in both arms and a candlestick under one arm.

"And now to the strongroom!" shouted the prince. "Follow me!"

They ran through the vestry to the rooms adjoining the chapter house. The door to the *armarium*, which a terrified monk showed them, gave way under blows from battleaxes. The Kondzioł brothers forced their way inside and soon after began to toss out loot. Chasubles embroidered with gold thread, silver bust reliquaries, chalices and patens, ciboria, incense boats, aquamanilia and even aspergilla. Kuropatwa and Reynevan hurriedly shoved everything into sacks.

The wagon was already standing in the courtyard. Achacy Pełka and Skirmunt—clearly horrified at the events—were harnessing to it two horses they had led out of the stable and were tying some free horses to the wooden sides. The Kondzioł brothers and Kuropatwa were tossing sacks of loot onto the wagon. Tłuczymost and Nadobny came running out of the church, the latter with an ornate homiliary under one arm.

An old Pauline monk was sitting outside the vestibule, his shoulders shaking with sobs. Mikoszka Kondzioł noticed him and drew a dagger.

"Leave him," said Reynevan. And the tone of his voice was enough to make the Pole desist.

Fedor Ostrog, already mounted, swung and tossed a brand onto the roof of a shed. Tłuczymost threw another onto the roof of the stable. Skirmunt and Pełka hopped onto the wagon; one seized the reins and the other cracked a whip above the horses' rumps.

"Yah! Yah!"

They fled down the Wieluń road towards Kłobuck. As fast as they could. The horses harnessed to the wagon, however, could not and did not want to run very fast. Neither shouts nor whips helped.

"Head over there!" said Fedor of Ostrog, indicating to the drivers a roadside glade near a fresh clearing. "Over there!"

"Do you mean we're dividing up the spoils here?" said Jan Tłuczymost, looking back restlessly, "and then every man for himself?"

"Only if you want to hang alone," sneered Fedor. "No, lads, we're heading together to Wieluń. Each man will receive his share there and then we ride on to Kuyavia and from there to the Margraviate or Prussia."

"And rightly so," said Kuropatwa, nodding. "We've robbed Jasna Góra, they won't forgive us for that. We need to get as far away from Poland as we can."

"And as quickly as we can," added Nadobny. "So let's ditch this fucking wagon. We didn't rob so much from the monastery that it won't fit in the saddlebags and onto the loose horses. Well, Fedor?"

"Unhitch them," agreed Ostrog, "and we'll repack it all. I have something else to do in the meanwhile."

He dismounted, took the icon from the wagon and unwrapped it. Pełka gasped. Jan Tłuczymost's mouth dropped open. Jerzy Skirmunt crossed himself mechanically. Jan Kuropatwa of Łańcuchów shook his head.

"If that's what I think it is," he said, "let's leave it here. Let's leave it. I wouldn't want to be caught with that."

"With or without it, what's the difference?" said Fedor, throwing the icon onto the grass. "It's only a painting on a wooden board. It's worth no more than those trinkets and baubles. Which we aren't leaving. *Herrgott!* Help me, one of you!"

Jerzy Skirmunt ostentatiously crossed his arms over his chest. Jakub Nadobny of Rogów and Jan Kuropatwa of the Szreniawa coat of arms did not budge. Only Tłuczymost and the brothers Kondzioł hurried to Ostrog's aid.

The Madonna of Częstochowa offered no resistance as they prised her out with daggers and stripped the gold leaf from her crown. She didn't make a sound or shed a tear when the crown was torn from her Son. Her dark face didn't twitch when the metal leaves were tugged from the sleeves of her gown. Her sad eyes didn't change their expression and her small, narrow mouth didn't move when they gouged out the pearls and precious stones.

The wood gave a crack when it was broken, and the canvas creaked as it was torn. The stolen icon snapped under their knives. Into two boards. A larger and a smaller.

Reynevan stood with his arms hanging limp and helpless. Blood was rushing into his face and his eyes were misting over.

In his head he heard the word "*Hodegetria.*" The one that points the way. The Great Mother, the Panthea-Pan Goddess. Regina-Queen, Genetrix-Parent, Creatrix-Creator, Victrix-Triumpher.

"Enough," said Ostrog, standing up. "Forget those little trifles, they aren't worth the trouble. We may go. But first, I just have to do what I was ordered to do."

Mother Nature, ruler of the elements, Queen and Lady of radiant heights. She whose singular divinity in many manifestations is venerated by the entire world under manifold names and in various rituals.

Prince Fedor Ostrog drew from a scabbard a single-edged

dussack with a straight cross guard. He walked over to the stolen icon.

Reynevan blocked his way.

"Find something else to smash," he said calmly. "You may not touch this."

Ostrog took a step back and narrowed his eyes.

"You never stop fucking things up, Teuton," he drawled. "All you do is fuck things up. Your fuck-ups are getting me down; I cannot stand your fuck-ups. Get out of the way or I'll kill you!"

"Move away from the icon."

Fedor didn't betray his intention either by his voice or the expression on his face. He struck all of a sudden, as swiftly as a viper. Reynevan dodged, surprising himself with the speed of his reaction. He caught the stooping prince by the arm and slammed him hard, head first, into the body of the wagon. He tugged the man towards himself, turned him around and punched him in the jaw with all his strength, simultaneously prising the dussack from his fingers. He pushed him away and smote. Ostrog howled and grabbed his head in his hand. Blood was pouring between his fingers.

"Ooooow!" he roared as he fell. "Kiiiiill him! *Baszom az anyat!* I fuck your mother! Kill him, kill him!"

Tłuczymost was the first to attack, followed by the Kondzioł brothers. Reynevan drove them back, swinging the dussack. Then Nadobny sprang at him from the side and stabbed with his sword, wounding him in the hip. Mikoszka Kondzioł leaped forward and slashed him across the biceps with a knife. Reynevan dropped the dussack, caught Kondzioł by the hand holding the knife and the blade cut his hand. Melchior Kondzioł went for him and stabbed with a dagger, the same one he had used to prise the gemstones from the icon. The blade slipped down over his ribs, but Reynevan still cringed in pain. Tłuczymost attacked and slashed him with a knife in the forehead near his hairline. Kuropatwa thrust his sword into Reynevan's arm and at the same moment Pełka struck him with a swingletree, on his upper arm and again in the lower back and on the back of the head. Everything went black and Reynevan's body went limp. He fell, grabbing the two halves of the icon and shielding them with his body. He felt blades stabbing and cutting him, felt heavy blows and kicks landing. Blood poured from his forehead, blinding him and dribbling down his nose into his mouth.

"Enough!" he heard Skirmunt shout. "Lord have mercy, that's enough! Lay off him!"

"Aye, we're wasting our time," said Kuropatwa. "He'll expire here anyway. Let's go. Wrap something around Ostrog's head, get him in the saddle and ride!"

"Ride!"

Hooves pounded and then faded into the distance. Reynevan vomited. And then curled up in a foetal position.

It grew darker. A light drizzle began to fall.

Pain.

Descendet sicut pluvia in vellus. She shall come down like rain upon the mown grass: as showers that water the earth. During Her days shall the righteous flourish; and abundance of peace so long as the moon endureth. And She shall have dominion also from sea to sea, and from the river unto the ends of the earth.

And thus shall it be until the end of the world, for She is the spirit.

The pain passes.

Cries and horses neighing pulled him out of his lethargy as the ground all around him shook with the stamping of hooves. Splashed with mud, Reynevan pressed the icon to his chest and screwed his face up; the blood sticking his eyelids together cracked and he spat blood clots from his mouth. He tried to get up but was unable to. He heard voices above him. He saw moustachioed faces, weapons, arms in iron vambraces and hands in armoured gauntlets. The gauntlets seized him, gripped him like pliers, he felt searing pain and everything went black. He cringed and curled up under the touch, writhed and flexed, retching, plunged into a chasm again, tumbling downwards.

They left him alone until he came around. Again, he heard the neighing and wheezing of horses, many horses. He heard voices. With immense effort, he raised his head. A well-built, chubby-cheeked man in a sable calpac and overcoat trimmed with sable fur cast a piercing gaze down on him from the saddle of a bay stallion with a golden trapping.

It was Zbigniew Oleśnicki, Bishop of Krakow.

"How is he?"

"They beat him, Your Eminence," a knight in a short tunic with the Pobóg coat of arms hurried to explain. "They beat him soundly. They stabbed and slashed him with knives. Wound on wound...God only knows if he will live."

"Arguing probably over the division of spoils?"

"Who knows?" said the Pobóg, shrugging. "Perhaps it was because he forbade them...from destroying it...When we found him, he was holding the Holy Mother, we could barely prise it from his grasp—"

"Why are you not pursuing the gang?" asked Zbigniew Oleśnicki and straightened up imperiously in the saddle.

"We stayed to guard the wondrous painting. It's a sacred thing."

"Be off and pursue them. Without delay!"

"Yes, sir, Your Eminence."

One of the bishop's men caught his horse by the bit, another held a stirrup and proffered a hand. Oleśnicki dismounted and gestured for them to move away. Then he approached. Slowly. Reynevan tried to rise, but his wounded arm failed him. He fell back onto the grass, not taking his eyes off the bishop.

"In Greek, *Hodegetria* means a guide," said Oleśnicki, not looking at him, but at the icon. "She who shows the way. I don't know if she showed you the right one. Or if she inspired you. For she did me.

"This painting," he continued, "is considered a true likeness of the Mother of God. It is reputedly the work of the first icon painter, Luke the Evangelist, supposedly painted on a board from the Holy Family's table. That explains its remarkable wondrousness and determines its immense value as a relic. And as a symbol. A symbol of the light of faith and the power of the Cross. A symbol of the strength of the spirit of the nation, its spiritual unity and its faith. Its steadfast faith, which will help the nation to ride out every calamity and will save its spirit in the most troubling of times. Symbols are important. Very important.

"The Holy Mother inspired me. She showed me the way and taught me what to do. And there will be no Polish intervention in Silesia. Polish help for the Czech heretics will cease. Heretical indoctrination will stop, heretical miasmas will stop poisoning Polish souls. The Czech Hussites and their Polish henchmen will become hated and reviled by all Poles, from the king down to the meanest serf. They will be hated as servants of the Antichrist. For only the hordes of the Antichrist raise their iconoclastic hands to strike symbols. And mutilate them hideously."

The bishop bent over and picked up Ostrog's dussack from the ground.

"I shall take this sin on my conscience. For my faith and for the fatherland. For the peace of God. For the future. *Ad maiorem Dei gloriam.*"

Heedless of Reynevan's groans and his desperate attempts to crawl over and impede him, Zbigniew Oleśnicki hewed the painted boards twice with the dussack. Twice, hard and deep. Across the Holy Virgin's right cheek. Parallel with the line of her nose.

Reynevan saw no more. He plunged into the chasm.

And fell for a long time.

He came to, covered in bandages, lying on sacks of straw in the back of a trundling wagon. The roadside elderflowers smelled so springlike that for a moment he thought he had gone back in time or that everything he had lived through during the previous two years had been a dream. That it was May 1428 and he was being carried, wounded, to the hospital in Oława. And that Jutta, alive and loving, was waiting at the Poor Clare convent in White Church.

But it wasn't a dream, nor a journey back in time. He was in manacles and fetters. And the soldiers riding alongside the wagon were talking in Polish.

He raised himself up onto an elbow with difficulty and realised that his whole body was sore and pulled tight from the sutures. He saw a hill lit by the setting sun. And a stone castle on top of it, a veritable eagle's nest, crowned by the column of a keep.

"Where..." he said, overcoming his dry throat. "Where are... you taking me?"

"Shut your trap!" growled one of the soldiers from the escort. "Talking's not allowed! It's against orders: if he begins to talk, knock his teeth out. So beware!"

"Give over," said another, appeasing him. "Have some kindness. For he's not talking but asking. And in any case, it's the end of his road. He may as well know where he's going to rot away."

Crows flew past, cawing.

"That, brother, is Lelów Castle."

I don't believe any of you have done time in a severe prison.

None of you, noble knights, none of you devout and pious monks here present in this tavern. None of you, gentlemen merchants. None of you, I expect, has ever seen deep cellars, dungeons aged by putrid water or stinking, pitch-black cells. Well?

None of you.

And there is no need, I assure you, to regret that.

During the reign of good King Władysław Jagiełło there were a number of severe prisons, terrible prisons. The Krakow Tower. Chęciny. Sandomierz. Olkusz. Olsztyn, where they starved Maciej Borkowic to death. Ostrężnik. Iłża. Lipowiec.

But there was one prison, the very mention of which made folk fall silent and go pale.

Lelów Castle.

You did your time in those other prisons; you suffered in them. You eventually left those other prisons.

No one ever came out of Lelów.

Chapter Twenty-Two

In which Reynevan, freed from the dungeon at Lelów, rejoices to see the light. And goes into battle for the last time.

There was an atmosphere of anxiety and nervous haste in the royal castle at Łęczyca. Guest apartments were being prepared in the Old House, and the grand hall cleaned, furnished and decorated. Information that Łęczyca had been chosen as the site of the peace talks had reached the burgrave late, almost at the last moment, and very little time remained to prepare everything. The burgrave was rushing around the Old House, swearing, fulminating, urging, scolding and endlessly asking if the entourage of the bishop and the Polish lords or the approaching Teutonic mission had been seen from the towers.

From the Order were expected, among others, Konrad of Erlichhausen from Malbork and Ludwik of Lausch, the Commander of Toruń. Franciszek Kuhschmalz, the Bishop of Warmia, was also meant to be in the mission. Of the Poles, Bishops Zbigniew Oleśnicki and Władysław of Oporów; the Castellan of Krakow, Mikołaj of Michałów; and the Castellan of Poznań, Dobrogost of Szamotuły, were thought to be coming.

The most important representative of the Polish side had already arrived in Łęczyca. Immediately after arriving, he had locked himself away in the chambers prepared for him. And the burgrave was informed that he received in them a strange, hooded guest. And gave instructions not to be disturbed.

A December wind banged the shutters and whistled through cracks.

"The Teutonic Knights are agreeing to a truce," said Rixa Cartafila of Fonseca, a spy in the service of Władysław Jagiełło, King of Poland, tossing her hair onto her neck. "They're afraid we'll saddle them with the Hussites again. They are also under pressure from the Prussian estates, which are threatening to withdraw their allegiance. The Chełmno knight, Hans of Baysen, is gaining in importance in the estates. I suggest that Your Right Reverend takes note of that name. The anti-Teutonic Order opposition is growing in strength and Baysen has the chance of becoming an important player. It'd be worth keeping an eye on him."

"I shall heed your advice," replied Wojciech Jastrzębiec, Archbishop of Gniezno, Primate of Poland and Lithuania. "I always listen to your advice, daughter. You render us invaluable service. Always remaining in the shadow. Never asking for anything, neither honours nor rewards."

Rixa smiled. With the corner of her mouth.

"The Right Reverend emboldens me," she said slowly, "to ask a favour."

"I pray you, ask away."

"Here we have the Teutonic Knights riding to Łęczyca to ask for a truce. There is a chance of lasting peace with the Order, with conditions convenient for Poland. There is a chance to recover Nieszawa and deprive Svidrigiello of Teutonic support. Certain Czechs deserve considerable credit for this. For example, Jan Čapek of Sány and the terror that his Orphans aroused in the Margraviate of Brandenburg and the Danzig region. The Pabianice Agreement and alliance between Poland and the Hussites has undermined the morale of the Teutonic Knights, the Right Reverend will certainly admit."

"Why such a long prelude? Tell me, daughter, what is it all about?"

"I have a request: that we celebrate the alliances, victories and successes with forgiveness. With an amnesty. Just one. An inconspicuous one."

"Who is it?"

"A prisoner at Lelów."

Wojciech Jastrzębiec said nothing for a long time. Then suffered a coughing fit. *It's thirty miles from Gniezno to Łęczyca*, thought Rixa. *He's too old for journeys like that. In weather like this.*

"The prisoner at Lelów," said the Primate finally, "is a prisoner of state."

"A political prisoner," she corrected him, head lowered. "And quite fundamental changes have occurred in politics recently, haven't they? Today it's clear to everybody that the attack on the Jasna Góra monastery wasn't carried out by Czech Hussites faithful to the Chalice—"

"But was an act of common thievery," Jastrzębiec finished quickly. "A simple plundering attack executed by common bandits."

"A mainly Polish—"

"A rabble without fatherland or faith," corrected the Primate with emphasis. "Slow-witted robbers who had no idea what they were raising their hands to strike. Who unthinkingly mutilated a miraculous painting."

"They ought to receive a divine punishment for desecrating something sacred," the agent interjected emphatically. "Most of them are said to have died. And died before a year passed after the attack on the monastery. Which is right and proper. They should all die. The ones in prison, too. By the hand of God."

Jastrzębiec brought his palms together as though in prayer and lowered his eyes to hide the flash in them.

"Thus the punishing right hand of God will reach the prisoner in Lelów?" he said, "Will the prisoner at Lelów also die? And will no one know where he will be buried? Will everybody forget about him?"

"Everybody."

"And what about the Bishop of Krakow?"

"The Bishop of Krakow," said Rixa softly, "is no longer interested in the Częstochowa affair. He has no interest in digging up corpses and awakening sleeping dogs. He knows it would be better if everybody forgot about Jasna Góra and the marred painting. Which, in any case, so I hear, is being restored in Krakow and will soon be hanging on the wall in the Pauline Order chapel, as before. As though nothing happened."

"May it be so," said Jastrzębiec. "May it be so, daughter. Though I admit I'd prefer you to be asking for something else. But you have rendered great services to the Kingdom of Poland. And you continue to do so, working with devotion and sacrifice. There are very few like you, particularly now."

Now, he thought, *since one of my best men met his death in Silesia. Łukasz Bożyczko, a good and well-concealed agent, a loyal servant of the Kingdom of Poland. He died, though the cut by iron he suffered was trifling. An irreparable loss. Where to find replacements?*

"So do what needs to be done," said the Primate, finally raising his head. "With my blessings. But consider whether the venture will incur expenditures. Whoever needs paying off at Lelów will have to be. I prefer not to involve in this the royal treasury, nor to deplete the Church's humble coffers yet more."

"In matters of finance," said Rixa, smiling, "please rely on me absolutely. I know how to deal with such things. It's in my blood, one might say. As it has been for generations."

"Yes, yes," said the old man, nodding. "Yes, yes. And since we're on the subject. Daughter?"

"Yes."

"Don't misunderstand me." The Primate of Poland and Lithuania looked at her, and his gaze was frank. "Don't perceive intolerance or prejudice in what I say. What I say, I say out of kindness, affection and concern."

"I know. I know, Reverend."

"Wouldn't you convert to Catholicism?"

Rixa said nothing for a while.

"Thank you," she finally answered, "but no thank you. Please don't perceive prejudice in that, either."

"I wish you a career. Promotion. As a Jewess you have meagre chances—"

"At present," said Rixa Cartafila of Fonseca, smiling. "But it will change one day."

"You're dreaming."

"Dreams come true. The prophet Daniel assures us of it. May God keep Your Eminence."

"God be with you, daughter."

First there were heavy steps. The clink of iron. Then the infernal, literally hair-raising rattle of bolts making Reynevan huddle up on the muck-covered straw. And the stark light of torches which made him cringe even more, tightly clenching his eyelids. And his teeth.

"Get up. Get out."

"I—"

"Get out. And look lively! Move!"

The sunlight stung his eyes painfully, blinding him. Making him dizzy. Making him stagger and lose his balance. He fell over.

Full-length, stiff like a drunk man, not even trying to cushion his fall onto the timbers of the drawbridge.

He lay prone and though his eyes were open he couldn't see anything. At first, he couldn't hear anything apart from the buzzing in his head, through the cocoon he was wrapped in, until slowly, very slowly, sounds began to penetrate and be discernible. At first incoherent and incomprehensible, they gradually began to assume cadences. Some time elapsed, however, before he understood that the sounds were words. Before he began to understand their meaning. And before he finally realised that the speaker was Scharley.

"Reynevan? Can you hear me? Do you understand? Reynevan? Don't close your eyes! Jesus Christ, you look dreadful. Can you stand?"

He tried to answer. But couldn't. Each attempt to make a sound turned into sobbing.

"Pick him up and carry him down. We'll put him on the wagon and go to town. He needs tidying up."

"Scharley."

"Reynevan."

"Did you...Did you get me out?"

"I played a part in it. The financial part."

"The black wagon?"

"Indeed."

"Where are we?"

"In the village of Niegowa, by the Siewierz road. At the back of the Demijohn tavern."

"What day...is it today?"

"Tuesday. After Quasimodogeniti Sunday. The sixth of April. *Anno Domini* 1434."

*

Ofka of Baruth rushed into the kitchen, her plait streaming behind her, and almost trod on the cat. She grabbed a large cauldron with both hands and flung it down onto the floor. She swept bowls and spoons from the table.

She kicked the waste pail hard, so hard it rolled under the stove. Finally, she kicked the cauldron, but it was solid and heavy and didn't yield. Ofka screamed, swore and hopped on one leg and sat down hard on a bench, holding her foot, and burst out crying, weeping tears of pain and anger.

The housekeeper observed it all with her plump forearms crossed on her chest.

"All done?" she finally said. "Is the performance over? Shall I learn what the matter is?"

"The ass!" yelled Ofka, wiping her eyes and cheek on her sleeve. "The clodhopper! The silly young pup!"

"Parsifal of Rachenau?" asked the housekeeper, who was observant and rarely missed a trick. "What about him? Has he declared his love? Did he finally propose? Or quite the opposite?"

"On the contrary," said Ofka, sniffling. "He said he can't marry me because his father won't permit it. His father is making him marry…Anooooother…"

"Don't bawl. Speak."

"…His father is making him marry another. Parsifal doesn't want her. Not now, not ever. But he can't marry me, either. He told me he can't. He won't oppose his father's wishes. He's entering a monastery. The idiot."

"As regards the monastery," said the housekeeper, nodding, "I agree. An idiot, indeed. But a father's wishes are a sacred thing. One mayn't oppose them."

"Not a bit of it!" yelled Ofka. "One may indeed! What about Wolfram Pannewitz? Did he wed Kasia Biberstein? He did! Although his father forbade him! They had their wedding, they had their celebration, now everybody is content, including old Pannewitz. Because Wolfram loved Kasia. But Parsifal doesn't looove me, waa-waa-waa…"

"Don't bawl," said the housekeeper, glancing at the door to make sure no one was listening. "That Parsifal of yours still hasn't led her to the altar, there hasn't been a betrothal. Much can still happen. Fate can bring much. And you ought to know that there are…"

Ofka wiped her nose with a sleeve and opened her hazel eyes wide.

"You ought to know," the housekeeper continued more quietly, "that there are ways…to help fate. But you need courage—"

"I'm prepared to do anything for him," said Ofka, clenching her teeth.

Elencza Stietencron shuddered and leaped up on hearing the grinding of stones under boots. She involuntarily leaned against a dry branch, which snapped with a loud crack. A muffled cry from the path answered the crack. Elencza froze, her heart beating in her chest like a bird struggling to escape from a cage.

A figure appeared on the path and Elencza sighed with relief. For it wasn't a brigand, a werewolf, a Baba Yaga, a dreadful forest spirit, a dangerous green-skinned alp or one of those notorious wandering monks bent on besmirching a maiden's honour. The figure appearing before her was a girl, younger even than she herself. With a fair plait, a freckly face and a retroussé nose. Dressed like a man and very opulently, at that.

"Oh my," said the freckled girl, sighing deeply to see Elencza. "Oh my, I was frightened. I was certain it was a werewolf…Or a wandering monk…Oh my. Greetings, whoever you are…I am—"

"Quiet…" whispered Elencza, going pale. "Somebody's coming…I heard footsteps…"

The freckled girl turned around, crouching and reaching towards the hilt of a dagger hanging from her belt. Her hand was shaking so much, however, that Elencza didn't believe she'd be capable of drawing the weapon. Elencza snatched up a stone, determined to sell her life—or whatever she would have to sell—dearly. But that day, it turned out, was one of ceaseless astonishments and surprises. For along the winding, steep, rocky path leading to the top of Radunia came a third girl. She also froze at the sight of the other two.

She looked the youngest of them all. Her face, her features and the colour of her hair all reminded Elencza of somebody, triggering anxiety in her. It was a vague and inexplicable feeling, making it all the more worrying.

"Well, well," said the freckled girl, recovering her composure at once and standing with arms akimbo. "What has brought you here, you minx? And all alone, at that. Don't you know it can be dangerous here?"

Elencza fought to stifle a snort. If the new arrival was younger than the freckled girl, it wasn't by much. But she was certainty taller. There wasn't a trace of fear or even embarrassment on her face. *Her face*, thought Elencza, surprised by the thought, *is older than she is.*

"I swear," said Elencza, "that we've all come here with the same intention. And since that intention is at the very top, we ought to make haste, otherwise we won't get back before dusk. Come on, girls. Follow me."

The freckled girl made a face, as though she was about to snort. But, ah well, every group must have a leader. And Elencza was the tallest. And who knew, perhaps the oldest.

"My name's Ofka…Euphemia of Baruth," said the freckled

girl proudly. "The daughter of Sir Henryk Baruth of Studzisko. With whom do I have the honour of speaking?"

"Elencza…of Wirsing."

The new arrival lowered her eyes when they turned to look at her. She didn't answer for a long time.

"You may call me Electra," she finally said quietly.

The elongated peak of Radunia was ringed by a stone embankment encircling a large boulder, a monolith resembling a catafalque. None of the three girls could have known it, but the monolith had been lying on the mountain when mammoths strode over the Sudeckie Hills and huge tortoises laid their eggs on the island of Piasek in the Odra, which was now a busy and densely built-up part of the great city of Wrocław.

At the foot of the monolith burned a campfire, its flames licking the bottom of a sooty cauldron spitting boiling water. Nearby, on a heap of skulls, lay a black cat, in a typically indolent, feline pose. It was busy licking its fur. It was the laziest licking Elencza had ever seen in her life.

Around the fire were sat three women.

One, a decrepit old hag, stooped and shrunken with age, was tottering, mumbling and humming, contorting her swarthy face. The one sitting furthest away appeared to be barely a girl. Feverish eyes shone in her pale, plain, somewhat vulpine face. Her tangled hair was being kept in relative order by a garland of verbena and clover.

The most important of them sat in pride of place. The *bona femina*. The one whom the three girls had come to see. Tall, stout, wearing a pointed, black felt hat under which flame-red hair tumbled onto her shoulders in luxuriant waves. A scarf of green wool was wrapped around the witch's neck.

"My thumbs are pricking," muttered the swarthy old woman. "My thumbs are pricking, which means—"

"Shut up, Jagna," said the one in the hat, quietening her down and then raising eyes the colour of molten tin towards the petitioners. "Welcome, girls. What brings you here? Don't say anything, let me guess. Unwanted pregnancies? No, I think not. Nor do you look to me sick; quite the opposite, I would say you all appear to be extremely hale and hearty. So it must be love! We are in love, but the love object is far away and unavailable, but moving further and further away and becoming more and more unavailable. Have I guessed right?"

The freckled Euphemia of Baruth was the first to eagerly and energetically nod. The first and the only one. Under the gaze of the red-headed witch, Elencza lowered her eyes, struck by a sudden conviction that it had been quite senseless, totally unnecessary and awfully foolish to come. As for Electra, she didn't even twitch, but stared vacantly into the fire.

"Did I guess right or not?" muttered the red-headed witch. "*Per Bacco!* It remains to be seen. Eliszka, toss brushwood onto the fire and herbs into the cauldron. Jagna, behave."

The swarthy one shoved a fist into her mouth to stifle a burp.

"And you will receive what you ask for," said the *bona femina*, bright eyes fixed on the girls. "Each in turn. Each one individually.

By the power of the Sun and the power of the Moon
By the power of sign and power of rune
Eia!

"Bubble, bubble, cauldron, and in it deadly nightshade, monkshood and henbane. Lower your head, Euphemia of Baruth. Breathe in the steam.

"Here is a looking glass; take it. When the moon begins to

wane, on the day of Venus and Freya, secretly catch in it your beloved's reflection. Wrap it in wool, lay it in a casket. Sprinkle on it a mixture of dried petals of rose and verbena. Add the herb *Agnus Castus*, also known as the chaste tree. Add a drop of your own *sanguine menstruo*. Hide the casket so that not a single ray of sunlight can fall on it. As you hide it away, utter three times the spell: *Ego dilecto meo et ad me conversio eius*, I am my beloved's and his desire turns towards me. Before the moon comes around three times, your beloved will be yours.

By the power of sign and power of rune…
Magna Mater, Magna Mater…

"Bubble, bubble, cauldron, and in it deadly nightshade, mandrake. Lower your head, Elencza of Wirsing. Breathe in the steam.

"Here is a knife of steel; take it. When the full moon begins to wane, on the day of Venus and Freya, go to an orchard before sunrise. Pluck the apple which seems most beautiful to you. Cut it in half with this knife, first rubbing into it a drop of your *sanguine menstruo*. Sprinkle on each half of the apple a pinch of dried knotgrass, then pin the two halves together with myrtle twigs. On the apple peel carve with the knife the initial of your beloved's name, utter his name thrice, each time repeating the spell: *Ecce iste venit*, behold, he comes. Hide the apple, so that not once does sunlight fall on it. Even if your chosen one be at the end of the world, he will return to you.

Eia!
By the power of the Sun and the power of the Moon
By the power of sign and power of rune!

"Bubble, bubble, cauldron, and in it deadly nightshade, fool's parsley, hemlock. Lower your head, breathe in the steam, you who wish to be called Electra. You have chosen a fell name, fell and terrible for somebody so young. Know you that I usually send away empty-handed maids such as you. I do not help maids such as you, I do not support them in their designs and intentions. I customarily tell maids such as you, Electra, to rely on time and fate."

The cat lying on the skulls hissed. The witch's eyes flared up with a baleful fire.

"Thus, as an exception," she uttered quietly, "I shall help destiny a little. And though your wish is full of evil, Electra, I shall make it come true. Hold out your hand. Behold, I give you…"

The red-headed witch whispered and Electra listened with her head bowed. The fire was dying down, the cauldron still bubbling and the boiling water hissing as it spat on the coals.

The cat miaowed.

"And now begone," said the *bona femina*. "Glory to the Pan Goddess! Aha, don't forget: after leaving here, no complaints will be listened to!"

"Don't eat so greedily," Scharley said to Reynevan. "You'll do yourself a mischief."

Reynevan raised his head above the bowl he was shielding with his forearm, and for a moment he looked as though he didn't understand. Then he resumed devouring the dumplings and fried pork pieces. Having finished them off, he slid towards himself a pot of *żurek* rye soup and tore a hunk of bread from a loaf. The penitent watched him in silence.

"How?" Reynevan suddenly asked him, with his mouth full. "How did you do it?"

Scharley sighed.

"After we parted, I didn't know what had happened to you for a long time. I heard about Częstochowa, naturally; everybody did. But how was I to know you were there? And that they threw you in gaol? To put it briefly: you owe your freedom to Rixa. To her information and her connexions."

"Even so, it was you," said Reynevan, putting down the spoon. "It was you who got me out of Lelów."

"That's what friends are for. Eat a little more slowly. No one's going to take the food away from you."

Reynevan glanced at him, his watery, festering eyes squinting. His eyeballs were bloodshot and covered in a dense meshwork of tiny red veins; he was clearly also suffering from intolerance to light.

"I need a barber-surgeon," said Reynevan, guessing what Scharley was thinking. "Or an apothecary's shop. Some medicament for my sore eyes. Eyebright, aloes, *faeniculum* or *herba sancta*... But first I need to eat, I must eat something. And you talk."

"What?"

"Talk," said Reynevan, reaching across the table for some white sausage from the Easter leftovers. "About what's been going on in the world while I've been away."

"Plenty has gone on. You've been away for exactly three years, though it feels like thirty. The times are historic. You can tell because a lot happens, and what happens, happens quickly. While you were inside, too many historic moments passed you by for me to bring you up to date; I'd have to talk till tomorrow morning, and I have neither the time nor the inclination."

"Find them both. Please."

"As you wish. Thus, in order: Pope Martin V died. A new one was elected—"

"Gabriele Condulmer," said Reynevan. "The heavenly She-wolf of the Malachy Prophecy. And the election took place on *Oculi*

Sunday, the fourth one before Easter. It was once prophesied to me. Apart from the name. What name did he choose?"

"Eugene IV. And the English burned Joan of Arc alive in the old town square in Rouen. A Vatican Council began in Basel. A crusade was launched against Bohemia—the fifth—and it was crushed at the Battle of Domažlice. Prokop sent the entire Duchy of Oleśnica up in smoke and then led a plundering raid all the way to Bernau, three miles beyond Berlin. Bolko, Duke of Cieszyn, died. Konrád of Vechta, the Archbishop of Prague, died. Bishop Jan Szafraniec, the brother of Piotr Szafraniec, died. Frederick of Aufsess, Bishop of Bamberg, died...Where are you going?"

"To throw up."

"*Dulce lumen*," Reynevan suddenly declared, "*et delectabile est oculis videre solem.*"

"What?"

"Truly the light is sweet and a pleasant thing it is for the eyes to behold the sun. Ecclesiastes."

"By which you mean," said Scharley, "that the medicine has helped a little?"

"A little. But that's not the point. At least, not the main one."

Having gorged himself at the demijohn, the recently released prisoner declared he'd had enough of taverns, complaining of the stuffiness. So they left in search of a medicament for his eyes. They eventually found extract of fennel, verbena, rose, celandine and rue, a dependable remedy for infections of the eyes and the eyelids, in an apothecary's shop in Siewierz, for there was neither an apothecary's shop nor any barber-surgeons in Niegowa. Not far from Siewierz, they stopped for a while in the open air, in a roadside birch wood. Reynevan applied the medicament himself, but they had to wait some time for it to take effect and had to repeat the treatment several times. Each time he washed his eyes with the fluid, he repeated as he did so the magical formulae, in order, as the recipe on the flacon announced: "For the natural potency of the medicine to be more effective in its treatment thanks to supernatural power."

Faeniculum, Verbena,
Rosa, Chelidonia, Ruta Lumina reddit acuta.

"Go on, Scharley," said Reynevan, pressing a poultice to his eyelids. "The last thing you said was that a few bishops died. Who else died while I was inside? Among the people of more interest to me?"

"Christine of Pisan, the French poetess. Does that ring a bell? *Seulete sui et seulete vueil estre...* Ah, Witold, Grand Duke of Lithuania, also died. Towards the end of October 1430."

"The cause?"

"He was injured falling from a horse and was then ill for a long time."

"Was he cut with iron when he fell?"

"I don't know. He may have been. Among other events: Sigismund of Luxembourg was crowned emperor. And King Władysław Jagiełło entered into an alliance with the Hussites and an offensive alliance against the Teutonic Order in Pabianice. Last June, the Orphans of Jan Čapek of Sány invaded the Margraviate of Brandenburg shoulder to shoulder with the Poles—"

"I happen to know about that," said Reynevan, peeling off the poultice and blinking. "The guards seldom spoke to me, but one was extremely badly disposed to the Teutonic Knights and had to share his joy at the victory with somebody. And here? Did Korybut carve out a kingdom for himself from Upper Silesia?"

"Not exactly. He was residing in Gliwice, which he had captured and meant to make into his royal capital. On the fourth of April 1431, three days after Easter, the Dukes of Oleśnica captured the castle using trickery and slaughtered the garrison. Korybut was fortunate not to be in Gliwice then. But his fantasy about a kingdom burst like a soap bubble. The duke returned to Lithuania. In other words, to obscurity and oblivion."

"Bolko Wołoszek?"

"He began ambitiously, enlarging his rule as he had planned, capturing castles and towns one after the next. But he didn't stay anywhere long, he was always driven away. Mikołaj of Racibórz took from him his final conquests, Bytom and Rybnik, a year ago. The chariot of history came full circle and Wołoszek is where he was at the beginning, that is in Opole. And there he will stay."

"Puchała? Bedřich? Piotr the Pole? The others?"

"Puchała invaded Kluczbork and Byczyna, from where—with one Kochłowski of Wieluń—he attacked, pillaged and burned, tormenting Silesia terribly. They fought against him, besieged him for weeks, but to no avail. Both sides finally grew weary of fighting and decided to solve the matter mercantilely. After bargaining, Puchała gave up Kluczbork for seventy-two thousand groschen and Byczyna for thirty thousand. He gave up the castles and left Silesia. He fought with Čapek's Orphans in the Margraviate and the Battle of Danzig. But he didn't return to Bohemia, he stayed in Poland.

"Jan Pardus is holding out in Otmuchów Castle, which he captured three years ago. While Bedřich of Strážnice and Piotr the Pole have headquarters in Niemcza and in Wierzbno, from which the Silesians are constantly trying to drive them. Unsuccessfully, for the moment, but it's only a matter of time."

"What do you mean? I don't understand."

"Weren't you listening? The plans to conquer Upper Silesia

came to nothing. Polish intervention never happened. The Silesians, left to themselves, will drive the Hussites from their lands. It's no use the Czechs hoping for reinforcements because the situation there has changed drastically."

"How, exactly?"

"Folk are tired. Of war, poverty, hunger, anarchy, the constant presence of armies, violence, killing and pillaging. So if any man begins to declare peace, a return to law, order and a system of values, if any man promises calm, stabilisation and the rebuilding of structures, he gains supporters immediately. And moderate advocates of compromise are declaring slogans like that and gaining support. At the expense of Prokop and the Orphans, who are losing support. Drunk on blood, the revolution has devoured its own children. The revolution has become too revolutionary, to the extent that it suddenly horrified the revolutionaries themselves. The radicals were suddenly horrified by radicalism, the extremists by extremism and the fanatics by fanaticism. And suddenly almost all of them moved to moderate positions. The Chalice—yes, but extremism—no. Hussitism with a human face. An end to war, an end to terror, out with the radicals, out with Prokop the Shaven, out with the Orphans, long live negotiations, long live pacts…"

"Pacts with whom?"

"With Rome, of course. Rome learned its lesson at the Battle of Domažlice, where the legate Julian Cesarini, the Spaniard Juan Palomar and the new Pope were defeated and driven away. They now know they will accomplish nothing with the Hussites by force but must use cunning. They know they have to take advantage of public feeling, win over the advocates of compromise and negotiate. Give up something in order to gain something. They are already talking. And will reach agreement. The Chalice will remain, but it'll be a tiny little one. Freedom of religion will be tiny. The extremists and incorrigible radicals will be exterminated. The undecided will be intimidated. And there will be compromises. There will be compacts. Rome will clinch the deal, the Pope will bless it, the new Archbishop of Prague will sprinkle it with holy water. The Church will recover its stolen wealth and estates. Sigismund of Luxembourg will regain the throne of Bohemia, because somebody has to be a guarantee of restoration and order, and how can there be order without a king? Thus Sigismund will take his seat in the Hrad! He will be the arbitrator between the peoples and will issue decrees for numerous nations. Then they will beat their swords into ploughshares, and their spears into sickles. And everything will be splendid."

"No, it won't. It won't happen. That would be treachery."

"It would be. And will be."

"Do you think the men who defeated five crusades and sent them packing will permit that? The victors at Vítkov, Vyšehrad, Sudoměř, Malešov, Ústí, Tachov and Domažlice? Will the Czech people, loyal to the Chalice, permit it?"

"The Czech people are paying a dozen groschen for a bushel of rye and one and a half for a loaf of bread. That's a dozen times dearer than before the revolution. That's what the Chalice and the war have given the Czech people. Reynevan, I don't want to quarrel. I summarised the current political situation for you and sketched out the perspectives comprehensibly, making predictions about the events of the coming months, if not days, with a large helping of likelihood. I know something about how you can lose contact with reality—often for a long time—when you're locked up. That contact occasionally returns, but one can't hurry the process. So don't. Rely on me, trust me."

"Could you be more precise?"

"Half a mile from here is a crossroads where two roads meet. We will ride southwards from here, down the road to Olkusz,

Zator and Cieszyn. We will cross the Jabłonków pass, and from there the way is straightforward. Čadca, Trenčín, Nitra, Esztergom, Buda, Mohács, Belgrade, Sophia, Philippolis, Adrianople. And Constantinople. The pearl of the Byzantine state."

"And you accuse me of a lack of contact with reality?"

"My plans are quite down to earth and cling to reality as tightly as a priest to his parish. And they are based on the actual economic power I possess. Come with me, Reinmar, and I swear on my old cock that before Advent, you'll see the sails on the Sea of Marmara, the Golden Horn, Hagia Sophia and the Bosporus. Well? Are we going?"

"No, Scharley. We aren't. Forgive me, but my plans are quite different."

The penitent looked at him in silence for a long time. And then sighed.

"I fear I can guess," he said finally.

"I'm glad."

"In March 1430, in the forests by Kłodnica," said Scharley, going over to Reynevan and grabbing him by the shoulders, "as you were leaving, you said you'd had enough. Frankly speaking, you didn't surprise me at all. And, as you recall, I didn't stop you. Your reaction was quite reasonable to me. You had known misfortune, and you reacted to it by throwing yourself into the maelstrom of the fight for true apostolic faith, for ideals, for social justice, for *Regnum Dei*, for a better world. And you suddenly saw that it wasn't a mission, but politics. It wasn't inspired, but calculated. The Word of God and apostolic faith are traded just like any other goods: with a view to profit. And you can see *Regnum Dei* on church frescos. Or read about it in the writings of Saint Augustine."

"I was imprisoned in a dungeon," replied Reynevan, quietly and calmly, "losing hope that I would ever get out. Tormented by the thought that my life lacked purpose. I was locked up for a long time, in the darkness, going as blind as a bat. *Dulce lumen*, I repeated the words of Ecclesiastes to myself. And finally, it dawned on me, I finally understood. I realised it is a matter of choice. It's either light, or darkness. I had no choice in prison; now I do. My choice is light, *lux perpetua*. I'm going to Bohemia. For I think that not everything has been lost there. And even if it has, it can't just be surrendered without a fight. If I want to give my life purpose, I will, by going into battle. For ideals, for *Regnum Dei*, for hope. But if *Regnum Dei* must die, if hope must fail, then I may as well die and fail, too. If it is all going to stay only on frescos, then they may as well paint me on those frescos, too."

Scharley took a step back.

"Perhaps you expected me to dissuade you from that idea; beg and plead. Not a bit of it. I won't. To every thing there is a season, and a time to every purpose under Heaven, as your favourite Ecclesiastes says. A time to receive, and a time to lose; a time to keep, and a time to cast away; a time to rend, and a time to sew. Destiny, Reinmar, sewed us together for a good few years, tossed us into the cauldron of history for a while and gave that cauldron a damn good stir. It's time to unpick those stitches. Before *Regnum Dei* arises, I want to put things in order here and now, for *patria mea totus hic mundus est*. I won't stand shoulder to shoulder with you in the last battle, because I don't like last battles and can't bear losing battles. I hate the idea of dying and fading away. I absolutely don't wish to appear on a fresco. I absolutely don't wish to appear on a list of the fallen in the decisive battle between the forces of Light against the powers of Darkness. So the time must come to say farewell."

"It has. So let's not drag it out. Farewell, Scharley."

"Farewell, Reinmar. Let's shake on it, comrade."

"Let's, old friend."

From outside resounded the clank of weapons and the metallic rattle of horseshoes on the stone courtyard. The garrison of Niemcza was preparing for a foray or a raid. Bedřich of Strážnice closed the window and went back to the table.

"I'm pleased to see you," he said. "Alive, at liberty and healthy. For word had it that—"

"I am also glad to see you," Reynevan interrupted. "And pleasantly surprised. The whole journey I was wondering if I would find you here. Whether you had followed Puchała's example and sold all your castles to the Silesians. Along with your ideals and God's truth."

"I haven't, as you see," replied the director of the Tábor positions in Silesia. "Nor did I give them away, although they put great pressure on me. Me in Niemcza and Pardus in Otmuchów. But they failed and departed empty-handed."

"I've heard the view that it's only a matter of time. That you won't retain the Silesian castles without the intervention of Poland and reinforcements from Bohemia. And apparently that can't be counted on."

"Unfortunately," Bedřich calmly agreed, "it can't. Though four years ago things were quite different. Quite different. Do you recall Szafraniec and his grand-sounding programme? The return of Silesia to the motherland? The sceptre of the Jagiellonians leading all the peoples *linguagii slavonici*? Conquering all the lands between the Baltic and the Adriatic? Ruthenia and Crimea? Great plans and huge ideas that fell through after some slight damage to one icon, which wasn't especially well painted, in any case.

"The Poles," he continued, "when their anger after Częstochowa had subsided, would gladly have seen Čapek join them fighting the Teutonic Knights, but they gave us no help in Silesia and will give us none now. After Częstochowa, even the enthusiasm of the Szafraniec family began to wane, even Spytek of Melsztyn, Siestrzeniec and Zbąski drew in their horns. We are alone here. Korybut has gone and Wołoszek is as quiet as a mouse. As for Bohemia…"

"Yes?"

"In Bohemia, things are going badly with the cause," the preacher began a moment later. "After the victory at Domažlice, Prokop had a series of setbacks. He lost a few battles, failed to best Plzeň and lost credit in the eyes of the brethren. That's human nature: your luck runs out once and they slander, hound and maul you to death; no one will remember your previous accomplishments and victories. It was exploited by the moderate wing, they that were always plotting to negotiate with Rome and Sigismund. Which meant, naturally, Prague Old Town and our old friend the plotter, Jan of Příbram. And the gentlemen of the nobility, who vied with each other to sew the Chalice onto their family arms for private gain and now vie with each other to unpick it. And not just the neophytes, such as Menhart of Hradec and Calixtines of the ilk of Bořek of Miletínek or Jan of Smiřice; now our old comrades, the Warriors of God from the Žižka years, are a model of moderation and compromise. They have gathered together in Prague and call with one voice for peace. And for good King Sigismund to ascend the throne of Bohemia. I do beg your pardon: *Emperor* Sigismund. For you ought to know that a year ago, at Pentecost, we had a great celebration. The new Pope, Eugene, the fourth of that name, after a Mass beautifully sung and celebrated in person by him, placed on the noble brow of Sigismund of Luxembourg the imperial crown before the Altar of Saint Maurice in the Church of Saint

Peter. In the process, the ginger-haired rascal became Holy Roman Emperor and Lord of All Christendom. To the delight of those who were always ready to kiss his foot. And when he ascends the throne in Hradčany they will be prepared to kiss his arse."

"And you?" asked Reynevan coldly. "How about you? Where will you kiss your new master, in order to ingratiate yourself? Or do you prefer to bargain with the Silesians for Niemcza to get the best price? And enlist for the Polish shilling? Is that your intention?"

"No, not that," countered Bedřich of Strážnice calmly. "Something different. I don't recognise the agreement between Sigismund and the Prague Compacts. I mean to assemble a detachment and head for Bohemia, to aid Prokop and the Orphans. It's not yet time to give up and hand over the throne. Not without a fight. What do you say?"

"I'll ride with you."

"But your eyes? They look—"

"I know what they look like. I'll cope. I'd even ride with you today. Who will you leave at Niemcza? Piotr the Pole?"

"Piotr was captured by the Wrocław men a year ago," said the director, grimacing. "They're holding him in the Tower and are squabbling over the ransom. I shall entrust Niemcza to somebody else. A new ally. Oh, talk of the devil..."

The door creaked and into the chamber, stooping under the lintel, walked a powerfully built knight with a jutting jaw and shoulders as wide as a cathedral door. Reynevan gasped.

"You've met, haven't you?" asked Bedřich. "Sir Hayn of Czirne, Lord of Nimmersatt Castle. Once in the service of Wrocław, for some time an ally of the Tábor. He joined us after the victory at the Battle of Domažlice. Where we triumphed resoundingly, indeed."

Reynevan detected a faint note of mockery in the preacher's voice. If Hayn of Czirne also noticed it, he didn't show it.

"Sir Reinmar of Bielawa," he said. "Well, well. Who'd have guessed I'd see you alive."

"Exactly. Who indeed?"

"I shall leave a garrison in Wierzbno and at Otmuchów Castle," summarised Bedřich, clapping for servants to bring wine. "And Sir Hayn in Niemcza. Well, unless Sir Hayn desires to ride with us to battle in Bohemia."

"Thank you kindly," said the Raubritter, adjusting his sword and sitting down. "But it is your—Czech—battle. I prefer to stay here."

The old chronicler monk from the Augustinian monastery in Żagań shooed away an intrusive fly and dipped his quill pen in ink. He examined it in the light before beginning to write.

It happened in Anno Domini 1434, on Sunday, in crastino Cantianorum, ipso die XXX mensis Maii. *The sun was in* signo Geminorum et luna in gauda sive fine Piscium.

When the Thaborites et Orphanos *left Prague New Town, the Catholic lords and those of the Calixtines who sought agreement with Emperor Sigismund gave chase. And they pursued them from Kouřim to Český Brod, and there were* nobiles barones et domini *Menhart of Hradec, Diviš Bořek of Miletínek, Aleš Vřešťovský of Rýzmberk, Vilém Kostka of Postupice, Jan and Burján of Gutštejn, Přibík of Klenové and Zmrzlík of Svojšín, with them the Catholic Sir Jan Švihovský, the Plzeň landfried, the contingent from Mělník, and also knights, squires,* clientes *and Oldřich of Rožmberk's domestic servants. In all there were thirteen thousand armed men, of which one and half thousand were heavy horse. And they formed up near the village of Hřiby.*

On the opposite side, at the village of Lipany, on the slope of Lipská Mountain, waited an assembled Taborite-Orphan force of ten thousand foot and seven hundred horse concealed inside a wagon fort built of some four hundred and eighty armoured wagons, protected by the barrels of forty cannons. And there was Prokop the Shaved, capitaneus et director secte Thaborensium, *and the preacher Little Prokop* dictus Parvus. *And likewise, the leaders: Jan Čapek of Sány,* capitaneus secte Orphanorum, *Ondřej Keřský,* capitaneus de Thabor, *Jíra of Řečice, Zikmund of Vranov, Jan Kolda of Zampach, Rohač of Dube and other* capitanei cum aliis ipsorum complicibus.

At first, they thought to be reconciled and end the matter peacefully; nonetheless there was too much hatred and bad blood between them. Bedřich of Strážnice, who had come from Silesia and was calling for agreement, was abused and almost killed, and had to withdraw from the battlefield with his men and go on his way. But they began to fire cannons, trestle guns and other pixides *at each other, making a tremendous roar and covering the whole field in smoke. And the Rožmberk knights charged at that smoke, but were repulsed and they fled. Then a great shout went up among the Tábor and the Orphans that the enemy was fleeing and that it should be pursued and finished off. They opened up the wagon fort and charged onto the battlefield together.*

And that was their end. And their destruction.

"Haaaalt! Haaalt!" roared Jan Čapek of Sány. "It's a ruse! Close up the wagons! Don't leave the wagon fort!"

His voice was lost in the roar of battle and the booming of cannon fire, for the gunners from the Taborite wagon fort were firing ceaselessly at the retreating knights. But the Taborites and Orphans rushed onto the battlefield, yelling and brandishing flails and halberds.

"Have at theeem!"

And then missiles showered down on them. A hail of balls, shot and bolts. The Calixtines' position was shrouded in smoke. And then the heavy cavalry rumbled out of the smoke. Charging towards the now unprotected wagons and the infantry dispersed over the battlefield.

Whoever could, fled; whoever had the fortune to flee from the swords of the knighthood reached the wagons where hejtmans, hoarse from yelling orders, were trying to close ranks and organise the defence. But it was too late for that. The Rožmberk troops feigning an escape turned back, forced their way between the deployed wagons and galloped into the wagon fort, stabbing the defenders with their lances and wiping them out in the gallop.

Ondřej Keřský and his cavalry attacked them. They were stabbed with lances and swept away; the light Taborite cavalry wasn't able to stop the iron-clad cavalry. Jan Čapek dashed to help, wielding his sword and calling the infantry. Reynevan also joined battle. He saw in front of him the bared teeth of horses, breastplates and sallets; he saw a forest of fixed lances, certain he was going to his death. A lance pierced a horseman and threw him from the saddle, but before the lancer could release the shaft, Reynevan had ridden over to him and slashed him with his sword, once and twice, and blood gushed from under the mangled spaulder. Another cavalryman struck him with his horse, made a broad sweep of his sword, and Reynevan saved his life by ducking down behind the horse's neck. The Rožmberk man didn't have time to slash again as Taborite infantrymen caught him with the hooks of their gisarmes and yanked him from the saddle. A third bounded forwards with a battleaxe, and Reynevan, seeing that he had no chance against him, yelled, jerked the reins and spurred his horse hard. The horse reared up, swung its forehooves, the horseshoes fell onto a cuisse and a plackart, buckling the armour, and the Rožmberk man screamed and fell to the ground. A savage fight was raging all around, sheet armour grating and bones crunching under horses' hooves.

Before Reynevan's very eyes the Rožmberk armoured cavalry tossed hooked chains onto the wagons of the fort, reined their horses around and pulled. The wagons were overturned, crushing gunners and crossbowmen. Into the breach charged the Calixtinistic cavalry, a river of horsemen forcing its way inside, stabbing, hacking and trampling. The broken wagon fort suddenly turned into a trap with no escape.

"It is the end!" yelled Jan Čapek of Sány, hacking left and right with his sword. "Defeat! We are done for! Every man for himself! Reynevan! To me!"

"To me!" bellowed Ondřej Keřský. "To me, brethren! Every man for himself!"

Reynevan reined his horse around. He hesitated for a moment, a short moment, a moment determining life or death. He saw the heavy horse cut down the Slány flailmen and the spearmen from Kutná Hora, saw the Orphans from Český Brod marching to their deaths. Saw Zikmund of Vranov tumble from the saddle. Saw Prokop the Shaven, fighting atop a wagon, fall, stabbed with lances and slashed by swords. Saw Little Prokop drop a monstrance and fall, mortally wounded. Saw the battle turn into a massacre.

And fear gripped him. Horrible, gut-wrenching fear.

He pressed his face to the horse's mane and dashed after Čapek. Through a gap in the wagons, under a hail of balls and bolts. Downhill, downhill, along a ravine, along a mountainside. To get away.

As far away from Lipany as possible.

*

"To Kolín!" yelled Jan Čapek. "To Kolín! Let's hope the horses hold up! Reynevan! What the bloody hell are you doing?"

Reynevan had dismounted. Fallen to his knees. Bowed his forehead to the very earth. And started sobbing.

"The purpose of my life…" he sobbed, choking. "Ideals…*Lux perpetua*…And I'm fleeing from the battle…Like a coward… I couldn't even…even fall in battle!"

Čapek wiped blood, sweat and soot from his face. Shook his head and spat.

"It's not the end yet!" he called. "We'll show them still! What? Should we have let them kill us? Like fools? He who fights and runs away, lives to fight another day! Stand up, Silesian, stand up! Do you see? We've reached the Kolín road! We riding to Kolín, they won't catch us there! Get up and ride! Do you hear?"

"Go on by yourself."

"What?"

"Go by yourself. There's nothing for me in Kolín."

The warm May rain was falling and rustling the leaves.

Yes, yes, noble knights, yes, god-fearing monks, believe me, gentlemen merchants, that the Lipany *conflictus* was harsh, the battle on the slopes of Lipská Mountain was fierce.

Men fought to their deaths until the late evening. Until the late evening, almost until it got dark, the brothers of the Tábor and the Orphans were dying in battle. Some were killed on the field, some in the wagon fort, some in flight. In total, they say that almost two thousand Warriors of God fell, among them Prokop the Shaven, called the Great. Many brothers were taken captive. The lives of the more notable were spared. But more than seven hundred captives were driven by the Rožmberk men to barns near Český Brod and burned alive there.

And it was a great victory for the Calixtines and the Catholics. And it was the end of the Taborite-Orphan field armies.

On the day after Lipany, however, the first day of June 1434, Władysław II, King of Poland, died in the arms of priests in the eighty-fifth year of his life, in Hrádek, on his way to Halič, where he was meant to receive homage from the new Voivode of Moldavia, Stefan. That year, on the day of Saint James the Apostle, Jagiełło's son, Władysław of Warna, ascended the throne in the Wawel at the age of ten.

There was a revolt in Lithuania. The rabble-rouser Svidrigiello, the uncle of the new king, supported by the Livonian Brothers of the Sword, the Ruthenians and Sigismund Korybut, the would-be ruler of Bohemia and Upper Silesia, took up arms against the union with Poland and everything Polish. In 1435, on the day dedicated to Saint Giles, on *dies Jovis*, fourteen days before the *equinoctium autumnale*, Sigismund Korybut fell, fighting the Poles. In a battle fought at Wiłkomierz, beside the Sacred River.

1435 was a fertile year. Perhaps you recall? After all, it was only five years ago. The harvest was gathered in before Peter and Paul in some places, and all the crops had been brought in by the time Peter and Paul was over. Vines in vineyards bloomed before Saint Vitus's Day, and soon after Saint Vitus's Day the grapes were already as large as peas and in some places as large as goats' droppings. The summer that year was extremely hot, so unbearable that people fainted in the fields.

That autumn, a bright comet appeared in the heavens with a fiery tail pointing towards the west. Astrologists pronounced it a bad sign. And they were right. A short time after, a great pox broke out in Silesia, in Bohemia, in Saxony and in other lands and many folk died of it. In Dresden, they say, they buried more than a hundred on a single day. Many, many notable people died. And Canon Gwisdendorff died in Wrocław. And it was a good thing, because he was a bloody whoreson, *oret pro anima sua, quis vult*. Pity that more like him didn't die, for life in Silesia would have been better.

In 1436, two years after the massacre of the Tábor and Orphans at the Battle of Lipany, the day before Saint Bartholomew's, Sigismund of Luxembourg, *dei gracia Romanorum imperator, Ungarie, Boemie, Dalmacie et Croacie rex*, rode into Golden Prague. Great crowds greeted him with cheers and cries of joy and led him to the Hrad with tears of happiness in their eyes. But there were those who didn't recognise Sigismund as king, but called him a ginger-haired rascal and King of Babylon, and some even declared war against him. That was the preacher Ambrož, Bedřich of Strážnice, Jan Kolda of Žampach, and above all the famous hejtman, Jan Rohač of Dube. The latter was such a vexation that soon the imperial army besieged his fortress Sion. The castle fell and Rohač, Wyszek Raczyński and their comrades were taken captive and delivered to the capital. They were tormented and tortured for a long time, on the orders of Emperor Sigismund, and finally hanged on a great gallows. It happened on Monday, the day after *Nativitatis beate Marie virginis Anno Domini* 1437.

And the people wept long and hard. Whenever it was mentioned, people wept.

Chapter Twenty-Three

In which the end comes to everything.

"My eye grows weak from sorrow," said Jan Bezděchovský of Bezděchov, the oldest, most experienced and most respected among the congregation of sorcerers at the Prague apothecary's shop at the House at The Archangel.

"My eye, strength and guts grow weak," he added, pouring aqua vitae from a carafe into cups. "Worry corrodes my life and sighing corrodes my years. Oppression has weakened my strength and my bones have grown feeble. In other words, Reinmar, there is no bloody joy in old age. But that's enough about me. Tell me how you are. Apparently, your lady…Is it true?"

"It is."

"And our good friend Samson…"

"True, too."

"Oh, I'm sorry, I'm sorry…" said the *reverendissimus doctor*, lifting his cup and taking a large sip. "A great pity. And you were at the Battle of Lipany, they say…They say men were burned alive in barns there, hundreds of men. The horror, the horror. And what now, tell me? What will happen now?"

"It is the end of an era. A turning point. Bohemia is like a boiling cauldron…"

"And the scum rises to the top," guessed Bezděchovský. "Right

621

to the very top, as usual. What about you? Will you fight on?"

"No. I've suffered defeat. In everything. I've had enough."

"It fell on us to live in interesting times," said the old man with a sigh. "Interesting indeed. And ridiculous and terrible... Fortunately, little of this life remains—"

"What do you mean, Master...?"

"Little, little. All that is keeping me alive is this beverage. This inebriating beverage. *Aqua vitae*," said Bezděchovský, raising his cup, "is quite simply *aether*, which removes impure substances from the body and restores fluidity and vibrance to viscous and indolent blood. An extract of the highest harmony is contained in vodka, as it is in the quintessence. *Aqua vitae* acts like its name. It's the water of life, a life-giving fluid which can extend our days—why, even drive away death and delay our demise... Oh, I've said enough! Let us drink!"

"Master."

"Go on, son."

"I shall not tarry in Prague for long. I'm returning to Silesia. I have...scores to settle there. I visited you because...I have a request. Curious enough that I dare not ask either Telesma or Edlinger Brehm...I can only ask you. In the hope that you will want to understand..."

"Fire away. What do you need?"

"Poison."

"I have everything you asked for, Master Jan," said the librarian, Štěpán of Drahotuše, glancing at Bezděchovský and Reynevan suspiciously as he dumped an armful of books on the table. "*Turba philosophorum*, that is a translation of *Mushaf al-gama*. *Sirr al-asrar*, or *Secretum secretorum*, in the original. Should you have difficulty with the Arabic, please ask for Teggendorf's help. Arnoldus of Villa Nova's *Epistoła de dosibus tyriacalibus*. And a rare find: Guglielmo of Corvi's *Questiones de tyriaca*. I wonder why you need those last two works? Do you mean to poison someone?"

"Behold your poison, Reinmar," said Jan Bezděchovský of Bezděchov, raising a flacon of iridescent green liquid. Reynevan said nothing and paled. Bezděchovský put down the flacon and scratched his purple nose.

"Your target, you claim," he began, "regularly imbibes liquid gold, *aurum potabile*. By so doing he is absolutely resistant to all known toxins and poisons in their fundamental form. It is thus necessary to use a *compositum*, a many-staged, combined poison.

"By itself, *aurum potabile* doesn't react with anything. Nonetheless, one ought to assume that the person taking *aurum* also takes other medicines for the purpose of maintaining an organic balance, somatic equilibrium and to suppress side effects. Medicines of that kind include *confectiones magnae*, *confectiones opiatae*, some *panacea*, such as, for example, *Hiera*, and some *athanasia*, such as *Theriak*.

"Our alchemic *compositum*, devised by *magisterium* Edlinger Brehm, uses tasteless *aqua fortis* as its *menstruum*, or solvent. The *simplicia* used here, if it interests you, include meadow saffron, or *colchicum autumnale*, and spurge laurel, or *daphne mezereum*. Nothing special or new here; Medea used meadow saffron in her poisons in Colchís, as can be guessed from the Latin name. The most innovative element of our mixture—and the most lethal —is bufotenin. A magically processed extract from the active substances in the secretions from a toad's glands."

Bezděchovský reached for the carafe and poured himself some liquor.

"When you administer the poison, after some time the target will experience the symptoms consistent with a negative reaction to *aurum potabile*. As usual, he will take the *panaceum*. The meadow saffron will react to the *panaceum*, causing diarrhoea. The diarrhoea remedy will react to the *mezereum*, intensifying the symptoms and considerably raising the body's temperature. The target will then take *Hiera* or *Theriak*, and the bufotenin will react violently to the reaction produced by all of this combined."

"Will death occur quickly? Painlessly?"

"Quite the opposite."

"I'm glad. My great thanks, Master."

"Don't thank me," said the *reverendissimus doctor*, knocking back more liquor. "Now go and poison the bastard."

People literally stopped dead, turning around, staring with mouths open in awe, whispering and pointing. The sight was deserving of being pointed at and admired. You'd have thought that legends, fairy tales and knightly epics had come back to life and arrived in Wrocław, in the thronged Castle Street. For down the middle of the street lined on both sides by Wrocław folk pranced a gorgeous dark bay stallion, adorned in a snow-white caparison, its neck decorated with a garland of flowers. A young knight in a black and silver doublet and velvet beret with a plume of feathers was mounted on the stallion. The knight was carrying before him on the saddle a maiden, as pretty as a picture, in a white cotehardie and flower wreath over her luxuriant fair hair, which flowed down loosely around her like a sylvan nymph's. The maiden embraced the knight and gave him a passionate, loving look, and every now and again a no-less-passionate kiss. The horse walked on, its horseshoes clattering rhythmically, and the people looked on in delight. It was as though characters straight from the strophes of a romance, from a troubadour's air or a bard's tale had come to Wrocław.

Behold, whispered the people of Wrocław, *look, Lohengrin is carrying Elsa of Brabant, Érec is carrying Énide on his pommel, look, Aucassin in the embrace of his Nicolette, look, Floris and Blanchefleur. See, Yvain and the Lady of the Springs, it is Gareth and Lioness, it is Walter and Hildegund, it is Parsifal himself, with his Condwiramurs.*

"They're staring at us," said Parsifal of Rachenau, tearing his lips away from his betrothed's lips. "They keep staring at us—"

"Let them," said Ofka of Baruth, soon to be Rachenau, shifting her position on the saddle and looking lovingly into her betrothed's eyes. "For you promised."

Parsifal of Rachenau had indeed promised. The two fathers— Tristram of Rachenau and Henryk Baruth—had been left by the betrothed couple with beer and wine following the official betrothal ceremony, while the mothers, Hrozwita of Baruth and Berchta Rachenau, had been left to dream about grandchildren. But the fiancé Parsifal honoured the promise he had given his fiancée. That he would carry her romantically from one side of Wrocław to the other. From the Town Square to the cathedral and back. In front of him on his saddle. On the dark bay castellan that Dzierżka of Wirsing had given him.

The people of Wrocław stared. Horseshoes thudded on the boards and planks as the betrothed rode onto Piasek Bridge. Passers-by parted in front of them. Ofka suddenly gasped aloud and dug her fingernails into Parsifal's shoulders.

"What is it? Ofka?"

"I saw…" said Ofka, swallowing. "I thought I saw…a maid I know…"

"A friend? Who? Shall we turn back?"

Ofka swallowed again and shook her head, blushing involuntarily. *Better not*, she thought. *Better not to return to old matters, better to erase them, eject them from memory. That afternoon on Radunia. Better that her beloved didn't know it was owing to white magic, that it was magic that bound them, it was spells that overcame the obstacles and brought them together, today and for ever, because what God joins no one can put asunder.*

I wonder, she suddenly thought, *if they succeeded, whether the magic had been equally obliging towards them.*

Towards Elencza…And towards Electra. Electra, whose face I saw in the crowd a moment ago.

"We barely knew each other," she explained, trying to appear indifferent. "Her name was Electra."

"I'm surprised at parents giving their children names like that," said Parsifal. "Call it superstition, but I'd be afraid that the name might prove to be prophetic and influence my child's destiny."

"What do you mean?"

"Electra was the daughter of Agamemnon, King of Mycenae. She adored her father; when he was murdered, she went insane with hatred and the desire for vengeance. She exacted revenge but she herself went mad. I wouldn't give a daughter of mine that name."

"Neither would I," said Ofka, snuggling up to her betrothed. "We shall christen ours Beata."

The bell of the Church of the Blessed Virgin Mary on Piasek Island tolled the Sext. Reynevan pushed his way through the crowd, nursing and protecting the flacon with the composite poison hidden under his coat. He was determined. He was looking out for an opportunity. As he had for a long time.

The Wallcreeper, guarded by Kuczera of Hunt and his men, walked down the middle of Piasek Bridge, greeting with a raised hand the citizens of Wrocław thronging towards him. His jacket was adorned with a heavy gold chain, a symbol of power. The Wallcreeper had power. Bishop Konrad had ceded to him the secular governorship of the whole of Silesia, appointing him *Oberlandeshauptmann*, steward, starosta and monocrat of Wrocław, elevating him above the town council and magistrate. Thus had Birkart Grellenort become the most powerful man in Silesia after the bishop. To unqualified approval and overwhelming joy. For a fierce war with the Hussites was being waged, Niemcza and Otmuchów were still in Hussite hands, bands of Hussite marauders and robber knights allied with them were still prowling around Silesia. Folk wanted power to be held in one strong hand, to have a decisive and unbending ruler. A man of the moment was needed, a leader and a defender. Wrocław people had faith in their defender, believed that he would protect them, raise them up from the ruins, bring them wealth and happiness. They trusted and admired him.

"Our saviour!"

"Our refuge!"

"Our benefactor!"

Flowers were tossed at the Wallcreeper's feet. Mothers held children up for him to bless them. Apprentices from the guilds knelt before him. The poor fell at his feet from where Hunt's men quickly and brutally removed them.

"We are in your care!"

"Be our hope!"

"Rule over us, O leader!"

Behind the Wallcreeper walked Father Felicjan Gwisdek, now Lord Gwisdendorff, promoted by the bishop for his loyalty and service to prebendary and the position of canon at the Collegiate Church of the Holy Cross. Father Felicjan smiled at the crowd, blessed them and dreamed…About how he would soon be striding at the head with the Wallcreeper behind him. Kuczera of Hunt also smiled, teeth clenched, shoving nuisances away.

"We will examine everything," promised the Wallcreeper with

a smile, pushing away the petitions and requests being held out towards him. "We shall examine everything in detail…We shall punish the guilty! The law will prevail! And justice!"

"Begone," hissed Kuczera to the petitioners. "Begone, or you'll get a kicking…"

"A golden age for Wrocław will dawn…" said the Wallcreeper, stroking the head of another little girl with a posy of flowers. "A golden age! After we have vanquished our enemies! But the battle is not yet over!" he announced in a loud voice. "The serpent is not yet defeated! You must be ready for renunciations and sacrifices—"

He broke off, seeing a fair-haired girl standing just in front of him. Her face reminded the Wallcreeper of someone. Worryingly. *Her face*, he thought, *is older than she is.*

He held his hand out in a gesture of blessing. Something made him withdraw it.

"Do I know you?"

"I am Sybilla of Bielawa," said the girl brightly. "The daughter of Piotr, called Peterlin. Die, murderer."

It happened quickly. So quickly that Kuczera of Hunt responded too slowly. He wasn't able to shove the Wallcreeper out of the way or overpower the girl. She, however, drew from under her mantle a short Prague "treacherous" handgonne and shot the Wallcreeper straight in the chest from close range.

Dense smoke obscured everything and the girl vanished in it like a ghost. Like an apparition. Like a nightmare.

The crowd parted, screaming, dispersing, scattering. And now Reynevan could see.

See the Wallcreeper, pierced by a ball, staggering, but not falling. See him look down at his soot-covered, bloody chest, at the links of the golden chain rammed into his body by the ball. See him cackle wildly.

"Seize her…" he grunted, catching his breath. "Apprehend her…I'll flay the bitch alive…"

"You are wounded!"

"It's nothing…I'm not hurt…It takes more than that to harm me…An ordinary ball is too—"

He broke off, choked and his eyes popped out of his head. Coughing violently, black gore gushed from his mouth. He yelled, screamed and cawed. He understood. Kuczera also understood. Canon Felicjan, cowering on the ground, understood. Reynevan, watching from a distance, understood.

It wasn't an ordinary bullet.

The Wallcreeper screamed. And croaked. And before the croak faded away, in front of the onlookers' eyes, he turned into a black bird. The bird flapped its wings ponderously, rose up and flew away, shedding drops of blood, above the Odra, towards Ostrów Tumski. It didn't fly far. Everybody saw the bird, as over the river it turned, with a macabre keening and croaking, into a large, shapeless winged creature, spurting blood, kicking its legs and flapping its wings. The metamorphosis took place before the eyes of everyone present, as the monster fell, now in human form, into the grey waters of the Odra. A dying man with a golden chain on his chest.

The waters closed over the corpse. All that remained was a patch of bloody foam which the current tossed around.

The Wallcreeper's body came to rest on the starling of the Long Bridge, caught by the branches piled up on it. It floated on the water, face down, rocked by the current, for a good hour. It finally drifted on, the water carrying it beside watermills, towards sandbars, where several times it was grounded on shallows. Then a stronger current took it, sending it again towards the left bank, towards Garbary, into the stinking waste from the tanning workshops. Turning around in whirlpools, it flowed to Sokol-nicki's weir where the water carried it over the crest.

In the deeper water beyond the island, the corpse, spinning around in whirlpools, attracted the attention of a monstrous Odra catfish. But the body was still too fresh to nip flesh from it, and the big fish jerking the body only managed to turn it over onto its back. So when the Wallcreeper flowed into the broad water near Szczepin, some terns landed on it. By the time it reached Bytyń it had no eyes, just two bloody holes in its face.

In Popowice, the shepherd boys watering their cows pointed it out to each other.

It was late afternoon when it reached Kleczków. And came to rest by a groyne reinforced with a fascine.

An angler in a straw hat was sitting on the groyne, holding a hazel rod. For a while, he looked at the body turning around in the eddy. At its black hair, billowing in the water like the tenta-cles of sea anemones. At the birdlike face and nose.

"At last!" cried the angler, leaping to his feet. "At last! Glory to the philosophers! You've come, Birkart of Grellenort!" shouted Wendel Domarasc, cavorting like a madman and waving his arms around. "I've waited a long time, patiently, yes, I've waited patiently by the river! And the Odra has finally brought you! And I can look at you! Oh, how glad I am to be able to look at you!"

The body bumped against the groyne, turned around and joined the current. The former Hussite spy waved goodbye to it.

"Pass on my greetings to the Baltic!"

And that would be the end of the tale. *Completum est quod dixi de Operatione Solis.*

Finis coronat opus. I have finished. And I am worn out. *Explicit hoc totum*, and you, gentle lass, *infunde mihi potum*! Pour away, pour away! I shall drink a mug of Świdnica ale for the road. Or two.

Farewell, noble and good gentlemen. May providence protect you from misfortune and misadventure on your travels. No, no, I told you that's the end, I shall tell no more tales. For force failed my high fantasy.

> *Here force failed my high fantasy.*
> *But my desire and will were moved already.*
> *Like a wheel revolving uniformly,*
> *by the Love that moves the sun and the other stars.*

L'amor che move il sole e l'altre stelle...

I can't seem to get that Dante out of my head...

That's the end of my speech. Because, as Ecclesiastes wisely states, although there is no end of making many books, I must end it. I am compelled.

It is time I went. It's a long way to Constantinople, and I'd like to see the sails on the Sea of Marmara, the Golden Horn and the Bosporus before Advent.

I want to see my dream. Before it vanishes for ever.

I wish you good health. And on parting…I say sincerely to you, to each of you: think on Ecclesiastes. *Primo*: *omnia vanitas*, all is vanity. *Secundo*: having listened to all of this, Fear God, and keep His commandments: for this is the whole duty of man!

For God shall bring every work into judgment, with every secret thing, whether it be good, or evil.

Whether it be good or evil.